A Spellster Novel

TO TARGET THE HEART

ALDREA ALIEN

Thardrandian Publications

TO TARGET THE HEART

For information contact:
http://www.aldreaalien.com

Cover design by Leonardo Borazio
https://dleoblack.deviantart.com

Map Design by renflowergrapx
https://www.fiverr.com/renflowergrapx

ISBN: 978-0-9922645-7-4
First Edition: April 2020

10 9 8 7 6 5 4 3 2 1

Dedicated to my
critique partners, my editor
and beta readers.

ENDLESS SEA
NOVYDOMOV
TIRGLAS
Haalabof
OBUZAN
TWIN LAKES
Annabar
NIHOLIA
MAMOGUCHABHAG
INDEPENDENT ISLES
N
THE KNOWN

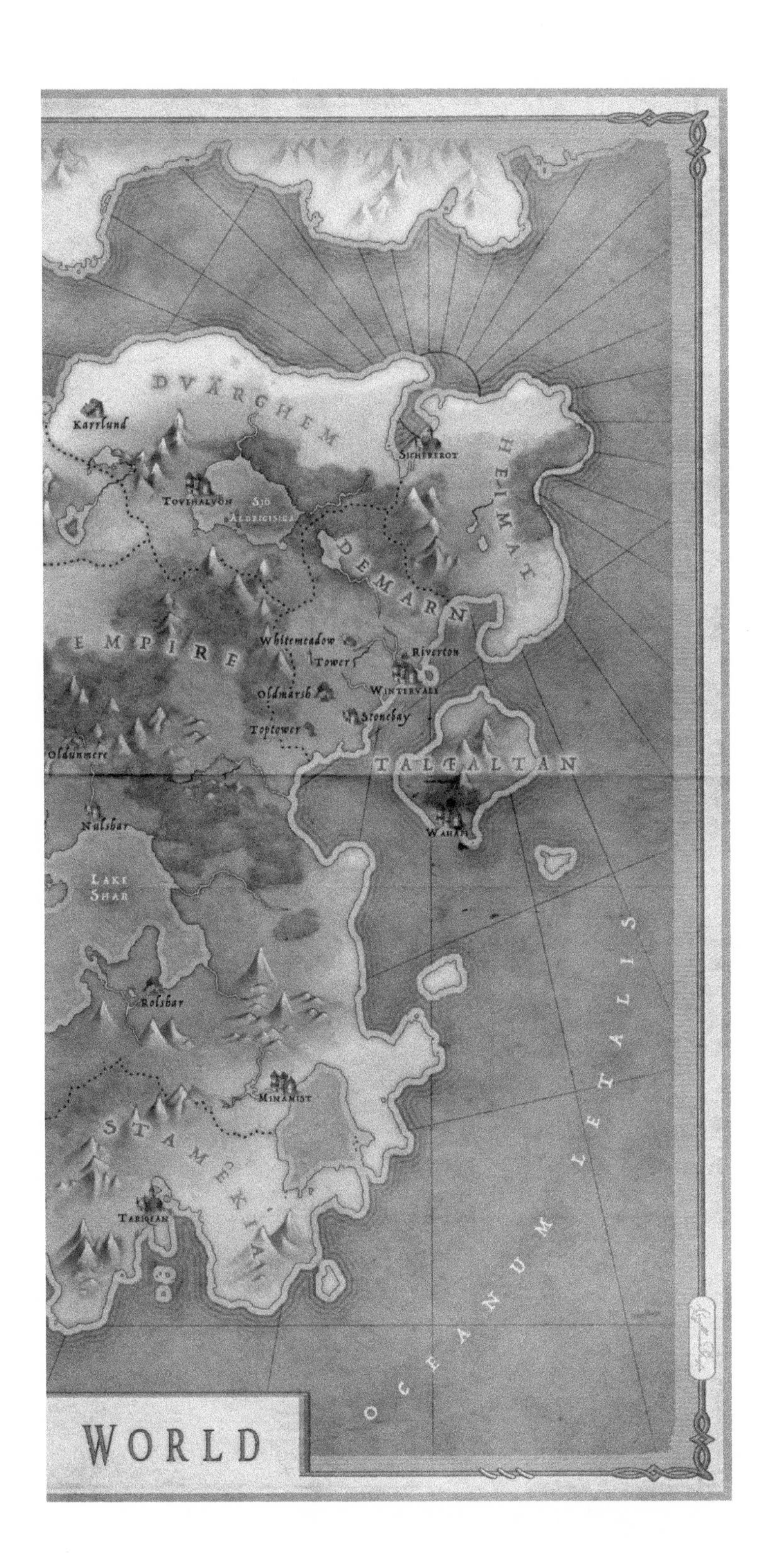
DVÄRGHEM
Karrlund
HEIMAT
DEMARN
EMPIRE
Whitemeadow
Towers
Riverton
Wintervale
Oldmarsh
Stonebay
Toptower
Oldunmere
Nulsbar
Lake Shar
Rolsbar
Minamist
STAMEKIAN
OCEANUM LETALIS
WORLD

Chapter 1

The boar fell, an arrow lodged just behind its shoulder. It kicked once, then was still.

Hamish allowed himself to breathe again. Precious few things were more dangerous than a wounded animal. He leapt across the fallen tree in his path, easily getting to the animal's side before the rest of his impromptu hunting party.

Close up, the size of the black-haired beast had him wishing he'd brought more men. The brute had given them a good run around as it was, leading them all over the forest of the western ranges, which was a challenge at the best of times. Getting the boar back through such terrain would be no small feat. The boar likely weighed as much as he did, if not more.

"By the Goddess' swollen tits," Ewan said as the rest of the farmers-turned-hunters reached the boar. He brushed back his dark hair. The day was young and, already, his hair clung in sweat-drenched clumps across his face. "Just look at the size of that monster. He's going to be a beast to carry."

The corner of Hamish's lip twitched at that. It would certainly feed a good number of the clan, perhaps even make up for the sheep they'd lost to the beast's tusks. *If* the five of them were able to get the whole carcass back to the farm, which seemed unlikely. "Are we certain this is the beast?" He'd never seen such a large boar descend from these woods and had been hesitant to bring so few into a hunt without proper preparation. His reservations had ebbed somewhat after seeing the downed fences. It would take a good-sized boar to break through the railing they'd passed downhill.

"Aye, this is the brute. See this here?" Ewan extended his spear and gave the boar a nudge in the belly. There were two prominent scratches along the animal's sides, about the right height for fence rails. "If this isnae the bastard that broke me fences, then he's keeping bad company."

"What does it matter now?" muttered one of the other men as he drew his hunting knife. "He's nae going to get any less dead, might as well get to gutting him before the bears come sniffing." The man bent over the boar's head before pausing and glancing back at Hamish. "I'd clean forget me head if it wasnae attached." He offered up his knife hilt first. "First cut goes to you, your highness."

Hamish took up the man's knife and made a swift cut across the boar's throat. Everyone knew not to take their chances with these brutes, especially when those tusks were sharp and a good doctor was some hour's march away.

It took the five of them manhandling the carcass, largely due to the fact they had to roll the beast onto its other side so gravity would help in the gutting. It left Hamish hot, sweaty and not the least bit covered in pig's blood. If ever there was a time to not get an itchy nose, this had to be one of them.

Done, they stood back and stared at the gutted beast. Usually, Hamish would have no qualms in chucking a smaller boar or deer over his shoulders and marching home with it, but this brute was nothing like the smaller prey on the edge of the woods. *Seems a shame to leave anything behind.*

"What I'd give for a cart," one of the farmers muttered.

Hamish glanced over his shoulder at where the steward, Lyall, sat upon his horse, clutching the reins of Hamish's own heavy steed. The animals had a hard time traipsing through this rough terrain without the hindrance of a cart. "I guess we lop off the good bits and be on our way."

"And—what?—leave the rest for the bears?" Ewan asked, his brows raised in incredulous horror. "Forgive me, your highness, but this winter's already been lean and me wife will go spare over the fact I'm leaving the offal behind. If I leave the bones too..." He shook his head, likely imagining his wife voicing her opinion.

"We're nae exactly equipped for carrying out everything." Not easily. None of them had been expecting to chase the damned sheep-gorer at all, let alone deep into the forest. They had no packs, no extra horses, not even a sledge. Even if they quartered the blasted thing, they would be trotting off to Ewan's home with the chunks balanced on their shoulders. Not the best position to be in if they came across a spring-hungry bear.

"Aye, that's on me." Ewan thumped a log with the toe of his boot. "Should've sent one of the lads back for proper gear."

Sighing, Hamish motioned for the steward to bring the horses closer whilst he wiped most of the blood off his hands. "Perhaps if we lash some branches together, we can drag it out." Unfortunately, there were no nearby roads. Even if they got stuck further along and had to break the boar down, then the men could hopefully come back for the rest.

Ewan nodded. "Aye, we should have more than enough rope between us for that." He hefted his wood axe and, with a jerk at a pair of the other farmers, headed for a tree with low branches.

The rest of them got to trussing the boar's legs together, their efforts punctuated by their grunts and the solid *chonk* of sharp blades hitting wood as the trio by the tree chopped down a few of the straighter branches.

There was the faintest disturbance of foliage behind him before the warm gust of a horse's breath heated Hamish's neck. He twisted to give his horse's muzzle an affectionate rub and moved on to check her saddle. "Soon, lass." Over the mare's back, Hamish caught the steward glaring at him from atop his horse. "Aye, Lyall? What is it now?"

Those pale blue eyes grew sharp and the man's lip quivered in derision. They both knew he'd only meant to visit the village to check on the damage done to Ewan's fences, not go gallivanting into the woods after the beast responsible. "It seems that his highness has forgotten that the ambassador is to arrive today. And that her Majesty expressly stated the presence of all her children was required when the ship comes in, which was sighted at dawn."

Hamish groaned. This had to be the third ambassador to visit Tirglas in a year. Clearly, his mother was being a little more aggressive in scouting foreign nobility for a potential bride to wed him off to. It didn't even seem to matter that the woman was also an uncloistered spellster. "I didnae forget," he muttered, turning his full attention back to the men lashing a crude sledge from the felled branches. How could he have possibly forgotten when the man reminded him at every opportunity?

With the sledge complete, they fastened the poles to either side of his horse before hefting the boar onto the framework and used every last length of available rope to secure the beast.

"You promised her Majesty you'd be there," Lyall pressed as Hamish swung into the saddle.

Hamish nodded, absently adjusting the straps securing his bow. "Aye, I did." He nudged his mare into a steady walk. Maybe the men would discover the tracks of yet another monster boar that could've been the fence-destroying culprit. So long as it was something Hamish could spend the better part of the day hunting down with them. By the Goddess, if the steward wasn't babysitting him, Hamish wouldn't have given a thought towards seeking home until night had well and truly settled in.

Lyall rode alongside him. He stroked his beard, curling the black and grey end around his finger. "You'll barely reach the castle before them at this rate. Forget meeting the ship at the docks." He shook his head. "Will you at least clean yourself up before greeting the ambassador?"

Hamish smiled at the old man. "I thought you said I didnae have time?" Maybe turning up covered in pig blood would help deter the woman from heeding any of his mother's daft plans. Then again, the ambassador was from the Udynea Empire, she'd probably mistake it for a proposal.

Their passage through the woods was slow, hampered every so often by the need to heft the sledge over the odd piece of treacherously uneven ground. The woods seemed to still with their passage, though he caught the occasional flash of bigger animals. Deer, at least he hoped so. With spring settling in, the bears would be wandering the valleys in search of food. If any were nearby, the hulking beasts would hopefully make for the gutted remains before bothering them.

They stuck to the gentler hills, making their way around the steeper sections they'd originally traipsed over to spare any extra strain to the horses. His mare might've been a heavy animal, capable of spending long days crashing through the woods after sprightlier prey, but she was no plough horse accustomed to dragging dead weight.

Slowly, the land they trod became less wild. Trees stopped pressing in on each other, the undergrowth thinned and the slope of the earth evened to a gentle downhill incline. The familiar bleating of sheep grew louder, punctuated by the fainter call of cattle. Hamish slowed his mare and allowed the men to lead the way to the farm, deferring to their knowledge of walking along paths frequently travelled.

The men picked up their pace and, before long, the shattered remnants of the fence became visible through the sparse trees. With a little rearranging of the already-broken rails to fit their crude sledge, Hamish continued on through the open field with the steward and Ewan whilst the rest of the farmers returned to their repairs of the fence.

Unhindered by brush or trees, their passage over the hills remained smooth and swift. The bleating of sheep grew louder as they neared Ewan's farmhouse. When he had first arrived, the locals were attempting to herd the remaining flock into the pens.

Hamish scanned the gently rolling hills. There could easily be a few tucked away in the hollows, but it seemed they'd been successful.

His mother would be glad, for the less sheep the people lost to wild animals, the less the crown had to reimburse them.

They crested the brow of the hill that'd blocked the sight of the farmhouse. Sheep milled around the buildings like impatient clouds. Children and dogs darted amongst the flock, driving some into the nearby barn and others into pens where adults waited for the animals.

The activity slowed as they neared and curiosity drew people's attention from their tasks.

One of the women—which Hamish presumed was Ewan's wife—hastened out of the pens to meet them. "Is that the blighter responsible for ruining me fences?" she asked of the man, tilting her torso to peer around Hamish's horse. "He's a fair brute, isnae he?" She turned her attention to them, swinging her head from side to side as she seemed to count them. "Didnae more of you leave this morning? Where'd the rest of you lot go to? Are they all right?"

"Aye, they're fine," Ewan replied. "They'll be back once they're done with fixing the fence. Until then, it'd best if we moved the flock to the lower fields. I could do with a few of the young ones to help me dress this beast. They could use the experience." He jerked a thumb at the boar.

Nodding, the woman strode back towards the pen to bellow orders at the people milling around there.

A few of the younger folk hurried over to help with removing the sledge from behind Hamish's horse. They dragged it towards the farmhouse, grunting all the way.

Ewan watched their efforts, a small smile tweaking his lips as he shook his head. Shielding the sun from his face with a hand, he looked up at Hamish. "Are you sure about leaving the boar behind, your highness? It's your kill."

"I'm sure." He lifted his gaze from the farmer's face to take in those of the man's family and neighbours. "You'll all need it more than I will. Especially once winter settles in." They'd a few months yet of growth and harvest, but the chance of them retrieving the stock they'd lost through the downed fence was barely worth the thought.

"Thank you, again. I'm nae certain we'd have caught the bugger so easily without your help."

Hamish laughed. "You thought that was easy?" Granted, he'd taken on tougher prey, but not after traipsing several hours through untamed woods for it. "Maybe I should be bringing you on me hunts."

The man ducked his head, but Hamish caught the faint gleam of delight in his eyes. "Anytime, your highness."

"If you need any extra help in dressing—" Hamish cut himself off as Lyall cleared his throat. He glared at the man.

"Has his highness perhaps forgotten he is meant to be meeting the Udynean ambassador?" Lyall asked, his face innocently neutral.

Hamish fought for his own features to remain so calm. *Why cannae you just forget?* If the steward would remain lax in reminding him, he'd be able to put off the meeting until tomorrow. "Aye, I had." It took some effort to not have his teeth grind on each word. "Thank you for reminding me." *Again*. Nodding his goodbyes to Ewan, he kneed his horse into a trot.

Lyall kept an easy pace with him. "May I also remind you that you are currently covered in pig's blood? You're nae going to reach the docks, so you might as well take the time to clean yourself up before the rest of your family returns to the castle."

Grumbling under his breath, Hamish kneed the mare into a canter. Whatever else Lyall said was drowned out in the thunder of hooves. By the Goddess' good graces, he was thirty-seven years old, not some child still tied to their mother's apron strings. As much as it would've amused him to see the look on the ambassador's face if he greeted her in his current state, it wouldn't be worth the bollocking he'd get for it later.

He thundered along the dirt roads leading towards home. Mullhind Castle loomed over them, a hulking stone beast atop the hill. Below her, and ahead of Hamish, lay Mullhind itself. The city sprawled across the western side of the harbour, sheltered by the natural hook shape of the land.

His horse veered around the outskirts of the city, taking a path they'd raced across many times, jumping a few fences and logs along the way. At his back, Hamish caught the tail end of the steward's exasperated cry. He ignored the man and urged his mare to go faster. If Lyall wanted to take the long, winding way through the city, he was welcome to it.

Hamish slowed his mare as her hooves clattered onto the cobblestone. They trotted along the streets that butted up against the cliff face. The castle sat just above them, a clear upward climb if he'd wings.

The streets fell away swiftly enough, opening out into the city square. Free of their confines, he nudged the horse faster to race up the slope leading to the castle gates. It followed the natural curvature of the hillside, sweeping to give him a full view of the city and harbour.

Hamish glanced at the docks far below him to confirm what he already knew. The huge Udynean ship sat proudly in the harbour, her sails furled and likely with all travellers disembarked. He urged a little more speed into his mare. He'd be cutting it fine, but he could reach the castle in time to swap his bloodied clothes for clean ones.

The castle gates came into view.

He slowed his horse. Far too many people milled near the entrance for his family to still be at the docks. That had to mean the ship docked early. He hadn't much chance of slipping by unnoticed, either. That meant meeting the ambassador as he was. *Bugger.* His mother was going to give him a right dressing down once they were alone.

No point delaying the inevitable. He nudged his mare onwards, hunching his shoulders as the gate loomed. Maybe he could duck into his quarters after introductions and avoid his mother's lecturing. For a few more hours, anyway.

A mob of people bustled about the courtyard, his family at the centre. His mother had her back to the gate, heavily invested in talking with a man in a long, silvery-white coat and red cape. Probably the ambassador's steward or whatever the Udynean equivalent was called. Of the ambassador herself, he saw no sign. Not that it meant much. A whole person could hide behind his father's enormous bulk.

Hamish quietly guided his mare along the stable front, skirting open stable doors and scattering the odd discarded piece of grooming kit. If he could get his horse into her stall, he might stand a chance of slipping into the castle before anyone noticed his presence.

He'd almost made it when his brother glanced his way. Gordon's mouth split into a wide grin as recognition lit his face. He jogged over, drawing the attention of a young stablehand who was instantly at Hamish's side to relieve him of the mare's reins.

"Good to see you could make it," Gordon said. "I thought for sure that you'd gone bush on us."

Hamish wordlessly dismounted.

His brother's brows lifted to their highest. "By the Goddess' sweet name, what have you been up to?"

"Ewan's farm," Hamish replied, jerking a thumb back the way he'd come. "Boar took out all the leeward fences."

His brother nodded. "Aye, I ken you were going to check the damage. But what's all this?" He gestured to Hamish's attire. The pig's blood had dried on the trip out of the woods, but it'd left dark marks all across the soft brown leather of Hamish's hunting jacket.

Hamish self-consciously brushed at where the tunic hem was unprotected by his jacket. His trousers, baggy in the traditional style, were also liberally smeared with blood and dirt. The laundry workers would no doubt give his ear quite the chewing once it was known. "We tracked down the boar. He'll nae be destroying much but a wee bit of hunger now."

Gordon clapped his hand on Hamish's shoulder. "Well, you missed the ambassador's arrival."

"Did I?" Hamish finally relinquished the reins to the waiting stablehand. He nodded his thanks to the lad and turned back to Gordon as his horse was led into her stall. "I'm fair heartbroken."

His brother beamed. "You might be when you see who they sent us."

Who? Hamish peered at his brother, trying to decipher just what had put that gleeful twinkle into his normally stark green eyes. "I thought it was just some countess?" He glanced back at his parents and the man they were speaking with. No woman at all beyond his mother. Including his sister. "Where did Nora scamper off to?" Granted, she wasn't much one for the false niceties of politics, but if Hamish was expected to be here, then so was she.

"Herding the troublesome trio to lessons, where else?"

"And your daughter?" At twelve years of age, Sorcha was more than old enough to begin the training that would eventually lead to her taking the throne after her father. Even if she did prefer stalking deer to politics.

"She's probably the one leading them astray, as always." Still grinning, Gordon shook his head. "Come on. Mum's head is practically exploding trying to be civil about the change." His brother chuckled and pulled him in close. "Let's see if we can still make that dam burst."

"Nae that I'm complaining about her absence," Hamish said, choosing his words carefully as they veered within earshot of his parents. "But did something happen to the original ambassador they were sending?" He'd admit to a few unfair prayers sent her way, but it wasn't her fault his mother played matchmaker with him and every single noblewoman.

His brother shrugged. "He said she couldnae make it."

"*He?*" Hamish echoed. His gaze flicked back to the man chatting with his parents, barely seen around his father's shoulder. *That* was the ambassador? They'd sent a man? After his mother no doubt requested the ambassador be a woman? Small wonder she was fair fuming.

He rounded the crowd, hoping to get a good look at the ambassador to determine just what sort of man their kingdom would be dealing with.

His silvery-white coat remained closed without any noticeable way of doing so. No metal buttons like Hamish's own attire, nothing visible at least. What Hamish had first mistaken to be a cape appeared to be a shawl. The red fabric hung over one shoulder, winding behind him to hang in the crook of his other arm. The way it draped spoke of him being very conscious that the golden thread embroidered along the edges be visible to everyone.

The man's whole outfit seemed to scream the same thing. Luxury. The silvery-white garb halted at his knees to reveal matching trousers that hugged his figure far more than the voluminous fabric encasing Hamish's own legs. All of it was heavily embroidered in a sort of floral motif with gems stitched into the design. The stones sparkled in the noon light and made the man look very much like a cheap trinket.

No one, not even Hamish's own mother, looked quite so… gaudy. If he planned on impressing anyone in Tirglas with such an obvious display of wealth, he'd quickly learn that bearing weapons and proving he knew how to use them would work far better.

"Aha!" Hamish's father bellowed. He'd turned sometime during Hamish's scrutiny and now singled Hamish out with one thick finger. "There's me missing son. Come, lad." His father beckoned him closer, clapping a hand onto the ambassador's shoulder, which had Hamish wincing in sympathy right alongside the man. To the uninitiated, his father had quite the grip.

The ambassador turned, his brow arched in curiosity, and froze. On his face sat an odd metal framework encasing a pair of small clear discs like windows for his eyes. From behind these eye-windows, the man's gaze flicked over Hamish in apparent disinterest, widening to reveal a multitude of colours as they slowly traverse back up Hamish's body before making eye contact. A ring of black darkened the edge of his eyelids, making the whites that much brighter and his eyes seem huge.

"This is our ambassador, Darshan *vris Mhanek*." His father fumbled with the foreign words. What could be seen of his face through the thick and greying, dark red beard was screwed up in concentration.

Hamish knew as much as any Tirglasian did about the Udynea Empire, which wasn't a lot. But he knew what those words meant, or at least in part. *Not just any ambassador, then.* The empire had sent a prince in place of the countess. He held out his hand and bowed slightly, getting his height as close to the man's and then a little lower. "Welcome to Tirglas, your imperial highness."

The ambassador continued to stare at Hamish. His eyes had glazed over, much like a deer stunned by a glancing arrow. One brow lifted and the slight twitch of his moustache suggested a restrained smile. There was the faint suggestion of a beard trying to break free, tamed to barely cover his chin and cleft. At least they hadn't sent some clean-shaven boy to negotiate these new trade agreements.

He waited patiently for the man's brain to catch up with his ears. He'd heard from the other ambassadors that the Tirglasian accent made it difficult for some foreigners to understand, that certain inflections took a while to grasp.

Then, Darshan blinked and a soft redness touched his olive-brown cheeks. His gaze flicked to Hamish's outstretched hand, which Hamish only now realised still showed traces of pig blood. The man's gaze shifted, clearly taking in Hamish's blood-stained attire.

Grinning sheepishly, Hamish wiped his palm clean on the side of his trousers and offered his hand again.

The ambassador slowly accepted the gesture, the rings adorning his fingers glittering in the noon light.

Hamish couldn't help noticing how the man's slim fingers lacked anything in the way of calluses. Not a warrior, then. Not in the traditional sense, at least. Udynean nobles were strong spellsters and a prince would certainly be one of the more powerful.

"H-hello," the man mumbled, his tongue barely able to utter the greeting. "Uh..."

"Hamish," he offered, giving the man's hand a reassuring squeeze.

The man cleared his throat, his face growing redder. He ducked his head, the soft curls of his dark brown hair bobbed. "Darshan." The word came out soft and crisp.

"So I've heard." Still, it was nice to hear the name spoken by its owner and not mangled by his father.

Another faint blush took the man's cheeks. "It is an absolute pleasure to meet you, your highness." He spoke Tirglasian quite smoothly, with the influence of his tutors lingering in the slight rolling tones. There was the hint of a musical note in the words that suggested his natural voice wasn't used to being quite this harsh.

Hamish straightened and slowly released his grip on Darshan's hand. "I do apologise for me absence. I was told your ship wouldnae get in before the afternoon."

"Yes," his mother interjected, coolly slipping between them. She glanced his way, the icy depths of her blue eyes flashing their customary warning whenever he was near a man of unknown background. "We were all taken aback by the unexpected fair winds that rocked the harbour this early morning."

"I am no sailor," Darshan admitted as if it weren't completely obvious that his perfectly-manicured hands had never held anything rougher than silk. "But the winds did seem to favour us towards the end." The longer he talked, the less stilted his accent became. Each word gained a rich, velvety tone and a softness that had Hamish's mind briefly meandering into forbidden depths.

It wasn't until Darshan cleared his throat a little louder than necessary that Hamish realised the man had still been talking. "Sorry," he said. "It's been a long day, you ken? You were saying?"

Brief panic flickered across the man's face before his expression turned neutral, although his gaze darted all over the place. "I… believe I understood that, yes. I merely mentioned that—"

"How oddly the sailors reacted," his mother interjected, her brow furrowing as she eyed Hamish. "Dinnae blame them. In all me life, I've never seen the winds shift eastward for another month or so." She placed a hand on the ambassador's back, turning him. "Come, your imperial highness. You must be weary after such a long journey. I'll have one of the servants escort you to the guest quarters."

Darshan eyed the castle with barely-concealed dismay. Had he been expecting it to look different? Or was he not yet ready to settle? If Hamish ever found himself in a foreign land, sleep would've been the last thing on his mind.

"Why doesnae Hamish show him the way?" Gordon suggested. "Since he missed the ambassador's arrival."

Hamish fixed his brother with a very pointed stare. What was he thinking? Their mother would never allow him to be alone with Darshan without her believing he was bending over for the man. He didn't want to be responsible for another ambassador's swift banishment. Especially when they were also a Udynean prince.

Their mother's head whipped around, causing the end of one honey blonde braid to slap her shoulder. She glared daggers at Gordon, who smiled innocently back. It was a facade that Hamish envied at times. Being the eldest, his brother got away with more than he felt was fair at times.

It didn't help matters that Gordon would use that leeway to needle Hamish and had done constantly ever since his brother found him kissing one of the stable boys back when he was a lad. Thankfully, Gordon always stopped short of outright suggesting anything that couldn't be innocently construed.

The ambassador continued to stare at the castle, oblivious to the silent berating going on in his midst. Hamish took the man's preoccupation as an opportunity to re-evaluate him.

If Darshan had been a Tirglasian, his attire would've been considered a frivolous waste, but the rumours of Udynea suggested they'd plenty of a great many things. It likely hadn't occurred to him, although there was a spark of cunning in his eyes that hinted at more. Especially in the way the man's stare didn't settle on one spot. That muddy-brown gaze roved across the castle walls, followed several of the servants and guards, and flicked towards the stables before sliding to the front gate. Calculating.

Hamish just wished he knew if the man was looking for weaknesses to relay in an attack or searching for a way out should his mother renege on the man's protection. Unlike Udynea, Tirglasian spellsters were sent off to spend their days in cloisters, their healing talents called upon only in times of dire need.

Trying not to startle a man that was likely capable of spewing fire, Hamish nudged the ambassador's shoulder. Attention got, he jerked his head towards the castle door. "Come on, it willnae take long to show you the way, then you can get back to staring at our defences."

A small, slightly sheepish, smile creased the man's eyes. He inclined his head and indicated Hamish lead the way with the sweep of one bejewelled hand.

Chapter 2

Darshan remained silent as he followed Hamish into the castle. Although he'd learnt the local language during the trip from his home on the other side of the continent to the Tirglasian capital of Mullhind, he wasn't entirely confident in himself to utter much coherently at the moment.

His father had also seen to it that he was briefed during the trip, but it had been in simple things, common customs alongside their current political and economic standings and the like. They'd even touched on a few cultural differences to help him avoid any major gaffes.

No one seemed to have had the wherewithal to prepare him for the introduction of the hulking man currently leading him through the castle corridors.

Confident his actions would be less obvious than his previous appraisal of the courtyard, he took another sweeping glance at Hamish. Tall, he'd wager a full foot more than himself, if not slightly more. Quite a bit of flesh on that frame, too. Muscle rather than fat, if those broad, brown shoulders and thick arms were any judge as to the state of the rest.

Even the man's hair didn't shirk at being big and bold. The whole glorious fiery, orange-red mass of coils had been gathered at the back of the man's head and, rather than hang down, it stuck out like a flag caught in a zephyr. Darshan could quite clearly picture sinking his fingers into those curls whilst—

No, he softly cautioned himself before his thoughts could meander into predictable places. *You can't go doing that to yourself again.* Nevertheless, his gaze indulgently slunk down the man's back, settling on Hamish's behind. He subtly unbuttoned the collar of his outfit. *Behave*. The gods might've had a sense of humour, sending him to the pit of the world then populating it with men like this, but he wasn't some savage with no self-control. *You're here for a reason.* He bit his lip and stifled a sigh. Sadly, that reason wasn't to sleep with the locals.

Not that such a minor detail had stopped him before. If this was anywhere other than Tirglas, he likely would've already propositioned the man. Perhaps even had a chance to feel what was under all that clothing.

"And here we are," Hamish announced, jolting Darshan out of his little fantasies.

Darshan scrutinised their surroundings. Nothing about the corridor suggested there was any difference to the rest of the castle they had walked through. It was all the same bare slabs of stone. Even the door Hamish gestured to sat part way down the corridor instead of at the end, which it would've done had Darshan ventured into the guest wing back home. How ever did the people get around without becoming altogether lost?

Hamish faced him as he opened the door to what Darshan could only assume to be the guest accommodations. "I doubt it's quite what you're used to, your imperial highness, but it'll be better than a ship's cabin."

Offering up a small smile, Darshan casually leant on the doorframe in a vain attempt at pretending his legs hadn't just weakened at the mere sound of the man's smooth brogue. At least he had gained a little more control over himself. Having his mind go blank on all bar one subject had been mildly mortifying, especially over a simple greeting. *Get a grip.* This man was likely married, with children. *What an utter waste.* Still, his father had made his stance on Darshan's dalliances with already-spoken-for men quite plain.

"It might be a wee while before you get your land legs back." One side of Hamish's beard twitched as the corner of his lips lifted with amusement. "I'd take it carefully for the rest of the day if I were you."

Before now, Darshan hadn't seen many thick beards. Not that men around Minamist didn't grow full beards if they so chose, but they were typically on much older men. Yet here… all the men seemed to sport one, be they working on the docks or guarding the castle. It somewhat served to make him feel a little underdressed, with his carefully-groomed moustache and goatee. None of his tutors had mentioned anything pertaining to an expected look.

"I guess I'll leave you be," Hamish continued. "You probably want to get settled in before someone comes to call you for dinner." That glorious sapphiric gaze lifted to briefly meet Darshan's, stunning him all over again, before falling away.

Like gems. Darshan used to scoff at those who dared such a trite comparison, but he'd never before met someone for whom the phrase rang true. The most lovingly cut blue aquamarine stone couldn't compete with the crisp shade of the man's eyes. Gods, it put the very ocean to shame. Coupled with the way they almost shyly peeked out from beneath the muted orange shade of his lashes, it rather seemed like Darshan had somehow sinned just meeting them.

With great difficulty, Darshan tore his gaze from the man to give a cursory glance around the room that would be his for the next few weeks. The bare stone walls were illuminated only by the light streaming through a single eastward window. Whilst his travelling chest had been whisked from the ship upon their arrival, he hadn't expected it to be sitting in the far corner. *Efficient*. The palace servants would've been hard-pressed to match such a speed.

Sparse came to mind as he took in the meagre furniture; a bed and a small table. Functional did, too. That rather sat in line with what his tutors had briefed him on. He should've expected the Tirglasian guest rooms would look more akin to the palace dungeons back home than his own lavish bedchamber.

Darshan turned back to his guide, stilling the man with a gentle hand on that very-much-toned bicep. The warmth of the man's bare skin sent a fluttering spark through Darshan's fingertips straight to his groin. He bit his lip to stifle a whimper at the passing thought of how easily the man would be able to lift a person. "Hamish, was it?" he managed.

"It is, aye."

"I was wondering..." Darshan mumbled before catching himself. Good grief, had that breathy tone actually come out of his mouth? *Really now, this is just embarrassing*. Next thing he'd find himself fawning all over the man like some simpering concubine. Pushing off the doorframe, he cleared his throat and tried again. "I would very much like to see some of your city." He had originally considered remaining confined to the guest quarters, but now he had seen it? The thought of remaining here more than he needed to felt terribly constricting. "And I think a guided tour would be best at this moment. If you are of a mind?"

"Sure." Hamish grinned as he spread his hands, indicating his bloodstained clothing. "But let me clean meself up first."

Darshan inclined his head, his cheeks heating ever-so-slightly. He had rather forgotten about the man's less than immaculate attire after the first word had left Hamish's mouth. Clearly, the man had been indulging in what Darshan's tutors had taught him was the local pastime here.

Hamish went to leave, then swung back around in the corridor to eye Darshan. "And you might want to change into something plainer if you have it."

He reluctantly lowered his gaze from the giant of a man to his own clothes. In cut, his sherwani wasn't terribly different from the overcoat Hamish wore, knee-length where the man's attire stopped mid-thigh. And, of course, the fabric was leagues apart. Hamish's overcoat looked to be made of soft leather whilst all of Darshan's clothing was either silk or fine linen.

"Do I look so out of place?" he finally enquired. He thought this particular sherwani *was* plain. It had very little in the way of gemstones and the embroidery was limited to the fabric edges and his shoulders. He had a few stark outfits in his travel chest, but he had packed them in the off chance he'd need to travel beyond the city limits. "You seemed shocked to see me earlier."

"To be fair, aye, you do. But by the way the court's been talking, everyone was expecting a woman."

"You mean Countess Harini." Darshan nodded. He'd had only brief conversations with her whilst in court, but he knew what had become of her. "She *was* supposed to take up this duty. Sadly, she had the poor taste to... uh..." He gnawed on the inside of his lip, trying to remember the correct word. "I do not believe I was taught the Tirglasian equivalent," he mumbled. His tutors had been diligent in focusing on more than the phrases he would need for the coming negotiations, but there were a few words they'd skimmed.

Hamish waited. Silently polite just as when the man had introduced himself.

A fresh flush of heat washed over Darshan's cheeks. He could stand there all day and still be no closer to the word he wanted. Technically correct would have to do. "She was... slain." He waved his hand, his mind racing for the words to explain. "A political affair. Terribly ill-mannered of her, of course."

"Political?" the man echoed, his brows lowering in thought.

Darshan rather wished they hadn't when Hamish's sapphiric gaze also disappeared beneath his lashes.

"You mean she was assassinated?"

"Ah!" Darshan grinned, immensely pleased he'd managed to get across what had transpired. "You *do* have a word for it, after all. *Splendid*."

"And that's ill-mannered?"

"Of course. She should have had ample power to counter any attack on her person." Unless those attacks had come from one of the Nulled Ones, who were immune to direct magic. But the Nulled Ones served his father. "It is not as if we are a bunch of barbarians." On the other hand, his father was the type of man to eliminate barriers for his son. And it had seemed a little too convenient for the woman to die at the precise time Darshan was to be sent far from his homeland.

"Says the slaver," Hamish replied, his voice flat.

Warning bells rang in his head. That was a topic he had been advised to speak sparsely on, if at all. "Heard about that, have you?" He wasn't surprised. Every northerner he had ever spoken to seemed to be fond of pointing out the same fact, as if Darshan had no idea in regards to the status of the people around him.

"Doesnae everyone ken Udynea is the centre of the slave trade?" Hamish asked. It could've been the accent, but the question certainly sounded sarcastic.

"The *centre*, yes. But not the only country that deals in it." Whilst his homeland's neighbouring empires weren't as large, Niholia and Stamekia both had a thriving slave trade. Yet, their trading in people also seemed to go largely unnoticed. At least by northerners. Geography likely had something to do with that, with the Udynea Empire taking up much of the continent.

"Do *you* have slaves?"

Darshan didn't bother trying to hide his wry smile. There went his hopes of a stay in pleasant company. "Going straight for the personal questions, I see." Sighing, Darshan rubbed at his temple. "I am certain you can deduce the answer there—and, should you wish to continue this conversation at another time, I will be quite willing to accommodate you—but I would prefer to discuss it when I have *not* just spent several months travelling aboard a wretched sea-going tub."

"Fair enough," the man muttered. "I'll meet you in the courtyard in about an hour. You can find your way back, right?"

Darshan inclined his head, not at all keen to admit he'd been far too preoccupied in studying Hamish's backside than the route they'd taken, especially not to the man in question. If it came down to it, he would enquire as to the proper direction from one of the servants.

He waited until the door closed and the sound of footsteps faded before he plonked onto the bed, grunting at the solidness of his landing. Already, he missed his bed back home with its goose down mattress. He dug the heel of his hand into the bedding. At least it didn't seem like straw. Wool, most likely. *Marvellous.*

Rubbing at his cheeks with a hand, he gave the room a more in-depth look. The window was at his back, throwing his shadow over an open fireplace set into the opposite wall. A stack of wood had been piled nearby. That looked freshly done. No doubt in preparation for his arrival. Or Countess Harini's, at least. Either way, he wouldn't be expected to freeze.

He had also missed the full-length dressing mirror upon his initial perusal and the sight did gladden him somewhat. Still… had this been home, the walls wouldn't have been able to breathe for tapestries, murals and paintings. There would've been tables and seats aplenty as well as an entire room for his clothes to hang. And, whilst this window at least had curtains, the imperial palace would have made a show of using the richest, gauziest fabric a man could make rather than what looked to be the remnants of a blanket.

This is going to be a long month. A blustery sigh bubbled against his hand.

Some ambassador he was. He had barely set foot on foreign soil and, already, the call to return home ran strongly through his blood. It wasn't just the luxuries of the palace he had left behind. The very air seemed off. *Wet in the wrong way.* Home could be humid more often than not, but this was the kind of damp that clung to stone and promised rain.

He had already spent several wretched months aboard the blasted rocking coffin they dared to call a ship—crewed entirely by women at his father's request. His stomach still hadn't quite settled from that journey, but he would gladly suffer it twofold for a chance to leave Tirglas sooner.

And he could, in all likelihood, get the trade agreements sorted within a few weeks, but that would vastly depend on Queen Fiona's willingness to accept the starting terms his father had laid out for him to offer. And that was unlikely.

Grumbling under his breath, Darshan hauled himself to his feet. If he was going to leave this wretched place swiftly, then giving the docks and markets a more thorough look would be a good place to start.

He dug into his travel chest and hauled out the plainest sherwani he'd brought. The silk was creased from its time folded into a neat parcel. *Wonderful.* He somehow doubted the local servants knew how to treat such fabric. What passed for royalty here certainly didn't dress all that extravagantly.

It took little effort to switch out one top half for another. The tiny, diamond-studded buttons parted as he wove his magic through them in a manoeuvre he had long since perfected. He shrugged out of the sleeves and tossed the sherwani atop the bed. The muted chill in the air nibbled at his skin through his undershirt.

He checked himself in the mirror as he fastened the plainer top's silver buttons, seeing his outfit properly perhaps for the first time. The cut wasn't too outlandish for the area; almost tunic-like simple without the heavy embellishment of thick embroidery and gems. Even without that, the shimmering white fabric would have him standing out like a black snake in the sand. If he'd been planning to stay for longer than a few weeks, he would've sought something closer to the native attire. As things stood, there was little point.

Garbed, he ventured out into the corridors. Finding his way down to the courtyard took far longer than he would dare admit to anyone, even after asking for the way… thrice. His every move seemed to be watched by someone, be they servants or animals—never before had he encountered dogs almost as big as himself.

The courtyard was no longer as full as it'd been upon his arrival. The horses the royal family had ridden all appeared to have been stabled. Of Hamish, there was no sign.

Darshan briefly considered that the man had gone looking for him, or had perhaps given up on waiting for his arrival, before venturing into the stables. Whilst Mullhind was the biggest city in Tirglas, it might as well have been a village in comparison to Udynean towns. He didn't believe he'd get easily lost, so if he couldn't get a guided tour, then a solitary one would have to do.

That, of course, depended on whether he could borrow one of the horses.

He poked his head around the open door. Rows of occupied stalls filled the building. His ears were greeted by the gentle sounds of animals eating and the heavy shuffling of hooves.

It seemed rather quiet for a castle stable. He had barely been near the palace stables, and even then only as a boy, but it was always bustling with stable hands attending to the tack or the horses. Here, there was no one.

One of the nearby horses, a heavy black and white beast of a thing, nickered at him with the curiously hopeful note of imminent food. He had travelled to the castle via cart, a simple one that likely served to carry sacks and barrels most of the time. It had been pulled by a massive beast such as this.

Darshan stepped into the building to give the place a more in-depth look. He couldn't even spy a single soul checking a hoof or leg for soundness. *Odd.* Had he somehow managed to arrive whilst everyone was on break?

The black and white horse stretched out its neck and lipped at his hand, sniffing at his clothes in heavy blasts of hot breath.

Chuckling, he gently rubbed the pink muzzle. "Sorry, greedy one. I have no treats on me."

A faint grunt came from the other end of the stalls.

"Hello?" His call echoed.

"Darshan?" Hamish's grinning visage appeared from the far stall. "I thought you were nae coming. Got a pony all geared up for you." He led out a hairy barrel on four legs. Like the beast Darshan stood next to, it was mostly black with splashes of white and great hair-clad hooves.

"You can ride Warrior," Hamish continued. "He's me niece's pony, but I'm sure Sorcha willnae mind you borrowing him." He gave the animal a heavy pat on the shoulder and grinned at Darshan. "Dinnae let the name fool you. He's as gentle as they come."

Darshan eyed the animal. Warrior might've been smaller than the monstrous horse Hamish had arrived on—with a little room to spare between Warrior's wither and Hamish's armpit—but if that animal was a pony, then he was an elf. The animal stood almost as high as himself. He could barely peer over Warrior's back. "Is everything in this kingdom so *frutzian* huge?" he muttered.

Hamish arched a brow in silent enquiry. Quite possibly in part due to the usage of a Udynean word that didn't generally get used in polite company.

Darshan waved his hand about. "I mean the horses, the hills..." His gaze slid Hamish's way and a flush of heat touched his cheeks as he mumbled, "The men." He cleared his throat, hoping the Tirglasian hadn't caught that. "A little forewarning that this was a land of giants would have been nice. Is it something in the water? What you eat? What—?" He stalled as the man started laughing. "Did I say something amusing?"

Wheezing in an attempt to halt his laughter, Hamish draped himself over the pony's back. "We're nae giants."

"I beg to differ." There were men of all heights in Udynea, but people this statuesque weren't considered the norm. "Your father must be over seven feet tall."

Hamish wiped his eyes with the back of a finger. "That's a good guess. I wouldnae say he was *over*, though. But they're all tall in his clan."

"Clan?" Darshan had vague recollections of such from late night lessons in his cramped quarters aboard the ship.

Hamish frowned. "They live out on the plains near the Cezhory border. Lots of cattle, I hear." He tilted his head, puzzlement furrowing his brow as he eyed Darshan. "But I thought you would already ken that? What with being an ambassador and all?"

"Yes," he admitted. And Countess Harini probably did have quite a bit more knowledge than what had been crammed into his head during the journey here. "But I *was* recruited at the last minute." If he hadn't been so foolish back home, he would still be there. And the countess would likely still be alive to do her duty.

"Oh aye?" The man grinned broadly, the expression shaping his beard until it mimicked the long-haired hounds Darshan had encountered on the way here. "Well then, this should be an education for you."

"I welcome it." Years had come and gone since anything as

challenging as this position had reared its head.

Leaving Warrior to stand placidly in the middle of the stables, Hamish disappeared into another stall and returned with the same massive horse Darshan had seen him arrive on. "Is there any place in particular you're wishing to visit or are we just doing a general tour of the area?"

"I would rather like to see the docks." Father often said that facts were better checked firsthand and, no matter how honest a people claimed to be, there was always something hidden in the dark.

The man glanced up from where he was adjusting the horse's tack. "But you just came from there. I thought you'd want to stay away from ships and waves."

Darshan inclined his head. He was utterly sick of both those things. "I would like to see a little more, if you do not mind." There were few places where he would get a better idea of the kingdom's commerce than the docks. But he'd seen very little of the area on his arrival. Queen Fiona had taken one look at him and whisked the entire greeting party back to the castle so fast that he was surprised he didn't have scorching on his heels.

Hamish shrugged and swung into the saddle. "Suit yourself. But if we're leaving, we should do it before someone realises we're missing and comes looking."

"Quite." The last thing he wanted was any manner of formal tour, especially involving guards. That would hardly give him the truest outlook of Mullhind.

Clambering onto Warrior's back, Darshan followed the man's brisk pace out of the castle gates. There were a number of guards at the entrance. But whilst the men eyed them, not a one made any move to stop them from leaving.

The road leading to the city wound down the hillside, clearly taking a path once trod by wildlife. In Minamist, this sauntering journey would never stand. The rock would have been moulded by labour and magic, these naturally easy curves eradicated in favour of stark lines and high-arching bridges.

Darshan's gaze swung towards the harbour. From their position high on the hillside, the ocean lay spread before them like an undulating rug. He breathed deep, taking some small comfort in the familiar salt tang in the breeze. *Too cold.* Even with spring rearing its head, he would need to invest in warmer undergarments if the negotiations dragged on.

Home might've boasted a fabulous view of the sea-green ocean in the south, but it was nothing as all-encompassing as this. The Imperial Palace had no clear line of sight to the docks. Nor did his homeland have any towering hills or cliffs upon which to perch on like a Niholian sea-diving hawk. It was a structure designed with only luxury and segregation in mind. Whereas Mullhind Castle was clearly built to withstand a siege inside and out. Even concentrated magic would be hard-pressed to do more than dent the walls.

When the next gentle curve in the road turned them away from the sea, Darshan let his gaze wander across the city itself. He tried to follow the roads with his eye, not an easy thing to attempt when streets would seem to stop without reason or curve off into a direction that appeared nonsensical. “I had no idea your capital was so winding.” Unlike Minamist’s straight, well-defined roads, Mullhind twisted towards the ocean like a shore-stranded eel.

“Aye?” Hamish replied, his heavy brows lifting. “She’s grown like any other city, whenever and wherever she’s needed to. Come on, if you want to see the docks before me mum sends guards after us, we best shift it.” With the click of his tongue, the man urged his horse into an easy trot with Warrior following at a slightly faster pace to keep up.

Chapter 3

Hamish glanced at the ambassador every-so-often as they rode through the middle of Mullhind. The man didn't seem the least bit interested in the stalls and shops they plodded by. Darshan had expressed mild interest when Hamish mentioned visiting a nearby pub, but insisted on the docks first.

Now they stood in the midst of the raucous. Black-backed gulls screamed as they circled the ships and stalls, seeking an easy meal. People shrieked to be heard over the birds and each other. One man nearby battled with one of the bigger gulls. It was precisely the type of noise Hamish often sought to avoid.

That and the smell. Unlike the earthy, alive scent of the surrounding forests and the dry, grassy aroma of grazing fields, there was nothing welcoming about the docks. When the fishing vessels weren't in, the breeze had an almost pleasant briny smell, but with them moored, their stench of death permeated the air.

Darshan rode wordlessly along the dock front. He seemingly paid little heed to the sound and, although his nose wrinkled at first, made no mention of the smell. His gaze was fixated on the larger trade ships moored along the northern half of the docks. The vessels sat in the water like summer-fat ice seals. Men and women swarmed their rigging and winched crates of wares onto the decks.

The ship Darshan would've arrived on still sat amongst the trading vessels in the southern half, the crew clambering all over it. Unlike the other ships, there seemed to be not a man in sight. "Is it common for Udynean ships to only be crewed by women?" Hamish knew from watching the ships as a boy that a large percent of the crews tended to be equal in gender. Those that weren't generally came from foreign shores.

Darshan shook his head. He halted Warrior once they were a good distance from the stalls and bird-swarmed fishing boats. "My father requested that particular crew. Said I would be less distracted from duties that way." He nodded at the ships and stalls. "I have been told that your people deal mostly in textiles; wool, linen and the like. I see very little of that here."

Hamish swung his head from side to side, taking in the rest of the ships and smaller fishing vessels lining the docks. Much of what came to Mullhind by sea also came out of the dark, icy waters. "I think you'll find they send a great deal of the linen by land. And there's nae an abundance of flax around Mullhind. Those fields are a wee bit more south."

Darshan frowned. "How much more? And do they have a suitable dock?"

Hamish peered blindly at the trade ships. "I cannae say for certain," he confessed. "Nora would be the one to ask there." His older sister was the one who knew the most about their economic state. Upon glimpsing Darshan's slightly puzzled face, he elaborated, "She's me sister and will be with me mum during the negotiations." She'd also be happy answering any of the ambassador's questions.

The man's brows lifted in mild surprise. At the reference of his sister being included in the trade discussions? Or was it because she wasn't a man? The latter did seem at odds with the Udynea Empire's decision to originally send the now-departed countess as their ambassador.

"Not your brother, then? I would have thought the heir would be involved in his kingdom's trade. Or did I misunderstand his ranking?"

"Nae, he's the eldest amongst us. And aye, he'll likely pop in at some point, but Nora is better suited to the task. She's good with figures and is sure to ken anything you want to ask about what we trade and where." Hamish still wasn't sure how she managed to keep all the numbers straight in her head. He had tried in his youth, and quickly gave up to instead pursue the more amiable task of mingling with those living on the surrounding farms.

Darshan nodded, seemingly to himself. "I look forward to availing her of such knowledge." He pointed at the crates and barrels still being hauled aboard the nearest ship. "So what are they loading? Do you know what comes out of Mullhind?"

Hamish swung his attention to the ship. Whilst he couldn't identify everything at a glance, he was well aware of what lurked in the barrels. "A lot of fish and salted pork." Hides, too. Leather, sheepskin, the occasional bearskin... "There is likely some wool already aboard. Only from the closest farms at this time of year, though."

"I would assume much of the exports from here go to Cezhory?"

He nodded confidently. "I cannae tell you how much, though. Nora can."

"I will be sure to ask her." The man swung Warrior about with practised ease. "I would like to see the markets now."

They rode down the streets, halting occasionally as Darshan eyed a stall or window front. He seemed especially curious of places involving wares that took some crafting—the smithies, cobblers and the like—but asked no questions. A shame considering Hamish knew a little more about them than exports.

"I notice a distinct lack of elves beyond the ships' crews." Darshan smiled. "Or are you keeping me away from their district?"

"There are nae districts. And there have never been a lot of elves in Tirglas. They always seem to be coming through." And most of them travelled further south. Kings and queens in the past had offered land for the nomadic elven clans to settle on, but they would always respectfully decline and move on. Their distrust of humans likely ran deep into their blood, all because of the Udynea Empire's greed. He peered at Darshan. The ambassador didn't seem overly eager for information. "Why?"

"Mere mild curiosity. The climate here must be similar to that kingdom they carved for themselves in the east. They run hotter than humans, did you know that?"

Hamish shook his head. He knew very little about elves, most of it from books or second-hand, and sometimes third-hand, recounting.

"I merely wondered how they had adapted to a cooler climate, it might have helped back home." The ambassador's words drifted, his attention seemingly drawn to the clanging of a smithy. Then his head snapped back around, all focus narrowed on Hamish. "You get snow here, correct? What is that like?"

"Cold?" Hamish mumbled. Just what sort of answer did Darshan expect from him? "Wet?" He'd a multitude of unpleasant memories consisting of days trudging through knee-deep snow, be it during his youth training alongside his father and siblings or searching for lost livestock as an adult. "It's difficult to move through when it first goes down and the whole world's muffled like you're hearing it through a thick blanket."

"I am almost sorry I shall not be around long enough to witness it."

"Do you nae have snow? The border of Udynea cannae be that far south that it avoids a harsher winter. Or do you spellsters alter the weather there?"

Darshan's mouth dropped open. "Gods, no!" he spluttered. "Only a madman who believes himself a god would tamper with something as complex as the weather. Never mind the vastness of magical energy that would be required, just one wrong action could throw an entire estate into a barren mess."

Despite the late afternoon sun warming Hamish's shoulders, coldness seeped through his skin. At no stage had Darshan said it was impossible. If a single man could cause a drought, then they could weaken a village without any loss of life on their side.

Was that why his mother seemed intent on forming an alliance with known spellsters and slavers, rather than constantly objecting to the presence of Udynean traders crossing the southern border?

The sky had turned into a mixture of dusty-pinks and yellows by the time their horses trudged through the castle gates. The change of guard meant there were twice as many eyes watching them enter. A few of the more knowledgeable men gave Hamish a smirk, whilst some others shook their heads as if he were some unruly child.

"I thank you for indulging me," Darshan said, his voice carrying across the courtyard where Hamish knew the straining ears of the guards readily collected every word. "Your escort around Mullhind was most insightful." The ambassador gracefully slid off Warrior's back, his head swinging from one side to the other in search of something.

It wasn't until Hamish caught the man fiddling with the end of the reins that he realised what Darshan was looking for. "Come on." He jerked his head towards the stables, leading his mare into the dark opening. "We unsaddle our own mounts here."

"Truly?" The word wobbled on a light tone, surprise making it almost incoherent. "How terribly rustic." Both pony and rider caught up to Hamish with a brief trot. "I am afraid you shall have to show me, your saddles are a mite more complicated than what I am used to. Our riding gear rather lacks the straps on the animal's chest, or under the tail, unless they happen to be carthorses."

Hamish halted in the stables. "They come off easily enough. Here, I'll show you." With a few quick movements, he unbuckled both the breastplate and crupper on his mare's saddle, waiting until Darshan mimicked him before leaving the man to the rest and returning to his mare do the same. "I take it that you dinnae do a lot of travelling on hills."

"Our roads tend to wind around the steep ones," Darshan replied between grunts as he fought to release the girth buckle.

After a few moments, Hamish took pity on him and undid that, too. He hauled off the saddles one by one and placed them on the racks with the rest of the horse tack before idly snatching up a couple of brushes and handing one to the ambassador.

Darshan looked oddly amused by the gesture, even as he took the brush. "Do you not have stablehands who do all this for you?"

“Aye,” he murmured, turning his back on the man to focus on grooming his horse. He softly hummed to himself as he worked. Most of the time, he left the stablehands to their jobs, but there was something soothing about brushing the accumulated dirt and sweat from the mare’s back after a long day. And it took time to get her spotless. Whatever lazy moments he wasted here was less he had to spend in the castle.

Hamish circled around to the mare’s far side and glanced over to the other pair as he continued to groom her back. Darshan was tending to Warrior, not perhaps as vigorously as the pony’s owner, but methodically.

What could he get away with asking in regards to magic before the man thought it as prying? There wouldn’t be many times afforded to him like this where he could enquire about any limitations. He wet his lips. “I noticed earlier that you didnae mention whether it *is* possible to control the weather.” He focused on his horse’s back as if brushing her was far more important.

Darshan jumped and a crackling sheen of purple outlined him for a heartbeat. He whirled to face Hamish, his face having gained the slightly sallow look of shock.

“I didnae mean to pry,” Hamish hastily said.

“No, that is not— I merely—” He laid a bejewelled hand on his chest. “My thoughts were miles away until you spoke.” His lips twisted into a strange smile, the mist of times long since past drifting across his face. When Darshan’s gaze met his own again, he almost seemed to be a different man. “What was it you wished to ask of me?”

Hamish repeated himself.

“It is all mostly theoretical,” Darshan muttered, returning to grooming Warrior. “I cannot rightly recall anyone in Udynea trying and, if there was a spellster that strong in imperial lands, I am certain they would have made their presence known to the emperor by now.” He shook his head, now just visible on the other side of the pony. “Like I said earlier, it would take a lot of power and the source is not endless. Could you imagine if it was?”

Hamish quietly sucked on his teeth. He hadn’t had a lot to do with spellsters beyond his younger sister—before she was sent to the cloister at least—but he could picture it well enough. *It’d be like a world full of gods.* Only without the Goddess’ divine will and wisdom to guide their actions. “And just what is the source of your power?” Spellsters appeared in Tirglas without reason. Some believed it the Goddess’ punishment, whilst others were convinced it was the work of demons.

“Well, it would be easier to explain with my childhood diagrams at hand, but it comes from here.” Hamish barely caught Darshan laying a hand on his chest and tapping with a forefinger.

"Your… heart?" he carefully ventured. He had vague memories of the days before Caitlyn was taken from the castle, of the priests suggesting his sister not force her magic. He didn't understand why back then. The spellsters in foreign lands had always sounded so powerful and demonic.

The man frowned at Hamish over the pony's back, his thick brows almost touching the wire frames adorning his face. "No, I mean my being. The energy I use to spark a flame is the same one you draw upon to fire that bow you were carrying earlier."

"You use your muscles?" He could see that applying to hurling objects or fire, but in the type of healing that was acceptable in the cloisters?

"Like I said," Darshan muttered. "Easier with diagrams." He tipped his body, peering at Hamish from beneath Warrior's neck, his face as eager and open as a puppy. "I could draw up some. I would be more than happy to explain to you in greater detail once we are inside, if you are of a mind?"

Hamish hummed, considering. Whilst he saw no practical use of such knowledge, he wouldn't have minded spending a little longer in the man's presence. There was a certain bounciness that came to light every so often, like his face was usually hidden beneath an ill-fitting hood that was always on the verge of slipping off his head. "I'd like that."

"*Really?*" The man perked up like a boarhound on a fresh scent. He smiled broadly, the glee on his face sitting on the verge of unnerving. "And here I thought magic was a taboo subject in Tirglas."

"I wouldnae say taboo. Discouraged, maybe." Hamish led his horse into his pen, the act mimicked by the ambassador. "But you will nae be able to do much explaining tonight. Dinner'll be ready." He indicated the doors of the castle proper with a jerk of his head. "Come on."

"Of course, the welcoming meal." Darshan dusted off his hands, frowning at his pale attire and swiping a few dark hairs off the no longer immaculate fabric of the knee-length coat. "I am not really prepared for food right now. Or dressed for it. I do not suppose something could be brought up at a later time?"

Chuckling, Hamish clapped a hand around the man's shoulders and led the way towards the castle doors. "Nae. First rule of dining around here is: You eat now or go hungry."

"That is about what I thought." Darshan sighed. "To be honest, I have not had the pleasure of eating any Tirglasian cuisine and I am unsure what—"

"Cuisine?" Fresh laughter roared out his throat, paralysing him for what felt like an eternity until he was able to regain control over his own body. "There's your first mistake," he said, wiping a tear from his eye. "We've food. *Grub*. Nothing fancy but it'll fill you up."

The man's easy smile had turned a little glassy. "How delightful," he murmured. "I look forward to it."

~~~

The dining hall wasn't as lavish or even as big as Darshan had pictured. Only a few tapestries adorned the otherwise dark grey slabs of stone. Heat roared from twin fireplaces situated on either side of the room and standing between them was a heavy wooden table with another, longer one intersecting lengthways at the far end. Both tables were laden with food and people already sat, enjoying the fare.

A quick, mental headcount of eight was enough to let him know this was close to the entirety of the royal family. They sat in an oddly-familiar placing, Queen Fiona and her husband, Prince Consort Duncan, sharing the heavy table at the head whilst the rest of the family was relegated to the longer one.

What Darshan didn't see was anything resembling a court. He leant closer to Hamish and whispered, "Should I perhaps be elsewhere?" Back home, evening meals were rarely shared without some nobility present. This seemed a far more intimate affair.

Hamish shook his head. He clapped his hand onto Darshan's shoulder and gave it a squeeze.

Queen Fiona glanced up as they neared the tables. That sharp, blue gaze latched onto Darshan, burrowing its icicle-like depths into his soul before settling on Hamish. "You're late." The crack of a whip couldn't have snapped any cleaner than her voice.

Hamish took up a seat between his older brother, Gordon, and a sandy-haired woman who Darshan had yet to be introduced to, but guessed was Hamish's sister. "Well, you see—"

"It is entirely my fault, your majesty," Darshan interrupted. There was little point in standing by and allowing the blame to fall on Hamish when the man had only done as Darshan had asked. "I saw very little of Mullhind on the journey up from the docks and I was eager for a second look. I am afraid that eagerness led me to taking advantage of your dear son's hospitality. I do hope it did not cause any trouble."

The queen's icy gaze swung to encompass him once again and Darshan was immediately thrown back to a time when his five-year-old self, still enamoured with his new abilities, had set the bed curtains alight with an errant magical flame. His father had pinned
~~~

him to the spot with a similar look.

"That is to say I—"

"You wanted to confirm our fiscal state for yourself?" Queen Fiona finished for him, her tone scarcely thawing. "I assure you, ambassador, everything is as stated. We dinnae make a practise of lying in Tirglas."

"Leave it be, lass," Duncan said, his soft voice rumbling much like a distant thunderstorm. Even seated, he was a large man. He laid a hand on his wife's shoulder.

A glance around the table was all it took to see how Queen Fiona stood out amongst her own family, her tan skin practically ashen in comparison to everyone else's.

Much of the children's features seemed to take after their father. Duncan's sons shared a heavy similarity in bone structure if not hair colouration—even if Hamish's was a touch brighter than his brother or father's greying auburn coils. And where only the elder two children had Duncan's rather startling green eyes, all three royal siblings were close enough in skin tone to each other, if not as dark a brown as their father.

Queen Fiona opened her mouth.

Her husband got there first. "You cannae stem curiosity."

Darshan took the only empty seat left at the table as his face warmed, glad that it was the farthest from the head table. Yes, he probably could've arranged the whole trip a little better, but he hadn't exactly been thinking straight at the time. "I did not mean to imply that—"

"Mum?" Hamish piped up. He glanced at Darshan, a not-so-subtle request for him to remain silent. Was the man hoping to spare him another icy glare? "I was thinking of travelling to the cloister tomorrow?"

Darshan sat a little straighter in his chair. "You actually visit the cloisters?" He'd heard about the Tirglasian custom of locking away their spellsters, most of the Udynean court had. But he had thought the people inside were imprisoned much like the Demarn kingdom did with her spellsters and that ghastly tower. "I would very much like to see one up close. Providing that is acceptable, of course."

Queen Fiona's brows shot to their highest. "You want to enter one *willingly*?" She was silent for a moment, chewing thoughtfully at a piece of pork crackling. "Tomorrow willnae be ideal. It's a fortnight journey to the nearest cloister."

"I understand," Darshan murmured. Whilst most nations often lavished foreign royalty, he did comprehend her desire to see an uncloistered spellster shown the way out of her kingdom as swiftly as possible. Hammering out the negotiations immediately would serve that purpose.

"Actually, 'Mish?" The prince consort swung to his son. "If you can hold off a few days, the ambassador could accompany you, along with a full escort."

Hamish stiffened, then bowed his head in acquiescence. The man seemed altogether uncomfortable with the idea. Was it the waiting? The prospect of an escort slowing him down? Or had he been looking to distance himself from Darshan's presence?

He ran a considering eye over the man. Hamish had shown little sign of unease whilst riding through the city. Not even shirking from laying a friendly hand on him. And if he was willing to travel to the cloister, then it couldn't be Darshan's spellster status. "I would not wish to intrude or put anyone out," he insisted.

One side of Hamish's mouth lifted, raising the hair on his cheek. His gaze rose from his plate to Darshan. "I can wait. The cloister isnae going anywhere."

The rest of their dinner continued amicably. On the edge of his vision, he spied Hamish glancing at him every so often, a slight furrow twitching between his brows. Quite likely due to the way Darshan picked at his food.

He could identify quite a number of the dishes spread out on the table, at least in part. Surprisingly, he spied very little in the way of vegetables, mostly mashed turnips and potatoes. Of meat, there was plenty. A leg of pork—that he respectfully turned down—another of what the small hoof told him was venison, and a pale lump with a honeycomb texture that was buried in creamy sauce.

The eels were a little more familiar and he didn't mind them, but back home they were usually served heavily spiced and lightly grilled. Certainly not in a pie. Fortunately, there was grilled fish to be had and he'd eaten a few mouthfuls of the flaky, white flesh before growing tired of the blandness. There was bread, too, in moderate abundance. Not as fanciful as back home, but serviceable.

What he couldn't identify was the crumbly brown mass currently adorning his plate alongside the mashed vegetables. It had a vague meaty scent with the pungent aroma of clove alongside other spices he couldn't quite put a finger on.

"You going to eat that?"

Darshan lifted his gaze from the plate, seeking the speaker from those sitting across the table.

There were four children sharing the long table alongside the queen's adult children, three boys and a young lady. The girl seemed intent on her food, her auburn curls obscuring her face. She would reach over her shoulder to stroke the near-bald head of a large bearskin draped over her chair every so often, but as far as she was concerned, his presence was of no interest.

The boys were another matter. They appeared to be different ages—although he would hazard a guess at there being a scant few years between them—but they all had the same flame-red hair. Darshan had caught them eyeing him through much of the meal, each face screwed up as if they expected him to burst into flame with the next breath. Any one of them looked brazen enough to have spoken.

"Pardon?" Darshan softly enquired.

The eldest of the trio pointed at Darshan's plate. "I said: are you going to eat that?"

"I cannot even be certain what *that* is," he confessed. "You are welcome to it." He went to push the plate the boy's way, but the boy leant across the table and snatched up the dish before Darshan could finish talking.

"Bruce!" the sandy-haired woman snapped, instantly getting the boy's attention. "Put that down."

With his ruddy-brown cheeks growing darker, Bruce immediately returned the plate to the table.

"I'm sorry about that, your highness," the woman continued, fixing the boy with a sharp look. Now that she had turned her attention to him, there was no mistaking her as being one of Queen Fiona's children, not with her face a replica of the queen's narrow jaw and high cheekbones. "The wee devils would starve you skinny and pick your bones clean if they'd half a chance." She gave the boys another stern look, although her glower quickly softened into a fond smile.

"It is quite all right," Darshan insisted, nudging the plate ever closer to Bruce until the boy was able to sneakily slide it on top of his own bare dish. "I rather doubt my ability to eat another bite." At least, not without it coming back up.

"Really?" The woman eyed him as if he were some wretch that'd washed up in the last storm. "Pardon me for saying, but you look like there's barely anything to you."

"Nora," Hamish growled, nudging the woman with his elbow. "Knock it off. He looks fine." Panic flickered across his face and he glanced at Queen Fiona before lowering his gaze to his own plate. "I mean in a perfectly healthy sense," he mumbled.

Darshan gnawed on the inside of his lip as he eyed Hamish's plate. *That has to be his third helping*. Where was he putting it all? The man ate more than a ravenous spellster returning from battle.

The sandy-haired woman giggled.

"So, you are Nora," Darshan said in an attempt to deflect the woman's interest from her brother. The name had been mentioned in passing as he'd exited the docks and Hamish insisted she knew more about the kingdom's trade than most. Odd how he hadn't met her when the other children had been expected to greet his arrival.

"Have me brothers been talking about me?" Grinning, Nora gave both of the men a light-hearted shove. "Good things, I hope."

"I believe so." He glanced at Hamish, looking for any sign that he should stop speaking, but the man merely gave a faint smile as he met Darshan's gaze before returning to his food. "I heard you have an excellent grasp on the trade records."

Nora beamed, pride squaring her shoulders. "Aye, I do!" She steepled her fingers on the table, all attention focused on Darshan. "Is there anything in particular you wanted to enquire about them?"

"He was asking about linen earlier," Hamish said around a mouthful of food.

"Linen?" Nora frowned at her brother, her brows knotting further in thought before she grinned. "You want to ken about the flax plantations? I can tell you a lot there." She leant over the table, very nearly putting her bosom into her food. "You see—"

Queen Fiona cleared her throat. "Rein it in, Nora dear. We can discuss all this in greater detail tomorrow."

Nora hung her head, a knuckle pressed to her lip. "Aye, Mum," she mumbled.

"There is one thing I did wonder," Darshan said. "Your brother mentioned much of the wares go by land, would it not be favourable to send them by ship?"

The gentle clink of plates and cutlery halted. Everyone grew still, some scarcely daring to chew the food still hanging out their mouths. One by one, their gazes left him to focus solely on Nora.

The woman's face, which had been so cheerfully expressive a mere moment ago, was now wiped free of all emotion. "If you will excuse me," she murmured, standing woodenly. "I'm a wee bit more tired than I thought." The woman didn't linger around for anyone to utter a word, opting to hurry out of the nearest door.

The three boys looked amongst themselves before scampering after her. Upright, they seemed a good deal taller than he had first judged, with the eldest looking as though he could easily rival the height of Darshan's twin sister. Or maybe even himself.

"Well," Queen Fiona said. "That was not quite the ending to dinner I was hoping for." She stood, along with her husband who still towered over her even though she was a good half-foot taller than Darshan. She halted as they went to leave the table. "Do send your wee lass to bed, Gordon dear. Just look at her, almost asleep in her food."

Gordon circled the table to gently shake the auburn-haired girl and whisper in her ear.

The girl jolted upright in the chair. Those wide, green eyes surveyed the table, her brows lowering and her lips pursing. "Where'd everyone go?"

"Bed, lass," Gordon said. "You should be off, too."

Nodding, the girl dutifully hopped out of her seat—her height not far off that of the eldest boy. She gave the ghastly bearskin a brief pat before trotting off towards the same door the rest of the family had vacated through.

If only my siblings were as complacent. He had lost count of the times the palace servants had been reduced to chasing his half-sisters through the corridors. Did a lack of magical talent make children less likely to be unruly, or did his father merely have the ill-fortune to sire disobedient offspring?

Darshan waited until the girl was well out of earshot before speaking. "I am dreadfully sorry for upsetting your sister." There was no question her exodus had been his doing. He stood and made for the main door alongside the two princes. It'd likely be for the best if he sought a different route back to the guest quarters. "But I must admit to a little confusion as to what I said wrong." Anyone would be forgiven for thinking he had suggested roasting children alive by her reaction.

"Her husband used to captain one of the bigger trade ships," Hamish replied, his voice low even though the room housed but the three of them. "It hit stormy weather just off the north-western coast some eight years back. He drowned attempting to rescue their daughter."

A gasp slipped through Darshan's lips before he could stifle it. "I... I had no idea she—"

Gordon clapped a hand onto Darshan's shoulder. "And why would you have? It'll be all right, lad." He gave Darshan a few hearty pats on the back that almost had him sprawled face-first onto the floor. "She will understand."

"It might be a touch difficult to discuss trade without mentioning ships, though," he murmured. Especially as that was what his father sought to rectify. If he could find a way to have Tirglasian linen enter Minamist cheaply without buyers having to deal with land cartage taxes, then Minamist would only increase its wealth.

The older prince nodded. "I just think you took her by surprise. She's usually more composed about it."

Darshan gave a noncommittal hum. If the woman was worried about sparing her people a similar fate as her husband and daughter, then perhaps he could offer a spellster for every ship. There would need to be rules, though. He rather doubted Queen Fiona would allow foreign spellsters to roam her lands unchecked. "I wonder..." Old tales of Tirglas spoke of their spellsters being permitted beyond the cloister confines during extreme medical cases. Perhaps there could be some convincing into letting them aboard the ships. "Do you usually have to ask Queen Fiona's permission to visit the cloisters?"

"Nae," Gordon said, releasing Darshan to clap his hands on Hamish's shoulders and give the man a little shake. "But me brother's just about got to ask Mum permission to piss. He certainly cannae leave the castle without someone tailing him."

Gnawing at the inside of his cheek, Darshan peered at Gordon. Whatever made the man think he would actually believe that? True, a lot of things about Tirglas had seemed mind-boggling until his tutors had presented him with proof, but that sounded a little farfetched. Surely the princes were allowed to venture into Mullhind unescorted. From what he'd seen of Hamish's arrival through the castle gates, the man had been alone.

"That's nae true," Hamish blurted, a faint bloom of colour brushing the tops of his cheeks. The man shot his brother a death glare that Darshan had witnessed on a great many of his own siblings' faces.

Chuckling and ruffling his brother's hair, Gordon twitched his head to indicate the corridor. "Come on, we'll escort you to your quarters."

"I did that already," Hamish said, rolling those sapphiric eyes of his. "He cannae have forgotten the way back that quickly."

Darshan slowly turned his gaze to the surrounding walls. *Grey, blank and dim.* Still, he'd vague recollections of passing by the dining hall doors whilst trying to exit the castle proper, but not during his original entry. Spending the night wandering the corridors in search of his bed didn't sound all that appealing. "I could do with an escort, if it is not too much trouble."

Gordon grinned and wrapped an arm companionably around his brother's shoulders as he guided them, with Darshan tailing the pair. "See, 'Mish? You're forgetting we grew up here and *he* was likely distracted by all the—" He airily twirled his hand before them. "—fine architecture." Tipping his head, he gave Darshan a wink behind Hamish's back.

The sight almost had Darshan stumbling as they veered up a flight of stairs. Yes, he had been very much distracted, but the older prince couldn't have known that, or what by. It had only been the pair of them then. Had he somehow given some clue? He hadn't needed to be discreet about his preferences so thoroughly before. Even so, how could he have possibly been noticed that quickly?

Clearly, he'd have to try harder to push such thoughts to the back of his mind. *I'm here for a reason.* He just needed to keep reminding himself that and get the negotiation details hammered out as swiftly as possible. Then he could return home where such things as the gender of his lover didn't matter.

Darshan stared at the back of Gordon's head. He toyed with one of his rings, twisting it back and forth. He couldn't have misconstrued the act, could he? It had definitely been a wink and not something else.

Then why, if Tirglasians were against the idea of men being with men, had the older prince winked at him?

Chapter 4

Thunk!

Hamish glanced up from checking his bowstring. That hadn't sounded like a promising shot. Putting aside his half-fletched arrow, he ran a scrutinising eye over the archery range.

All three of his nephews stood before him, they had the range to themselves this morning and took advantage of that by spreading across its width. He leant against the low stone wall separating the area from the rest of the castle's training ground.

His niece was meant to have joined them, but Sorcha was content being tucked against one side of the range, at the end farthest from her cousins where she could sulk in peace. She was well past the point of needing lessons from her uncle, but Gordon refused to let her hunt alone after the lethal fate that had befallen her mother and sister.

Hamish wouldn't typically be here either, but he had promised his sister that he'd keep an eye on them to ensure they didn't do something foolish like shoot one another in the foot. Which now seemed like less of an issue than Nora had led him to believe.

Bruce might've been just shy of a dozen years old, but he followed the rest of the family in being quick to master the bow. And Ethan, having only a year's difference between them, would catch up to his brother sooner than Bruce likely thought.

Mac, however, was another story. With the boy being only eight years old, the weapon was new and unruly to him. Unlike the toy swords he had waved about since he could stand. But as Hamish's mother was so fond of saying, a prince who relied on one weapon was a fool.

Hamish had heard snippets of the boy's brothers trying to teach him the lessons they'd learnt, but Mac was too busy sulking to take in their words.

Watching the older pair try again reminded Hamish of his childhood days in this same range, when Gordon or Nora would attempt to correct him. He hadn't been much for listening to his older siblings either.

"I cannae do it!" Mac roared, although the sound was far less fearsome than he likely intended; a bit like a puppy yapping next to the baying of a boarhound. He tossed the bow to one side and aimed an inefficient kick at it.

Shaking his head, Hamish dropped off the stone wall and strode towards the trio. "Is that any way to treat your bow?"

"I cannae hit the target," the boy continued to wail. "I'll never be good enough." He glared at the abandoned weapon sitting in the grass. "Thing's a bloody menace."

"Language," Bruce murmured, casting a covert glance at Hamish.

"There's your problem," Sorcha bellowed from her place beside the left wall. She waved a hand in their direction, pointing with an arrow that she gripped almost daintily between her middle and index fingers. "You cannae use your bow if you're nae holding it." Giving a decisive nod, she nocked the arrow, drew her bow full and loosed to the muffled *thack* of the target.

Shielding his eyes, Hamish peered down the range. The girl's arrow had met the target about a few inches shy of centre. Given a year or so of training, and a good deal more hunting trips than she was currently allowed, she'd a fair chance of becoming more skilled than her mother. Just the sort of tale for a future queen.

But her abilities weren't the ones currently being contested.

Scooping up Mac's discarded bow from the dew-damp ground, he turned back to his nephews. "She's right, you ken," he said to the sulking boy.

"What does it matter?" Mac muttered. "It willnae shoot straight whether I'm holding it or nae."

"He's shaking all over the place," Ethan said with his older brother nodding over his shoulder.

"Really?" Hamish offered the bow to Mac. "Show me, lad."

His nephew glared at him through a mop of gingery red curls. All three of the boys had more-or-less the same hair colour, several shades darker than their mother's almost reddish blonde locks.

Seeing that further insistence would only serve to frustrate the both of them, he knelt at Mac's side. "You ken, I was pretty rubbish at this when I first started."

His nephew eyed him warily, likely trying to picture a time when Hamish had ever not been capable of loosing an arrow and hitting his target dead-centre. Admittedly, the boy hadn't even been a glimmer in his dad's eye when such a statement was true, but maybe it would motivate him.

"Aye," Hamish continued. "I wasnae much younger than you. Your mum was just a wee bit better than Sorcha is now and she was always dragging me down here. Didnae matter how hard they tried, I just couldnae do it."

Whilst the wariness remained, a glimmer of curiosity danced across his face. "What changed?"

"I tried one more time." He recalled the day of his first centre-hit quite clearly. Seven years of age, frustrated and harassed almost beyond reason, his thoughts had been only on the target and getting it right, even if it was just the once. He couldn't explain how, but it had all just fallen into place and he'd been able to down his targets on the first hit ever since.

Hamish gently pressed the bow into Mac's hand. "That's all I'm asking of you. One more and I promise I'll nae ask you to do it again if you nae want to."

"He's nae going to listen to you," Bruce piped up. Both the older boy and Ethan had abandoned their own training to lean against the range border wall. "Even granddad cannae get him to try when he gets this worked up."

That sounds familiar. He had rather strong memories of his father attempting to teach him and giving up in the face of his stubbornness. "Then it's a good thing I'm nae his granddad. And you two should be practising as well." He pinned them both with a hard look until they returned to their previous spots. "Now, what do you say, lad? One more?"

Sullen brown eyes continued to watch him. Mac's fingers twitched along the bow's leather grip. The bow dangled in his grasp, but at least he hadn't let go of it.

"Come on." Hamish grinned. "Just once for your favourite uncle."

Huffing, Mac plucked an arrow from the ground. He pulled back on the bowstring. "See?" The bow did indeed wobble in his grip. His fingered tightened, knuckles paling as he fought to keep the arrow steady.

"That's because you're holding on too hard, lad." The bow was a simple recurve, the type most of the hunters around Mullhind used. "You're stronger than your bow, you dinnae need to fight him. Relax your grip some."

"I've tried," Mac insisted, his jaw setting stubbornly. "It willnae work."

"Trust me."

Muttering what Hamish was certain had been a few breathless curses, Mac finally loosed the arrow.

Hamish held his breath, all his focus trained on the arrow. It wobbled along its path, reaching the height of its arc a quarter of the way down the range. *Not enough*. It didn't need to hit a decent mark, or even reach much farther than the foot of the target. Anything less and Mac would give up on archery completely. He wouldn't be allowed to leave on hunts without that training.

The arrow straightened, sailing down the range in a flat line to bury itself into the centre of the target.

"I did it!" Mac crowed, bouncing in a small circle and flapping his arms like a startled chicken.

Hamish frowned. "So, you did," he murmured. But how? There was no logical reason the arrow should've reached the target, but the proof sat deep in the straw, trembling slightly in the cool breeze. "Good job, lad." He absently patted his nephew on the back.

"That was awesome!" Ethan barrelled into his younger brother, almost knocking Mac off his feet. "Did you see the way it flew?" He clasped Mac's head, his brown eyes wide as he pressed their foreheads together. "Can you do it again?"

"I dinnae ken," Mac drawled.

"Seems like a fluke to me," Sorcha muttered, prodding Ethan away from his brother with the end of her bow. She snatched up one of Mac's discarded arrows and stared down its length. "Or a trick. Nae arrow flies like that. Have you been holding out on us, Maccy me lad?"

The boy hunched his shoulders, rubbing at one arm. "I—"

"Got a few extra skills up our sleeves? Or are you going to keep telling me it's just more plain luck for the lucky duck?"

Hamish laid a hand on his niece's shoulder, stilling her. "That's enough." Mac was clearly uncomfortable with his cousin's line of questioning. And well he should be being that Sorcha was borderline accusing him of being a spellster. "We've all had our share of luck, lass. Doesnae mean foul play."

"Some more luck than others," she muttered. He didn't blame her for being a touch bitter. Ever since her mother's death, she had to fight hard to get her grandmother's permission to train, to be seen as something more than the fragile and precious next in a long line of rulers. Even then, it'd taken her father threatening to train her in secret for her grandmother to relent.

"Aye, some people do get more." His younger sister, Caitlyn, seemed to have copious amounts of luck allocated to her. At least, back before she had been forced to protect him from the bandits attempting to take both their lives. Decades later and he could still recall the furnace heat of the inferno her untrained magic had brought to their defence.

And it was true that the boys seemed to have the Goddess' good fortune smile upon them a fair bit, especially when together. But the same could've been said of Gordon and himself when they were young.

Sorcha harrumphed.

Hamish fixed his niece with a stern glare. "Lass, are you questioning the Goddess' judgement on who is worthy of what?" Even as he asked, he knew what her answer would be.

Her brows lowered as those big eyes glared right back at him, the inherited dual stubbornness of her parents sparking to light in their green depths. Then she glanced away and, with her lips barely moving, managed to mutter, "Nae, uncle."

"Right." Giving her a firm nod, he gently ushered his niece towards her previous position before the targets. "Back to it, lads," he shot over his shoulder.

Mac scooped up another arrow and, with his chest puffed out, returned to his training. His brothers flanked him, no doubt trying to figure out how he had managed the last attempt.

Hamish also kept his attention casually trained on the boy. Sorcha was right; arrows just didn't fly like that. But Mac was eight years old. Surely any sign of magic would've made itself known by now. From what he had heard about the cloistered spellsters, most had been around four or five.

Caitlyn had been found out at eight, but had shown some proficiency in what she had done, meaning she must've been of similar age when her magic manifested.

"So," said a familiar musical voice, "is *this* how Tirglasians occupy themselves?"

Hamish turned on his heel to find the Udynean ambassador leaning against the range wall. "I thought you were meant to be negotiating with me mum?" Just how long had Darshan been there? Was *his* magic the reason the arrow had reached the target? That would explain things, not that it would help the boy in the long run.

"I was," Darshan replied with the tilt of his head. "And we were, I believe, making some headway into it. At least, up until a man marched in blathering on about boars, some farmer and fences." His brow lowered, twisted slightly in puzzlement. "Your mother went off muttering words I failed to catch. Your name was amongst them."

Hamish winced. After meeting Darshan, he had forgotten all about Ewan and his fences. He had thought the steward would've seen to all the necessary paperwork required to compensate the man's family. Apparently not. *I'm going to get such a tongue-lashing.* Especially once his mum learnt he had spent the afternoon wandering the city alone with the ambassador instead of tending to his duties.

He slowly became aware of the presence of small bodies behind him. The boys milled at his back, all eyeing Darshan with the same level of expectancy they had displayed at last night's dinner. They nudged each other and whispered amongst themselves, their voices just on the edge of hearing.

"You ask him," Bruce said, shoving Mac forward.

"You're the oldest," the other boy objected. "*You* ask him."

Around the three of them went, badgering one another to step forward.

"I believe I told you lot you get back to your archery practise," Hamish shot over his shoulder. They wouldn't have much longer here before other duties called them.

Darshan chuckled. He leant to one side, peering around Hamish. "Seems like one of you better ask me soon before you lose your chance."

Ethan stepped forward, blushing and clearing his throat as he clutched his bow before him like a shield. His chubby, brown face stared up in awe at Darshan. "Is it true that you're a spellster? We heard that everyone in Udynea has magic and—"

The ambassador laughed. "Not every *one*, dear boy. Magic is a thing of bloodlines and breeding. It is not like your bows. You cannot teach such a skill to all."

Hamish frowned. *Bloodlines?* How did that explain his sister when there were no other spellsters in his family?

Ethan nodded, as he'd been doing since Darshan first spoke. His fingers danced nervously on his bow grip. "Are you?" He glanced back at his brothers as Darshan bowed his head. "We were wondering if you could... That is—" His head snapped back around with enough speed that Hamish was almost convinced it would break. "Can you really shoot fire from your fingers?"

Smirking, Darshan flipped his hand with a dramatic flourish. A flame flashed to life in his palm. It snaked and twirled, slowly forming the shape of a person, a man. Just the torso, but it waved its wispy arms as it swayed from side to side in some sort of dance.

Mac inched forward. He reached out, one finger extended towards the fire.

"Do not touch." Raising his other hand before him in warning, Darshan withdrew his hand. The form of the dancing man dissipated into ordinary fire. "It will burn you as quickly as any other flame." With another, more exaggerated, flourish of his hand, the spellster snuffed the flame completely.

Ethan brushed at where the fire had been, then his brothers and cousin joined in. All that remained was a thin wisp of smoke as evidence of it ever being there. Hamish couldn't help but wonder if the flame had actually heated the air. He hadn't felt anything. Or was the heat more subtle, like a candle?

Sorcha turned to face Darshan. Unlike the boys, curiosity had cloaked her in a sheet of courage. She cradled his hand, examining the palm. "If it burns things, then why didnae it burn your hand?"

Darshan smiled, weathering both unasked-for contact and question with equal grace. "Because, dear girl, it is mine and what is yours does no harm to you. Once it touches something it can burn, *then* I am a touch more vulnerable. But I have means to counteract the inevitable."

"Meanwhile," Hamish said before either of the children could bombard the man with more questions. Darshan might be good-natured about it now, but that could change as swiftly as a rain cloud. "You four will inevitability run out of time to do more training."

"But—" Ethan began to whine, halting when Hamish held up a finger.

"There'll be none of that, lad. He's nae going to vanish in a puff of smoke once your back is turned."

The boy eyed Darshan as if he wasn't entirely convinced that couldn't happen. Hamish wasn't certain of it himself. The sailors were always bringing strange stories of magical feats. Sifting the truth from the tall tales was often a mission in itself.

"Go on, see if you cannae get a few more into the target before you're off to Mrs Maggie."

Groaning, the trio returned to their practise. Sorcha remained at Hamish's side, her quiver empty and the target full.

Darshan seemed to eye the boys with a smidgen of curiosity. His gaze flicked from them to Hamish. "Yours I trust?"

Hamish blinked, then laughed as he realised what the man was asking. It had to be the hair. It was always the hair. He had the same colour, but the boys had inherited their flaming curls from their sun-tanned, freckled-faced father. "These wee bairns? Nae." He hoisted his niece, the smallest of the children despite being the eldest, onto his shoulder. "Sorcha here is me brother's daughter. The rest of the terrors are nephews on me sister's side." He smiled fondly at the three boys all lined up before their targets. For once, Mac seemed to be putting the proper amount of effort into the task.

"Who are you calling wee?" protested a voice at his ear. Sorcha still didn't weigh much, having taken after her rather petite mother.

Although, having seen them next to the spellster, Hamish was sharply reminded of just how tall all the children had grown over the past year.

"I'm almost as tall as me mum," Sorcha continued. "*And* I can shoot a bow just as well as she could!"

"Aye, lass. That you can." Like her daughter, Muireall had made up for her lack of size in attitude. Hamish was certain her sheer commanding presence was why his brother had fallen for the woman, especially when his marriage to her brought little in the way of a connection to a strong clan. He set Sorcha back on her feet. "But she also would've collected her arrows by now. Make sure the rest do as well."

With an excessively toothy grin, she trotted over to the boys. A few quiet words were all it took to have them running for their targets, urging each other on with taunts of reaching theirs first.

Hamish glanced towards the sunrise, shading his eyes with a hand. The light had crept over the outer castle wall, meaning it had to midmorning. "Hurry up, you four, then shift your bums to Mrs Maggie for your lessons. You dinnae want to be late again."

Laughter and the clatter of discarded weapons answered him, followed swiftly by the thunderous pounding of booted feet as all four of them raced by.

The spellster continued to side eye Hamish as the last of the four ran out of sight. "You have children of your own, though?"

Hamish shook his head as he gathered the bows and now-filled quivers.

The answer had the man's brows lifting. "Really? I know my lack of understanding when it comes to your culture is less than thorough, but—"

"Did they nae give you lessons?" Hamish enquired, shouldering the quivers and heading for the armoury. "I wouldnae have thought they'd let you be an ambassador without some idea of the people you were to deal with."

Darshan smiled, tagging along. "I am endeavouring to close the gaps in my knowledge, have no fear there. Nevertheless, I do know that your people marry at a young age and tend to have a great many children."

"Oh, aye. Me mum would very much prefer if I followed that tradition."

"But you have chosen not to? No children? No… wife?"

Hamish shook his head.

Darshan halted in the middle of the courtyard. "If you will excuse me?" The man was already making for the castle door before Hamish could enquire further.

~ ~ ~

The door to the empty room clicked shut. Darshan leant back on it, barely seeing the shelves of books lining the walls. He had come here only because he didn't think himself capable of remembering the way to the guest room, much less making the journey.

His heart hammered, his thoughts twirling off into multiple spirals of possibilities. He needed to slow down, to think straight.

No wife. That thought ran through his mind the loudest. He latched onto it, trying to anchor himself, only to be caught by an eddy of questions and suppositions.

Did that mean what he thought? Could it? Whilst his tutors had taught him everything they believed he would need to know during the journey, there were only so many hours in a day and so much knowledge a mind could handle.

Nevertheless, he knew that a lack of wife or child at Hamish's age would be rare indeed without good cause. And there were a limited number of reasons as to why not.

Could it be that Hamish preferred men? Tirglasians had a peculiar notion about men enjoying each other, a distinct aversion to the idea if his father could be believed, but it would be foolish indeed to think there were none such as himself in an entire kingdom.

Still, for a prince to be that way inclined...

No. He was clearly reading too much into it. Why, he had gotten none of the usual signals from the man in that regard. All this was far more likely to be nothing but idle hope in the face of blind lust. He couldn't do that to himself again. Hamish certainly didn't deserve to be dragged into Darshan's self-inflicted implosion.

Then again...

Frowning, Darshan tipped his head back against the door. This wasn't Udynea. What passed for a signal there would be far too blatant here. And Hamish might not even be aware of it himself or, far more likely, in denial over his attractions.

There was really only one real way to be sure and, ordinarily, he would just outright ask whatever man he had taken a fancy to if they were likewise inclined. Doing so here ran the risk of having his teeth knocked in.

He pushed off the door, pacing between it and the thick wooden table filling the centre of the room, absently toying with his rings at each turn. What to do? His curiosity wouldn't simply leave it be. He had to know one way or the other.

He would have to be careful, though. Subtle. Hamish seemed a laid back sort, but he didn't want to offend the man.

Perhaps if he got Hamish alone, like out in the city. A neutral place where the man felt comfortable. Somewhere like—

One of those pubs of theirs. Hamish had pointed out a few on their excursion around Mullhind. They could tuck themselves into some quiet corner. A little alcohol would help loosen the man's tongue; in a multitude of ways should his hunch prove correct. And should his gentle questioning turn sour, he could always shamelessly blame it on the drink.

But when? He halted, staring blindly at the door. That was a harder decision. He had his duties and Hamish no doubt had responsibilities of his own to attend. Would an evening stint raise too many brows? What of during the day? It was custom amongst the desert tribes in Stamekia for alcohol to only be shared amongst family and lovers during the day. Did Tirglas have any such taboo?

His gaze slid to the books, then the shelves, before moving on to finally take in the room. He was alone, mercifully. Large windows filled the wall to his left and a pair of low-backed chairs had been positioned near them to maximise the light. Had he stumbled upon the castle's library? He should've realised by the smells of leather, parchment and the dry dust of a room kept warm.

Breathing deep, he strode to the nearest shelf. A peek into one of the books—the pages crackling with neglect and age—revealed little that he understood. Another offered a gleaning of an old tale involving an attack on Mullhind Castle or perhaps a historical record. It was hard to be sure, even when his grasp on the written language was far better than the tenuous hold on verbal communication. It didn't help that the words were all but smashed together.

Maybe if he brought Hamish here, the man could help him decipher the words and, in the process, give Darshan a less conspicuous opening.

The door rattled, jolting him from his vaguely-interested attempts to make out the tale the book spoke of—something about a lone prince, he had lost track three times already. He turned as the door opened, revealing the queen's bubbly daughter.

Nora stared at him, those blue eyes at their widest. One of her hands alighted on her chest, clutching tight the scrolls and journals she had been pouring through during their meeting earlier; the other hand had fallen to her belt knife and was now merely resting on the hilt. "I didnae expect to find you here."

"Am I intruding?" Darshan hastily replaced the book where he had found it. "I can leave. Or were you sent to fetch me?"

Shaking her head, she strode into the room to rest her burden on the table. "Nae, on all counts. Me mum—" A small smile tweaked her lips. "I mean, Queen Fiona has been regrettably called out to duties and willnae be back until this evening."

"That is a shame," Darshan replied. "Will we be reconvening afterwards?"

Again, Nora shook her head. She shuffled the scrolls into some semblance of order, glancing up at him. "What were you reading?" The question came so lightly, almost absentminded.

"I cannot rightly say." He picked up the book and brought it to her side. "History, I believe. Unless the castle library is big on fictional works?"

"We've a number of them, aye." She flipped through the book in question at a speed that barely gave her time to glean more than the occasional word. "This, however, could be considered a bit of both. It was a long time ago, but it happened."

Taking the book from her unresisting fingers, Darshan thumbed through a few pages. "I admit I find it a little difficult to read."

Nora nodded. "Formal text. They're all like that."

He hummed, turning another page. The script was almost legible. "I wonder... would you be willing to assist me in parsing? If you are free, that is? I would very much like to learn."

"I dinnae see why not. We were meant to be in negotiations, so I've nae a thing beyond that planned."

"Excellent. Where do we start?"

She gently took the book from him and laid it on the table. "With something a little simpler."

Chapter 5

Darshan wandered down the corridors with no actual destination in mind. He had spent quite a number of hours in the library with Nora and his head swam with everything he'd read. Some of the text referenced old clan battles, feuds that still festered to this day. He was familiar with such animosity and had, regrettably, been the cause of one before his father shunted him off up North.

Other books seemed more folk story than history. The one he'd discovered on his own had certainly walked the border between the two with wide-scale murder of the royal family, leaving only the youngest son of the King's youngest child alive. That the story expected him to believe a boy of five could mount an attack on his own castle was laughable, but Nora seemed to take the tale fairly seriously.

His feet had taken him to a spiralling flight of stairs. Up led to the guest quarters, where the only thing awaiting him was a few hours of boredom before the evening meal, whilst the prospects of going downstairs held rather much of the same, the only difference being he would be bored in public.

Darshan plodded down the stairs. Perhaps he would get lucky a second time and find people training, or become luckier still and have those people be fighting fit men. His speed increased at the idle thought. Ordinarily, he wouldn't bother searching the training grounds—the deliciously-sculpted soldiers in Minamist Palace didn't do much training in the afternoon heat—but with Tirglas being much cooler, there was always the possibility.

Maybe luck would be even further in his favour and he'd find the men training without any bulky armour obscuring their true physiques.

Footsteps echoed from the corridor on his left as Darshan reached the foot of the stairs, brisk, purposeful and steadily growing closer. He slowed, curiosity swivelling his head, then drawing his feet. Whoever could be in that much of a hurry around here?

Hamish appeared from one of the many corridors branching off the one they stood in. "There you are," he said, his arms and smile wide as if welcoming an old friend. "I wondered where you'd scuttled off to." He clapped an arm around Darshan's shoulders, squeezing tight in the same good-natured fashion he had witnessed from the man's brother last night. "Thought I might've said something to upset you this morning."

"What?" Darshan blinked up at the man, still a little dazed. After spending hours confined in a small library, anything earlier was a distant, foggy memory.

"Archery range?" Hamish supplied, clearly searching for a hint that Darshan understood him. "You asked if I was married?"

"Oh! No, I am merely a bit out of sorts." He had almost forgotten the reason he had begun his little jaunt through the castle library. Sadly, he had garnered no useful information on that front, at least not from the books Nora had chosen as his starting point. Further perusal would probably lead him to the answer, but he hadn't ever been that patient.

Hamish slowly slid his arm off Darshan's shoulders, the absence leaving him cold. "You're nae ill, are you?"

Darshan shook his head. Illnesses and injuries were for people without healing magic. "I must not be entirely over the journey here, that is all. I have heard travelling over water can do strange things to a person's insides." Dwarves especially hated it. At least, when it came to the hedgewitches of ancient lore. Something to do with the mysterious magic they once had and their ties to the earth.

The admission seemed to ease the tension from Hamish's broad shoulders.

"I had the most delightful time with your sister, though." His ears grew hot as he realised just how that must've sounded. *Yes, that'll really endear me to him.* Rubbing his temple, he added, "We were reading some of your history and folktales. Something about an attack on this very castle and a single boy surviving." Already, the details were fading, picked clean of relevant information.

"Aye? She has a fondness for that one. Tried to do the same with me when I was a young man, but I was never one for spending too long indoors."

Darshan nodded. Although he had only been here a few days, he'd picked up a distinct liking of the wilderness from the man. That could work in his favour in regards to questioning Hamish, but asking those sorts of questions whilst alone in the woods might very well have the man bolting. "I had the most interesting midday meal, too. One of your sister's favourites as I understand it." It had consisted of thickly-cut meat between two equally-thick slices of bread.

"That'd be the library special. She used to eat wee pies and pasties in there, but grew tired of dropping pastry everywhere." Hamish shook his head, smiling fondly at some distant memory. "I can still remember the look of horror on the cook's face when Nora entered the kitchen to make the first one."

"What were *you* doing in the kitchen?" Perhaps it was different here, but the royal family didn't tend to venture anywhere near such common amenities back home. Darshan wasn't even certain he could lead the way to any of the palace kitchens.

Hamish grinned, boyish mischief glittering in those blue eyes. "I was there as punishment. Cook had me peeling tatties for several hours."

"Peeling—?" Darshan laughed at the imagery. "What did you do? Flog off the silverware?"

"Something like that. Where were you headed?"

He shrugged. "Nowhere, really. But I was wondering... I am interested in taking you up on that offer of showing me one of your pubs."

"Now?"

Taking in the slight confusion on the man's face, Darshan decided some reassurance was in order. "Not a date." He wouldn't presume anything until he had gotten to know Hamish a little more. "Just a... cultural experience, if you would."

The man's puzzled expression deepened, scrunching his nose. "Date? As in a set day?"

"No," he drawled. He hadn't been taught the actual word for such socialisation. Finding out if he'd a like-minded individual nearby hadn't exactly been on his intended agenda, certainly not according to his father or tutors. Only now did it occur to him that such outings might not even be a done thing in Tirglas. "I meant as in an excursion involving a romantic couple. Which I was trying to stress my suggestion is most certainly *not* that," he babbled, mentally kicking himself.

Hamish scratched at the underside of his chin. "I dinnae ken..."

Darshan scoffed. Perhaps there was a sliver of truth in Gordon's words about his brother last night. *The poor man*. "If you are thinking of first garnering your mother's permission, then I am rather afraid you have missed her. According to your sister, Queen Fiona will not return home until evening."

"Nora said that?" He bit his lip, his gaze settling on a window set deep into the corridor. "Evening, hmm?" Grinning, his focus turned back to Darshan, that boyish mischief reigniting his face. "Sure, then. We can be back well before she arrives. You go change into that plain outfit you wore to the city yesterday whilst I saddle the horses and I'll show you one of me favourites."

"Wonderful!" Darshan fought to hide a grimace of wearing the same attire behind exuberance. It had been laundered as to his requests—by a most amused middle-aged woman—but to be seen in public wearing the same outfit so close together would've turned him into a pariah back home.

Hamish paused as he took a few steps towards the stairs. "Oh, and Darshan? The date thing? We call it ducking out."

"Noted." His heart pounded. Excitement or anxiety? Either seemed plausible. If things went to plan, he would know where he stood on certain matters. He just hoped Hamish didn't react poorly should the answer be negative.

~ ~ ~

The Fisherman's Cask was situated near the docks and served as a sort of hub for all sailors, be they locals in search of a drink close to work or travellers from afar. That was what had first drawn Hamish to this place in the distant past, beyond it being the farthest pub from the castle.

Propositioning men here had been easier on his conscience. Sailors were often more willing to bed another man than other like-minded land-working Tirglasians. They'd also the added benefit of being off home with the tide.

The smell assaulted his nostrils first as Hamish opened the door. Always did. It was a sort of briny stench that spoke of fish guts and seaweed drying on the shore. He didn't know where it came from as the pub interior was immaculate, its flagstone floors kept clean of dirt and drink in equal measure.

Whilst he had learnt to ignore the smell, he glanced at Darshan to gauge the spellster's reaction. The man's nose wrinkled slightly, but he voiced no objection towards venturing further so Hamish led the way into the room.

Smoky lantern light greeted them. It glowed dully on the battered wooden tables and muddied the mortar clinging to the assortment of stones that made up the walls.

Despite it being mid-afternoon, *The Fisherman's Cask* already had a wide assortment of patrons. Some nearer the door were deep in their drink and oblivious to all else. A group to their left played darts, the dull *thunk* as each one hit the target was greeted by collective groans or cheers. At the back of the room, another bunch tossed wooden rings onto the tusks of an old boar head.

Darshan froze at Hamish's side, his expression one of uncertainty. "Well now," he breathed. "What a quaint place. Not exactly a high-end establishment, is it?" He arched a meaningful brow at Hamish.

Heat flooded his face and he offered up an apologetic smile. *Maybe I should've chosen another pub.* Something a little more suited to serving an imperial prince. The man's attire, although absent of the embroidery and gems of his arrival garments, practically glowed in the low light. Hamish wouldn't be surprised to discover it was silk or finely woven linen.

On the other hand, they were here now, leaving would likely generate more rumours than having a few pints together could ever hope to garner.

Darshan must've come to a similar conclusion as he seemed to gather himself and waved Hamish on. "Please, lead the way."

Inclining his head, Hamish strode across the room. Curious eyes, some already deeply fogged with drink, tracked their passage. More likely, they watched the ambassador. He would need to be mindful of opportunists attempting to accost the spellster once they left.

They settled on a couple of barstools, where Hamish flagged down the barkeep, Ewan.

Unlike the farmer of the same name, this man had a sickly grey complexion that matched his greying blonde hair. He'd a sparse beard and, through it, a disapproving frown had permanently etched itself into his face, dragged down further by heavy jowls.

Still, there was a hint of youthful curiosity gleaming in his dark gaze as he eyed Darshan. "This is the ambassador I've been hearing so much about?" Ewan asked Hamish, jerking his head towards the man in question.

Hamish fought to hide a smile as one of Darshan's brows twitched upward. The spellster continued to stare at the assortment of kegs and casks sitting behind the bar as if he hadn't understood a word. It was possible. The barkeep had a thicker brogue than most around Mullhind, the kind that spoke of him coming from the northward mountains across the harbour.

"Aye," Hamish answered. "He's here to sample some of Mullhind's finest."

"Oh ho!" Ewan slapped his hand on the counter. He gave Darshan a wide grin, the smoky light turning his teeth yellow. "And what does his lordship wish to taste first?"

Darshan remained silent for a time, likely trying to decipher the accent.

Just when Hamish thought he might have to translate, Darshan said, "Wine would be good, right now." The words came slowly, almost wistful. "Any will do, but a nice Nulshar Red would be preferable."

Ewan frowned. He glanced at Hamish before leaning across the counter. "Is he serious?" He jerked his thumb towards Darshan as if the ambassador wasn't a mere few feet away.

"I assure you, I am quite serious," Darshan snapped back, the reply raising Ewan's thick brows. Heat flashed in the ambassador's eyes, his narrow-set nostrils flaring.

Hamish clapped a hand on Darshan's shoulders. There was a lot of tension in that slender frame. Just what would the man do if he considered himself slighted? What was the spellster capable of? "You're in Tirglas, your imperial highness." Out the corner of his eye, he caught Ewan's face growing greyer. "You should drink like a Tirglasian."

His gaze swung Hamish's way, becoming far warmer. "Then, what would you suggest?"

"How about we start with a couple of pints of me usual?" Hamish said to the barkeep.

"Getting him right into the strong stuff, your highness?" Ewan chuckled, a nervous edge weaving its way into the notes. He eyed Darshan warily. Did he understand that the ambassador was a spellster? Or was it the royal address Hamish had unthinkingly uttered? "Two usuals it is then." The man tottered off back to a barrel crowding the other meagre ales. He returned bearing two wooden tankards with creamy white heads of foam and set them on the counter before moving on to other tasks.

Hamish took a swig of his drink, watching Darshan's reaction out the corner of his eye as the man mimicked him.

Darshan smacked his lips and delicately wiped the foam from his moustache. "Tastes like sucking on an iron bar."

Hamish chuckled quietly into his tankard. The man wasn't wrong; there was a certain hint of iron in the aftertaste. Perhaps not to the extent Darshan suggested, but if all he usually drank was wine, then any Tirglasian drink might take a bit to acquire a taste for.

Regarding the tankard as if it was poisoned, Darshan took a slightly less bold sip before wrinkling his nose and setting the drink back down. "What absolutely ghastly stuff this is. Did I hear you proclaim this was your usual?"

Hamish nodded. "When I can escape the castle for a few hours." His mother didn't mind him spending time amongst the locals—he *was* the public face of his family, after all. But it had been some years since he'd been able to venture off unescorted.

"Then you, my friend, must have an iron stomach to match this swill. If I ever brought this home, they would likely use it to strip paint off the walls. This simply cannot be the best Mullhind has to offer."

"If it's that bad, then why are you still drinking it?" The spellster had been taking one hesitant gulp after another, almost punctuating each sentence.

Darshan glanced down, his brows lifting as if he was surprised the tankard was still within reach or so empty. "Why I do believe my senses are in shock. I must have gone catatonic for a while there. Or perhaps I simply cannot believe it is truly as bad as my tongue proclaims, but alas..." He took a long swallow, set the tankard down and shuddered.

Hamish ordered a second round.

Darshan treated it in much the same fashion, swallowing in small, shuddering sips. The ambassador seemed to sway on the stool, but he couldn't possibly be drunk already, he hadn't even finished his second tankard.

Hamish twisted in his seat, indolently leaning on the counter to take in the pub.

More people had filled the room. They crowded tables and jostled each other in games. Music had started up at some time between the two drinks, the source being a man plucking the string of a Udynean lyre and another beating a hearty tune on a drum. A few drunken louts danced in the centre of the room, some singing off-colour songs, the words garbled but vaguely Cezhorian.

He turned back to the ambassador, who sat with his back hunched to the crowd, idly swirling his drink. "I was wondering, what—?"

Darshan held up a finger as, with the other hand, he knocked back his drink before setting down the empty tankard. "Right, I believe I am sufficiently lubricated for questions." He grinned up at Hamish. There was definitely a touch of cockiness to the quirk of his lips. "Ask away."

"What's with the eye windows?" Glass was expensive, with the best stuff coming from Niholia, maybe it was different in Udynea, but he'd never heard of people putting small circles of it in front of their eyes.

The man peered at him, those dark brows squeezing together in confusion. "The *what*?"

"The thing on your face." Hamish twirled his finger near his eye, just in case the man still didn't understand what he was enquiring about.

"You mean the glasses." Smiling, Darshan touched the side of the frames where they seemed to curl behind his ears. "The lenses help me see. I am as blind as a mole without them."

Hamish had heard of farmers struggling in their later years to pick out their stock on the fields, but never thought it could happen in younger people. What would a Udynean prince need to see so badly that he would be tied to such things as glasses? "And here I thought a powerful spellster would've had his slaves fetching him everything he could possibly need," Hamish said, the words escaping perhaps slightly more acerbic than necessary.

The man blinked owlishly at him.

Unable to bring himself to rescind the words, Hamish pressed on. "I'm assuming that, being the emperor's son, you would have slaves. Or do they all belong to your father?"

Darshan frowned into his empty tankard, likely lamenting that state. "No, I have a handful. Gifts accumulated throughout my childhood, for the most part, which I share with Anjali. My twin sister," he clarified, swirling his tankard then tipping it to drain the last few drops. "The nobility likes to make a show of gifting imperial children with their best and brightest. There were quite a few when we were born; wet nurses, valets and the like."

"*Gifts?*" Hamish echoed, the word barely passing through his lips, shock near stealing his breath. He knew about the barbaric practice of buying and selling people like cattle, but *gifting* another as if they were mere trinkets? "They're people."

"Yes." Darshan gave a bittersweet smile. "I am well aware of that, thank you." He twirled his tankard, letting it rock on the counter without him laying a finger on it. The act got a few stares from nearby customers, but little else.

Hamish bit the inside of his cheek. The details he had heard of the Udynean slave markets was that the people weren't considered as such. They were ranked as animals and—to his surprise and disgust in himself—he had been expecting such a response from their imperial prince. "I notice you didnae bring any with you."

Laughter rumbled out the man's barely-parted lips. "No doubt some kind-minded soul would have tried their hand at convincing them to stay." He flashed another mirthless smile. "Simply put, a great deal of them are quite elderly, I would not have them risk their lives taking such a journey."

"Elderly?" He supposed, given that the man looked to be in his late twenties, that the wet nurses and valets were likely to be at least a decade or two older. "*All* of them?"

Darshan gently rocked his head from side to side. "I do not like to consider their children as in my ownership, although they technically are, but yes. That neither I, nor my sister, have purchased younger slaves to replace those who are getting on in years is a topic that often circulates the court's gossip wheel." He snickered and flapped a hand. "Besides, even if I had done so, I can survive without people waiting on me."

"Then why dinnae you free them?"

The man grew silent, running his tongue along his top lip as he clearly searched for an answer in the countertop's beer-stained wood.

Hamish set his drink down.

"I will confess, the thought has crossed my mind." The words grew quieter the longer Darshan talked, as if he dared not speak them. He swung about on his seat, all focus trained on Hamish like a boarhound on the hunt. "But it is a little more complicated than simply signing their freedom papers. There are laws in place for such acts. Mitigating factors on how many can be absolved of ownership at once, the amount they must be paid, where they must live afterwards, the sort of jobs they can take up..."

Hamish hadn't ever considered there'd be any laws involved in slavery. Or that once being a slave would carry such a stigma. Yet Darshan spoke as if he expected any of his people to be treated in a manner akin to those branded with the Black Mark. *Like criminals.* His mother had abolished the punishment, which often didn't fit the crime, before he was born, but people still eyed those carrying it with great suspicion.

"Not to mention the likelihood of them becoming victims to exploitation," Darshan continued. "Without the tie of my ownership, I am uncertain what would become of them. I would not like to think my father would see them shuffled onto the streets, but the palace chamberlain might. The very reason as to why they were given their freedom can often turn a dedicated, hard-working slave into an impoverished free being."

"But they would have their freedom."

Darshan frowned. "Do not mistake it as twisted excuses. If there is one thing Udynea fosters in all her people, it is pride. And I know of many a poverty-stricken citizen who has preferred to die in the Pits than accept a helping hand in return for their freedom. But the very thought of my Nanny Daama relegated to the streets of Minamist..." He clapped a hand over his mouth, the lantern light flickering on his rings as he took a shaky breath. "I would be foolish indeed to think an elderly elven woman like her would survive long on her own, even if she is a strong woman."

Hamish remained silent. It seemed the wisest option given that the man looked on the verge of tears. It was far from the reaction he had been expecting. It had to be the drink opening him up.

He ordered them another pint. He certainly needed another, what with the way the conversation was going, and having Darshan carted back to the castle draped unconsciously over the back of a pony might be preferable.

Darshan knocked back a few hearty swallows of his drink with barely the bat of an eye. The tankard slammed onto the counter, slopping more over the rim. "Alas, I think Daama might actually give me another of her clips over the ear if I tried to free her. She is a bit of a traditionalist."

An odd expression took Darshan's face. It was almost as if he spoke not of a slave, but of family, such as a cherished aunt or grandmother. Perhaps he did see her as such.

Hamish tapped on the handle of his tankard. His memories of his grandparents before the plague took them were dim, but he could imagine having a part of his family sent away without warning. The priests had done that when they'd cloistered his younger sister.

"I suppose there are also others who would react poorly to losing her," Hamish murmured before drinking deeply. He peered at the ambassador out the corner of his eye, trying to gauge Darshan and finding the man favoured not reacting. "Children, maybe? It must be hard being so far away from your family." The Udynean capital of Minamist was literally on the other side of the continent. He couldn't imagine having such distance between him and home.

Darshan shook his head. "I have no children." Chuckling, he scratched at the side of his nose with a thumb. "And what a bone of contention that is."

"Your wife must be eager to remedy such an oversight." Hamish knew without an ounce of doubt that he would already be a father if it wasn't for the truth of what he'd have to do to turn that into a reality.

A weak, and slightly queasy, attempt at a smile stretched the man's lips. He snatched up his tankard and mumbled into its depths, "Not married."

"Oh?" The man was perhaps a little too pretty and foppish for Hamish's tastes. And a little on the lean side, despite his protests at Nora pointing out the same thing at dinner last night.

"There *is* a very good reason for that." Darshan set his mug on the counter and, giving a smirk, motioned him closer. "It is something of a secret."

Intrigued, Hamish closed the already small distance between them. Amusement danced in the man's eyes. *Hazel.* This close, the separate rings of brown and green in Darshan's eyes were clear in the pub's light, colours muddied only where they met and merged. *That's nae fair.* Of course he would find the prettiest eyes belonging to a man he shouldn't consider being alone with.

He also couldn't help noticing the ring of black around the rim of Darshan's eyes seemed slightly smudged in the inner corners, near where the glasses sat. Was it some sort of powder? The clans would sometimes plaster dyes and paints across their skin during war, but he had heard of men in foreign lands using such things in a more civil setting as fashion and tradition dictated.

The ambassador clapped a hand on Hamish's shoulder, tearing his attention back into the present. "It goes a little something like this..." In one swift move, Darshan slid his fingers into Hamish's hair and sealed their lips together.

There was no hesitation in the act, nor any forceful prying open of his mouth to invade with a tongue, just the bold press of his lips. There for a blissful moment then gone.

"Oh," Hamish breathed. "I... er..." In all his years of fooling around, of rutting with strangers in the dark, he'd never met a man that forward.

Darshan returned to his drink, his face flushed by more than alcohol. His gaze slid back to Hamish as he drained the last of his drink. There was certainly something of an invitation lurking in that multi-coloured depth.

Hamish wet his lips. Should he dare to answer such an invite? It could cause a lot of trouble for the both of them if it was found out they had done anything more than a kiss. *Probably best to leave it.* The ambassador didn't need Hamish's past stirring up the future prospects for their countries.

He opened his mouth, prepared to tell Darshan as such.

"Oi!" a man roared from the other side of the room. "Udynean!"

Chapter 6

Hamish hunched his shoulders. He recognised that voice. *Big Billy.* He winced as Darshan turned at the cry with one brow raised in question.

The man was one of the dockmasters, built like a bull and belligerent when drunk. He was also responsible for several people needing to be rushed to the cloister for healing. If Billy objected to Darshan's presence, then things were going to get messy.

Please, dinnae be right. Hamish twisted in his seat, hoping that having to defend the ambassador wasn't going to be necessary. His hopes sunk as he spied Billy stalking his way through the hastily parting crowd, flanked by two of his lackeys.

"You," Billy growled, jabbing a thick finger at Darshan. "Just what did you think you're doing planting your filthy mouth on our prince?"

Smirking, Darshan stood to face Billy. "What did I think I was doing?" He squared up before the three men, swaying slightly with his arms akimbo. "I was kissing him."

Hamish groaned, leaning on the counter, his head in his hand. There went any chance of leaving without a fight.

Billy laughed coldly. He loomed over the ambassador, his shoulders squaring, his work tunic barely containing them. "You looking to die today, lad?"

The two men flanking the dockmaster gave twin chuckles. One rolled his shoulders, clearly eager to begin such a task, whilst the other cracked his knuckles.

Hamish laid a hand on Darshan's shoulders. "Come on, the drink's clearly gone to your head." A drunk spellster. He thought the man's magic would've kept him from reaching such a state. "You cannae win a fight with him. He makes two of you."

"As if that matters," Darshan replied. "I can still kick his arse." Even so, he lowered his fists.

Billy's lips parted to reveal broken and stained teeth. Hamish had seen similar expressions on starving feral dogs. "As if I'd let you near me arse, rutter." He cocked his head and spat onto the flagstones at Darshan's feet.

Hamish held his breath, tightening his grip on the spellster's shoulder. *Please, dinnae understand him.*

The whole pub seemed to grow still the longer Darshan stared at the man, his expression blank.

"Bill," Hamish hissed at the dockmaster. "That's enough." The man must have realised it would be the grandsire of all bad ideas to piss off someone capable of setting things on fire with a thought.

Ignoring Hamish, Billy continued to give the spellster a smarmy smile.

Darshan returned the grin, his tongue snaking out to run along the underside of his teeth. He calmly unhooked his glasses from behind his ears. "Hold these, will you?" he asked, waving the frames in Hamish's general direction.

Hamish took a cautious step backwards. He couldn't be certain if Darshan was merely posturing or actually planned to attack the man, but it would be better if he stayed out of it. After all, he couldn't haul Darshan back to the castle if they were both unconscious.

He delicately reached for the glasses.

Darshan barely waited for Hamish to properly grasp them before he swung at Billy, clearly aiming for the man's head.

Billy jerked back, too late in mounting a defence against the attack.

The spellster's fist—heavily bedecked in jewelled rings—connected with Billy's face like a hammer. The definite snap of breaking bone was almost an exhalation.

The dockmaster fell back, howling. Blood poured from beneath the man's fingers, staining his blonde beard. At first, Hamish thought the ambassador had only broken Billy's nose, until he caught sight of the dockmaster's jaw. One side bulged alarmingly, whilst the right, the side Darshan had hit, was caved in.

The two men flanking Billy lunged at the spellster.

Sneering, Darshan flicked both his hands as if brushing the dust from his outfit. The men went flying, smashing into the walls. Neither one got up.

More men jumped up from their seats, agog. One ran out the door screaming. Not a one of them seemed to know what to do about the spellster who had made short work of three men; a foreigner who still stood over Billy without a care as to the bleeding state of his hand.

Hamish wasn't entirely certain it was even Darshan's blood. Surely, with the force he'd hit the dockmaster, he must've broken something.

Darshan turned. He squinted at Hamish, then held out his bloodied hand. The fingers and knuckles seemed normal enough. No twists or swelling that suggested any harm had come to them. "My glasses, if you please?"

Hamish returned the item in question back to their owner. "I think this might be the best time to leave." There'd be trouble once word of this got out—and a lot of questions Hamish wasn't looking forward to answering. But if they returned to the castle now, then Gordon might be able to help him wrangle a more palatable version of events for his mother.

With the glasses once more firmly in place on his face, Darshan glared at Billy. "One moment." He strode over to the howling man and grabbed his head. "Do not move or I will leave you injured. And I would advise against trying to talk."

Billy stilled. Panic and fear flashed in his tear-redden eyes.

It had been some years since Hamish had last been in the presence of healing magic. But he'd been in no position to objectively watch either. Seeing the man's face slowly reform to its previous state was something he'd never thought he would witness.

Billy's cheeks shifted alarmingly, like a bubbling pot of porridge. The skin constantly changed colour, from the pinkish-red of freshly-struck to the bruised rainbow hues of blue, purple and green, then fading to trout-brown before regaining its natural wrinkled and heavily-tanned state.

Throughout it all, Billy's eyes grew wider. He whimpered and fisted at his trousers. If Darshan hadn't already stipulated stillness, he likely would've bolted from the spellster's grip.

When Darshan was done, he released Billy's head and let the man tumble onto the floor. "Call me that again and I shall do the same," he snarled as he bent over the dockmaster. "Only next time, you can keep the broken jaw. Understood?"

Billy nodded. "Aye, your lordship." He back-crawled across the flagstones, pausing only to rub his jaw and standing once Darshan was well beyond physical reach.

Dusting his hands, the ambassador returned to Hamish's side. "As entertaining as that was, I think you are right, we should return to the castle."

Hamish expected them to be attacked as they left the pub. Hindered by guards or a small mob, at the very least. That the streets were empty certainly didn't bode well. He caught flashes of life on the edge of his vision as he removed their mounts from the pub stables; little more than figures at doorways and windows, looking out for possible danger. No one appeared, much less dared to approach them.

The streets began to fill out the further they got from *The Fisherman's Cask.* People bustled about their tasks, children played amongst their elders with some wrangled into working alongside them.

They rode in silence, partly because the noise around them made any sort of conversation beyond shouting at each other impossible. That Hamish couldn't think of a topic not pertaining to what had happened in the pub didn't help matters. It certainly wasn't the type of thing he wanted to discuss where others could hear.

Their journey was halted several times; once for several men pushing rattling barrows laden with goods, and again as a cart packed with bleating sheep passed through the main street, heading for the southern hillside.

Hamish barely noticed they had left the rest of the city behind until they'd begun the upward path towards the castle gates. He eyed the man on his periphery. Away from everyone else, the silence didn't quite sit right with him. Not after that kiss. *And the brawl.* Although it seemed ridiculous to call it such when only one punch had been thrown.

But that kiss...

He rubbed a hand across his mouth as if that would scrub the memory of how Darshan's lips had felt against his own. *Sure and supple.* Dominating, but not to the point of overbearing.

He had heard strange things about Udyneans. Whilst on some things it was hard to parse out the fact from the fiction, he was relatively certain that men being openly affectionate with other men was something that *did* happen there.

Whether Darshan had been pulling his leg with such an act was a different matter. The man hadn't seemed shy about admitting it in the pub. Had he somehow known Hamish wouldn't react badly to the act? Had someone told him? *Gordon.* If his brother had put the man up to this, then Hamish was going to kick his arse.

He flipped a tuft of his horse's mane to the other side of her neck. *Best nae to linger on it.* What difference could one kiss make in the long run? "So," Hamish squeaked before clearing his throat and trying again to fill the quiet with idle noise. "You're a healer?"

Darshan chuckled, a wicked sound that conjured visions of secret spells woven in the darkness. "Repairing that man's jaw gave it away, did it?" He grinned warmly. "I am indeed. Most Udynean nobles have some rudimentary knowledge in that area, enough to have an innate healing ability. It keeps us from being poisoned so easily."

"Poisoned?" Hamish latched onto that morsel of new information, desperate for anything that would keep his mind off the man's lips.

"That's a common occurrence in Udynea?" He had thought Nora had been attempting to fool him when she mentioned something similar all those years ago. *I guess I was the daft one there.*

Darshan rocked his head from side to side. "Not at the moment. There are a great deal more recreations to occupy the mind, but it becomes fashionable every now and then. New mixtures are concocted and those lower in the ranks are always looking to ascend by way of permanent elimination of the upper nobility."

Hamish frowned. Disputes amongst the nobility in Tirglas generally involved whole clans feuding. Eliminating those higher up was often a cause of battles, not the end. Clearly, the people had no loyalty for their leaders. "Have you ever been—"

"No," Darshan replied before Hamish could finish asking. "Any poisons that make it as far as the palace do not have a habit of bypassing my father's personal guard. But he likes to ensure all his children are capable of defending themselves."

Hamish nodded. Whilst it was harder to grasp the idea of deliberately poisoning an enemy, being able to defend against an attack was an easier concept. His whole life, from the moment he could wield a weapon, had been forged around the idea that history could one day repeat itself and he would be forced to defend the castle, or even become the only one left like in the old tales his mother always spoke of.

"Wait a minute," he mumbled, his thoughts circling back to what the ambassador had said earlier. He nudged his mare closer to Darshan. "If you can mend bone and clear poison from your blood, then why are you so dependent on those?" He indicated the man's glasses with the twirl of a finger.

Seemingly taken aback, Darshan pushed his glasses further up his narrow, hook-like nose. "Well, it is not that simple. I can heal, yes, but I am no healer."

"The difference being?" He could understand there being a difference if magic wasn't involved. Hamish had long since been brought up on the idea that cloistered spellsters were only allowed to leave their cloisters to work healing magic, and only then during epidemics or wars. During ordinary times, most people had to make do with medicine men and sawbones. "I thought magic could do anything?" Hamish would often have his ear bent with feats performed by spellsters in other lands.

Darshan turned his attention towards the view of the harbour.

Hamish slumped into his saddle. Clearly, he wasn't going to get much from the man there. They rode on, the only noise breaking the stillness between them coming from the muffled crunch of hooves on the road.

After a while, Darshan cleared his throat with a mighty cough. "I think you are confusing magic with a tool. It can be that, it can also be a weapon, but it is, first and foremost, an extension of the self. Which is why some things come easily; shields, minor deflections, the small heat of a flame. They are little more than the will made solid."

"And healing isnae one of these easy things?"

Darshan shook his head. "Would you say your bow was easy the first time? Or a sword? Healing is skill and training and art all bundled into one immensely twisted knot. Just starting down its path demands one completes an extensive study on what is required for particular parts to mend."

Hamish peered at the ever-nearing castle gate. He couldn't spy any extra guards or a sign that anyone was waiting on their return. Maybe they could linger a little longer, learn a little more of what spellsters were capable of. "Such as?" he pressed, gently encouraging this horse into a shuffling plod.

The ambassador adjusted his own mount's speed to match almost subconsciously. "Take our skin for instance." He twisted in his saddle. An eager spark lit his eyes, making his whole face glow. "That is the easiest healing magic and usually the first taught. Our bodies are built to repair it quickly—not as much as elves, of course." He waved a hand, seeming to dismiss the fact. "But healing any species only increases the body's natural process. Bone is a little harder, but considered as basic field training. Organs are trickier, best left to experienced minds, and even then their successes vary wildly. Not having just enough knowledge, or the wrong kind, can kill a patient as cleanly as any blade."

"Or blind them?"

They passed through the castle gates. Guards on both sides saluted them. Hamish returned the gesture with a warm smile and a nod. None of the guards seemed twitchy or mildly concerned with their appearance so late in the day. That had to mean his mother hadn't yet returned from the farm.

"Eyes are all but impossible to get right," Darshan continued, seemingly oblivious to the men and women around them. "There have been attempts, but the success rate is not exactly sparkling. The idea of having otherwise serviceable vision lost for vanity has never sat well with me. There is far less risk in a good pair of glasses."

Dismounting, Hamish led his mare to the stables. "Unless you're brawling a great deal?" he shot over his shoulder. How many of those glasses did Darshan have with him? He'd be daft to think the man had travelled so far with just the one pair. "And you clearly have been in a few scraps before." Or at least come up against a man like Billy before to know he would have to throw a punch like that to keep the dockmaster down.

Darshan grinned, wide and feral. The cockiness that'd fallen away when he spoke of healing now snapped back into position. "I have been in a few. More than my father would like me admitting. *Strike first, if you must,*" he deepened his voice, clearly mimicking someone. "That is what he would say. *Hard, fast and first. Then make sure they stay down.*" That dark chuckle returned as he slid from the saddle. "Won a lot of scraps that way. Although, it probably helped that most of them knew who I was."

Hamish glanced up from handing his own mount over to a stablehand. It hadn't occurred to him to explain that detail to the dockmaster, not that it would've stopped Big Billy if he was itching for a fight. "To be honest, I didnae think you were that strong." He had witnessed others trying their luck with the dockmaster. Not many could beat the man, but those who could hold their own were generally just as bull-like as Billy.

The spellster's grin wavered, growing a little shy as he peered around Warrior's back. "If you promise not to tell anyone… I sort of cheated there. You can, if one is as well-practised in healing as I, bolster natural strength with magic. Just for time, a very *short* time. Pushing that boundary can run the risk of tearing the very muscles apart."

Hamish clapped a hand on the man's shoulder, steering him out of the stables and towards the castle doors. "Then it's just as well you laid him out with one punch."

Darshan winced, then visibly collected himself. "I suppose you expected to be carrying my broken body back. I did have a shield up, not that you would have seen it. If he had tried to hit me, he would not have made it far."

A shield? They could make those with magic? No wonder the spellster had faced Billy so calmly. *And an invisible one, to boot.* Hamish scratched at his chin. If he could hunt knowing he couldn't get hurt, he'd probably go after more of the troublesome bears and boars. "What I actually thought was that you didnae understand him," he confessed.

The ambassador shook his head. "I have no idea what he said, but I assumed it was derogatory by your reaction."

"Then why'd you heal his jaw?" Most brawlers would've been more than content in leaving Billy broken and bleeding. Doubly so if the man had insulted them.

Darshan mumbled something as they entered the castle proper.

"What was that?" The snippets Hamish had caught hadn't sounded like any of the Udynean he'd heard. Just a long word that he couldn't say with all certainty wasn't actually the man cussing.

"Just an ancient Domian motto. Translates to *Offer mercy to the wounded, it confuses the enemy*. My father still trots that one out whenever my sisters squabble." He glanced up at Hamish, the inner corners of his brows lifting in concern. "I suppose I should apologise… for my behaviour."

Hamish scoffed. "Dinnae fash. Nae many people can say they've knocked Big Billy down a peg or two. It was actually kind of fun watching you kick his arse."

"No, no. That was—" The man bit his lip, his brows lowering slightly in thought. "I meant what transpired before then. It was completely my fault and I—" Huffing, he tucked a lock of hair behind his ear. "I am usually better at this."

"At kissing men in pubs?" Hamish gently prodded. He had been trying—and failing terribly—to forget that part had happened. His lips tingled at the mere mention.

Darshan laughed, the sound light and with a hint of nervousness. Had he been told what had happened to the last man Hamish had been with? "Well, I *did* just spend several rather wretched months aboard a ship, so I cannot say it is something I have indulged in recently. But I usually conduct myself with a little more decorum before it gets that far. In public, at least." He rubbed his neck. "It would seem your Tirglasian drinks loosened me a little faster than I had believed."

"Oh aye?" On the edge of his vision, he spied the unmistakable sight of his mother storming around the corner and coming their way, flanked by two of the guard. His stomach dropped. He'd been hoping to avoid a confrontation, at least until morning. "Hold that thought."

"What did you think you were doing?" his mother screeched before she had fully walked the length of the hall. "I cannae believe that after our agreement, you would kiss—"

"Actually," Darshan blurted. The man stepped between Hamish and his mother, the majority of his body turned to the side so as to not quite be seen directly confronting her. "*I* kissed *him*."

His mother didn't miss a step. She bore down on them, her forefinger raised like a dagger. "*You?* How *dare* you bring this corruption into me home."

The ambassador straightened to his full height. Although his face had settled into a mask of haughty indifference, fire and anger flashed in his eyes. Still, he didn't fully face her.

"Mum," Hamish interjected, shame burning his cheeks. He wasn't a boy of ten stealing kisses from stable boys. However he felt about Darshan kissing him—and he was still trying to process everything that had happened—he was quite capable of dealing with it.

"Bad enough that I must still deal with your sort under me roof, but that you think you can lay your filthy hands on me son and corrupt him with your ungodly influence is unacceptable."

Darshan's mask wavered. His nostrils flared and there was the twitch of his jaw speaking of a retaliatory tongue barely restrained.

"*Mum*," Hamish pressed. It couldn't be a good idea to upset a spellster, certainly not one strong enough to bring down a man twice his size. Surely Darshan was going to crack at any minute and she was going to end up stuck as a slug.

His mother jabbed a finger in his direction. "*You* are to be escorted to your quarters." With a twitch of her head, she ordered the men flanking her. "See to it that he doesnae slink off elsewhere tonight."

"What?" Darshan snapped, his voice tight with disbelief. "You are putting him under house arrest for a *kiss*?" All colour had drained from his face, turning his olive-brown skin a sickly shade. Those hazel eyes darted between Hamish and his mother, frantically seeking the truth.

"Aye," Hamish's mother snarled back. "For his own good."

The guards' hands had barely touched the back of his arms before Hamish shrugged them off. "I'm going." He glanced over his shoulder at Darshan. A soft twinge of regret tightened his chest at the sight of the man weathering further berating at his mother's hands.

I shouldnae have let him kiss me. He should've pulled away or pushed Darshan back. Anything to show he wasn't a willing participant.

But no, he had just sat there like a lump, enjoying himself.

It'd been so long. Years—over a decade, at least—of denying himself any intimate contact. To know, after all that time, that he was still desirable... It had stolen all rational thought.

The guards led him to his quarters in silence. The dull thump of his door closing at his back might as well have been the metallic clang of a cage.

Hamish flopped back onto his bed. He stared at the ceiling, watching as the last of the evening sun set. The room slipped into darkness, save for a single sullen candle grimly glowing on his dresser. He rolled his head and turned his attention to the tiny flame. *His had burnt brighter*. Had it really been just this morning gone that Darshan had shown his niece and nephews the ability to create fire from nothing?

His stomach rumbled a sullen inquiry as to the whereabouts of dinner. Someone might eventually remember to send some up, but it wouldn't be enough. It hadn't been the last time his mother locked him in here.

A faint knock broke the quiet.

Hamish lifted his head. There were only a few who would dare venture near his door after his mother's tirade and he wasn't certain if he wanted to speak with any of them. But then, they might also have food. "Aye?" he called out. "What are you after?"

The latch clicked and, as the door slowly opened, Gordon poked his head in. He glanced around the room before entering fully, bearing a covered tray. "We havenae been indulging in spontaneous decorating this time?" Shaking his head, Gordon shut the door and set the tray on the bedside table. "Must be serious."

Grumbling under his breath, Hamish half-heartedly flung a pillow in his brother's direction. "What do you want?"

"I was out and about, fetching dinner for me dear incarcerated brother, when some interesting news caught me ear. Something about you and the ambassador locking lips down at *The Fisherman's Cask*."

"And you just so happened to be drifting by to hear the whole thing?" Hamish couldn't help laughing. *There* was the real reason why his brother had come a-calling. "You're almost as bad a gossip as your wife was."

"So," his brother drawled. "Is it true? Did you actually kiss him?"

Hamish scoffed, pushing himself upright until he sat on the edge of the bed. "I wouldnae say that. More *he* kissed *me*." Resting his elbows on his knees, he fisted his hair. "It's nae fair, you ken? *You* slept with your wife well before she even won the union contest and you didnae get in trouble."

Chuckling and shaking his head, Gordon plonked onto the bed. "I think your memory of events are a wee bit different to mine there. I got a right bollocking for it." He bumped his boot against Hamish's. "And, from what I hear, you didnae exactly stop him."

Closing his eyes, Hamish's thoughts drifted back to how Darshan's lips felt against his. So very sure of himself. *I should've kissed him back.* That would've made being locked in here a little more bearable.

"Be careful, 'Mish, you ken what Mum will do if her guards catch you."

"It was just a kiss." But how he wanted more. In one moment, that man had reignited something he had thought long-snuffed. "And Mum's already well aware of it, so there's nae need to fash yourself over that. And I've nae plans to take it further. He willnae thank me if Mum has him kicked out of the kingdom." The last thing Tirglas needed was to enter into a war with the Udynea Empire because his mother had offended one of the emperor's children.

"I'm surprised you were nae subtler about it than last time."

With his head still firmly resting in his hands, Hamish glared at his brother. "He asked to see a pub and I showed him. I didnae exactly expect him to snog me once he got a few drinks in him."

"To be fair, you probably should've."

He glared harder, pursing his lips for optimal glowering. *Probably right.* Not that it mattered. The fact Gordon would've thought of it whilst Hamish hadn't was just another reason not to let his brother off easy.

"Dinnae look at me like that." His brother gave his arm a shove, almost tipping Hamish off the bed. "Did I hear right in that he also fought Big Billy?"

"Aye." A grin tugged at Hamish's mouth, much has it had done in watching the belligerent man go down to someone half his weight. "And then dealt to a pair of Billy's lackeys."

"They say he broke Billy's jaw?" His brother was clearly needling for more details.

Hamish was more than happy to give them. "Billy was doing his usual intimidation tactic. If I'm honest, he probably would've tried it even if we'd only had a few drinks. But Darshan, he took Billy out with one punch." He swung his fist, mimicking the spellster's action. "I didnae think Billy was expecting it. And then, Darshan went and healed the man."

Gordon frowned at him. "What'd he go and do a thing like that for?"

He shrugged. "They believe mercy confuses people or something like that." It certainly confused him. The reasoning behind it, at least. "I just think he was trying to show off. There cannae be many places in Udynea where you can scare a man with magic."

His brother clapped an arm around Hamish's shoulders. "Correct me if I'm wrong, but it sounds like you had fun."

"I'll nae lie, I did." A long time had passed since he'd been able to venture into a pub and not have one of his mother's lackeys breathing down his neck. To just relax with a congenial companion was something he didn't get outside of joining his brother.

"Do you want to see if I can arrange things so you two could...?" Gordon's brows lifted suggestively. "Be alone? Together like?"

Hamish shook his head. "I cannae risk it again." This wasn't like the last time he was caught with a man. Yes, prematurely evicting the dwarven ambassador from Tirglas had resulted in a bitter response from their Coven of hedgewitches, but ultimately nothing further.

To do the same to a Udynean ambassador? A *prince*, no less? He didn't want to be the cause of a war between his kingdom and a powerful empire. Whilst the mountainous Tirglasian terrain would be an inconvenience for any army in the short term, it wouldn't matter if their spellsters chose to burn the forests.

His brother squeezed Hamish's shoulders. "Listen to me when I tell you it's nae healthy for you to spend the rest of your life like some virginal prince locked in a tower."

Scoffing, Hamish rolled his eyes. "I'm nae locked away." Most times, at least, he was free to roam the castle grounds. "I leave the castle every day. I hunt." Sometimes, he'd camp out in the woods for days. "I even visit Caitlyn." And it was a two-week round journey to the Cloister, a place that had become his sister's home ever since the blossoming of her magic. Granted all that generally involved an escort, but where he went was his choice.

"But you always return."

"You ken why I stay." Leaving the castle on a permanent basis might raise a few eyebrows, but his mother would've found a way to cover it up. Likely by claiming he had been killed. Yet it was better to have his mother's disappointment aimed at him than his nephew. Not that the lad's time wouldn't come, at least he would've lived his childhood not hating himself.

"All I'm suggesting is, if the man's confident enough to kiss you in public, then maybe—"

Hamish was shaking his head before his brother could finish the sentence. "That's nae happening. You remember what became of the last ambassador I took a liking to?" It had been over a decade ago, when the dwarves were in need of experienced hunters to keep them safe as they roamed the old ruins up on the mountains behind Mullhind.

His brother chuckled. "Aye. And I can still hear Mum's shrill tone over *that*."

And well he should. Especially since the guards had found Hamish in the guest quarters, on his knees orally servicing the dwarf. That the pair of them had gotten no further didn't seem to matter. A kiss, it seemed, was too far for her liking. "He said I was phenomenal."

"Sweet Goddess' teats!" Gordon cried, clapping his hands over his ears and shooting him a disgusted look. "Did you have to—?" He shuddered. "Nae. *That* goes straight on the list of things I nae want to hear about, or *from*, me brother. Right at the top."

Hamish snickered and waved his hand. "You can put your arms down, idiot. You only deserve that for letting your ears flap far too often."

Gordon cautiously lowered his hands, eyeing Hamish as if suspecting foul play. "So, if you're nae going after the man, what do you want to do about all this?" He waved a hand around the room. "You cannae sit here the whole time they're negotiating."

His brother was right on that last point. Whilst the only way he could avoid another incident with Darshan was to remain in his room, that wasn't an acceptable solution. He still had his own duties and the ambassador could be here for weeks. "Visit Caitlyn?"

That had been his original plan. Especially after seeing how coolly his mother's response had been to Darshan's arrival. If he had gone immediately and spent the two-week round trip to see his younger sister, then the ambassador would've likely hammered out the details of the trade agreements and been off. It would've suited everyone perfectly.

He would've already been on his way if Darshan hadn't expressed an interest in seeing a cloister and his mother had agreed to let the man go with him. That certainly wouldn't be allowed now. "I just hope Mum doesnae do something daft."

"You ken Mum," Gordon said. "She'll nae let it go easily." He stood, giving Hamish a hearty pat on the back. "But I'll see if I can talk her into us taking that trip. Or, at least, letting you out of your cell. In the meantime, dinnae forget your grub. I brought you extra."

Hamish nodded his thanks before his brother left the room. *I should never have let him kiss me.* His brother was right in that he should've seen it coming. *I'm a right idiot.* Thirteen years and he went and screwed it up with the first man who had expressed an interest in him.

Chapter 7

Darshan lay still on the bed, staring up at the ceiling. He had discarded his sleeping garments sometime during the night and, still, sweat beaded off his brow. The mattress beneath him was firm, unforgiving and overall hard. He rather wished it was the only thing that could've been described thusly, for it certainly didn't help matters.

Groaning, he rubbed at his temple. His head might not ache from that ghastly concoction Hamish had dared to call alcohol, but ridding the after-effects of such toxins taxed his healing magic. He never much liked the weak feeling that came over him from an excessive use of his power, but he hadn't any control over the latent healing.

How much of the damn stuff had he drunk? He had lost track after the second tankard, but it'd certainly not been enough to forget how much of fool he had acted.

So much for subtle. What had he been thinking, kissing the man in public like that?

Chuckling, he flung an arm across his face. Who was he fooling? "You knew exactly what you were thinking," he muttered. *Get an answer*. Yes or no, one way or the other, he had to know his chances.

But what a response.

Even if Queen Fiona hadn't blown the entire scenario all out of proportion, he would've known the truth. He had kissed men who weren't as interested in him as they'd claimed. They didn't lean into his kiss like Hamish had, and certainly didn't flash him hot eyes afterwards.

It didn't help that he used to have wet dreams about strong and gentle men like Hamish. The untamed but docile sort. Tall, rugged and hairy men just didn't seem to exist back home. He hadn't truly believed they existed at all until reaching Tirglas.

Grunting, he rolled onto his side to glare at the stark grey stone wall. It wasn't fair. Sending him to this dismal place where men couldn't enjoy themselves with a chaste kiss.

And to do anything a little more physical?

His thoughts were more than willing to spiral into knowingly forbidden depths. It already had a fair approximation, but what he wouldn't give to know more...

He slid his hand down, taking a firm hold of himself. It'd been a long time since he had done anything as tame as use his hand on its own, but he'd been ruthlessly denied any of his usual toys. Being sent to Tirglas was meant to be his punishment after all.

Closing his eyes, he furiously moved his hand. Imagining it was a certain delicious redhead took some effort. Hamish's hands were bigger—he recalled that much from their first meeting—calloused from years at archery.

A small moan eked through his lips. It wasn't enough. Imagery could only get him so far.

If he had but one of his toys to—

Darshan bolted upright. Surely one must have made its way past keen eyes and aboard the ship. He jumped to his feet to rummage through his travelling chest, desperate. He had spent months aboard that wretched ship, surrounded by women and with nothing better to idle away the days than to learn of this stodgy kingdom.

Anything would do.

Yes! Buried at the very bottom was a small wooden box, still wrapped in one of his drawers. Disturbing the toy inside revealed a small vial of oil tucked into the velvet cushioning. The toy itself wasn't much to look at; reputably modelled on the average man back home and curved just slightly to hit the right spot. It couldn't replace an actual hot, flesh-and-blood being, but it would do for now.

His hands shook as he hastily applied the oil, spilling some onto the dark wood floor. Then he was back on the bed, no longer lamenting the mattress' lack of give as he lowered himself onto the toy. A soft grunt wisped out his nose at the slight burn as eagerness overtook his usual care. He worked through the feeling, which quickly faded thanks to his innate healing abilities.

If he were home, alone and with no desire to seek out company, he would've settled down to a little reading be it a saucy story or some naughty poetry. The kind that'd make prostitutes blush. But those had all been confiscated along with the rest of his toys.

He tipped back, squirming ever so slightly across the blankets. Arching on the bed, he slipped one hand beneath him. His fingertip touched the smooth metal disc nestled in the toy's base, pushing the final inch in.

Steadying his breath, he sent a small pulse through the metal. A tiny amount would be all he'd need at this point.

The toy vibrated deep inside him, amplified by the metal core, slowly fading and eking out a shuddering groan from his lips. Another pulse, longer, just enough to let the vibration build, to push him that little bit higher.

He turned his thoughts towards Hamish. Maybe he wasn't allowed to touch, but he could certainly imagine. He ground his rear on the bed, convincing himself it was that delicious hulk of a man who was currently in him. A soft moan slipped from his lips, his imagination easily conjuring up visions.

His finger on the toy slipped. Darshan hastened to readjust, grinding against it. With his free hand, he grasped himself and stroked, each movement trembling. He sent a fresh burst through the toy, a spark of lightning this time. The buzz it set off had his hips bucking.

There was no chance of lasting after that.

He lay still, unable to do more than tremble and pant as the residual magic in the toy petered out. *Wow*. He hadn't reacted so strongly to one in quite some time. Perhaps there was some merit in that denial theory some of the scholars back home preached about.

This wouldn't rid himself of the dreams, though. No more than it had in the past. But it had taken the edge off. It might even let his mind think clearly on other matters after his heart stopped pounding through his temples like an ancient dwarven war drum.

A timid rap on the door broke through his reverie.

He stared at the door handle for several thundering heartbeats, his chest heaving. Had he actually thought to lock the door last night? Or was the servant just too polite? Either way, he didn't think he had the strength to decently cover himself.

"Yes?" he managed.

"I didnae mean to wake you, your highness," a small voice replied. "But Her Majesty is waiting for you in the study."

"Of course." He leapt to his feet. A dull thud heralded the toy hitting the floor. *Blast*. Years had passed since he had been that forgetful or used so much oil. "Inform Queen Fiona I shall be forthwith." Scooping up the toy, he bundled it into a rag and threw it into the travelling chest. He would deal with it later. Right now, it'd be best to not have such an item lying around where innocent eyes could just stumble upon it.

He made his way to the royal study only after he could be completely certain he had scrubbed away the smell of exertion down to the smallest trace. Applying the customary kohl around his eyes was a far more taxing task than usual, with his hands still shaking, but leaving without it just wouldn't do.

The study was small, practically minuscule in comparison to the vast chamber his father used back home. He supposed the fact there were only two people to deal with rather than the imperial trade coterie helped in that sense.

Queen Fiona glanced up as he entered, those ice-blue eyes harder than yesterday. "I see we have deigned to join us," she haughtily announced as if she hadn't been the one to cut their talks short yesterday.

Wonderful. His gaze darted to Nora. The woman might sit at her mother's side, but she certainly didn't seem on it. "My apologies. I overslept." He settled into the chair positioned on the opposite side of the table and thumbed through his notes. "I believe we were discussing the tariffs on linen?"

"We had gone past that," Nora tapped on a piece in her own notes, which were scattered between herself and her mother. "We had even agreed on a percentage."

They had? Frowning, Darshan shuffled madly through his sheaf of parchment. *There.* A note scribbled in a corner to confirm with his father's council on the lowest amount he could negotiate with. "Ah, I believe I am still waiting on the pigeon with the official response." Fortunately, the bird would only need to make the nearest Udynean town. They had faster methods of communication, but alas, being that they relied heavily on magic, he had been barred from bringing such a convenience into the kingdom. "Should we move on to the wool or the leather?"

"Actually, I'd like to focus on the imports, if you dinnae mind? Specifically, iron."

Darshan nodded. He recalled that, whilst the mountainous Tirglasian countryside might offer an abundance of ores, iron was rather scarce. That would've been fine some centuries back, when even the Ancient Domian Empire had only mastered bronze tools, but not in this day and age. "Yes, I have been authorised to trade raw iron and steel ingots from the mines and mills in Oldunmere."

"That's..." Nora swivelled in her seat to glance at the large tapestry on her right. Someone had taken great pains to stitch out an elaborate map of the known world, right down to the small plague islands dotted beyond the shores of the Stamekian capital city.

At any other time, Darshan would've marvelled at such work. Now, he had to resist the urge to fidget. "You will find Oldunmere is above the Shar, your highness. The big lake in the middle."

"Ah." She turned back, one sandy brow arched. "That's quite a distance. And inland at that."

He inclined his head in agreement. "The mines closest to your border are regrettably absent of the materials you seek and the ones near Minamist are, as I understand it, not on the table."

"And what if we really wanted them?" Queen Fiona murmured. "Could we nae just go in and take them?"

Darshan stared at her. It almost sounded as if she was suggesting her people would invade the Udynea Empire. For iron the imperial citizens would gladly trade. He had to be missing something. "I do not understand."

"I welcomed you into me home. We dined together as allies."

"*Mum*," Nora said, her stern voice an absolute joy to hear after her mother's sharpness. "I ken you're pissed, but could we get back to discussing the actual reason he's here?" She tapped on the pile of scrolls and loose sheets of parchment. "This is in everyone's interest."

Queen Fiona continued to bore her icy gaze into Darshan without a hint she had heard her daughter. "You repaid me hospitality by defiling me son."

Scoffing, Darshan rolled his eyes. One kiss, it seemed, was enough to have him thrown in the same dank category as criminals. "Your son was hardly shocked by the act. I would even hesitate to say he was mildly stunned." And Hamish wasn't the only one to exhibit a rather reduced level of surprise. Queen Fiona had been angry, yes, but not in the least bit taken aback. "Honestly, it was a kiss. You are acting as if I bent him over the counter and had my way with him then and there."

No sooner than the words had left his mouth did he spy Nora trying to hide a wince.

"Nae doubt, if it hadnae been for one of me people causing a ruckus that is exactly what you would've done next."

Darshan shot to his feet, the chair crashing behind him. How dare she! He was not some animal. He had morals. Limits.

The air, especially directly around his hands, was far too hot. He fussed with his sleeves, trying to calm himself. Any greater a temperature and there would be combustion. He couldn't risk that. Not here, surrounded by at least a dozen flammable, and very important, objects.

"It would seem you are not in the mindset to discuss things civilly." As much as his pride demanded he didn't let the insult slide, allowing the queen to calm down would surely be a far better outcome for his land in the end. He turned to face Nora and bowed. "I do apologise, your highness, but I doubt any negotiating can be done until your mother has composed herself. I will take my leave until then." Graciously giving Queen Fiona a slightly deeper bow than he had offered her daughter, he strode out of the room.

He hadn't gone more than a few steps when the sound of pursuit caught his ear. He whirled about to meet the threat head-on, the purple shimmer of his shield snapping around him.

What he came face to face with was Nora.

She stared at him, wide-eyed and a touch fearful. Then her gaze grew slightly unfocused as she reached out to lay a hand on the barely-visible barrier between them, jerking back with a gasp once she met resistance. She peered at her fingers as if not quite believing what they had felt. Had any of the royal family met a spellster before?

Darshan let the shield dissipate. If the woman had any intention of being a threat to his life, she likely would've made an attempt on it yesterday, when they were alone in the library for the entirety of the morning. "Has Her Majesty calmed herself so quickly?"

Nora shook her head. "Me mum doesnae do calm very well." She glanced over her shoulder, then without moving her head, peered at him out the corner of her eye. "I ken things are done differently in Udynea, but—"

"No." He cut the woman off with a swipe of his hand in the air. No matter whether or not she would be more reasonable in her tone, he wasn't about to listen to the same lecture. "I am getting thoroughly sick of having to repeat this, but it was a *kiss*." Such an innocent act wouldn't have been given a second glance back home.

But he wasn't in Minamist. He wasn't even in Udynea. *I really should've thought it through*. Well, he hadn't and now he had to deal with the consequences. "I will speak with you and your mother when she is ready to talk trade."

Darshan stormed down the corridor, pounding his rage out through his heels. If they were going to treat him as some debauched heathen set on corrupting the entirety of the royal Tirglasian bloodline, then he was more than willing to accommodate them in acting like one.

~~~

Hamish tied the final loop around the fletching in his arrow. He held it up to the light, checking the binding, before setting it into the basket with the rest. The feathers would need trimming later, but that task wasn't as time-consuming or relaxing as the initial binding. In any case, whilst he was allowed to have much of the tools for fletching in his room, a knife wasn't one of them.

His stomach gurgled a rough demand of food as he picked up another arrow shaft. Ignoring the reminder that breakfast had been quite some time ago wasn't easy, but he managed to concentrate on
~~~

his task.

The faint creak of his door opening unannounced drew his attention.

Hamish glared at the handle, waiting for the person on the other side to speak. Had the guards finally come with lunch? *About bloody time*. He squared his shoulders, readying himself to give whoever was on the other side one hell of a verbal bollocking. If anyone thought they could sneak into his room and leave without him noticing, he was going to leave them with no doubt there.

A mop of dark brown hair preceded the soft glint of glasses and the brightness of gem-studded silk.

Darshan? Hamish leapt to his feet, knocking over the basket of arrows and scattering its contents in his wake.

The man winced as he quietly closed the door. "I am dreadfully sorry. It was not my intention to startle you, but I thought it prudent not to shout out my whereabouts."

Hamish dropped to his knees, shaking his head as he hastily collected the arrows. Whilst he appreciated the caution, that wasn't his immediate concern. When the last arrow was back in the basket, he cast a furtive glance around him. The spellster was *here*. In *his* room. Alone. "How…?" he rasped in answer, shock stealing his breath for the brief moment it took to clear his throat. "How did you get by the guards?"

Darshan frowned and indicated the door with his thumb. "There are meant to be guards out there?"

Hamish bolted for the door. Sure enough, jerking it open revealed nothing but empty corridors. How long had they been gone? They generally made an announcement of their departure from guarding his door at dawn, but he'd been under the impression that his confinement would be until the ambassador had left. Especially seeing they had brought him breakfast.

He'd bloody missed lunch for nothing.

"Are you often kept locked away?"

He turned back to Darshan, shutting the door behind him. The man seemed genuinely concerned. "You shouldnae be here." If Darshan was discovered in Hamish's room, then that would be the end of any negotiating.

Like a scolded child, Darshan rubbed at his arm. "I gathered that, but I wanted to apologise. Properly. I am not entirely certain what I was thinking."

Hamish leant back on the door, folding his arms. "*Really?*" Amazing that, even with a whole continent separating them, a Udynean prince could come up with the same paltry defence as a common Tirglasian sailor. "Pretty sure I ken where your mind was at."

Darshan chuckled mirthlessly. "Fair enough." He paced before Hamish, his hands fluttering as he spoke. "I suppose you also expect me to blame it all on my intoxication, but when is that an acceptable excuse?" He shook his head. "In all honesty, I still had the wherewithal to know kissing you was a bad decision. I did know how unacceptable such actions are viewed here before it was made absolutely clear by certain parties. I chose to do it anyway."

Hamish remained silent. The stance had already proven effective in eking out more information from the man when he was drunk. Perhaps he would be likewise willing now he was sober.

Sure enough, Darshan continued, "I could wrap up my reasoning in pretty words if you like, but the core of it was that I needed to know if you would be amenable to further proposition. I am aware it is a wholly selfish reason. I make no excuses for it." He bowed slightly, a mere dip of his head and shoulders. "And I deeply regret any suffering my actions may have caused you."

"Aye?" Having a man apologise for their actions was certainly a first, and he had typically indulged in more than a chaste kiss with them. "Well, apology accepted."

Darshan inclined his head a little more. "That is not the only reason I came here." That hazel gaze lifted, barely seen through the upper half of his glasses. "I was worried about you."

"*M-me?* Why?"

"I saw you flinch when you heard..." A faint tinge of distaste twisted his lips. "...*her*. Granted your mother fell upon us like a hell beast, but you had a look in your eye that spoke of enduring far worse than the tongue-lashing she gave. I came here to see if you were all right."

"If I'm—?" He shook his head, trying to clear it. Was he dreaming? He must be. But Darshan still stood there, extremely real and concerned. No one else beyond his siblings, and occasionally his father, ever expressed any unease over his mother's treatment of him. "Aye, I'm fine."

"Was she aware about—" He indicated Hamish in his entirety. "—your preference before we kissed?"

"Preference," Hamish grumbled. "I've never liked that word. It always comes with the intonation that another option is still viable. I've a preference for pork over venison, but I'll eat either. It's nae the same with this."

Darshan slowly nodded. "I gathered as much. Allow me to rephrase, then. Is she aware that you like only men? I am assuming it is only."

"Aye, it is." Otherwise, he would've been married with children like his siblings. "And she is, although she'd prefer otherwise." He peered at the man. "What of you?" He could assume they were the same, but he had long dismissed the idea of relying on assumptions when came to men's desires.

"Well," he drawled "To use your analogy, I am definitely a one-kind-of-meat man." He looked about him. "If you are all right, then I guess I should leave before I make things harder for you." He bowed and turned to the door.

"I'm sorry about what she said," Hamish blurted as the man's hand touched the handle. "I know she's a wee bit harsh, but dinnae turn her into a slug or anything." He peered at the spellster's face, marking the slight confused furrow forming between his brows. "You cannae do that, can you?"

"Not that I am aware of."

The tightness in Hamish's chest eased some. That didn't erase the possibility of a dozen other gruesome attacks, but it was one less to worry about. *I cannae wait to tell Gordon.* His brother had always believed spellsters to be capable of anything. "I'm still sorry that—"

"No, no." Darshan held up his hand. "You need not waste your breath. The fault is mine. I admit it freely and I apologise again for putting you in that situation. I had rather forgotten where I was, but that should not excuse me."

"But still, what she said was—"

The man dismissed the words with a flick of his hand, his gaze deflecting to skim the room. "I have been called far worse. Being a bad influence is the least of my sins." He flashed a wolfish grin, one brow arching. "Although, judging by what I heard, you are somewhat less innocent than I thought you were."

Hamish chuckled. The man really had been ignorant if he had thought, for even a moment, that Hamish was at all innocent. "That I am."

"So," Darshan purred. "I admit I have been wondering..." He sauntered across the space between them, slowly stroking the small amount of hair on his chin. "If the naughty prince has been bad before, just how bad does he want to be now?"

Swallowing, Hamish took a step backwards. That the answer of 'very' almost slipped from his lips nearly had him bolting for the door. *If we're caught.* Well, they still could be just standing here doing nothing. "I hope all this hasnae given you the wrong idea about me. Especially me mum."

"She was very loud, I will give her that." Darshan halted before him, his dark brows lowering in thought. "But I think it is more a case of your mother's tirade over an innocent little kiss that has given me the right idea, namely that you have locked lips with other men in the past."

"Aye." Hamish managed, the word little more than a gust of breath.

"And, if I am not mistaken in that you *have* done something like this quite a few times..." The man's gaze finally settled on Hamish's face, those hazel eyes warm, wanting and that little bit uncertain. "Then perhaps, you have done quite a bit more?"

"That too." Although there would be a lot more bulk to the men he usually rutted with. He would've been concerned that Darshan might actually break if they attempted anything, but the vision of the man knocking out Big Billy was still fresh in his memory.

"Well, the mind positively boggles." He slowly walked his fingers up Hamish's undershirt. "Just how far have you gone?"

He shrugged, his face warming. Was this how most Udyneans acted around each other or was it just how Darshan did? "Far enough to get me into trouble," he admitted.

Darshan wet his lips. "I would like to explore this further, *if* that is what you also want, of course."

If? This was not a matter of *if*.

The spellster frowned. Whatever action he seemed to have expected from that declaration, Hamish clearly hadn't done. "Would you rather not? I would never—" He held up his hands in surrender. "I do not want you thinking you are obligated to a positive response." Sighing, he hung his head. "My apologies, I am not usually the one doing the propositioning."

I can believe that. A son of the emperor would likely only need to express a mild interest in a person for them to throw themselves at his feet. Hamish shook his head. "It's nae that."

"Am I not to your taste, then?" There should've been heat in that question, or at least a little bitterness. But Darshan's voice remained light and calm.

"I have nae taste." The words were out before Hamish could consider them. Hearing them aloud had his cheeks flushing hotter than any summer day could make them. "That's— I didnae mean— *That* came out wrong."

Darshan laughed. He might've given a little snort and tried to quickly cover his amusement by clearing his throat, but it was definitely laughter.

"Sure," Hamish mumbled, his face heating further. Was that what this was going to be like? He'd fumble and the man would laugh at him? "*That* you understand straight away."

"I do not need you to tell me. I can *see* the lack of taste." The man spread his arms wide and spun on the spot, gesturing at the room. "One only needs to take in the ghastly decor."

"Hey!" Yes, carved figurines from his childhood still lay scattered about various shelves, along with small trinkets his niece or nephews had brought him during their excursions. Only his bow, gifted to him when he'd reached manhood, had an actual place where it belonged, but he would hardly call it horrible.

"Not that it is entirely without redeeming features," Darshan added, a mischievous smile plumping his cheeks. "A few throw rugs, some gauzy curtains... getting rid of the antlers."

Hamish's gaze swung to the pair of antlers set above his bed. They had come from a magnificent twenty-pointer three autumns back. It had fed a good portion of the nearby village, too. He turned back to find Darshan grinning at him. "You're nae serious, are you?"

"A bit." Those hazel eyes lowered, creasing at the corners. "Forgive me." The man's whole chest shook in mirth as he spoke. "Do continue. It has been some years since I got anyone flustered."

"I find that hard to believe."

"Oh?" Darshan rocked back on his heels, mock surprise lifting his brows. "He does flattery, too? You are most welcome to continue babbling nonsense at me, if you like. I can wait."

For once, Hamish wished he had the time to spare. Then he'd find out just how much patience the man really had. "Do you think I have nae experience in this?"

Genuine surprise danced in Darshan's eyes and raised just a single brow. "No, I—" His lips twisted sourly before he ran a hand over them, mussing his moustache. Huffing, the man turned from him. "The thought did cross my mind," he confessed, the words muffled. He waved his hand flippantly. "One can hardly determine much from a single kiss." His gaze settled on Hamish, uncertainty flickering to life in their depths. "Am I moving too quickly for you?"

Hamish shook his head. If anything, this was the slowest he had ever gone with a man since his first time.

"Allow me to make myself perfectly clear on the matter. I am aware of how this is viewed in your kingdom." He reached out, a timid hand alighting on Hamish's chest. Warmth soaked through his undershirt. "I want you, make no mistake about that, but not if it means further strife for yourself. If you want me to bac—"

He cupped Darshan's jaw, marking the faint hitch in the man's breath. "What I want..." A smirk took his lips upon recalling Darshan's original question. Hamish wrapped an arm around the ambassador's waist, drawing them closer together. "...is to be very bad." He caught the soft gust of Darshan's gentle laughter and a flash of a grin before he claimed the man's mouth with his own.

Darshan sagged against him. He made a small noise in the back of his throat. Not quite a whimper, but not deep enough to be a moan.

The sound raced down Hamish's spine, running straight to his groin. He hadn't heard a noise so unashamedly needy in years.

"Your mouth tastes like sin," the spellster purred against his lips.

Hamish grinned. "I'd hold off on any such declarations. I havenae started sinning, yet." He drew the man's lips back to his, prepared to make good on that promise.

Chapter 8

Hamish slanted his mouth over Darshan's, their tongues twirling around each other. This was familiar, like a dance. Dim though, as if it were a distant memory or dream.

Still, he recalled the steps.

Darshan's hands slid up Hamish's shoulders, a soft moan escaping the man's mouth. The gentle kiss Hamish had started with was met with unabashed passion. It set his head spinning.

When he paused to catch his breath, the raw desire pouring off Darshan seemed ready to ignite the very air.

The man's fingers slunk up Hamish's neck and carried on to entwine into the thick coils of his hair. Darshan pressed against him, necessitating that Hamish grab the man's hips. The spellster seemed to take it all in stride, grinding against Hamish.

That was new. Any other man would be halfway through with hauling down his trousers. Was Darshan waiting for some sort of signal from Hamish? He hadn't ever actually taken the lead before, always being the receptive one. And he'd thought after the man's boldness in the pub…

His hands shook as he tightened his hold on Darshan's hips and took the first step back. Terror and expectation mingled in Hamish's muscles as the spellster practically flowed after him into the centre of the room and towards the bed. *His* room. *His* bed. Not once had he ever been brave enough to let anyone take him here.

His gaze slid cautiously to the door, as if it might swing open at the mere thought. Nothing could stop that. It may remain closed at the moment, but he couldn't lock it. *We shouldnae do this.* Not here. The guards could, theoretically, return at any time.

And if they found him with the Udynean ambassador?

"Hamish?" They had broken the kiss at some point. Darshan

stared up at him, the corners of those hazel eyes creased with concern. "You *do* want to do this now, do you not?"

If nae now, then when? They might never get another chance like this and he would only wind up kicking himself if he let this opportunity slip away. "Sorry. I was just—" Hamish took another few steps back towards his bed, coaxing Darshan to follow with a gentle tug of the man's arm. Maybe if they were quick.

Darshan's cocky smile returned. No trace of nerves. He'd likely never concerned himself about being caught in the act, probably indulged in his desires on the regular. Still, his bejewelled fingers seemed to tremble slightly as he picked at the few buttons holding the neck of Hamish's shirt closed.

Hamish stepped back again, this time, ensuring the man didn't follow him. The back of his knees touched the bed frame. "What are you doing?"

"Undressing you? Generally, nakedness is involved." Darshan fussed with the collar of his knee-length coat—a sherwani he had called it—undoing buttons Hamish still couldn't make out amongst the embroidery running down the front of the outfit. "Unless you would prefer to do it yourself?"

"Fully?" Most of his times had involved no more undressing than the quick downing of trousers and smalls.

Darshan paused in tugging one of his boots free. "Are you certain you have experience with this?"

"Aye." Was that the something the spellster had expected from him? "Just... nae here." He spread his hand, indicating the room. A large percentage of his time rutting involved a dark place in a pub's storage. "And nae fully naked."

Frowning with his other still-booted foot awkwardly held in his hands, Darshan shook his head. "That simply will not do." He hauled the boot off and tossed it to one side. There was a shimmer in the air between them.

Firm, but gentle, pressure from the very air hit Hamish's chest, tipping him off-balance. Having no chance to right himself, he fell back onto the mattress. He propped himself on his elbows. Had that shimmer been magic? *Aye.* The act had been so precise.

Darshan planted himself between Hamish's parted knees. He stared down at Hamish, his arms folded and a wolfish grin parting his lips.

The sight sent a shudder through Hamish that tingled and pooled in his groin. Every dark story he had ever heard of spellsters flooded his mind, rendering him incapable of speech. How much of what he had been told was true? It was a bit late to worry about having his soul stolen through a kiss, but what of other things?

The man bent over him, laying a hand on Hamish's thigh. "If we are doing this, I would prefer no barriers between us. So, either you take that shirt off." That grin was back for a heartbeat. "Or *I* do."

Nae barriers. Not even linen. Just bare skin wherever they touched. "I think I can manage that." He stood with Darshan backing away to give him room. With the buttons at his neck already undone, it was a simple matter of untucking the shirt from his trousers and pulling it over his head.

The action was met by Darshan's whispering gasp.

"My word." The man's gaze ran over Hamish. Barely-restrained lust burned in those hazel eyes. The tip of his tongue brushed across his upper lip ever so slightly. "You are practically a walking rug." His fingers reached out, returning to clench at his side before they could land on skin.

Hamish looked down at his chest and shrugged. Yes, he carried a dog's-worth of dark red hair there, but it was hardly anything noteworthy. "I guess it's a Tirglasian thing." All the other men he had ever been with—the only exception being that one ambassador from Dvärghem—were native to his country. And even the dwarf had been just as hairy as himself, if not more so.

"Yes?" Darshan cast another hungry glance over Hamish and sighed. "I rather think I grew up in the wrong kingdom. Minamist lacks men like you." He bit his lip, seeming to consider the statement. "Well, maybe the docks, but I suppose I cannot count the few Tirglasian sailors who make port."

Frowning, Hamish paused in untying the cords of his trousers. Had he imagined that jittery note in the man's voice? "Do you usually talk this much?" His past experiences had all been rather quiet beyond grunts, and the occasional pained hiss from himself upon their entry.

The man's cheeks darkened. "Not generally." One side of his mouth hitched up. "But then, I have never been nervous about this before." He ran his fingers through his hair. "Which is surprising in itself seeing that this is most definitely *not* my first time. But I am afraid you might find me rather lacking in certain departments. I am no sparsely-haired elf, but I am hardly a rug either." He laced and unlaced his fingers, toying with a ring or two along the way. "I hope you actually do find me to your taste after all this."

"You're a man, you've a pulse." Too late, he clapped a hand over his mouth. He hadn't actually said that out loud, had he? *Well, there goes me chance.* When the words weren't immediately met with Darshan's departure, he lowered his hand. "I dinnae mean you were—" He fisted his beard, tugging at it slightly, letting the pain help clear his head. "What I meant was—"

Darshan's laughter stilled Hamish's his tongue. It was a dark sound that seemed to relax the man's shoulders. "Oh dear," he murmured, laying a hand on Hamish's chest. "Is the bar truly set so low?" His other hand slunk up Hamish's side, the faint brush of nails digging in as the man's touch wandered across Hamish's back.

Heat flooded his face. Of all the corners to back himself into. "I'm nae exactly in a position to be picky."

Pity flashed in those hazel eyes and flattened Darshan's mouth for a heartbeat. "Well, neither can I, since we are being honest. But even with a choice, you would have been high on the list."

"Likewise." If he had ever been given that mythological chance to choose, like his siblings had, it would've been someone bold enough to chase him even knowing the consequences.

"Since we seem to be getting our tongues horribly tangled." Darshan wrapped his arms around Hamish's neck. "How about we go back to something a little easier on them?" He coaxed Hamish down, their lips brushing each other for but a breath.

Hamish drew back to eye the man. "You're really nae bothered?"

Sighing, Darshan's fingers returned to roaming Hamish's neck, sliding up to thread into the thick hair near the nape. "No." Those hazel eyes lifted. The hot and wanting glaze to them had vanished, replaced by something far softer. "I am not exactly a stranger to being… a port in a storm as it were and if that is all you require, I am happy to oblige." His hands slid down to the waist of Hamish's trousers. "But I do find these being still on as bothersome. Allow me."

Before Hamish could speak either way, the man set to work on the cords. Hamish's trousers dropped at a phenomenal rate.

Darshan's gaze slunk down Hamish's body, clearly tracking the very direct passage of his fingers. A soft groan escaped the man's throat as he caressed Hamish's length through his smalls.

Hamish's legs trembled at the touch, threatening to dump him where he stood. It had been far too long since any but his own hand had ventured so close. "Wait," he gasped, breathless. He was almost naked whilst Darshan, bar his boots, was still fully clothed. "Do I nae get to undress you?"

Darshan grinned. "If you like. Allow me to make it easier for you. These buttons can be fiddly." He waved his hand down the sherwani and the front unfurled like a butterfly.

More magic? The man had clearly just used some to undress himself. Was there anything those spellsters didn't use as an excuse to show off their power?

Shrugging out of the sherwani, Darshan tossed it to one side and spread his arms in open invitation. "When you are ready." Underneath sat a short tunic very similar in design to what the farmers wore out in the fields. Likewise, the trousers—although cut in a manner that hugged the man's legs and tented eagerly at the groin—were merely fastened by a simple cord. Removing both would be an easy matter.

Hamish's fingers fumbled to untie the knot at Darshan's waist and failed. *Focus, you idiot.* He could perform better than some novice. Sucking on his teeth, he tried again to similar effect.

His gaze flicked to the door as he finally loosened the ties, it helped keep the heat dominating his face in check, but brought back far more sinister thoughts. "I dinnae suppose you've a spell that can keep that shut." He indicated the door with a jerk of his chin.

Darshan wrinkled his nose. "Excusing the fact I do not do *spells*—" He all but spat the word. "—I am going to say yes… and no. I *could* place a barrier in front of it," he continued before Hamish could ask, tugging himself free of his trousers as he spoke. "Very easily, in fact."

"But?" Hamish pressed.

The spellster offered up a smile that bordered on embarrassed. He laid a hand on Hamish's arm, steadying himself whilst freeing his other leg of clothing. "It would fail once my thoughts turned to other matters."

"Ah." It had never occurred to him that, whilst spellsters could weave incredible and terrifying feats at a whim, it was intrinsically linked to their thoughts. Or what that really meant when distracted. "Bit like archery, then. Part instinct, part focus."

"You could say that."

Hamish made swift work of discarding the man's tunic. He rocked back on his heels. Rather than be faced with a man clad only in his smalls, there was another tunic beneath. "Just how many layers are you wearing?"

Darshan lowered his gaze, but not before Hamish spied him blushing. He fingered the tunic as if surprised to find it there. "Only the three." He hauled the final article off over his head. A faint shudder ran through his body. "Tirglas is a touch colder than back home."

"Aye?" Hamish drew the man closer. Their chests touched at every breath, Darshan's vaguely hotter. He tipped the man's head back, caressing Darshan's chin with a thumb and struggling to think of anything beyond kissing the spellster senseless. "How about I help you warm up, then?"

Humour creased those hazel eyes and a brief chuckle shook Darshan's torso. "I thought you would never ask." He leant hard against Hamish, rocking them off-balance.

With one hand, Hamish gripped the bedpost. "That was more of an offer than a question."

Snickering and shaking his head, Darshan gave a gentle tap on Hamish's chest that had him landing back onto the bed. "Are you really going to quibble over semantics right now?" He grasped the waistband of Hamish's smalls, tugging the front down just enough for the afternoon air to slink its way into his short hairs.

His length strained against the soft linen. Crawling a little way up the bed allowed his smalls to slide off that little bit more. He tugged them down further still.

A faint whimper greeted him being fully naked to the world. Breathing heavily, Darshan assisted in fully removing the smalls, tossing them to one side. Those bejewelled fingers gently wrapped around Hamish's length. A soft groan parted Darshan's lips.

Hamish fisted the blankets, fully reclining as Darshan's hand moved. His touch was soft and warm, definitely practised at jerking off another man. *Just as I'd imagined.* He pushed the thought away, letting it slink back into the forbidden depths. This wasn't the time for thinking. This was only about the moment.

Darshan silently withdrew his presence.

With an objection fighting its way along his tongue to be heard, Hamish sat up only to discover the man was pausing merely to remove his own smalls. Now that Darshan stood there, completely naked like himself, Hamish finally took in what his roaming fingers had already told him. He had thought the spellster might've been a weedy man beneath all those layers, but he was pleasantly toned. Just the sight had his tongue sticking to the roof of his mouth and set his heart pounding.

"Shall I take that look as your approval of the view?" Darshan enquired as he crawled onto the bed to sit upright, straddling Hamish's thighs. The cocky smile was back, but quivering slightly at the corners.

"Aye," Hamish managed, his voice thick and his mind very much focused on how the man's semi-hard length brushed across his own with every breath. He reached out, running a finger up the spellster's arm. Each brush tingled. Was that more magic? Or just his imagination?

He had thought the olive-brown tone of the man's face and hands might've been sun-darkened, but Darshan was a similar shade all over, not even a hint of the sun-lines he'd seen on paler men. And, true to his word, Darshan wasn't all that hairy, but Hamish's questing fingers found a pleasing amount as they ventured across the man's chest, especially heading south.

His length certainly wasn't typical— it seemed to be missing the usual bit of loose skin near the tip—but it reacted no differently at his touch, growing harder under his ministrations.

Darshan rolled his hips. His bejewelled hands landed firmly on Hamish's chest, digging into his hair as the man thrust against Hamish's palm. His breath rasped. A word slithered out his lips, heavy and rough. Then, as his breath was beginning to grow erratic, he gently removed Hamish's hand and leant over him, curls of dark brown hair framing his face.

Their lips met and parted as the man moved on to roam Hamish's neck and shoulders, leaving messy, wet kisses along his path.

A small sound escaped Hamish's lips. Not quite deep enough to be a moan. He didn't think he had the breath for it. Was Darshan trembling? Or was that himself?

Slowly, clearly reluctant to stop, Darshan pushed himself upright again. "Before we go any further…" He bit his lip. "I know you are of age, but I need—"

"Of age," Hamish echoed, incredulous. Just how young did Darshan thing he was? "I've bloody seen thirty-seven summers. I'm *of age* twice over."

Darshan's brows shot up. He mouthed the numbers, then smiled, his eyes crinkling at the corners. "Well now. I do not believe I have done anything with an older man for some time. Not since I was in my teenage years, anyway."

"You dinnae look much younger than me." Yes, the lack of a full beard had thrown him for a while when they'd first met, but there couldn't be that much of a gap between them.

Darshan scoffed. "Oh, the difference is negligible. Four years, give or take a few months. But that is not what I was going to ask you. And I probably should have done so before we got this far. I just—" He rubbed at his neck, his whole face flushing. "I need your consent before we go any further."

Hamish peered at the man, then laughed. Darshan had to be having him on. "I'm lying naked on me bed." And just about ready to explode before they'd gotten very far. "How much more consent do you need?"

"A *lot* more." He breathed deep before the words rushed out. "Granted, you already know what I want, and I believe we are in agreement there, but I need to be certain."

Hamish shook his head, still unable to control his mirth. "You Udyneans have some strange rules." Not a single man had actually asked for his consent. Tearing off each other's trousers and wrestling him over whatever was handy generally counted as that.

Darshan closed his eyes. His brows lowered, encroaching on the metal edging of his glasses. "This is a little more personal," he whispered. "Anything less than an empathetic yes from you will be taken as a no."

"Bad past experience?" He had more than his fair share of those.

A faint hum of agreement thinned the man's lips.

Hamish grasped the man's hand. "Look, I'm nae drunk. Me wits are about me. I fully understand what's happening and I want it. Is that enough for you?"

Those hazel eyes opened. Smiling, Darshan lifted Hamish's hand and gently pressed his lips to the back of Hamish's fingers. "More than enough," he whispered. He returned to his previous position, stretched out atop Hamish.

Darshan's hips rocked, slow at first, then with a determined rhythm.

Hamish followed suit, although it was a bit difficult with the added weight. He hadn't ever had the hot press of another atop him. Not like this. The needy contact of skin on skin, rubbing against each other as they shared breath. Their broken moans and half-swallowed murmurs ate up the quiet.

The spellster's kisses wandered, sharp and quick down Hamish's neck, then open and sloppy along the shoulder. A sudden bony pressure spoke of teeth sinking into the flesh where shoulder met neck. Not enough to be painful, but strong enough to wrench a guttural sound from Hamish's throat and set a fresh wave of desire through his gut.

Darshan reached down between them. His fingers wrapped around Hamish's length. That hazel gaze lifted, eyeing Hamish. Gauging his reaction, he was certain of it. Darshan's hand moved with practised speed.

Try as he might, Hamish could do nothing else but thrust into the man's hand, utterly compliant to Darshan's firm and steady touch.

Before too long, the only sounds escaping him were small, rather telltale, pants. *Nae now. Nae like this.* With great effort, he clasped Darshan's wrist, stilling the man's hand a little too late. Already, his body emptied itself, spilling into the afternoon air.

Bugger! He laid there, burying his face in his hands even as he continued to twitch in the spellster's grip.

Darshan's weight shifted.

Cold air filled the gap between them, sending a shudder through Hamish's stomach. Darshan hadn't left, but Hamish didn't dare lower his hands. He didn't want to see the man's face. To see the disappointment. The derision. The utter disgust.

"Did you just…?"

"Aye." His cheeks burned against his palms. For the first time, in a good long while, he had finally found someone as willing to be with him as he was with them… and he'd blown it. Wetness soaked his fingers. Tears? Was he actually crying now? *Aye.* A few, but well too many. He squeezed his eyes tight and sniffed in an effort to contain them. *Shit.* Turning into a sodden, blubbering mess over all this was the last thing he needed.

Soft and lean fingers curled beneath his, lifting his hands. "Hey, now." The words were light and carried no hint of what he feared.

Hamish peered through his lashes, opening his eyes wider once he was certain of the expression he was faced with.

Darshan knelt next to him, his brows scrunched and raised in the middle. "It happens to everyone now and then." That hazel gaze continued to evaluate Hamish. Did it pick out signs of tears? "We can always give it a little while and try again, right?"

Hamish scrubbed at his face. Had he heard right? The man was willing to wait and make another attempt?

If only. He wanted nothing more than to spend more time with Darshan, but if his judgement towards the angle of the light through his window was correct, they would have nowhere near the amount of time they would need to get the man out unseen before the guards arrived. And once the guards had taken up their positions in the hall directly outside his door, Darshan would be left with the choice of being caught in an hour or in the morning.

Still, he couldn't have the man leave without something.

He silently rolled them over, marking how Darshan's demeanour changed as the man was pushed deeper into the mattress by Hamish's weight. Of the way he bit his lip and flushed right down to his neck. Even his gaze suddenly seemed more interested in settling on anything but Hamish.

Propping himself on his elbows had Hamish witness the man's cocky grin and daring stare return, along with his feather-light touches down Hamish's sides. Did Darshan *like* being pinned down? Hamish gently lowered back onto the man to a similar effect. *He does.* If he just had the time to play with that bit of information.

Sighing, Hamish slid off the spellster and the bed to kneel on the cold floor. Darshan sat up in his wake, one brow raised in silent query. Hamish answered by parting the man's legs and caressing Darshan's length in soft, slow movements of his thumb, eking out the man's trembling moans.

Hamish wet his lips. This should be easy. Whilst he had orally pleasured men who could choke a horse—and weren't exactly gentle with it to boot—Darshan was in the range that Hamish had labelled as pleasant. It was almost a shame that this was likely to be a one-off. "Just so you're nae expecting miracles from me, it has been a while."

Darshan laid a hand on Hamish's shoulder, kneading with his thumb. "And exactly how long is a while?"

Years. His stomach fluttered. Hamish wordlessly lowered his head, sliding his tongue over the man's length before wrapping his lips over the tip and sucking.

With a loud open-mouthed moan, Darshan arched his hips. His hand slid from Hamish's shoulder and up, digging into Hamish's hair. "Gods," he slurred. "Would you be offended to know that is just as I imagined?"

Hamish glanced up to find his gaze locking onto Darshan's. He released the man, ignoring Darshan's faint, disappointed whine. The spellster would more than get what he wanted soon enough. "You've imagined me sucking you off?"

Darshan's answering blush was all Hamish needed for confirmation.

He adjusted his position, abandoning sitting passively back on his heels in favour of a more upright kneeling stance. He kissed along Darshan's inner thigh even as he hoisted both of the man's legs over his shoulders, grinning at the spellster's surprised grunt. Sliding his hands beneath Darshan's buttocks and lifting him higher allowed Hamish to return to his previous actions with full control over them.

Darshan shuddered in his grasp. The spellster struggled only to contain his deep moans. The slap of his hand clapping over his mouth spoke of stinging skin. His fingers wove through Hamish's hair once again, trembling and vaguely attempting to guide. Words escaped the Darshan's lips, mumbled past his bejewelled hand and colliding with his moans. One such word, sibilant and long, repeated over and over.

Hamish slowed, listening as the soft tone of the man's voice grew thick with need, before he registered the words were also entirely foreign. He lifted his head. "I cannae understand a word of Udynean, you ken."

Darshan gave an exasperated huff and, as he altered his grip on Hamish's hair, Hamish found his head directed back towards the spellster's crotch.

That he understood.

He opened his mouth wide, letting Darshan's gentle thrusts dictate how fast he went, and swallowed the man whole. Hamish couldn't see the spellster's face, tipped back as it was. But he heard him.

Darshan no longer tried to muffle his moans—which grew deeper with every downward bob of Hamish's head—opting to plant his shoulders in the mattress and thrust his hips. The spellster's legs tightened around Hamish's neck, using him as leverage.

Words escaped between the pure noise, mostly gibberish to Hamish, but his name came warbling out. Hamish almost stopped the first time. He hadn't ever heard it spoken in such a rich tone, almost on the verge of begging. Only a handful of those he'd been with had known who he was and, of those, just the one beforehand.

Darshan stiffened. His backside, still firmly in Hamish's grasp, clenched. With the man halfway down his throat, Hamish only felt the faint pulse of Darshan's length against his tongue as the spellster emptied himself.

Only once Darshan's body began to sag did Hamish pull back. Breathing deeply of the cool air, he lowered Darshan back onto the bed with far more care than he had hoisted him up and sat back on his heels.

A strange scent drifted on the air, like the sea after a thunderstorm. A glance at the window confirmed only clear sky with the shadows indicating it was far later than he had originally presumed.

Beyond time his guest left.

Darshan slid his fingers into Hamish's beard, cupping his jaw and tilting Hamish's head up. The man's thumb stroked from the corner of Hamish's mouth, continuing on across his cheek, following the natural lay of his beard. He bent forward, their lips close enough to share breath.

Reflexively, Hamish withdrew. "Have you forgotten where me mouth's just been?" No man he had ever been with had wanted to kiss afterwards.

Darshan shook his head, his eyes creased with amusement. "Come here." He threaded his fingers into Hamish's hair, holding him fast as their mouths met. Darshan's tongue parted their lips, moving in gentle strokes.

By the time Darshan let them separate, Hamish was breathless.

He wobbled on hands and knees to the bed post, using it to steady himself as he stood. The man's smalls were draped over the edge of the bed. Hamish gently tossed them back to their owner. "You have to go."

Darshan blinked up at him, those hazel eyes still dazed with pleasure. "Go?" he echoed, frowning. "I just got here."

Hamish nodded. How he wished he didn't have to do this. But if there was any chance, any minuscule possibility, of Darshan being more than another one-time fling—even if only for the duration of his stay—then the ambassador had to leave now. "Tomorrow, climb up the cliffward tower at noon. I promise, I'll explain everything then, but you have to leave now."

On legs made uncertain by excessive kneeling, Hamish crossed the room to the door. Pressing an ear to it revealed nothing. Peeking showed only empty corridor. They had time.

Glancing back revealed Darshan still lounging on the bed.

"*Please*," Hamish stressed. "Before the first guards arrive for the evening shift."

"You will have sentries outside your door? *Still?*" Even puzzled and questioning, the man hastened to dress.

I always do. Yesterday's kiss wouldn't have changed anything beyond making them more vigilant. "Tomorrow. Noon. Cliffward tower."

Darshan pressed a hand to Hamish's chest. "I shall be waiting." Adjusting his glasses, he slipped out the door, trailing the room's heat and that strange thunderstorm scent.

Hamish leant on the door. If Darshan hastened down the corridor, then he would avoid the guards. That would just leave tomorrow. Bubbling uncertainty joined the mixture of relief and lingering lust already churning in his stomach.

How, in the name of the Goddess Almighty, was he ever going to explain his predicament to a man who'd never had to hide himself?

Chapter 9

Darshan stared out at the view his elevated position afforded him. The city of Mullhind stretched out far below, buildings set in clumps rather than the strict curves and lines of home. To his left, the remains of a large building tentatively peeked out from the treetops. The breeze drifted in from the sea, colder and sharper than the warm salty tang of Minamist's onshore winds. He clutched the parapet and breathed deeply nevertheless.

This small space atop the western tower seemed almost remote. He hadn't met another soul on his way up here.

An explanation. That's what he'd been promised. Did he really want one? Was it even needed? It seemed pretty straightforward. The man was terrified of being caught, of his mother and her punishments. Which, if he wasn't mistaken, must have involved locking Hamish in his room for days on end.

If he could find a way to get the man far from here…

Darshan dug his fingers into the edge of the parapet. *This is not your fight.* From the way others around them had reacted to a simple kiss, it was clear enough that what he'd done was seen as unacceptable. *Practically criminal.* Any further interference from him could only make things worse. Hamish didn't deserve that.

So, he lingered.

All this would've been simpler back home. His father might not approve of him bouncing from one fling to the next, but he was at least permitted to be himself. *To a point.* There was a line. Crossing it was how he had ended up in Tirglas.

The faint creak of hinges heralded the arrival of another.

Darshan squared his shoulders. He twisted part way around, peering over his shoulder to check that it was indeed Hamish who shared this small space, an excuse on his tongue in the faint off chance someone else had seen him come up here.

Hamish stood halfway out of the trapdoor, those sapphiric eyes wide and his mouth gaping like a stunned fish. "I didnae think you'd actually be waiting."

"Well, I am apparently owed an explanation."

"Aye." Hamish rubbed at his neck. "About that. You see—"

"I have been thinking," Darshan interrupted. If he let Hamish just explain, then the man might not stay to discuss anything else and he wasn't ready to leave it at that. "The other day? When your mother called me ungodly… amongst other things?" he mumbled, turning his gaze on the harbour. He would *not* let those words bother him. He'd been called far worse in the Crystal Court, some of them even to his face.

Another glance behind him revealed Hamish had climbed the rest of the way out of the trapdoor. He looked a touch off-colour. Clearly, not at all prepared for a theological debate. But then whoever was? Beyond those who dedicated their lives to service of their deity, at least.

"I am well aware we have different beliefs," Darshan continued. "But I will admit to some curiosity. Your people worship a single Goddess, correct?" His tutors hadn't considered such information important enough to more than touch on it during his briefings, but he remembered that much.

Hamish slowly nodded as he joined Darshan at the parapet, his heavy brows lowering in quiet confusion.

"And what does your Goddess think of…?" He waved his hand, indicating the both of them.

Hamish leant on the parapet. "I see," he murmured, causing Darshan to raise his brows. Was he truly so transparent? The man cleared his throat. "They say nothing specifically on the subject. At least, nae that I'm aware of. Most of the sermons are about the usual things, of how her strength can be found in birth, creation and the harvest."

Sounds familiar. A few deities—amongst the several dozen the Udynean citizens worshipped—were associated with various stages of growth and vegetation, with the oldest and most widely accepted being the High Mother. But making such comparisons blindly could very well lead him to the wrong assumption. "Who taught you about sex, if I may ask?"

Hamish sighed. "That would've been me dad. And before you ask if he was aware I'd nae interest in women…"

"He was?" An easy assumption to make. Someone eventually had to be the first to become aware of Hamish's lack of desire in pursuing women.

He nodded.

"Did *he* ever—?"

"—tell me it was wrong?" Hamish finished, shaking his head. "He's never said such in those words. But then, me dad's always been more puzzled than against it like me mum." He shuffled his weight and scratched at his jaw, his fingers all but disappearing into his beard. "I ken what you're looking for. There isnae some rule written down saying men cannae be with each other, it's just... you pick up what's considered acceptable behaviour and... that's nae part of it."

Darshan swallowed, his throat far tighter than it should've been. He could've handled a rule. They came with ambiguous clauses that enabled people with the right knowhow a way to ignore the law without technically disobeying. That's how things happened in the Udynea Empire. His father, and the senate he oversaw, had slews of legal scholars at their command, their task always to be one step ahead of those seeking to skirt the law.

"I ken there are other men living normal lives out there who have nae interest in being with a woman," Hamish continued, staring vacantly out at the city. "The priesthood is pretty unilateral on whom they frown upon and they tend to focus on any couples without children regardless of whether they are two men, two women or nae. They make it clear that two men alone cannae create anything, but they're nae demonised any more than any other childless couple."

Darshan sucked on his teeth. Already, he could see a few flaws in that statement. *No more than.* That didn't exactly mean they weren't. "One would be hard-pressed to deduce I was not some sort of rock pool slime based on your mother's reaction."

Hamish nodded, his gaze lowering further. "That's because me mum adheres to the ancient scriptures, which say—"

Darshan sneered. "Now there is a phrase that could not make me shudder any further if it tried." The imperial library boasted hundreds of ancient texts. Not only of when Udynea had yet to become the empire it now was, but from the fallen Domian Empire and other lands few even remembered the names of. They had rather polar outlooks on how a person's life should be lived.

Hamish leant further over the parapet, his head hanging well out from the edge. How he was able to do so knowing the drop should he misjudge his balance was beyond Darshan's comprehension. "Plainly put, me mum's aversion is largely due to the fact it willnae produce children. If it did..."

That sounded far more familiar than Darshan would've liked. "It always boils down to children and heirs, does it not?" Everyone seemed so unreservedly obsessed with the idea. Even his own father had trouble understanding Darshan's utter disinterest in siring another chain in the imperial bloodline.

Hamish's head cocked to one side, but his attention seemed rooted to the world far below them. "By your tone, it sounds like you've nae interest in becoming a father."

"That is because I—" His tongue froze. Once, he would've been certain of the answer; a most empathetic no. But that'd been when there'd been only one way to make children. There'd been whispers in the Crystal Court as of late, rumours coming from Niholia of other means. "—do not know," he finally managed.

Hamish lifted his head to frown over his shoulder at Darshan. "Oh?"

"Do not get me wrong. I have met some absolutely charming women, but they just… fail to spark something in me." That included Rashmika, a dear young lady who he had once considered living a lie for; an idea that had come from a place of pity for a friend rather than any desire to sleep with her.

They'd first met when he was but six years old. Although she had spent much of her early teenage years being groomed to become his twin's handmaiden, they'd grown close with time and she had been one of the first he had informed of his desire for men. With her noble bloodline, she was also strong enough to be considered worthy as a future imperial bride by the senate. His father had made numerous rumbles about Darshan marrying her.

Ultimately, it wouldn't have been fair to either of them and she was far happier with her current husband than she ever could've been with himself. He was content knowing he'd helped her find a man worthy of her gentle nature in a distant cousin of his. "But then I have also met brutes of men who elicited a similar reaction." Including Rashmika's father, who used to take great delight in beating his daughter.

The wretched man didn't do anything now. Darshan had made certain of that, his wedding gift to the happy couple.

Hamish nodded. No doubt he had met his own fair share of men not worthy of his time. "To be honest, *if* I didnae have to lay with a woman, I'd nae mind the father part. I adore me wee niece and nephews. And, sure, I have thought about adding a child or two to the clan. Except…"

"And therein lies the rub, yes?" There was more than the obvious driving Darshan's lack of interest in siring an heir of his own. But it was a formidable hurdle nevertheless.

"Aye." Hamish's head drooped. "Call me daft if you want, but I've been hoping me mum would come around. Eventually."

"No doubt she has been thinking the same thing. How old did you say you were?" He had vague memories of what they'd spoken about during his far-too-short-a-time in the man's room. Most of it had been eclipsed by the mind-wiping pleasure Hamish had offered. "Thirty-five, was it? Six?" Older than himself.

"Seven," Hamish gently corrected. "I've been thirty-seven since the midwinter just gone."

"Right, of course." Midwinter? When the land would be enveloped in snow and the very air was rumoured to freeze the lungs. How ever did they manage to keep babies warm enough to withstand such a time without magic to heat the air? "You are that old and she still insists on you marrying a woman? I am sorry, but I do not foresee her changing her mind. Ever."

Hamish returned to frowning at the land below. He said nothing. Although, judging by the tension running from his squared shoulders to the fist he clenched and unclenched, there was a definite battle raging through his thoughts.

Darshan's stomach turned leaden at the man's continued silence. He had come to the same conclusion with his father years ago, and it'd been a hard lesson to swallow, but he hadn't faced it alone. He sidled up to Hamish. "How long have guards kept a close eye on your door?"

"Dinnae your people worship a divine being?"

Darshan jerked back, momentarily dumbfounded by the sudden swing. *Very well.* He knew better than to press a topic best left alone. "*A?*" He chuckled softly, hoping a show of amusement would ease Hamish's mind. "We have several gods and goddesses. Araasi sits at the top of the pantheon, their queen as well as the Goddess of Home and the Hearth." One of the more widely-worshipped deities alongside the High Mother.

"Queen?" Hamish echoed. He lifted his head. Those blue eyes, slightly red around the edges, trained on Darshan. "Does she have a king?"

"She does." Not that anyone took him seriously. Where Araasi was the welcomer of departed souls, he was the doom of anyone found unworthy. Those who found themselves in Jalaane's embrace faced an eternity of suffering in the icy depths of the Forgotten Place. "And a once-mortal lover," he added.

Hamish frowned. "How does that work?"

He grimaced. This wasn't at all the direction he wanted to take. "I feel a little ridiculous reciting a love story I learnt in the *fānum* to you, but it goes something like this." Keenly feeling his face warming, he cleared his throat. "Araasi was supposedly intrigued by the beauty of a woman's artistic craft and she entered the mortal realm in disguise to watch this woman work up close, spending a great deal of time in the woman's presence and, eventually, they fell in love. And that—"

"All right," Hamish interrupted as he returned to standing upright. "We've similar legends about people falling for demons. They dinnae generally end well for the mortal, though. I cannae imagine your god king was pleased with such an outcome."

Darshan shook his head. "Jalaane—the 'god king' as you put it—is just as powerful as his wife. He caught wind of their affair and, no, he was most definitely *not* pleased. The priestesses say he chased after the woman, seeking to remove her from existence, but his wife was always one step ahead and would hide her lover from his grasp. The tale goes that the chase continued for years." Sometimes, the priestesses would insist it was decades, but everyone knew that a mortal life was only so long. "Finally, there was nowhere in the world left for the woman to hide."

Frowning, Hamish leant back on the parapet, his arms folded. "I dinnae like where this 'love story' is going."

Darshan rolled his eyes. *Trust me to find the impatient listener.* His sisters were much the same way, wanting to know the end before the story could naturally reach its conclusion. His twin was the worst offender, sometimes going so far as to snatch whatever he was reading from his hands to skip ahead. Only the presence of a magical shield had ever stopped her.

"I'm getting to that." He cleared his throat and continued, "Unwilling to relinquish her lover, Araasi turned the woman into a ball of fire and mounted it atop her crown. According to the priestesses, she's still there, hovering above the queen's brow for all eternity. The first Flame Eternal."

Hamish stared at him, those stunning blue eyes bulging. "*What?* How is that a love story? Your goddess had an affair, then when her husband found out, she turned her lover into a ball of fire and *then* mounted her like some sort of jewel... forever?"

"I—" Darshan gnawed on his bottom lip. "Well..." He'd never thought of it that way before. Everyone had always just accepted it as the priestesses said. The Flame Eternal was seen all over Udynea as a symbol of love and devotion. "I guess so. I do recall the priestesses mentioning that Araasi would see her lover returned to human form whenever it was safe."

Hamish threw up his arms and paced a few strides across the tower roof. "And that makes everything better."

"I can think of worse fates than to be the immortal lover of a gentle deity," Darshan mumbled. Not that he had any experience of anything beyond flings from those who attempted to use him to climb the ranks. He humoured the more attractive ones, using them whilst offering nothing in return.

The tale of Araasi and the Flame Eternal was meant to be something to aspire to. Beyond that, he had no examples to compare against. His mother had died birthing his twin, his father slept with any noblewoman in the hope of siring another son to take the burden off Darshan. Even his wedded half-sisters married for power over all else.

He couldn't imagine what it would be like living for love. It had been made plain early on in his life that such things were rare amongst the nobility.

"I trust there is an explanation to my hurried escort out of your room," Darshan said, knowing he could easily be setting himself up for a volatile response. *Please, don't be the whole 'not you, but me' dribble.* "I must confess, I do not understand. Did I do something wrong?"

Hamish shook his head. "I was hoping you'd nae ask." Sighing, he tugged at his beard. "And you didnae do anything wrong. *I* did. I should nae have led you to believe we were free to rut in me room."

Darshan frowned. There was that word again. The one the man back in the pub had uttered, or something that sounded very close to it, at least. He hadn't been given the translation and he had thought it was derogatory, but for Hamish to say it... "What do you mean we were not? It *is* your room, correct?"

"Aye." Hamish hung his head, his shoulders hunching like a chastened hound. "But the guards—the ones who escorted me after we kissed?—they are under orders to search me room if they've any reason to believe I'm nae alone."

"Search?" Darshan echoed, scarcely believing the man. "Like you are some sort of delinquent? Rather indecent of them."

Hamish nodded. "It's been that way ever since I was seventeen."

He could almost understand having an eye kept on a young man still fumbling his way through the final years of adolescence. "But you are a grown man, now."

"Nae according to me mum. I'm nae married. I have nae bairns of me own. As far as she's concerned, I am still her wee lad." He peered at Darshan out the corner of his eye, an act Darshan was rather envious of—glasses had always made judging things on his periphery hazy at best. "I'm sorry I led you on. That's actually what I came here to say. *That* and yesterday is as far as we can take this."

Darshan wrinkled his nose. The act dislodged his glasses, forcing him to push them back into their normal place. "Sorry?" he mumbled, recalling old words his father had spoken to him decades back. "I do not know how it is in Tirglas, but in Minamist, little boys apologise, men make amends."

Hamish leant on the parapet. He clasped his hands, resting his lips against them. But not before Darshan caught the twitch of a smile and the faint snort of laughter. "And how would you have me do that?"

"Well, as satisfying as yesterday's appetiser was, I will admit to a… mild disappointment. Stopping now is hardly fair when we barely got anywhere." He pressed closer. "And I had rather been looking forward to the main course."

The spark of amusement that had illuminated Hamish's eyes suddenly fizzled. "As much as I'd like to—and, believe me, I want to a *lot*—the risk that she'll exile another ambassador isnae worth it."

"*Another?* You have done this before?" Small wonder Queen Fiona was upset with his arrival. She had probably guessed everything they'd already done, and then some.

"Once," Hamish confessed with a brief bob of his head. "The last time I set foot in the ambassadorial suite was when we entertained a visitor—a man, to be precise—from Dvärghem and…"

"Let me guess," Darshan supplied. "Your precise entertainment involved tumbling the man into bed?"

Hamish nodded. "Those guards found me bed empty and searched the castle. Once they discovered us, I was dragged back to me chamber." He hung his head. "It wouldnae have been any more embarrassing than if they paraded me through the halls as naked as the day I was born."

Darshan mentally shook himself, scattering the image of Hamish being bodily hauled through the castle's tight corridors whilst stripped bare. "I beg your pardon, but did you just admit to getting a *hedgewitch* into your bed?" Even he hadn't been successful there. Dwarven hedgewitches tended to be very serious about remaining celibate. "You naughty man."

Shock took Hamish's face for a moment before a wide grin split it. "Well, I wouldnae say *into*. And it was quite a few years ago. Thirteen, if we're being precise. I was cocky and foolish back then. Dinnae think me mum would do anything about it." His gaze dropped and he picked at his nails. "She had me locked up for three days. By the time I was allowed to leave, the ambassador had been sent away. I spent the next month under house arrest. I've nae been with anyone since."

Darshan's brows shot up in astonishment before he could control the expression. "Not in thirteen years?"

Hamish vigorously shook his head, his hair bobbing behind him like a pennant snapping in the breeze. "Before yesterday, that was the last time it's been anything other than a solo affair."

Darshan took a deep breath, his cheeks puffing as he exhaled. The very idea of going without sex for so long weakened his knees.

"Yesterday evening? When you said it had been a while? I did not expect it to have been so long."

The man grunted.

He silently stared out at the harbour for some time in some vain hope that the deep blue waters would hold an answer. His father might have made a number of attempts towards convincing him to lay with a woman—conceding from him having a wife to just long enough to sire an heir—but not once had he been made to feel that he couldn't enjoy himself with another man. "I think I understand now. You do not wish to repeat the error of getting caught?"

"Amongst other things," Hamish muttered. "I willnae lie, yesterday was fun. But I wouldnae blame you if all this is more than you planned on dealing with."

It would've been, if Darshan had been back home where he had a myriad of options. If Hamish had been any other man beyond one from his darkest fantasies. If the man's reaction to a simple kiss hadn't been so explosive.

Common sense told him to back away. "This is a jest, right?" He clasped Hamish's arm, much to the man's surprise. "If you want me to be more careful, then I shall."

Hamish stared at him as if he'd suddenly sprouted extra eyeballs. "Have you got rocks in your head? I just said we cannae do it."

"I heard you, but what if we are discreet?"

The man's fiery-red brows twisted with disbelief.

"I *can* do discreet."

"You snogged me in the middle of a pub," Hamish pointed out. "Forgive me if I find to idea of *you* being discreet a little hard to swallow."

Yes, some years had passed since it had been required of him, but that was hardly a basis for his abilities. "All right, that was not one of my finest moments, but I was drunk and… curious."

The confusion-etched wrinkles around those brilliant, aquamarine-blue eyes deepened as amusement took over. "And horny?"

Laughter bubbled through Darshan's throat. "That, too." Not that he had much hope of completely quashing the feeling once it dug its claws in, one of the barbs of being born into a strong magical bloodline.

However, letting those emotions command his actions was inexcusable. *The tales they would've told at court.* Not that he had lived his life back home in any way free of scandal. "Do let me know if I get a bit much, I cannot always tell."

Hamish remained silent, but his brow twitched briefly in puzzlement. Over what, exactly? Just how well-informed was the

Tirglasian population about spellsters in general much less their quirks?

Darshan cleared his throat. He'd never had to explain this to someone before, they'd just known. "The current scientific theory is that strong magical bloodlines tend to also come with a heightened libido that lends itself to a greater chance of thinking with the loins rather than the head in... certain situations."

"I didnae say—" Hamish trailed off, his gaze distant as he stroked his beard. "I thought the Udynean court was full of strong spellsters? It must be interesting having them all in one place."

Only during the soirées. There was that one orgy in Madaara's temple that had gotten quite out of hand during the yearly blessing of the Goddess of Wine's bounty, although the unexpected potency of the alcohol imbibed at the festival could also be attributed to such hedonistic acts. He certainly hadn't meant to unleash his magic when he had braced himself on Madaara's statue, much less reduce twenty feet of carved marble and gilding to rubble.

"It is not as bad you might think," Darshan murmured, struggling to ignore the unfamiliar flush of heat invading his face over the memory. "Restraint is a highly prized trait." One he routinely failed at displaying. "And, as you can see, I am more than capable of not ravishing you whenever we are alone."

Hamish laughed with a deep throaty rumble. "That's a shame. I've nae been ravished before."

"How about starting small? It seems to me that sneaking more than a few kisses behind your mother's back in the vein of a pair of horny teenagers is a thing that is long overdue."

"And you're how old again?" Hamish's open smile took off what could've easily been a harsher edge to his words.

Grinning along with the man, Darshan bumped their hips together. "You are never too old to attempt sneaking things past your parents."

Whilst there was definitely a smidgen of agreement in the curve of his mouth, Hamish's thick brows lowered. "You'd risk getting caught with me again and possibly exiled?"

That last threat would've held more weight if exiling him, an ambassador offering only peace and trade, didn't also carry the definite recourse of angering his father and the Udynean senate. And that was without factoring in his royal title. "Would *you*?"

Hamish's frown deepened.

Darshan held up his hands, pleading forgiveness. "That was a poor comparison. You need not answer." He rubbed at his temples with a single hand. "How about you come to my quarters tonight?"

"*What?*"

He tilted his head, peering up at the man through the outer edge of his glasses' lens to find Hamish staring back at him. Those blue eyes should not have been so wide, especially after his actions last night, nor should they carry that hint of trepidation. "I would suggest your room, but I get the distinct impression that you would prefer it maintained its off-limits aura." He could work with that. It would make things tricky, but interesting.

Hamish nodded.

"And, whilst I might not have had someone I could actually claim was my lover before, I—"

"Neither have I," Hamish blurted as if such a fact could be open to contestation.

Darshan inclined his head in acknowledgement. "Then this will be somewhat virgin ground for the both of us." He stressed those last few words, making sure that detail had reached Hamish. "And we have yet to figure out each other's tastes beyond a few fumbling moves." On his part, at least. Hamish certainly knew what he was doing orally and Darshan was more than happy with *that* performance—the very thought of it sent a pleasant shiver through him—but it wasn't much to base any sort of relationship on, even one forged solely for sex. "If we are to become paramours, we should perhaps see if our previous attempt at intimacy cannot be improved upon."

"Aye, but *tonight*? It's nae that I'm averse to the idea, it's just... real soon like."

Darshan bit the inside of his cheek, chasing his thoughts. He supposed engaging in a second night of intimacy in a row *would* seem an extremely short time after being forced to abandon any sort of sexual act for... How long had Hamish said?

Thirteen years.

He still couldn't quite get his head around that scenario. To have to pretend, to constrain his emotions, to keep any friendship with another man at a distance least the worst was thought of such closeness... Darshan had some experience with the latter, but the rest was foreign. Not once had he ever been made to feel that he needed to hide any part of his being from the world.

Punishment he understood—being in Tirglas *was* his punishment—but it was what he'd done and with whom, not that the act had been with a man.

He gnawed on the inside of his lip as a frustration-laced sigh whistled out his nose. Why—*Gods, why?*—couldn't the man he found utterly irresistible have been someone who had *not* spent almost two-thirds of his adult life forced into celibacy by their wretched mother? *Their damn queen, no less.* With a head full of ancient scriptures and her intentions only on ensuring her brood filled the world with more of her clan. Disgusting.

I could walk away. That had been an option since he had first kissed the man. Not that he'd been able to shake Hamish from his dreams no matter how hard he tried. Were a few nights of pleasure worth dragging Hamish into a worse situation than the man was already in?

He wished he had an objective enough stance on the matter to answer that truthfully.

Darshan took hold of Hamish's hands, coaxing the man to turn from the tower parapet. It wasn't his choice to make alone, if at all. "I would understand if your preference is to remain as you are." He wouldn't be pleased, but he'd rather not begin at all than to prematurely part because he had made life worse for Hamish. "You just have to say 'no' and that will be the last you hear of it from me. I am not in the habit of forcing those who decline the offer into my bed." Not that he generally had to offer. Or even try that hard when looking for a little fun. Someone was always willing to lay with their *vris Mhanek* and they generally weren't backwards in coming forwards about their intentions.

Hamish bit his lip, his mouth disappearing beneath his ruddy moustache as both it and his beard seemed to merge. "Dar..." The name escaped in a gentle puff of breath. Soft and intimate, the sort of sound Darshan could listen to over and over. "I think I made meself pretty clear that what I prefer rarely comes into it." So quiet, those words. "I always make the wrong choice." So convinced and dejected.

That simply won't do. If Darshan had been made of weaker stuff, maybe something inside would've cracked slightly. His chest did ache dreadfully, but it was an old sullen anger that bubbled in the depths. How dare they twist such a gentle man like Hamish and make him believe he couldn't be trusted to do what felt right to him. *The very nerve.*

Any lingering thoughts of taking the easier path with backing out boiled away.

He cradled Hamish's head, urging the man lower until their foreheads touched. "I shall leave my door unlocked until midnight. If I do not see you, then understand I will press the matter no further. If it were my choice alone, I would have you at my side well before then."

Hamish wet his lips, the act shifting his beard enough to tickle Darshan's chin. "If we're found out..."

"I have no fear of retribution." What was the worst Queen Fiona could do to him, the *vris Mhanek* of the Udynean Empire? Kick him from her country? He'd damned well take Hamish with him if the man let him. "If you need me to, I shall stand at your side." The statement was out before he could stop to think the words through. Damn his fool pride. But he was not leaving this land whilst Hamish believed himself the one at fault here. “And I trust it to be the right choice, whatever you choose.”

The man’s hand caressed Darshan’s jaw, tilting it. Their lips brushed together. Soft. Hesitant. Hamish’s beard tickled however much Darshan tried to ignore it. He leant gingerly into each touch, barely breathing between kisses, fearful Hamish would pull away if he pushed.

Their tongues entwined. Firm and insistent on his part, sweet and submissive on Hamish’s. It wasn’t quite enough. Darshan found his thoughts plunging into the idea of dropping to his knees and swallowing a great deal more than the man’s breath.

No. With great reluctance, Darshan relinquished Hamish’s mouth. *Not here.* A part of him—the sensible and wary side that tended to reign over his actions back home that had all but melted at the sight of those blue eyes—now snapped back into action. “Does that mean I shall await your arrival?”

Hamish chuckled, the sound heavy and mirthless. “You talk big for someone who’s only been here a few days.”

Darshan grinned. It was hard to remember only two days had passed since that kiss in the pub. His soul was so at ease around Hamish that if felt like he’d known the man for years. “And I relish the thought of spending many more in your presence, getting to know you.”

“Tonight then.”

He would need to tread with utmost care. Patience in these matters wasn’t his forte, not when he truly desired something, but he would do his best to contain himself. It could only work in his favour. *Be discreet.* And wait. “Tonight.”

Chapter 10

Darshan practically jogged down the stairs, skipping off the final step and into the corridor. He hadn't felt this giddy since his teenage years. He'd never had to anticipate sex before. Not for more than an hour, anyway.

Surprisingly, the mere thought of it set his heart racing. He foresaw very little chance of them not being compatible.

Calm. If he got himself too worked up over tonight's possibilities, he would never make it until then. He would have to ensure everything was ready. As well as account for the likelihood of an interruption.

Fortunately, the castle chamberlain had gifted him with a key to the guest room on his first day here. Locking the door should slow the guards if they turn up as Hamish feared. What he'd do then, Darshan wasn't entirely certain, but he swore he'd make good on his promise to stand by his lover's side should things turn sour.

Potential lover, he staunchly reminded himself. They weren't quite there yet, but he was rather optimistic. And eager to please.

His thoughts drifted back to yesterday, of the hot press of Hamish over him, his weight passively pinning him to the mattress. He had almost lost his mind when Hamish had manhandled him, lifting him like he weighed nothing. And the ferocious way he'd claimed Darshan with his mouth, consuming like a starving man. *To have to contain himself for over a decade…*

Well, he did like his men feisty and there was a definite keenness lurking beneath the uncertain facade. If Hamish made love with the same passion simmering under the surface, Darshan would either find himself faced with a lust-hungry beast or something more akin to a giddy virgin. *Best prepare for either option.* Although, the latter seemed more likely given the man's temperament.

Darshan slowed to glance up at the sky as he sauntered by a window. He never could quite grasp the art of telling the time of day beyond a few basics. What had Hamish claimed the hour was before he had descended? *Late afternoon*. That left him with precious little time to bathe and make himself presentable.

Had they really spent so long talking? They'd mostly spoken about frivolous things; like how the ruin Darshan had seen poking through the trees in the distance were the remains of a cloister, or that Hamish wasn't fond of the colour blue. That last bit had been a surprise, any noble back home who'd been blessed with eyes as vibrant as Hamish's would seek out ways to complement them. And there were so many ways.

He was vaguely aware of rounding a bend in the corridor, his thoughts lost to the possibilities.

Already, he could picture the man sporting a sherwani that accented such a trait. Understated. Off-white with a bit of ice-blue brocade. Or just the gems themselves, sparkling out between the silver and pearl needlework. He would need a scarf to match, although that might take a little persuading. Perhaps a deep ocean blue—not quite black, but close—would be best. Or something in slate.

"Your highness," a familiar woman's voice called out, jolting him from his reverie.

Darshan glanced over his shoulder to find Nora trotting after him, clutching a leather satchel that seemed to contain quite a few pieces of parchment. He slowed, but made no effort to stop. He wasn't exactly in the mood to talk trade, especially not with Queen Fiona.

"Where were you?" Nora demanded as if he were a wayward child. She fell into step with him. "I looked everywhere for you."

A quick survey of their surrounding confirmed they were alone. "Evidently not, but to answer your question: I was on the eastern tower."

She shot him a confused look. "Not that one near the cliff edge." Her nose scrunched further as he nodded. "What were you doing up there? They abandoned that tower years ago in favour of the new watchtower. I wouldnae think it'd hold much of interest, it's practically a shell and the view is nothing to harp about."

He smiled. Similar words had once left his lips of the view back home, until he had stumbled upon a visiting dignitary from the northern edge of Udynea admiring the docks. Familiarity leant itself to blindness. "I would disagree on that front. There was a great deal to look at and I thoroughly enjoyed the view."

"Of the harbour?" The corridor they were travelling down split into two. Nora took the left one and Darshan idly trailed her. "I thought

Minamist was also a port city?"

He inclined his head. "You are correct there." Although, comparing the two was a little like oil and water.

The bay of his home city was huge, although not quite as massive as the Shar, a lake which took up a good portion of the lower half of the Udynea Empire's land. Called *Sinus Luminis* when under the control of the Domian Empire, a civilisation that had fallen centuries ago, the Bay of Light was now the territory of both the Udynea Empire and the neighbouring imperial lands of Stamekia. Only a small strip of shallow water, nicknamed the Throat of Death by sailors, kept the harbour from being an actual lake.

To compare that bay to the hook-like inlet that shaped Tirglas was almost an insult. The deep blue waves that lapped at the shores here were nothing in comparison to the crystal-blue waters of home. To look upon the Bay of Light was to bear witness to how the gods could take the essence of a simple jewel and turn it to liquid.

His gaze dropped pointedly to the satchel. It looked a great deal like the one she'd had sitting beside her during their last attempt at settling trade. Had Queen Fiona managed to reel in her poisonous tongue so quickly? It seemed at odds with what Hamish had divulged. "How is it I may be of assistance?" Whilst he was in no mood to deal with the woman's mother, shunning Nora as a matter of course sounded more like something one of his petty sisters would do.

"I was thinking that we could retire to the library and discuss trade."

Darshan fought down a groan. If he allowed Nora to steal away what time he had left to him before Hamish's arrival at the guest quarters, he could quite possibly return there to find the man had already visited and left.

But, as much as he would've liked to, putting pleasure before duty was how he had gotten here. "You do realise that, without the queen's final approval, anything we agree on here is ultimately fruitless."

"Perhaps." They reached an intersection in the corridor and Nora indicated for him to take the left passage with the gentle sweep of her hand. "But if we hammer out the fine details, then we can limit the time you need to be in me mum's good graces."

Darshan grunted. Given what he'd heard so far of the woman's behaviour towards her son, and the more recent outburst at his innocent kiss, being able to avoid extended exposure to her toxic presence would be a boon. Of course, that didn't stop her from making this whole negotiation difficult by simply refusing his terms.

"I do not exactly have the paperwork on me," he mumbled as if it wasn't obvious he'd have the sheets locked up in his travel chest whenever they weren't required. He could collect them easily enough, but that would only chew through more of his precious time.

Nora patted her satchel. "That's nae a problem. And, since this is unofficial until me mum signs, we can renegotiate if me figures dinnae match yours." She veered off to open a door that Darshan now recognised to be the entrance to the library. "Nae one will be in here at this hour."

He followed her into the room, slightly amused. How long had she been quietly directing them here? It seemed a little too fortuitous to be coincidence.

Inside, Nora dragged a second chair over to a table situated near the window. A heavy bronze candlestick sat in the middle of the table.

"It is awfully dim in here," Darshan remarked, his focus falling on the candle. A faint mischievous, and slightly childish, impulse itched its way through his palms. "How about a little more light?" With the snap of his fingers, a flame flared to life on the wick.

Nora jumped back, a hand pressed flat to her chest. She stared at the candle, her moss-green eyes wide and slightly muddy in the dancing light. Swallowing, she lowered herself onto one of the chairs before setting her satchel on the table and pulling out its contents. "We," she mumbled, her gaze seemingly tethered to the candle's flame. "We were discussing the tariff on..." At last, she glanced down at her stack of parchment. "...iron imports before you left."

"You mean before your mother made it quite clear that she would disapprove of me being in any way involved with her son?" Darshan quipped, plonking himself onto the other chair. He propped his bootheels on the table and leant back until he had the front chair legs off the ground. "I believe so."

Nora's lips pursed and she frowned at his boots with a disdainful glare that his Nanny Daama would've been hard-pressed to match, but ultimately the woman ignored his lack of decorum. Instead, she plucked a quill and inkwell from the table's recess. "Shall we start there, then?"

"I suppose it is as good a place as any." He held out a hand, gently coaxing a sliver of air to brush the topmost sheet of parchment into his grasp. It was a mess of notes and numbers, largely to do with the already agreed-upon tariffs of various ore exports. The amount of coal the Tirglasian mountainside held was almost sinful. Copper, too. Whilst both were in high demand throughout Udynea, the latter was in relatively short supply.

He stared blindly at the page. Had it really only been two days since that first negotiation attempt? If Queen Fiona hadn't been called away then, leaving him to his own devices and, ultimately, the pub where he had kissed Hamish, he might've spent a week here at most.

Now?

"How soon do you think you shall be able to converse with your mother over these numbers?" Surely if anyone knew how long it would take for the queen to compose herself enough to not spew filth at him, it would be Nora. He could be here for weeks, maybe even months if the woman chose to be exceptionally petty and refuse whatever agreement Nora and himself came to.

Gods willing. He may have little desire to be stuck here at the whim of one person, but what waited for him back home? The same old transparent deceptions, substandard assassination attempts and trysts that had seen him sent here. He didn't know if being with Hamish would be any different, but the chance to try was certainly an alluring one.

He slowly became aware of the distinct lack of response from the sole other occupant of the castle library. The uneasy silence drew his gaze up from the muddle of numbers and script to the woman.

Nora still sat on the other side of the table, although she'd gone terribly stiff and her face had definitely lost a certain amount of colour. She eyed the parchment in his hand as if he held a live man-killer serpent. He hadn't witnessed such a reaction in all his life, not to painfully simple magic. Even Hamish and all three of her sons had only displayed polite curiosity at the presence of his laughably effortless flame trick.

Relishing in unnerving someone with such parlour tricks as floating paper was considered bad form back home. Still, he couldn't stop the faintly amused twitch of his cheek. "We could discuss the linen percentage," he said, hoping to shake her out of her shock. "I have a response from the trade council." Not that he had it with him. "Although, I notice little mention of textiles. Is that on another page?"

"Text—" She frowned at the loose pages, shuffling through them in a daze. "Aye, they're here." She lifted a page from the middle of the pile, holding it out.

Again, he extended his hand and allowed a wisp of air to slide the page from her fingers into his grasp. Sure enough, the figures for linen took up a generous half of the page with a great many percentages crossed out. One set of figures was circled. It looked like what they had agreed upon. "Everything seems to be in order."

"You could've just asked for it," Nora muttered, barely audible.

Darshan tapped the side of his boot on the other. Where to start that wouldn't lead them down the path of quibbling over a single percent? It was one thing to be fair on the tariff over linen—and the council had given him leave to be quite generous indeed—for their own flax fields were woefully incapable of handling the demand.

His eye caught mention of a textile he didn't think Tirglasians would have much to spare. "You do, of course, realise that our need for wool is nowhere near as voracious as linen." He handed the page back in a similar manner. A warmer climate, coupled with the local supply made the need for importing wool almost unnecessary, but he'd been tasked with setting up a beginning trade line for every resource the Tirglasian crown was willing to part with.

Nora inclined her head. "I also ken that the wool our sheep produce can be spun into a finer quality yarn than your breeds. The way I understand it, Udynean sheep are bred more for meat."

He arched a brow at her. He hadn't expected such a reply. Just how much did she know of his homeland? "You would be correct in that assumption. Clearly, our people are more concerned with being fed than donning woollen garments."

"Your northern lands are nae much different from ours."

Considering some of those very lands bordered Tirglas, mostly separated by a line of mountains, he wasn't surprised. However, he doubted their presence alone would tilt the scale of demand for imported wool. "I shall need to send another messenger pigeon to the border, but I rather doubt they will wish for me to agree on anything as generous as my previous offers."

Nodding, she slid the topmost page aside. "There was some mention of medicinal aid? Something our doctors would be able to utilise?"

Darshan gnawed on a thumbnail. He had arrived with a list of various medicinal herbs and their uses, which was in the guest rooms with everything else. Not being a doctor, he hadn't paid much attention to their names, let alone the usage of each one. "To be honest, I would much rather discuss those after visiting a cloister."

The woman pursed her lips as if sucking something distasteful. "You dinnae think me mum would still allow you to travel with me brother?"

Probably not. If he was to be honest with himself, then it would most certainly be a definite no. "I made no stipulations that it *had* to be. But since you brought it up, one travelling party, and thus one escort, would be a far more efficient use of your guards." The gods knew that there wasn't much chance of being alone with Hamish whilst on the move, but he'd settle for getting the man away from the confines of the castle and out from under Queen Fiona's poisonous gaze. Even if it was only for a little while.

Nora set down the quill with a sigh. "Dinnae hurt me brother. Please? I ken he looks fearsome, but he's as gentle as a wee lamb."

Darshan steepled his fingers on his stomach. Had he become that transparent so quickly after leaving the Crystal Court's deadly intrigue? And how far could he trust Nora with the truth given her closeness to Queen Fiona? "Your highness, I have no intentions of doing any such thing."

The subtle tightening of her lips spoke several volumes towards her disbelief in that statement. "I meant what I said; I ken what it's like in Udynea. He's nae a plaything. You hurt him and you'll be answering to the whole clan."

He had already surmised as much. Still… "I do not take kindly to threats." Not that he'd had many levelled at him. Most of those with enough status to attend the Crystal Court also had enough wits about them to be aware that threatening the *Mhanek's* son could only end badly. Sadly, that didn't include his half-sisters, the title-grabbing locusts that they were.

"And I am nae the kind of woman to give them lightly." Nora straightened in her chair. "But whilst me brother and I continue to share blood, I would be doing him a great disservice to let you walk all over him."

Darshan hummed to himself, tapping a boot heel on the table. "I have changed my mind," he murmured. "I have no need to consult the council. I want double the percentage on wool that we agreed upon with the coal." He could no longer remember the exact figures, all thoughts of trade eclipsed by the rage of Queen Fiona's ranting.

"D-double?" Nora sputtered. "That's outrageous!"

"As were your mother's words." Not to mention the abuse she had heaped upon her own son. Hamish deserved far better than that.

"I ken you're upset over what me mum said, but you cannae take it out on our economy."

"Fine, I shall lower the tariff to a more agreeable range, on the stipulation that I get your brother. The younger one," he clarified, knowing full well she would be aware he meant Hamish.

If he thought the woman had been sitting straight before, he was proven wrong now. Any more so and she would have to learn how to levitate. "This is *Tirglas*, we dinnae trade in *people*."

He lowered his feet, allowing his chair to return to supporting him on all four legs. However carefully he maintained his balance on the two back legs, it simply wouldn't do to fall now. "Those are my terms." Even if Hamish didn't wish to make their rather new arrangement a permanent one, having the man in Udynea would leave Hamish with a far wider range of opportunities. Not just in bed partners.

Nora snorted. "You're going to be this bull-headed because of a few harsh words?"

Darshan slammed his fists onto the table. "*Harsh words?*" he whispered. "She insulted something that is an intrinsic part of me. Just as your traits make you." The aroma of scorched wood tickled his nose. He lifted a hand to discover the wood grain directly beneath bore the distinct impression of his curled hand.

Nora's faint intake of breath was enough to shake the cobwebs of shock from his mind.

He slowly lowered his hands, shaking them to cool off once he could be certain they were out of the woman's immediate sight. *Control it.* Lighting a candle was one thing, letting go of his magic any further would only end in disaster.

Confident he wasn't about to burst into flame, Darshan stood. He loomed over Nora, fixing her with a stern glare. "I am *vris Mhanek*, you would do well to look that up, refresh your memory on what it means. When your Queen insulted me, she insulted Udynea and it cannot be allowed to stand without recompense."

Nora matched his glare, but she squirmed in her seat. "Me mum is a stubborn woman."

"Then you may need to remind her that my ancestors have brought hellfire and ruin to lands for less. These negotiations are at the behest of my father. Best you remember that, princess, and not take his desire for peace as a weakness." He pushed his chair back, leaving the table and stalking past shelves of books and scrolls.

"Is that a threat, your imperial highness?" Nora called after him.

Darshan halted in the doorway. *A threat? Him?* He chuckled. "Of course not. I have never threatened anyone in my life." Those who displeased him rarely lived long enough for mere words.

~ ~ ~

Hamish waited a good hour before descending the tower. Whilst he knew he hadn't been followed, he couldn't say the same for Darshan. It'd be just his luck to have this clandestine, but ultimately innocent, meeting be what had him confined to his quarters again.

You are a grown man. Darshan's words rang through his mind.

He was right, of course. His mother had never sought to manage his siblings as viciously. *He* was the stubborn one that wouldn't step into line, the one who had the bad grace to be attracted to men and not bend on that position. Every time he fought against her wishes, she'd play the same tune of how she only wanted the best for him, to see him happy and married with children of his own.

Years had gone by before he had realised that all she really wanted was the assurance that there'd be another generation to rule should another attack on the royal line come. Once, such a fear would've had merit. Now? When his siblings had four living children between them?

Hamish sighed as he closed the trapdoor and descended the tower steps to aimlessly wander through the castle. What real hope did he have in going against his own mother, a woman who would often remark how lucky he was to not have been cursed with magic as his younger sister?

Sometimes, he wished he *had* been like Caitlyn. Spending a lifetime in a cloister learning how to heal people had to be better than this.

The conversation at breakfast tumbled over in his head. All he had done was casually enquire towards Darshan's absence at the table. He had thought it a simple question, neutral and fitting given the ambassador's spat with Hamish's mother.

"He's most likely in the guest room," his mother replied, skewering a sausage with unnecessary force. "Stubborn brat refuses to share the same room with me until I'm ready to continue negotiations, so he dines in his quarters like the uncultured swine he is."

Hamish winced. It wasn't the first time she'd spoken ill of Udyneans. Why did she choose to accept the extended offer of peace between them in the first place? *He mulled that thought as it ghosted through. Their trades with the Obuzans and the Cezhorians had been satisfactory for years.*

"Mum," Gordon piped up. He set down his utensils and steepled his fingers. "Are you nae being a little childish?"

"He assaulted *your brother," she snapped, slamming her fork down into a thick slice of roast mutton. "I honestly thought you'd be more upset over that."*

Ethan gasped. "He did? *But he seemed so nice."*

Nora wrapped a consoling arm around her boy, shushing him.

"It was a kiss, *Mum," Gordon growled. "And the only one harping on about it is you."*

"I should have him shipped back to his heathen people, just like that dwarf."

Hamish's heart thudded an extra beat. Exiling a dwarven ambassador was one thing. To do the same to a Udynean prince? Did his mother have any idea as to the ramifications of such an act?

"We need *this treaty," Nora said, still keeping her son in a tight hold. "They're extending a hand in peace. We knock that aside and the next gesture we see will be our forests burning."*

"We cannae afford a war with them," Gordon added.

Hamish had left after that, unable to stomach the thought of a war with people capable of pulling the same feats he had witnessed from Darshan. The man could conjure a flame like it was nothing, and brush aside full-grown men as if they were no more than leaves in the breeze. Battling an army of spellsters would be impossible without releasing every single one of those in the cloisters. He knew from his younger sister that Tirglasian spellsters were only trained in healing, none of them would be prepared to use their abilities for violence.

He stepped out into the courtyard.

Something heavy careened into him. He staggered along with them. Familiar hands grasped his shoulders, aiding in keeping them upright. When they'd both stopped, he found himself staring straight at his brother's grinning mug.

Movement over the man's shoulder drew his eye. His nephews. All three sullenly carried their bows and not a single one seemed any more pleased to see him. Less, in fact. Mac had a particularly sour look on his face.

"Did something bad happen?" He could well imagine the two older boys being a little too quick to show off without factoring in their brother's current limitations.

"You could say that," Gordon replied. "You missed the lads' hunting practice."

"I… did?" He'd never missed a chance to hone his niece and nephews' hunting skills. He could've sworn it was tomorrow, though.

"Aye," Bruce chipped in, his already squared jaw jutting out further.

"You promised to be the prey," Mac added.

Hamish dropped to a knee before the trio. "I'm sorry, lads. How about I make it up to you tomorrow?" He cast a conspiratorial glance at his brother. "You've— What lessons do you all have in the morning?"

"History," Bruce groaned.

"Mum's going over the Great Slaughter," Mac added, stabbing the air with an arrow as if he brandished a sword.

"The one where this castle's attacked? I could tell you that one." Hamish knew the tale well enough. His mother was obsessed with the time and insisted they went over it in their history lessons enough to damn near quote the whole scripture in their sleep.

It had been centuries ago, when the clans were still feisty enough to fight with each other at the very hint of missing sheep. The king back then had been a loud-mouthed sod. He had pissed off one or two of the clans—or maybe it was more, his mother had never been specific on which clans had been involved—who retaliated by murdering every royal child they could get their hands on. It had all ended with those very clans laying siege to the castle. In the end, all that was left of the royal bloodline was a small boy from the king's youngest son—their umpteenth-great-grandfather.

"I hate the story," Ethan announced. "She only trots that out when she cannae think of anything else for us to study."

"Your mum's probably got her hands full with the trade negotiations." Hamish stood, dusting off his hands on his trousers. "And I'm sure missing a day in favour of hunting willnae hurt. Nae as if history's going anywhere. For now, how about we try the forest run?" He glanced over his shoulder at his brother. "You up for it?"

Gordon nodded.

The boys raced ahead of them, making their way behind the archery range where a secret entrance that led to the foot of the cliff lay. To look at, the door tucked between the outer wall and the temple merely opened to the back of the building. Only in entering did it reveal its actual nature.

"Be careful!" his brother yelled at their dwindling backs, the boys pulling ahead even as they ambled along after them. "That was sneaky, 'Mish, having them take the same path spoken of in the tale."

"I thought so." He didn't know if it was true that their ancestor only survived by fleeing through the secret tunnels out into the forest below, but it wouldn't hurt the boys to know of alternative exits should the unthinkable happen as his mother so often foretold.

Far ahead of them, the door clanged as the boys vanished through the top entrance and into the tunnel.

"I hope they remembered to take a lantern," Gordon muttered, casting a glance at the ceiling. This section was relatively bare of cobwebs with a scant few in one corner.

"Like we didnae do the first time?" It had been night, both of them still far too young to venture out of the castle grounds unescorted. They'd made it halfway down the tunnel before it occurred to either of them that travelling down would've been so much easier with a light source. That'd also been one of his brother's more memorable experiences with a spider. "Thank you for what you said at breakfast, by the way."

His brother shook his head. "You shouldnae have to thank me. *I* shouldnae have to stand up for you anymore. Mum should ken by now you're nae going to change."

Hamish kept his mouth shut. They both knew *that* was never bound to happen.

Gordon sighed and idly scratched his cheek. "Trouble is, if she pushes too hard, she could start a war this time. They may be willing to trade, but they've the clout to take if they so choose."

They entered the tunnel. A pair of oil lanterns sat on a shelf just inside the entrance. The soft glow further down the tunnel spoke of the boys having already made off with a third. Hamish lit one with his flint, squinting at the sudden brightness.

They descended the stairs after their nephews. The tunnel ceiling could've easily allowed his father—a man that stood at seven foot—to walk without stooping and had a breadth wide enough to let the pair of them walk side by side. Unlike most of the caves and little hidey holes dotted across the cliff face, the grey stone beneath their feet was relatively dry.

"So..." his brother drawled after a dozen-or-so steps. "Does your lack of presence this morning mean you've gotten him out of your system?"

"Him who?" he replied, trying to act nonchalant. Cobwebs clung to the ceiling, just low enough to occasionally brush Hamish's hair. Although sure that whatever spiders made these webs would've scuttled off at the first hint of smoke from the lads' lantern, he ducked his head to avoid them anyway. The last thing he wanted to fish out from the coils of his hair was a spider. Fortunately, the tunnel looked to contain only the tiny web-spinning sort rather than the bigger, and far more deadly, arrowback variety.

"You ken precisely who I—" Gordon jerked back, sputtering and flailing at his beard as he brushed a mouthful of sticky webbing free. "Bloody creepy little..." he muttered under his breath, hunching his shoulders and glowering at the ceiling. "I meant our magical, princely ambassador."

Hamish smiled. If Gordon ever decided to side with their mother, he would be screwed as far as keeping things secret went. "Nae as yet."

"Aye?" Even though Hamish saw no evidence of remaining spider web in his brother's beard, Gordon continued to distractedly pluck at the hairs. "Well, be careful, 'Mish. Udyneans are cold bastards, I nae want you getting hurt over this."

His thoughts went back to last night as they walked in silence, settling on Darshan's gentleness and compassion. Maybe that coldness was only a front. Being a prince of an entire empire couldn't be easy. Where did the spellster sit in the order of succession? Second? Only men inherited the Udynean throne. He had learnt that morsel of information from Gordon. And they undoubtedly wouldn't send their heir to a foreign land.

The glow of the boys' lantern ahead of them steadily grew. They rounded the final bend in the tunnel to find the trio already waiting at the entrance.

"Are we doing this or what?" Bruce yelled.

"We'll be there in one flick of a deer's tail, lads." He turned back to Gordon. "I dinnae suppose I can get a wee bit of assistance with the guards tonight?"

His brother raised a brow at him, one green eye squinting. "Tonight?"

Hamish nodded. His face steadily grew hotter the longer Gordon mutely stared at him. An act he was well aware his brother did to elicit such a reaction. But knowing that didn't exactly help him control his blushing.

After what certainly felt like an eternity, his brother chuckled. "That man of yours doesnae drag his feet, does he?"

Hamish bit the inside of his cheek. Darshan wasn't his by any stretch of the imagination.

Gordon clapped a hand on Hamish's shoulder and squeezed. "Try nae to have this one go sour, you hear?"

"Come on!" Ethan called, rattling on the bars that made up the gate blocking their path. "It's locked!"

"Aye, we're on the way!" Hamish shot back before frowning at his brother. "You still got a key on you?"

"Hang on," Gordon muttered. He patted himself down, his search growing more frantic until he produced a heavy key. "Thought I'd lost it for a second there."

Hamish eyed the key enviously. He used to own one—everyone in the royal family was gifted a key once of age—until his mother had confiscated it under the guise of protecting his interests, whilst also claiming he would use the tunnel to set up affairs in the city. An act he had never even thought to attempt.

Gordon trotted down the final few steps to the locked gate. Through the bars, they were greeted by only the cold stone face of an alcove. Out in the forest, this entrance was hidden from the casual observer. No tracks, no sign of manmade structures.

The old lock groaned, then offered up a heavy clonk. The boys filed through as soon as the gate had swung wide enough for them to pass with his brother on their heels, leaving Hamish to put out the lanterns before he followed.

Beyond the alcove, old targets hung just along the forest edge. How many months had he spent with his siblings shooting those same painted slices of tree? He had lost count. "All right, lads," Hamish said. "Show us what you've got."

Chapter 11

Hamish stood before the closed door of the guest chambers. His stomach churned. Nerves or hunger, it was all the same. Dinner had been a short time ago, but the fluttering in his gut had him far too distracted to consider food.

The mere thought of being with Darshan again, especially so soon, had his heart thundering. All of his past encounters had been the single night kind. Any attempt on his part for a repeat performance—if he could find the men, given that most mysteriously vanished—was always harshly dismissed.

What if he screwed up? Maybe his reaction last night repeated itself and he went off early? Darshan might've understood about it then, but the man would have limits. Especially when heaped atop everything else.

Absently wiping his palms on his tunic, he all but crushed the door handle in his fingers. *Turn,* he commanded his hand. *There's nae point standing out here all night.*

The hushed patter of feet reached his ears, echoing from down the halls.

Hamish glanced over his shoulder. No one was there, but his heart still skipped several beats, he was sure of it. "You've nae been followed," he murmured, trying to stop himself from shaking. If anyone was near, it would be a servant and they had long learnt to keep their heads down about matters like this.

Gordon would see to it that the guards wouldn't think to look for him until much later and, by then, he was to meet up with his brother to concoct a viable excuse. The very fact he needed to do so at all set a bitter taste in the back of his mouth, but if skirting the rules was what it took to live as he wanted, then so be it.

He gently opened the door, not entirely sure what to expect.

Warm light bathed him, the source a half dozen candles. His eye was immediately drawn to Darshan. The man sat on the end of the bed, leaning back on his arms with one ankle propped on a knee.

"H-hello," Hamish mumbled, his face growing hotter with each thunderous pulse of his heart. Darshan might not have been naked—nor was he wearing the embroidered sherwani, leaving only the plainer clothes beneath—but that didn't help. If anything, knowing he would have to remove those flimsy barriers to the man's bare skin only served to have his heart pound harder.

Darshan silently beckoned him closer with one crooked finger.

He took a few halting steps forward. His heart leapt into his throat as he crossed the threshold. He hadn't fully entered this room since that disastrous night with the dwarven ambassador, hadn't even ventured near here in all the years between then and first escorting Darshan to the door.

The room didn't appear to have changed with the years. The walls were the same bare stone, the natural grey turned ruddy in the candlelight. The bed was no different, even the worn bearskin rug looked to be the one he'd been kneeling on when the guards found him all those years back. There *was* a little more heat in the room, courtesy of the furnace the spellster had just about made of the fireplace.

"Are you going to shut the door?" Darshan enquired. "You are letting all the heat escape."

Hamish complied. The faint scrape of a key drew his attention. He glanced down as the lock clicked. It should've reassured him, but he had witnessed this very door fall. At least the guards' initial thud against the iron-banded planks would give him enough time to attempt hiding. Maybe Darshan's magic was capable of turning a man invisible.

"Turn around." The instruction came just as softly as the man's previous question, but somehow managed to roar through Hamish's head.

Following the command had him turning to find Darshan standing right before him, his brow furrowed with concern. Those hazel eyes seemed intent on burrowing into Hamish's skull, seeking what, Hamish couldn't be certain, but definitely in search of something.

He recalled the man's words yesterday, of the explicit request for consent. Was Darshan still worried about Hamish's willingness?

"You seem tense," Darshan finally said. His weight shifted. Whether the subtle movement was a conscious act or not, it was definitely a readiness to step back should he need to.

This wasn't like when Darshan had turned up unannounced. Hamish had been given no time to think, barely enough to act. Now all his thoughts crowded to be heard. "It's been a while," he replied, wincing at the faint quaver his nerves made of his voice.

Darshan's mouth twitched; a soft curve that wasn't a smile, but held a kindness that strummed something deep within Hamish. "We shall take it slower this time." He clasped Hamish's hand and led him deeper into the room. "I promise."

"That's nae me concern." Although, he did appreciate the gesture. "I dinnae have a lot of pleasant memories of the last time I was in this room."

"If it bothers you to be doing this here, we could try to find another place?" His gaze didn't seem to quite meet Hamish's as he spoke, likely not relishing the thought of delaying.

Hamish shook his head. "There is naewhere else."

"I see," Darshan murmured, running his thumb over the back of Hamish's fingers. "They will not catch us, you know." The words came laced with such assurance.

Hamish wished he could be as confident. *Maybe I should leave.* Return only once the thought of being discovered by the guards wasn't all-encompassing. Although, that was looking to be unlikely without Darshan's departure. "You say that now, but—" His voice stuttered as Darshan wet his lips. All Hamish could think of was kissing them again. Would they still be soft? Or would their combined need turn them rough?

In one silken move, Darshan pressed close. His hand glided up Hamish's chest, around his neck and into his hair. The gentle pressure of the man's grasp had Hamish bending enough to drop a whispering kiss upon Darshan's lips.

No sooner than he had done so, did the man's grip tighten. Darshan dragged him down further, deepening the kiss, each move desperate, raw and brimming with power. Hamish's legs trembled.

Just when he thought he might drop, Darshan stepped back.

He stared at Hamish, wide-eyed, his face frozen in a mask of mortification. Then, all at once, he clapped a bare hand over his mouth and turned on his heel. "That was terribly uncouth of me."

"I didnae mind."

Darshan whirled back, grinning. "I can tell. Those trousers of yours might be voluminous in appearance, but they leave little to the imagination up close."

Dear Goddess. Hamish buried his face into his hands. His cheeks burned against his palms. Yes, he had noticed how hard he'd grown, but never had it been so casually mentioned. It didn't help that he'd opted to go without his smalls to speed things along.

He risked a peek between his fingers to find the spellster hadn't moved.

Seeming to notice Hamish's scrutiny, Darshan pressed his hand to his chest. His fingers certainly looked a lot longer and thinner without the thick rings. "Forgive me, I will endeavour to show a little more decorum. But I warn you, that might be difficult what with yesterday still running through my head since I left your room."

"Is that so?" Knowing that Darshan couldn't get that time out of his head any more than Hamish could forget did much to soothe his nerves.

The spellster wrapped his fingers around Hamish's belt, pulling them close once again. "I guess, if there is nowhere else we can go, the only recourse is to make some new, and extremely pleasant, memories for you to dwell on."

"That sounds preferable." Hamish cupped the man's jaw, tilting it at just the angle he desired. Their lips met, a little more restrained on Darshan's part.

How long they stood there, he couldn't be sure. The kiss never grew in intensity, just lingered in that strange balance of tender and full of raw emotion.

Darshan's deft fingers tugged at Hamish's clothing, first loosening his belt before moving on to the ties at the neck of his tunic. Hamish had been careful to wear only enough to get him through the halls without raising suspicion. Sadly, that meant wearing a great deal more than he would've preferred.

"You know," Darshan muttered whilst assisting Hamish in hauling off his undershirt. "As much fun as undressing you is, you might want to consider wearing less clothing next time."

"Oh aye?" Hamish levered off one boot with the other as he undid the ties to his trousers. He stepped out of them and pushed them aside with the flick of a foot. "And just how much less would you suggest?" He might be able to get away with no undershirt next time. Although, with the faint spring chill in the air, it would make the return trip to his quarters a bit on the cold side.

Darshan hummed thoughtfully, the flash of a playful smile all but concealed as he hauled off his own attire. It seemed the man had opted for the one layer this time instead of the three he'd worn whilst in Hamish's quarters. "If you could manage the journey here in your drawers..."

Laughter burst from Hamish's throat upon realising that the man meant for him to walk the halls in his smalls. "There's nae way that's happening." By the smirk on the man's face, he seemed well aware of that.

"A pity." Darshan shed his trousers and Hamish realised that the man had also thought to forsake the extra layer of clothing there. "The sight of you wandering the corridors in nothing else would be a privilege you would find me quite willing to pay for."

Hamish pressed close, wrapping his arms around the man's bare shoulders. Darshan's skin was hot, beyond what could've been attributed to the warmth in the room. Did magic turn ordinary men into furnaces?

That was a question to ask later. He dropped his head, not to kiss again, but to nuzzle at the spellster's neck.

A soft moan, almost a squeak, escaped the man's lips.

Darshan clutched at Hamish, arching his elegant neck in a fashion that allowed greater access to that expanse of olive-brown skin. All sorts of obscene murmurs and hushed groans rumbled through Darshan's throat.

He smelt good. At first, Hamish had thought the scent came from the man's clothes or the candles, but it was Darshan himself that emanated a freshness like the winter seas or grass after the rain, mixed with a sweet aroma he couldn't quite place, likely something from the spellster's homeland. Had the man bathed between their talk on the abandoned cliffward tower and now?

A flush of guilt washed over Hamish. After the journey down the castle's secret exit, he'd barely any time to do little more than scrub the essentials. Most of him likely still smelt of dusty tunnel and wet soil.

"Hamish?" Darshan murmured.

He halted his exploration of the man's neck and shoulders. The way his name had left Darshan's lips—gravelly with need, but also a little frantic—had his insides doing all sorts of strange flips he hadn't realised them capable of.

"I meant to ask," Darshan continued. "Seeing that it has been years for you... How would you like this to go?"

"What?" Hamish straightened. "I thought we'd already agreed on why I came here?" Although, if he didn't slow down, his visit would be a repeat of yesterday. He stepped back from the man, putting some distance between them to try and cool off.

"Yes, yes." Darshan waved his hand. "But what position do you prefer? Riding or being ridden?"

Frowning, Hamish settled on the bed. *Position?* That he'd understood and, truth be told, he had experience with only the one. The rest?

He flopped back, stretching out across the bedding and staring up at the ceiling. "You ask a lot of questions." Ones they probably should've gotten out of the way during their time on the tower fortifications rather than him prattling about various points of interest in their scenic view.

He caught only a few hushed footsteps from the spellster crossing the room before Darshan's weight shifted the mattress and the man's concerned face came into sight. "I *am* rather averse towards hurting you."

Hamish wriggled, trying to get comfortable. The mattress was a little softer than what he was used to. A good surface to lean on whilst rutting, though. "Isnae it supposed to hurt?" He'd never known a time that hadn't left him unable to sit properly for a few days afterwards.

Darshan sat back on his heels, his already furrowed brows trying their best to deepen the lines. "Exactly how much experience do you have with sex?"

"None."

Those hazel eyes bulged, wide and round enough to fill the lenses of his glasses. "None?" Darshan echoed.

"It's nae that I dinnae ken about sex," Hamish drawled, quietly dreading the turn this conversation had taken. Why were they even discussing this? "Because I do." More than he really wanted to know when it came to intimacy between a man and a woman. "I just havenae done it." As the man must've known.

There was a faint twitch of Darshan's upper lip, the minute narrowing of his eyes and the overall overt drawing of his brow. He looked for all the world like a man trying to decide if Hamish was really that ignorant.

As if he has ever done it. What had the man said up on the tower earlier? That he'd no interest in women?

When the silence had almost become too much for Hamish to take, Darshan spoke.

"You..." he mumbled. "*Never...?*" He shook his head. "I must have misunderstood you. You really have not had sex? You certainly cannot tell from the way you kiss. But yesterday... In your quarters... The way you pleasured me. We—"

"What does kissing have to do with lying with a woman?" Hamish snapped. Or even what he'd done to please the man for that matter? "We really dinnae have a lot of time, you ken? So, are we rutting or nae? Because if it's nae happening, then I best be going."

Hamish went to get off the bed when the spellster's hand pressed against his chest.

Darshan grew still. Those hazel eyes seemed to bore into Hamish as the spellster hovered over him. "That man in the pub said something similar and you said it earlier, but I am afraid the word was not in my Tirglasian language studies."

"Aye." He had forgotten that, even though Darshan had acted under the principle of what Billy said was derogatory, the Udynean hadn't understood all the words. "It wouldnae have been," Hamish mumbled, acutely aware there would likely be a number of words Darshan's tutors wouldn't have mentioned. He scrubbed at his face, letting his hand slide over his beard and down his neck. "Look, all I need to ken is, if we're doing this, what do you want me bent over?"

Darshan sat back, his brows raised to their highest. "Nothing. Your current position is more than adequate."

Hamish scoffed. "You cannae rut like this." Not face to face. That was a position for wedded couples; husband and wife specifically.

The spellster's handsome features contorted, those immaculate brows lowering in confusion. His lips parted to silently mimic the word. Then slowly, like clouds parting, clarity came to light in his eyes. "Am I right in thinking that you *are* referring to sex? But rough sex, specifically? The kind where one slams himself into the other until he is done?"

"Aye?" What other kind of act between two men could there possibly be?

Something flitted across Darshan's face, too quick to be certain of, but it had the soft air of pity about it. "And that is the extent of your experience?"

"It is, aye."

Darshan's eyes narrowed as he scrubbed at his chin. "I am wondering..." He crept closer until he hovered over Hamish. "...how much of a mood are you for indulging me? Just for a moment."

"That would depend on what you want."

"A mere question, I assure you." The man cleared his throat. "These other men you have been with?"

Hamish swallowed. The last thing he wanted to talk about was them.

"Was it rather a case of arse up, head down and not speak a word?" Darshan cocked his head even though Hamish hadn't answered. "Are you certain they actually like men that way? Or have they all just been looking for a convenient place to stick it?"

Hamish shrugged, a queasiness bubbling in his gut. He had known a few that had felt the same, but generally? "I dinnae ken much beyond most of them being sailors who were likely to leave port within the day." If not the hour.

Again, something flashed across Darshan's face. There for no longer than the first time, but definitely pity.

He peered at the man. If Darshan pitied him, did that mean... "Is it nae the same for you?"

Darshan's expression melted into one of sorrow. "Not at all," he whispered. "There is so much more." He crept up the bed, one knee slipping between Hamish's thighs to gently part them. "Allow me to show you what sex between two men can be like."

Hamish rolled his eyes. "Men cannae have sex with each other," he mumbled. Maybe it was the language barrier, or twisty Udynean thinking, but the man couldn't be aware of what he was implying.

Amusement snorted out Darshan's nose. He smirked, the act skewing his moustache. "What utter nonsense they teach you Northerners." He laid atop Hamish, stretching out so that his whole body touched. "Would you like to discover if that is entirely true? Because I do not believe I have heard any disapproval."

Hamish wet his lips. Dare he agree and find out just what the man was jabbering about? He desperately wanted to agree, but past disappointment cautioned him against hoping too much. How many times had men declared they would show him a good time only to be more concerned about their own pleasure?

"My word," Darshan snickered, propping himself up on his elbows. "You need not say a thing. I can practically see the dice rolling around in your head." He grinned. "Do they land in my favour?"

"Do whatever you wish," Hamish finally managed. He had come here for this very reason. What point was there in backing out now?

The spellster shook his head, the brown curls of his hair bouncing with the exaggerated movement. "Oh no, no, no. That simply will not do, my hirsute friend. Since it has been *years* for you, I would rather make it about your wants." He sat back, the grin turning cheeky as he winked. "Although, if you insist on keeping mum about it, I might just decide to flip you over and have my way."

Hamish's heart thumped a few heavy beats at the very idea. He shrugged, trying to remain nonchalant, aware his length twitching against the man's thigh had likely given him away. "I wouldnae mind." It wasn't as if he hadn't been manhandled before.

"I see," Darshan murmured. "Well there is an ocean of difference between not minding an act and explicitly desiring it." His hand ran idly up and down Hamish's forearm, the action oddly intimate. "You never answered my original question, you know. I can rather deduce how the past has gone for you, but I am far more interested in your desires now. Do you want to ride or be ridden? I am open to both, if that helps."

He slowly rocked his head from side to side. Whilst he wasn't entirely sure what Darshan meant, he *did* know what he wanted. "You in me."

"Riding it is, then." It might've been a trick of the candlelight, but Hamish could've sworn he'd seen a flicker of disappointment in his response cross the man's face. Before he could muster the courage to ask, Darshan hopped off the bed and sauntered to his travel chest.

Hamish rolled onto his side to find Darshan's back facing him. The man's olive-brown skin appeared unmarked by ink or blemishes, save for a single star-shaped scar halfway up his torso. He hadn't noticed if there was a matching mark on Darshan's chest, having been far too distracted with other thoughts both now and earlier, but the scarring looked reminiscent of an arrow wound. Couldn't spellsters fix any fault?

Darshan bent to rummage in the travel chest's depths, seemingly ignorant of how the act gifted Hamish a full view of that perfect backside. Whatever he searched for took far too short a time, but he returned to Hamish's side swiftly enough with a brown bottle.

"And that is?" Hamish jerked a chin at the bottle. Some sort of liquid sloshed inside, just visible through the cloudy glass.

"This?" Darshan stared at the item as if surprised to find it in his possession. "Just oil." He uncorked the bottle and poured a little of the almost transparent liquid onto his fingers. "It was perhaps a little presumptuous of me to bring so much, I wasn't exactly anticipating meeting anyone like-minded during my stay." A faint smile creased his eyes. "But here we are."

"I'm still nae sure why you need it." Was it a Udynean thing? He knew they had dozens of olive groves and typically used the oil all the time food-wise, but he'd never considered it might have other applications.

Darshan scoffed as he set the re-corked bottle on the floor. "If you want me in you, then you shall need preparation, especially since you have not done it in so long. Surely, you do not expect me to enter you dry… do you?" He seemed to almost cringe at the question, staring down at his oiled fingers. Was he dreading the answer?

Hamish frowned. None of his previous rutting partners had ever prepared him. Often, there wasn't the time for more than trousers down, get off and leave. And those last two acts were generally the other way around for him.

His silence must've tweaked something in the man's thoughts, for when Darshan met his gaze again, those hazel eyes were clouded with concern. "You *have* actually done it this way before? I *am* willing to ride you." His hand, slightly slick with tepid oil, caressed Hamish's length. "If that is what you would prefer?"

Hamish flopped his head back onto the bed. There hadn't ever been any other way. It would always be him bent over a crate or barrel in the shadows of some pub storeroom, trying not to cry out as some random, and usually drunk, man took him whilst he scraped together what small amounts of pleasure he could from the act. "This way is fine." He wouldn't know what to do with himself if he had full control of the act.

"Well, seeing that we, apparently, do it a little differently in Udynea." Darshan offered up a small, lopsided smile as his hand snaked from Hamish's length to slide between his buttocks. "I am afraid you shall have to indulge me here."

"Aye?" he breathed. Already, he felt the man's oil-slick finger gently circling his point of entry. Oddly pleasurable. Taking a deep breath, he sought to relax, despite the faint tremor of hesitancy in his gut. "Then indulge away."

With his gaze set on Hamish's face, the spellster pushed his finger in. The slide was slow but sure, meticulous in execution. There was a familiar whisper, the faintest echo of an ache that vanished as Darshan slid in and out. "You certainly were not jesting about it being years for you." His free hand stroked Hamish's length in tandem.

Hamish mumbled something, the words coming of their own accord rather than through any conscious effort. He could feel himself slipping on the gentle rhythm of those lean fingers sliding up his length whilst that single digit pushed in, only to have Darshan's hand move down as his other withdrew. They could do no action other than this and he'd be more than content.

Before long, Darshan shifted the finger inside him, changing the angle. A soft frown tweaked his brow. His gaze lifted from the silent, passive survey of Hamish's face to the wall, then the ceiling as he bit his lip.

Hamish lifted his head, trying to see something beyond the man's shoulders to no avail. "What are you doing?" The words escaped slurred.

Darshan's attention returned to him, a faint flush of red tingeing his cheeks. "Trying to, um..." He changed the angle of his finger once more as it slid in. "Trying to find your... uh..." A different expression took his face. One Hamish had grown familiar with as Darshan sought out words to replace those he hadn't been taught. "...your spot?"

"Me spot?" he echoed, chuckling. There was only one spot he'd been taught about and he doubted he had one of those. "I'm pretty sure I dinnae have a spo—" The word melted into a groan that sucked the air from his lungs. Flecks of light glittered in front of his eyes. Warmth suffused him.

The man's low snicker filled his ears. "Found it, have I?"

Hamish mumbled words that he was certain were of the affirmative kind. He tipped his head back onto the pillow, his hips rocking ever so slightly against Darshan's hand. Whatever magic the spellster wrought, it was good.

The finger moved again, pulling back. He felt stretched. Although pleasurable, each gentle shift of that digit also carried a methodical air about it. Was this what Darshan had meant by preparing him?

Not just the oil to ease entry, but allowing him the time and means to relax and be ready for something bigger?

"Hold a moment." Darshan held out his hand and the bottle of oil flew into his grasp. Prising the cork free with his teeth, he poured more out.

Hamish shivered as the cool oil hit his skin, leaving a trail from his balls to where—

Was that another finger seeking entry? He wriggled, testing the feeling. Definitely extra pressure.

"I see we are eager for more," Darshan purred. He moved his finger, sliding it in a half-circle around the one still in Hamish. "Do you think you could handle it?"

Hamish's breath shuddered from him. That question, the silken honey tone of the man's voice. He wasn't certain if he could actually go over the edge with Darshan's current actions, but if that tone continued he might be capable of it.

" 'Mish? Are—" A flicker of uncertainty seemed to slap across the man's face. "Can I call you that?"

He nodded, his body bouncing as he struggled to contain a laugh. Why would he mind his name being shortened? *Of all the daft things to concern himself with at this moment.* Maybe it was different in Udynea. He hadn't taken much interest in politics to bother with the minutiae, but now wasn't the time. "Dar," he gasped between breaths. "More."

Those hazel eyes, so focused only moments ago, slid closed. Darshan bit his lip and bowed his head. A faint gust of the man's breath hit Hamish's stomach. A groan?

Hamish levered himself up onto his elbows. As pleasant as it had been, they must have gone on long enough with this preparation. He clasped the man's shoulder, squeezing just enough to ensure Darshan didn't mistake it for him seeking the removal of the spellster's presence. "Dar?"

Darshan's eyes flicked open, that dark gaze locking with Hamish's. Lust burned in their depths. Only now did Hamish notice how Darshan's breath rasped. "Are you certain you will last long enough?" His languid strokes along Hamish's length grew stronger, rougher.

It pulled a throaty moan from him. Hamish tipped back his head, trying to find the will to stop Darshan and failing. His hips bucked with each down stroke. The edge wasn't that close, but if the man kept it up… "Please," he managed.

"Please what?" Darshan murmured, lifting Hamish's hand off his shoulder to tenderly kiss the palm. "Please continue? Please stop? Please slam yourself to the hilt in me and screw me blind?"

"Aye!" he blurted before Darshan could move on. "That one!

Goddess…" The sensation seemed to ebb, the edge slipping from his immediate grasp.

All at once, the spellster withdrew, taking the glorious feeling with him.

Hamish sat up, propped not quite in a fully-upright position by his outstretched arms. "What is it?" He eyed the room's only exit, a gentle bubble of uncertainty boiling away in his stomach. Had the guards been alerted? *Nae that.* Then… "Are you having second thoughts about this?"

"Not at all," Darshan said, patting the side of Hamish's thigh reassuring. "And there is no cause to look so alarmed." The bottle of oil was back in the spellster's hand only, this time, Darshan was applying it to himself. He winced and hissed slightly as he slathered the oil on his very-much-erect length. "I just— I have no desire to end this too quickly. I want it to last as long as we are able and would certainly prefer if you did not go off before the main event as it were."

Hamish mumbled his agreement on the final point. *Goddess, dinnae let this be like the others.* Although he was confident he could still handle a bit of roughness like the old days, he would've vastly preferred if the initial entry wasn't. He rather liked Darshan. At least, what he'd seen of the man so far. It would be a shame to end this at the beginning. "So we are actually going to do this?"

"Well, yes." Amusement hitched up one side of the man's mouth and tweaked his moustache. He slowly crept up Hamish's body, pausing to kiss every so often and not once losing eye contact. "And you better tell me if it starts hurting."

He huffed. "I'm nae some pansy," he grumbled, the declaration surprisingly gruff even to his ears. "I can handle a bit of pain."

"And as *I* already told you, I am in no hurry to hurt you." Resting up on his elbows, Darshan removed his glasses and set them on the bedside table. Without the barrier of lenses dulling their hues, the rich multi-coloured irises were laid bare. Although the pupils were blown wide, the separate rings of brown and green were still clear.

"How well can you see me without those?" Hamish asked, indicating the glasses.

"This close?" Darshan placed a wet kiss in the centre of Hamish's chest. "Well enough. And I do not plan to get far enough from you for it to matter. Shall we continue?" The question was thick and heavy with need.

Hamish nodded. He pressed deeper into the mattress as his legs were gently assisted into position by Darshan's touch. His hips tilted, putting him in a slightly angled pose. He felt the spellster against him, the man's warmth sitting just at the entrance.

His gut quivered, barely constrained excitement shuddered

through his lungs. That was new. Usually, it was a war of doubt and lust, where experience told him this would hurt and it would take a mixture of desire and drink to herd him to the point where he didn't care.

He tipped his head back, closed his eyes and tried to remain relaxed.

"No slamming in, I am afraid," Darshan murmured. He pushed against Hamish, the pressure gentle and steady.

Hamish fisted the sheets, struggling to keep his breathing even and his mind from thinking on the past. He'd had plenty of men in those times who'd taken him suddenly enough. Never without his consent, but certainly without a care towards his readiness or wellbeing.

Risking a peek between his lashes showed Darshan's face to be nothing but care. *For me*. The rasp of the man's breath was laborious and sweat already dripped from his hook of a nose, but he maintained the slow pace.

Try as he might, Hamish couldn't help the faint hissing inhalation as Darshan slid in—to the hilt, just as he had promised—and the building pressure finally gave way to fullness. He could typically remain silent whilst in the act, even through some of the most vicious pain. But this... *It—*

Darshan groaned. His eyes slid closed and he halted all movement, save for the slight shift of his heavy breaths. An air of patient waiting surrounded him.

It doesnae hurt. That was the first fully coherent thought to surface. It usually burned in the beginning and he generally spent much of the night after smarting. This was warmth, a dull ache that couldn't quite make up its mind whether it should hurt or not, and—

Darshan tilted his weight, leaning on one bent elbow, whilst he slid his free hand down Hamish's side. An uncontrollable flush of heat burrowed into Hamish's body, emanating from the man's fingertips. Rather than burn, it soothed.

"Wha—?" Hamish squirmed, trying to see just what the man was doing to him.

"Hush," Darshan breathed, the word little more than a hiss of air. "Just a bit of precautionary healing." As gravelled with desire as his voice was, it also came tempered by concern. "Are you all right so far? I can wait if you need the time to adjust."

He shook his head, an unfettered grin stretching his mouth wide. "I'm just *grand*." Was that why the man had stopped? *For me?* A hectic mixture of emotion tightened his chest and filled his eyes, threatening to spill. He blinked the tears back lest Darshan thought the worst of them. No one had ever waited for him to be ready. "Is this what sex is usually like for you?"

"Honestly?" The corner of Darshan's mouth lifted. "It is typically a lot faster."

He'd had fast before. Strong, hectic thrusts that had almost brought him pleasure. To have this sensation on top of that... "I can handle fast."

Darshan chuckled, bouncing the both of them as his mirth vibrated the mattress. "You say that *now*, but I have yet to actually move. And I have no desire to push your limits tonight."

"What if I want me limits pushed?"

"Not tonight," he whispered, bending over Hamish to plant a single chaste kiss on his lips. Darshan lifted his hips, withdrawing until he was almost free, before sliding himself back into Hamish with the same steady determination. A little rougher, but still far gentler than others had been.

A quavering moan left Hamish's lips. He closed his eyes, his grip on the sheets tightening. His back arched involuntarily, lifting his hips off the bed. Such an act seemed to gift Darshan a better angle that the man was all too happy to take advantage of. The spellster sat back—a world away after their previous closeness—and started thrusting his hips in earnest.

Grunts and soft groans filled his ears. Not solely his own. Soft and measured like the way Darshan moved inside him. Hamish's hips rocked in tandem with those thrusts. Or they at least tried to, his movements ungainly and inexperienced. Usually, he was in too much pain to do anything but lay there.

"You are allowed to touch me, you know."

He opened his eyes, searching wildly for Darshan as if he wasn't right there. With great difficulty, Hamish uncurled his fingers from the heavy linen bedding and reached for the man. "Closer," he mumbled.

Darshan's rhythm faltered, surprise darting across his face. He slunk back on top of Hamish, resting on outstretched arms. Their lips met; clumsy, wet and with a great deal more passion than Hamish had expected.

Hamish sighed into the man's mouth. His soul floated. If this was sex—real sex as opposed to what he had experienced in the past—then he had missed so much.

"Still good?" Darshan asked between soft grunts.

Nodding, Hamish wrapped his arms around the man's shoulders, pulling him closer. He needed the contact, needed that mouth back on his.

The spellster chuckled breathlessly. "Is that little moan all I get?" he mumbled into Hamish's beard. "I cannot recall ever leaving someone at a loss for words *during*."

Hamish bit his lip, a groan bubbling in his chest. Even if he could form more than a single word, he was confident that most of them would escape as animalistic grunts. Pressure was building deep inside him. A fire he had only felt when pleasuring himself. It spread through his veins, numbing all thought. Any moment, any thrust, could be the one to finally push him over the edge.

There was even a certain look in Darshan's gaze, a far-off gleam that spoke of the man far down the path towards chasing his own pleasure. The easy rhythm his hips set increased in pace. Not rough or uncaring. Darshan certainly wasn't ignoring Hamish's needs in favour of his own, but there was determination.

Hamish reached back to grip the headboard, clinging to it in search of a way to ground himself. Usually, he would've one hand firmly wrapped around himself by the time this sensation was upon him. Would Darshan object if he did so now? Most men in the past preferred he didn't. "Dar?" he panted. "Can I—?" He let go of the headboard with one hand, slinking between them.

"Do not be coy." The answer came gruff and heavy with the efforts of the night. Darshan slowed, each thrust less controlled than the last. His head sagged, obscuring his face with a mess of dark brown curls. The frantic huff of his breath still rasped in Hamish's ear, the heat of it hitting his chest.

Hamish grasped his length, pumping hard. His body tightened like a spring. His head tipped back as did his eyes. His mouth dropped open, his breath coming in heaving gasps.

The bottom fell out of his world, sending his senses freefalling into bliss.

The heat in his veins consumed him, shuddering through his limbs, lifting his hips as he emptied himself between their bodies.

There was the gentle brush of Darshan's lips against his clavicle. Then up further. "I did not take you for a quiet finisher," he murmured, the heat of the words warming Hamish's already sweat-soaked skin. The man nuzzled at Hamish's beard, seeking. "Your neck is in here somewhere."

Hamish tilted his head, allowing the man unfettered access. He stared up at the ceiling as Darshan nibbled up his neck, still not certain what he had experienced. He'd had orgasms before, just not with someone. And never during. But that had been far better than anything he ever remembered doing, like he had somehow forged a connection between them in a way he had never known with any other man.

Was that what sex was meant to be like? Euphoric?

"Wow," he finally managed.

Darshan chuckled, the sound low and smug. "You are most welcome." There was a tightness to the words and his right arm still moved, his bicep flexing against Hamish's chest.

Slowly, he became aware that the man had pulled out? When? Why?

There was the gentle blast of breath against Hamish's neck—a whimper—and then Darshan went still.

"You could've finished in me," Hamish mumbled. It wouldn't have exactly been a first.

"Now he tells me." Darshan surfaced from beneath Hamish's beard, grinning. His usually fluffy hair had gone flat with sweat. "Well, there is always next time," he murmured against Hamish's lips.

Next time? Still slightly dazed, his mind latched onto that one thought. He hadn't ever been with the same man twice. Although, he supposed this technically counted as just that if he also included the previous night's botched attempt.

Pressing a soft kiss to the tip of Hamish's nose, Darshan slid off the bed.

He tracked the man's passage across the room as Darshan collected a small bowl. Ice formed on the outside as he neared, only to melt like a spring frost.

Darshan glanced up from his task to frown at Hamish. "Am I being too presumptuous? My apologies." He set the bowl down on the bedside table, water slopping over the rim, before sitting back on the bed. "But if you would allow me the luxury of being so bold... You seemed to enjoy yourself."

Hamish grinned, biting on his lip to keep from openly laughing. "Aye, I—" Warm wetness caressed his abdomen. He lifted his head enough to spy Darshan running a cloth over him, cleaning the mess he'd made of himself. "What are you doing?" he mumbled, heat flooding his face like a burst dam. Usually, he would tend to this himself with a quick clean, then a more thorough one once safely back in his room.

Those hazel eyes flicked up from his task. "Did you really expect me to let you leave like this?"

He stared back at the man, puzzled. "Did I...?" The words trickled away. What *had* he expected? *Nae a damn thing.* It was far easier to anticipate indifference once the deed was done, for he was right more often than he wished to admit.

Judging by the man's hesitancy and tender movements, Darshan didn't do this very often. Hamish couldn't imagine an imperial prince cleansing himself, let alone others. Still, he appreciated the effort.

Darshan tossed the cloth over his shoulder, where it hit the floor with a slap. He laid the hand that'd been holding the damp cloth onto Hamish's stomach. The palm radiated warmth.

Hamish inched up the bed. "What—?"

"Hush," the spellster whispered, gently withdrawing his touch as if Hamish were a spooked colt. "It is merely a little heat. Nothing to worry about, but I will stop if you prefer."

Hamish shook his head. He'd already had magic performed on him once tonight, what was a little more? And now the moisture on his skin had been given time to cool, his stomach felt rather exposed, despite having the obvious advantage of a denser patch of hair than other parts.

Darshan resumed applying gentle heat. "Since, I assume, we agree on compatibility?"

"Aye," he murmured, still focused on what the magic was doing. It seemed to be drying his skin far better than cloth could manage. "That we do."

"Would you… like to continue?"

"Now?" He tore his gaze from Darshan's hand to stare mortified at the man. "I dinnae think I have the strength."

Throwing back his head, Darshan laughed long and hard. "Nor do I," he clarified once he was able to do more than chuckle and wheeze. "But I meant in the sense we continue our little clandestine affair."

"I'd like that." Hamish went to sit up only to have the man's weight firmly pin him back onto the mattress. "Just so we're both clear on where this is heading, given that this is uncharted waters for me, what happens now?"

"I shall leave that up to you," Darshan replied, sitting back. "I have some experience in being considered as just another avenue for pleasure and I would understand if you wish to take it no further than that. But if you would prefer something a little more formal—a relationship, for example—I am open to that possibility."

"What?" Hamish grinned. "Actually be lovers?"

"If that is what you want from this, then I am willing." There was a peculiar energy to the man's position, almost a readiness to spring out of the way should need be.

"That sounds—" Something about Darshan's expression halted his tongue. Was that a faint flicker of concern across the man's face? Or was he projecting his own uncertainties? Did he actually think Hamish would reject him? Now?

He caressed Darshan's cheek. "I'd like to try." It would all be gone once Darshan's ambassadorial duties were done. He wasn't daft enough to believe otherwise. But for now, he'd settle for a piece of what his siblings once had. No matter how small that time would be.

Darshan smiled, tension visibly melting from his whole body. "I had rather hoped you would." He shuffled further onto the bed, snuggling on top of Hamish and pillowing his head atop Hamish's chest. "Just for a while," he murmured. "If you do not mind."

Hamish released his breath in one long, contented exhalation. Reason warned him that he couldn't stay any longer, but the man's comforting weight, his warmth...

"Aye," he whispered, wrapping his arms around Darshan so that his hands sat comfortably in the small of the spellster's back. "A wee while will be fine." If this was what it meant to have a lover, he definitely didn't want to lose the man any sooner than he had to.

Chapter 12

The comfortably warm body beneath Darshan lurched. Before he could drag his thoughts out of the groggy sludge of sleep, he found himself thrown unceremoniously off the bed. A shield enveloped him as he hit the floor, his healing magic taking over soon after to ease the smarting of his bare arse hitting the old wooden planks.

Darshan scrambled to his knees, groping for his glasses even as he clicked his fingers to have a flame flicker to life in his hand—a childish act, but one he leant on in times like these. He peered at the scene before him.

Hamish bumbled about the room, gathering up his things in preparation for a hasty retreat.

He watched his lover race to don the bare minimum of his clothing. He had witnessed a few hurried exits from his chambers in the past, but never with this much fearful urgency.

" 'Mish?" The word came slowly, his tongue still stiff with sleep. Even to his ears, his voice was heavy with concern. "What is it?" Had their affair been discovered so quickly? He glanced at the door as his questing fingers found his glasses. The iron-bound, wooden panels were still intact and closed, whereas his ears picked up only the hurried scuffle of a man dressing.

"How could you let me sleep that long?" Hamish replied, hopping on one leg as he hauled on his boots.

"Surely, we cannot have slept for more than a few minutes." He recalled closing his eyes only moments ago.

"The moon's well up." Hamish waved a hand at the window. Sure enough, the sill was illuminated in pale light. "Midnight, I'd wager. I should've met up with me brother hours ago."

Darshan continued to stare at the window whilst putting on his glasses. Now that he could see, a glance over his shoulder confirmed that the candles had burnt down and the fire was naught but a dim glow of coals. "Then you had best be careful leaving here." He gathered up the man's tunic, the final piece of his lover's attire, and thrust it into Hamish's hands. "Is there anything I can do?" There were a number of distractions he could hurl from the window that would likely send every guard clamouring for the battlements. "I am very good at sky sparks." It wasn't as dangerous or loud as some of the other options, but the flashes of light above the castle would be cause for alarm.

Hamish shook his head. "Nae magic. As far as the guards are concerned, you've been asleep this whole time."

"Understood." He bowed his head. "I am sorry. It was not my intention to have you linger for so long."

A soft smile fattened Hamish's cheeks and creased the corners of those sapphiric eyes. "Me too," he breathed. He swung to the door, his hand on the key.

A knock came from the other side of the door before Hamish could unlock it. Three precise bangs on the wood; brisk and verging slightly on the presumptuous side. Someone who had come for a purpose and wasn't afraid to show their authority.

Hamish froze. Terror drained all the life from his face. Those wide eyes surveyed the room, taking in what Darshan already knew. There was nowhere for him to hide.

"Ambassador," a deep voice commanded from the other side of the door. "Let us in."

Hamish's fear-struck gaze settled on him, imploring.

Darshan wordlessly padded to the window. The curtains weren't long enough to reach the floor and the guards were bound to look behind them. Same went for under the bed.

He flung open the windowpanes. Cold air rushed to greet him. He could practically feel the hairs on his bare chest straining to stand straight.

Sticking his head out the window had him bearing the full force of the night wind ripping up from the sea. The salt air stung his nose and watered his eyes, but he still sought for a place Hamish could hide. Hanging onto the window ledge was unacceptable and dismissed with barely a thought. There were no cracks to cling to, either. No chinks in the mortar or bricks out of line far enough for a decent handhold.

Any other time, he would be amazed how Tirglasian masons managed such uniformity without magic. Right now, he was rather disgusted by it.

The guards still hammered on the door.

He pulled his head back in and eyed his lover. "How much do you weigh? Three hundred pounds? Four?"

"Probably?" Hamish snapped, the word hissing through his teeth. "There are a few boars me size, but I dinnae exactly weigh meself on the regular. Why?"

Nodding to himself, Darshan stepped back from the window. *A large boar*. Whilst he wasn't sure how big those got, he had lifted a solid carthorse off the ground in the past. Not very high, though. It would take a fair bit of concentration, but he could manage that weight for a time. "Do you trust me?"

Suspicion narrowed his lover's eyes and knotted his brows. "Do I have a choice?"

The hammering at the door grew heavier. Were the guards actually trying to knock it down? "You've until the count of ten to open up, Ambassador."

Hamish's gaze swung to the door. The doubt moulding his face crumbled into naked fear. If Darshan didn't know better, he would've sworn the men on the other side were here to kill them.

Darshan wove his fingers between his lover's, squeezing. "If you do not wish to get caught in my company..."

"One!" boomed the voice outside the room.

"I trust you," Hamish whispered.

"Then do not move and try to keep your breathing shallow." Like capturing a fly in the hands, he cupped a shield around Hamish. It was a small one, barely big enough to hold his lover, and dense through necessity.

"Two!"

Hamish's mouth moved, his voice silenced by the shield. Definitely a question.

Darshan motioned him to silence. Lifting Hamish, shield and all, was far harder than he had originally counted on. It rose sluggishly, but wholly under his command. Hopefully, he wouldn't lose control over it before the guards left.

"Three!" the man continued to count.

Sideways movement was far easier. He pushed Hamish, shield and all, out the window. It stuttered as Hamish rocked, flattening himself against the wallward edge of the invisible shield. Darshan persisted, gliding everything to one side of the window. Hiding Hamish above the frame would've been better should the guards think to look beyond the room's confines, but he didn't think he could manage any higher.

"Four!"

Darshan quietly shut the window once Hamish was tucked out of sight. "Just hold on," he shouted back. "I am coming!" After a few frantic heartbeats, he also closed the curtains. No need to make them suspicious.

He hurried across to the door, pausing only to extinguish a few of the candles and snatch up a cushion. He refused to seek a means to cover himself any further. If he could make the guards uncomfortable in his naked presence, then perhaps they would leave all the sooner. He wasn't certain how long he could hold Hamish in the air, even pressed against the castle wall. Already, the pressure of it pounded in his brain. Akin to a nagging headache at his temple that threatened to burrow deeper should he choose to ignore it.

Darshan unlocked the door and jumped back as three guards stampeded through the doorway. They spread out around the room, filling the space and then some like mongooses attempting to track a hooded serpent.

"Is there a problem?" he asked, keeping his voice light. He clung to the door with one hand, clutching the cushion in the other.

"His highness," one of the men rumbled, his dark gaze keenly surveying his surroundings rather than focusing on whom he addressed. Like most Tirglasians Darshan had seen, the guard was a big man; dark of hair and pale of skin. "Prince Hamish is missing from his quarters."

"And you naturally assumed he would be here?" They'd likely been ordered by Queen Fiona to search the guest quarters upon Hamish's marked absence, but no harm in crediting the guards with minds of their own. "As flattering as that is, I am alone." He waved his hand, indicating the room. "As you can see, there is only us. No prince beyond myself."

"We'll be the judge of that." In one smooth motion, the guard ordered the other two, who immediately began checking the obvious places Darshan had already ruled out as effective hiding spots.

The pressure in his temple throbbed that little bit harder. Was Hamish moving? He didn't think his lover could hear the guards through the shield's density. "As you can see, I was quite alone before you arrived." A lancing pain hit the left side of his brain. Darshan grimaced and cocked his head slightly. It alleviated the pressure, but not by much. *Stay still.* He needed the guards to leave now. "I am afraid I cannot be of any more help," he muttered between clenched teeth.

The head guard looked him over, seeming to finally notice Darshan's lack of clothing. "I find it suspicious that you're alone, naked and with a stiff one."

Feeling a little self-conscious, Darshan adjusted the cushion. How could he have missed himself growing hard? *How completely inappropriate.* Still, apart from the gnawing pain in his head, he couldn't deny that this was quite exhilarating. Being caught with men back in Udynea hadn't the same thrill behind it and never had he needed to hide a lover before.

He straightened, tipping his chin up and glared down his nose at the guard. It was a look he had perfected from his years in the Crystal Court and served him well back home. "Do you see me querying your night-time activities?"

The man sneered.

Behind the guard, Darshan caught one of the others flinging open the curtains. His heart skipped. The pressure in his head deepened like a chisel tapping deeper into marble. All it would take was for the man to open the window and look to his left.

Mercifully, the guard turned back around. "There's nae another soul here, sir."

"As I told you," Darshan snapped. "If you could now leave me to my slumber?"

The head guard nodded, his thin lips pressing together until they were but a line peeking out from beneath his beard. "That you did, your imperial highness." He bowed. "Our apologies for disturbing your sleep."

Darshan bit his cheek with the effort to remain silent. He hadn't imagined the faint pause in the guard's speech that suggested the man didn't believe Darshan had slept a wink. And the bastard had actually been hoping to catch Hamish here.

If he didn't have the vicious pounding in his head as a constant reminder that a life hung on his abilities, one of these men would certainly not be casually strolling off out the door.

Shadowing the guards' movements, he slammed the door on their backs the instant he was able to and deftly locked the smug bastards out.

He held his breath, counting to ten before hastening to open the window. Poking his head outside confirmed Hamish still stood flat against the brickwork.

His lover flinched as Darshan moved the shield. He could've lifted only the man, but directly hefting people with magic was a little different to the average rock or piece of decor. Inanimate objects tended not to protest if squeezed that little bit too hard, nor did they wriggle about in transit. This high, one ill-timed twitch could mean death.

The shield's faint purple sheen flickered. Darshan's heart stuttered. *No.*

Almost before he could finish the thought, the shield reformed to encapsulate Hamish once again. Darshan draped himself over the windowsill, half in an attempt to reach his lover and partly due to his wobbling legs.

The shield might've reappeared in the same spot, but Hamish had dropped at least a few feet in that time and now his legs, from the knees down, dangled in the air. Fortunately, the shield had returned not as dense or the man would've lost the lower half of those very limbs.

Squirming along the windowsill to get as close as he could manage, Darshan held out his hand. The shield buzzed along his forearm. He could no longer risk moving or altering the barrier lest it vanished again. They mightn't be so fortunate a second time.

"Take it!" Darshan ordered, his voice all but lost to the wind. There was a risk in Hamish's shifting weight causing the shield to fail, but that couldn't be helped.

His lover lurched for Darshan's hand, those rough fingers closing around his forearm. Unadulterated terror filled Hamish's eyes. He flailed with the other hand, searching for something to grasp.

Darshan strained to reach him. Their fingertips touched. *Just... a little... more...* No matter how hard he tried, he couldn't get any nearer.

There was nothing for it. He would have to pull Hamish closer and hope the shield held.

Holding his breath, Darshan gave the most minuscule of tugs. Maybe if he did it slowly enough...

The shield sputtered and died.

All of his lover's weight hit Darshan's arm at once. Lancing, *searing*, pain tore a scream from his throat. Hamish dangled below the window. Only his grip on Darshan's forearm and the desperate way he clung to the edge of the windowsill kept him from falling.

Fire and daggers burrowed into Darshan's shoulder. Magic flooded his body, seeking to heal the damage. He tried to haul the man up to no avail. His feet slid across the floor, finding no purchase in the old wood, then abandoned it altogether. If he didn't haul Hamish to safety or let the man go, they would both wind up falling to their deaths.

Darshan struggled to focus, to redirect his magic's involuntary persevering stance on healing him. Sweat beaded on his brow, dripping onto his glasses. Blinking furiously, he tightened his hold on Hamish's forearm. Letting his lover die because he couldn't see was not an option.

A surge of strength poured into his straining muscles. His questing feet found purchase on the wall, allowing him to brace himself. He had only a small timeframe before the magic would tear his body apart.

He latched onto Hamish's other wrist and pulled with every ounce of strength his magic could give.

Hamish inched up the wall, able to assist once his torso was balanced on the windowsill. He clambered the last few inches back inside under his own power, tumbling into the room to lie still on the floor. Just the steady rise and fall of his chest gave any indication that he lived. Had he passed out?

Darshan dared to take a single wobbly step from the wall before his legs opted to dump him where he stood. He slid to the floor, upright only thanks to the wall at his back. He released his grip on his magic, letting the passive healing once more flow through his body. " 'Mish? Are you all right?" His lover didn't appear injured, but he was prepared to spare some of the precious little energy he had left if that was the case.

His lover stirred, waving him off with the flap of an arm. "I'm fine. That's quite the trick you have there." There was a touch of acidity to Hamish's otherwise light tone. "Did it occur to you to—I dinnae ken—*warn me* before you shove me out a bloody window?" he growled, finally sitting up.

"I would have if there had been more time." His gaze slid from the man's back to the door. After everything, he half-expected the guards to burst into the room. "That was a little more intense than I was expecting."

"Aye and close, too." Groaning, Hamish got to his feet and brushed the dust from his clothes. "I better get back before they've searched everywhere else."

"What?" Darshan scrambled to get his legs back under him. He grabbed his lover's arm as Hamish neared the door. The act did little to stop him. "They do not believe you to be here. Surely, you do not have to leave just yet."

"I should though." His calloused hand cradled Darshan's jaw, the pad of his thumb caressing Darshan's cheek in one wide sweep. "I'll make it up to you next time."

"I certainly hope so."

Smiling, Hamish leant forward.

Their lips barely brushed together before Darshan pulled back, a hand over his mouth. "You do not wish to kiss me right now, my breath is probably atrocious." In comparison, and despite the several hours they had slept, his lover's breath still smelt quite sweet.

Hamish shook his head. "Dinnae be so prissy." His arms encircled Darshan's waist and pulled them together.

A gasp slithered through Darshan's teeth at the iciness of the man's belt buckle against his bare abdomen. Before he could compose himself, his lover's lips were upon his, powerful and yearning.

Darshan parted his lips slightly, a shudder passing through him when the expected passionate invasion of Hamish's tongue wasn't forthcoming. Instead, his lover tilted his head and obliterated all thought with several slow, open-mouthed kisses.

His legs wobbled anew and he became exceedingly aware that the only reason he stood upright at all was because of Hamish. Not that he would've minded dropping to his knees. His lover's trousers might be on now, but such a state could be changed swiftly enough.

Darshan closed his eyes. With any other man, he wouldn't have dared allow them such leniency with his person, but there was something about this one that echoed inside him, made him feel... safe. A foolish thought given they had met only a few days ago.

Nevertheless, he wrapped his arms around his lover's broad shoulders, clinging to the linen at the nape of Hamish's neck, and basked in the warmth surrounding the man.

Once they had parted enough for more to leave their lips than muffled attempts at sound, a single word slipped free of Darshan's mouth. "Stay." It escaped on a breath. A wisp of a wish. A plea.

Hamish stepped back. "I cannae do that."

Fool, he silently berated himself. Darshan pressed his fingers to his lips as if it would rescind what had already been spoken. Of course Hamish couldn't linger. Even though their previous search had turned up nothing, the guards could return. "You know," he mumbled around his fingers. "If you joined me when I returned to Udynea, you would never have to worry about this sort of intervention again."

Hamish paused in opening the door. "You daft?" he enquired, laughing. He smiled over his shoulder, the curve of those full lips weary and restrained. "I cannae leave."

"Why not?" Despite her own judgement on the matter, surely a Queen could see merit in allowing one of her children to have connections in the heart of political allies. "Is it the language? Our history? I could teach you everything you would need to know." Oh, if one of his tutors could hear that. He'd never been the most diligent student, focusing only what he absolutely had to, but he was more than capable of teaching the man how to speak Udynean.

Further amusement deepened the fine wrinkles around those sapphiric eyes. Hamish shook his head. "Goodnight, Dar."

"Meet me in the library come sunrise," he called out as his lover slipped from the room. His Nanny Daama would've thought that a riot, too. Especially given that he rarely stirred from his bed before midmorning back home.

He barely knew Hamish, was painfully aware of that fact, but the thought of leaving him here to live such an uncertain life almost broke his heart. Witnessing the guards hunting such a gentle man as if he was a petty thief only solidified his resolve.

~~~

Hamish swayed a little as he made his way through the halls. That'd been quite the drop the man had suspended him over. Thank the Goddess the spellster's shield had held out as long as it had. But where had Darshan gotten the strength to pull Hamish back through the window?

And what had been behind the sudden talk of leaving to the Udynea Empire with the man? Had Darshan been serious about that? To be somewhere he could be himself without reprimand or judgement. But what would he do there? He could hardly rely on Darshan's generosity forever.

And what of Ethan? He couldn't leave his nephew. Not now. Not when he had promised Nora he would be there to direct all of their mother's attention away from her grandson, to let the boy have the innocent life Hamish hadn't the luxury of living. He shouldn't have to be a shield for the lad, but if she found out…

Well, neither of his siblings was entirely sure what their mother would do, only that it wouldn't bode well for the boy.

The murmur of voices caught his ear. *Guards.* He flattened himself against the wall, resting his head back on the stone as he listened to the chatter. Not quite loud enough to make out more than the odd word. Not getting any louder, either. Nor, sadly, fainter.

That could only mean, rather than continue to scour the castle for him, they had returned to their post outside his room to wait him out. He had become accustomed to waking and readying himself for the new day before the guards could burst in, so knew they'd still be there hours later. And it was possible they believed him to have returned to the room before them, for they didn't regularly check if he was inside, but he couldn't be certain until later.

How was he going to make it past them?

"Still out on our little night-time foray, are we?"

The sound of his brother's voice drew his gaze. A shadow moved in the gloom of the corridor leading towards the rest of their family's quarters.

Relief weakened Hamish's limbs. "I thought you would've gone to bed." Unlike Nora, who preferred late nights of silence in the library, Gordon leant towards rising with the sun.

Gordon smirked and leant in the archway. "Well, I figured you'd need the help and, that if you were to come back here alone from his imperial highness' room, this would be the fastest route to take. I also came to the conclusion that you were too busy enjoying yourself to
~~~

bother sticking to the plan."

Hamish grinned. "Nae exactly, but you see I—"

His brother held up a hand as he straightened. "You ken I dinnae want to hear what me brother's been up to." Gordon peered around the corner. "I see Mum's guards are still in place. I'm surprised they havenae started looking for you."

"They did." In hushed tones, he regaled his brother with what had transpired with the guards back in the guest quarters, omitting just how Darshan had hidden him. And the fact it had also nearly gotten the both of them killed. "But if I'm nae in there before sunrise, then I'm going to be in trouble." The next stage of his mother's punishments would likely involve a permanent escort *in*, as well as outside, the castle grounds.

"I wouldnae be too sure about that. If you can promise me to be a little more discreet in future, I'll help get you past them."

He nodded. More discreet was something he could certainly do. Although, getting Darshan to cooperate there might take a little trial and error on both their parts. "How are we doing this? Injury?" No, that might be a little tricky to pull off this late.

His brother hummed thoughtfully. "That depends... How drunk can you act?"

We're going for that one, are we? It had been a favoured excuse ever since they were young men. And generally a truth of sorts when Hamish used to frequent the pubs. Not that he'd been in such a state recently. "Right now?" Grinning, Hamish draped an arm over his brother's shoulders. "Immensely well, but acting willnae get us anywhere without smelling the part."

Gordon narrowed his eyes. He pulled out a small flask and uncorked it. The heady scent of dark ale drifted up between them. "A little drink ought to be enough." His brother took a few deep swallows before handing it over. "Be sure to spill a little on yourself."

"I can figure that out for meself," he mumbled. This wasn't the first time they had duped the guards this way. Whether or not they would be caught was highly dependent on their mother's orders. "What do you think?"

Gordon wrinkled his nose and took a hesitant sniff. "You smell like a brewery." His brother eyed Hamish's clothes. "And you *look* like you've been brawling. What in the name of the Goddess happened to you? Did you fall down some stairs on the way back?"

Hamish shook his head and lightly brushed the dirt from a sleeve. "Tumbled in through a window." Glancing up, he spied the faint tightening of the wrinkles around his brother's eyes, that deep green colour almost lost beneath his lashes. "I'll explain later," he added before Gordon demanded the whole story right then and there.

"You had better," his brother growled, his lips barely moving beneath his thick moustache. Gordon wrapped one of Hamish's arms around his neck. "Dinnae hang on me too much, I'm nae as spry as I used to be."

"Bollocks," Hamish replied, laughing. Even after a little over four decades, his brother could keep up with the best of the guards and outmatched a good deal of the rest.

They rounded the corridor corner with Hamish deliberately swaying and bumping into his brother. The guards were already facing them, illuminated by the warm light of two lanterns hanging either side of Hamish's bedchamber door. No doubt the men had been tipped off by the noise of his unsteady stomping.

Ranulf, a warrior of the royal standing army that their mother had elected for the post, seemed particularly disgusted with their arrival. Those dark eyes narrowed further as Hamish neared until the man peered at him through slits. He carded his fingers through his black beard, but said nothing.

"Hello there, lads!" Gordon called. He tugged slightly on Hamish's belt, pulling them to one side and back in what could only be seen as a drunken-looking stagger. "Has me mum got you guarding empty rooms now?" They lurched to a stop before the trio. "Or did you think this sot was inside?"

Ranulf straightened. "Your highnesses." The warrior snapped a salute, likely more for Gordon than Hamish. "We were nae told your brother was with you."

"Did you think to ask? We've been down at the *Roaring Stag* for a good part of the night." Gordon patted Hamish's chest, thumping just hard enough. "Would've been home sooner, but as you can see, me brother took a tumble off his horse on the way up. At a walk, nae less." He barked a laugh and opened the door into Hamish's room.

"Sure," one of the other guards mumbled as Gordon guided Hamish through the doorway. The man's face wasn't one Hamish recognised. The unadorned band of leather around his bicep indicated him as a lowly swordsman in the army.

Had the man seen something earlier? Terror clogged Hamish's throat. He didn't believe anyone had seen him clinging for dear life outside the guest chambers, but it wasn't exactly implausible. All it would've taken was for someone to look up.

Gordon halted in the doorway, fisting Hamish's clothes in an effort to keep them steady as he slowly faced the guards. "A mighty piece of insinuation you've got in that tone there, lad. You dinnae believe me?"

Frowning, Ranulf nudged the man. "Answer your prince, swordsman."

"N-nae, I—" The man shook his head, his barely-tanned face losing all colour. He bowed low. "I wouldnae dare accuse you of such, your highness."

Gordon gave the man a curt nod. "I'll just see me brother to bed, then. Cannae have him collapsing in the middle of the room." He took up one of the lanterns and shuffled Hamish through the doorway.

The door clicked shut behind them.

"I cannae believe you got away with that," Hamish muttered. He released his brother, taking a few lurching steps towards the bed before regaining his balance.

"Neither can I." Gordon leant against the bedpost. "So, we've had our fill now? Because when you said you'd be sneaking off to spend time with him, I didnae think it'd be *all* bloody night."

"It's still dark." After midnight, sure, but that meant only a few hours over the agreed-upon time. "And it wasnae meant to be that long." Certainly not long enough to be in the position of almost being caught in the guest quarters. "I sort of… fell asleep."

His brother arched a brow at him. "Was he that boring?"

Hamish shook his head, laughter bubbling in his chest. Boring was as about as far from how he would've described it as language went. He flopped back onto his bed, his arms spread across its length. "I think I'm in love."

"*Love?*" Gordon echoed, pushing off the bedpost. "You met him four days ago." He held up as many fingers in emphasis. "In that time you two have spent—what?—maybe the grand total of a day in each other's presence? What you're feeling is nae *love*."

Maybe his brother was right, but Gordon hadn't kissed the man. He hadn't tasted the ancient fire in Darshan's touch; a flame hotter than the sun, burning through sheer desperation and determination, radiating warmth from its very core. Nor had his brother felt the strength in which the spellster had clung to Hamish after dragging him through the window, heart-stopping fear lingering in those tight muscles.

"Fine," he muttered. "If the lack of time with him bothers you, then find me way to spend more with him. I've already got tomorrow morning solved. He wants to meet with me in the library."

"As if that doesnae sound ominous or anything."

Hamish chuckled, throwing an arm over his eyes. "He said… something before I left," he mumbled. Had Darshan meant it, though? Or had he just been trying to see how Hamish would react? "He was talking about me travelling to Minamist with him after the negotiations." Whenever that finally happen depended largely on his mother opting to be in the same room as the ambassador she now seemed to outright loathe.

Perhaps backing off for a few days would give the illusion of Darshan abiding by her rules. It had always been the reasonable way to alleviate any suspicions his mother might've had about him and his brother sneaking out to be with whichever man fancied a few minutes with Hamish.

"Do you want to go?"

Hamish peered at his brother from beneath the crook of his elbow. *Do I?* He'd be far from home, literally on the opposite end of the continent. But like Darshan had said, he wouldn't be constantly looking over his shoulder for his mother's guards, wouldn't need to worry at all.

He shrugged. "Maybe." There were other reasons to stay, one very small and impressionable reason.

"What makes you even think it'll work?" his brother pressed, annoyance creeping into his voice and creasing his forehead. "You go to Minamist with a man you barely ken and then what?"

"You sound like Mum," he grumbled, pushing himself upright until he was perched on the side of the bed.

"I'm trying to be practical. What would you do in Udynea?" Gordon nudged him. "Besides the obvious. Or do you fancy yourself just as his bedwarmer?"

He glared at his brother. Darshan wouldn't traipse him all that way just for one reason. *Although...* What had the man said? Never worry about any intervention on his sexual preferences? Darshan hadn't specified Hamish's time there had to be spent with *him*. He wasn't entirely sure if that meant the man wouldn't care if Hamish chose another over him, but he didn't see any reason to find out.

"We dinnae have an ambassador in their lands," Hamish mumbled, his mind only half on the topic. That was part of the reason why Udynea had sent one to them, why his mother allowed a foreign spellster to enter the kingdom. Nora had offered to travel to Minamist—via horse, which would've taken several months—but their mother had refused. "I could go." There was nothing to tie him here; no wife or children. "He could teach me the language."

His brother gave a noncommittal grunt. "Even if you could convince Mum to let you travel such a distance from the castle..."

Hamish hung his head. The occasional trip to the spellster cloister was at the limits of their mother's tolerance of her children's journeys. She had only gotten worse with the death of her older grandchildren—taken at the hungry jaws of bears or the watery talons of the sea. Whilst the strict nature of the rule often fell on him, none of the royal family could leave the castle confines for more than a few weeks.

Gordon scrubbed at his face. "Did you tell him anything?"

"Aye," he sighed. "I told him I cannae leave." There was more keeping him here than his mother's arbitrary rules.

"I dinnae see how you could without Mum dragging you back, but I ken you're nae happy here, 'Mish. Everyone can see that. Maybe you *should* go."

Hamish shook his head. "You ken why I cannae just up and leave. If Mum finds out about—"

"Ethan?" His brother scoffed. "The lad's barely seen ten winters. You cannae use him as an excuse for the past."

Hamish ground his teeth. His brother was right. Being both diversion and shield to keep their mother's attention off her grandson had only given him an easy excuse to remain.

He could've run a long time ago, back before Gordon's wife and eldest daughter had met their grisly fates, before the trade ship, *The Princess' Fortune,* had fallen afoul of a storm and taken more of his family with it. *But—* "Where would I have gone?" This was the first time he'd been offered a chance at a life that wasn't just running and hiding.

Gordon sighed. "Look, Mum will learn eventually that Ethan likes his own sort and when she does, you'll have wasted your life for nothing. Do you really think that's what he'd want?"

Nae at all. If anything, the boy would be disappointed in him. "I dinnae ken what to do."

"How about starting small?" Gordon clapped him on the back. "And perhaps leave out any romantic declarations until you ken a little more about him?"

Hamish inclined his head. He could keep his mouth shut on that subject well enough. More time getting to know Darshan would either see him repelling such feelings or strengthening them. And he could start with whatever conversation the spellster wished to have in the library come sunrise.

Chapter 13

Hamish pushed open the library door. He wasn't ashamed to admit he hadn't ventured into the room since his childhood days, preferring the freedom of hunting and ensuring the people in the surrounding farms had a means to air any misgivings. The library always seemed dark. It also bore a mustiness that he couldn't help comparing to a closed mind. This was a tomb to history and tradition. New ideas weren't formed here.

In the early light of dawn, the richly dark wood of the bookshelves were illuminated only by the glow of a single lantern resting atop a table. Darshan stood near the light source, his attention taken by a particularly thick tome. He alternated between tapping his forefinger against his lips and chewing on a nail as he read, pausing only to turn a page.

Almost reluctant to disturb the man, Hamish padded through the doorway and inched the door shut behind him.

Darshan glanced up, visibly startled for a breath before a wide grin took his face. "You came." He snapped the book shut and trotted to Hamish's side. "I was beginning to think the worst." That hazel gaze scrutinised him, small and quick, but definitely with a degree of worry tightening the edges. No mistake there. "How are you this morning, *mea lux*?"

"All right." What had the man just called him? Although he couldn't seem to grasp languages like his siblings, he had picked up a smattering of what Udynean sounded like, mostly from sailors passing through. Whatever Darshan had uttered, the words didn't have the same resonance of any language he'd heard before.

"No trouble with the guards last night, then?" Darshan swung to indicate the lantern-lit table before Hamish could answer. "Come."

"Me brother showed up before the guards became a problem," he mumbled, eyeing the table as he tailed the man. A few books were scattered across the dark wood surface. What had Darshan been researching?

"I did not expect him to have waited so long."

"Neither did I," he admitted. Not when he hadn't recruited Gordon's aid for some years. The fact Darshan was both an ambassador and an imperial prince likely set a fire under his brother's arse when it came to them being caught.

As briefly as Hamish could manage, especially with Darshan snickering at some parts, he relayed what had transpired after leaving the guest quarters.

Sighing, Darshan settled into a padded chair. "It is a relief to hear you made it back to your bedchamber all right. I would not have been able to sit idly by if you were punished for my mistake."

Hamish shook his head. "We made that mistake together."

"Still... I shall endeavour to be more careful." The faintest twitch of Darshan's fingers had a stool skittering out from underneath the table. "Please, sit. I shall get a dreadful crick in my neck if we talk for much longer this way."

Smirking, Hamish straddled the stool. "Were you studying?" Now he was closer, he could spy several of the books' spines. Customs, for the most part, and a few slim books that he'd hazard a guess were either on the topography of Tirglas or outlined her various ore resources. "I dinnae think you asked me here for that." Darshan had to know that Nora was far better at trade. "What was it you mentioned me doing last night?" He remembered bits of it since waking, the rest floating on the edge of comprehension like a dream.

"Ambassadorship," Darshan replied, thumbing through the book he had been reading when Hamish arrived. He continued in a rambling tone whilst searching. "Throughout all the talks of peace and trade between our lands, there has been no offer of a Tirglasian taking up the rather vacant ambassador position in Minamist and..." He trailed off. In the ruddy lantern light, it was difficult to tell if Darshan was blushing, but there was a glassy edge to his smile. "And I am probably just repeating common knowledge to you, correct?"

"Somewhat." He had always thought there was an envoy of some sort in the beginning, but that might've been the Udyneans once again extending a hand in peace.

Nodding, Darshan halted in flipping through the book to lay a hand on the open pages. "I have been looking for—hoping to find, I guess is the better term for it—something in your customs to aid me in convincing Queen Fiona that your kingdom's ambassador should be you." He slid the book to one side. "Of course, it would require you to learn the language, an ambassador who needs a translator is more hindrance than help, but I thought I could... Well, teach you."

Hamish rocked on his seat, catching himself as he recollected the stool had no back. "Me?" So the man *had* been serious. "I dinnae ken the first thing about politics." That was never what he had been destined for. His brother would be king and Sorcha, Gordon's daughter, would follow. "Nora would be better." Even she would only take the throne if both his brother and niece died before the girl could birth an heir, and there were all three of Hamish's nephews who were in line well before himself.

"I did briefly consider enquiring about having your sister fill the position," Darshan confessed. "Seeing her verbally battling it out amongst those in the Crystal Court would have been a marvellous sight, make no mistake there. However..." He tapped his thumb on the page. "If we are to think logically on this, that choice does come with certain complications. Three of them, to be exact. The distance is great and I would never consider asking a mother to leave her children, but I rather doubt bringing them with her is a viable option."

"You'd be correct in that thinking. Those of the royal bloodline dinnae leave the castle for more than a few weeks at any given time." It was a tradition that his mother had been lax on, up until the death of two of her grandchildren. She had then clamped down harder than most in the past.

Where he had once been allowed to venture well beyond the lands belonging to the royal clan, now he could barely reach its border. Even the nearest cloister was just within range and, given the road leading there was a small one used by farmers, reaching it in time largely depended on not being held up by weather or injury. Not that his mother cared. She liked that the cloister was far from them. It meant the spellster influence was well out of reach.

Frowning, Darshan gave a noncommittal hum. "I read as much. I must say, it is a most peculiar stance to make. If you had attempted such in Udynea, the *Mhanek* could swiftly lose all his heirs in a single coup. It is far harder for any conquering force to maintain power after usurping the throne when they must contend with the prospect of being attacked by the rightful heirs from anywhere across the land."

Hamish shrugged. There'd been plenty of revolutions on the royal bloodline. Granted, a few centuries had passed since the last attempt, but his mother preferred to be vigilant. "Is that why your father sent you here? Because it's far?" Only in crossing the icy waters between Tirglas and the frozen lands of the north could a man get any further from the Udynean capital of Minamist.

A faint smirk curled Darshan's lips. "In a way," he murmured, his gaze sliding back to the open book. "I was hoping you would be able to help me or, at the very least, I could teach you a few simple Udynean words."

"I cannae help you with any of our laws." If he could trust Nora not to go blabbing the idea of him as an ambassador to their mother the instant she was out of sight, then maybe convincing her would be worth a try, but attempting it alone would be a waste of time. "In all honesty, I'm shocked you've given it this much contemplation." Scratching at his jaw, a burst of uncontrolled laughter escaped his mouth. "I thought you were joking."

Like a door slamming shut in the wind, soft emotion fled Darshan's face. He sat stiffly upright in his chair, eyeing Hamish as if the man expected him to turn into a surly mother bear. "I... can see how my words could be interpreted as jesting, but the issue of an ambassador for your people in the Crystal Court is a serious matter. Our compatibility aside, you are the best candidate for the position. I requested your presence because I thought it prudent to be aware of any angle, especially those that might work in my favour, before I consulted the queen."

Hamish shuffled in his seat. "It wouldnae be a good idea to tell me mum." He could well imagine her reaction to Darshan requesting Hamish leave with him to a distant city. "She would never allow me to leave our clan lands much less Tirglas."

"I would be lying if I denied wanting you to come with me. But I want *you* to want this because you... well... want it. Not because it is what you think I want."

"Right," Hamish mumbled, his head still spinning.

Darshan gave an apologetic smile. "I am rambling, I know. I am not typically known for doing so when I am nervous, but I guess you bring out all my bad habits."

"*You're* nervous?" His stomach was almost close to tying itself in knots. "Why?"

Darshan inhaled deeply. He closed his eyes and spoke in a rush, "I really like you, probably more than would be considered appropriate given the short amount of time we have known each other."

That's fair. Hadn't his brother mentioned as much?

"So understand I am not being entirely altruistic when I ask, do *you* want to go?"

"Aye." The answer was out before he'd a chance to consider hedging either way. He had thought a fair bit on the topic himself since his brother had left him to while away the rest of the night and had slept only fitfully in between.

"That is... a relief to hear." Darshan relaxed slightly in the chair, although a touch of hesitance still lingered in his eyes. "I have enjoyed your presence thus far and I do not mean just the sex. Even so, I would hate to think I was merely projecting my desires upon you, but I would require your mother's blessing on the matter in order to have your ambassadorial position considered official. Otherwise..." One side of his mouth twitched upwards, shifting his glasses. Mischief glittered behind those lenses. "I might as well just kidnap you."

It may come to that. If it had been the original ambassador, the countess who Darshan claimed had been assassinated, then his mother might've been content to let him leave. With Darshan? *Nae chance.* "I wouldnae ken a thing about your desires," he mumbled.

Frowning, the man's gaze shifted from Hamish to the books on the table. His mouth moved, clearly repeating the words he'd just uttered. "Forgive me, but did I misspeak? It was my understanding that the word *desire* has several meanings in your tongue beyond the sexual. If I have been misinformed, I—"

Hamish held up a hand, a little surprised to find that was all it took to silence the man. "You've nae been misled. It meant exactly as you thought, but that doesnae change what I said." He peered at Darshan. The emotionless mask had fractured some, uncertainty and concern peeking through the cracks. "I just need to ken one thing: What are you seeking from me?"

Darshan was silent for quite some time. His focus drifted off into the surrounding gloom whilst a single thumb tapped almost thoughtfully on the table. "I must confess to ignorance. I thought we had already agreed as to the nature of our affair?"

"In the short term, aye." He waved a hand at the books piled up. "What you're discussing is far longer than I was expecting."

"Our relationship need not affect your position in the Crystal Court." What cracks there had been in that stone-like expression slowly smoothed over like plaster on a wall. "I am not asking for the stipulation of us to remain together, if that is what you would prefer, any more than I would expect you to put your romantic affairs above your political obligations. If you were to come to Minamist, you would be free to court whomever you fancy."

Heat flooded Hamish's cheeks. *He said it all so coldly.* Maybe he had been wrong about the man. He swallowed. What he wouldn't give for a pint of... anything really. Thank the Goddess he'd had enough brains to heed Gordon's warning about blurting out his feelings.

Darshan continued, the emotionless tone cracking at every other word, "That is not to say I would not find us continuing our affair back where we could be more open as the preferable option, but I leave the choice of that in your hands."

Hamish shook his head. Leaving it up to him was a bad idea. "I've nae examples of a long term relationship." Or anything more than a single night's fling. His thoughts slid to his siblings and their long-dead spouses. "Nae personal ones," he amended.

Darshan laid a bejewelled hand on Hamish's knee. "Trust me, I did not lie when I said this is very much untrodden ground for myself as well. We can take it as slow as you wish. Nothing formally announced unless you want it to be. I know better than to push and it will do neither of us any good to rush a new relationship of any sort." There was a kernel of sorrow lurking in those words, struggling to stay hidden.

"Speaking from experience?" Hamish asked, trying to keep his voice light as his focus drifted surreptitiously over the table. A jug sat tucked out of the way on the other side of the books. He sniffed under the guise of scratching his nose. No hint of wine or any other alcohol. That ruled out the man being drunk.

His lover hummed in agreement. "My longest time with any one man lasted a week." He closed his eyes. "I found him in bed with a family enemy." One side of his mouth twitched into a bitter smile. "My own bed, no less."

"That's... unfortunate." And foolish on their part, unless their plan *was* to be caught.

Darshan's head lifted, his gaze snapping back to Hamish. By the Goddess' breath, a kicked puppy would've looked happier than he did right now. "You are a good man, 'Mish," he breathed. "Sometimes to your detriment, I would think. Men like you are scarce in Udynea. You could almost say they are extinct, especially amongst the nobility. The Crystal Court tends to change those who dare its depths, like little glass sharks chewing them up and spitting them out just for fun."

"Yet you're still looking to take me there?" Surely the man wouldn't dare if it was truly that bad. "And you must be pulling me leg. *You're* part of their nobility."

Sitting back, Darshan laughed softly. "I never said I was a good man, *mea lux*."

There were those words again. They almost resonated, tugging at something deep inside him. What did they mean?

Before Hamish could ask, Darshan continued, "I am extremely selfish, fairly debauched, too—possibly bordering on hedonistic, even. And let us not forget that I am far too used to getting my own way."

Hamish grinned down at where Darshan's hand still lingered on his knee. Yes, he could see all of that in the man, but... "You're also patient and careful." Especially if last night could be anything to go on. "Tender, too."

Scoffing, Darshan shook his head. "I can choose to be that easily enough. You have no idea if that is the norm for me."

He understood quite a few things, perhaps a bit more than Darshan believed. "That's kind of me point. You may think you're selfish, and you could've been all you wanted with me being none the wiser, but you chose differently."

Those hazel eyes had grown bigger the longer Hamish spoke, widening until they looked like they might overflow the man's lenses. The darkening of his cheeks was barely perceptible in the dim light. "Only with those who deserve it," he mumbled, reaching out. The tips of his fingers grazed Hamish's forearm, the touch barely perceptible through the heavy woollen sleeve. "You looked so frightened the night I came to you, so scared the guards would find us. No one deserves to live like that."

Hamish gently clasped his lover's hand, entwining their fingers. In the brassy lantern light, the rich olive-brown tone of Darshan's slender fingers almost matched Hamish's own weathered hands. "If we are to do this, then I need to ken how we are to go about it. What do you want out of it, physically?"

"Oh, one of those conversations." Darshan smiled, a faint huff of laughter flaring his nostrils. "Why did you not just come out and ask that to begin with? Although, to be frank, you satisfied most of my desires there well enough last night."

He rolled his eyes as he fought a losing battle to keep the heat in his cheeks from consuming his face. It wasn't that he hadn't had men compliment how good he was, just not generally the day after. "Dinnae pander to me. I'm aware I did feck all last night. I want to ken what you like."

Nodding, Darshan twisted in his seat until he faced Hamish square on. "You wish to lay down some ground rules before we continue this? I am perfectly all right with discussing that. Probably something we should have hammered out earlier."

"Rules?" Hamish echoed. He hadn't come across that one before. Wasn't an eagerness to participate the only rule? Had he been missing some crucial detail all this time? *That cannae be it.* Or could it?

Darshan inclined his head. "Discuss each other's limits, if you prefer to think of it that way. Shall I go first?" His brows rose expectantly, waiting for a response.

Hamish waved his lover on. Perhaps having something to compare would allow him to gauge just what he had misunderstood.

"Let me see..." Leaning back in his chair, Darshan tapped one forefinger against his lips. The ruby ring adorning the digit glittered with each movement. "Simple things first, I suppose?" He cleared his throat. "I do not do bindings, no matter how good I look in rope—and, believe me, I am an absolute vision. Sadly, I tend to panic if I cannot free myself. Almost burnt down a lord's house the last time I participated in such an act."

"Fair enough," Hamish mumbled, a sinking sensation growing in his stomach. Just what was the man talking about? Why would rope ever be involved with sex? And— "Did you say *burn?*"

Darshan winced. "I *did*. Not intentionally, you understand," he continued, the words almost climbing over each other in their rush to be heard. "The bonds were tied a little too snugly and my hands had gone numb. He really did his best to free me, poor thing. I was already frantic by the time he tried to cut me free and—" His gaze dropped and he scuffed the toe of his boot along the floor. "Well, the coldness of the blade against my wrist was the final straw, so to speak."

He recalled Darshan's apologetic insistence in being unable to hold the door to Hamish's room closed whilst they were intimate. Not being able to focus enough to maintain certain magics sounded plausible. It hadn't occurred to him that a spellster might inadvertently use his power. *And in such a destructive way...*

"If you are looking for a way to restrain me, I have no quarrels about being held down... physically anyway." Darshan's voice had turned husky, those hazel eyes glazing over, before he shook himself. "Toys are a big yes in my books, as long as I have a degree of control over them. Blindfolds, too. Not gags, though—you could say I like the sound of my own voice far too much to restrain it."

Hamish frowned. Toys? Blindfolds? *Gags?* Listening to his lover calmly list everything only served to have him feel even more ignorant. None of the old lectures he recalled on sex ever mentioned anything beyond two naked bodies.

Darshan continued, clearly heedless to the confusion he was causing, "And although I do not allow it to be used on myself, I am adept in several magical tricks, if you ever find yourself feeling adventurous. Although, I suppose that might be quite the leap for you."

"Sex magic?" he mumbled, his mind frantically struggling to catch up with his ears. They *were* actually still talking about sex? He had begun to wonder. "That's an actual thing?" He had heard rumours, there were always strange stories about what spellsters were capable of, but he tended to dismiss those mentioning sex magic.

Grinning, his lover nodded vigorously. "We do not call it that, but yes. What of you?" Darshan returned his hand to Hamish's grasp, his fingertips caressing Hamish's palm like it was the most natural thing to do. "Where do your limits lie?"

"I—" He'd only ever repeated the one act and with Darshan unwilling to cause him any pain, it was a stance he more than appreciated… "I dinnae ken."

His lover's fingers halted. Confusion fluttered across Darshan's face, then vanished. "You must have some idea."

Hamish rocked his head from side to side. "Me entire experience has been people bending me over things and having their way." And half of that wasn't exactly enjoyable. "Beyond that act, I honestly have nae clue."

Darshan shuffled closer, perching on the edge of his chair. "We could find out together, if you would like?"

"Starting with what?"

Darshan ran his forefinger down Hamish's palm. It radiated unnatural warmth. "How about I show you a little *sex magic*?"

"Here? Is that a good idea?" Whilst there were a number of bookshelves they could duck behind, the door didn't lock. "What if someone comes in and sees us?"

"They will see very little. I have no plans to strip you…" He cocked his head. "Not below your waist, at least. I shall require you to sit down on something a little steadier than a stool, though. You are certainly far too tall to stand for what I am thinking of." Leaping to his feet, Darshan dragged a nearby armless chair away from the table. "Strip to your skin and straddle this."

Curiosity had Hamish obeying before he could properly think of all the ways this could go wrong. He peeled each layer off one by one, the mute chill in the air digging into his flesh as his undershirt finally hit the floor. Throwing a leg over the seat had him facing the chair's back. A few quick adjustments to his position by Darshan's thankfully warm hands left Hamish with his arms propped on the back of the chair.

A hand, gentle and smooth, slid across his shoulder before gliding back up. His hair shifted, then a single strand snagged. A hiss slithered between his teeth. He could handle a tug at a clump of hair—he wouldn't be able to hunt in half the places he did if he couldn't—but this was like being stabbed in the scalp by a needle.

"*Frutz*," Darshan grumbled, the word almost too quiet to make out. "Hold on."

Hamish tilted his head, letting the mass of coils fall either side of his neck as Darshan untangled the rest. The presence at his back faded and the clatter of metal hitting the table filled the silence.

"My apologies," Darshan said as he returned. "I had rather forgotten that ring is somewhat carnivorous." He laid his hands on Hamish's shoulders. "Now, you should feel a slight tingle…"

Warmth soaked through his skin like a damp cloth, accompanied by a deep buzz that could only be his lover's magic. It *did* tingle. Soft and low, it put him in the mind of a tiny kitten purring happily away.

Hamish relaxed against the chair back, resting his chin on his crossed wrists. A contented sigh whistled through his nose.

The breath of his lover's chuckle skittered across Hamish's back. "Shall I take that sound to mean it is all right? Not too much?" There was a sliver of concern in the question. "I can decrease the vibration a little further."

Hamish shook his head. "This is good," he slurred.

He sagged further as sure and sinuous fingers swept over his back, finding each knot in his muscles like a boarhound on the hunt. The warmth and gentle kneading did much to relieve the little aches he hadn't previously noticed last night's tumble through the window had caused. Was it healing magic? There was a faint familiarity to the tingling.

But that didn't explain what Darshan had said earlier. Massaging his back wasn't new, although this was different in execution by being magically assisted. The nagging thought continued to tug at his slush-ridden mind. "I dinnae see how this can be seen as sex magic," he half-mumbled against his forearm.

"Like this?" Darshan gave a contemplative hum. "It is not generally considered as such, I will give you that. I merely thought it prudent to start low given this was your first time."

"Of what? Having magic used on me?" A hearty laugh bubbled in his chest. "This is nae me first time there." Granted, a good two decades had passed from the last time he'd been in a position to require such healing from spellsters, but it seemed Darshan had forgotten he had used magic on him last night. But then, other thoughts had surely swarmed his mind since.

"Oh?" Such rich delight and surprise tinted the word that Hamish wished he could see his lover's face. "Then, would you be agreeable to me increasing the strength?"

Nodding, Hamish garbled something that he hoped the man took as acquiescence and a crackling surge of heat washed over his body in answer. The tingling intensified, burrowing deeper into his flesh.

"Of course," Darshan murmured. "Even now, it is a shadow of what the real thing is like. I am afraid you shall just have to imagine it..." His hand slunk down Hamish's side, angling around to the front, the tingling touch sliding further until his fingertips slipped beneath the waistband of Hamish's trousers. "...lower," he purred.

Hamish swallowed. Imagining wasn't in it. Even with his lover not lingering long, the light vibration running through his abdomen was enough to stir him. "Aye?" he managed, the word thick on his tongue. "I can do that rightly enough."

"My apologies," Darshan whispered, his voice husky and failing at sounding in any way remorseful. His fingers returned to the warm massaging of Hamish's shoulders. "It was not my intention to tease so much. I shall stop before this gets awkward. Just allow me to turn down the heat first." Like the breath of a frost giant from the stories of Hamish's childhood, a wave of coldness slipped down his back.

An involuntary gasp filled his lungs with the library's musty air. The hair on his bare skin swiftly lifted. Jumping into Mullhind Harbour during the midwinter festival was a ghost of a comparison.

Chuckling wickedly, his warm breath only serving to make Hamish feel colder, Darshan planted a firm kiss onto Hamish's shoulder. "We call that the *auk-maardin.*" Heat slowly returned to the man's fingers. His lover hovered them over Hamish's bare skin, his fingertips brushing Hamish's skin fleetingly as the radiating warmth returned him to normal. "You are welcome to ask for it any time you desire to cool down."

Hamish whistled as he reached for his undershirt and pulled it on. "I dinnae think me tongue will get around a fancy word like that." And if it was always so bitterly cold, then it sounded like something uttered only after it was done to a person.

"Fancy?" Darshan scoffed. "It is merely common Udynean. Loosely translates as *the change of seasons.* It only sounds strange because it is foreign. How do you think I felt when I was learning your language?"

"Aye, but still..." He shrugged into his overcoat. Languages had always been his older siblings' speciality. For Nora, it made trading easier, whilst Gordon found any disputes along the border were often settled through conversing rather than the use of the weapons their mother preferred to brandish whenever the moment arose.

Darshan leant against the table, cocking one hip as he casually drummed his fingers on the old water-stained wood. "The things I have witnessed your tongue get around, a few fancy words should be little bother. However..." He breached the space between them, his hands gliding up Hamish's chest, those seeking fingers already entwining themselves into the cloth. "If you insist otherwise, I could loosen it for you."

Their lips touched and there it was again; ancient fire radiating a bone-deep warmth. It shuddered through Hamish, drawing strength even as it gave plenty more in return. His lover clung to him, restrained desire shaking through his grip.

He pulled Darshan closer, trying so very hard not to snicker as a small whimpering moan escaped the man.

The door creaked open.

Hamish all but shoved Darshan away. He glared at the man as he noticed how dishevelled his clothes were. He hastily tugged them into some semblance of order. Could the spellster not do something as simple as kissing without pawing at him like a bear seeking to break open a chicken coop?

"And just what are you two doing?"

Nora's voice had Hamish whipping his head around to the dreadful twinge of objecting muscle.

His sister stood in the doorway, clutching a small stack of books. She arched a brow at them, the quirk of her lips suggesting she already knew the answer. "Or should I say *were*?" She shook her head. "Nae exactly the ideal spot for it."

Heat flooded Hamish's face. Being almost caught snogging in the library by his sister... He groaned. Was there any worse fate the Goddess could've thought up? *Mum*. At least his luck hadn't turned *that* sour. "You've got it all wrong. We were just—"

"I am tutoring him," Darshan blurted. Unlike himself, the spellster looked as immaculate as ever. His focus seemed to be on donning the many rings he had discarded earlier. "Teaching him my native tongue, as it were. As I mentioned to you this morning."

Nora's eyes remained fixed on Hamish, narrowing the longer Darshan talked. "You ken that Mum doesnae wish for you to leave Tirglas, right?"

Hamish grunted. If their mother had her way, he wouldn't seek a breath unless she told him to. "Doesnae mean I cannae learn the language." There would be plenty of chances to use such knowledge within Mullhind, especially once the trade negotiations were finally agreed upon.

His sister's entire bottom lip disappeared into her mouth as she shook her head. Setting the books down amongst the others already on the table, Nora swung her attention to Darshan. "This is all we have with any Udynean translations, your imperial highness. *And* I'm meant to inform you that me mum wishes to see you in her study."

All at once, the library seemed colder. Had his mother been told about his disappearance last night? Did she believe he had been out drinking with Gordon or had she seen through the lie? Nora's tone had been hopeful. Perhaps she saw a means to have the negotiations end.

Disappointment settled in his gut at the thought of Darshan leaving so soon. Was there a way to delay finalisations that wouldn't also see the man banished from Tirglas like the dwarven ambassador?

"Thank you," Darshan replied. "And, please, inform her that I shall be there presently."

Inclining her head, Nora shuffled back out of the library as swiftly as she had entered.

Hamish waited only until the door closed before speaking, "Teaching me *your native tongue*?"

Darshan chuckled. "Abysmal, I know. I simply could not resist." His gaze slid back from the door. "What's with the head shake? I do not believe I misspoke. The word also means language, does it not?"

"Aye. Although, I dinnae recall much usage of this..." Hamish stuck out his tongue at the man and pointed to it.

A small smile curved his lover's lips. "Well, you hardly need tutoring in it," he breathed, leaning back against the table. "But if you insist, I could refresh your memory." He stretched his arms out behind him in what had to be the most nonchalant manner Hamish had observed in a long time.

The stack of books sitting just on Darshan's left chose that moment to slide unceremoniously across the table, seemingly without a soul touching them.

Hamish tipped his head to one side, trying to see around his lover without being too obvious. Darshan's hand had knocked a long, thin box that'd been tucked against the books.

A blush in full bloom spread across Darshan's face. He straightened, surreptitiously tucking the box behind his back. "Oh, I actually came bearing gifts. Well, *one*," he swiftly amended.

"The box?" It might've been big enough for a child's belt knife or boot dagger, maybe even a few trinkets at a stretch, but they were the type of gifts children were given during the midwinter festival.

Shock swiftly dropped Darshan's jaw. "How did you—?" Sighing, he produced the box and offered it. "Yes, this. You are most welcome to open it here, but I would advise against waving it around."

A strange gift. He had passed the point of trinket collecting and his hunting dagger was far too large to fit inside. Nevertheless, good workmanship had been involved in the box's design. It was fairly nondescript, though. No markings or latches marred the smooth, fawn grain. Nor was there anything about it to denote its usage. "Thank you?"

Darshan's jaw twitched. He pressed his lips together, his top lip disappearing completely beneath his moustache. That hazel gaze remained rooted to the box. One brow lifted expectantly.

There *was* something inside? He hadn't heard anything when he had turned it over.

Curious, Hamish lifted the lid. Inside sat a—

He slammed the box closed, his face burning. "What is this? I mean... I ken what it *looks* like." His face grew hotter still. *Dinnae wave it around indeed.* Thank the Goddess no one else was in the library. "What the hell am I supposed to do with it?" he hissed.

Darshan chuckled, a wicked timbre that shimmied its way

straight to Hamish's groin. "You poor, sheltered thing." He gently peeled back the lid. "It happens to be one of my toys. I did say I liked them."

"Toy?" Hamish echoed. He rubbed at his neck, the skin beneath his fingertips an inferno. *This* was what his lover had meant by that? He had thought—

Nothing. Toys had always brought up the image of dolls or wooden blocks and swords for children. The suggestively-shaped, leather-bound *item* nestled inside the linen-lined box wouldn't have been a consideration.

"Sadly, your lack of magic means you cannot make full use of its abilities, but..." A bejewelled finger rang across the toy's length. "You just oil it up and—" Darshan grinned, a faint hint of redness touching his cheeks. "Do I really need to explain further?"

Again, Hamish closed the lid, gently this time. "Nae."

A slightly puzzled frown creased the skin between Darshan's brows. "No, you do not want it? Or no, you have no need for an explanation?"

"The last one." He had already gathered its usage. "But why are you giving this to me?"

His lover ran a hand up Hamish's arm almost idly. "So you can have a little fun when we cannot play together." His soft smile fell. "Or if your mother finally catches us and throws me out of your... simply lovely kingdom. It is far less damaging to yourself than propositioning uncaring strangers."

Hamish stepped back, his hip bumping into the padded arm of a chair. "Have you really used this?" He shook the box. "I thought— I mean... you like it that way, too?"

"Do *you* not?"

"Recently, aye," he confessed. They might've only engaged in sex the once, but it had certainly been the best Hamish had ever experienced. He ran a thumb over the lid. His stomach knotted at the thought of trying it out.

Then an altogether wicked idea sprang to mind. "Could *you* show me how to use it?" The question was out before Hamish could reconsider.

His lover beamed, impious glee twinkling in his eyes. "I was hoping you would ask. Would you prefer this demonstration to be on you or myself?"

"To be honest, I hadnae thought that far." He shrugged. "You?"

Darshan widened the distance between them and, for a moment, Hamish thought he'd been too presumptuous. Then one corner of his mouth lifted. "Bring it to me on your next visit. I would suggest sooner, but I believe your sister might still be waiting for me outside."

He smiled warmly and readjusted his glasses. "Sadly, trade agreements lack the ability to negotiate themselves. At least, not in a way that shall make my father happy."

Hamish nodded. As much as he hated the thought, there were other obligations they both needed to ensure were met outside of each other.

Pausing at the door, Darshan waved a hand at the books. "Try and see what you can glean from those in the meantime. I shall return when I am able." With that, he slipped out of the library.

"Great," Hamish muttered to himself. "I'll just start here, then." He opened one of the books his sister had brought in and flipped through the pages, skimming the shifting text for something less familiar. Another language sat alongside the Tirglasian words, strange glyphs that ran in a dizzy line of loops. *Udynean.*

Huffing and clicking his tongue, he twisted the book one way, then the other. It made no difference. But then, he had trouble with written words at the best of times. The letters rarely stayed in the exact same order as when he first read them. This though?

He flicked back through the pages, searching for a simple phrase. This was worse. Everything looked the same save for the odd vertical line here and there.

How did Darshan expect him to learn *this* jumble? What way did these words even go?

He stared at the word before him, his eyes straining as the letters shimmered and changed. There was pressure on the right and a failing of the ink towards the left in the same manner most inked words ended. *Right to left, then.* Precisely the opposite direction he was used to. That wouldn't make things any easier. *Might as well get on with it.*

Sighing, Hamish settled back onto the stool and pulled the lantern closer. He could only try. It certainly couldn't be any worse than any other time he had been forced to stick his nose into a book.

Chapter 14

Darshan stalked along the corridor, his displeasure pounding out along the stone. How foolish he had been to think suggesting Hamish taking up the position of Tirglasian ambassador in the Crystal Court would be readily accepted by Queen Fiona.

I should've listened to him. Or, at the very least, given a few days thought on how to approach the matter. Sadly, the mere mention of it had gone about as badly as his lover had cautioned.

Queen Fiona stood at her desk, turning as he entered the study. She brandished a slip of paper as if it were a Stamekian starblade. "These figures you've negotiated with me daughter. I trust that, if I agreed to them, you would take your demonic influence out of my kingdom sooner?"

Darshan bowed his head. A bitter mixture of rage and sadness briefly clogged his throat. He would regret having to leave so soon, for more reasons than the dreadful sailing journey he would need to take, but that couldn't be helped. The far greater concern was how could he leave a man like Hamish here with a mother like her? *The very thought of it was...*

He choked down the ire battling to leap from his tongue. Getting himself banished would do no one any good. "I would have to convene with the council that the percentages are indeed agreeable on their part, but yes."

"Very well, then. I accept your terms."

At the queen's side, Nora shuffled on the spot, clearly uncomfortable. As she should be, given the harshness of some terms he had declared in a childish fit. "Mum, they're nae in our favour. If we could just—"

Queen Fiona waved her daughter into silence. "I said I accept and that is me final word on the subject."

Darshan cleared his throat, garnering the queen's attention. "If our lands are to be allies," he drawled. If he was ever going to get a moment to discuss this, then now seemed as good as any. "Then sending an ambassador to Minamist would be a prudent move."

She remained silent. No hint of suspicion or anger lurking in that cool, blue gaze. If anything, she seemed to almost be in agreement with the idea.

He breathed deeply and, in a rush, added, "I would recommend that person be your second son."

"That is nae possible." The words fell like shards of ice. No hint of her previous outrage with him showed anywhere on her face.

"Pardon me, your majesty, but I ask you to reconsider. Whilst I cannot claim to know the mind of my father's court down to the smallest quibble, I do *know they would listen more to someone of noble blood better than the keenest, but ultimately common, member of your clan." It was a terrible truth and he hated it, but if it worked in Hamish's favour...*

There *was the flicker of the rage he had expected from her. It burned coolly across those blue eyes, but no deeper. "The answer is still nae. Me son stays right here."*

"Hamish is *the more viable option of the three. I would have suggested your daughter first, if it were not for her children." He indicated Nora with a wave of his hand and the woman straightened, surprise lighting her face. "Seeing your younger son has none, I thought it would be—"*

"—easier to throw him into your bed?" Queen Fiona snarled. "I ken exactly what you're after. The royal line does nae venture so far from its roots and his lack of wife or bairn is a temporary phase, nae a constant."

He had tried pushing harder only to have her refuse to even acknowledge the matter, much less speak on it. What was wrong with the woman? Did she not understand that her son would be infinitely happier without her judgement breathing down his neck?

What had she meant by temporary phase, anyway? He hadn't missed Nora's sudden uncertainty at such a declaration, fleeting though the expression had been. Hamish had already regaled him about Queen Fiona's incessant insistence when it came to marriage and siring children, but she had been hounding the man since his mid-teens.

According to Hamish, she had even planned on arranging a marriage between him and Countess Harini, the ambassador who was supposed to have been here to negotiate the trade deals. As if any

Udynean noble would settle for anything less than the heir to a throne, especially when a marked lack of a magical bloodline was involved.

So why would Queen Fiona believe her son would change his stance decades later? It made no sense.

Maybe it was nothing, maybe Darshan had spent too many years around those who did nothing except conspire against him, but her words smelt of a plan that wouldn't bode well for Hamish. *I have to speak with him.* If this was back in the imperial palace, his first step would be to send Daama out amongst the servants and slaves, for most of the nobility had a habit of forgetting those under them still had ears and mouths. If only doing that here was an option. As grossly optimistic as it was, perhaps together they could reach another means of convincing Queen Fiona.

He had taken several steps into the library before the marked lack of light grabbed his attention.

Darshan slowly swivelled on his heel. The prickling of a shield not yet formed hummed around him, ready to appear at a moment's notice.

The room was a mass of looming shadows, bookshelves illuminated only by the reedy light peeking through the window. The stack of books he had left on the table was relatively undisturbed, save for a few that Nora had brought in.

No sign of Hamish.

Grumbling under his breath, he let the magic fade. He didn't expect to be ambushed in such a place—unlike back home where quite a few of his half-sisters would rejoice in seeing an end to his life—but that was no reason to become complacent. He had no way of knowing if one of the family's rivals had sent an assassin to these frigid lands and he would rather not find out via way of a dagger to the heart.

He lingered by the table, running a hand over the spine of the top-most book in the stack. Where Nora had dug them up from, he'd no idea. A few of the slimmer tomes appeared to be missing. Taken by Hamish or another? Thankfully, the man appeared to have taken the box containing Darshan's toy.

Nothing he had found within the books here gave him a way to free Hamish from this place, but maybe an answer lurked in this pile. Or perhaps they'd hold only more dead ends and empty promises.

Humming an old song to himself, he relit the lantern and opened the topmost book. A skim of the pages revealed the usual laws of his homeland with both Udynean and Tirglasian translations. Serviceable for someone learning about the empire and what was acceptable in her borders, and possibly why Nora had them in her possession, but not much help elsewhere. He put it aside and thumbed through the next book down. That seemed to be more of the same with a smattering of geography.

The third was the slimmest and largely in bulky Tirglasian writing. Like the first time he'd seen the language written down, Darshan was instantly drawn to the similarity between Tirglasian and the Ancient Domian script. Admittedly, there lacked a fluidity to the former's writing, but that could've easily been the fault of the writer. What drew his eye were the additions. All sorts of dots and flicks above the letters that the writer couldn't quite seem to be unified on which way they went.

Where else could he find what he needed? Who else could he seek assistance from? Nora? She seemed pretty close to her mother. Could he trust her that far? *Too risky.*

What of Hamish's brother? If his lover trusted Gordon enough to have him privy to their relationship, then maybe the man might also know a way around this law of keeping the royal line close to home.

He flicked the book shut, extinguished the lantern with a click of his fingers and strode out of the library. Finding Gordon would be a simple matter as the man oversaw the guards and their training. Getting him alone long enough to converse might be trickier, but doable.

He passed several servants on the way to the courtyard. Unlike his first foray beyond the guest quarters, they all eyed him with a cold wariness. That he could handle well enough. It wasn't the first time, after all. Being the *vris Mhanek* carried a certain reputation he'd been expected to uphold since his early childhood years.

That a few felt brave enough to sneer in his wake was commendable, although back home it would've meant the mines if not a beheadal. One, grey-haired man even spat on the floor under the pretence of cleaning away a stubborn stain—at least, he hoped it was a pretence and they didn't regularly employ such a method.

Still, none seemed brazen enough to outright ignore him when he spoke, nor did they shirk from divulging Gordon's whereabouts. Not the training grounds as he had assumed, but found within the courtyard nevertheless. He knew the way.

Rather than exit via the large main entrance, Darshan opted for the modest door that backed onto the archery range and led to the stables. His attention slid over the empty range and glided by the stables, which appeared devoid of people save for a few young men tending to the stalls. Even the courtyard was relatively quiet for a—

"Got him!" a small voice cried.

The buzz of danger on his periphery tingled through Darshan's skin. He jerked back, a clear shield flashing to life around him before momentum had finished with him.

Something bulbous smacked into the gossamer barrier, dispensing a great cloud of blue powder.

Darshan stared at the patch of dust still clinging to the faint static emanating from the shield's surface. What had been the intention? The voice had sounded young, but children had been used as assassins before. He peered around the blotch, hesitant to release his hold on the shield just yet.

Three small figures rushed his way, their bows held at the fore and waving arrows tipped with what looked remarkably like balls of coloured cloth. Rather than have them run straight into his shield and risk breaking a nose or an arm, Darshan stepped back into the doorway.

A swarm of tiny shocks shuddered through Darshan's body. He swayed back and bumped into what was most definitely a person.

"Whoops," a familiar deep voice behind him chuckled. Sure hands clasped Darshan's shoulders, steadying the both of them.

Regaining both composure and balance, Darshan turned to face the man he'd unfeasibly collided with. *Gordon?* Impossible. Nothing should've been able to pass through his shield. Not here. *Unless...*

Nulled Ones could, being the antithesis to spellster abilities. But their presence required the same thing as those with magical gifts: A spellster heritage. There were no records of their kind in Tirglas, not even a whisper of the occasional weak spellster cropping up within the royal bloodline.

Gordon turned his attention to the three children, seemingly unaware a shield surrounded him. "Come on, lads, show a little more decorum and watch where you're aiming."

All three of Nora's children slid to a halt and swung about to hang their heads like berated hounds.

"Congratulations, you idiot," snarked the eldest—*Bruce?* The name seemed like it should've been familiar—his baleful gaze settling on the youngest boy as he gave his brother a nudge. "You just dusted the Udynean ambassador."

The smallest of the trio attempted shrinking even further into his tunic, those big brown eyes wide with fear.

Darshan's stomach flipped at the sight. Even back home, where people knew who he was and what theoretical horrors he could rain upon them, the children never looked so terrified. Not even the slaves. "No harm done." He let the shield drop and the fine blue dust drifted off on the breeze.

"See there, Macco-boy?" Gordon gave Darshan a hearty pat on the back. "Our resident spellster is in one piece. Now, why dinnae you three run off and see if you cannae find your missing quarry?

Remember, lads, you've only got until the noon bell sounds. Or do you want him to win again?"

Casting each other meaningful looks, the boys dashed off across the grounds.

Darshan picked up the arrow that had struck his shield. The head was wrapped in linen and discharged dust in a garish shade of blue. "What is this?"

"That would be one of Mac's. The lads use them for hunting practice. They're nae tipped and the dust temporarily marks their clothes." He chuckled. "Good thing that shield of yours came up so fast. Works on instinct, I hear."

"You heard correct." He waited for some offhand mention of the man passing through it and was met with silence. "So what quarry are the boys missing?" He hadn't seen a sign of anything that would constitute as prey within the castle walls.

"Hamish," Gordon replied rather matter-of-factly as if having his nephews racing after his brother was the most common thing in the world. "It's a game we used to play with our dad. Makes target practice a little more interesting when the target can move and hide."

"Hence these." Darshan waggled the cloth-tipped arrow, sprinkling a fine blue powder into the air.

Gordon beamed. "The dust was Nora's idea. We'd always row over who actually hit our dad until her first attempt." The fondness of old memories glazed his eye. "You should've seen the look of horror on me brother's face the first time she struck our dad. She used red powder, you see? And it had started to rain about an hour into the hunt." Laughter, loud and strong, roared from the man. "Scared the two of us half to death before she'd a chance to explain."

"I can imagine." Although, he saw little hilarity in the memory of believing a parent was bleeding to death before his eyes. Tirglasian humour was apparently a little stranger than he had been told.

Still wheezing and chuckling at every other breath, Gordon wiped his eyes. "Sorry about me nephews almost dusting you. They can get a little excitable when hunting. I keep telling them that the aim is to only hit your prey, not everything that moves, but..." He shrugged.

"Does your daughter not participate in this game?" He had witnessed her at the archery range on the same fateful day as his innocent kiss with Hamish. Although his judgement of the girl's talent was perhaps rather less than professional, she seemed to have a fair bit of skill with a bow.

"She used to," the man confessed, inviting Darshan to walk with him along the courtyard as they spoke. "Me wee lass was damn good at it, too." Paternal pride puffed out his chest. "But just like it's me job to keep the country on an even keel and war free, she has to learn how to handle a great many things until the boys catch up and can help her out." His head turned, his attention drifting to the courtyard, as he half-heartedly added, "I reckon she'll be with Nora by now."

"Forgive me, but you do not sound all that happy about it."

Gordon grunted. "I'd prefer she'd time to find her feet like her sister had." He rubbed at his neck, his fingers disappearing into the bushy mass of his dark-red beard. "*But* there are certain ways she needs to ken about and it's best to get it all into her head now, before she's old enough for me mum to see her married off and Sorcha has to spend her days chasing her own bairns instead."

"So young?" The girl couldn't be more than in her early teenage years. He had heard Tirglasians married early and tended to have several children, generally straight away, but he hadn't believed it to be *that* early.

"Aye." Gordon scuffed a boot along the flagstones. "It never used to be this way. I think grief took its toll after me niece and her father drowned."

He could see that happening, especially with an older child. His own father wasn't immune to the call of siring spares should his heir die. "Even so... I have sisters in their twenties who are still unmarried." Granted, some of that had more to do with his half-sister, Onella, and her schemes.

"But are any of them lined up to be the heir?"

Laughter, far louder than he had expected, burst from him. Darshan shook his head, unable to calm down enough to explain. Judging by the man's scowl, he didn't need to.

"A woman cannae inherit the title of *Mhanek*, then?"

Clearing his throat and fighting off a few lingering giddy hiccups, he shook his head again. "That title always goes to the closest male in the bloodline." Darshan was well aware the same couldn't be said of the Tirglasian throne. At times, he wished that was true back home. It would've made quite the difference. *Fewer sisters for one.*

"And if there is nae male?"

"Then there is generally a scurry to produce one." A number of his half-sisters had already gone down that route. Onella—the oldest of his sisters excluding his twin—had married some poor lord in Nulshar some years back and had practically paraded her newborn son through the streets of Minamist.

Gordon's frown deepened, but he said nothing further.

Their little foray around the courtyard, silently tailing the children whilst not appearing to do so, ended at the back of the stables. All three of the boys circled various stacks of hay, their bows half-drawn. Was the hunt almost at an end?

Darshan peered at their surroundings. He didn't see anything large enough for a man to hide behind, unless he was in one of the haystacks, but surely that would've made this game far too difficult for the boys. Not to mention leave a trace. "How long do these hunts usually take?"

Gordon's shoulders bobbed. "Depends on where he hides."

Not helpful. That could mean anywhere from now to noon. He glanced up. The sun sat high, shaded by the occasional, fast-moving cloud. How was it not noon already? How did they even tell the hour here? *I'd kill for a portable timepiece.* The palace courtyard had been constructed as a huge astronomical sunclock, the ancient dwarves that'd designed the building taking advantage of sun and shadow on a phenomenal scale. There were other devices, like the recent mechanical marvel of wheels and weights that was the council room's chronometer, but none of them were small enough for travel.

"So," Darshan said as he watched the boys continue their search for Hamish. "If you handle the army and your sister manages trade, what does your brother usually do with himself? On the days that he has not become prey for his nephews, that is." As much as he would like to imagine Hamish having to actively search for something to fill his days, he rather doubted his lover was allowed to be idle for long.

" 'Mish?" Frowning, Gordon scratched at his chin. "I suppose you could say he's the face of the crown to the locals. He typically spends his days wandering the farms, helping where he can, listening to their troubles, righting wrongs and all that." A small, fond smile tweaked the edges of his mouth. "When he's nae the one kissing fools and causing trouble."

Cunning. Send out the youngest to make the crown look benevolent and eager to please the people. "And where exactly is he at the moment?"

"Around." Cupping his hands around his mouth, Gordon bellowed, "Sun's getting higher, lads."

Darshan eyed the haystacks. Did one of them just move? He peered at the left-most pile. He was certain he had seen a twitch that couldn't be explained by the wind.

The haystack moved, Hamish erupting from the centre like a vengeful god of the harvest. Hay scattered on the wind, getting caught up in his clothes, hair and a ridiculous pair of antlers tied to his head.

The boys loosed their arrows, easily hitting Hamish at so close a distance.

Coughing and laughing, Hamish swatted at the air. It disturbed the dust, but did little to deter the boys who were already nocking another arrow. "All right, lads, you got me. Fair's fair." He knelt before them. "I yield."

The boys cast glances at each other before scooping up the discarded projectiles. Giggling, the trio raced around their uncle, batting at him with the linen-tipped arrows as if he was a drum.

"Hey!" Hamish ducked his head, wrapping his arms around his face. He wore the assault for a few moments. "I already yielded. Lads— That's enough." One of the arrow tips hit him in the mouth, exploding dust everywhere. "All right," he spluttered, grinning and spitting out flecks dyed a disgusting green. "You asked for it." Roaring, Hamish leapt to his feet, arms up and hands clawed. "Who wants to be eaten first?"

"Bear!" screamed Mac, the youngest. He brandished his arrow like a sword. "I'll save us."

"It's worse than that," Bruce replied, already scrambling across the ground, his green-tipped arrow forgotten as he legged it. "It's a stag-bear!"

Growling, the sound somewhat akin to a sick dog, Hamish scooped up Mac and tucked the boy under an arm before barrelling on past Gordon and Darshan in his quest to capture his other two nephews.

The two older boys ran around the courtyard, squealing and giggling as they dashed from one bit of shelter to the next.

"He made it back to his room just fine, by the way," Gordon said, returning his attention to Darshan. "Nae thanks to you. You shouldnae have kept him so late."

Whilst he had been accused of leading men astray before—and some of those claims might've had more than a grain of truth to them—no one, not even his father, had ever berated him for the lateness of his activities. "Did he not tell you the reason was a very innocent, albeit entirely truthful one?"

"That you two fell asleep?" He scoffed, although the ghost of a smile crept along his otherwise stern face. "Aye, amongst other details, like you almost dropping him whilst trying to get him back through the window?" Gordon arched a brow at him, but continued before Darshan could open his mouth. "I ken you've probably got a reasonable explanation on how me brother wound up outside the room to begin with, but he's already told me everything. *I* am far more interested in how you plan to rationalise threatening me sister."

Darshan stared at the man, slightly taken aback. "When did I do that?" He certainly didn't recall issuing any major threats. It would explain the coolness of her response to his earlier request for books with Udynean text. "I might have suggested she reacquaint herself with what my title means. I might have also been a little sharp about it."

"To hear her say it, you said more than that."

Yes. Now he thought on it, he'd said quite a bit more than he had intended. "I may have also mentioned how it could lead to unpleasantness should Queen Fiona decide banishing me from her kingdom would be a valid recourse. I shall be certain to apologise when I see her highness next. She spoke to me at a bad time and, I am afraid, undeservedly caught the brunt of my temper."

"A temper you seem more than willing to flash when it pleases you. I'm going to go out on a limb here and say you *are* aware your father pressed for peace. Yet, you swan about in a manner that could lead us all to war." Those green eyes, suddenly far sharper than Darshan recalled, narrowed at him. "Is that what you're after?"

"Of course not." He bristled at the very idea. It had been a long time since the Udynea Empire had truly done more than bicker with itself. Even the border disputes were more likely to involve a lord's personal retinue than any imperial army. The only exception being their seemingly eternal battle with the spellster-slaughtering Obuzan kingdom. "I am here only to settle the trade between our peoples."

"And I suppose the negotiation now requires extra conditions to be met?"

Darshan bit his tongue. Gordon couldn't possibly know about his disastrous talk with Queen Fiona, not if the man had been with his nephews the whole time. Had Hamish mentioned leaving for Udynean lands? *Last night or this morning?* He thought his lover would've kept such talk closer to his chest. "Is having your brother happy and free to pursue whomever he wants that big of a stipulation?"

"Allow me to make something quite clear to you." Gordon swung from watching the boys still race around the courtyard to face Darshan square on.

Darshan had taken a half-step back before realising he had moved. The man was only a tad taller than Hamish, but he certainly cut an imposing figure when riled.

"I dinnae trust you."

"That is… fair." He'd been here a scant handful of days and, when it came to Hamish, had done nothing apart from upset the queen whilst simultaneously putting the man squarely under her suspicious eye.

Shock darted across Gordon's face. Whether he was aware of it or not, he recovered well. "Me brother told me all about you asking for him to return to Minamist with you. He willnae go."

"I beg your pardon?" That hadn't been the impression Hamish had given him earlier this morning. Had he told his brother something different or was that Gordon's opinion?

"Me brother willnae leave his homeland, even if it was in his best interests. There's too much tying him to here."

"Like what?" The only obstacle he had witnessed was a rather controlling mother and he was willing to bet that was the *only* impediment to Hamish living however he wished.

"His family. We're very important to him."

Darshan's gaze slid to where his lover chased the oldest boy, the other two firmly tucked under an arm or balanced over his shoulder like sacks. Hamish would certainly lose these moments if he travelled to Minamist. "Like a mother who abuses him every time he is himself?"

Gordon fell silent.

"You *do* know what she does to him, I assume?" More had happened than Hamish's one-time incarceration. Such an act might've left the man slightly hesitant to repeat his transgression, but Hamish had been terrified of the queen's guards.

"Do I—?" the man snapped before his voice dropped into a menacing rumble. "You've known 'Mish—what?—four days? You think I have nae seen, that I've been *blind*, to how she treats me brother? Because I assure you, what you have witnessed is the mere graze of an arrow."

"And?"

"And what? What do you expect me to do about it?"

"Intervene?" Even as the suggestion left his lips, he knew it wasn't usually as simple as that. And to challenge a ruler's word… Maybe it was different enough here to give them some breathing room but, back home, the *Mhanek's* word was law. "Stand by him. Stand up for him. Whatever it takes."

Laughing mirthlessly, Gordon threw up a hand. "And there it is. The imperial prince comes to educate the barbarians on how to deal with all matters." The smile he gave was one of crocodiles and jackals. "That *is* how you see us, right?"

"I assure you, I have no idea what you are referring to." That wasn't entirely true. *He* might not see Tirglasians as such, but he had heard enough grumbling from those in the Crystal Court to know there was a general discord on allying the empire with the backwards little kingdom from up north.

Gordon grunted. "I've read enough stories of your people coming in and taming so-called savage lands. Your lot are just as bad as the Obuzan fanatics hammering at our shores," he muttered.

Darshan calmly refrained from uttering a word. His thoughts refused to be so generous. *We share a border with them, too, you know.* And they clashed with Obuzaners quite frequently despite it being mostly mountains. There was a pocket of sorts north of the range where the Obuzaners had erected a rather impressive wall to keep out the filthy spellsters who had, in their minds, followed the devil down the path of shadows. Never mind that Obuzan had once been a part of Udynea back before the latter could be considered an empire.

"Is that how you see me brother? As some savage thing you can tame and parade through your city?"

He stared at Gordon for some time before the words soaked in. "Of course not." Steepling his fingers before him in supplication, he continued, "Look, I understand how it must appear from the outside."

Gordon sneered but said nothing.

"I am a chaotic unknown in the largely stable equation of your family's life, correct? And I admit to miscalculations on my part. I did not mean to create such an upheaval, nor did I factor in the queen's reception of matters that are seen in a less than favourable light. Asking Hamish to journey with me to Minamist is a big step, I am aware of this. You may think I have an ulterior motive, but I truly only wish to—"

"*Intervene?*" Gordon snarled just under his breath. "And just what do you think I've been doing for the past three decades? Twiddling me thumbs? I have spent years standing between me mum and 'Mish. And you undo all of it in one day."

Even with Gordon's apparent deflection, Hamish had still spent decades of being tailed by his brother or guards like a naughty child. "An aviary gives a bird more room to fly, but it does not mean it is free."

Gordon frowned and opened his mouth.

His youngest nephew collided into his leg before he could say anything further on the matter. "Did we win?" Mac asked between pants. His curly red hair was a sweaty mass clinging to his face.

"Of course we won," Ethan answered, trotting up alongside his older brother. "We got him before the bell. That's a win."

"Right you are, lad," Gordon replied, further ruffling the two older boy's hair. "Although I cannae say the hunt was an entirely fair one. Deer dinnae tend to bury themselves in piles of hay, do they, 'Mish?"

Hamish stumbled to a halt before them, grinning sheepishly. "Nae typically." Hay still clung to his clothes and he plucked a few pieces free as he spoke. What drew Darshan's eye were those ridiculous antlers. They bobbed with the slightest motion, threatening to come loose. How were they even staying on? "But they found me all the same and it does them good to think beyond the confines of ordinary every once in a while."

A bell resounded somewhere deep within the city, echoed by another within the castle proper.

"Come on, lads," Gordon said. "Let's go see if we cannae cadge some grub off the cooks."

Cadge? Were princes treated so differently from back home that the heir to the throne couldn't enter the kitchen and request a piece of whatever was on offer?

"*Or*," Hamish added, casting a sideways glance at Darshan. "We could ride down to the market square and see what's on offer at the spring festival?"

Like ruddy-haired grasshoppers, the boys bounced around their uncles to cries of "Aye!" and "Can we really?" with the occasional "Let's go!" from Bruce.

Darshan's heart stuttered at the sight. He had to be roughly the same height as the eldest of the three brothers, he was well aware he barely reached Hamish's shoulder and that the children came from a line of equally tall ancestors. Nevertheless… Was that how he looked standing next to Hamish?

Surely he conducted himself with more dignity.

Hamish grinned at Darshan. "Want to come with us?"

"I would love to." Truthfully, he would've accepted any excuse to leave the castle confines, but an actual festival did hold some merit. Darshan nodded at the pair of small antlers still somehow affixed to the man's head. "But are you planning on wearing those down there?"

Confusion took Hamish's face before the expression was consumed by a deep blush. He hastily removed the antlers, tucking them behind his back.

"Well, *I* was planning on a somewhat more peaceful afternoon," Gordon rumbled. "But if you lads would rather go to the festival than study…" He waited, grinning, as the boys chorused an empathetic assurance that they certainly did wish to go. "I'll go get the horses ready, then."

"*Really?*" Hamish asked, the beginning notes of a whine creeping into his voice. "We're only heading down to the city. It's nae far."

"And neither was the pub," the man shot back over his shoulder, earning a mixed cry of giggles and mock gags from the boys. Clearly, the young trio knew what had transpired there. "You ken the rules, 'Mish. You are nae allowed beyond the castle walls unescorted, especially with *him*." He jerked a thumb at Darshan. "So where you both go, I have to follow. Or I can grab one of the guards and you can have *them* tailing you for the rest of the day?" He gave a sly grin. "Or maybe you'd prefer Lyall? I dinnae think our old steward is doing anything noteworthy today."

Hamish grimaced. "It's just out to the markets," he clarified. "Me and the lads will show Dar what a real spring festival is like and be back before sunset."

Gordon nodded. "Nae doubt you will do just that, but you ken Mum. If she caught wind that you'd been out of the castle without someone to keep an eye on you." He narrowed his eyes at the boys. "And the Mischief Trio doesnae count." The man strode over to the stable entrance. "So, shall we?"

Darshan's shoulders sagged. There went his hope of a quiet, and completely innocent, time wandering the stalls with Hamish and their three young tag-alongs. And here he'd thought Gordon to be on his brother's side. *Hamish's perhaps, but certainly not mine.* He hadn't had to prove himself worthy of someone's time before.

It was a challenge he was quite prepared to accept.

Chapter 15

From afar, the city looked no less busy, but Darshan caught a central flow to the crowd that hadn't been in evidence the last time he had ventured beyond the castle walls. They descended the road winding into Mullhind on five horses. Whilst the two older boys each rode an animal almost as broad as the shaggy mare Hamish rode, Mac shared a single mount with his older uncle.

"Can we go to the docks first?" Mac asked, bouncing on his perch before Gordon. The animal didn't seem to mind the placement, perhaps well accustomed to such, but the boy's uncle stilled him all the same. "I want to see the sinking ship race."

"That's nae until tomorrow, lad," Gordon said. He shaded his eyes and stared out at the harbour. "I only see fishing boats right now."

"Sinking ship?" Darshan enquired, kneeing his horse closer in the hopes of an explanation.

"It's the final race of winter," Mac said. "They take a ship full of people out into the harbour and everyone jumps into the water." He paused and seemed to think for a bit, twirling a coil of hair tightly around his forefinger. "Well, nae *everyone*—nae the people sailing—but they jump in and swim back to the docks."

Darshan could understand abandoning a sinking ship, could even grasp the idea of a quick dip off a boat in warmer waters, but to jump off a seaworthy vessel when the harbour had to be freezing at this time of year... "Why?"

"Because the fastest to make it to the docks gets a whole side of boar," Hamish replied.

"It didnae used to be such a draw, mind you," Gordon added. "The race started off as a way to honour the original Mathan chieftain, see who could brave the same waters he swam and all that. And before then, it was just an old tale of our clan, before it was more than a single family set adrift by—"

Ethan groaned loudly and rocked back on his horse. "Nae this story again. Mum tells it to us every spring. Can we nae hear a different one?"

"You poor thing," Gordon mumbled. "You're right, it is a boring story. It's nae like the chieftain's act of saving his family didnae see you as a prince and fourth in line for the throne..."

"He *is* right, though," Hamish piped up. "It was boring when Dad told us and it's downright sleep-inducing when *you* tell it."

"You're nae supposed to agree with the rats!" Gordon snapped as they reached the bottom of the road. They clattered through the square, which seemed far too empty for a spring festival happening. "All right, lads, where to first?"

All three of the children answered at once, each with a seemingly different response. How anyone could distinguish distinct words from the garbled noise was beyond Darshan's understanding, but Gordon nodded as if he had made them out perfectly.

"May I suggest a place?" Darshan enquired once the boys had quietened. After the scuffle in the pub some days back, and the subsequent chewing out by Queen Fiona on where his lips should not land, he had sent a pigeon bearing his seal towards the nearest Udynean city. A letter had returned this morning, along with an address to acquire funds should it be necessary. Whilst he might not need money for a swift departure, wandering stalls with an empty coin purse was never much fun.

He fished out the note he had scribbled the address on and handed it to Gordon without a second thought, only realising his error when the man's face scrunched in confusion. Whilst the original might have once been in Tirglasian script, it had been translated and then copied word for word into his native Udynean. "I believe it is called Aged Priest's Manner."

Gordon frowned at the parchment, twisting it sideways and then upside-down. "Is that was this says? There's nae streets named—" He lowered the parchment, arching a brow in Darshan's direction. "Do you by chance mean Old Priest's Way? Everyone kens where *that* is. It's nae far from the central market square, as a matter of fact." With the click of his tongue, he urged his horse at the fore of their little group as they ambled through the city. "Why there?"

"I was informed there is a guild on that street."

"The merchant guild?" Hamish replied. "Aye, they've secure stables. We leave our horses there all the time. Me sister's husband was a member, before the—" He froze in the saddle, his gaze darting to the boys who were more absorbed in nattering amongst themselves. Nevertheless, Hamish whispered, "Before the sinking."

Merchant? He had assumed the guild would've been tied to a bank or some such like Udynea. "I take it this guild works like a...?" The question died on his lips as he considered the great mental lexicon of words his tutors had stuffed into his brain during the trip here. Any equivalent translation for bank wasn't amongst them.

Did Tirglasians not have banks? The thought hadn't occurred to him before. It seemed so natural for people to place their trust—and copious amounts of money—in banks and their guild posts. Only the imperial treasury, and a few stubborn nobles, stood separate from the financial guild. Admittedly, the communication network was vastly superior to the Tirglasian reliance on pigeons and horse messengers, but surely those in the capital city relied on something more substantial than personal vaults and chests to store the entirety of their wealth.

"Works like a what?"

Shaking himself out of his musing, Darshan became sharply aware of Hamish staring at him as if he had somehow dropped out of existence and popped back. "A financial establishment," he mumbled, his face heating. "One that deals in loans and investments. Perhaps even exchanges of currency?"

Hamish's ruddy brows lowered at the last example, but the spark of recognition in the rest did give Darshan some hope that he was stepping into somewhat familiar grounds. "I dinnae have much to do with money," he confessed. "So, I couldnae rightly tell you about that last one, but the merchant guild deals with the trade and loans within the city."

"They're a pest," Gordon muttered over his shoulder. "I'm honestly glad Nora deals with that lot. I would've run the buggers out of town by now. Remember their last demand? That their leader be named Mayor of Mullhind? And you ken what?"

"That he wasnae even of the clan," Hamish replied, rolling his eyes and shaking his head. With one hand opening and closing like the beak of a duck, he mimed his brother's chatter. Clearly, a conversation they'd had many times before.

"Precisely. I thought poor Muir was going to have a heart attack when he found out. Almost caused a massive upheaval in trade throughout the city, would have if Nora hadnae convinced Muir that an extra tax on all goods wasnae going to help settle matters."

Perhaps there was a little more in common to the merchant guild and the banks Darshan frequented for funds. The man who ran the central bank in Minamist also oversaw the guild district and did a fine job of keeping them organised. Then again, he was imperial property. Keeping the empire running smoothly was expected of them. "I take it the guild failed to get what they asked for?"

Gordon shook his head. "Nae a scrap. I dinnae ken why they even tried. The mayor always comes from the local clan. It's the same all over Tirglas."

Their chatter grew broken and less frequent the closer they got to the central market square. People and carts crowded the streets, the former loud in their efforts to be heard and move on.

Animals also joined in with their cries. The resonating rumble of cattle at his elbow—the brutes big enough to feed a large family with one leg—near deafened Darshan. Thankfully, the driver directed them down a nearby side street. Sheep heavy with wool bleated as they passed by, mercifully in carts often towed by horses as the woolly beasts all brandish curled horns and seemed rather eager to butt them against their wooden cages.

There was a mighty crash to his left, sending people skittering from the chaos. Darshan had barely turned his head at the noise before several crates tumbled onto the road, spilling wizened apples everywhere. Hamish's horse slid on one, the mare's rump swinging Darshan's way as it struggled to remain upright.

Darshan's horse bunched beneath him in a most alarming manner. *Don't kick.* No telling what, or who, those hooves might connect with. Whilst he could heal most injuries, having a face caved in by a well-placed hoof was not one of them.

He gave the animal a few reassuring strokes on the neck. What had Hamish said the animal was called? "Easy, Warrior," he murmured, pleased when the horse flicked his ears back and listened to him rather than the shrieking of the apple seller, who berated a rather harried young man with a toppled hand cart. "Steady boy."

After what seemed like an age, the horse relaxed enough for Darshan to guide the animal around the disaster scattered across the street and down another, less hectic, road. Their group wove through a few more relatively empty streets before entering into one a little wider than the others.

Large buildings dominated either side of this street and they halted before one that, like most of the surrounding buildings, started off with a few brick levels before climbing up several more with the aid of timber. Windows jutted out all over those upper levels. The bottom level was clearly reserved for horses, carts and cargo, with plenty of each crowding a space that would've rivalled the imperial ballroom had it been empty.

Two sets of stairs led the way into the building. People clattered up and down them, lugging small chests or sacks. Unlike back home, there was no signage above the archway leading into the area beyond a simple iron wrought sign of what he presumed was a sack.

Not waiting for any sort of signal, the boys leapt off their horses and eagerly dragged the long-suffering beasts into stalls. Darshan followed their lead with the dismounting, but waited for an indication of where his horse should go.

Rather than dismount, Gordon merely waited for Mac to slide down the horse's shoulder onto the street. "Right, I'm off to the *Roaring Stag* for a few pints." He chucked a small pouch Hamish's way, it jingled with the telltale rattle of money. "Meet me there when you're done."

Darshan peered at the man. "I thought we were to be chaperoned?" Gordon had certainly made enough noise about it in the courtyard and whilst passing through the gates. He wouldn't be surprised if the whole castle knew where they were and with whom.

Smirking, Gordon toyed with his reins. "I can if you want, although I think a certain person would much rather I vanish from the land." His gaze slid towards Hamish.

Darshan followed the look, ducking under the horse's neck to see in full, and bit his lip in order to refrain from laughing. If mere looks were capable of hurtling a person into the atmosphere, then Gordon would've reached the moon by now.

"But so long as you dinnae snog me brother in public again," the man continued. "I dinnae see why you shouldnae be fine walking around the stalls without me shadowing you. Besides, there's me nephews to keep you in line, right lads?"

"Yes, Uncle Gordon," all three children chimed in unison. Darshan wasn't sure how the man could believe the boys. Their expressions certainly didn't lend themselves to any sort of dependability.

"By the way, 'Mish, we'll be travelling to the cloister in the morning," Gordon announced as if it were an afterthought. "Keep that in mind."

Hamish froze, half out of his saddle. "Mum actually agreed to let me go after everything that's been going on?"

"Aye." Gordon swung to eye Darshan, kneeing his horse close enough to keep his voice low. "If you'd like to come with us..."

"You are actually *asking* me to come along?" That seemed awfully at odds with the man's previous stance. "I thought I was untrustworthy."

Gordon inclined his head. "I am asking. Wouldnae normally, but 'Mish insisted I extend the invitation after your interest in visiting." He glanced over Darshan's shoulder and, seemingly satisfied, added, "Personally, I'd take you there and leave you."

"Would the queen not stop me? I cannot imagine your mother would be amenable to having me in Hamish's presence for such an extended period." Especially after their mid-morning meeting.

"It's nae as if you two will be alone. I'll be there, as will a handful of guards. Besides…" he added, shrugging. "…she's got to ken, first. By the time she realises you're with us, it'll be too late to send extra guards. If you're coming, be at the stables before sunrise." Clearing his throat, Gordon gave the boys a stern nod. "Behave for your uncle." With that, he nudged his mount into a steady trot back out into the street.

"We shouldnae be more than a few hours," Hamish said, having finally dismounted. The boys took up his mare's reins, along with those of Darshan's mount, and vanished into the stables with the two horses. "If you're after funds, then I'd recommend trying the small door." He jerked a thumb at the narrower set of steps leading off to their left. Although far less crowded, there was an air about it that put Darshan in the mind of a servant's entrance than the double doors opening onto the whole of the courtyard. "Dinnae be too long. I'm nae sure how long I can keep the lads here before they start complaining."

"I shall attempt to be swift," Darshan promised before trotting up the narrow stairs. A quick rap on the door had it swinging open to the flat clank of an old cowbell.

A young man stood on the other side of the door. He bowed as Darshan stepped inside and indicated the hallway sweeping off to Darshan's right as if the left option held more than a blank wall.

Bowing his head in thanks, Darshan strode down the hall. A few closed doors dotted the left side. The interior of the building was lit by oil lanterns, their ruddy light throwing a warm air over the wooden walls. He had expected a little more show of opulence, perhaps a few rugs or some curtains that didn't look quite so threadbare. Maybe he really had entered through the servant's entrance.

He glanced back the way he had come and bumped straight into a door that he was certain hadn't been open a moment ago.

"Oh really," a harsh voice snapped on the other side, the top of a grey head of hair just visible around the edge. "You clunking louts ought to take more care where you're—" The voice's owner glared at Darshan for all of a moment before shock stilled her tongue. Steel-grey eyes swept over him, no doubt taking in the heavy embroidery on his sherwani and the multitude of rings adorning his fingers. "Can I be of assistance, my lord?" Now that she wasn't growling like a hellhound, her voice had a slight musical note about it that was common amongst the dwarves.

"I certainly hope so." He rummaged through his belt pouch, searching for the letter. "I was told to ask for an… Aggie?"

Her light brown skin darkened slightly at the name. "Agnetha, my lord. That's me." She waved him into the room. "If you've been sent to me, then you're after funds." She settled behind a large, wooden desk and dug through the piles of paper already strewn across the surface to pluck her quill pen from its inkpot. "How much, exactly?"

"I am not entirely certain how much I shall require." If pressed, he could hazard a guess in Udynean coin, but Tirglasian? "I suppose—" By the firm look in her eye, he'd need an acceptable amount and a reason. Not too specific, mind. "Well, the fact of the matter is, my stay here is looking to be longer than planned. I merely require enough to see me through until I can return home."

"To Udynea?" Her full lips curved into a smug smile, likely to his surprise. "The accent gives you away, my lord."

"No doubt my clothing, too," he said, settling into the chair opposite the desk. "Whilst we are on accents, and if you will excuse my curiosity, you would not happen to have dwarven ancestors, would you?" The name certainly didn't seem of Tirglasian origin. Although, there were other reasons beyond heritage for that alone, coupled with the slightly stilted way she spoke, a foreign origin was a far better possibility.

Agnetha smiled. "I *am* dwarven. The guild invited me to work for them."

"I was of the opinion that dwarves preferred not to stray from their homeland for long." At least the hedgewitches didn't. Although he had never come across a dwarf outside their lands who wasn't part of their Coven. Maybe they did and the hedgewitches just never talked about them. "I do hope I caused no offence by that statement. My ignorance shows, it would seem."

"You've caused nae offence and you're right, we typically dinnae leave home for long." Sighing, she put down her quill pen. "And this establishment also doesnae make a habit of loaning to those from beyond the city. Makes it harder to reclaim should the deal fall through, you understand?"

He did. But he also had ways around that little barrier, which he hoped the guild would accept. Darshan worked one of his rings loose and placed it on the table. "I believe this should be adequate recompense."

Agnetha took up the ring, gasped and dropped it back onto the papers. "I can't take that as collateral," she cried in her native Dvärg tongue, a language slightly more pleasant on the ears. "That's the royal sigil... uh..." That wide-eyed gaze darted from him to the ring and back. "My apologies, *vris Mhanek*. I should've realised that the Udynean walking through my halls was the ambassador everyone's been talking about."

"That is quite all right, I—"

"How much did you say you needed?" she blurted, snatching up her quill pen and writing furiously on the first scrap of paper that entered her hand. She scoffed before he could answer and continued to babble in Dvärg. "I'm sure you don't need me bothering you with specifics." Snatching up his ring, she thrust both jewellery and paper towards him.

"Do you not need to keep the—?"

"*No*," she all but screamed. Gasping, Agnetha dropped the items and clapped a hand over her mouth. She stared at him, frozen like a mouse before a Niholian hooded asp.

Darshan remained just as still, making no effort to speak or even twitch in any way that might be taken as aggression. He'd never come across a dwarf that was frightened of him before. They were usually curious people, especially around spellsters, always inquisitive about magical abilities and their limits.

Had she picked up that fear from the local people? Was this how Tirglasians viewed all spellsters? Or was it Udyneans they feared? He was never entirely certain people shouldn't.

Perhaps his position in the Crystal Court was more to blame. What gossip had circulated that he might not have heard? That was an avenue to think on should any more people display Agnetha's level of discomfort around him.

Slowly, she seemed to regain a modicum of composure. "Take this to Fib down the hall." She held out the paper, seemingly unaware of how much it shook. "You can't miss him. Big man. Bald and with a black beard to make up for it. He'll give you whatever you want."

Standing at a pace that would make a dead man look lively, Darshan relieved her of the paper. "And the ring stays?" He could hardly have the woman's livelihood threatened because she feared him.

Agnetha shook her head and picked up the ring. "Take it. Please." Her eyes were huge, her skin shiny with sweat. Had he not known better, he could've been mistaken for thinking she was begging for her life. "Just take it and go."

He did as she asked with her collapsing in apparent relief once the ring was back on his finger. "I am sorry to have troubled you," he murmured before exiting the room. Whatever had happened to make her fear him, it wasn't something he could fix there and then, as much as he wished that were so.

Chapter 16

Finding Fib had taken longer than conversing with him. The man had shown no hesitancy at Agnetha's letter, merely doling out the amount requested of him.

Darshan trotted down the stairs to join the others, the pouch of gold coins tucked securely under his belt. It was a modest amount, enough to afford him some comfort and no more. Whilst it nagged at him that he was taking it without offering anything in return, he made a mental note to have a suitable repayment sent from his private coffers back home.

"You took forever," Mac moaned once Darshan joined the group waiting near the gate. He tugged on Hamish's overcoat. "I'm hungry," he said, his voice suddenly small and teary.

"Then I guess food should be our next stop." Hamish ruffled Mac's hair and laid a guiding hand on the boy's shoulder as they stepped out onto the street. "Lest you lads waste away before me eyes."

On foot, the distance to the central market square seemed far longer. Darshan did his best to remain close to the others, his legs burning with the effort to mimic the brisk pace the boys kept. He considered himself as a fit sort of person, unlike some in the Crystal Court, but the trio were easily able to put him to shame.

They wove through carts caught at a standstill and skirted groups of people crowding various stalls, their individual voices lost to the general clamour of noise. He peered around a few elbows, curious as to what could draw so many, but caught only glimpses of colour.

The stench of animals was far more of an assault on the senses than it had been on horseback, bordering on knocking him out at one point when a pair of cattle sauntered by and deposited their own cargo. He started paying a little more attention to the cobblestones after that.

Eventually, the boys chose to crowd around a stall stocking dark loaves of bread and gleaming buns. The heady aroma of baking bread filled Darshan's nose, emanating from the building just behind the stall. He breathed deep, sighing and casually wiping at the corners of his mouth.

His stomach issued an embarrassingly loud query. When had been the last time he'd eaten? He had no memory of breakfast.

As one, the boys twisted to shoot Hamish a lip-quivering plea.

"I dinnae think so," Hamish replied, folding his arms. "I ken what you're after and you're nae stuffing yourself with honey cakes. Your mum would kill me if I let that happen."

"Who said she has to be told what we ate?" Bruce suggested. The boy waggled his brows slyly and Darshan had to cough or forsake his neutral face to laughter.

Fortunately, his lover seemed a little more hardened to the act. "Now lad," Hamish warned, shaking his head. "You ken that mums have ways of finding out. Even if we dinnae breathe a word, she'll ken."

"But—" Mac blurted, instantly silencing his protest as his uncle raised a finger.

"Dinnae think I'm at all willing to go toe to toe with your mum over this. She'll want good food in you and that's what you lads are going to get. You want honey cakes? You have something else *first*."

Three heads lowered in the most dejected stance Darshan had ever witnessed. He had never seen anyone other than his father manage to wrangle his siblings with barely an argument. How ever did Hamish manage to quell them so deftly?

Catching Ethan eyeing him, Darshan swiftly backed up with his hands held high. "I do hope you are not thinking of dragging me into this. As far as I am concerned, what your uncle says goes."

One by one, the boys' shoulders slumped. They each grabbed what looked to be a rather inedible clump of pastry and began to unenthusiastically devour them whilst their uncle paid.

"Here," Hamish said, offering up one of the pastry clumps. "I ken it's nae your usual palace fare, but you'd do well to get something in your belly."

Darshan accepted the food, although still slightly hesitant to call it such. A glance at the boys revealed that the clumps were pies with thick crusts. Whatever lurked inside had to be cold, the outer crust certainly was. He bit into the pie.

The aroma of meat hit him. Hard to tell if it was meant to be beef or mutton. Flakes of pastry and a tepid, claggy substance filled his mouth. Coughing and fighting back the bile rising in his throat, he choked down the mouthful.

"I didnae think they tasted *that* bad," Hamish said, attempting to hide a smile behind his hand.

Darshan discreetly wiped the corners of his eyes, sniffing in an effort to clear his head even with an echo of his old Nanny Daama berating the uncouthness of such a sound. "Not so much the flavour," he clarified, his voice a little hoarse. "More the consistency. The pies back home are a little... firmer." And with meat he could readily identify. Even looking at the pale brown, minced mess sitting mournfully in its crumbly shell told him nothing.

A gentle nudge in the ribs drew his gaze up to meet Bruce's eyes who flicked his gaze down to the pie like a ravenous crow.

"If you're nae going to eat that..."

Darshan wordlessly handed over the remainder of the pie, his stomach bubbling at the sight of the boy happily devouring the slop. He rather doubted his ability to take another bite from anything containing meat for quite some time.

Hamish clapped an arm around Darshan's shoulder. "Sorry about that. Let me get you something that'll have the taste out of your mouth."

A kiss would be nice. The thought surfaced and sank almost immediately. If the mere sight of Bruce eating the pie was enough to turn his stomach, then kissing his lover after the man had finished one would definitely not be a good idea. The last thing he wanted was to throw up. "One of those honey cakes sounds interesting."

It took only a mention of them for the boys to start clamouring for their own promised treat. They circled Hamish like fledgling birds whilst the man made good on his word.

They strolled along the street with the boys silently munching away. The honey cakes were more bun-like than Darshan had expected. Spongy, soft and incredibly sweet. After a few bites, he could see why Hamish insisted on other foods first. It wasn't as sweet as the cane syrup they produced back home, but it was filling nevertheless and quite sticky. Not that the latter bothered the boys, who merely licked their fingers clean and wiped them on their shirts, much to their uncle's disgruntlement.

"Try and show a bit of decorum, lads," Hamish grumbled at the trio. "You're in the public eye, for Goddess' sake. What would your mother say seeing you lot dirtying up your clothes like wee pigs in a pen?"

Darshan discreetly covered his hands with a faint layer of ice and rubbed until it melted. It didn't remove all of the stickiness, although the remainder was more tacky bits of crumb that he could easily—

The street opened out into what had to be the central market square.

He slowed, the remnants of his honey cake all but forgotten. With what had to be the vast majority of Mullhind crammed into such a space, Darshan had to stand on his toes and crane his neck to see more than a few feet in front of him.

It wasn't that there weren't similar squares dotted across Minamist's merchant quarter, because there were a great many that were more expansive and draped in far richer trappings. Nor did the elements of a spring festival faze him for, with as many deities as the Udynea Empire had, there was bound to be some sort of celebration each month. Sometimes there would be two or three festivals within a few days of each other.

But nothing back home had the same warm rustic air about it. Shops with their lush awnings and signage lined the outer edge whilst temporary stands crowded the middle of the square, rubbing shoulders with more permanent stalls.

Darshan remained rooted to the spot, hesitant to move on and be disappointed by what he would find amongst the stock. *Oh Ange, how I wish you were here.* His twin would've adored this. She'd a fondness for all things... "Quaint." Could he perhaps find a trinket for her amongst these stalls? He swung towards the children. "Right, boys. I have gold burning a hole in my money pouch and siblings to buy for. Where to first?"

"I know!" Ethan declared, grabbing Darshan's sleeve and towing him through the crowd. The boy moved with an agility that spoke of numerous times dodging around those far taller than he and with a distinct air of determination.

They halted roughly a third of the way into the centre of the square. Stalls bearing all manner of wares flanked him just as expansively as other stall spread out before him. He perused a nearby stall from a distance. Sadly, they had little more than the same trite baubles he'd seen echoed amongst the festivals markets back home. Cautiously hopeful, he strolled along the stall fronts, with the other two boys and Hamish easily catching up to them.

"It would probably help if you told us what you're looking for," his lover suggested. "Otherwise, you could be hours here and find nae even a sign of a gnat's knee."

"I wish I knew," Darshan confessed. His twin was perhaps the hardest to find a gift for, if only because she already boasted a great deal. Modest trinkets were always greeted with delight, but—

He halted before a stall displaying a number of carved chunks of stone. Animals were a favourite of Anjali. She had a few crudely-carved statuettes from Cezhory, a finely-spun glass figurine of a dolphin leaping from the water that'd survived a heart-stopping trip all the way from a prominent glass baroness in Niholia, and a scrimshawed shell gifted to her by the ambassador of the Independent Isles. What would fit best amongst those pieces?

"What about this?" Mac asked, holding up a painted, stone statue of a tortoise almost as big as his head. If the merchant had also made it, then the man had some skill for both the fine detail in the stone carving and the paints. Combined, it gave the piece an unerringly life-like air. "It's pretty."

Extremely. The habitual noncommittal grunt passed his lips before Darshan could check it. "You have quite the eye. However, my oldest sister has a real one."

Mac's eyes widened. "*Real?*" he squeaked. "*Really* real?"

Darshan grinned. The boy couldn't have looked any more amazed if he had been told dragons were real. "Yes. She calls him Mani. He came from the Independent Isles about ten—maybe twelve—years ago." Anjali had acquired quite a number of gifts back then, before the man courting her realised she wasn't at all interested in... anyone really. Whilst most of his sisters sought marriages, Anjali preferred her animals and her books. "I would say it is about the size of the average dog now. Looks quite like that, actually." He tapped the stone tortoise on the nose.

The boy stared at the statue as if he held a live animal rather than stone. "Uncle 'Mish," he said, his voice little more than a peep in the crowd. "Can I have this?"

"You already have three," pointed out Mac's oldest brother.

"And you broke those within a day," Hamish grumbled. "The last thing you need is another one to destroy."

"Have a heart, Uncle 'Mish," Darshan purred, batting his lashes and nudging his lover. "It *is* the Spring Festival after all; a time for frivolity and excess." At least, that's how the nobles in Minamist celebrated the Fresh Year. He assumed they were comparable. "Who actually spends their festival money on necessities, anyway?"

"*I* do," Hamish shot back. "And *you* should think about acquiring something a wee bit warmer than *that.*" He indicated Darshan's modest attire of fine linen and silk. "Especially if you plan to journey with us tomorrow."

Darshan flapped a hand, dismissing the idea. If he was cold along the way, then his magic could serve to warm him well enough. "I am certain Mac will take good care of this one," he said, returning to his original point. He handed two gold coins over to the merchant. "Especially with it being a gift from a friend afield."

If he thought Mac's eyes couldn't get any larger, he was wrong. "I can keep it?" he whispered. The boy hunched his shoulders, almost fearful that the answer would be negative.

"Of course you can keep it," Darshan insisted, gently taking the stone animal from the boy. He turned back to the merchant, who was still staring at the coins, and handed the statue over. "See that this makes the castle in one piece, would you? Let them know it is a gift for Prince Mac."

"A-aye, me lord." The merchant snapped a salute, his dark eyes darting to the boy and back. Had the man not realised who stood before him? "I'll oversee it meself. Watch the stall whilst I'm gone, lad," he added to a young man, waving the boy over. His son, judging by the similarity in their features and tanned skin. Packing the tortoise into a box already sitting on a handcart, the man pushed the clunky thing off into the crowd.

Darshan perused the rest of the stall's offerings. Little caught his eye. What scant pieces did draw his attention certainly weren't suitable gifts for his sister. He laid his hand on the brow of a sitting stone dog. Cool, polish stone greeted his palm. It sat about as high as his hip, its nose pointed up and its floppy ears perked in anticipation of a command. Whilst the piece was carved as finely as the tortoise, he feared the journey to Minamist would see it reach her broken. *A pity*. Anjali was quite fond of their father's lanky hunting hounds.

There was a stone mouse tucked behind a pair of black, polished seashells, white as pipe smoke. He plucked the creature from its mournful place to find the piece was almost round. The carver had chosen a pose that had the dear thing on its haunches and peeking over its shoulder, its cheeks stuffed with food and a crumb of bread still in its little paws. In the full light of the afternoon, the stone had a translucent quality. A chunk of marble, perhaps.

"Why a mouse?" he mumbled to himself. The little things were both pest and pet in Minamist—and sometimes also training aide for falconers, although he'd never had the heart to feed them live to his father's birds. But surely mice could only be considered as pests in Tirglas.

"For good luck," answered a soft voice disturbingly close to his ear. "Stone ones, anyway."

He glanced over his shoulder to find Ethan staring adoringly up at him. The boy was perhaps half a foot shorter than himself, and he appeared to be bouncing on his toes to gain a smidgen of extra height, but there was no mistaking that slight tilt of his head that suggested mischief or an attempt to curry favour. Had the boy been older, he would've labelled him as smitten.

Darshan looked about for the others, spotting them two stalls down, before returning his focus to the boy. "Luck?" he queried. "Are they not vermin?"

Ethan gave a disinterested jerk of his shoulder. "Sure. But the priests say mice always pop up in times of plenty and, when Great

Ailein was trapped in the cave of the Grey Bear, unable to leave, it was mice of ivory and onyx that the Goddess sent to him with food."

"Great Ailein, huh?" he murmured, handing over a silver coin to the merchant's son and ignoring the young man's gaping mouth. It sounded like common folklore. His knowledge of that was sadly lacking. If only he'd had the chance to immerse himself in the nuances of Tirglasian culture before arriving then he wouldn't be left feeling wool-headed over simple things. But his father had opted to give him little time to prepare.

"Do you nae ken the tale?"

"Not a bit," he confessed. A glance down the row of stalls revealed the rest of their group was steadily moving further away. "You must tell me it. But at another time." Popping the mouse into the small, rather empty, pouch dangling beside the one bristling with coin, he hastened to catch up to the wandering trio.

Ethan trotted at his side, bouncing past the stalls without a care towards losing sight of his siblings or uncle. "Does your sister *really* have a tortoise the size of a dog?"

"Yes." He thought of the hounds wandering the castle. Did they come in any size apart from massive? "Although, maybe a touch smaller than you are imagining," he conceded.

They meandered around the stalls, pausing every so often to peruse the more likely establishments and finding little in the way of suitable offerings. *I could return with nothing.* He often did for his half-siblings, preferring not to show favour to any lest one of the others targeted them. But if he came home empty-handed after such a journey, Anjali would never let him forget it.

A ramshackle stall almost tucked away around the corner of a building drew his eye. He sidled closer, hesitant to show any obvious interest to what could amount to little more than utter filth.

An old woman sat behind the rickety table. Her dark eyes seemed to light up as he stopped to survey the little wooden ornaments scattered across the cloth, each piece glittery with scraps of metal and bits of seashell cobbled together. "See anything you like, love?"

"No, I think—" A tiny bear no bigger than his thumb lay at the feet of far chunkier works. Darshan plucked it from the table. Where the carving of the other pieces was crude, this had the sheen of time and care. Small black stones had been worked into the paws, held there by fine pieces of wire.

She doesn't have a bear. He couldn't be certain of the other animals, but there were no bears amongst Anjali's collection of Cezhorian figures. They considered the animals akin to demons and ill omens to have in any form. "This one." Not taking his eyes off the creation, he handed over a coin before slipping the bear into the pouch with the marble mouse.

Content with his purchase, he relaxed a little and ambled along the outer ring of stalls and shops. The storefronts were largely walls with a single doorway. It was most unlike the merchant square back home, where the more exclusive shops boasted large glass window displays with people modelling whatever was sold within.

Darshan halted at a store bearing the familiar sign of a solitaire ring. *A jeweller's store?* He poked his head inside. He didn't often get the chance to peruse the ones back home. All the good jewellers were under house commission for this or that noble and the rest generally weren't worth bothering over for more than gaudy trinkets.

A man stood at the counter, buffing the dark wood. He glanced up as they entered and resumed his task.

It was a small room, barely big enough to squeeze the five of them in. The counter stretched across one end. Displays sat nested into the wall behind it. Silver and gold, bearing gemstones of every imaginable colour, glittered back at him from behind thick glass.

"All right," Hamish grumbled. "I'll bite. What are we doing here?"

Darshan hastened to shush his lover with the flap of a hand. His gaze fastened on an array of silver rings in a box propped up just enough to lure the curious customer. One fat ring sat proudly in the middle, its light blue colour almost lost against the silver backing. "May I?" he enquired, pointing at the box. "The blue one."

At his back, Hamish issued a faint groan.

Nevertheless, the jeweller looked over him, no doubt taking in the gold thread embroidery and gems of Darshan's attire, before producing a set of keys and unlocking the cabinet. It took all of a few moments for the man to fish out the ring and lock the rest away. "This is a good one," he rasped, each word sounding as if it had to escape a grinding before being spoken. "Carved each line with me own hand." He shook out a cloth from his belt and laid it onto the counter.

The ring's diameter was quite large. Far bigger than Darshan's thumb, at any rate. The design that curved down the side was one of leaves and vines, so detailed that he almost believed they'd move in the gust of his breath. Sitting proudly on the top was a sparkling, oval-cut aquamarine gemstone, its colour the crystal shade of blue that reminded him of the tropical ocean waves of home... and a certain man's eyes.

Darshan went to pick up the ring only to have the jeweller's hands slam down either side of the cloth—one hand, at least, the other appeared to stop at the wrist.

The jeweller glared at him, his shoulders seeming to triple in size. "You dinnae touch unless you got the gold to buy."

Wordlessly, Darshan placed the pouch of coins on the bench. The neck opened, the warm glow of the lanterns reflecting off the gold.

The man plucked one of the coins from the pouch and examined it with a wary eye. Whatever he searched for, the gold seemed to almost disappoint him. Grunting, he waved his arm at Darshan in an offer for him to inspect the ring.

He snatched up the ring, holding it so that the candlelight glittered off the gem. "Gorgeous." He swung back to Hamish and held the piece up beside the man's face. "A perfect match. You simply must get it."

Hamish huffed and rolled his eyes. "And it's a sapphire, nae doubt."

"Nae at all, your lordship," the jeweller blurted, the deep-set wrinkles on his pallid forehead lifting in alarm. "That there is the finest aquamarine. I had it imported all the way from Udynea."

Darshan smiled. He had thought as much. Aditi, his youngest half-sister at ten years of age, had once commissioned a hair comb incorporating a vast array of aquamarine stones. Although, none of them could compare to this blue beauty. "You should buy it," he murmured to Hamish.

His lover looked from the ring to Darshan and back. "I dinnae believe me allowance would be enough for such a bauble."

"*Allowance?*" He scoffed. "You are not a child. Why are you still stuck on an allowance?" Darshan hadn't been able to count his years in double digits the last time he had been restricted in such a fashion. Yes, he had private coffers—all his unmarried siblings did—but even that held a sizable amount.

Hamish opened his mouth.

Darshan waved his hand, stalling him. "No, no. Do not say another word, something tells me the reason will only serve to upset me and it is too nice a day for that." He rummaged through his coin purse and tossed a handful of gold on the counter. "That should be adequate."

With the jeweller's mouth still gaping soundlessly, his eyes bulging enough that they might very well pop, Darshan grabbed his lover's left hand and went to thread the ring onto Hamish's middle finger.

His lover gently shrank out of Darshan's grasp. Hamish remained silent, the faint darkening of his cheeks the only clue as to his discomfort.

"Is something wrong?" Did people not buy each other gifts? That seemed unlikely. Or was it the type of gift? Clearly men wore jewellery or there wouldn't be such a demand for a ring so large.

A small tug at his sleeve drew his attention to Ethan. "That's the wedding finger," the boy whispered, cupping a hand over his mouth as if revealing a great secret.

"Oh?" Heat took over his face. Why hadn't he considered that? He glanced at the jeweller to find the man still fussing over his payment. "Forgive me, I did not know. Back home, it is the one next to the little finger on the right hand." Instead of trying to guess what was acceptable, he placed the ring firmly in his lover's open palm, much to Hamish's obvious consternation.

"Is that why you've nae rings on that one?" Mac asked, holding up Darshan's right hand as if he had forgotten what his own fingers looked like. Surrounded with an abundance of gold, silver and gems, the third digit was conspicuously naked.

"Sort of." How could he explain to the young boy that it was a silent protest against his father's persistent nagging about him marrying some young woman and getting down to the business of siring a son? Over the years, his father had conceded to only harassing him about the fatherhood portion, but Darshan's refusal remained strong.

"It's lovely," Hamish murmured, turning the band over to examine the design. "But you shouldnae have bought it for me." He held out his hand, trying to offer the ring back to Darshan.

Darshan clasped his hands behind his back. "It is my gift to you, *mea lux*. I shall not accept its return." Hamish would have no choice beyond keeping the ring or selling it. Whilst he would've preferred his lover kept the trinket, either way suited him fine.

The man's bushy brows lowered slightly, furrowing the skin between. But he made no more effort towards relieving himself of the ring. His gaze dropped back to it, his thumb caressing the stone. "You dinnae think me eyes are like sapphires?"

Darshan shook his head. "If I was to make an accurate comparison, I would say they remind me of the crystal blue waters of Minamist's harbour."

Hamish eyed the ring, then him, before slipping the band onto his right hand with a grunt.

Well aware his face burned, Darshan attempted to remain casual. The ring truly did fit quite nicely on the third digit. *It's just a finger*, he sharply reminded himself. *Doesn't mean anything here*. Not like back home.

"We should return to the horses and meet up with me brother." Hamish swung back to the shop entrance and was out it before Darshan could think to follow.

The children were far quicker, disappearing after their uncle and leaving him alone with the jeweller.

"He your piece?" the man asked, jolting Darshan out of his stupor.

"Of course not," Darshan scoffed. Had the jeweller been listening to them the whole time? That couldn't be good. *What if Queen Fiona finds out?* That was a thought he wished would've surfaced sooner. It was just a ring, but it had been just a kiss, too. "Just a friend eager to see me enjoy the festivities." He scooped up his coin pouch before the man could pry further and trotted after the group.

Chapter 17

Hamish lay flat on his bed, twisting the ring back and forth on his finger. His room was the black of cellars and sealed tunnels. Not even the moon dared to show its face in this early hour. He had barely slept all night, despite the journey ahead. He did so better in a tent anyway and would rest well during the next fortnight.

Memories of last night's dinner floated before him in the dark. So vivid that the minty scent of roasted lamb still tickled his nose.

Darshan had opted to join them that night, the first since his arrival dinner. His lover had settled at the far end, right beside Hamish. That had likely drawn his mother's attention. It had certainly given her cause enough to be caustic about his sudden appearance.

If the spellster hadn't been there, would she have noticed the ring? The silver band had shone brightly in the candlelight, but not enough to draw the casual eye. Still, he should've known she would spot it. His mother was like a hawk in that respect.

Hamish lifted his hand before him. In the dark, he saw only the faintest impression. The crush of her fingers as she had twisted his hand one way then the other still lingered in his mind. He'd only himself to blame for being cloth-brained enough to keep wearing it. He could've removed the ring before entering the hall and avoided any queries.

Why had he let Darshan buy the accursed thing in the first place? *Especially blue.* She knew he hated the colour and its presence on his hand had drawn her attention all the more. "*Exquisite*," she had called it. And it was.

Then his mother had asked the very question he had been dreading. Those piercing eyes had dug deep into his soul, seeking to snatch up the answer like a gull did fish. How had he afforded it when they were both aware Hamish had no access to that amount of coin? The very moment the question left her lips, he knew he had screwed up.

Fortunately, Gordon saved him from their mother's scrutiny, just like he always did, by owning up to purchasing the ring. His brother had seen it well enough back in the *Roaring Stag* to describe it.

What would he have done had Gordon not stepped in? *I dinnae ken*. He could only be thankful that his brother chose to stand by him over and over.

In the stillness, the faint shuffling of guards outside his door was like rats scuffling through the rafters. They thought their job of keeping him in was almost done for the night. Little did they know he had visited Darshan in the early evening at a time usually reserved for mingling with his family. Whilst he couldn't bear their presence at that moment, he could spare his lover the time.

Hamish rolled onto his side, in an effort to find even a brief moment of proper sleep. His arm hit the little wooden box Darshan had gifted him. The toy still lay within. He had originally returned to his room with the intention to use it, but settled for the familiarity of his hand.

He wrapped his fingers around the box, drawing it close to his chest, and let his mind slip away into the far more pleasant recollection of last night. *Bring the toy*. Hamish closed his eyes, his skin prickling at the memory of Darshan's voice; silken and dripping with wisps of promised pleasure.

An oath his lover had most certainly upheld.

Hamish slunk his hand down to his groin, letting his fingers massage himself through the soft linen of his smalls until the simple act was no longer enough. Untying the drawstring, he slipped a hand beneath the cloth to fist his length as the image of the man's little demonstration tumbled over and over in his mind.

Darshan sat in the middle of the bed with Hamish perched half-off the side near the foot. Wetting his lips as he opened the box, his lover removed the toy in slow, almost hesitant, movements. Need or nerves had Darshan's fingers trembling. Or perhaps it was...

Shyness? *Hamish silently re-evaluated the way his lover glanced up at him, that hazel gaze not quite hidden by the rim of his glasses. "Are you sure you want to do this?"*

His lover's already faintly ruddy olive-brown cheeks darkened further, noticeable even in the dim light of the fireplace. Despite having the time to, he had apparently opted to keep the candles unlit. "Yes," he breathed, taking up the bottle of oil and pouring a generous amount over the toy's head. "It just occurred to me that I have never done this with an audience."

"Really?" The man had sounded so confident just this morning whilst suggesting he gave Hamish a demonstration. "I thought you'd—" He clicked his teeth shut on the rest of the sentence.

The faint, upward twitch of his lover's brow took away any hope that the man hadn't understood what he had intended to say. "You thought what? That I had done everything under the sun?" There was a hint of a barb beneath the sweetness of his tone, a veneer of geniality much like his toothy smile.

"Nae every thing," Hamish mumbled, scratching at his jaw. His mind frantically searched for the right words and came up sadly lacking. Darshan had quite a bit more experience than himself on a larger number of topics, but that didn't mean he thought the man was of loose morals.

Darshan's shoulders shook in silent laughter, the previous tension in them draining. "I suppose in comparison..." He sat back, critically eyeing the toy. It shone in the light like a freshly-waxed boot. The leather had taken much of the bottle of oil to turn slick, but there was no sign of resistance as Darshan stroke the toy's length. "It is a pity you lack magic or you could use this to its full effect."

"Such as?" Most magic in Tirglas fell under two categories, dangerous and curative. He couldn't see the first being applied, but the latter option seemed even less viable.

"The casing holds a metal core. Not all the way, you understand? Just near the base. See?" He tilted the toy and revealed a metallic disc. There were scratches all around the leather base and crescent-moon imprints that could only be done by nails. "Here, feel for yourself what it is capable of."

Curiosity had him shuffling further onto the bed to kneel just before his lover. Darshan wordlessly took up Hamish's hand, entwining their fingers and wrapping them around the toy. The leather was vaguely warm, but the simple touch of a hand could do that without any magical involvement. "I feel nothing."

Darshan smirked. "Because I have yet to do this." He pressed a finger to the metal disc and a soft buzz ran through Hamish's hand. The hairs on both their arms stood upright as if they were on a hill during a thunderstorm. "Or this." A second digit joined the first.

Hamish jumped as the whole toy vibrated in their grip. A little on the violent side for something the man planned to have inside him. Surely, the strength of it would turn his pelvis to dust.

Something must've shown on his face, for the intensity ebbed until only a pleasant tingling ran against his palm. Reminiscent of the early morning massage Darshan had offered back in the library.

He gently untangled his hand from his lover's. "That's some trick," *he murmured, the words coming out a lot hoarser than he had expected.*

"I could always sneak into your chambers and assist you there?" There was a cheeky light to his eyes. They both knew he'd never get that far. Not again.

"But if I had you *in me chambers, why would I need anything else?" Even without using his power, the spellster had proven capable of showing him a magical time.*

"You say that now, but I warn you: It can become quite addictive."

All the more reason nae to start. *Especially with the prospect of the source of such addiction departing for the other side of the continent. When? He didn't know. If Darshan chose to join them on their excursion to the cloister, then two weeks was a given. If not, then he could return to find the man already on his way home.*

"Are you going to give me this promised show of yours or nae?" The question came out rougher than he had intended, but he didn't want to stand another session clinging to the outside of the castle wall whilst his lover chased away the guards.

Biting his lip, Darshan rocked back and onto his side. With his fingers still slick from the oil, he slowly prepared himself.

Hamish shuffled from one knee to the other, his smalls already quite a bit tighter. His lover hadn't insisted he remain fully dressed, but Darshan hadn't suggested otherwise either and this display wasn't meant to involve Hamish doing anything more than watching.

"You are welcome to participate in this part, if you so desire."

He silently shook his head, afraid that any word he voiced, however brief, would give away his true feelings on the matter. He hadn't any experience with this type of intimacy. What if he inadvertently hurt the man with his fumbling?

Shrugging, Darshan reached for the toy. He let forth with a soft moan as it entered him. The languid way his eyes closed, the lids fluttering, and that petite bite of his bottom lip almost had Hamish forsake his personal resolve to remain a spectator.

When the toy had only a handful left to go, those hazel eyes snapped open, fastening on Hamish as his lover slowly started working the toy in and out with one hand gripping the base like a lifeline. Darshan's hips lifted slightly at every inward stroke, a grunt escaping, before he let it gently slide out.

That hazel gaze remained fixated on Hamish, even as continued pleasure glazed the outer edges. Darshan held out his hand imploringly.

Hamish crept closer, gasping as his lover latched onto his wrist. Rather than the expected guide of where his fingers should touch, Darshan pressed his lips to Hamish's knuckles.

Nuzzling his palm, his lover's hand slunk up Hamish's arm to settle behind his neck. The gentle pressure of those fingers at the nape coaxed Hamish closer still until he practically lay stretched out atop the man. Darshan sighed as he placed a chaste kiss on Hamish's nose.

Words tumbled out his lover's mouth, a whisper that could barely be heard above their breaths. It carried a tangled air of promise and hushed desire.

Hamish desperately wished he knew what any of it meant. "You've nae taught me a word of your language, you ken."

Smiling blissfully, Darshan smoothed back a stray coil of Hamish's hair. "I imagined you, you know." He took up Hamish's hand and guided it down to the toy, wrapping their fingers around the base. He moaned as, together, they resumed his previous motion. His breath grew fast and hoarse like a stag in autumn.

The heat in Hamish's cheeks grew with each sound. "Imagined me?" he mumbled.

"Taking me just like this," his lover panted, releasing Hamish's fingers to leave all movement of the toy entirely up to him.

Hamish continued in a similar motion, keeping the rhythm steady even when Darshan's hips started to move along with him.

More words poured from the man, obscene even without translation. Hamish took that as the cue to take matters into his own hands. He grasped Darshan's length, working it in tandem with the toy, to the surprised gasp of his lover.

With his mind still fixed on Darshan's panting figure, Hamish continued to stroke himself. Slow at first, then faster as the man in his thoughts neared the end of their time together, his lover bucking and cursing in what Hamish suspected had been several languages.

In the darkness of his room, his breath rasped loud in his ears. Between the memory and his hand, the edge didn't sit far from reach. Once he was spent, he laid still upon his bed whilst waiting for the furious pounding of his heart to slow.

Three heavy thumps connected with the door.

Hamish launched himself upright in the middle of the bed. His heart hammered anew, fear driving each quivering beat. He sat there like a cornered mouse, staring at the door, waiting for someone to throw it open and find him with a hand still down his smalls.

Who wanted him at this early time? Not the guards, for they would burst in with nary a care. Nor would Darshan be lingering on the other side. He doubted the man would bother with knocking, either. His brother? It couldn't be time to saddle the horses yet, could it?

When no one immediately burst through the entrance, he slunk off the bed and padded across the room. Opening the door revealed only the trio of guards. Two of them eyed him with their usual disdain until Ranulf cleared his throat.

"I thought I heard a knock," Hamish mumbled. Was he that far gone to be hearing things now?

"Your brother," replied the swordsman who Hamish still hadn't caught the name of. "Prince Gordon, your highness," he added as if Hamish had somehow forgotten the name of his sibling. "That is... I meant to say, the knocking was his doing. Said a few bangs would be enough to wake you. Also said to let you ken the guards are readying the horses for your journey."

Nodding and thanking the man, Hamish closed the door and set about his usual morning routine, bemoaning the lack of a fire in the hearth and some warm water to bathe in. Still, nothing chased any residuals of sleep from the brain like freezing water on the essentials.

He had gotten quite good at finding most of the items in the dark, too. His personal pack of clothes and other travelling effects were already packed and waiting, leaving him with only the need to don his warmest clothing and be off.

Except there was one thing he hadn't done earlier...

Scooping up the box from the bed, he tucked it into his private chest of effects. Unlike the rest of his quarters, only he possessed a key. If his mother sought to rummage through his belongings whilst he was gone—and he was in no doubt that she did just that—then the toy would be safe.

He twisted the ring, sliding it up and down the finger. Should he remove that, too? Seemed a bit late for it. The band was snug enough to hold no fear over casually losing it. Hamish shook his head. If anything was likely to go missing, it was the ring. The safest place for it would be on his person.

Fastening the lock and grabbing his pack of personal belongings, Hamish vacated his room. The sun had yet to crest the horizon and warm the skies, which meant the hallways were dark save for a few lanterns spaced out far enough for the servants to see without wasting fuel.

His breath misted in the early morning air as he strode into the stables and fell into the familiar routine of gearing his mare. Around him, the guards and his brother did the same to the other horses. Although the travelling preparations were adequately lit by storm lanterns, their heat was nonexistent.

A cursory glance at the men revealed them to be the same three Gordon favoured for the journey; Sean, Zurron and Quinn. *Good.* Sean wouldn't bat an eye if Darshan chose to be less than discreet about his affections. Quinn might make a few course jokes but, being the youngest of them all, he'd be even less of a bother. And Zurron—

Hamish frowned. The pale-skinned man might be a bit of a prickly one given the company. He often forgot about Zurron's elven heritage. The man's parents were one of the few families who had chosen to settle this far north. Most elves came to Tirglas only after fleeing Udynea and seemed content to move on, likely pressing for the elven land of Heimat, rather than remain amongst largely-human settlements. *We'll make do.* It wasn't as if the man was likely to start trouble with Darshan.

He rubbed his arms, his thoughts idly turning to the bed he had abandoned what seemed like a lifetime before. He could easily leave the stables to slip beneath the blankets, content and warm. No one would stop him if he chose to stay.

On the other hand, returning to bed wouldn't grant him a fortnight of reprieve from looking over his shoulder every time he dared to be that little bit too friendly with Darshan.

Providing the spellster actually showed his face.

Hamish glanced up from tightening his mare's girth to eye the stable doors. Still no sign of his lover. Gordon confessed to waking the spellster, so it couldn't be a case of Darshan not knowing when they were leaving.

Had he chosen to stay? Hamish wouldn't blame the man, not after his mother's prying on where the aquamarine ring had come from. Thank the Goddess that Gordon had the brains to lay claim to the purchase or they'd never be allowed in the same building as each other.

"Staring at the door willnae make him appear."

His gaze slid to his brother, heat pricking his cheeks and amplifying the chill air. "Can we nae wait a wee bit longer?" Given that his niece's pony, Warrior, was geared and ready, it wouldn't take much out of their time to lash a few of Darshan's effects to the rest of their belongings and be on their way.

Gordon's mouth skewed to one side, his lips thinning. "If he's nae coming—"

"Maybe he got held up," Hamish blurted. He wrung his hands and toyed with the ring, twisting it one way, then another. "Or overslept." After last night's exertion, he wouldn't be surprised. They might not be able to wait for hours, but a moment longer was doable.

Gordon scoffed. "Or maybe he's a soft lout who'd prefer to sleep the morning away than set out on a fortnight long journey."

"Well now," purred a familiar voice. "I do believe my ears are burning."

Hamish ducked beneath his mare's neck to find Darshan leaning in the doorway with a small, leather pack slung over his shoulder. "I take it that you're joining us, then?"

"Indeed." He sauntered into the stables, his gaze casually taking in the mounts and people with equal interest. He zeroed in on Warrior and lashed his pack beside the other supplies already attached to the gelding's saddle. "Do forgive my tardiness. One of the servants had to track down a spare pack for my things."

"Did you nae already have one?" Hamish couldn't imagine travelling anywhere without a place to store his belongings. But now he gave it some attention, the bag seemed a little worn. Possibly one that had been stored in a corner somewhere for a long time.

Darshan shook his head. "I did not exactly expect to travel during my time here. Not on a fortnight-long excursion to a cloister, at any rate. Could have insisted we bring my travel chest along for the journey, but I anticipated we would not be taking a cart with us." Again, he took in the stable's interior, seemingly vindicating his choice. "And I am not that much of a prick to suggest otherwise."

"Just a wee bit of one, then?" Gordon shot back, grinning.

The spellster smiled up at him. It was the smile of winter wolves surrounding prey. "*That* depends entirely on my motivation. Those who cause me too much bother quickly find out just how much of a nuisance I can be."

"Nae doubt," Gordon murmured before clearing his throat. He lifted his head and in a far louder voice said, "Right lads, mount up. Let's see if we cannae get some distance under us before the sun's fully up. I'd like to reach Old Willie's by tomorrow morning."

Hamish climbed into his saddle, waiting for Darshan to do the same before they exited the stables.

"What is at Old Willie's?" Darshan asked, leaning over in the saddle to practically whisper in Hamish's ear.

"It's a small farming community," he replied before the combined racket of their horses on the cobbles blanked out any chance of talking further. "Gordon prefers to supplement our provisions whenever we can. He typically purchases whatever they can spare from their stock."

"And they will have enough?"

Hamish shrugged. "Always seem to." They had made the journey to the cloister often enough that he wouldn't be at all surprised to hear the folks at Old Willie's Farm deliberately kept a certain amount of provisions back expressly for their party to purchase. The people probably got more for it at home than selling at market, too. His brother tended to err on the generous side when it came to payment.

They approached the gates with Gordon at the head and the three guards bringing up the rear. The guards manning the gates saluted as they passed.

Free of the castle confines, they settled into an easy trot down the road leading to the city, their way lit by the last vestiges of lanterns staggered along the winding path. Their pace would slow once they reached the forest road and the surface became less predictable, but for now, he was content to let his mare have her say as to the speed in which they travelled.

Chapter 18

They had left the city far behind by the time the sun had fully crested the horizon. Hamish tipped his head back, letting his mare plod with the group whilst he basked in the quiet. Few people shared the road, enabling them to spread out along its breadth for a short while. Warbling coos picked up with the light; male grouse calling for a mate.

The lofty trees flanking the road were a mix of those that lost their leaves and ones which kept them. It left the forest with the effect of looking like a moulting chicken. A pity they weren't travelling in the summer when the foliage was thick and their height provided shade for a traveller. They tended to pose as a risk during the winter what with branches falling only to be noticed after the snow had melted.

Given the number of carts that had used the road for the Spring Festival, they could be certain of the main passage being clear. The road to the cloister would be another matter. Few went there unless they absolutely had no choice, even the priests overseeing the spellsters seemed to dislike being reminded where they were.

"Why do some of these trees have wispy leaves?" Darshan asked. His gaze hadn't left the trees since entering it. Hamish had mistaken the intensity of the man's look for apprehension. "Are they sickly?"

"They're nae sickly," Gordon replied, his brow furrowing. "It's what they always look like in the spring. They shed their leaves every autumn and start growing new ones after the snow melts. Is it nae like that in Udynea?"

"There are very few trees in Minamist, but we've an estate just near the border of Stamekia. Spent a few winters there in my youth. The trees near our house were lush and green all through the winter. Except for some of the nearby orchards. Are these fruit trees, perchance?"

Shrugging, Gordon glanced Hamish's way. His brother could march a company of soldiers through the densest of forests, but he was terrible at remembering much about the different trees beyond their uses. "It's just your usual forest," Gordon mumbled.

"Do none of the trees in Udynea lose their leaves, beyond the fruit trees?" Hamish asked. It seemed a bit farfetched, but the kingdom of Obuzan lay just across the strait south of them that the locals called Freedom's Leap and he had heard plenty of tales about their lands being nothing but untameable jungle in places.

"Some do, of course," Darshan confessed, shooting him a glance that clearly queried Hamish's acumen. "But it is more typically in the dry season—what I believe you refer to as summer—not winter." He frowned at the trees anew, seemingly disgusted with their lack of leaves.

Carts started appearing on the road as the sun rose higher. Some travelled alongside them for a spell, idly chatting about the weather or this and that rumour. But the larger flow of people were those hastening towards the city with their wares, likely trying their luck at the Spring Festival before buyers' coin pouches grew lean.

Gordon took the opportunity to buy a few supplies from a handful of the merchants, ambling beside the carts to bargain, then trotting back with his haul to divide it amongst them. For the most part, that haul consisted of withered fruits from the last harvest along with a few loaves of day-old bread.

They halted on the side of the road come midday to rest the horses.

Darshan groaned as he slithered to the ground. He took a few wobbly steps, massaging his backside and thighs as he stretched. "Well, that certainly tenderised the old buttocks." Even so, he made swift work of the saddle, unbuckling it and setting his gear at the base of a tree with the others.

Hamish reached for a loaf of bread stashed in his pack, giving a hunk to his mare to chew before her questing mouth could slobber over the whole thing.

"I'm surprised you've managed so well," Gordon said as he unwrapped a block of cheese bound in wax cloth, a parting gift from the castle kitchen. He broke off a sizable chunk and handed it to Hamish, swapping the cheese for some of the bread. "Wouldnae have thought you'd have many opportunities to spend the day on horseback."

Darshan laughed. "Not as much as I used to, sadly." He tethered the pony with the rest of the mounts, leaving them to quietly graze in the dappled light breaking through the branches. "But do you honestly think one gets to look this good just lazing around the palace? If I ate but only half of the rich food back home without some form of training, I would be the *size* of the palace by now."

"To be honest," Gordon mumbled around a mouthful of cheese and bread. "I wouldnae have a clue what you lot do down in that empire of yours."

Humming, Darshan broke off a piece of cheese as the block passed to him and popped it in his mouth. "Granted," he said after he had finished chewing. "We are not as ravenous as elves when it comes to sustenance, but magic certainly demands much of our energy."

"Aye, take Zur," Sean piped up, clapping a hand on his fellow guard.

Zurron grimaced and tugged at the hood of his cloak in an attempt to pull it over his head. Both Sean's arm and one of the elf's own ears seemed to hinder him.

Sean continued, oblivious to his companion, "I've seen him devour a whole lamb leg and *still* go looking for more."

"I have no doubt he has done so many times," Darshan replied, a faint smile lifting the corners of his mouth. He'd likely seen his fair share of elves and their eating habits, more than Hamish could say. "The dwarves have many theories about elves and food. I believe the current one is that, due to the sharpness of certain teeth, the original elves had a diet primarily of meat and they would have consumed a lot of it."

The elf fingered one of his canines, then ran the tip of his tongue over the points.

Odd. Hamish hadn't noticed their sharpness before. *Or their length.* Akin to that of a young bear in being slightly longer than the rest.

"The dwarves think elves were predators?" Sean mumbled, his brows pulled low in thought. "As in hunting down things bare-handed and all that?"

Bubbly laughter shook Darshan's body. He wiped a finger beneath his glasses, composing himself with a sigh. "I doubt they were anywhere near that primitive, not if they built the massive ships of legend. They would have had tools and weapons, same as us. Magic, too I believe. Although, hunting with a bow and arrow would have been far less taxing."

A deep rumbling chuckle emanated from Gordon, followed swiftly by a cough as he thumped on his chest. "If you think archery isnae challenging, then you've never loosed a single arrow."

"Not since my youth, but I do know that just having magic burns through energy at twice the rate of a normal man and using it can easily increase that to thrice again. Even then, it could cause a spellster to drop unconscious in their tracks if the strength is not controlled."

"I dinnae ken you could grow tired from using magic," Hamish said. There were plenty of childhood stories cautioning those who tried to take the easy route, often with the people in the tales always coming a cropper after taking that advice of some suspiciously-helpful spellster, but such tales had rung false to him once he deduced that the person *with* magic always seemed to win out. "Or that it caused that much of a toll on the body." Magic had an air of effortlessness about it.

"How else do you think we were capable of anything beyond the mundane? The power has to come from somewhere, but there is only so much magic a person can do at any one time. No matter how much people try to prove it wrong, magic is not an infinite source. It comes from inside us, as innate as your ability to breathe."

"But nae as natural," Gordon pointed out. "Or it wouldnae be difficult."

"And your breathing has never become laboured?"

His brother grinned. "Only when I've pushed meself well beyond me limits."

"Then you will understand when I say that magic is, in essence, a constant battle to remain within one's limits. It takes its toll. Severely, at times. Recuperation is required if used to excess. Your people are familiar with healing, correct? That is all your spellsters are allowed?"

Gordon nodded, clearly waiting for Darshan to reach his point. He likely recalled the exhaustion of their younger sister, Caitlyn, far better than Hamish could, being the first to find them in the charred undergrowth.

"Healing is simultaneously one of the most simplistic and difficult magics. Easy to begin, but hard to direct. Harder still to stop without training. In its natural state, it can tear the body apart whilst attempting to repair itself. Learning is not recommended for those weak in magic."

Hamish frowned. According to his younger sister, every spellster within the cloister was expected to learn how to heal others, for occasions where their talents might be needed. Did they also know the limits?

"Fire, ice, shields..." Darshan continued. "These are generally one of the first to be attempted by a young spellster. Their application is easy, but they take from within before using any means from without."

"How so?" Hamish queried.

"Fire." His lover held out a hand. The thin tongue of a flame danced on his palm. That hazel gaze remained focused on his conjuring, curious like he held a living thing. "It is a simple process, requiring heat, fuel and air. Any novice can do it. But the initial spark of that heat is generally from within themselves rather than the safer method of manipulating outside forces. Offering too much body heat can freeze a spellster where they stand."

Hamish rubbed at the scar hidden beneath the coils of his hair, recollecting the first time he had witnessed his younger sister using her gift. It had all been so fast. They'd been alone in the forests below the castle when ambushed. He had tried to protect them, but he'd been so young and their attackers were many. One had struck from behind, or maybe he had turned, then...

Fire. His memory was patchy in places afterwards, but he remembered flames pouring from his sister's hands like the breath of a demon and the men running in their wake. *And cold.* Caitlyn collapsed not long after the flames went out. He had crawled to her side, too dizzy to move any other way. Her skin had been deathly cold, as if she'd spent a winter buried in the snow. He hadn't ever considered she would've died had Gordon not stumbled upon them soon after.

"Ice is a little different," Darshan continued. "But it requires minimal effort to crystallise the water in the air." He held up his other hand and a thin veneer of frost coated his fingers. "It is rather similar to how nature forms such things." He shook his head and the frost melted away. "There are other, more complicated, forms of magic, but those three are widely considered as the basics."

"You never explained shields," Hamish pointed out before taking another swallow of water.

"Well, they are not something that is taught. The appearance is considered an instinctual reflex to danger but..." His eyes became unfocused for a breath. A shimmer of a filmy purple sheet of light surrounded him like a blanket. "It starts close to the skin and can, depending on the spellster's strength, be extended further to encompass a great deal to protect others as well as ourselves." The filmy barrier spread from Darshan's body, growing distorted until it had become a sphere. And still, it grew. The tingling edge slunk over them until everyone sat within. "However, the former is as much as a newborn can manage and all most rely on."

"A bairn?" Sean blurted, spraying food. "You mean a spellster new to this world can do *that*?" He waved a hand at Darshan's shield.

"Only in reaction to a pain stimulus. It is how we test for the ability in noble bloodlines."

Gordon's face darkened, a smouldering anger lighting his eyes. "You inflict pain on a newborn? Just to see if the bairn has magic in their blood?"

Darshan held up a hand. "A pinprick. No more. It is over in a heartbeat and causes no lasting ill effects." As quick as he had formed it, the shield was gone. "Not even to those who lack the spark."

Hamish tipped his head up to eye where the crest of the sphere had been. Raising a child who was capable of this had to be vastly different to the way childrearing was done in Tirglas. *Nae paddles on the arse, for one.* Certainly not after the first crack. "How do you stop wee bairns from burning down your houses?"

"That sort of magic does not manifest itself until about five years of age."

Quinn gave a low whistle. "That's a young age to have that sort of power."

Extremely young. Especially when most Tirglasian spellsters discovered their abilities in their seventh or eighth year.

Darshan chuckled. "Strength is something that typically grows with time and practice, but there have been cases of a young child's inexperience being behind a tragedy." His expression had sobered the longer he spoke until he stared at his meal from beneath heavy brows. "I believe that was the theoretical cause of a fire that gutted half of the Pits in Nulshar some years back."

"The Pits?" Hamish echoed. "What's—?"

"They're slums," Zurron answered, sneering. "Mostly full of former slaves and elves. Those who are sick or injured, who cannae work well enough for a better home, live there."

"And not generally safely," Darshan added. "Or with much degree of health. My father has spent the better part of his life as *Mhanek* trying to find a way to improve the lives of people there. But I fear it may take the rest of it to see any sort of movement there."

The group fell silent. They munched down the rest of their lunch, watching the odd cart go by and occasionally speculating what was within the sacks. Once everyone had eaten their fill, they threw the gear back onto the horses and returned to the road.

They encountered a few carts heading towards Mullhind—sadly carrying no more food than a traveller needed—but the vast majority seemed to have already passed by. Fewer still came by as they veered off the main stretch for the less-maintained road that would lead them to their destination.

"I would like to query one small detail," Darshan eventually piped up, glancing over his shoulder at the guards who had, since lunch, been silently trailing them. "Will three men be enough to keep us safe?"

"Why wouldnae they be?" Gordon replied, his brow furrowing in confusion.

"What if we are attacked? You must admit, three princes is a respectable target."

"I dinnae think the wildlife care who we are. And the bears are nae too much of a problem at this time of year, you'd be lucky to *see* one let alone have it bother you. Plus, with me brother around, we'll be fine."

"Why?" Darshan's cheeks fattened with humour. "Does he speak bear?"

Gordon laughed. "Nae, but he can shoot them dead in the eye on the first go."

Darshan swung his head around to shoot Hamish an incredulous look. "Really? Well, I hope we have no cause for you to use such a skill. But what of brigands?" he asked Gordon. "Would they not seek to rob us?"

"You'd be hard-pressed to find folk like them around here. It's easier for them to find honest work in the farms, where food and a warm bed are part of the deal, than trying to pick out a living hiding in the forest. Those few who dare are soon caught or find themselves picked off by nature."

"I find that highly implausible. The roads leading to Minamist are generally the worst for banditry."

"Does your army nae patrol the imperial roads?"

Hamish held his breath. That question came perilously close to fishing for defence and tactics information.

Darshan laughed. "The imperial army patrol roads? The general would not have them be seen doing something so mundane. He only tolerates them getting involved in feuds only at the behest of the *Mhanek*." He shook his head and gave a hiccupping snort. "No, the empire has an entirely different sector responsible for her roads and the safety of the people on them."

"And yet, people still try the bandit life?" Gordon pressed. "They're *that* desperate?"

"Desperation comes in many forms. Your first thought was of hunger and the home comforts of a bed. We must contend with war-broken families, slaves who have been abandoned or fled, even those who have been set free without the proper freedom fee..." He wrinkled his nose and pushed his glasses back up it. "People are doing that more and more, you know. It is a disgusting trend, worse than abandonment."

Hamish shook his head. He didn't understand one piece of what Darshan was saying. Leaning back to give his brother a surreptitious glance revealed Gordon to be none the wiser, he frowned at Darshan as if the man had lost his mind.

Darshan huffed and rolled his eyes. "When a slave is unwanted by their owners, a large portion of them are sold at market, *but—*" He held up a silencing finger as he audibly strained his voice in emphasis. "—there are a few who choose to free them. A fee is then paid to both the empire and the ex-slave. It is supposed to be enough to see them settled into a new life, but it often barely covers a single meal, if they see a single coin at all."

"I ken all about what can happen to slaves, your highness," Zurron muttered behind them.

Hamish twisted in the saddle to eye the pale-skinned guard. "Were you nae born in Tirglas?" He had spent so many years travelling alongside the man that he sometimes forgot Zurron had different experiences of the world, but surely the man would've mentioned being from another land.

"I am," Zurron replied. "As is me mum. It's me dad who came from the empire. He was just a wee lad still clinging to his mum's apron, granted, but the memory of scraping by for weeks with only a few straps of hide to feed him isnae one that goes away easy. His mum probably would've sold herself right back into slavery if it hadnae been for him."

"An all too common tale, I am afraid," Darshan murmured. "The empire is in a constant race to help her people. But there are only so many resources, so many hands willing to aid. A lot of people fail to see the problem, or simply do not wish to see, until it becomes theirs."

"And some sit up in their gilded towers seeing all and nae caring about a thing," Zurron muttered.

Darshan's lips flattened, but his gaze remained on the road before them.

The daylight had gained a grey edge by the time they turned off the road and aimed for a clearing they'd used a multitude of times during their journey to the cloister. Quinn led the way, as he always did, scratching fresh marks into the same trees as he went.

The clearing came into view and Hamish sighed. Winter hadn't been at all kind to this patch. An oak had succumbed to the weather, its fallen branches stretching across much of the space like the bones of a giant. The branches of other trees had also snapped off, dotting the edges of the clearing.

"Well, this is less than ideal," Gordon muttered, swinging down from his saddle. "Looks like we've a fair bit of work, lads."

Hamish dismounted and secured both his mare and his brother's gelding to one of the heftier-looking fallen branches whilst Gordon unpacked the axes. He had expected the branches, there was always at least one every time they settled here, but trying to shift an entire felled oak? They could be at it for hours and not make a dent.

If their sleeping arrangements had consisted of a single tent, then there was already ample space cleared and far from any tree. But given they all couldn't cram into one tent, they would need to make more room. *At least there'll be some wood.* Not much, given that most of the branches would be sodden from their winter on the ground, if not starting to rot.

Hefting his axe, Hamish set to chopping off some of the larger branches to a substantial log. If he could cut close enough to the main piece, then he might've been able to roll it clear or even to the centre camp for a seat.

He eyed the oak after each swing. Even if they left the main trunk alone, they could be here for some time moving the branches from the middle of the clearing. *A shame.* There was a small cliff-side view not far from here that he wanted to show Darshan before the sun set. *Guess I'll nae be doing that.* Perhaps on the way back to the castle.

"How can I help?" Darshan asked as the rest of them secured their horses and set to work on the smaller branches.

"Just stay out of the way, your imperial highness," Quinn replied, his usually gravelly voice oddly light. "We've got this." A few of the branches were easily dealt with, being small enough to drag under the trees, but the vast majority of them would require sectioning into more manageable chunks before attempting any sort of movement.

"We would've had a better handle on it if we'd brought a few lines of strong rope," Zurron muttered. He tugged at a branch end almost as big around as his middle. Although the elf was the shortest of their group—by how much, Hamish didn't know, but it had to be over a foot of difference from himself—his strength and stamina in hunts often made up for the lack of height. Even so, the branch didn't budge. "The horses could've moved these bastards nae trouble."

"You're welcome to go back for some," Sean quipped as they continued to chop at the wood.

"Feck off," Zurron snapped back. "I'm nae riding back in the middle of the night."

"But I thought elves could see in the dark," the other guard needled. They were all well aware just how much better the elf's vision was at seeing even in the blackest night when compared to theirs. Zurron often boasted about it.

Muttering and swearing under his breath, Zurron stormed over to a smaller branch and started hauling it towards the tree line. "Just because I *can* be," he growled between tugs as the branch snagged on bush and grass. "Doesnae mean I *want* to be out in the dark on me own."

Darshan shuffled on the spot near the horses. The silvery off-white shade of his sherwani practically glowed against the shadowy backdrop of the forest. "I am quite certain I can assist with—"

"Quinn's right," Gordon said. "Staying put is your best course of action. You're nae built for this task and I wouldnae want to have you break something trying." He swung his axe at one of the oak branches. The outside caved in to reveal the powdery white core of decay. Giving a disgusted grunt, his brother moved on to the next branch. This proved to have a little more substance. "Mind the horses if you feel the need to be useful."

Hamish winced. Yes, Darshan would likely get hurt if he dared to attempt something as foolhardy as moving a branch as big as himself, but Gordon could've delivered that with a little more tact.

Sean let out a strangled yelp.

They all spun to find the thick branch Zurron had abandoned was wobbling in the air. It swung on its axis, ponderous and deliberate. When the length of the branch was finally lined up with the trees behind it, the branch sailed backwards to land amongst the undergrowth with the hearty thump.

He glanced at Gordon, praying his brother had witnessed the same spectacle. By the way everyone eyed the branch, he could be certain it wasn't just him seeing things.

"As I was saying." Darshan still stood by the horses, his arms folded with his hips and shoulders tilted cockily.

"That's a neat trick right enough," Gordon drawled, rubbing his chin.

Hamish rolled his eyes and hacked off another piece from the branch he worked on. Trust his brother to act as if he hadn't just witnessed a spellster effortlessly heft around a branch almost as big as himself.

Gordon jerked a thumb at the oak. "But *that's* the bugger we have to contend with. So unless you can lift that out of our way, I'd suggest—"

"Watch the horses," Darshan said, marching past Gordon to eye the oak close up.

"Excuse me?"

Even as his brother argued with the spellster, Hamish quietly abandoned his axe in favour of untying his mare.

"You heard me," Darshan retorted over his shoulder. He laid a hand on the fallen trunk, pressing against it. "Naturally, I would not dream of telling you how to control your animals, but this is going to make a lot of noise."

"You're pulling me leg, right? You're nae going to be able to lift *that*, magic or nae." Nevertheless, Gordon edged towards the tethered horses. As did the three guards.

Darshan planted himself before the tree. "I can certainly give it a try."

Hamish thought back to the night his lover managed to suspend him outside the window. Lifting Hamish seemed to have demanded quite a bit of effort on Darshan's part. He'd rather the man didn't strain whatever the spellster used to focus his power. "You really dinnae need to." If they chopped off the bothersome branches, then Darshan could aid in their removal.

The tree shifted slightly, groaning and dropping pieces as the fragile, hollow shell that remained of the trunk slowly crushed in on itself with the pressure. A faint purple sheen surrounded the tree—a shield?—there for only a moment before failing, much as it had when trying to contain Hamish. A crack, akin to the shattering of dry bones, echoed across the clearing.

Hamish tightened his grip on the reins as his mare launched backwards with a snort. Her focus remained on the tree, her eyes wide enough to show white all around. "It's all right, lass," he murmured, sure his attempts to soothe her weren't getting through.

The others struggled similarly. Sean and Quinn both fighting to control not only their mounts, but also Darshan's pony. Warrior lived up to his name, pulling back on the reins and kicking out at the bigger horses. Mercifully, each strike missed, if by mere inches at times. The last thing they needed was for one of the horses to break a leg.

"Let me have him," Zurron said. He tossed the reins of his placid-in-comparison gelding to Gordon and vaulted onto the pony. Warrior reared, shaking off the other two men, and took off into the forest with the elf clinging to his saddle.

"Leave him," Gordon commanded as the other guards went to follow. "He'll be back when the noise stops." Like the horses, the elf was capable of hearing far better than the average human. If anyone would know when Darshan was done moving the tree, it'd be Zurron.

We should've gone with him. Although, hearing the dreadful cracking without seeing the cause might've been worse for the horses. How much longer would it take? He risked a glance over his shoulder at Darshan.

The oak trunk sat suspended a good few feet in the air. Hamish blinked hard to clear his eyes. Lifting a branch that probably weighed as much as himself was one thing, but an entire tree?

"By the Goddess," Gordon breathed. His brother's mouth hung open like a broken trap.

Rocking and groaning, the tree rotated to line up with the clearing's edge, much like what the man had done with the branch. Only this time, Darshan swayed along with the motion. He no longer stood quite so confidently, his knees sagging to the point where they leant against each other.

Would the tree also fall if Darshan dropped where he stood?

Thrusting his mare's reins into Quinn's hands, Hamish hastened to his lover's side. "That's enough." He laid a hand on the spellster's shoulder, gently least he startled the man.

Darshan's body trembled, straining as if he lifted the tree not by magic, but with his entire body. By his rasping breath, Hamish would forgive anyone for thinking the man had sprinted all the way here from the castle. Those hazel eyes were glazed, focused only on what was ahead of him, and the angle of his jaw suggested clenched teeth. Hamish wasn't even certain he had been heard.

The tree rocked away from them, branches snapping against the ground. The main trunk drifted closer to the ground with every foot it neared the tree line. It continued on that way until returning to the forest floor where, with a final grunt from Darshan, it rolled against the other trees. Some of the sturdier branches still encroached on the clearing, a mere handful compared to the main bulk.

Darshan sagged to the ground as if he were boneless. Sweat ran down his face, dripping from his tuft of a beard. "I trust," he said, puffing at every other word. "That is a sufficient amount of room for the tents?"

"And then some." There were a few spindly branches scattered around the clearing, but the rest of the group would be able to make swift work of them. "You really didnae have to lift the whole thing."

Although his lover's head remained drooped, Hamish was certain he caught the edge of a glare. He knew that expression well, had seen a similar one on Nora's face right before she proved some unbeliever wrong.

Darshan exhaled in one long sigh, his exhaustion seemingly slipping away. "Yes, well." He got to his feet and adjusted his sherwani, brushing the dirt off the hem and his knees. "As much as watching you get all sweaty and exhausted whilst chopping wood would have been entertaining, such effort was uncalled-for."

Effort? Hamish wordlessly wiped his lover's brow. His skin was a blotchy mix of ruddy and pallid. How much had this little display taken from the man? He wrapped an arm around Darshan's shoulders, subtly assisting the spellster as they casually wandered to a branch that looked strong enough to hold the man. "How about you rest here for a bit and leave the cleaning up to us?"

A small, slightly amused, smile tweaked one side of his lover's moustache. "That sounds adequate."

Hamish returned to the middle of the clearing. Already, Quinn had dragged a few of the more troublesome branches to one side. They'd likely use what they could from them for firewood, but a lot of the rubble was a crumbly mess.

Hamish glanced over at the horses as he helped the other guard. A few of the less-spooked mounts were tethered with both Sean and Gordon busy reassuring the rest. There was no sign of Zurron, but the elf was likely deliberately taking his time to calm the pony and cool him down. *As long as he gets back before dark.* Warrior still had one of the tents strapped to his saddle and Hamish didn't fancy wrestling with it in the light of a campfire.

Chapter 19

Zurron had returned by the time they had cleared a sizable patch for camp. The pony was sweating heavily and needed to be dried off, but he seemed to have more-or-less settled, calming further once amongst his fellow horses. A good thing, otherwise they would have no choice but to waste tomorrow returning the pony to the castle. *And Mum will insist on several more guards.*

With all the horses content to graze, their gear was stripped and tossed into a pile in the middle of the clearing. Gordon and Quinn wasted little time in pitching the tents, whilst Zurron vanished back into the undergrowth on his own two feet in search of more firewood.

Sean squatted before the campfire, feeding twigs and splinters of kindling into the flames. Soon, the man would set about preparing dinner. It wouldn't be anything fancy, likely a light broth to soften the remainder of the stale bread, but it'd help keep them warm once the light faded and the spring chill encroached.

Nevertheless, Hamish's stomach grumbled at the thought of food. He still had the last few pieces of cheese and a hunk of bread in his pack. It wouldn't be enough to feed him but it would serve as a morsel to tide him over.

Dumping the last of the good wood near Sean, Hamish idly made his way to where Darshan still sat on the thick branch. The piece had clearly fallen from the rockbark tree encroaching on the clearing and, even though it would be a challenge, they had debated hacking it up for the fire before abandoning the idea. Whilst it appeared to be dry enough, the main section was covered in knots that could break the strongest of axes.

"So," his lover said as Hamish settled on the branch. "Will all our nights be in such crude shelters?"

"For the most part. There's a few farms along the way, we might be able to spend a night in their barns."

Humming, Darshan propped his chin on the back of an upraised hand and watched as Quinn and Gordon pitched the second tent. "How terribly rustic."

"I take it you've nae slept in anything beyond a bed." He wouldn't be surprised to find the man had never been beyond the confines of the imperial palace. It would help explain how the Udynean thought his thin, silvery-white sherwani was a good choice for travelling.

"Not since I was a child and it was more of a novelty even then." A frown drew his dark brows even with the edge of his glasses. He twisted in his seat, his head still leaning against his hand. "I thought your people had inns? Or was I told wrong? Travel down any Udynean road long enough and you are bound to come across one before sunset."

"On the main roads, aye, there are inns everywhere. If we kept travelling past Old Willie's for a half-day, then we'd strike one at a wee village." He had only been there the once whilst travelling with Nora on their way through to her husband's lands further north. All he remembered was a view of the sun sinking over a steel-blue sea.

He couldn't journey that far from the castle anymore. None of them were allowed such freedom, but he could show Darshan a sliver of that same beauty. Hamish eyed his lover. Whether that time was now or on the way back depended on how well the spellster had recuperated from his tree-lifting attempt. "You seem to be feeling better."

Darshan inclined his head. "I am."

"Come with me, then." In one smooth movement, Hamish bounced upright and tugged Darshan to his feet. "Quick, before the light fades altogether." He strode across the clearing before his lover could object, towing the man by an unresisting arm and halting once they reached the opposite tree line.

"And just where are you going?" his brother called out.

"We willnae be long."

"Dinnae expect your tent to be ready and waiting when you get back."

Hamish waved off the threat. As much as his brother blustered and nagged, Gordon wouldn't leave him to wrangle with the canvas sheets on his own any more than he would allow Hamish to sleep out in the open all night.

They pushed through the undergrowth. It wasn't thick, mercifully, but Darshan still clung to the lower half of his sherwani. Hamish paused every few feet to cut a fresh marker in the bark of each tree he past. Even though he was certain he knew the way back without such a trail, it was better to err on the cautious side.

The trees grew stunted the closer to their destination, eventually giving way to hardier bushes that they were forced to skirt or squeeze past. The crash of waves beckoned them on.

Darshan cut a path through the denser patches in the bush. How? Hamish wasn't entirely sure, seeing just a flash of purple slice the air before the offending foliage fell only to be swept away by a magical blast of wind.

Finally, pushing through the last of the brush, they halted on a small patch of weedy grass and rocks.

Hamish breathed deeply of the sea air. The hook-like curve of the harbour was more noticeable here, dominating the left horizon. *We're nae too late.*

Twilight turned the ocean into the shade of rich whiskey. A hazy band of clouds, flushed an orange-pink, hovered on the horizon. The sun peeked through them like a fiery jewel. If he shaded his eyes and squinted, the other side of the harbour came into view as a dark line near the water's edge. "Isnae she beautiful?"

Like the trees at their back, Darshan remained silently standing at his side. The waning sunlight glinted off his glasses, but his lover's smile was clear enough.

"Do you have views like this back home?" He knew Minamist was situated in an almost lagoon-like harbour, but not if there were any cliffs to get a decent view of the sun sinking into the horizon. He would often watch the day's end from the tower, eking out the most from each ray before the guards came for him.

"Ocean views, yes. The imperial palace has a magnificent one. Not wholly clear all the way to the harbour pass, though. And it looks nothing like this." He finally tore his gaze from the sunset to face Hamish. "Is this what you wanted to show me?"

Hamish nodded. "I thought you might like a last look at something familiar before we head inland tomorrow."

"So soon? A pity." His gaze returned to the sunset, although his head cocked Hamish's way. "Can we linger here for a while? Just until the sun goes down?"

"Sure. The campsite's nae far." And, even if it had been, the spellster was more than capable of lighting their way until they reached the others. He held up a small sack of wax cloth and waggled it. Dinner would be some time regardless of where they waited for it. "I already nicked some grub. I was saving this for tomorrow, but I reckon you need it more after the tree." He peeled back the cloth to halve the remainder of the cheese and hand a piece to his lover.

"I could have survived until dinner, but thank you. A picnic on the cliff edge is a welcome relief from the forest." He settled on the ground, patting the earth next to him in invitation and smiling when

Hamish sat close by. "I do not believe I have seen so many trees for some years." He waved his piece of cheese around like a lecture stick. "This would all be farmland in Udynea. Has no one tried to tame these forests?"

Hamish shook his head. Maybe if the people had ready access to magic like it seemed most Udyneans did. It took a lot of men and sheer grit to maintain the farms already out there. Adding more would only spread people thin. And when it came to some dangers, superior numbers was often the one factor towards victory.

They chatted sparsely whilst eating. Darshan dared to attempt teaching him a smattering of Udynean to describe the sunset. It wasn't the easiest language to mimic. Hamish's tongue mangled quite a number of the words until his lover was laughing uncontrollably, trying to explain what he had actually said whilst tears continued to stream down his face.

Eventually, he gave up at Hamish's promise to practise.

"I see you are still wearing one of my gifts." Whilst that hazel gaze hadn't left the view since they had settled amongst the rocks and mossy grass, Hamish swore he felt the man's eyes boring into his hand all the same. "Are you not afraid you will lose it?"

"Are you nae concerned about losing your multitude of rings?"

Darshan lifted a hand, seeming to consider the wealth of precious metals and gems it bore. "I have worn these for long enough that I know losing them is somewhat difficult. Even consciously removing them takes some effort. I cannot imagine that ring has such a tight fit."

Hamish fiddled with the band, well aware the action was being noted. Maybe he should've left it back home. He could've tucked it into the box with the toy. Although the risk of losing the ring to prying eyes whilst he was gone seemed far more likely than having it slip off his finger out here. "Seems snug enough."

His lover casually lifted Hamish's hand to examine the ring. "A perfect fit, I would say. Without any need of adjustment, either. If I was a priestly man, I would say the gods rather declared it was meant to be."

"I honestly thought you were going to swallow your tongue when Ethan pointed out you were trying to put the ring on the wedding finger." The memory of Darshan standing there, shock draining the warmth from his olive-brown cheeks and turning his eyes as vacant as a pole-struck steer, was one that would be etched into his mind forever.

"I hope you will forgive me for putting you in such a spot."

"Nae harm was done." *If Ethan hadnae said...* Well, he wouldn't exactly have taken it as a proposal, but he could have. The difference in marriage traditions should have been one of the cultural differences Darshan's tutors would've focused on. Or were they really so inept as to not know? "As you said then, you dinnae ken."

Darshan muttered something under his breath. It sounded Udynean.

"What was that?"

"The gods suffer an act of ignorance the once," his lover dutifully translated. "It is from the *Book of Kailin*. He was a prophet of sorts. Mad as the God Jalaane. They say he spent a year in the desert bordering Stamekia towards the end of his prophet-hood, subsisting on nothing but sand and fresh air. Absolute poppycock, but people do like to embellish legends. He was rumoured to have returned home and slaughtered his wife because the gods told him to."

Hamish wrinkled his nose. "I dinnae think it wise to take advice from a murderer."

"Not in family matters, certainly." He peered at Hamish out the corner of his eye. "But I have been thinking… you and I would make quite the pair."

"In what sense?" Hamish mumbled around his final piece of bread.

Darshan shot him a meaningful look, one brow arching as if he couldn't quite decide if Hamish was that dense.

"Oh," Hamish murmured. "Oh!" His face fast grew uncomfortably warm. Darshan couldn't actually be meaning that they should make their dalliances a little more permanent. Or could he? Hamish cleared his throat, gagging on a few remaining crumbs. "You'll have to excuse me, I was nae expecting a proposal."

Shock widened those hazel eyes and naked terror slackened his lover's jaw. "I—"

"You were nae meaning it in that sense, I ken that." Still, even saying it aloud did little to hush the bitter whisper of disappointment that flooded his thoughts in the absence of relief. Only now he was faced with a negative answer did he realise he had been hoping for a different one. How long had *that* desire been lingering beneath the surface?

Darshan laid a bejewelled hand on Hamish's knee. "Do not misunderstand, *mea lux*. If I thought my father would approve of me bringing home a husband…" The words trailed off, a shy smile taking their place.

A warm flutter started up in Hamish's stomach, spreading until it suffused his whole body. He turned his gaze to their surroundings. It was the only way he could think of anything beyond kissing the man breathless. "*Mea lux*," he mused aloud. "You've called me that before." Several times whilst they were in the library. That'd been on the morning after their night together in the guest quarters. He had dismissed it since. "But you've nae given me a translation."

"Have I not?" Darshan cleared his throat when Hamish shook his head, his cheeks quickly turning a deep red. "It is a term of endearment."

"I gathered that by the tone." Did he mean it as genuinely as it sounded? All light and sweet? "What does it mean?"

If Hamish didn't think the man's cheeks could darken further, then they seemed happy to prove him wrong. "My light," Darshan whispered.

He ran the words through his head. "But you just told me the Udynean word for light is *haalen*." Did that only refer to sunlight? He hadn't said as much, but it was possible. Or was he lying about their meaning? That seemed just as likely.

"It does mean that," Darshan rambled, twisting around until he sat cross-legged before Hamish. "In Udynean. There are other words for it, of course, but *haalen* has a more widespread usage. However, *mea lux* is from the Ancient Domian tongue."

Wonderful. Yet another language Hamish had no experience with that the man seemed fluent in. He was really starting to feel like a barbarian. "How many languages can you speak?" And was Darshan going to attempt to teach him every single one?

"A number of them. Ancient Domian is..." His lover waved one hand in the air, rolling it at the wrist. "How do I put this? It is my mother tongue, the first one I spoke. You see, the Udynea Empire rather overran the Domian lands some hundreds of years ago."

"Your ancestors conquered, you mean. I ken about that." Udyneans were well-known for taking over lands, removing the nobility and planting one of their own at the top to continue running whole cities without disturbing the lives of common folk. He'd even heard tales of them adopting certain customs from the very lands they had conquered.

Wincing, Darshan bowed his head. "Yes, well the empire no longer seeks to expand her borders. But for some time now, being able to speak Ancient Domian fluently has become somewhat of a social status symbol amongst nobility and is taught first to all children of high birth. Naturally, we learn Udynean soon after, most times together."

"That's it? On top of Tirglasian, obviously." Three languages, two from childhood, didn't sound nearly as intimidating.

Darshan gave a sheepish smile. "Not entirely. I also speak Niholian and pick up a smattering more of Dvärg each time their hedgewitches visit the palace. I can also wish good health to the herd of a Stamekian nomad, although their language is a little more complicated to learn."

An incredulous huff escaped Hamish's lips. The man spoke all those languages, even only in part, and still considered *Stamekian* as complicated? "I hope you're nae planning on teaching me all of them, because I dinnae think there'll be time for additional lessons before you leave."

His lover fell silent, frowning at the ground. He plucked a budding daisy from the scrags of grass and rolled the stem between his thumb and forefinger. One by one, the petals fanned out and seemingly leapt off the flower to drop back amongst the dirt.

Hamish watched wordlessly. Speaking of Darshan leaving wasn't why he had come here, but there wasn't anything he could say to change the fact his mother was a stubborn woman and most certainly would refuse to let him go. If he had sired children, given her another royal line to cling to, then maybe. But if he had ever felt the desire to lay with a woman, then he wouldn't be here with Darshan now.

"Truthfully," his lover whispered. "I am still holding out that leaving will not be a solo affair." He glanced up at Hamish, peering over the rim of his glasses. "Despite her dislike of me, your mother seems genuinely eager for an alliance and the Crystal Court *is* lacking in an expert of Tirglasian culture. It is not as if you would be expected to share my quarters. There are entire wings set aside for our ambassadors."

Hamish nodded absently, his focus still mostly on the flower steadily losing its petals. His mother probably knew that. It didn't matter. He was a prince, he belonged in the castle.

Darshan shuffled closer until their knees casually touched. "Of course, with us so far from Tirglas and your mother's guards, we could continue our affair a little more openly."

And that was precisely what his mother suspected would happen. "Would your father nae object to his son fooling around with a man?" He knew things were different in Udynea, but his lover was still a prince. Surely, the *Mhanek* expected Darshan to have children of his own should he need to take the throne.

Just how far down the line of succession was Darshan?

Before he could ask, his lover chuckled mirthlessly. "If you had asked me a few months ago about whether or not my father cared when it came to who I slept with, I would have agreed with you. He rather despairs over the fact." Darshan ran a considering gaze over Hamish.

Heat started to warm his cheeks despite the cool ocean breeze.

"But," Darshan purred. "Not this time, I would think."

"So, he's objected in the past?" He should've known travelling to Minamist with Darshan sounded too easy. His lover would be bound by his own obligations to his family. Hamish wouldn't exactly factor into plans likely years in the making. "You dinnae strike me as the type to fash himself over what his father wants."

Darshan leant forward until his lips almost brushed Hamish's ear. "Can I tell you a secret?" his lover whispered conspiratorially as if they weren't sitting alone near the cliff edge. He waited until Hamish nodded before continuing. "Being sent here was somewhat of a punishment."

"Punishment?" Hamish echoed. The emperor thought sending his son to the other side of the continent, where Darshan was far from under his eye, could be considered in any way as a reprimand?

Tipping back, his lover nodded energetically. "Oh yes. I will admit, I was less than thrilled with the idea of venturing to a foreign land on my own, especially given that I was to learn what I could about your lands whilst journeying to it. But father insisted I take Countess Harini's position." He tipped his head, glancing over his shoulder at the forest as if to reassure himself they were alone. "Between you and me, I am certain he was the one to have her assassinated. Almost." If he was expecting Hamish to be shocked, he didn't seem disappointed in the lack of reaction.

"But why send you here?" Had Darshan's father been anything like Hamish's mother, he would've found himself under constant watch, not being allowed to stroll through a whole other kingdom.

All at once, Darshan straightened, his chest puffed out and his nose tipped to the sky. "*There are no men like you in Tirglas.*" His voice took on an inflection that Hamish guessed was meant to be his lover's father. "*It shall teach you discipline and respect for the law.*" His lover grinned, laughter hissing through his teeth. "And then I met *you* pretty much within an hour of setting foot in Tirglas. The gods have such a sense of humour."

Hamish remained silent. The Goddess didn't meddle in a single man's life like that. She was more focused on the balance of the world, keeping the sun rising and the tides flowing. People were just ants busying themselves through the years.

His lover's smile faded, bitterness darkening his eyes. "And then what do I do with my good fortune?" He threw his arms wide, rocking back to the point where he almost tumbled down. "Same as always. Mess things up for everyone but me."

"To be fair, things were going south before you arrived." Hamish had long since made peace with the knowledge that his life had more-or-less stagnated into a routine that saw him waking only for duty.

Darshan snorted. "That does not excuse my actions. Not then, not now."

"So, what happened that was so scandalous? Did you kill someone?" It didn't sound like something that would be of concern to an emperor, but if it was someone of equal importance, such as an ambassador or… "Did it have something to do with the one who wound up in your bed with another?"

Wrinkling his nose, Darshan flapped a hand as if shooing a midge. "That one was years back. My last foray involved a man who I had no idea was…" He frowned, his lips pursing. "No, that is not entirely truthful, I knew he was engaged and kept fooling around with him. Long story short, we got caught. Or rather he did. Word got out and it set a few noble houses against each other. Minor nobles, granted, but troublesome nevertheless. Father thought my attitude towards what I had done was unbecoming of a prince."

"I would think so. A prince has a duty to his family to assist in keeping the land running smoothly." At least, that was what his own father would've said.

Darshan chuckled. "He would be rather enamoured with you. I am…" That hazel gaze slid off into the distance, his shoulders sagging. "Not really what he wanted in a son."

"Sounds familiar."

His lover hummed an agreement. "Right down to him wanting me to marry and have children."

"You dinnae seem any worse for it." If anything, the man had been relatively shameless in his pursuit of Hamish and likely hadn't been hiding his wants in Udynea either. *Nae like me.* He had done his best to quash any desire towards men to no avail.

"Unlike your mother, my father saw little merit in curbing my desires. And he understands that even marriage would not have altered my affairs. It is not exactly unprecedented for a noble to have a lover, sometimes the same one for years."

"Is that what you have planned for me?"

Smiling, Darshan shook his head. "Of course not. You would be there as an ambassador, being my lover would be considered a perk rather than an obligation. I would not even ask you to stay exclusively mine if you found someone more to your taste."

"I thought we already established that I dinnae have any taste?"

Darshan grinned. "Besides, my father gave up on me marrying years ago—he just wants grandchildren now—so you most definitely would not have to worry about my wife." He whispered those final words, shuddering as if the mention was more of a curse. "I do not suppose we could turn this conversation to something more pleasant?" His lover pointed out at the sea, where the sun had half dipped beyond the crest of the hills. "Like that land over there perhaps?"

Hamish shrugged. "That's the Goddess' Hook."

"A name like that sounds to me like something with a legend tied to it."

"Aye." As old as the land itself. He turned to face the view, his heart skipping when Darshan sidled up to him, his face practically aglow with interest. "Do you really want to hear the story? It's a long one." And Gordon told it far better, but his brother wasn't nearby and probably wouldn't be inclined to crash through the brush just to tell the tale.

"I do not mind lingering here whilst you tell it, especially when staying includes such a magnificent view." He grinned rakishly, one brow arching as he gently elbowed Hamish in the side. "And the sunset is quite marvellous, too."

Heat flooded Hamish's face, even as he rolled his eyes. "I hope you're comfortable, because it really is a long story. Starts a long way back."

"That suits me fine, really." Darshan ran his fingers up and down the underside of Hamish's forearm, the caressing touch faint through the thick woollen sleeve. "I could listen to your voice all night."

"M-me—?" He clamped his mouth shut before making a bigger fool of himself. His voice was no different to anyone else's in Tirglas. Not especially deep like his father's or even close to the soft, melodic tone of Darshan's. Having his lover listening to him drone would likely put the man to sleep. "It's nae as long a story as *that*," he promised.

"Pity," Darshan breathed. "Although I am certain you could draw it out."

His face was already hot enough to rival the sun. Any warmer and he would melt. Try as he might, he struggled to think straight. *Breathe.* If he was going to tell any sort of story, being able to talk with some semblance of sense would be a must. He coughed in an attempt to clear his throat. "Like I said," he rambled. "Back before there was earth, there was the Goddess."

Darshan smiled, those hazel eyes glittering like a child at a festival. "A creation myth." The words practically purred with his delight. "I thought as much. They stopped telling them back home, too many contradictions." He clasped Hamish's knee, all but climbing him to get closer. "Do go on."

"All right," Hamish mumbled. He was going to keep things brief, but he had a suspicion that, even if he tried, his lover would tug every piece Hamish remembered free. "But next time you want to hear a legend, you can ask me brother."

Chapter 20

The sun had all but set by the time they left the cliff edge, only a thin crescent remained to light the sky a brilliant pink. Hamish glanced over his shoulder as he stepped beneath the trees. It was a shame to leave the last vestiges of daylight unwatched, but Darshan's shivering body necessitated they return to camp.

They could've lingered had he asked for his lover to heat the air around them, but the man had already done so much. And his own grumbling stomach needed more than a few crumbs to sate it.

Under the trees, darkness already reigned. His lover took the lead, holding a small globe of light aloft to illuminate the forest, whilst Hamish practically travelled at his hip to search for the marks he'd made and point out the direction. Not that he needed to indicate much for large chunks of the way, what with the path Darshan had cut through the bushes earlier.

Hamish eyed the globe of light during those times. It shone like a miniature sun, hovering just above Darshan's outstretched hand with no other apparent connection to the spellster, yet put out no heat like the flame the man had shown the children the other day. He wished he had known the spellster was capable of such things before they had left camp, then he could've alerted the others.

The light of a campfire broke through the undergrowth. Hamish tapped his lover on the shoulder. "You may want to put that out." He pointed to the globe. Entering camp like this was likely to have them full of holes from the guards' bows before they could be recognised. "Safety's sake."

Darshan said nothing, but the globe dimmed and vanished.

They stumbled through the rest of the bush in the dark, with only the campfire to guide them. After their seemingly brief jaunt through the clearly-lit bush, traversing the rest of the way had the feeling of an age passing.

Eventually, Hamish broke through the last of the trees with Darshan on his heels.

Four tents took up much of the clearing. Despite his brother's words on not setting it up for him, Hamish's tent squatted amongst the others. Whilst big enough to sleep two people, Gordon had stopped sharing the space with him after one too many nights of being jostled awake by what his brother had dramatically referred to as the demons struggling to escape via the portal in Hamish's mouth. *I dinnae snore that bad.*

Regardless, Gordon insisted on bunking alongside one of the guards—usually Zurron—whilst the other two also shared a tent. That left the fourth tent for Darshan. He hadn't seen it packed, but it looked to be the same one Gordon used when he took his daughter camping. It was a tiny thing, considered as being more suited for a child, but the spellster should fit.

Darshan sniffed as they neared the campfire. "What is that smell?"

On impulse, Hamish also inhaled. The vaguely meaty aroma of mushrooms greeted his senses, almost hiding the less pungent scent of turnips. He savoured the smell, peering into the pot at the bubbling brown liquid. Bits of chopped vegetables and fungi bobbed in the soup like half-sunken ships. He sat before the fire.

"That'd be dinner," Sean said, he stirred the pot, bringing the ladle up for a taste. "A bit longer ought to do it. Your people eat mushrooms, I trust, otherwise it's going to be just bread for you."

"Mush—?" Darshan frowned. "You mean fungus? Yes, but generally only the spotted ones and truffles are served at soirées. The rest is considered peasant food."

Sean's gaze slid from the spellster to Hamish as he leant closer to whisper in Hamish's ear, "Do you think their spotted mushrooms are poisonous like ours?"

Hamish shrugged. It was possible that Darshan wasn't meaning the brown and white ones that were known to cause hallucinations before a careless person spent a half-day vomiting and gasping for breath in-between, being lucky to survive beyond that.

"Are you forgetting spellsters can heal themselves as well as others?" Zurron said, settling down next to Sean. "Do you really think a bit of poison would bother him?"

Darshan's frown deepened, his gaze darting between the two guards. Clearly, he hadn't heard the first part of the conversation.

Bloody elf hearing. So often Hamish forgot that elven ears picked out sounds far better than any human—or even dwarf. And for all the conversations to barge in on... "We're nae trying to kill you," Hamish blurted, his face growing hot as his lover's brow twisted into a puzzled arch. "That is…" He glanced wildly over the others, searching for an out. "Have you lot nae eaten?"

Sean shook his head as he gave the pot's contents another stir before gingerly tasting a sip from the spoon. "About to, though." He sidled up to Darshan, giving the spellster a friendly nudge in the side with an elbow. "Speaking of magic, I dinnae suppose you'd care to give the fire a little kick in the guts for me?"

Darshan arched a brow at the man, likely wondering how the guard dared to be so familiar. Hamish couldn't imagine many common Udyneans having a chance to casually converse with an imperial prince, much less doing so.

And to ask for him to do such a mundane task, to boot. Hamish was surprised his lover showed only slight scepticism. Perhaps rumour did exaggerate on how poorly Udynean spellsters treated those ranked beneath them.

Nevertheless, red flushed across Sean's face, turning the man's ears a dusky pink. Had he realised just who he'd jostled and requested such an act from? "I— If you would be amenable to doing so, your highness. I've nae seen magic fire before."

Pursing his skewed lips, Darshan extended a lazy finger at the campfire. The flames leapt higher, licking at the pot suspended above it.

Sean whistled loud and long, eyeing the flames much like Hamish's nephews had done back in the archery range. "Right, lads," he announced, ladling a spoonful of soup into his bowl. "Grab yourself a bowl if you want some." He filled Zurron's bowl as the elf practically shoved it under Sean's nose. "You ken, before our resident bottomless pit goes for thirds."

Gently cuffing his fellow guard over the back of his head, Zurron sat down nearer to the spellster than Hamish thought the elf would want to be. Rather than devour his food with a single-minded determination like he had done during lunch, he slipped a hand into his pack in search of something.

Hamish fished out his own bowl from his pack, motioning Darshan to quickly do the same. If there were any leftovers after they'd all had a first fill, then Zurron would most certainly go for the rest.

Quinn was next, the man slurping his meal straight from the bowl almost before he had finished settling back on the ground. Gordon followed swiftly on the last guard's heels, leaving Hamish scurrying to aid his lover in relieving Darshan's pack of the single dish within. Like most of the times they journeyed to the cloister, Sean insisted they pack only the essentials. Anything beyond one bowl was apparently what the man considered as a luxury during travel.

The remainder of the bread was divided amongst them as they ate. A disjointed hush fell over the camp now that everyone had their dinner, broken raggedly as Quinn slurped his soup, smacking his lips every now and then. Sean drank much the same way, but far quieter. Gordon sipped at his meal, his gaze intent on the elf and spellster. Neither of the men had swallowed a bite. Zurron still wrangled with whatever he searched for in his pack, whilst Darshan had set his meal aside in favour of doing a similar amount of rummaging in his own pack.

"Lost something?" Hamish asked of his lover. Was it important? Something the spellster would need over the next fortnight? Could they get another at Old Willie's Farm or was it a specifically Udynean object?

Darshan grunted, pulling out a cloak from his pack before diving deeper into its dark depths. "I am merely looking for a spoon, but I cannot seem to—"

"A *spoon*?" Quinn laughed explosively, spraying droplets of soup. "We travel light. Nae a lot of necessity for spoons when you can slurp straight from the bowl. You want fancy, then you picked the wrong group to travel with."

Next to the spellster, Zurron silently withdrew two spoons from his own pack and handed one over to Darshan.

"Really?" Sean sneered. "I thought we agreed to only pack essentials?"

"They *are* fecking essentials," the elf snapped back. "Nae all of us are bleeding animals. Dinnae mind him, your highness," he said to Darshan, jerking his head towards his fellow guard. "I'm pretty sure he strains everything through that hairy creature he has living under his nose."

Hamish muffled a laugh under the pretence of rubbing a thumb across his upper lip. Like all the human men in Tirglas, Sean sported a thick beard, but his moustache spent a great deal of the time being fished out of the man's mouth due to the ridiculous length he allowed it to grow. Only his wife seemed capable of getting her husband to trim the wild thing.

"That may be so," Sean shot back, caressing his moustache as if soothing an offended beast. "At least I dinnae look like some wee, bare-skinned lad."

The elf spluttered, dribbling soup down his chin and back into his bowl even as he set his meal aside. Coughing and struggling to form a rebuttal, he glared at Sean.

"That is hardly a fair standard to hold him to," Darshan interjected. "No elf can grow facial hair. I would have thought you would be privy to such knowledge given that, as I understand it, you all travel together on a regular basis."

Zurron threw up his hands. "*There*, you see? It's just as I've been telling you all this time." He returned to his dinner, spooning mouthfuls in at a maddening pace.

"Isnae your dad half human, though?" Quinn murmured into the silence.

Over the elf's squared shoulders, Hamish caught Darshan wince. The man covertly increased the distance between himself and the two guards, keeping his attention furtively locked on Zurron.

Hamish hadn't given much consideration as to how the spellster actually viewed elves, and from what little he knew about Udynea—largely the rampant magic and slavery—nothing seemed to mesh with the thought of elves being given any sort of high standing, let alone actual notice by an imperial prince. But if Darshan thought such a question would cause conflict, then perhaps he paid more attention to them than Hamish had given the man credit for.

Returning partial focus to his near-empty bowl, Hamish kept one eye on his lover whilst mopping up every last drop of soup from the inside of his bowl with a crust of bread.

"What did you say?" Zurron asked of his fellow guard, his voice as frigid as the northern trade winds coming off the icecaps. "What has me dad's heritage got to do with you?"

Quinn shrugged. "Just wondering, can you technically be considered as elven if you're part human?" There was a shifty edge to the way Quinn eyed Darshan. What interference could the spellster do in the time it would take the two guards to come to blows? Would a shield be enough to stop them? Would it hold long enough for the men to cool down?

Zurron rocked back, his eyes growing wider and his pale skin turning a ghostly shade.

Darshan brushed back a lock of hair, the surreptitious rubbing of his temple with a little finger almost lost beneath the strands. He cleared his throat, but otherwise remained silent.

"Quinn!" Gordon hissed before Zurron could react or speak. "Did I nae warn you about bringing that up?"

"I'm just saying," the man replied, his sun-weathered face nothing but strained innocence. He held up his hands in peace. "I hear those snooty buggers up in Heimat willnae let the pointiest-eared elf past the border if they're half human. I only want to ken, exactly how much of an elven bloodline does it take before they're nae considered an elf?"

Zurron's face was no longer starkly pale. Instead, it had taken on an equally unhealthy shade of purple. His arms strained as if he fought something invisible, but Darshan showed no sign of constraining the man—the spellster even seemed somewhat sympathetic towards Zurron. So, was the elf actually restraining himself?

Hamish tried to recall the last time the pair physically clashed. He couldn't remember what about, only that it was a trivial matter coming to a head.

The elf had taken a fair number of blows from Quinn, who probably knew he had won only because he'd struck first and was a far bigger man. Most humans were. Even some of the children towered over the tallest of elves and Hamish would be surprised if Zurron was an inch over five foot. But the elf hadn't looked anywhere near as angry back then as he did now.

Quinn huffed and picked something out of his teeth. "You dinnae have to get all prissy about it. I dinnae care, I just thought you'd ken your own people." He shrugged, his dark brown gaze flicking Darshan's way. "But I guess you're nae interested in hanging onto that knowledge."

Wincing, Hamish set his bowl aside. He wasn't all that keen on having to restrain Zurron, especially if the man slipped free. The one thing he knew for sure about the guard was that he'd a kick like a mule and had broken various bones on people down at the docks with a well-placed foot. He'd vastly prefer not collecting it.

Zurron leapt to his feet, an echoing heat of the campfire raging in his dark eyes. The promise of murder twisted his lips, baring those uncomfortably long canines. If it wasn't for the fact the elf grappled for his belt knife, Hamish would've sworn the man intended to tear Quinn's throat out with his bare teeth.

"That's it!" Gordon roared. "Zur, sit down before I have him—" He jerked a thumb at Darshan, who sat in bewildered silence with his mouth wrapped around the head of his spoon. "—restrain you."

Quinn snickered, earning him a glare from every pair of eyes in the camp.

Swallowing his food, Darshan gestured at the two guards with his spoon. "I would vastly prefer not to have to break up a fight, but if it is needed..."

The elf sank back to the ground. He continued to glare at Quinn over the campfire. The heat in that gaze had dulled, although his eyes had gone harder than the chips of obsidian their colour mimicked.

"*Quinn,*" Gordon said, his voice dripping venom and blood. As always, the tone pinned the man in question to the spot without a single hand being laid upon him. "You will return to the castle at dawn and turn yourself in for disciplinary measures. And dinnae think you can sidestep that like a snake because I *will* be sending a pigeon once we arrive at Old Willie's. We'll make the trip fine without you."

"But I was just—"

Gordon cut him off with the dismissing wave of a hand. "I dinnae care what you thought you were just doing. You've been warned. Be lucky I'm nae sending you on your way now or without a horse. Because I can and will order it if you continue. For now, I think it's best if you retire for the night."

Quinn clamped his mouth shut so tight that his lips disappeared beneath his beard. He rose, slowly and eyeing Darshan the entire time, before stalking off to the tent he shared sleeping quarters with Sean.

Zurron's sharp gaze followed the man and he glared at the tent for some time after.

The rest of them returned to their meals, occasionally peeking at either the elf or the tent. Hamish dared to glance at his brother in an attempt to gauge his thoughts on the matter. As commander of the royal guards, he had the power to send either guard wherever he deemed acceptable.

Gordon sat with his back pole-stiff. He chewed with that dead-eyed, brow-knitted expression that spoke of wheels turning. Unlike the rest of them, his gaze never left the elf.

Were they going to have to restrain Zurron until the morning? The man didn't seem the type to start anything violent. As a whole, elves didn't have an altogether decent reputation, with those outside of the nomad caravans often labelled as troublemakers and murderers.

With the majority of the elves passing through, those who stayed in Tirglas bore the brunt of such a reputation. More often than not, it led to them proving certain opinions right. Zurron was one of twenty-four elves in the whole guard—often sent on their duties in pairs to limit this sort of behaviour.

But if this was how a man like Zurron got treated by someone Hamish had thought was the elf's friend, then he wasn't surprised some elves retaliated violently. No man should be expected to weather being constantly pushed down.

Only when Quinn showed no sign of leaving the tent confines did Zurron relax. "What kind of world do we live in?" he muttered shaking his head. "I expected a remark like that to come from someone like..." The elf waved his hand, gesturing in Darshan's general direction. "Well, like *you*, nae me own kinsmen." He wrinkled his button nose, turning the tip upwards, and added, "Nae offence, you understand?"

Darshan hummed consideringly. "I do. Although, I would not have spoken so crudely even if I did not already know the answer. At least when it comes to the outlook of Udynean elves."

"Oh aye?" Zurron arched a brow and tipped his head back. "And what do they believe?"

"You understand this is merely an outlook by those working in the imperial palace?" Darshan cleared his throat once Zurron nodded. "You see, once particular defining elven features have vanished to the point where they can pass as humans, most within the palace—even the city, really, there are quite a few part-elf, part-human children—seem to consider themselves as human. Takes around two generations of breeding with humans. Or three, depending on how virulent the elven bloodline is."

The elf squinted, the faint gleam of light twinkling on the thin slit between his lashes the only evidence he saw anything. "What features would they be?" The words pierced the air with a note of already having been answered.

Whilst the pointed ears were a strong feature of elven blood, it wasn't the only one. Beyond their short stature and the elongated canines, there was the eerie length of their fingers. Although not noticeable at any great distance, once Hamish had first spotted it on a stablehand several decades back, he hadn't been able to keep himself from staring. They weren't creepily long, just an inch or so, but it was enough to lift the hairs on his neck that time. Learning it was natural and not some monster of lore trying to pose as an elf had also helped.

But to see such a feature on an otherwise human-looking person would certainly bring stares and speculation in several circles. Enough to ostracise the individual? He wished he could be certain of the outcome there.

"As you seem to have already guessed, the point in the ears is generally the last thing to go," Darshan murmured. "It is not uncommon to see some attempting to hide the smaller tips." His lips curved into a smile slightly on the watery side. "Although, I am quite certain that, if one of them ever felt the need to travel there, they would be welcomed into Heimat regardless."

Zurron's jaw twitched from side to side as he appeared to mull over the words. "Are they ashamed to be part elven?"

"More, I believe, searching for a better life. There are still places, social heights, barred for elves." Darshan bit his lip and toyed with the tuft of his beard. "I think your father and grandmother would know that better than I. It *is* changing, albeit very slowly. The current council rather considers it as anathema."

"Nae doubt because of the rampant slavery in your lands," Sean murmured. The man had silently inched closer to his fellow guard. Seeking to protect. Who? Hamish wasn't entirely certain there.

He glanced over his shoulder at the tent. *No sign of Quinn.* That ruled out one scenario.

Darshan's eyes slid shut. "*That...*" His whole body seemed to deflate at the word, his breath gusting through his barely-parted lips. "Certainly does not help matters. It may come as a surprise, but not everyone in Udynea is happy with the current situation in regards to slavery and the number against it rises with each generation. Will they abolish it within our time?" He spread his hands wide and shrugged.

They finished their meals in silence, beyond a brief bicker between Sean and Zurron over who would polish off the remains in the pot. As always, the elf won and happily consumed the spoils of victory. The act was almost normal enough to make Hamish forget all that had happened since sitting by the fire.

Talk turned to the usual discussion of which duo went on night watch and who with. Zurron, as always, opted for the final watch. He preferred taking it alone so that there were, as the elf put it, no clumsy humans to distract him. The other two guards generally took the first watch together, leaving Hamish and his brother to take up the midnight hours. That would likely change after tonight with Quinn returning to the castle.

Hamish stood, stretching the kink out of his spine. He grabbed his pack and, with a nod to his companions, sauntered off to bed. They'd be up at first light and he aimed to get as much sleep as possible before his time on watch.

The inside of his tent held only a few woollen blankets folded near the entrance. Tossing his pack to one side, he laid one blanket on the ground. To look at, they weren't anything fancy, but they were sturdy, practical and, above all, warm.

He bundled himself up in the other blanket and pillowed his head on an arm. The light of the campfire danced across the tent wall before him, throwing odd shadows as the men outside moved. Closing his eyes was enough to throw the world into darkness, but as much as he tried to sleep, his mind raced faster than a boarhound on the scent.

Tomorrow, they would reach Old Willie's Farm around midday. By the middle of the afternoon, they would've taken their first steps on the road leading towards the Crowned Mountain, where the cloister nestled in the foothills.

Would their path be clear? Whilst there were no actual villages, the land between here and the cloister had a few sizable farms. The farmers might not have magic to aid in the removal of downed trees, but Hamish found it hard to imagine they'd suffer much blocking their way for long.

Sleep had just begun to claim him when a thump from within the tent jolted him awake.

Scrambling to sit up, he came face to face with Darshan kneeling just inside the entrance. The tent flap fluttered in the wind, thin streams of moonlight peeking through the gap. "What—?"

"It is *freezing*." Darshan was wrapped in a thick blanket and still trembled as he crawled along the ground. Although Hamish couldn't quite make out the man's expression, there was the distinct energy of a glare directed his way. "How can you travel like this?" his lover demanded.

Even with his heart hammering, a puff of laughter shook Hamish's body and eased his muscles. He leant back on his arms. "It's nae that bad. You should try it in the winter, when there's snow." They didn't typically travel far then, but there'd been a few times in his youth where braving the cold had sounded like the sort of challenge worthy of a man.

Via a flicker of moonlight, he caught Darshan pull a face as the man imperiously flapped his hand. "Move over. If we are to traverse through this frigid clime, then you are keeping me warm." He flopped onto the ground and rolled over to present his back. "I swear this bloody place is going to be the death of me."

"Aye," Hamish chuckled. "Pay nae mind to the bears and rogue boars that can gore a man to shreds in seconds, it's the cold that'll kill you."

A soft, unamused grunt emanated from the bundle of blankets.

Hamish wrapped an arm around the pile. The sweet scent of whatever Darshan put in his hair still clung to the strands. Had he brought it along with him? What of other lotions? "I could warm you a lot better if you were naked, you ken," he murmured into the man's ear.

Silence greeted his suggestion.

He waited for some sly remark or a comment on his boldness, but nothing was forthcoming. *Maybe he really is cold.*

"That is some sort of Tirglasian trick, right?" Darshan wriggled deeper beneath the blankets. "You shall not get me to shed a single layer."

Still chuckling breathlessly, Hamish slithered beneath the blankets to the muffled squeak of Darshan's protests about letting the night air in. "Then I guess I'll have to come in after you." He felt his way along his lover's side, searching for the hem of the man's undershirt. However much Darshan protested, he had discarded at least the outer layer of his garments.

At last finding a gap in the soft fabric, Hamish worked his fingers beneath. His lover's skin was chill against his fingertips. "Goddess' breath, you're as cold as an orphaned lamb."

"What did I tell you?" Shivering, Darshan scrunched tighter on himself. "And *you* are letting all the heat out," he grumbled.

Hamish pressed himself against Darshan until his chest was flush with his lover's back. He rubbed at his lover's arms, using the friction to work some heat back into the limbs. "Can you nae heat up the inside of a tent with magic?"

"I can," Darshan conceded. "But *not* when I am asleep. Not safely." He squirmed beneath the blankets, twisting around like a rebellious pup on a leash. "How can you sleep like this? The ground does not exactly have much in the way of give."

Hamish continued to rub furiously at his lover's arm and back until heat slowly returned to Darshan's skin. "You get used to it, I suppose." He had spent a good portion of his youth roaming the hills surrounding Mullhind, sometimes opting to sleep out under the stars with the castle just an hour's walk away. And, whilst the ground didn't have an ounce of give, his bed wasn't much softer. "Did you nae go camping as a lad?"

"We had beds." The gentle tremor in Darshan's voice was starting to fade along with the cold radiating from his body. "Wooden frames with strong linen hung between. And *pillows*."

Hamish chuckled. No mistaking the emphasis there. With Sean's decree to pack only the essentials, anything resembling a pillow with no other function had been the first thing to go. "Lift your head." When his lover obeyed, Hamish gently slid his arm into the space beneath and urged Darshan to relax onto it. "It's a wee bit firmer than a wool-stuffed sack, but—"

"I will take it, thank you." Although the lower half of Darshan still sought out whatever comfort eluded him, his torso remained relatively still. Eventually, even the man's legs calmed down, reaching back to entwine themselves with Hamish's. Mercifully, he had discarded his boots somewhere between entering the tent and burrowing under the blankets. That he still wore socks was a blessing, too.

Hamish closed his eyes. He dozed, drifting to sleep only enough to jerk himself back awake before repeating the cycle. Anything deeper eluded him like a fish taunting the bait line.

" 'Mish?" a voice hissed.

He peered through one eye. Had he dreamt that? It sounded almost like Gordon, but it couldn't be their turn to take the watch, he had only slept for a short time.

A figure lurked by the tent entrance, bent over but still the right size for his brother.

"Wake up, you lump," the voice growled before Hamish could move. The command was swiftly followed by a *whump* as a hand came down onto the blankets.

A shriek erupted from the covers. Darshan sat upright to face his assailant.

Hamish flinched. He would've been prepared to weather the usual good-natured slap on his thigh. His lover, not so much.

The spellster's shimmering barrier slammed around them, enclosing only half of Gordon's body. His brother launched back through the tent flap, cussing every word he knew. The shield trembled at the action.

Hamish thought nothing of it until Darshan groaned and pressed a hand to his temple. "Are you all right?"

"I will be." He glared at the entrance. "Kindly request your brother to not wake me in such a manner again. He was fortunate my first thought was a shield otherwise we would be short one tent."

And one brother. He'd only witnessed one moment of magic being used violently, but he had heard plenty of stories about battling spellsters and could well-imagine the damage a provoked spellster could do, especially when startled awake by a slap to the flank.

Hamish hauled on his overcoat whilst his lover returned to his woollen blanket cocoon. A yawning sigh, followed by Darshan's barely audible breathing, was the only way Hamish knew the man had resumed his slumber.

He sorely wished he could rejoin his lover.

Gordon glared at him when he exited the tent. His brother stood not far from the campfire, which neglect had seen it burn low during the previous watch. "You could've warned me he was in there."

"Warn you?" he echoed, his voice high but hushed. "You didnae give me a chance. You just belted the blankets."

"I didnae bloody expect him to be in there with you." His brother eyed him, then the tent. "I wasnae interrupting anything, was I?"

"Only our sleep."

The look his brother shot him was one of complete and utter disbelief. "We're nae home, you ken, you dinnae have to hide the truth. Lad moves fast, I'll give him that. We've only been on the road a day. I expected him to wait at least for a few more before getting his end away."

"We were nae having sex," Hamish hissed, struggling to keep his voice low.

Gordon crouched by the fire to give the barely-burning wood a few pokes. Flames flared up between the pieces then died. "Bloody wet wood," he mumbled, chucking a thin branch onto the coals. "You'd think Sean would ken better than to..." The words trailed off into a stream of grumbles and curses as he worked on getting the wood to burn.

After a couple more encouraging prods and a handful of dry

branches, the fire sputtered back to life.

His brother brushed the dust from his hands, looking immensely pleased with himself. "Now then, what's this? I thought two men didnae do sex, that you called it something else?"

"*I* do." So did every Tirglasian he'd been with. "Apparently, Udyneans dinnae differentiate. And I'm nae pulling your leg. It really was innocent. He was cold and so—"

Deep, belly-shaking laughter erupted from his brother. "By the Goddess' swollen teats." He slapped his knee. "They use that one in Udynea, too?"

Hamish frowned. What, in the Goddess' good name, was his brother on about?

"*I'm cold sleeping all on me lonesome*," Gordon clarified before Hamish could ask, his voice pitched abysmally high. He clasped his hands at his chin and batted his lashes. "*Can I come warm meself with you?*" His brother arched a brow at him. "You *sure* I wasnae interrupting a little late-night warming session?"

"Gor…" he growled, his face growing hotter the longer Gordon talked.

In response, his brother gave a wicked chuckle. "Did you offer to warm him up from the inside? That was my standard answer with Muireall."

Hamish wrinkled his nose and, with a hearty shove to his brother's shoulder, tipped Gordon onto his smug arse. "I dinnae want to think about you and your wife."

Gordon lay on the ground, cackling like a merchant who had swindled a buyer. "Oh, so it's all right if *you* talk about getting it off with your latest piece but, Goddess forbid, if *I* say a word…?"

"It wasnae some ploy to get into me smalls, he was freezing." Outside of the tent, the wind had the usual toothy bite. He knelt by the flames and warmed his hands. Maybe they should've waited a few more weeks for the weather to warm up. Darshan couldn't have faced these sorts of temperatures before. How cold could it possibly get in a land that bordered deserts?

Grunting, his brother righted himself. "Easy enough to remedy. We're already stopping at Old Willie's. Nae hard to see if we cannae find a lad the right size with some clothes to spare whilst we're there. Will your man wear clothes that've been on another?"

"He'll live." Darshan didn't strike him as the type to have ever worn hand-me-downs, but the chill air should suffice as a rebuttal to any protests. Given how cold he appeared to be, Hamish doubted there'd be any objection. "And he's nae me man." Sure, they had both agreed to being lovers whilst Darshan was here, but a couple of days wasn't enough to be sure of anything.

"You might want to tell him that, then, because I dinnae think he understands you're staying right here in Tirglas when it's time for him to go."

Maybe. What could he possibly do when that time came? And he didn't doubt it would come sooner than either of them expected. Naturally, his mother would do her best to keep him home. On the other hand, short of locking him in his room until he was old, what else could she do to stop him from leaving?

He had considered running away before, a great many times. It always fell back to where and how. Money would be an issue. As would the ability to travel far before his mother's lackeys caught up.

With Darshan at his side, he could leave. Maybe not be an ambassador, but perhaps the Udynean court would have a place for him nevertheless.

It would mean leaving everything behind, though. Not just his mother, but the rest of his family. His siblings, his nephews and niece. His father. They'd all been there for him in some manner. Could he really leave everything behind for one man?

He sorely wished the answer wasn't so muddled.

Hamish stood. "We should get to searching the perimeter."

Mercifully, his brother nodded and dusted off the seat of his trousers before they parted ways to loop the outer edge of the campsite.

Like so many times he had been on the night watch with his brother, the midnight hours proved uneventful. The night-time noises were muted and unthreatening. The horses dozed where they'd been hobbled, barely stirring as he paused nearby on his way past.

Finally, Hamish was able to return to his tent whilst Gordon went to wake Zurron to watch for the final hours before dawn.

Inside the tent, the smell of dangerously warm wool wadded his nose and set his eyes to watering. His gaze darted about the bedding, checking for any sign of ignition. No flames, no patches, not even a single ember glowing in the dark.

He knelt next to Darshan, gently pressing a hand to his lover's temple, then his hands. The fingers were like ice. In comparison, the man's head was hotter than a furnace.

Darshan mumbled something. *Taandha?* It sounded familiar. Was it one of the words the man had tried to teach Hamish back in the cliff edge?

Aye. Something about wind. Cold? When his head was burning up? "Here." Kicking off his boots, Hamish wriggled beneath the blankets. He tucked himself up against the man's back, sliding his arm under Darshan's head once again. "Better?"

A grunt that sounded like it could be acquiescence rumbled

through the man. He seemed no warmer.

Hamish fell back to administering the same friction he had used earlier. "You really should've listened to me yesterday," he murmured. If Hamish had been given anywhere near the same amount of money as Darshan had doled out from that blasted tortoise, then buying warm clothing would've been his first stop. Not indulging in trinkets. Even if it had been something as simple as a thick undershirt or a pair of trousers. "Dinnae think on it though, we'll see you're warm enough for the rest of the journey."

Goddess willing, there would be a boy Darshan's size with extra clothes and a willingness to part with them for a few coins.

Chapter 21

Darshan stood in one of the barn stalls that made the central building of the little farming community known only as Old Willie's. He pulled on yet another pair of trousers. *Too short*. A pity as the rest was a decent fit, if only the leg length had halted a foot further down. An unbidden sigh whistled out his nose. Whilst the collective families living here had dug up whatever scrap of clothing they could part with, he was fast running out of options.

A suitably warm undershirt had been an easy find, if a bit long in the arms. Nevertheless, coarse linen now sat snugly around his torso, his undershirt the only barrier between the fabric and having his skin scrubbed raw. Although his sherwani might fit over the pair, he had also selected an overcoat from the bunch in the off chance that it didn't. He would've also picked through the cloaks the locals had thoughtfully added to the pile had he not arrived in one.

If only finding a decent pair of trousers was as simple.

Already, various pieces of clothing lay piled in the corner. He had picked through several of the trousers and shirts, immediately tossing aside those that were just too small and reconciling himself with the idea that nothing amongst the dwindling plausible pile would fit as finely as his own attire.

He relinquished himself of the trousers, tossing them into the far corner, and picked up another pair. Dangling in his hands, this new pair looked far too long in the leg, but he could suffer that over freezing his ankles.

Although just how warm this particular pair would be was debatable. The fabric felt more akin to hessian than linen. Wearing such coarse fabrics was unheard of in Udynean nobility. *And for them to be someone's hand-me-downs...* Like many of the higher nobility, every stitch and cut made in his clothing had been done specifically for him.

He struggled to tie the frayed rope that served in lieu of a front fastener for this particular pair of trousers, grunting and heaving the pieces together. No matter how much he forced them, the front refused to close. *Well, I certainly can't parade around with my undergarments showing.* People would have conniptions all over the place.

Stripping and flinging the trousers into the pile with the rest, he reached for the penultimate pair. If neither of these last two fitted, then they would have to make a detour to the nearest village before travelling to the cloister to ensure he didn't freeze during the rest of their trip.

The stall door creaked behind him, a mass of bright-red hair preceding a head poking through the gap. "You're still trying them on?" Hamish asked, incredulous. "You only need one or two. Or do none of them fit?"

"So far, sadly not." This current pair was far heavier than the rest. Hopping awkwardly on one leg, he slipped the other into the trousers. Wool lining greeted his skin, soft and luxurious. *Please fit.* He hauled them higher.

Fastening them was a touch on the tricky side, the set of rather chunky buttons a menace to feed through holes that were a touch too small. They slipped from his grip as his fingers fumbled, dropping faster than a priest's morals. "I see how you would be amenable to a quick screw in these trousers. They hit the floor rather quickly, do they not?" And being bound closely against the leg all the way to the knee would have them stay in easy reach of retrieval.

"Th-that's nae why—" Hamish stammered, his face growing increasingly ruddy in the smoky light.

Darshan turned his attention to the icy shard he had formed from the trough for use as a mirror. He'd already come to terms with the fact most of the undershirts were on the threadbare side and the overcoats had large patches in them. But the way the trousers billowed most uncomfortably between his legs was disconcerting to say the least. He'd manage. He wasn't as precious as all that. Although, it might take a few days of checking that his trousers hadn't actually fallen to be fully comfortable with such a style.

"What's with the face?" his lover asked. "Are you nae warmer?"

"Hush," Darshan mumbled, continuing to check his reflection. He was indeed quite toasty now his legs were clad, but that wasn't what drew his eye. Standing swathed from neck to ankle in the local fashion, he could almost be seen as a Tirglasian. His glasses somewhat spoiled the illusion, but that couldn't be helped.

He'd be happier if the clothing was actually flattering. The trousers had his backside looking rather shapeless. *Just as well I won't be in court.* Fortunately, the animals cared not a whit as to what he wore. Nor did his travelling companions, providing he didn't complain.

Melting the ice back into the trough, he turned to Hamish. "These will suffice." His gaze traversed his lover's form. How did the man look so delectable whilst wearing practically the same type of clothing? Shaking his head, he shoved his trousers into his pack along with the rest of his clothes.

His lover peered at him as Darshan strode up to the stall door. "You seem to have lost those thin dark rings around your eyes, too."

"I left my kohl back at the castle." Bad enough trying to apply it with the smoky candles and lantern oil they used there, but to attempt it whilst travelling and without a decent mirror? *Madness.* It didn't help that leaving his face bare gave him the sensation of being half-dressed, even with the hefty amount of thick wool and linen weighing his shoulders.

They exited the stables together, before Hamish jogged off to climb aboard his mountain of a horse and wait with the guards whilst Darshan sought out the man's brother.

Not that searching would take long. Old Willie's was little more than a few sheds and houses surrounding a large barn. Built entirely from stone and roofed in thatch, they huddled together, almost cringing against the elements. Most of the buildings had the air of age around them for Darshan to suspect that, whoever old Willie had been, the man this place had been named for had certainly been in the ground for some years.

He found Gordon still chatting with the woman in charge of the main farmstead. They'd already bargained for the supplies the folk here could spare and waited only for Darshan before moving on, but it seemed the man wasn't beyond trying to squeeze extra from the people. Although Darshan rather doubted these folk were the kind to lie about their possessions.

"If you're able to spare just a little more," Gordon said, even as the woman shook her head firmly.

"We can nae give up even another crumb, your highness." Whilst she might not have the wrinkles or grey hair of an old woman, her voice certainly had her sounding like one. "The winter's been lean enough being short on hands and with extra mouths to feed now young Aggie has birthed her twins." She crossed her arms, an affectionate smile daring to curve the no-nonsense line of her thin lips. "Lass'll have her hands full if she's nae careful, third lot in five years."

Gordon bowed his head. "I understand."

The woman looked ready to say something further when her attention swung to Darshan. "You're looking warmer, me lord."

He bowed his head in silent acceptance. What a sight he must've looked when they had arrived, with him perched atop the pony, his legs completely scrunched up beneath the thick cloak in search of shelter from the icy wind that had picked up midmorning. It'd been the lazy type, preferring to go through a body rather than around. Although he could easily heat the air of a room or the immediate area outside as he had professed to Hamish last night, to do so whilst on the move with the wind was nigh impossible.

"Took your sweet time about it," Gordon added, arching a brow and peering out the corner of his eye at Darshan. "Was beginning to think you were personally weaving new clothes."

Darshan spread his arms wide. He had only the truth for the length of time he'd taken in finding suitably-fitting attire. Debating it would only waste more. "I am here now, am I not?"

"That you are." The man jerked a thumb at the rest of their travelling companions. Both of the remaining guards held a horse each; Gordon's beast of a mount and Darshan's pony. "Mount up, we'll be leaving shortly."

Inclining his head, Darshan fastened the bundle of his clothes to the pony's saddlebags and clambered aboard. The trousers shifted uncomfortably, bunching beneath his thighs and requiring a few tugs to have them back into a position that meant they wouldn't have a stranglehold on his privates.

After a few more words with the woman, and an exchange of coin, Gordon finally joined them and they were able to return to the road.

Unlike through the majority of their travels yesterday, the wide road leading to Mullhind was sparsely populated. A few carts creaked their merry way, mostly leading north, away from the capital. None appeared to carry any wares that might've come from a festival.

Gordon twisted in the saddle, eyeing all of them over his shoulder. "Once we turn off the intersection, we'll be keeping to the road as much as we're able. Naebody leaves the camp for long, nae alone." He waggled a finger at Hamish and Darshan. "Especially nae for hours on end."

Darshan snorted. "And I thought we had nothing to fear from brigands."

"It's nae them I'm worried about. Bears are my greater concern. The closer we get to the mountain, the more likely we are to find some. And I'd rather nae disturb them."

Darshan rolled his eyes. He'd never seen a bear, not a living one anyway. The Udynean landscape—at least the southern part he was personally more familiar with—was rather devoid of such predators.

Where the jungles of places like Obuzan had slinky spotted cats lurking in the canopies, and the southern lands worried over jackals and wild dogs, the untamed lands of Udynea belonged to the tigers.

"I dinnae think you comprehend how dangerous it can be out here."

Darshan smirked. "To be fair, I am used to *being* the most dangerous thing in the vicinity." His magic could frighten off the biggest of creatures. He had proven that in his late teens when frightening off a curious tiger from the family's country estate near the twin lakes when one had slunk into the gardens. True, the beast had been more interested in going after the herd of spiral-horned deer that grazed there, but his young half-sister, Nita, quite likely would've died attempting the same thing had he not acted.

A sigh escaped him at the memory. *Dear Nini.* He often believed she would've been much like Anjali had she the chance to grow up. To think, he had saved her from a potential tiger mauling only for her to fall prey to their half-sister, Onella. Unfortunate timing, the council had eventually ruled. That'd been a decade ago. He still didn't believe a sturdy bridge could just collapse without warning, especially at the precise time for Nita to cross it during her usual morning ride.

But having faced a hungry tiger, he rather doubted a bear posed much of a threat. Granted, bears were bigger—much bigger if the stuffed examples in the palace study were to be believed as the norm. But even if something so big and clunky managed to land the first blow, he'd a moderate chance of having enough wits about him to protect himself and the others until the so-called danger left.

Frowning, Gordon opened his mouth.

"Rabbit!" Zurron blurted before the man could speak. The elf pointed at the road ahead even as he scrambled for his bow.

The guard's cry set off a flurry of activity. Like Zurron, the rest of the men went for their bows. They urged their horses forward, shuffling Darshan to the rear whilst spreading out across the road's width.

Darshan craned his neck to see beyond their shoulders and flailing arms. Sure enough, one of the fluffy-tailed creatures was bounding up the road in a haphazard zigzag pattern, likely flushed out from the underbrush by the noise.

Several arrows flew through the air, skimming across the ground or digging point-first into the dirt. Unscathed, their prey continued bounding ahead of them.

"Got it!" Hamish cried, loosing his arrow.

The rabbit abruptly changed direction, bounding right over the arrows the rest of the men had fired before racing in the opposite direction. The erratic path it took stopping only once Hamish's arrow hit. It dropped like a windfallen apple.

Odd. He could've sworn that arrow had veered off its natural arc, twitching along with the rabbit's zigzagging movements. By all rights, the man should've missed.

The guards congratulated Hamish's speed as they collected both the rabbit and their arrows.

Darshan gnawed on the inside of his lip as Hamish plucked the arrow from the animal's heart. First the fluke of Gordon being inside his shield back at the castle—an act that he couldn't quite be certain had also happened last night when his backside was walloped—now this?

Could it be that the royal line had magic in its blood? None of the empire's usual sources had dug up any such possibility. Still, it would be foolish to not consider it before a proper test. But how to go about that? All the tests he knew of were done on infants, whose abilities responded on an instinctual level, and usually only to determine spellsters from Nulled Ones.

To attempt the same examination on a grown man?

His lover could very well have learnt to suppress any abilities without knowing. Darshan couldn't exactly outright ask Hamish for the same reason, not even in private. Never mind the risk of offending the man should his querying prove false.

"—nae halting to cook one measly rabbit," Gordon was saying, his hands raised placatingly towards the guards. "We wasted too much time at Old Willie's. If we're lucky, we might be able to add a few more to the pot for a decent supper." He nodded at his brother. "String it up for now."

Hamish tied the rabbit to his saddle, letting it hang down one side of the mare's shoulder, and mounted his horse. "Supper? Dinnae we usually wind up sharing the farmhouse's fare?"

"I dinnae think we'll make it to the guard tower before dark never mind a farmhouse. Maybe if someone hadnae taken so long or had chosen to wear suitable clothes for the journey." Gordon shot Darshan a meaningful look.

Darshan returned the expression with a carefully neutral one. He was no mind reader, nor did he masquerade as such, unlike some. If their journey was operating under time constraints, the man really should've mentioned it earlier.

"We couldnae have been that long," Hamish said. He tugged his mount's head away from a tree branch, growling unintelligibly at the animal. "That's enough of that, lass." He urged the horse down the road with a firm nudge of his boot. Pine needles still hung out the mare's mouth as she continued to placidly chew.

"An hour or so," Gordon clarified. "It's enough to see us still on the road come nightfall." He bent over his horse's shoulder to peer at the road. The ruts and holes forced them to remain in the middle or trudge along the dubious footing in what little strips sat either side of the road. Still, there was plenty of room for two horses to ride abreast. "The footing should improve the closer we get to a farmstead, but beyond that, we cannae risk the horse's tripping in the dark. Zurron?" He shot over his shoulder. "Keep a lookout for any more rabbits."

They rode on in silence, the rest of the men hesitant to relinquish their bows, especially after the third rabbit poked its nose out from the undergrowth. They halted briefly at a creek just around mid-afternoon, letting the horses drink and rest for a bit whilst they ate a meagre meal of crumbly, almost biscuit-like, bread.

Darshan eyed the trio of rabbits that'd been strung up by their feet in the low branch of a nearby tree. Hamish and the guards had taken their rest as an opportunity to field dress the animals, leaving the hides largely intact. Little in the way of blood had drained from the animals on account of each one having rapidly bled out when shot.

They had Hamish to thank for that. Every time there was prey, it would be his lover's arrow that downed the animal. It didn't matter the man was often the last to draw or even when the final of the rabbit trio had nipped back into the bushes at the last moment, Hamish still managed a hit. And each arrowhead pierced the heart in the exact same place.

He would definitely have to discuss the prospect of magical power within the man the next time they were alone.

The rest of their afternoon journey was somewhat less eventful. No more prey revealed itself for Darshan to witness another perfectly-placed shot. They slowed as the light began to wane, Zurron taking the fore as his elven eyesight enabled him to pick out details far better in the gloom. The elf peered at the roadside, seeking for a suitable place to camp.

Kneeing his pony into an amble in order to keep up with the two brothers' far bigger mounts, Darshan cleared his throat. "That was an impressive display of archery back there."

His lover twisted in the saddle, glancing at him over a well-muscled shoulder. Even if the possibility of the man possessing magic was true, only actual physical exertion could've sculpted that frame. "You've a little experience with a bow, then?"

"Very little," he confessed. "My father rather insists on all his children mastering several types of weaponry beyond the magical." But even with magic to aid him, he had been handier with a blade than any sort of projectile. The skill there went to his eldest half-sister. He'd a scar on his torso that could attest to the trueness of

Onella's aim. "Quite frankly, I am astonished you managed to hit, not only one but, all three rabbits directly in the heart, especially with the way they were bounding about."

Hamish brushed aside the remark with a swipe of his hand. "I just got lucky."

"You mean lucky *again*," Gordon said, leaning across the gap between horses to clap a hand on his brother's shoulder. He very nearly missed, leading to him waving his arm in search of purchase even as he hauled himself upright in the saddle. "Dinnae listen to Lord Humble here, 'Mish has nae missed a mark since we were wee lads."

"*Never?*" Even magic occasionally missed a target if the proper focus wasn't applied.

"Nae even one."

Darshan rolled the bottom tuft of the pony's mane around a forefinger. Perhaps the man's aptitude for a clean kill was merely skill. On the other hand, he had heard of extremely weak spellsters specialising in but a few abilities. If Hamish was one of them, then it would certainly be harder to prove. Perhaps starting at the beginning would help gauge the truth. "How young?"

"Seven," Gordon replied. "It's the normal age to begin training." He eyed Darshan, seeming to consider his next words.

"This way," Zurron declared before Gordon could speak further. The elf steered his mount off the left side of the road. "Wait here." He dismounted and, chucking his reins at his fellow guard, swiftly vanished into the undergrowth to leave the rest of them waiting on the edge of the shadows.

"Since we were on the topic," Gordon said. "When does your average spellster start training their magic? I assume you have to learn to control it."

"That is what they teach at the cloister, correct?" Only healing, which took considerable years to perfect to the point where, like a physician, a spellster could be certain of not harming the patient through the attempt to mend.

The man nodded. A few shorter lengths of ruddy hair had escaped the cord confining the mass of curls at his nape, they gave an extra bob. Without a pause, Gordon huffed them out of his eyes.

"There is a touch of truth in those words, although some of the power is more instinctual. I cannot speak for other lands, but most of the spellsters in Udynea start at around the age of five." There was the occasional late bloomer, typically discovering their magic at the far later age of nine, but they were few and often too weak to protect themselves from those looking to use them as a way up the ladder of political power.

"That'd be for minor things, though?" Gordon pressed. "Those shields and the lifting of objects. Nae dangerous magics like fireballs and all that, right?"

Darshan shook his head, biting the inside of his cheek to keep from laughing. It was a crime for these people to be so ignorant. "Actually, for many, fire is often the first controllable force. They do not call it the easiest magic for nothing." Sometimes he wondered if it was considered as such simply because their tutors told them it should be. Whilst he had mastered in within the expected timeframe, his twin had struggled. Instead, she had taken far more swiftly to the complex art of forming and directing ice.

"That's nae exactly—" Sean said, cutting himself off as the rustle of bushes and the definite thump of an axe preceded what Darshan hoped was the elf's return.

Sure enough, Zurron appeared from the bushes with the same ease as he'd entered. "I was right," he announced, jerking a thumb behind him. "There's a gap in the brush a little ways back. Nae all that big, but it'll get us off the immediate roadside."

They forged a path through the undergrowth effortlessly enough; the ease helped by the fact Zurron had already cleared some of the troublesome branches out of the way. True to the elf's words, the space was small. To call it a clearing at all was being generous. Darshan had envisioned something like last night, but a little more snug. This was barely big enough for a few tents.

His thoughts must've shown, for Gordon clapped a consoling hand on his shoulder. "We'll make do for the night," he said as the two guards set about pitching the first tent. "Since you're obviously fine sharing sleeping space with me brother—and I dinnae ken how you can get a wink with that row rattling in your ear—I'll share with Sean and Zurron."

"Still not willing to put up with me snoring?" Hamish snickered over the top of the horse he was unsaddling.

Darshan frowned. He hadn't recalled any such noises. But then, being curled up in the man's embrace had been the deepest sleep he'd had since he was a small boy. "Will that not be a bit snug?" Darshan enquired of Gordon. "All three of you in one tent?"

The man shook his head. "Shouldnae be any trouble. Sean'll take first watch, I'll be taking the middle and Zurron the last like always."

"Alone?" Sean added, his head popping out from behind the second tent he was currently in the process of fixing into position. "Nae that I'm complaining, but I do prefer company on a watch."

Gordon hummed for a bit, then clicked his fingers. "Hamish?" He pointed a forefinger at his brother. "You'll share the watch with Sean tonight." The digit swung towards Darshan. "And you can join me, I assume you're capable."

"Of course." It might take him a moment to distinguish the unfamiliar night sounds, but that wasn't anything he hadn't attempted before. "I thought you would've preferred sharing the watch with someone you are more familiar with."

"And who is also nae a spellster?" Gordon grinned, the starkness of that likeness to Hamish's expression rather eerie. "I dinnae think you're about to do anything untoward. Besides—" Gordon's gaze slid to his brother and back. "I'd prefer the pair of you to be watching the forest rather than each other. I dinnae fancy having me face chewed off because you two were snogging when you should've been focused on your duty."

"And when have I ever done that?" Hamish demanded of his brother.

"How about the summer of your eighteenth year? At the foot of the castle cliff, if I recall correctly."

Darshan glanced at the guards. Neither man gave any indication they had heard Gordon. He could've dismissed it there, if he wasn't entirely certain that Zurron most definitely would have. Maybe the elf already knew about Hamish. And, perhaps, Sean did, too. Knew and didn't care. It stood to reason Gordon would fill his travelling party with those who wouldn't judge his brother.

"Arse," Hamish muttered, his expression darker than the jesting tone suggested.

Gordon merely stuck his tongue out at his brother.

"Come on," Hamish said to Darshan. "Let's leave me brother to his fanciful delusions and see what wood we can find."

"Nae much in the way of dry stuff, I'd wager," Sean grumbled, most of his attention directed to tying down the second tent. "Dinnae wander too deep into the forest, either. I think I saw tracks further back."

"You *think*?" Gordon asked, swinging around to face the guard. "Did you also think to confirm that? Or what sort of tracks they were? Or did your thinking just consist on praying to the Goddess' left tit that you were wrong?"

A tap to Darshan's shoulder had him turning from the conversation. Hamish jerked his head at the tree line to his right before striding off into the brush.

Darshan jogged to keep up with the man. "Are you all right?" he asked once he could be confident none of the others would hear. "You seemed upset by what your brother mentioned."

Grunting, Hamish brushed it off. "He surprised me is all. I did something foolish years back, I just didnae ken he was aware of it. Dinnae pay it any mind."

They picked their way through the undergrowth in relative silence, scrounging for whatever bits of wood they could find that were dry enough to burn. Darshan likely could've ignited even the wettest of pieces if he put any actual effort into the act, but it seemed counterproductive to use up what energy he had when simpler means were at hand.

At first, the forest seemed reluctant to relinquish any remains of its fallen brethren, but after a little more poking and prying around some of the bigger trees, they were able to gather a modest amount to tuck under an arm. They made their way back slowly, rechecking the undergrowth in the off chance of a bigger haul.

"Well," Hamish mumbled around a piece of bread he had produced from a ball of cloth tucked into his belt pouch. "We can rule out any bears from this direction. I've nae seen a single sign."

Darshan grunted as he poked around the bushes huddled beneath a gnarled pine. After being warned of the danger they posed, he rather wanted to see one up close. Just for a moment, as irrational as he knew that desire to be. *Anjali would be so jealous.* He didn't get many chances to tease his twin, and most of them were too cruel to consider. Letting her know he had seen a Tirglasian bear up close would ruffle her feathers for a month and she would be begging their father to let her travel here by the end of it.

"Dar?"

Blinking, he lifted his head to find Hamish looming over him, concern creasing his features. Darshan straightened slightly, the nape of his neck tingling although he could discern no immediate threat. "Is everything all right?" The hum of a shield not quite formed ran through his body and vibrated the air.

"That's what I was going to ask you. You've been staring into that bush for a while now." He frowned and reshuffled his load of branches and twigs. "Have you nae heard a word I said?"

He released his hold on the half-formed barrier with a sigh. No danger, just a man concerned he hadn't been heard. "Something about bears?" His thoughts might've wandered a touch, but it couldn't have been for too long.

The expression on Hamish's face spoke of it being the wrong answer well before the man opened his mouth. "That was several sentences back. I was asking if last night was what you'd call one of these dates of yours?"

Darshan chuckled. "Not like any date *I* have had." Unlike the men who attempted to woo his sister, few sought anything more than a few hours of pleasure and, occasionally, a little favour. He'd be stretching to call any of that a date. "But the ones in our folktales tend to start out that way... generally just before the lord's lover vanishes under mysterious circumstances. And thus begins the saga of adventure and battles leading to a glorious culmination and much rejoicing."

"Would you have counted it as one?"

"Perhaps," Darshan replied as he resumed poking around the bush, spying a short length of tree branch tangled within the budding leaves. He certainly wouldn't shirk at the idea of spending more time passively consuming food in such company, the ocean view had been a bonus. *A shame we had to leave.*

"And now?" The words might have been muffled by the rustle of leaves and crack of dead twigs, but the wariness in his lover's voice was thick enough to taste.

"If you wanted it to be." Darshan surfaced with his haul. He slid the piece into the bundle tucked snugly beneath his arm. "Although, I believe it is typically more intimate than this."

The forest echoed with the clunk and clatter of wood hitting the ground. His lover pressed close, scooping Darshan into his arms, then up against a tree before Darshan could think to react. The wood that'd been tucked neatly under his arm tumbled to the forest floor, the tip of one branch scraping his shin on the way down.

Hamish hovered over Darshan, one muscular arm corralling him either side. "You mean like this?"

He barely heard the words over the rhythmic beat of his pulse marching in his ears. His mind blanked terribly. The hissing pain of the injury and the soothing warmth of his healing magic clashed with the jumbled knot in his stomach.

Nevertheless, Darshan found himself biting his lip even as a small groan of acquiescence escaped his throat.

His lover bent to kiss him. Soft skin whispered against his own, feather-light and nothing more.

Still, his body shuddered. Darshan grabbed for the man, his legs embarrassingly weak. With his fingers full of the man's overcoat, he hauled himself up to deepen the kiss, parting his lips just slightly.

Hamish moaned, pressing harder against Darshan's mouth, but not taking the unspoken invitation. Firm hands fell on Darshan's hips, lifting him until his toes barely touched the ground. Their hips met clumsily, the force slamming Darshan's back against the tree.

With a low guttural sound that was half pain, half desire, Darshan took possession of his lover's mouth, greedily deepening the kiss. His hands twitched, longing to traverse the expanse of chest and shoulders before him, but to release his handhold risked a rather painful slide down the tree trunk.

Darshan opted to abandon the forest floor completely, wrapping his legs around Hamish's waist to grind against him, his thoughts bent only towards chasing pleasure. His lover thrust chaotically in response. Each movement crushed Darshan against the tree, but he no longer cared.

Their lips parted far sooner than he would've liked, both gasping for air. Darshan tipped his head back, resting it on the tree.

"You ken," Hamish murmured, humour huffing out with his trembling breath. "For someone who speaks about control so much, you give it up quick enough."

Heat flooded his face. Few back home would knowingly entertain the idea of playing anything but the submissive for their *vris Mhanek*. Fewer still actually restrained him with any intent. And none turned his limbs to water with a rather straightforward kiss.

Gods, was that would it took to get him off now? Simplicity? Clumsy innocence?

He squirmed against the tree, looking for a way to wriggle out of this position. Just when had Hamish pinned him so tightly against the trunk that he could do nothing but grind against the man? And, if he wasn't mistaken, his lover was rather enjoying Darshan's bid for freedom.

Far from innocent, I see. That was a mild relief. He would certainly need to work on not falling apart every time his lover touched him though, especially if he was to have Hamish join him in Minamist. It would be all too easy for the Crystal Court to exploit such a weakness.

Hamish's warm breath gusted against Darshan's neck as he gave freedom one last attempt. "You're nae even trying now," he murmured, the words thick and hoarse. He nuzzled that dear little spot just below Darshan's ear, freeing an embarrassingly whimpering moan. "You didnae happen to bring your bottle of oil along for the journey, did you?"

"No?" He'd been told essentials only. If his shaving equipment and kohl failed to meet the criteria, what made his lover think a bottle of oil would've?

Hamish stepped back, letting Darshan slip to the ground.

A twinge of disappointment struck him in the chest. How he wished he could say otherwise, if only to dispel the sudden absence of Hamish's touch, but to speak anything beyond the truth would be a ridiculous stance to take. "I did not believe you would be comfortable enough to attempt sex in a tent with others so near, especially your brother." He rather doubted *he* could perform under such circumstances, let alone expect his lover to be ready for it. "And the thought of having sex in the wilderness is not one I have given much contemplation to. Ever."

"*Ever?*" Hamish echoed, snickering. "I cannae believe I just found something you've nae done that I have."

"*You* have had sex in a forest?" Darshan blurted, realising the foolishness of such a statement when he had very nearly emptied himself into his drawers only moments before.

His lover shrugged as if it was the most common thing in the world for a man to be intimate in the wilderness. "Near the edge of one, sure. That's what me brother was alluding to. We were meant to be hunting and—"

"Let me guess." Darshan rubbed his back. The bruised flesh and abraded skin had mended almost as soon as it happened, but all that healing magic layered over itself itched something fierce. "The only prey he stuck was *you*?"

"He had me arse naked up over a log as soon as we realised we both fancied men." His brows lowered as his gaze slid downward. "Are you all right?"

The concern slathering that question curved his lips. "Quite fine." He wasn't against being manhandled over an object, so long as there wasn't anything to dig or scratch him. "I must admit, over a log sounds like several types of uncomfortable."

Hamish grinned. "A little, but I was an impatient lad of eighteen years. You remember your late teens, right?"

"Rather fondly in parts," he murmured. Like that time he had engaged in a masked orgy. His stewards had found him draped over a marble statue of the wine goddess, Madaara, being filled at both ends by a pair of well-built men whilst a third fellated him. "Not so much in others. And there are a few I still cannot recall clearly." How he must've run his father's lackeys ragged as they scrambled to cover up whatever escapade had taken his fancy at the time. They were likely relieved he'd mellowed with the years.

His lover snickered. "I can imagine."

Darshan hummed to himself, considering the options laid before him. "If you desire it, we do not require oil to have a little fun."

"To be honest, I prefer when it's involved."

"As do I." Why else would he have insisted on using it? "But that was not quite what I meant." He slunk up against his lover, gliding his hand across Hamish's groin.

"A hand job?" His mouth twisted, pursing and not in the slightest bit impressed. "If I wanted that, I could do it meself."

"Such insolence," Darshan murmured. As if he'd offer something so mundane as that. He focused on the flesh directly below his hand, sending a soft vibrating pulse through his fingertips.

Those sapphiric eyes widened, then rolled back. "All right," he said on the wings of a moan. "I cannae do it like that."

"I am afraid that, if you want more, you shall have to wait."

Darshan ducked to gather up his share of the fallen wood. "We really should head back, they will be expecting our return. Surely, you do not want them to catch you with your trousers at your ankles, do you?"

"You bloody tease," Hamish muttered. Nevertheless, he followed suit in gathering up his share of the wood before leading the way back to camp.

Chapter 22

Darshan tugged his cloak tighter around him, although the new clothes aided a fair bit in staving off the chill that had settled in his fingers and face. Last night had been the warmest one he had experienced since arriving here.

Nevertheless, he rather wished he was still abed, wrapped in his lover's arms as well as their blankets.

Like the previous morning, they had broken camp with the rising sun and made for the road. Their group couldn't have been placidly travelling along for more than an hour when they came upon a squat tower standing proudly at an intersection. By the battlements and thin windows, it had to be a guard's outpost. Was it an occupied one?

Darshan peered at the battlements. He couldn't spot anyone. Perhaps this was a relic of old borders from back when the clans fought for every scrap of land. His companions certainly had a complete lack of care about them. If it was occupied, it was clearly manned by allies.

His attention turned to the road. Whilst both routes were equally as wide, the one leading straight ahead had the smoothness of excessive use. Whereas the left was pitted with water-filled ruts and holes.

Gordon turned off to the left, giving barely a glance at the tower as they rode on by.

"Who goes?" a voice bellowed from somewhere up above before a white-haired head poked over the battlements. "Identify yourselves."

Gordon swung his horse about, grinning up at where the voice had come from. "I think your eyesight's failing you if you cannae recognise us."

More of the white-haired head poked over the brickwork, along with the heads of two other guards who seemed to be equally as grey-haired as each other. "Prince Gordon? Ah and Prince Hamish, I see. Off to the cloister, your highnesses?"

"That we are," Gordon replied.

The door to the building swung open, permitting the exit of four men, all with swords at their hips. The men marched out to the roadside; three halting just behind the one who had to be their leader, whatever his rank.

The man on the battlements continued to talk as if it were normal for armed men to approach barely armoured travellers. "We were expecting you yesterday, your highness."

"Nae one here sent any kind of message," Gordon said.

A thread of unease wove its way through Darshan's gut. Did that mean what he thought it did? Had Queen Fiona sent word ahead? What of at their backs? Could they expect to be beset upon by guards ordered to drag Hamish back to the castle?

"You might nae have, your highness," said the guard at the fore. He was a broad-shouldered man, with a thick streak of white through his black beard. "But we've an order from her majesty."

"What order?" Hamish snapped.

Bitterness coated Darshan's tongue. Of course she had sent an order to detain her son. Even out here, she wasn't content with letting Hamish be.

"The one that specifically mentions *him*." The leader pointed directly at Darshan. "The Udynean ambassador. Dinnae think you can disguise him with a change of clothes."

"And what does me mum want with him?" Gordon demanded.

"Naething much." The guard clasped his hands at his belt. His beard was thinner than the others and did nothing to hide the smugness tightening his smile. "Just a wee escort back to Mullhind."

Darshan straightened in the saddle. "Forgive my ignorance, but am I under arrest?"

The guard shook his head. "But you should be," he growled. "The corruption of a prince is treason."

Hamish rolled his eyes and sighed. "Nae this again," he muttered. "He hasnae corrupted me."

"And I can hardly be committing treason when I am not Tirglasian," Darshan added. "Nor is Queen Fiona my monarch."

One of the other guards—the one with a bushy grey beard that made up for the lack of hair atop his head—nudged their leader. "This is what I've been saying for years. Do away with the hunts and the world goes to shit. Some traditions shouldnae be allowed to die. Did she specify alive?"

Their leader shook his head. He raised his hand in a clear signal.

"Now wait a minute," Gordon said.

Pain lanced through Darshan's chest. He slumped in the saddle, his breathing suddenly a strain.

"What the—?" someone exclaimed.

"Stand down!" That was Gordon, no mistaking the authority in his voice.

Through the sudden wash of tears blurring his sight, the fletching of an arrow danced on the edge of his vision. The shaft grated against his ribs with every shallow huff of air.

Already, his healing magic rushed to repair the wound. It couldn't do a thorough job with the blasted arrow still in him, but it would staunch most of the bleeding and dull the pain.

"Dar!"

'Mish. Darshan clutched the arrow shaft. He had to get the bloody thing out.

"Nae." Hamish's hand landed on Darshan's shoulder, helping him stay upright atop the horse. "Dinnae try to pull it out. We'll—"

The hiss of another arrow flew by, leaving a sharp pain in his shoulder. A mere graze in comparison to the fire still blazing in his chest.

Hamish cursed and jerked his mare back, causing the horse to rear. He appeared uninjured. That could change with the next arrow.

Darshan snapped his head up, his focus settling on the men still up on the battlements. One man stood closer to the edge, his bow drawn full. *You.*

A blast of air was enough to tip the man off the top of the tower. He hit the ground with a crunch.

"He's a fecking *spellster*?" someone bellowed. "Naebody told us he was a spellster!"

"Forward men!" roared their leader, drawing his broadsword. "He cannae take all of us. Avenge your fallen comrade!"

"Halt!" Gordon commanded, even as he swung his horse about to put the full length of the steed in their path. "You cannae do this!"

The men barrelled straight past him, heedless to his words. Animalistic growls and grunts escaped their bared teeth.

Darshan pulled on his pony's reins, urging Warrior back as fast as his hooves could take them. What had he done to deserve their ire? To deserve death?

The leader reached Darshan first.

Darshan jerked the pony to the side. Warrior staggered back, his rear legs sliding and giving. His rump hit the ground. The impact jolted right through Darshan and sent a fresh flare of fire through his chest.

The man swung his sword up, the arc clearly aiming for Warrior.

Not the pony! A shield flickered to life before him even as Warrior screamed and fought to right himself.

The man's blade struck and, mercifully, bounced off the shield.

Zurron leapt onto the leader's back before the guard could recover. The elf wrapped his wiry arm around the old man's neck. The guard flailed wildly, then with less force until he finally collapsed.

Warrior continued to kick and thrash beneath Darshan. The pony rolled to one side, throwing him to the ground as it regained its footing.

"Grab him!" Gordon bellowed, the command sending Sean galloping after the pony.

"You bastard!" another voice roared from atop the tower. It was all the warning Darshan got before arrows hit the ground near his head.

Without looking, Darshan flung a bolt of lightning in the direction of the battlements. The crack of shattering stone rumbled alongside the muffled boom of thunder.

No more arrows answered his attack.

The grunt of fighting filled his ears. The others, Zurron and the two brothers, fought to keep the three men on the ground from closing on Darshan. But even with the latter not using lethal force, they were armoured and all bearing broadswords. Whereas Darshan's companions carried nothing bigger than hunting knives. Neither side seemed at all willing to mortally injure the other, but if they didn't restrain the guards soon, Darshan was certain he would wake up dead.

"Filthy elf!" one of the men snarled, throwing Zurron to the ground. The guard dealt a kick to the elf's gut and, collecting his sword, charged for Darshan. "You die here, rutter."

Darshan struggled to sit up, to keep a solid shield around himself. His chest was ablaze and bleeding despite his magic's frantic attempts to staunch the flow. He could feel the strength draining from him with the attempt, clouding his sight, slowing his movements.

"Nae!" Hamish screamed.

The cry pierced through the swiftly descending fog of Darshan's mind in time for him to register the sword bearing down on him.

Unbridled terror overrode his senses. Darshan flung up his hand.

Raw magic flowed from his fingertips. Wild and deadly, it followed only instinctual command, rushing at the guard.

Wisps of smoke and heat encapsulated the man, searing the flesh from his bones. Greasy smoke filled the air. The sickening stench of charred meat invaded Darshan's nostrils, fuelling his wrath.

His magic carried onwards, heeding the most basic of thoughts. These guards wanted him dead. Never mind that nobody harmed those of the *Mhanek* and breathed for long, this had clearly been personal. He wasn't about to give them a chance to regroup for a second attempt.

Under his command, the wind gained speed and power. It bowled the two princes off the ground, brushing them aside and tearing the remaining attackers from the earth in one almighty blast.

The guards slammed against the tower. There they remained, pinned by glistening shards of ice and the shimmering forms of broken magical constructs Darshan hadn't the focus to craft in full. The guards screamed, their agony echoing into the forest.

Only once the pressure crushed the breath from their bodies did they fall silent.

And still, Darshan held them in place. Waiting. Pushing them harder against the tower until the stone surrounding them began to crack.

By the time he thought to stop, the men were as limp as corpses.

Darshan lay there, panting and shaking. He had ordered quite a number of deaths as *vris Mhanek*, but they had all been through the usual method of contracted assassinations. He hadn't actually killed anyone since his early teens. "Are they dead?"

Gordon scrambled to his feet. He knelt beside the guards, checking one and then the other, before nodding. "Aye, they've passed on to the Goddess' bosom."

Darshan didn't know if the man had actually whispered or if the fall had also affected his senses. Nevertheless, he shook his head. "Not them," he wheezed. He already knew his magic had done a thorough job if not with its usual finesse. The sting of it sang through the air. "The others." He pointed at the shattered battlements, his arm trembling.

He had only meant to scare the archers into hiding, but there was no hint of anyone up there. Not even a cautious arrow launched his way. Not that he wished there was. He rather doubted his ability to do more than sit here. A shield dense enough to stop an arrow was out of the question.

One by one, his companions turned their attention to the battlements. They waited in silence for someone to poke their head over the edge. Nothing.

Darshan eyed the windows, hopeful of spying a glimmer of light, a darker form within the shadows. But the arrow slits were designed to keep those within unseen.

"I'll go see," Gordon offered. Slipping his hunting knife free of its sheath, he strode into the tower. It wouldn't be much use against something like the broadswords these guards had used, but the men inside had been very particular about avoiding doing any harm to their princes.

"I'll secure the horses," Zurron offered, already backing up to where the majority of their mounts stood under the trees on the opposite side of the road. At least none had sought to follow Warrior or Sean.

Darshan inched himself into a seating position. He felt along the shaft jutting from his chest, surprised to find it still whole. At least the arrow hadn't appeared to have moved too far.

Hamish knelt beside him. He clapped one steadying hand on Darshan's shoulder. "Is it as bad as it looks?"

How could it not be? Just what sort of injuries had his lover witnessed to think an arrow in the chest might not be all bad? "A little," he admitted. The shaft was deep and grated against his ribs with every movement of his chest. Now he was able to focus a little more on what his magic had healed, it seemed that his shortness of breath had been due to a nicked lung. Had it been just a little bit further to the left? Well, then he most certainly wouldn't have be sitting here chatting. "I am sorry you witnessed that. It is not usual for me to—"

Hamish stilled him with a drawn out, sibilant hush. "How about we get you patched up?" One side of his mouth twitched into a nervous smile. "Then you can apologise if you still think it necessary." He slipped an arm beneath Darshan's shoulder, preparing to lift him.

Darshan batted away the man's hands. "I can heal this readily enough once I get the arrow out." Judging by the other arrows scattered about, removal would likely require pushing the head through to the other side. He rather doubted he had been struck by the only arrow without a barbed tip.

His lover's lips flattened. The knowledge of what needed to be done seemed to dull his eyes. "That's going to hurt. A lot."

"I do not doubt it." Likely more than the arrow's initial entry, if past experience with such an injury was anything to go by. "But I cannot repair the damage unless it is removed."

"Then let's at least get these clothes off you." Hamish grasped the arrow and, with a quick warning nod, snapped off a large chunk of the shaft.

Shrugging out of the overcoat was easily done, once his belt was released. The shirts were a little trickier, requiring Hamish's assistance in manoeuvring the fabric around the arrow shaft as well as having his lover pull each one over Darshan's head. Each shift and tug sent a fresh ripple of pain through him. The chill air gnawed deeper into his skin with each layer removed.

At last, his second undershirt was free. Darshan hissed as the removal from around the arrow shaft also tore away a chunk of congealed blood. His magic hummed through him, resealing the wound. He shuddered, trying to prepare himself for what was to come.

Hamish returned his bracing grasp to Darshan's shoulder. His other hand clasped the broken arrow shaft. "Ready?"

Not at all. He had only been a boy the last time he had suffered such a wound as this, but the searing memory of that extraction was not one to be easily forgotten. There was nothing else that could be done. Leaving the arrow in would only continue to nibble at his magic until there was nothing left to give.

Darshan gave his lover a curt nod and prepared himself as best as he could for the pain. At least the arrow's downward angle would aid in its, hopefully swift, removal.

With his lips pressed into a tight, grim line, Hamish drove the arrow further in.

White-hot pain clawed its way through Darshan's gut, tearing a cry from his lips. His body shook as he desperately fought the urge to pull away from the source. His magic battled to mend the barb's slicing path even as the cuts were made.

Gritting his teeth, Darshan slumped against Hamish's hand. He was grateful for the solidity found in that grasp even if the consoling squeeze the man gave did little to ease the agony burrowing its way through him. He wasn't sure if the pain had turned the world to white light or his tears had.

There was only agony and that hand.

The pressure at his back grew. He arched involuntarily, desperately seeking to shrink from the barb breaking through his skin. A whimpering gasp parted his lips, his lungs too exhausted to breathe deep enough for more.

Hamish lowered Darshan, exchanging the hand that had braced him for one of those broad shoulders. He reached around Darshan's torso to feel what Darshan already knew. The arrowhead sat just beneath the skin. "It willnae be much longer," he whispered. "Just stay with me, all right? One more push ought to do it."

Be strong. His father's voice echoed through his mind. A memory of another time with another arrow.

He fisted his lover's overcoat. Waiting. Dreading.

Be strong.

At first, he thought he could bear it. The pain was no worse than already, the addition of a mere pinprick. It grew with each heartbeat, tearing the skin with all the finesse of a mace. It burned through his senses like ice, stealing breath, voice and thought.

Then it was gone.

His magic rushed to fill the void, itching and prickling through his body. When the last minuscule nick was gone, the buzz of healing subsided to bone-gnawing exhaustion.

Darshan sat back on his heels, steadied only by Hamish's grip, and delicately wiped his fingers across his cheeks. Unsurprisingly, they came away damp. He had to be halfway to crying himself to a husk.

Without the heat of pain and magic, the chill air ran icy tendrils across his bare skin. Shivering, he reached for his shirt before catching sight of the tear in the threads. Already, his blood had dried to a dark stain around the holes.

"Here." Hamish threw a cloak over Darshan's shoulders, followed swiftly by a second. "I ken healing takes its toll. Stay warm and rest for a bit, then we'll see about getting you dressed again."

Nodding, Darshan eyed the outpost's door. How long had it been since Gordon had ventured inside? The archers must've been dead.

Uncertain his legs would obey him if he tried to stand, Darshan wrapped the cloaks tighter around him. There was nothing he could do but wait.

Gordon exited the tower. He shook his head, his lips pressed into a thin grim line.

Definitely dead. Hopefully, the archers had succumbed to the faster death of the lightning's power rather than the debris his wild aim had created.

The prince beckoned his brother and the elf to his side. The trio conversed in hushed tones amongst themselves and then strode into the tower.

Darshan didn't bother to move a muscle. Whatever they were about, they clearly didn't think him up to the task.

He heard them before long at the top of the tower. Zurron's booming exclamation of the sight did little to convince Darshan that the archers had met anything less than a gruesome fate.

The truth of it was only confirmed as the trio dragged a crushed body out of the tower and laid them beside the other two guards who had met a similar end. Of the charred remains lying not that far from him, none seemed willing to touch.

He didn't blame them.

Sean had returned, the pony in tow, by the time the trio had brought down the second archer. "What the feck happened?" he asked, halting his horse at the edge of the road.

"Our resident spellster ambassador," Gordon replied, waving a hand his way. "How else? Was it really necessary to kill them all?" That final question was directed Darshan's way with an accusatory glare as if he were an unruly child new to his power.

Darshan gestured to the bloody arrow, then to the skeletal remains of the guard. "Was I supposed to let him lop off my head?" He returned his attention to the ruined overcoat and shirts, fingering each tear. *A shame.* Tossing the overcoat aside, he staggered to his feet. "I need to eat." The tower larders should have something. Maybe there was a change of clothes inside or, at least, the means to wash and repair his attire.

And myself. His blood had congealed upon his front and he didn't dare doubt his back looked a similar gory mess. *Food first.* He could bathe once his body didn't feel like it was sucking itself dry.

"How can you think about food after doing all this?" Sean asked, incredulous.

"It is *because* I did all this that I need sustenance." It wouldn't matter if he was currently walking through the deepest pile of putrid filth, his body would still cry out to replace what he had lost. He slapped a hand against the door. The hinges creaked, but gave freely.

"Hey," Zurron called out, drawing everyone's attention. The elf stood near the leader he had managed to incapacitate. "This one's still alive. What do we do with him?"

"Truss him up and wait until he wakes," Gordon replied. "I want to hear what that message from me mum really said." His gaze slid to the rest of the dead guards. "I suppose we should bury them."

"Bastards dinnae deserve to be resting on the Goddess' bosom after what they attempted," Zurron growled. "I reckon we burn them. Let their souls be lost in the ether."

"I'm nae sure I want to be responsible for that."

The elf shrugged. "You're the crown prince, but I reckon they committed treason trying to take down the ambassador, nae matter their reasoning."

Gordon scrubbed at his chin, burrowing his fingers deep into his beard. "That is true. But we've nae the wood or the manpower to make a pyre big or hot enough for seven men."

"Give me some time to recuperate," Darshan said. "Along with nourishment, and I shall be able to do it." They would still need fuel to burn—it was always easier that way—but once the pyre got underway, keeping it at a high temperature would take very little effort.

"Fair enough," Gordon grumbled. "You were the one to suffer the most out of all this." He shook his head, mumbling inaudibly to himself. "Come on, there ought to be plenty of food in the tower for you."

"And perhaps some fresh clothes?"

Gordon grunted. "These sods sure dinnae need it anymore." He pointed a finger at Sean. "Secure the horses and be sure he—" Gordon jerked a thumb at the unconscious leader. "Stays put until we're ready to talk to him. And let us ken when he wakes up."

Sean snapped a salute and set about his task as Gordon waved

Darshan into the tower. After the sun-soaked forest, the inside of the tower was dark and smelt faintly of mould. That didn't bode well when it came to the condition of their food.

Nevertheless, Darshan raided the entirety of the outpost's larder whilst Gordon and Hamish picked through the guards' chests in search of clothing and answers.

What they hadn't found was any sign of a message from Queen Fiona.

Darshan pondered over the absence as he sat in the warmth of the doorway, toasty in his new—although admittedly slightly oversized—attire and munching on his haul whilst the rest waited for the leader of these men to awaken. His meal consisted of simple fair; mostly stale bread, cheese that had gone hard around the edges, a few smoked sausages that hadn't looked terribly suspect and the wizened lump of an apple.

He intended to consume every last bite.

If there had been any message, it could only have reached here via messenger pigeon. Even if there were no signs of the feathered rats within the tower. Anything reaching by foot was preposterous. The lack had to mean the leader had disposed of it. Had that been part of the queen's orders? Leaving no trace of suspicious, and possibly illegal, acts.

Hamish stepped through the doorway, his arms full of firewood, forcing Darshan to scrunch against the door pillar. "This is the last of it," his lover declared, dumping his haul beside a pile near the charred remains of the guard Darshan had already halfway cremated.

Rather than move the bones—an act not even Darshan was willing to attempt—the others had piled the bodies, along with the split wood from within the tower, atop the remains. All it would take to ignite was a little push from his magic.

They just had to wait now.

"Do you think the queen ordered a hunt?" Sean murmured to his elven companion, shaking his head. "I cannae believe she would suggest such a thing, but do you?"

"Maybe nae her," Zurron growled. "But they clearly had nae qualms. Still..." He glanced towards the charred remains of a guard. "They got theirs. Should've been flogged for even suggesting it, but the punishment fits."

"What *is* this hunt?" Darshan asked between bites of the last sausage. One of the guards had mentioned it before the leader had ordered their attack.

Heavy silence followed in the wake of his question. Hamish looked as though he might vomit at any moment, whilst the rest of them all looked at each other as if trying to decide which amongst them would be the unfortunate one to answer him.

Sighing, Gordon scratched at his cheek with a thumb. "It's an archaic form of punishment. Something from the ancient scriptures. You ken of them?"

Darshan raised a brow at that. Were these the same scriptures Hamish claimed Queen Fiona followed? "I have heard them mentioned," he admitted. Dread seethed in the depths of his mind, backed by a slow-burning anger.

"Were you also told what those scriptures entail? What they used to do to men like you?"

Darshan shook his head. The conversation he'd had with Hamish atop that disused castle tower—a time that seemed an eternity ago—had moved on and he had forgotten to ask. He could guess readily enough, though. All this time, he had thought the gathering of spellsters had been a gentle thing. But to hunt them like animals?

"Gor," Hamish warned. "Dinnae you dare tell him what those bastards used to do."

"He deserves to ken," Gordon snapped back at his brother. "I'll be brief. The scriptures hold the laws of the clans. Of what should be obeyed for a happy life. Much of it has been scrubbed from the new version, but the old one was... nae kind to people like you. They were seen as detrimental to the Goddess' will."

"Spellsters?" He could see how the people wouldn't want entire families of magically gifted folk, but they were used as healers and were considered as vital resources during plague.

Hamish shook his head. "He means men like us."

Gordon cleared his throat but said nothing further.

"That..." Darshan glanced from one brother to the next. Shock wiped his mind, sending him adrift. "Sorry, I believe I misheard there. You mean they were *killed* for loving other men?" Was Hamish really suggesting that, had either of them been born in those times, then they would've been hunted and slain?

"Aye," Gordon replied.

"I honestly have no idea what to say to that." There had been no such restrictions in Udynea, not even when the empire was young. "How old are these scriptures?"

"Me mum was a wee lass when the law was finally struck from Clan Decree. I reckon it's been about five decades. A lot of folks dinnae care much about who other folk are sleeping with, providing they keep their heads down like everyone else. But there's plenty who are nae so forgiving."

"Clearly." Enough to use him as target practice, at the very least. "I..." Even knowing the wound was gone—the trace of its entry fading the longer his magic worked at the spot—he still ran a finger across his chest. It could've just as easily been his heart. There was no coming back from an injury as grave as that.

"He's awake," Zurron called.

Wiping the greasy residue of sausage off his fingers, Darshan stood to join the others at the elf's side.

The guard sat against the tower wall, surveying their surroundings. His greying brows lifted upon spying the pile of bodies before sinking to their lowest. "So," he snarled, his dark gaze settling on Darshan. Perhaps it was the murderous ire warping his face, but he seemed to be a good few decades younger than the other guards. "You survived at the expense of me men."

"Never you mind him," Gordon said, squatting between the man and Darshan. "You mentioned receiving a message from your queen. Was that the truth?"

"And what happened to it?" Hamish added.

Darshan bit his tongue. He was certain of the answer there.

"Aye, your highness. A pigeon arrived a few days ago, likely nae long after you lot started your wee journey." He grinned broadly at Hamish, showing a row of mostly gaps with a few teeth. "It said to burn the message afterwards, so I did. All right and proper. Cannae fault a man for following his queen's orders."

Gordon jerked the man's head around with a tug of the beard. "What did the message say?"

The man harrumphed, further ruffling his beard. "I already told you."

The older prince folded his arms and continued to silently glare at the guard.

Those dark eyes clouded with uncertainty. "I spoke nae lies. We were only following Queen Fiona's order. Find the ambassador and escort him."

"As what?" Darshan snapped. "A corpse?"

The man spat in Darshan's direction. "Filth like you deserve death. Your kind are poison, spreading your corruption across the land, sickening everyone you touch."

"And what would you have told that queen once I turned up dead?" Darshan enquired.

The man shrugged. "Bandits... Bears... Boars... There's plenty of mishaps that can happen to the unwary traveller."

"I've heard enough, Gor," Hamish said. "Do it."

Gordon opened his mouth as if to object, then closed it and withdrew a slim dagger from his back sheath.

"Do?" the guard demanded. Panic widened his eyes. "Do what? You cannae harm me. What would you tell the queen?"

"You knowingly injured," Gordon replied, laying a hand on the man's head. "And attempted to kill, an imperial ambassador who also happens to be a prince of the Udynea Empire. They are our allies and that means you wilfully committed treason."

"This is nae Udynea," the man growled. "The only treasonous ones here are you for letting this filth freely wander the lands."

"May you be granted all the mercy you show others." Gordon plunged the dagger into the man's neck, holding it there even as the guard jerked and only removing the blade when the man had stopped moving. "Throw him with the others." He stepped back, letting the body fall to the ground.

Blood continued to pour from the wound, staining the grass as Zurron and Sean hefted the leader onto the pile of bodies and wood.

"Light it," Gordon commanded.

Darshan breathed deep and focused on the straw packed around the wood. He hadn't regained as much energy as his healing had burnt through, but with luck, he would need only a spark. The air grew hot. Thin curls of smoke, almost indistinguishable in the haze, drifted up from the straw.

Then, with a mighty *whump* and a billow of pale grey smoke, the whole pyre flared to life.

"By smoke and flame," Gordon said as the fire twirled and danced before them. "I cast you from the Goddess' bosom. Through dust and char you are condemned to wander the endless darkness of the ether."

They stood vigil as the pyre burned. Darshan maintained a tentative hold on the fire, manipulating the intensity to a furnace-like heat. The air all around it shimmered in the dull afternoon light. The wood crackled and snapped, not quite masking the sizzle of flesh. He took care to manipulate the wind, too. Not a terrible amount, just enough of a gust to feed the flames and keep the stench from invading his nostrils.

When there was nothing of the guards but ash, they smothered the embers and mounted their horses. Whilst it would've been more convenient for them to use the tower's facilities, especially with dusk approaching, none of them had been at all keen to sleep where dead men had lain.

"We're going to be in so much trouble when we get back," Hamish mumbled as they returned to the road.

"Sounds like we already are," Gordon replied. "I just hope Mum hasnae done something foolish."

"Perhaps this was all a misunderstanding," Darshan suggested. He certainly hoped so. Whilst the idea of someone plotting the end of his life wasn't new by any measure, that a foreign queen sought his death carried complications he didn't want to think about. "I doubt she would seek to throw her people into a war."

"Nae rational ruler would prefer war over peace," Gordon said, the uncertain twist of his frown not instilling Darshan with much confidence that the man considered his own mother as befitting the description. "I guess we'll have to wait and see. If more guards come after us, then we'll ken her true intentions."

"I fecking hope not," Zurron muttered. "Last thing we need is a bloody war."

"And it is the last thing my father wants," Darshan assured the man. That didn't mean Udynea wouldn't be ready for one. The empire fought with herself more often than not. Squabbles amongst lords that were only settled after imperial forces moved in. It certainly kept the army sharp.

He glanced over his shoulder. The tower stood dark against the blushing peachy hue of the sky. Surely, with the speed they travelled and the time they'd wasted, any troops sent to fetch them would've already arrived. *They were acting alone*. There would perhaps be additional tongue lashings for the two princes, and further ignoring of his own presence, but nothing further.

At least, he could hope.

Chapter 23

Every time he saw the cloister on Crowned Mountain, Hamish was in awe of its ability to remain in place. Hewn from the very cliff face, it clung to the side of the mountain. Slashes of green broke up the grey-brown monotony of the mountainside, gardens to supplement the tithe gifted to them by the very farms their group had visited on the way.

It had taken them seven days to get here since leaving Mullhind. All of them without a sign of being followed.

He thought the delay at Old Willie's, and the messy business at the guard outpost, would've left them too far behind to make the trip today worthwhile. But they had made up the lost time by way of Darshan's globe of light illuminating the road as dusk drew near. Just a half-hour here and there had swiftly added up, leading to them spending less time in the dubious safety of tents and more in the security of barns and sheds.

They had halted just off the road winding up the mountainside. A spring lay in the clearing, the warm water bubbling up from somewhere deep in the ground.

His lover stood at his elbow, staring up at the building. Darshan seemed unimpressed with the structure, but then the cloister was an old Domian outpost. Given that the southern half of Udynea was once part of the ancient empire, it undoubtedly had dozens of such buildings. "How far away is it?" Darshan asked. "Will we be required to climb?"

Hamish shook his head. Whilst the cloister had a solid rope and pulley for hauling supplies up the cliff face in a half-hour, few were willing to risk their lives to such a contraption. The road stopped at the foot of the cliff where a narrow path snaked its way up to the cloister gates. "It's an hour or two via horseback." They would spend the night there before heading off for home come midmorning.

"Then why are we stopping?"

"To cleanse ourselves," Gordon replied. "The priests prefer visitors to be unsoiled before entering." He jerked his head at the pond from which their unsaddled horses currently drank. "A little dip usually suffices. We'll eat on the way up."

"Bathe in a natural pool in the middle of nowhere? How terribly rustic." Although Darshan continued to affect a casual air, a hint of trepidation lurked in the flatness of his lips and the dull way he eyed the pond.

With the horses tethered, they shed their clothes and leapt into the water. The pond was deep enough for even his father to relax sitting down. Although, just how tall his father stood was a bit of a mystery to them. He had fond memories of him and his brother attempting to measure their father's height as boys without him knowing. Seven foot was their estimate.

Hamish slithered into the pond, tepid water enveloping him like a warm sheet in winter. He sank until only his chin sat above the surface. Closing his eyes, he tipped his head back against the edge of the pond. The act of bathing usually took a few minutes of scrubbing to ensure all the dirt was gone, but no one was exactly in a rush to clamber up the mountain.

After a while, he became aware of the presence not far away on his right. *That better nae be you, Gor.* His brother had a wicked sense of humour when it came to water games. Most were harmless enough if both parties knew how to swim, but he wasn't in the mood for a dunking.

Opening his eyes revealed Gordon to be bobbing amicably on the other side of the pond with the two guards chatting to his left. *And Dar?*

He twisted to find his lover sitting quietly at the side of the pond, not that far from where Hamish floated. *Odd.* The man had been bemoaning the lack of a decent tub to bathe in all the way here.

Hamish pushed himself off the rocky bottom of the pond, drifting closer to Darshan without looking like the man was his goal. Halting at his lover's feet, he rested his arms on a flat rock. "Are you nae going to join us?"

With his lips curving into a watery imitation of a smile, Darshan shook his head. "Thank you, but I shall politely decline the offer. I am perfectly all right staying dry."

"It's nae cold."

Silent laughter creased the corners of those hazel eyes. "That is not my concern."

Hamish clambered onto dry land. Water dripped from his beard, trickling down his chest in a freezing trail as the spring breeze cooled the drops and nipped at his bare skin. "What is, then?"

That hazel gaze darted down then back up and Darshan's tongue peeked out to wet his lips. Still, he remained uncustomarily silent. During much of their travels, the man had barely stopped talking, be it to attempt teaching Hamish the Udynean language or natter with either Gordon or the guards. Much to the latter two's consternation at first.

Was it the naked part that bothered Darshan? The man had been slightly apprehensive the first time he had undressed in Hamish's presence. "Do men nae bathe in front of each other in Udynea?" It seemed a little at odds with what he'd been told countless times in the past, but not everything about the empire had lived up to his expectation.

The question seemed to shake Darshan from his stupor. "No, there are several public baths within Minamist alone, not including the one within the palace. I just—" He huffed, frowning. Red bloomed in his cheeks. "I am not generally the self-conscious type, but it has occurred to me that all of your bits are uncut whilst I—"

"We're just bathing," Hamish said before Darshan could finish talking. *Uncut?* His lover was clearly the opposite. Did that mean they had actually put a blade down there? A shudder passed through him at the thought. "Nae one stares at another's dick whilst they bathe."

"I beg to differ. You turn up to any public bath in Minamist with that monster and you would garner nothing but stares." He cocked his head, his brows twitching into a considering frown, before adding, "And perhaps a few proposals."

Hamish laughed, heat flooding his cheeks. "Remind me to never visit a public bath during my next visit to Minamist."

"Are you two joining us?" Gordon bellowed from the other side of the pond. "Or are you going to cluck at each other like two old chooks?"

The pit-sized lump at the fore of his lover's throat bobbed. "All right," Darshan grumbled. He flung his arms wide. "If you gentlemen would be so good as to turn around, I shall get in."

"Get a load of Sir Modest, here," Sean crowed. Submerged to his neck, his surfacing hand sprayed water everywhere as he jerked a thumb towards Darshan. "What are you going to show us that we dinnae already have?"

Darshan muttered something in response as he peeled off the layers of clothing. Although the words were just loud enough for Hamish to hear, they were also spoken in the Udynean tongue. He recalled a few words from his daily tutoring with his lover on the language, but not enough to string the sentence together.

Finally, Darshan divested himself of his smalls and tossed them atop his pile of clothing.

Hamish couldn't help the appreciative sigh tightening his throat. His lover might not have been a solid man, nor was he as thickly carpeted as every other man Hamish had been with, but what was there was... *Perfect*. The priests said the Goddess had a hand in creating each being, if that were true, then she could've put Darshan forward as her masterpiece.

"Fecking hell," Sean blurted, breaking Hamish's quiet adoration. "You've had a good inch lopped off your pecker."

Hamish groaned. Yes, the look of Darshan's nether region was a little odd with the foreskin missing, but he couldn't believe any of them would be crass enough to point it out.

Before anyone else could say a word, Gordon lazily swept his arm in a wide arc, splashing the guard. "Nae more than the inch of floppy skin you've got hanging there."

"I'll give you an inch," Sean shot back.

Hamish faltered in the act of getting back into the pond, slithering into the water by way of inertia. Of all the words to come out of the man's mouth, he hadn't thought it would be those.

Gordon laughed, deep and hearty. "Just an inch? I ken you were small, but you didnae have to measure it for me."

Snarling, the guard practically leapt across the pond like a surfacing fish. The man barrelled straight into Gordon, dragging the pair of them under. Water splashed everywhere.

"Come on, lads," Hamish grumbled, fighting the urge to strangle the both of them. "Have a little restraint."

"They are," Zurron piped up from his new vantage point on Hamish's left. "It's a *lot* of restraint you want them to have, nae a little."

"I really do not mind," Darshan said. He had slipped into the pool whilst the two men continued to wrestle and splash each other, and now bobbed at Hamish's right elbow. "Reminds me a little of home."

Frowning, Zurron leant forward to address Darshan around Hamish. "Seeing two lumbering men fighting in water reminds you of home?"

"Naked wrestling has always been quite the popular sport in select circles. It is actually gaining a wider audience at present."

"Two men actually wrestle naked?"

"Or two women. And yes."

"Are they doing it... willingly?"

"You mean are the contestants slaves?" There was a grim edge to Darshan's otherwise congenial smile. "Some of them might be—there are very few sports slaves are forbidden from competing in—but not the majority."

"And what does the winner get?"

"The usual, I would suspect." Darshan shrugged. "Money, women, men... prestige. It is all largely in good fun. Except for those betting on the wrong outcome, I guess."

"I'm picking there are rules, then?"

"Rules for what?" Sean asked. The pair had surfaced and now gave them comically identical squints of confusion. "Loping a pecker off? I can tell you the first one: nae mine. Nae whilst I'm still breathing."

Darshan's expression soured.

"Actually," Hamish said, diverting his lover's attention. "Since Sean brought the topic up and all... I've been meaning to ask about..." He waggled a finger downwards whilst rubbing at the back of his neck. Deciding how to breach a clearly delicate topic was one of the reasons he hadn't done so. What was the correct way to speak of it? "Why *are* you... cut?" He thought it might've been an unfortunate accident, but if it was common enough for a man such as himself to garner attention, then maybe that was the way in Minamist.

"We call it *Khutani*," Darshan replied. "Both for the act and the coming of age practise where it is done."

"You cut it off *deliberately*?" Sean mumbled, his cheeks losing their usual slightly golden tone.

Hamish glanced at the other two men, both Zurron and Gordon looked equally as sick as Sean. What earthly reason could an entire culture have to remove pieces of themselves? Especially a region such as that.

"It has been around for as long as the Udynea Empire. Probably back before we were even truly an empire. The foreskin is removed when a boy is..." Darshan scrunched his face in thought. "Thirteen? Fourteen years of age. *When* rather varies by city. I was done when I was twelve."

As one, the rest of the group hissed in sympathy, grasping or covering their privates.

Hamish winced right alongside the others, certain everything had just attempted to retract right up inside him. The mere thought of letting a blade anywhere near that region... "Ouch."

His lover laughed. "*Yes.* Although, not for long if one has access to a healer or has been in training long enough to acquire innate healing as I had."

Hamish hadn't seen any healing beyond what had been used upon himself. He *had* heard tales of the plague that'd happened a few years before either him or his siblings were born. So many lives had fallen to the sickness by the time his grandfather had allowed the

Tirglasian spellsters to leave their cloisters. Once magic had intervened, the plague had ground to a halt faster than a dry waterwheel, but what had intrigued him was how the stories explained the utter lack of fear those spellsters were rumoured to have shown. They spent days surrounded by death and illness and never once felt the slightest bit unwell.

"Then, wouldnae it just have grown back?" Gordon asked.

"No?" Darshan arched a brow at the man. "Healing magic does not work in such a fashion. It uses the body's natural ability, just expediting the process. That is, typically, why scarring still occurs. Given that neither humans, dwarves nor elves can regrow severed parts like a lizard, the best the body's capable of in such a circumstance is the usual crude method of knitting everything together. Scarring and all."

"I dinnae see any sc—" Hamish said before catching himself, his cheeks burning. No one here minded that he liked men, but being so free with his tongue in their company could mean a slip up back home.

Out the corner of his eye, he caught Zurron's sly smile. "I bet you've had a good long look," he snickered, his grin widening when Hamish splashed him.

Darshan cleared his throat. If he had heard the elf, he made no indication. "The one thing the healing magic does well is reduce most marks to a few fine lines, if it does not mend seamlessly. As you can no doubt tell, the latter is a far more common outcome." He indicated the shoulder that had been shot only five days prior, which showed no sign of the injury. "I could show you all the full effect on a more noticeable part, if you would like?"

Hamish shook his head before anyone could suggest otherwise. "We've all seen healing before." Granted, in his case, only when he had been the patient. "You mentioned something about it being innate?" He had thought all healing was instinctual, whether there was magic involved or not, just that the non-magical type was far slower and didn't always save the life it was trying to mend.

His lover frowned and Hamish scrunched deeper into the water. Had he asked something he shouldn't have? He would be the first to admit how woefully ignorant he was in what information could be shared, especially around magic.

"It is harder to explain to those lacking the ability." Darshan gave a considering hum. "Once there has been a certain—" He waved his hand, the right words clearly escaping him. "Healing magic is an intimate skill. It requires sufficient training and understanding of how the body works—not to mention constant usage of the ability and all that. It is through that training that the body begins to draw upon magic to heal injuries without conscious thought."

"Handy," Sean murmured. "I suppose, being aware your magic can mend any injury makes taking the reckless option less dangerous."

Darshan's lips twisted wryly. "Not really. There are exceptions to most things and healing has its limits. Whilst comforting in some situations, the magic cannot differentiate between a simple pricked finger and a broken leg, reacting with the same urgency either way." He shrugged, rippling the water. "It is but one of the immutable norms, much like elemental magic must obey certain rules."

"Such as?" Hamish coaxed. His lover had seemingly relaxed, talking about a topic obviously a great deal more pleasant than their previous one. If Hamish was capable of keeping the conversation going in the same direction, then the others would likely forget too.

"Fire requires heat, air and fuel if not feeding off a spellster's magical energy. The apparent conjuring of water from nothing is little more than the act of drawing moisture from the air—rather tricky in dry climates. That sort of thing."

"I dinnae—" Hamish fell silent, just like the rest of the men. He likely wore the same considering frown as well.

Darshan chuckled, submerging himself until the laughter became just bubbles burbling beneath the hook of his nose. "Do not tell me you all thought magic happened just like that." He snapped his fingers, flicking droplets in all directions.

But that was it. Hamish had given no thought towards how spellsters created the terrors and miracles they performed. Likely no more so than their ancestors had the day they bound and cloistered their once-revered chiefs. Magic was a thing best left alone.

Forgotten.

He shouldn't be intrigued by the idea of watching Darshan display more of his abilities. Nae after seeing just how dangerous the man could become when riled.

~ ~ ~

They continued to bathe in relative silence, the heads of the other men no doubt swimming with new information. The quiet suited Darshan just fine as it enabled him to turn his focus to the cloister. Whilst it clung rather impressively to the side of the cliff, the building looked to be the size of the academy him and his siblings studied at. Being a place of prestige, the academy typically had between fifty to seventy students.

He couldn't see the cloisters operating on the same low ratio of students to teachers, but perhaps the same number of spellsters walked those halls as did in the academy. It made sense, if he viewed it from a Tirglasian standpoint, for small groups of spellsters to be contained across the land rather than something like the massive prison setup they used in Demarn.

"They're nae expecting us," Gordon said. "Or *you*."

Darshan frowned at the man. Had he heard a note of reassurance in Gordon's voice? Did the man think Darshan held reservations about entering the cloister after asking to visit in the first place? Under ordinary circumstances, he supposed the average spellster would be at risk of confinement. Not that they called it as such. "It is kind of you to be concerned, but I already gathered my ambassadorial status grants me immunity from such laws. Was I wrong to think so?"

Gordon hastily shook his head, his flushed face having nothing to do with the mild heat of the pond.

"And I trust we shall be camping somewhere nearby after our visit?" He spied several places with room enough for a tent. Their camp might be a little more spaced out than usual, but it was doable.

"We'll nae need to do that," Sean said. "They've beds to spare."

Bless. Actual beds with mattresses and pillows. He would even settle for something as lumpy as the back-aching bed he had left behind in the castle's guest quarters. Anything to stall another night sleeping on the unforgiving ground.

"Single beds," Zurron added. "One per room, typically. You'll nae be able to sleep coiled up to your walking heat source." The man waggled his brows suggestively. It was no secret that Darshan shared a tent with his lover, but the others clearly thought more was happening within than mundane slumber.

Gordon splashed the elf. "Dinnae you start again. Shut your gob and get out." Taking his own advice, the man hauled himself out of the pond and started drying off.

One by one, the rest abandoned the warm water and hastened to their separate piles of clothing. Darshan lazily followed suit, turning his power to forming a barrier just around his body and heating the air within. It was an old trick that enabled him to dry off far quicker whilst also keeping the cool wind at bay.

He abandoned the Tirglasian-made attire in favour of his original garb, with the exception of the thicker undershirt. His sherwani was wrinkled from a week folded within the depths of his pack, but nothing a little moist heat couldn't fix.

His gaze returned to the cloister as he did up the last few buttons. The priests must've had ways of keeping their charges within the walls. Hopefully, it would be made clear that he wasn't to be a new addition to the spellster ranks.

Once clothed, the rest of the group returned to their mounts with a wordless syncing that spoke of a great many travels together. They'd done similar actions along the way.

Darshan strolled along behind them, his thoughts mostly elsewhere as he checked Warrior's straps and tightened the pony's girth. "I must admit," he said, trying to maintain a light edge to the words. Not an easy task when the Tirglasian language already sounded quite harsh on his tongue. "I am surprised that all of you are quite laid back about me and…" He glanced his lover's way, trying to gauge the man's feelings on the matter of speaking openly when it came to who he desired.

Hamish showed none of the usual signs. No wincing, however minute. Not even the slight shifting of his gaze to suggest Darshan remained silent. Hamish merely went about his usual task of checking his horse's straps before mounting, as casual as if Darshan had remarked on the cloudy nature of the sky.

"That is to say, the current sleeping arrangements," Darshan continued. Although they hadn't spent many nights sleeping in tents, he still felt the warmest snuggled against his lover. Not that they'd done more than slumber—no different to the rest of the group—but he supposed cruder minds would wander below the belt far more often. "I would have thought that such things were rare and—"

"Frowned upon?" Gordon finished. "Aye, and I wouldnae blame you for thinking it the truth after those bloody guards attacked you. Or what with how me Mum's treated you. She's certainly nae trying to be open-minded there."

"Gor picked us because we're nae likely to judge," Zurron said, clambering aboard his horse.

"Your head's full of tar if you think that's the only reason," Gordon snapped back at the guard.

"Aye," Sean said. "We ken there are others, but it was a factor, you must admit that."

Gordon shook his head. "The point these two lugs are trying to make is that they've personal experience with those who prefer the same gender. Zurron's brother is a bit like you and 'Mish."

"A bit?" Darshan echoed.

"He's married to a nice human lass from up in the northern farms now," Zurron added. "But he's always been just as fond of chasing men."

Gordon bridged the gap between mounts to nudge his brother. "Didnae we try to have the pair of you step out for a bit?"

Hamish sneered whilst picking at his teeth with a fingernail. "Dinnae talk to me about him," he grumped. "Nae offence, Zur, but your brother's a prick."

The elf laughed, rocking back in the saddle. "You cannae offend me there, I've called him far worse."

"And Quinn's brother was exactly like you two," Gordon continued.

"*Was?*" Darshan echoed, his stomach twisting with the all-too-familiar queasiness of dread. He never liked that word. There'd been far too many instances of its use with his half-sisters. Had the man been a victim of that now-illegal practice innocently referred to as a hunt?

"He hung himself just last autumn." There was just a little bit too much of a flippant edge to Gordon's voice, an echo of the crown prince's mother. "And Sean here." He jerked his chin at the brown-haired man, who'd become solemn at the mention of their comrade's brethren. "His sister has a wife and they're expecting their first in…" Gordon frowned. "Is it two months now? I've lost track."

Sean nodded. The hint of a prideful smile tweaked the corner of his mouth. "About that, aye. They're hoping for a good strong lass."

Darshan frowned. "She has a wife?" After learning they had hunted men for what had been seen as a corrupting act only half a century ago, the notion of those same people being allowed something as official as marriage was a surprising one. "Same gender couples can marry?"

Again, the guard bobbed his head in affirmation. "Nae many choose to and most priests dinnae like the idea, but coin generally changes their tune."

"Dinnae let the priests hear you saying that," Zurron quipped. "They'll see you strung up for slander."

Darshan held his tongue as the pair continued to squabble good-naturedly amongst themselves. He had preferred not thinking about how much of a hold the priests had on people's way of life here. Not as badly as the kingdom of Obuzan, where the people lived in fear of their priesthood.

"Sean?" Darshan interjected during a lull in their chatter. "Did I mishear or was there a mention of an impending pregnancy?" Even before the rumours of a new child-making method whisked out of the Empire of Niholia, there were women in Udynea who bore children without seeking a man's aid. However, he was uncertain if that was what either of the men meant.

"Dinnae ask me how," the man insisted, waving his arm. "I've enough brains to nae enquire how a woman got in the family way, especially when that woman's me sister."

"Fair enough." He could rule out the Niholian method, which required magical healing knowledge on a level that boggled him, and he didn't think Tirglasians as a people would be the kind to impregnate without sex, but it was possible. Without those, that left Sean's sister as being also willing to sleep with a man or the woman's wife had done the deed herself. He couldn't see any of those options being open to any sort of dialogue. "I could not see myself asking the same of my sisters." Perhaps a few of the younger ones, but that would've been a completely different conversation given that the youngest was ten.

"You've sisters?" Gordon interjected, arching a brow at Hamish who just smiled and shrugged; the man had been there during the hunt for a special trinket to gift Anjali, after all. Gordon slapped his knee before Darshan could respond. "That's right. You said some are still unmarried. Are they all younger than you?"

Darshan inclined his head. "Although, in the case of my twin, just barely." Two hours. That was all it had taken for their mother to turn from having a healthy birth to dying in distress.

"How many?"

"Several more than I would like," he muttered, garnering a laugh from the group. In truth, he had lost count of them. If they had all survived, then the total would be a great deal more than the current dozen. At least, he hoped it was still that. Onella had made quite the contribution towards thinning the royal line, not that anyone could actually pin anything on her. Assassination studies had been the one place she had rather shone in the execution thereof.

Darshan glanced up at the cloister. The closer they got to the cliff, the more that building loomed over them and he found ignoring the cloister's presence wasn't a simple task. "I wonder if you could indulge me in a question?" he asked of Hamish. "Why *are* all your spellsters cloistered?"

"Did you nae learn that when you were taught the language?"

"Well, yes but I—" He grinned sheepishly. "I rather drifted off." Only his elderly nanny, Daama, could make the learning of history engaging enough to absorb, but he wouldn't have dreamt of asking her to come along. "There was a war? Or am I confusing your history with that of the Demarn Kingdom?"

Hamish shrugged and turned to his brother.

"I cannae say much about Demarn's history," Gordon confessed. "But aye, there was a war. Spellsters like yourself had full reign of the land."

Sounds familiar. It seemed to be a common theme in most of the lands where spellsters were either imprisoned or outright slain on sight. "I suppose they enslaved people, too?"

Gordon's expression soured, but he shook his head. "There wasnae a need. The entire kingdom was under their thumb, each clan blindly following their chief. They were considered blessed by the Goddess and untouchable. Right up until the first king of the people challenged his chief in battle and won."

"Against magic?" Could there really be a Nulled One that far back in the royal line? "I take it he is your ancestor?"

"We're nae direct descendants. Our line comes from a civil war five hundred years back."

After his tutelage, Darshan had been left with the impression that Tirglasian rule had been stable for far longer. His own bloodline's influence rather fluctuated, holding power on and off over the past thousand years, with his great-grandfather being the one to wrest the crown back from a usurper not even a century ago. "I cannot imagine the spellsters of that time were pleased with the idea of whiling their lives away in cloisters."

"They were prisons first," Hamish mumbled.

"Like the Demarn tower?" Reports of what transpired behind those thick walls were few. Rumours ran rampant about the place, with Udynean parents using the horrid imagery of the tower complex to frighten young children into line. *To spend one's whole life from birth to death in one tower*. The imperial palace was bad enough at times and he had the choice to leave its walls should he desire.

"I dinnae ken about their tower, but the stories mention a lot of death. On both sides."

Darshan could imagine that. A single, moderately-powerful, spellster was capable of wiping out a small village if riled. One against an army would fight with every scrap of power if they knew only imprisonment or death were their options.

"Those who submitted were said to be... bound?" Hamish glanced at Gordon as if seeking confirmation from his brother, relief relaxing his shoulders as the man nodded. "I dinnae ken how, though."

"Nae one does," Gordon added.

Darshan already had a suspicion there. *Infitialis*. The rare purple metal that had a reputation for exploding at the slightest miscalculation during its processing and also nullifying a spellster's abilities, providing that person was encircled by it—a collar being the most foolproof method. He could think of nothing else capable of binding a spellster.

That spoke of Domian influence.

If the ancient, and now very much eradicated, empire had reached as far as Tirglas, then how much had it influenced the land? How he wished he knew the answer there, for it would certainly explain the lack of trust in spellsters. Not that the actions of his ancestors within Udynea would've soothed any minds.

His gaze slid back to the cloister. Perhaps the answers he sought lay within.

Chapter 24

The road led up the foot of the cliff. Buildings sprawled around the base; stables, storerooms and what appeared to be a few huts sitting on the edge of the undergrowth. Darshan hadn't expected to find much out here beyond the cloister, perhaps a few buildings to serve as a resting point for those bringing wares, but this almost amounted to a small hamlet.

Much of the cleared space was taken by carts and cargo. Whilst most of the men and women bustled around the carts, loading barrels and sacks, others stacked more of the same onto a wooden pallet sitting innocently enough on the ground.

Gordon jerked a chin at the workers. "They'll nae doubt send up a missive with the cargo, letting the priest ken we're coming.

A few of the men were lashing the barrels and sacks to the pallet, which seemed to be attached to a crossbeam via heavy ropes. Darshan followed the ropes up to where an even thicker one led straight up the cliff. A wooden structure jutted out from the edge like a laughing fisher bird over the southern end of the twin lakes. He almost expected it to swoop down after them. *Any second now.*

Behind him, Zurron grumbled. "That pulley system gives me the willies every time I see it." Darshan caught the man visibly shudder. The elf shot a disapproving glance up at the structure, a worried frown creasing his forehead.

"Do you see something wrong?" Darshan asked. Perhaps there was a fault in the mechanism that superior elven vision could spot. "Dangerous, perhaps?"

"Nae more so than usual." The man shrugged. "But what do I ken about how they work? Me dad just spends his days designing the sodding things."

Darshan drew his pony in until he rode beside the elf. "You have expressed concern to them before?"

"Aye," Zurron muttered. "Every time we come here, they're overloading it. You can have all the muscle you like at the other end, but if the pulley's nae built to take the strain, she'll give. I can only pray that she doesnae take someone with her when it happens."

They turned onto a narrow road winding up the mountainside. The necessity of keeping to a single file stalled all but the most important of conversations, lending Darshan's mind far too much time to consider the unimpeded drop should his pony stumble. Not what he wished to think about—even if he'd little fear of heights—but once his thoughts latched onto the notion, it was somewhat reluctant to consider anything else. He could certainly see the merit behind why those in the buildings below preferred the pulley for carting their goods.

Their journey upward seemed to travel at a snail's pace, but the path they trekked wasn't eternal and the cloister entrance loomed over them in due time. The archway seemed to be made half from hewn blocks and half carved directly out of the cliff. Each man-made slab was pitted by the centuries of rain, the edges no longer sharply defined, if they ever had been.

His gaze slid to the building itself. It was like no cloister he had ever seen before. Seemingly a repurposed fortress, much of the structure was embedded in the mountain. And it carried on higher up than he'd imagined, too. The front had been carved splendidly, but all the effort seemed to halt several levels up and what he'd first thought to be cracks in the mountainside were actually windows.

An elderly man garbed in a simple willow-wood brown robe of the Tirglasian priesthood trotted over as they filed through the gate. "Your highnesses." He bowed low to Gordon and Hamish in turn, seemingly flustered. "We were nae expecting your presence."

Darshan couldn't help but raise an eyebrow there. Such a thing was unheard of when he or his sisters travelled. Every man and his dog seemed to know precisely where the *Mhanek's* children were at any given time, even throughout Darshan's moments of spontaneity. But then, he supposed that getting word to this remote section of mountainside would be difficult without the magical technology the Udynean government had access to.

"We're here to see our sister," Gordon said, dismounting. A woman scurried up to take hold of the man's reins and led the horse into what appeared to be a stable hewn into the bottom level of the cloister.

The rest of their group dismounted, Darshan following suit. He stood next to Warrior, patting the pony's neck and attempting to decipher his next move. Both the princes had been relieved of their mounts, whereas the two guards were leading theirs into the stable.

Someone must've decided he was of some importance as a man scampered to his side with a cascade of apologies and relinquished the pony from his charge.

Darshan took the opportunity to stroll to Hamish's side, casting an eye across the courtyard.

A massive wheel took up one side and the nearby wall had been demolished, letting thick wooden beams jut out into the abyss. Hanging off them was a rope as thick as his thigh. The business end of the pulley system, no doubt.

"This is his highness, Darshan *vris Mhanek*," Gordon said by way of introduction to the man. "He's a spellster from Udynea and has expressed interest in the inner workings of our cloisters." Gordon's expression grew dark for a heartbeat. "He will be returning with us."

The old man's face scrunched as if he had bitten a lemon. "It isnae our policy to let those with magic just wander out our gates."

"It would be prudent for you to make an exception here," Darshan said before either prince could reply. "If only for the good of your kingdom. My father would be rather vexed if he was forced into a war to recover me."

The old man peered at him. Then the reality of the situation seemed to seep into his mind as his ruddy face slowly drained of colour. His dark eyes darted to Gordon, finding only confirmation. "As always, your highnesses are welcome to come and go as you please. Will you be staying long?" There was a hopeful note in the man's voice of the answer being in his favour.

"A day or two," Gordon replied. He made his way up the stairs leading inside, tailed closely by the old man. "We should make our sister aware of our arrival. Where will we find her?"

The man's bony shoulders bobbed. "The study hall, where else?"

"Still? I would've thought she'd have learnt all she could by now."

"There is always more to be learnt of the body, your highness. Some of our texts speak of reviving the dead, but none so far have ever been able to successfully duplicate the act."

Darshan frowned as he followed the men into the cloister. What did the feats from spellsters of old have to do with a Tirglasian princess? Was she ill? Deathly so? Or was there some ailment that wound through the countryside that he hadn't heard of? It wouldn't be the first time a plague had come to Tirglas. He'd been quite shocked to find one had ravaged the land only a generation ago.

Inside, they strolled by the men and women also walking the corridors with little fuss. A few were in the same drab robes that the man who led them wore. The vast majority of the people were clothed in modest attire that appeared no different to any he had seen on those walking the streets. Whilst a casual glance revealed that a number of clothes appeared threadbare—mostly on a few of the younger subjects—there was nothing else to suggest their position.

He eyed the necks of several, finding them bare. *Odd.* After hearing they'd bound the first cloistered spellsters, he had expected to find the current ones also leashed by *infitialis*. Perhaps they weren't spellsters, but the cloister's caretakers.

On the other hand, there seemed a great deal them, ranging from young children to white-haired elders who would surely be retired from their duties rather than bustling through corridors. "I would love to know the number of years it takes to indoctrinate them all into staying."

"A lot of spellsters turn themselves in to the local chapel," the old man replied, his chin lifting indignantly.

"So this obedience is something taught as a child, then?" It stood to reason. "Are there any active hunts for them?" Beyond Obuzan's merciless pursuits of spellsters by their priests, he knew only of one other land that seemed so intent on ridding their populace of magic. *Demarn.* His nanny had told him wicked tales of the King's Hounds stalking through that kingdom, corralling their spellsters like wayward cattle.

But where people like Demarn's hounds sounded as though they were specifically chosen and trained to deal with their rogue spellsters, the Obuzan priests were mere men. Spending a lifetime believing magic was sinful or made a person dangerous beyond measure would certainly aid in their compliance. Nobody wanted to think of themselves as the very monster they'd been taught to fear.

"You mean witch hunts?" Gordon asked. "Nae that I'm aware of. We're nae like our neighbouring lands."

"The Goddess had a plan in sending her power to mortals," the old man added. "Even if our minds are nae capable of discerning what that plan is. The chieftains of old might've abused their power, but we've grown humble with the centuries and the whims of magic no longer rule our clans. If we keep our faith in the Goddess absolute as scripture decrees, her divine plan will be made known to those who are in need of guidance."

Darshan chewed on the inside of his cheek in an effort to keep his true thoughts from showing on his face. He wasn't an overly religious man and none of the deities throughout the Udynea Empire required unfailing devotion. Coin, perhaps. Maintaining temples and feeding the various priesthoods wasn't free.

The man waved them through a doorway that appeared to house only an array of tables and chairs.

Darshan eyed the bare stone walls. Only the presence of the two brothers kept him from heeding the itching urge to form a shield around himself. Even so, if this was a study, then where were the books? The scrolls? Even a few diagrams would've put his mind at ease.

A lone woman occupied the space. She sat at one of the tables, her shoulder to them and bent over a large book spread before her. Her head rested on one hand, the fingers disappearing beneath the mass of gravity-defying blonde curls that crowned her head.

She glanced up as they neared, then lifted her head, beaming. " 'Mish? Gor?" She stood, one delicate finger pinning her place in the book. "I didnae think I'd be seeing you two until the summer. Is Mum being that much of a pain that you've had to escape already?" Her features didn't bear the same stark resemblance to the two princes as their other sister—clearly favouring her mother's bloodline in the sharpness of her chin and the narrow, downward tilt of her nose—but Darshan didn't doubt this woman shared blood with the men.

A far more pressing matter busily scrambled to find sense in what he saw. The woman didn't wear the light brown robes of priesthood, but rather a common gown and sleeveless vest. As much evidence as there was for her to be Hamish's sister, he could scarcely believe it. Yes, both princes had divulged that a sibling lived with the cloister, but in all the conversation they'd engaged with, never had either man mentioned their sister was...

A spellster.

That meant there *was* magic within the bloodline. Clear and strong enough to be made known. Gordon bumping through his shield wasn't a fluke. The man had to be a Nulled One and Hamish—

Well, Darshan had used direct magic on his lover before. Hamish clearly wasn't immune to it like his brother, which left only one option.

The woman swung to face Darshan, seeming to finally realise he was there. One sweep of his attire was all she gave before a veil of suspicion fell over her face. "Can I help you?"

Hamish cleared his throat. "I'd like you to meet his Imperial Highness, Darshan *vris Mhanek*, me—" He stalled, clearly flustered. "Me... uh..."

"Your yours?" the woman said, a soft smile crinkling her blue eyes. Not as aesthetically crystalline as her brother's, but dark like the oceans he had travelled to get here. "I see." Her gaze darted to Gordon, then Hamish, before she extended her hand to Darshan. "Nice to meet someone who is me brother's."

Darshan swiftly re-evaluated the woman's clothing. She indeed wore a shirt beneath the vest but the sleeves were tight along her arms and the same tawny shade as her skin. He clasped her hand

and offered a small bow. "Your highness."

She giggled. "I've nae been called that since I was a wee lass. You dinnae get to keep your titles when you're cloistered." She gave his hand a hearty shake. "Caitlyn is fine. I wouldnae have thought they'd allow a *vris* of the *Mhanek* to leave the Udynea Empire."

"He's me *friend*," Hamish blurted, his cheeks having gone an adorable shade of plum red.

"What would you ken of Udynean politics?" Gordon asked of his sister whilst simultaneously giving his brother a sympathetic pat on the shoulder, the man's jovial tone taking the edge off his words. "I dinnae recall Mum teaching us anything about them when we were bairns."

"There's more than a few mentions of Udynea in the older texts. Any decent study of the body requires slogging through the dregs of old rivalries and rumours of far off wars. Of course, there are the translations, but only a right idiot believes those. Nae that they cannae be called *technically* correct, but..." She rolled her eyes, rocking her head from side to side.

"I hope we were nae interrupting any serious studies," Gordon said.

Caitlyn shook her head. "Just giving meself a wee refresher of basic human bone structure. We'd a lad with a snapped thighbone and an absolutely shattered hand just a few weeks back. It was touch and go at finding someone with the power and proper understanding of how fingers work to mend him."

"It must've taken some doing for the lad to break it."

"Aye. But they mended his leg easily enough. Just a clean break. It was his hand that gave the most trouble."

Darshan nodded his agreement. They were some of the trickiest bones in the human body to mend correctly.

"He'll be walking with a limp now, but at least he still has full use of his hand. Certainly learnt his lesson on horse thieving." She jerked her thumb back at the book. "Anyway, I should be taking this one back. The information is good, but the diagrams are piss-poor compared to the ones in the archive."

"You've diagrams of human anatomy in your archives?" Darshan blurted before his manners could take command of his tongue. He smiled woodenly at the trio, secure in the knowledge that none of them could've possibly understood him. To the uninitiated mind, Udynean was often a garble of noise.

But whilst both the men stared at him with the almost identically confused expressions Darshan had expected, the twinkle in Caitlyn's eye suggested she had understood his every word.

"Would you like to see them?" she asked.

"Very much," he managed in Tirglasian. He hadn't been in a space dedicated to sketches of human, or elven, anatomy since his years training as a healer. Seeing the difference between what he remembered from the academy and here would be quite the education. "If you do not mind."

~~~

Hamish watched as his lover trotted off at his sister's side. "I guess I'll stay here, then," he mumbled. It wasn't as though he would understand half of what they spoke about. When it came to medicine and ailments of the human body, his knowledge didn't go much beyond splinting broken limbs and applying pressure to wounds.

Gordon chuckled, drawing Hamish's eye from the empty doorway. "What did you expect?" He leant back on a table, his arms casually bracing himself. "He's new and exciting; a spellster from another land. We're just her brothers. She sees us at least once a year."

It used to be every week. Back when there'd been a cloister within a few hours' march of Mullhind, before their mother had forced the priesthood to abandon it. They were fortunate Caitlyn had been sent this close as it was, for many of the spellsters had been spread out over the southern cloisters.

"In the meantime." His brother reluctantly pushed off the table and jerked his thumb at the door. "I should probably make sure the priests ken to bunk us all near each other tonight. I dinnae want to try explaining once we get back home why our return trip lacks a certain ambassador."

"Do you really think they'll try to keep him here? Or could contain him?" Darshan was right in that none of the spellsters, once cloistered, seemed at all eager to leave. He'd noticed similar during his brief stay at the old one near Mullhind. Back then, it had been explained to him that it just wasn't done. Spellsters didn't leave the cloisters without the consent of both priesthood and crown.

Gordon shrugged. "I couldnae rightly say either way there. And I'd prefer to nae find out." He halted in the doorway, peering back over his shoulder. "Speaking of ambassadors, have you made up your mind what you're going to do once Darshan's on his way?"

It might've been ten days since he'd confided in Gordon of how he felt about the Udynean, with the last week being consumed by their travels, but he was only surer of his answer. "I want to go with him."

"I thought that might be the case, but have you—"

"I ken it hasnae been long," he said before his brother could trot out the usual warnings. "How much can I possibly ken about him in
~~~

that short amount of time?" He peered at his brother. "You're staying unusually silent. Are you nae going to give me one of your stern warnings of how I should be listening to the right head?"

Gordon pulled a face and shook his head. "You pretty much covered most of it in your ranting. But I suppose you've probably enjoyed getting it on the regular."

Even though he knew his brother only jested, a part of him still bristled. "I'll have you ken that we've done nae more than innocent slumber during the whole journey. Or have your ears heard fairy-fancies since we've been travelling?"

Gordon held up his hands. "Nae a thing and for that, I am grateful, because the last thing I want to hear is me brother getting some."

Thoughts of Gordon actively cringing as his brother passed the tent Hamish shared with Darshan fluttered through his mind. He pressed his lips together, staving off a snicker. "Does that mean he's passed your test?"

Gordon grinned. "I've nae been testing him."

Huffing through his nose, he glanced at the table beside him for something to toss at his brother. "Dinnae give me that rot." He settled for a dollop of cooled candle wax some clumsy soul had left on the table, peeling it off and deftly lobbing it across the room. The wax shattered on his brother's upraised arm. "I ken you far too well."

Gordon peered over his wrist, his grin in no way diminished. "What I *was* going to ask before you interrupted me was whether you've spoken to him about it recently. Does he still want you to come back with him?"

Hamish rolled his eyes. "Of course he does." Even if their stint as lovers didn't last in the Crystal Court, he would still have his duties as an ambassador. And he'd be in a land that granted him far more freedom of self.

"He might've had his full of our little family's song and dance. After all, getting Mum to agree to you leaving will take some doing, especially if it's in his company."

Hamish flopped into the chair his sister had abandoned. He glanced at the book she'd been so intent on, but couldn't make out a single word. "I'll have a better chance of cracking a mountain with me skull than I do with convincing Mum. She nae listens to me anymore." Just one word, one piece of acknowledgement that she understood him. That was all he had ever wanted.

"We might need to call on Nora for help there."

"Nora'll throw us in the deep end and leave us floundering."

"I dinnae ken about that. Nae if we explain the situation to her. Ambassador, he said, right?" Gordon slapped his thigh when Hamish answered with a nod. "Nora will love that. She's been bemoaning the lack of the position since this correspondence began. Maybe if we can get her to convince Mum how badly we need someone in Minamist, she'll cave. I'd suggest getting Darshan involved there, but I dinnae see that happening amicably."

"Let me think about it on the way back. Coming at Mum from all sides without cause willnae endear us to her."

"Just dinnae take too long, you ken how stroppy Nora gets when she's left in the dark."

"Aye," he mumbled. There'd been the time Hamish had dared to be intimate with the dwarven ambassador where Nora had sworn a few words would've been enough to placate everything. He couldn't see how. Their mother had been pretty angry at him. Maybe Nora had meant a more lenient sentence than being imprisoned within his own room. But that talk never happened. He had left it too late for his sister to attempt anything.

I cannae make that mistake again. Who knew what his mother's response would be if she realised he had involved himself with the man beyond a kiss? There were worse punishments than being confined to his bedchamber.

Chapter 25

Darshan turned on his heel, taking in the room under the cool light of a magical globe. So many anatomical diagrams and murals adorned the walls, some in detail he hadn't seen since his childhood healer training. And it wasn't in mere dusty patches, everything within the room seemed to be polished and mirrored from one side to the other, be it the rows of books filling shelves carved from the stone walls, the heavy-set tables bearing gigantic tomes or a cabinet containing—

Was that an actual elven skeleton?

He stepped closer to the object in question, lifting his hand to coax the ball of light nearer still. It was indeed no mural or illusion. The longer he stared at it, the more the hairs on his arms lifted. Of all things, he never considered the image of a skeleton unnerving, but this…

This wasn't any ordinary framework of bones. The elves of now, the ones he had grown up alongside, were over a thousand years separated from that image. "Is this real?"

"Aye. One of the original elven arrivals, or so I've been told. We'd a human one just as old, but we were able to trace that back to their kin and give them a proper burial."

"Just look at it."

"I try to avoid that. It gives me the creeps."

"Such a petite size…" He laid a hand on the glass at chest height for the skeleton. The ribcage wasn't too dissimilar in shape to that of a human, although bearing the customary thirteen ribs. Much like some other creatures, all but the final pair of ribs were attached to the sternum via cartilage. "The broadness of that sternum, the elongated finger bones."

"It's the teeth that get me."

Darshan lifted his gaze from examining the foot bones to the skull. Although common rhetoric stated that the sharper the canines the purer the elf, he'd never encountered one with teeth any more than marginally different. The canines of this skull were a good inch from the base of the jaw. "You hear nobles back home boasting of how pure their elven slaves are, but this is what the first settlers were like." Whoever this specimen had been, those teeth could rival a tiger's.

He stepped back to take the skeleton's frame in its entirety. *If the theologians could have this for but a day*. Even an hour would suffice for a new wave of theories to spread throughout the academic circles. "This place has much in common with the average Knitting Factory."

"Excuse me?"

Darshan frowned. What part of what he'd said had confused her? "Of course, my apologies. It is a somewhat colloquial term for our healing academies." With apprentice healers being slightly cheaper than even their non-magical counterparts, common folk often sought aid. It didn't seem to matter that it ran the risk of getting an inadequately trained healer and dying. "How did this collection come to be?" She had mentioned translations earlier, but not the language.

"This used to be a Domian outpost, back when Tirglas couldnae even be classed as a kingdom."

He strode to the opposite side of the room. There was a space in the shelving, big enough for a cabinet of similar size to the one the elven skeleton sat in. That had to be where the human remains had resided. But there was also a similar structure on a third wall, the shelving there was also bare. Had there been more than two skeletons? *Another elven specimen, perhaps?* What had become of the third one?

"When the clans finally joined as a kingdom and ousted the Domians, a lot of their studies remained."

"I am surprised they left the building standing, much less the work within. Do you, perchance, know what sort of studies they were doing here?" As much as some within the Crystal Court liked to idolise the ancient empire, Domian had a rather distasteful underbelly. Not that his own land was clean of atrocities, some of them had likely come from Domian during the invasion several centuries back. But the rumours of what the Domian people could do, what they had known... quite a number of their feats defied the natural order.

"Medical notes, mostly. A lot of that was a few generations before me time."

Nodding distractedly, Darshan turned his focus on the tome dominating the table on the left side of the room. The yellowed pages were already opened to a section on the musculature that made up the forearm. Although age had faded the angular Ancient Domian script and constant use had darkened the page edges, the words were easy enough to make out. "I trust your people have a translated version?"

"Some sections have been—we keep those in the library downstairs. Most here still choose to work with the original text."

"All these?" He waved a hand at the rows of books. Age had ravaged a handful of the leather spines, cracking the edges, but most looked no more than a century old. "Each one is Domian in origin?" It seemed impossible. The ancient empire had fallen centuries ago, but perhaps a pocket had survived. And if heretofore unknown knowledge rested within these walls, then maybe he could bargain for copies.

"Each one," Caitlyn echoed, a small smile creasing her eyes.

So many. Only the royal library in Minamist boasted more than a half-dozen and here was thrice that all lined up in one spot. Strange to look upon them and know hands had crafted them almost two millennia ago, back before the Udynea Empire had been given a chance to properly form into an empire. "I never thought your people would possess this much knowledge on the inner workings of the body."

"We've little else to turn our attention to."

"Of course, my apologies." Back home, the tales his tutors would tell of Tirglasian cloisters, of being confined to a place such as this. Those stories had always carried an undertone of dread, but how different was this place to the hermit towers of the priesthood? If these books were all as detailed as the ones used back home, then Tirglasian spellsters could very well be the most skilled healers in all the lands. *Such a waste.*

He carefully lifted a few pages. Much of the Domian text he had read about the body focused on one or two species, usually human and dwarf. It seemed the same here, both in the text and sketches. "Are these all human-based?"

"There *are* elven ones." She pointed to the opposite side of the room where the mirrored layout of books and diagrams sat alongside the skeleton. He hadn't even noticed them. From afar, little seemed different beyond a few less books and some additions to the diagrams. "I'll warn you, they're nae as detailed."

They wouldn't be. Elves were a relatively new arrival to the continent in regards to the time the various races had spent here, with only the dwarves being native to the lands. Seeing any evidence at all did date the information. *Not much older than nineteen centuries.* Elven bloodlines hadn't yet been around for two millennia.

"We'd a few dwarven records, too. But—"

"Permit me to guess. The hedgewitches claimed them?" It wasn't uncommon. After the wars that uprooted the vast majority of the dvärg clans, the Coven sent out their hedgewitches to acquire all and every mention of their ancestors. Domian had refused, as had Udynea when the empire was young.

Caitlyn nodded.

He gave a cursory glance to the papers on the table next to the tome. Half-completed translations and direct copies for the most part. One caught his eye. He picked it up, trying to identify the object inked on its surface.

It appeared to be a vaguely egg-shaped maze of some kind, with no discernible opening or end. That the page was here suggested it had to do with the body, but he'd never seen anything like this during his healing tuition. Turning the page around did nothing to help make sense of the image. "What is this meant to be?" He handed the page over, affecting his usual nonchalant expression. Maybe the woman would mistake it for being tested.

"That's a brain."

As soon as the word left her mouth, Darshan saw it. They had touched briefly on the subject back in his tutored years, but no healer worth his coin would dare to apply more than the weakest probing. Delicate organs were often left to themselves. He'd never seen an image of a brain that wasn't stylised. Or symmetrical, as the current theory was on what the perfect specimen should resemble. "It seems rather..." He tapped his upper teeth with the tip his tongue, hunting for the right word. "...lifelike."

"It's probably from one of the specimens they jarred. The majority of the Domian studies done here were on the diseases plaguing complex organs. We've still got the jars. They're kept in the secondary basement."

"How gruesome," he murmured, his thoughts elsewhere. *Studies on brain disease.* Never mind the ancient elven skeleton, he knew of several healers who'd give their right arm for a chance to peruse any studies involving the brain.

He would need to find out who was in charge and discuss the herbal remedies he had been given leave to use in the trade agreements. Although, if their texts were this detailed, then maybe...

Darshan shook himself and smiled at Caitlyn. "Can I see them?"

Shrugging, she beckoned him to follow as she vacated the room.

Their downward passage required retracing their steps through the same winding route, the stairs seemingly narrower and the corridors that little bit emptier. The time of day likely had a hand in the latter. His stomach certainly seemed to be of the opinion that a midday meal should be forthcoming.

They strode by the study where he had met Caitlyn. He peeked into the area, idly wondering if the woman's two brothers lingered there. Alas, no.

Probably enjoying a nice lunch. He briefly considered suggesting to Caitlyn that they follow suit before dismissing the idea with barely a creak. Eyeballing antique organs on a full stomach likely wasn't the best plan.

Caitlyn led the way out the cloister's main entrance. He trotted down the stairs leading to the courtyard at her heel, casting an eye around the space in an effort to spot just where they would place something so fragile. But he caught no hint of anything he would class as a basement.

In contrast to the emptiness within the cloister, the courtyard practically bustled. Especially around the pulley. A good dozen men worked around the massive seven-levered capstan, their faces pulled tight with effort as they hoisted whatever goods the people below had loaded. The wooden beams groaned along with them.

Caitlyn slowed, her head tilted towards the mechanism. A distant look took her eye. She halted with a gasp, then raced towards the men. "Reverse the wheel! Lower the platform!"

The men hesitated only as long as it took to see who issued such an order. They hastened to follow her demands, shuffling around to unwind the capstan. More men rushed to the edge and yelled for those below to get clear before likewise fleeing the immediate area.

Darshan eyed the pulley, searching for whatever had spooked Caitlyn. The beams continued to groan and bend, but they didn't show any sign of breaking anytime soon.

Through it all, Caitlyn hopped from one foot to the other. "Please," she whispered. "Goddess, please let it hold out just a little long—"

Slowly, like the unfurling of a rose, the rope snapped.

Unthinking, Darshan lashed his magic towards the frayed end. His grasp held for but a moment before the rope slithered free, vanishing over the edge in a second that took an eternity.

A heart-stopping scream punctuated the crash of wood.

People rushed to the cliff edge, yelling down at those working there, struggling to get a cohesive answer. Above them, the beam continued to shudder, the vibration running the length of the pulley's framework. But it seemed to be holding together.

Rather than attempt to forge a path through the press of bodies around the cliff edge, Darshan followed Caitlyn to the capstan. A handful of men sat nearby, clutching their chests. They smiled sheepishly up at Caitlyn, grimacing only slightly as she healed each one in turn.

"You have the gift of premonition?" Darshan enquired. There was no mistaking she'd been aware the rope would fray. *If only it had come sooner*. He pressed his lips together lest the wrong words escaped. Hopefully, her actions had reduced the fatality of any injuries. "It is a rare skill, even in Udynea." There were plenty of old elven stories of how they had fled their homeland at the behest of their Oracles. Quite a few scholars insisted those Oracles must've had the same power, but no one had ever seen it manifest in any elf.

Caitlyn shrugged and moved on to the final injured man. "It's nae like I see things all the time. I just ken certain *dangerous* things are going to happen. That's how I sensed Hamish and me were in trouble all those years back."

Trouble? Hamish had never mentioned having a spellster sibling, let alone getting into some sort of trouble with one.

"Rouse the spellsters!" a woman screamed before Darshan could enquire more from Caitlyn. She came rushing out of the crowd, her hair in utter disarray as she waved her hands about. "We've wounded coming up!"

Several of the younger men examining the pulley's frame hopped down to race through the entrance. More people increasingly withdrew from the cliff edge to bustle around the pulley and help the recently-mended inside. A few greeted those exiting from the cloister's main entrance to speak with priests and spellsters alike, the latter of which often had those same people scurrying off for supplies.

Not a single face was familiar.

He turned his attention to the stable entrance. Zurron stood amongst those staring at the pulley, although the look on his face was far removed from the shocked expressions of those around him.

Darshan strode to the elf's side. Even from this new vantage point, he saw no sign of either Tirglasian prince. "Have you seen Gordon or Hamish recently?"

The man failed to answer his query, forcing Darshan to repeat himself.

"Nae since we arrived." Zurron's gaze barely left the pulley as he spoke. He shook his head. "I warned them. Why did they nae listen?" His dark gaze fastened onto Darshan. "Any word on the wounded?"

"Only that there are some on their way."

"Any deaths?"

The ache in the elf's eyes was almost enough to pull an instant 'of course not' from Darshan's lips. Only in glancing away did he manage to regain his composure. "I cannot rightfully say." Until the wounded arrived from below, all they could realistically do was hope Caitlyn's warning had been soon enough to limit the chance.

The wait for those from below went by swiftly enough. The massive Tirglasian cart horses trotted through the gate, each one heaving and dark with sweat. Behind them, several makeshift litters dragged along the cobblestones. Other, more mobile, wounded persons sat atop the horses, some clinging to the riders to keep from falling.

Darshan hastened to lend a hand in the dismounting of the latter whilst others swarmed the litters.

"I told them," Zurron muttered, seemingly to himself, as he aided Darshan in assisting a limping woman to a nearby bench. "I bloody told them."

Darshan knelt before the woman, laying a hand on her knee and let his magic seek out the source of her pain. *Fractured tibia.* That explained her rather pallid appearance. Nothing beyond his capabilities and repaired within moments.

Issuing a few precautions at the woman, he scanned the courtyard in search of others who required his help. The men who'd been dragged here were still strapped to their makeshift litters and each one had at least a single spellster tending to them. He wove through the swarms, stopping beside Caitlyn.

She was bent over a man who bled from his chest. Already, her hands were dark with his blood. Unlike most of the others, little sound came from the man.

Darshan knelt at the injured man's side. "Can I be of assistance?" Although she seemed to be struggling, it was potentially life-threatening for a spellster to assist another in healing without warning.

"I cannae stop the flow," she mumbled. "Goddess, there's so much blood. I try and... there's something deeper. I..." She shook her head. "I cannae do this, nae without me diagrams." Withdrawing her touch, Caitlyn stared longingly at the cloister entrance. "I need to—"

"Stay put," Darshan snapped. He laid a finger on the man's neck. There was a pulse. Weak, but there. "He cannot wait whilst you scan your notes." *All that knowledge.* It sat in books and on walls... How could they be so reliant on them? Did the priests not let their charges study enough without conferring with old pages?

"But I dinnae ken how to mend this. We do bones, skin and muscles, nae—"

Darshan grabbed her hand, keeping her palm pressed hard against the man's shoulder. "The body knows what it needs. You only have to aid it."

Nodding, she closed her eyes. The strain of healing swiftly lined her face.

"You must push harder." Even without trying, a tendril of his magic had seeped into the man through the finger Darshan kept on the man's neck. As horrific as the gash in his chest was, mending such injuries was child's play to an adept spellster. Something had to be underneath all that to reject Caitlyn's attempts.

"I cannae do it!" She jerked her hand back. "It's too much. We're nae supposed to put ourselves into the effort. The Goddess' claim to him is stronger than I."

"What you are jabbering about? He—"

The heartbeat under his forefinger stuttered.

Without a thought, Darshan flooded the man's body with his magic. The man's very being seemed to latch onto the power, feeding off it like a leech.

The force of it tore a gasp from Darshan's lungs.

Like a line-caught fish, he fought against the pull to no avail. His only chance laid in directing the flow of magic towards the injuries. Caitlyn had repaired a few, namely the broken rib, but a lung was still punctured. Not terribly, just enough to let blood in. He focused there first.

Sweat poured down his brow, blinding him. Still, he pressed on. Something else was feeding off his magic, something that the body required more than a mere lung.

There! Fluid seeped around the man's heart, squeezing whenever Darshan tried to wrest his power back. He probed further and found a tear in the thin membrane surrounding the organ. Nothing seemed to be the likely cause of the wound.

He directed the fluid back through the tear to dissipate elsewhere. His head spun with the effort.

Sealing the membrane was a far easier task and done in an instant. And yet, the heart refused to stay at a reassuring rhythm. *Don't you dare die on me now.* But what else could he do? What had the healing professors said on this?

There'd been that one case... It had been years ago. The old lectures little more than a wisp of a memory.

"Everyone stay back!" Darshan screamed. He crossed his hands atop the man's chest. A tendril of lightning, barely more than a static spark, zipped from his palm. The man's body leapt, causing Caitlyn to squeak in surprise. The man's heart twitched, taking a few ungainly beats.

Another zap. A little more precisely aimed this time.

Finally, the man's heart seemed to resume a steady beat. Darshan fumbled for a wrist, holding it close to his chest whilst measuring the pulse. *Regular.* Relief relaxed the constraint on his magic and it flowed through the man, mending the remaining minor injuries.

Darshan sagged, barely able to keep himself from falling to the flagstones. He thanked the gods for already being on his knees, for he certainly would've dropped to them.

People collected the litter, lifting the now completely healed man and carrying him through the crowd. Others who'd suffered lesser and similar injuries were also being escorted inside.

Drawing upon every ounce of his strength, Darshan hauled himself to his feet and followed the litter. His body cried out for sleep, for food. He couldn't indulge in either yet. That wasn't how Nanny Daama had raised him. He'd a duty to his patient first.

~ ~ ~

Hamish raced through the halls. He hadn't heard the crash that'd been the pulley system failing, but the bustle around it stirred the whole cloister. Spellsters and priests poured from the entrance, rushing to aid the wounded or assist in those who already were.

He trotted down the stairs, tailing his brother. The pulley was absent of people, but seemed strangely intact for something to have caused so much trouble. Especially when people lay groaning and bleeding like—

Darshan.

The Udynean knelt in the middle of the crowd, slumped over beside one of the makeshift litters. The sleeves and chest of his sherwani were stained with blood. His own? Had he been struck by the pulley? What had he been doing out here, anyway?

One of the litter bearers bumped him, jolting him into the realisation that he'd been standing on the steps like a statue.

He hastened through the crowd, forging a path to his lover.

The crowd closed in before Hamish could reach Darshan's side. When it parted again and allowed him through, the man was nowhere to be seen. Neither was the litter.

A quick survey of his immediate surroundings also revealed a complete lack of the man. *Where...?* He wouldn't have gone beyond the courtyard gates. But the cloister was big and he had looked injured. Would those carting the wounded inside care that his bloodstained attire wasn't of this land?

What if Darshan mistook a healer's attempts to aid him with danger? Would he fight them? How would the priests react to such an action? With his imprisonment? His *death*?

He whirled on the closest person, realising he had grabbed his sister only when her face was inches from his. "Darshan?" he blurted, clutching at her shoulders lest she also vanished. "Where is he? I saw him, but he's gone."

"He followed one of the workers inside." She jerked a thumb up the stairs as if he hadn't just descended them. "Said he was heading to the infirmary."

Followed. Not taken. He could move under his own power, then. Maybe the wound had been superficial. Something that he could—

Heal.

Hamish bowed his head, relief and embarrassment at his own stupidity quaked through his gut and squeaked out his mouth. Whatever injury Darshan had suffered, it clearly hadn't killed him, so his magic would knit him back together. Just like it had with that arrow wound back at the outpost.

That didn't explain why Darshan was going to the infirmary, but it was a question easily satisfied. "Can you take me to him?"

Nodding, she trotted up the stairs. He followed at her heels, silently taking in the number of bloodstained and battered people being led inside. It had to be half the workforce stationed at the cliff base. What had happened?

"I must say," Caitlyn said over her shoulder. "He's nicer than I thought a *vris* of the *Mhanek* would be. A little morbid, but polite."

"Dinnae let him hear you say that, I think you might actually offend him. Especially seeing as he describes himself as being arrogant and selfish." Whilst Darshan didn't seem overtly proud of the fact, he was quite insistent that he had no redeeming qualities. Even with evidence to the contrary.

They passed Gordon on the way through the main entrance. Their brother fell into step beside Hamish, a faint query tightening his brow.

"Well, your selfish man just risked his life to save another's." Caitlyn shook her head as if Darshan was only a child having returned from a successful, but ultimately foolhardy, hunt. "I've nae seen a spellster throw themselves into a healing so thoroughly. Nae one who has lived more than a few minutes, at least."

"Should I take that to mean you approve of 'Mish's new man?" Gordon rumbled.

"Well, he—" Caitlyn swung to eye their brother before turning her gaze on him, continuing to backstep her way down the corridor. "I was only having a lark before, but he *really* is?"

"I guess so," Hamish mumbled, his face burning.

"You *guess*?" Gordon quipped, playfully nudging him in the ribs. "He followed you into a cloister, I dinnae think many foreign spellsters would do that."

Hamish shot his brother a death glare, but Gordon had long built up an immunity to such looks and merely grinned back.

"Your man is quite reckless, in a fearless sort of way."

"How so?" He had witnessed Darshan's healing abilities on others before. Granted that had been a broken jaw rather than the crushed ribcages or shattered limbs he had witnessed in these injuries, but his lover hadn't seemed any worse for wear.

"We're instructed to be careful when healing another. The old writings' warnings about the risks of draining the self to mend another are quite explicit. Put too much effort into it and your body starts cannibalising itself for fuel. That man was on the brink of death, I felt it trying to take me with him and yet…" She shook her head, disbelieving. "Most who've tried healing those that close—of those in Tirglas, at least—have nae only failed, but it cost them their own lives."

"Dar's stronger." The admission didn't do much to shuck the unease from his stomach, not after witnessing his lover looking like he'd run the whole way here from Mullhind, but at least he knew the cause.

Grunting and rolling her eyes, Caitlyn turned back around and increased the pace in which they traversed the crowded corridors. "Strength doesnae come into it. He seemed to ken what he was doing, but if he had slipped up then you would've been explaining to the *Mhanek* just how his son died at a cloister."

And *that* wouldn't have had repercussions.

They descended a short flight of stairs where Caitlyn slowed to walk level with him. "So, how are you managing to have your little whatever you call it with him without Mum being aware?"

"About that…"

"They're doing an abysmal job of it," Gordon piped up, grinning anew as Hamish aimed another glare at him.

"You mean she *does* ken?" Their sister exhaled mightily. "Bloody hell, she's calm down some."

Their brother shook his head. "Nae really. She just cannae send him home without cause." Not if she wanted to avoid a war.

They entered the infirmary to the accompaniment of groans and the hushed conversations between healer and patient.

In the middle of it all stood Darshan. He had stripped himself of his sherwani, as well as both undershirts, somewhere between now and the courtyard, leaving him completely bare from the waist up. And yet, despite the slight chill in the air, he seemed content with leisurely drying his hands and conversing with one of the priests.

Caitlyn froze. Her gaze solidly focused on Darshan, who seemed oblivious to the scrutiny. There was little point in denying that there was something about Darshan that drew the eye, whether he was garbed in his silks and jewels or half-naked. But the current aura he projected seemed diminished from the man's usual confident stance.

"See that he gets plenty of fluids," Darshan continued saying to the priest, the clip of authority in his tone enough to have the priest bobbing in agreement at every other word. "A light broth, if the kitchen can manage it. I would not recommend allowing him to do any heavy work for at least a few weeks, a month just to be safe."

Hamish tipped his head closer to his sister's ear. "Mine," he whispered. "So stop staring."

A bloom of pink darkened her cheeks. "I… I wasnae—" she spluttered, shoving him and giving his shoulder what he supposed she considered a solid punch. It might've hurt back when they were kids, but he had connected harder with animals and trees since then.

At their backs, Gordon snickered.

Darshan turned, finally noticing them. His face was drawn and slightly on the grey side. Even his smile was a pale imitation of his usual energetic grin.

Before the spellster could take a step towards them, a young man in the robes of early priesthood scurried over to Darshan's side with a bundle of clothes and a cup of wine. He spoke to the Udynean, low words Hamish couldn't quite make out.

Darshan wasted no time in downing the whole cup in a few gulps before taking the shirt and overcoat. Only then did Hamish notice a ripple of heat surrounding the man. Had he been using magic to keep himself warm?

"That's an interesting scar," Caitlyn said whilst Darshan donned the clothing. "How'd you manage it?"

"This old thing?" Darshan brushed a hand over the star-shaped mark on his chest. "A mere token of a hunting accident I was unfortunate to be a part of in my youth."

"Most who are able to heal to the level you attained dinnae typically scar that badly," she continued.

"Yes? Well, my half-sister liked to hunt with *infitialis*-tipped arrows."

Caitlyn peered at the man.

Hamish wasn't certain why. He had seen firsthand how an arrow through the chest affected a spellster, even if any sign of the wound Darshan had suffered a week ago was long gone. It had been quite the feat to come back from without any special arrowheads. *Lucky it wasnae nearer his heart.* Did *infitialis* have an effect on the healing process? He knew very little about the metal other than its rareness. He'd never even seen a piece.

Instead of pressing Darshan on the matter, Caitlyn silently tailed him as he went about tending to a man lying prone on a nearby bed. He placed his fingers on the man's neck, checking for a pulse, and seemed satisfied enough to peel back the blankets to expose scarred skin still stained with blood.

"You seem to know your way around a patient," she said.

Darshan glanced up from his examination. "As they say back at the academy, you never really stop being a healer. Although, to hear Anjali tell it, you would think I have a personal vendetta against mortal injuries because of what happened to our mother."

"Was she gravely injured?"

"You could say that. She died giving birth to my twin."

Caitlyn jerked back, a gasp lingering in her wake. "I—"

"—am sorry to hear that." Darshan shot her an understanding smile. "I know. It's all right. I made amends there some time back. Yes?" This last word was given with little more than a glance to the head priest.

Hamish looked about him. Just how had the man managed to slither to Darshan's side with barely a hint of his presence? The doorway was at their backs. He would've had to walk straight past them. Was there another entrance or was he losing the ability to tell when other people were in his immediate proximity?

"Your highness." The man genuflected with a flourish of his hand before him. "The cloister is indebted to you for this man's life. And I am doubly so for you wresting my son from a premature greeting to the Goddess' bosom. How can we repay you?"

Darshan was silent for some time, his hand resting on the unconscious man's chest and those hazel eyes unfocused.

What do you see? His sister had tried to explain the sensation of healing another, but he could never grasp the concept.

"Zurron," Darshan blurted, making everyone around him jump. He turned to the head priest. "It has come to my attention that the man has warned you as to the potential of this outcome in regards to the pulley on numerous occasions. You would do well heeding his words. Knowing you have taken measures to ensure this never happens again shall be payment enough."

Flustered, the head priest bowed in a similar manner as before. "You humble me, your highness."

Darshan waggled his finger. "I am not quite finished. I require a meal, preferably one with a lot of protein. And a full account of whatever arcane healing knowledge you could share with Udynea, who is all too happy to reciprocate in kind."

The priest bowed once again, taking a step back towards the door whilst still bent over. "I shall see to those promptly. Please, wait here whilst I send someone up with food." With that, he scurried off out the door, the susurration of his feet echoing down the corridor.

Hamish took one final glance around the room. Apart from the sleeping wounded, they were alone. His gaze landed on Darshan, who had opted to claim one of the precious few chairs in the area. His lover looked for all the world as if he was about to fall into as deep a sleep as those surrounding them.

"I think," Gordon said. "You two should start explaining just what happened."

Chapter 26

Hamish stared down at his hands, currently doing nothing extraordinary beyond holding his mare's reins. The horse plodded alongside the others, her shod hooves clopping sharply on the cobblestones that paved the road leading to Mullhind. They would veer off from the road in time to travel the less-trodden path that snaked along the base of the cliff. Home would come soon enough, no point in speeding the inevitable.

Because of their delay in getting Darshan warmer clothes, coupled with the attack on the spellster at the guard outpost, they had been only two days to spare at the cloister before further dallying would have his mother issuing the call for is retrieval.

Darshan had spent a great deal of that time conversing with the priests and older healers, even through the evening and morning meals. Whilst the grey pallor that'd claimed the customary olive-brown tone of Darshan's cheeks had vanished during their stay in the cloister—a point Hamish was more than delighted to witness—the act certainly hadn't dulled the man's keenness. It had been an intoxicating sight.

One that Hamish wished they hadn't needed to be done with so swiftly.

When the time to leave had arrived, they had lingered at the base of the cliff for a few more hours whilst Zurron finished assisting with the pulley's reconstruction. Even though that had been a week ago, Hamish could still hear the elf stressing the mechanism's limits as he worked. Unlike in the past, his words seemed to garner more attention and less eye-rolling. Hopefully, it would also mean no repetition of the accident.

The week-long trip back home had been its customarily uneventful passage. Despite his brother's concerns, they met no guards on the way back down the road. Not even when they reached the outpost at the intersection, which had been eerily absent of a single soul.

Hamish wished all their days could've gone as placidly as they did now. But in the days since leaving the cloister, a far more insidious thought had plagued his mind.

It had started out so innocently. And only on their second night away from the cloister. The farmer hadn't been able to spare room in his stables and Hamish had gone to fetch wood to stave off the night chills. Darshan had tagged along, helping mostly by keeping an eye out for any wildlife that could've posed as deadly.

The stint in the cloister seemed to have made the man impatient. Or perhaps it was the bundle of papers he now carried, copies of ancient texts and strange drawings. He hopped from one foot to the other like a child itching to head out on their first hunt. "Surely we need but only one armful of logs to carve up for the night."

"It's going to be an icy one."

Darshan pulled a face. Whilst he had never verbally complained during the sodden days their group had spent on the road towards the cloister, his distaste for the less-than-agreeable weather had been palpable. "I see. Well, cold or not, I look forward to resuming our prior sleeping arrangements."

"Was there something wrong with your bed in the cloister?" He found them a little on the softer side, but serviceable.

"It is not so much that—although I have certainly slept in better and the blankets could have been thicker—it is more the fact I have never spent a night in a mountain." He glanced over his shoulder, as if somehow able to see any evidence of the Crowned Mountain through the dense canopy. "And I shall be quite happy to never do so again."

"You're still meant to sleep in your own bed." Hamish's thoughts swung back to their first five days of travel. Of how his lover would snuggle against him, shivering with the cold even through three layers of clothing whenever Hamish dared to move any more than a few inches away. How warm were Udynea's southern lands? Hot enough along the border of the Stamekian deserts. *Nae wonder he keeps the fire lit in the guest quarters.*

"I vastly prefer being entangled with you in yours."

"Nae sex, though. Nae here." He'd never live down knowing his brother had actually heard them.

"What?" Darshan chuckled, his moustache twisting as his brows lowered in bewilderment. "*Mea lux*, I would not dream of proposing sex in the middle of the wilderness, nor am I looking for it. I meant only that I find the comfort of your presence preferable." He rubbed the very tip of his nose with a forefinger. "And I missed your warmth."

"Sharing me blankets I can do." Beyond the first night, his brother had made little comment on Darshan's chosen sleeping arrangements. No one would deem it strange if the man continued to sleep bundled in Hamish's arms.

"Exceedingly well, in fact."

Hamish bent down to collect another worthy-looking length of bare branch, hoping to stave off the heat growing in his cheeks. Goddess, how did the man manage to make him blush so effortlessly?

They walked for some time in silence, picking up whatever suitable wood they could carry. Darshan stopped every-so-often to glance his way, his lips parting as if to speak, but never quite giving breath to the words.

"You ken," Hamish drawled, attempting to keep his voice neutral as he filled the quiet. "It's been over a week since we started this... whatever you want to call it."

Darshan jerked upright from his hunt beneath a scraggy bush. "Really?" he squeaked before clearing his throat with a hearty cough. "Has it been so short a time? I feel as though I have known you forever."

Fresh warmth infused Hamish, the source starting from his chest. "Aye." He hadn't realised that feeling of lifelong kinship was mutual. "I guess it also means I'm now your longest lasting sexual relationship."

His lover chuckled breathlessly. "I must admit, the thought did not occur to me, but it would appear to be so."

Hamish tucked his bundle of wood beneath one arm and draped the other companionably over Darshan's shoulders. "And how do you think this one will end, given both of our histories?" No matter how he looked at it, he couldn't see any other path other than the one that led to them separating once Darshan's purpose in Tirglas was over.

"Amicably, I hope." Darshan smiled up at him, but a faint bitterness lingered in his gaze and it echoed through his voice. "I would hate to think I could hurt you."

"What makes you think *I* wouldnae do the hurting?"

"Truly? You are not that kind of man."

Probably nae. But he doubted Darshan was either. "I've been meaning to speak with you. About journeying to Minamist?"

"Oh?" His lover bumped Hamish with a hip. "Made up your mind, then? Simply cannot wait to be free of all this?" He indicated the whole forest with one broad sweep of his hand.

"I *do* want to leave with you when the time comes." If he left, the land would be the only thing he missed beyond his siblings and their children.

Darshan's answering smile fattened his cheeks and increased the wrinkles around his eyes.

"*But*... if I was to play the part of ambassador, I'd need me mum's acceptance of me position to make it official."

The corners of his lover's mouth dropped faster than a stunned bird. He stared out into the forest for a long time. Enough for Hamish to collect two more branches. "I have been doing some thinking of my own," he confessed.

"I thought you look like you'd something else on your mind." Hamish laid his haul of branches on the ground and dusted off his hands. "Tell me. Is it the cloister?"

Darshan gave an affirmative hum, but the lines in his face only deepened. "In a matter of speaking. I wish to enquire about something personal, although I am unsure how to go about that without offending you or your family."

Hamish shrugged. "Just ask."

"Your cloistered sister? She is—? That is to say... you share a full parentage?"

"Aye." Why would Darshan even need to ask such a question? Let alone be puzzled by it? "All my siblings share the same bloodline. You cannae be considering that as strange. You've a sister you share full blood with."

"Trust me, *that* is not the part of my query which stumps me. You see, there is one definite in creating a spellster, they must share the bloodline of another spellster or their antithesis."

Hamish scoffed. "There's nae such a thing as an opposite of spellster powers."

"There most certainly is. They go by many names, but my people call them Nulled Ones. Their bodies... ignore direct magic. Throw a fireball at them and they feel only a touch of heat, healing fails to mend the smallest of scratches, and magical barriers are nonexistent to them. I believe your brother is one."

"*Gordon?*"

"Unless you have another brother I have yet to meet, then yes."

Hamish stepped back. "You think me brother is some sort of... of..." What had Darshan called them? "Anti-spellster?"

"A Nulled One, yes."

"You're saying me brother could die with a spellster inches from him?" That couldn't be possible. He had witnessed Gordon's return from the cloister with his arm merely in a sling after a horse had thrown him. Neither of them could claim their years were in double digits at the time, but the way his brother had howled, he had certainly broken his arm. That wasn't something a mere week of bed rest could fix. "All because nae magic will work on him?"

Darshan inclined his head. "Regrettably so."

"Bollocks. Magic can fix anything."

His lover laughed softly. "I dearly wish that were correct." He perched himself on the remains of what looked to be a stone wall. "I told you my mother died giving birth to my sister and I, did I not?"

Hamish nodded. It hadn't been him specifically, but he'd been within hearing range.

"My grandfather saw it as a needless death. She was a purist, you see, a spellster who believes magic should be used sparingly. They never use their god-given gifts except in the most extreme of cases. Where most of the court use their talents to heal themselves, she refused to even learn."

"I thought magic could do everything."

One side of Darshan's mouth twitched into a melancholic smile. "It is true that magic can push the limits of... normal capabilities. But it is bound by far more rules than those without the power believe."

Hamish arched a brow at the man. "Such as?"

"Take healing. An ordinary person sees us wave a hand and the wounded are mended, the sick are cured. That sort of skill takes years of study, just as much as a common doctor. Without it, a single stray thought could kill a patient or leave them in agony for years to come."

"I..." He hadn't ever given the ability much thought. Everyone knew spellsters could heal, no one before Darshan had mentioned anything about them needing to train that talent. "I thought it was instinctual."

"To a point, but fire is generally considered as such first and foremost."

"Because it's the easiest of magics?" Hamish replied, mimicking the man's words from a week back.

Darshan inclined his head, a small smile tweaking his moustache. He conjured a small flame in his hand and let it dance on his palm. "But then we are taught what heat is at a young age. We know fire burns and how hot it should be."

Hamish thought back to his siblings teaching his nieces and nephews the dangers of fire. That'd been back when the children were barely able to walk.

Another thought bubbled up amongst the rest. The raging heat Caitlyn had brought to life when he had been overcome by the bandits that'd been out to kidnap or kill them. The heat had been immense. The air almost too hot to breathe. The screams of men dying...

He shook his head, scattering the memory back into the depths. It had been so long ago. They'd both been so young and him bordering on unconscious. The only one who knew the full truth was Caitlyn and she refused to speak of that day beyond vague mentions.

"But you know the most amusing part?" Darshan continued on, oblivious. "What you do with your arrows? That is some of the hardest magic. There are powerful spellsters out there right now who can command all sorts of wonders, but can barely lift a pebble an inch off the ground. And you manage far more without a thought."

"I am nae a—" Hamish spluttered. A spellster? *Him?* When had Darshan come to *that* conclusion? "I cannae do magic." What could possibly possess the man to think he could?

"Your arrows never miss," Darshan whispered.

"That—" He could see where a person unskilled in a bow would think it some spell or trick, but... "That's just skill through years of training. I focus on where I want the arrow to go and that's where it hits."

"Precisely!"

"That doesnae mean I can do magic."

His lover scoffed. "Any spellster in Udynea is taught how to manipulate the forces around an item." He scooped up a palm-sized stone and bounced it in his hand. "You see, everything wants to fall, just as the wind wants to buffet them around. Manipulating these constants is tricky."

"How so?"

Darshan held out his hand and the stone floated above his palm. "Push too little and it falls." True to his word, the stone dropped back into his grasp. "Too sudden and it grows uncontrollable." The stone leapt into the air like a flea. "But try to counter these forces too much..."

The stone shattered into dust.

"And you do it all without a thought," Darshan murmured. "*Incredible.*"

"I am *nae* a spellster," Hamish growled. If he had been one, then his life would've taken a far different course a long time ago.

Darshan lifted his head, those hazel eyes glittering with confidence. "Prove it. I know you cannot be a Nulled One, but if your sister is fully related to you as you claim, then you must have magic in your blood."

He spread his arms wide. "How can I prove I dinnae have an ability?"

His lover stood and after a bit of rummaging through the undergrowth, came up with a length of branch. A few quick swipes with the spellster's magic were enough to cut a section from the piece. "Aim at this and we shall see."

Easy enough. He unslung his bow and nocked an arrow, his fingers unconsciously settling into their customary places. "Nae when you're standing there, though." Whilst he'd never consciously aim at the man, there was a chance his arrow might stray. Not that it ever had done so. There was always a first time, though.

Darshan chuckled. He waved his hand and the section rose just below the branches. "Try it now."

Hamish focused on the centre of the slice. It was quite small, now he looked at it, perhaps as big around as a single one of his mare's hooves. He loosed his arrow.

The tip smacked into the piece with a hollow *thunk*.

He waited, shuffling from one foot to the other, whilst Darshan examined the slice of wood. "How is this supposed to prove I've nae magic in me?"

"Patience, *mea lux*." Once again, the wood rose into the air, still carrying the arrow. "Now focus on the same spot and loose only on my command."

Sighing, he nocked another arrow. The slice wobbled a little more now its weight was uneven, but his focus remained just as sharp. *The same spot?* He'd done that plenty of times. What did Darshan expect to see?

"Now!"

His fingers twitched. The arrow slipped from his grip, tension carrying it across the clearing towards its target. But the slice of wood moved as the fletching of his arrow past the bow's belly. *Feck*. The wood sat no longer directly in front, but to his left. When had Darshan shifted his target? His arrow would completely—

Thunk!

The world slowed, his heart along with it. His breath was almost nonexistent. There was no possible way the arrow could've hit that target. He had aimed straight. The slice of wood was even turned sideways and still...

When Darshan returned the slice of wood to their side, the gap between the two arrowheads was negligible.

"That's nae possible." The only way that arrow could've struck was if it had defied gravity, defied inertia, defied all the bleeding laws of nature. If he had— If he was—

A spellster.

"Do it again," Hamish whispered.

"I rather doubt I—"

"Chuck it in the air, then! Throw it behind any one of these bloody trees." He spread his arms wide, indicating the clearing as a whole. "I'll show you how much of a fluke that was."

"And how many times will it take until you accept the truth?"

Darshan let the slice of wood fall to the ground. "There is no shame in having magic, not even in your own culture. Being a spellster is not considered a sin like in Obuzan. I am not leading you down some shadowy path."

Tears pricked his eyes. *Nae shame?* When spellsters all across Tirglas were shuffled off into distant cloisters or slain if they attempted to leave without permission? When his own mother refused to accept she had given birth to two daughters? "This is nae Udynea and you're nae saying it's just me." His niece, his nephews, even Nora... they could all potentially have the same spark. They could already be using it unaware of the danger to others, to themselves. "You're saying that I'm some weak spellster who—"

"Actually," Darshan interjected. "Spellsters with minuscule magic such as yourself are referred to as specialists."

"I dinnae care what they're called!" he screeched. *By the Goddess...* He was going to burst. Every part of his being felt ready to rend itself from his bones. "You're saying I deserve to be in there." He jabbed a finger in the direction of the cloister.

"No," his lover breathed. He clasped Hamish's hands, turning them palm-side up. "I am aware that would have been your fate, had you more power, but I would never suggest you deserve to be there."

"Where else would a Tirglasian spellster belong?"

If he hadn't been so intent on Darshan's face, he certainly would've missed the pity that welled in his lover's eyes and tightened his features.

Darshan turned from him, one hand fastidiously smoothing down his moustache, although the hairs along his jaw were at least a half inch long. "Forgive me, I should not have brought this to your attention." He bent to gather a small armful of the branches Hamish had collected and abandoned in his quest to prove Darshan wrong.

"Nae, you shouldnae have. But now I ken and you cannae take that away." Even if it were possible, he wasn't quite sure he wanted to forget.

Darshan paused in bundling up the rest of the branches. "We should get back to camp before the others think we've been beset upon by a bear and come to our rescue."

"More like our burial." He didn't know if they had bears in Udynea, or how large they got, but the ones he had faced were big enough to bleed a man out with one bite.

"It is somewhat of a shame. I was hoping to see one that wasn't stuffed and mounted."

"You wouldnae be saying that if you'd ever seen any of the full-grown mountain brutes." His brother certainly wouldn't be thrilled to come across one on the way home. He shrugged. "But our journey's nae over, maybe you'll be fortunate to see one in passing." His family always had the worst kind of luck. Why wouldn't it hold back now?

His gaze slid to the segment of wood still holding two of his arrows. *Luck.* Just a few moments ago, he would've considered all his feats as a mixture of mere happenstance and skill.

Now?

Knowing the truth behind his records?

That he had...

Magic.

His mare stumbled, jolting Hamish from his musing. Snorting, she righted herself and carried on. Hamish glanced up to take in their surroundings. Nothing but trees and the castle looming through the leafy canopy.

His gaze dropped back to his hands. They held the reins a little tighter, but were no different than before.

The better part of a week had passed and he still couldn't say with absolute certainty that his lover was wrong. Hamish couldn't force the arrow to move in any fashion but how the Goddess had intended such projectiles should fly. He had tried shifting his focus to a completely different patch of undergrowth as he let go of his arrow. It had still hit his first focus point.

No matter how he tried, all of his attempts to replicate the trick he had witnessed in Darshan's presence had failed. That had to mean something.

I cannae be a spellster.

Why did Darshan seem so certain? Did his lover attempt to deceive Hamish under the delusion that it would help Hamish leave Tirglas for good?

Would his mother believe it? Would he become another Caitlyn in her eyes, tainted and unworthy? And if being a spellster was all it took for her to forget all ties to her daughter, would she care if her son left for Udynea rather than the cloister?

He had expected Darshan to make several more attempts towards convincing him of his status as an extremely weak spellster—a specialist—but the man hadn't spoken a word. Perhaps he waited for their return to Mullhind and the chance to test his theories on the rest of Hamish's family.

Or perhaps his lover believed to have already made his point.

Maybe knowing also hindered the testing. How many rabbits, deer and wild pigs had he downed over the years? *Always in the heart.* Not even the most precise of hunters could make such a claim. How had he not seen it sooner? Why had no one else suspected more than pure skill on his part?

Where had the spark come from? That'd been the only question Darshan had asked since. Not his mother, that much was certain. His father's side was the only other option but…

Were there any spellsters in his ancestry? Darshan's words echoed through his thoughts. His father was an only child, raised in the midland sheep-fields. What little he knew of his grandparents on that side came only through stilted tales from his father.

What he did recall was a warning given the first time Hamish had turned his hand to shearing. His grandmother had cut herself and had fallen down dead. The other shearers had deemed it unfortunate, but not terribly uncommon amongst the impatient.

Except… The healers in the nearby cloister had claimed one of her veins had mysteriously collapsed and that had been the true cause of her death. Any enquiries by himself or his siblings had always led to his father shrugging and confessing she'd never fared well after the smallest of injuries.

Could it have been through her that they were doomed to bear this magic? From a woman who had died because she didn't know her power?

Was that also their fates?

"Something's nae right here," Gordon rumbled.

Hamish glanced up from his hands. They were almost home, their chosen path taking them around the cliff rather than through the middle of Mullhind. Nothing about their immediate surroundings suggested anything was off.

His brother's attention was focused on the castle where swathes of fabric and thick braids of spring foliage adorned the entrance. "That cannae be good."

"Looks like preparation for spring festivities to me," Darshan said.

Gordon shook his head, sweeping aside any coils of hair foolish enough to impede his vision. "They wouldnae start without us." His brother glanced his way.

Instantly, Hamish's stomach dropped. There'd been two other instances where the castle had been decorated outside of the usual festivals. Both times had involved the union contest and had culminated with his siblings getting married.

She promised. He had expressed his reluctance for women to go through such a competition for him multiple times. His mother had always insisted she wouldn't dare send out the word until he had chosen a woman he found worthy. "Do you think she's—?"

"I didnae see any sign of camps on the way in." Uncertainty pinched his brother's face. Just because they hadn't witnessed the calling of the clans didn't mean much. There were a number of reasons as to why, starting with the possibility that their mother hadn't yet sent the call.

The guards at the castle gates offered only their customary salute. They were garbed no differently from any other day. Surely if other clans were around, or expected, then the castle guards would be dressed in their finest armour. The courtyard also seemed to have the right amount of bustling about for mid-afternoon and there was a distinct lack of strange horses in the stables. Maybe it really was just early spring festivities.

"Finally," Nora blurted from the castle entrance. She trotted across to them as they halted their horses in the middle of the courtyard. "You lot chose a bad time to wander off."

"Why?" Gordon asked before Hamish could open his mouth. "Did something bad happen?" His brother dismounted faster than the rest of them. He grabbed their sister's shoulders, almost lifting her off the ground. "Is Sorcha injured?"

"Your daughter's fine. But you should've been here." Nora turned to Hamish and grimaced. "You're going to want to see Mum. She'll be waiting in her study."

Apprehension tingled along his skin. His gaze darted to his brother and was met with only a stony expression. He had considered that word of what had transpired at the guard outpost a fortnight ago might reach here before them, but he couldn't see how. And his mother wouldn't be asking for him. "What for?"

"Just go to her study," Nora repeated.

"Tell me she hasnae done something foolish," Gordon begged, as Hamish strode up the stairs.

Nora's silence knotted Hamish's stomach. It could only mean one thing. *She has.* Opening the door, he glanced over his shoulder at his siblings.

Gordon had tightened his hold on Nora's shoulders, forcing her to face him. "Tell me what she's done." The command boomed across the courtyard.

If their sister replied, it was lost to Hamish as he entered the castle. Whatever their mother had done, he would find out from the source soon enough.

Chapter 27

T*hunk!*

The arrow veered too far to the left of centre, joining its kin on the edge of the target.

Grumbling, Hamish nocked another arrow and took aim. *Just a fluke, is all.* He never missed. Not since that first day of training so long ago.

He recalled back then as if his boyhood self stood right before him, frustrated after a long day of practice. Even as young as seven, he could hit the target. But there'd been no consistency to those hits, each mark scattered around the outer rings like a drunken man's game of darts. Not like his brother, who could put three of every four arrows near the middle of the target. He had been so angry, then. So jealous of his brother's talents.

And now, *he* was the one surpassing everyone he had ever competed against.

Except it wasn't so easy at this moment, not when his mother's words kept playing in his mind. *How could she?* She had promised him.

He knocked on the door to his mother's study and stood waiting, the desire to burst into the room close to overwhelming. His stomach was leaden, cramping and ready to expel his meal. No actual clue as to why he was here other than she wanted to speak with him.

Answers. He needed them. Craved to know, to assuage the fear bubbling in his chest. What could she want? What had she done that would send Nora into a tizzy?

Not daring to breathe, he loosed the arrow. Again, it fell short of its mark.

Curse Darshan. It was all his doing, filling his head with talk of magic. He wasn't a spellster. He *couldn't* be. He just needed to focus. On the moment, not the memory of the mess he had left behind in that study.

He flung the door open at the first pealing call of her permission to enter. His mother sat in her usual padded chair near the fireplace, casually working a needle through a small piece of hooped linen. Although she had plenty of servants that could've done her needlework for her, his mother had a fondness for such tasks.

"You wanted to see me?" Hamish shuffled in the doorway. His gaze flicked over the room. Nothing unusual.

His mother glanced up from her needlework. "I did." She carried on with her sewing as if it was far more important than their conversation. "About your lack of enthusiasm in finding a wife. I—"

"It's taking longer than usual," he blurted, hoping to stave off her usual lamenting of him not adhering to custom. "I ken that. I..." His mind desperately worked to find the right words that would see him leaving without angering her. Floundering, he latched onto an old excuse. "I just havenae found the right one."

"Well, then." She finally put the hooped fabric aside. "I'm sure you'll be pleased to hear you can stop looking."

"I... can?" Relief stuttered in his heart. Had she...? Was she finally seeing what she was doing to him? "Is this because you've decided to make me the ambassador at Minamist?"

His bow shook and another arrow missed its mark, glancing off the lower edge of the target and spinning away. He should've known right then. Should've realised her intentions and left.

But no, he'd been stupid enough to believe she would keep her word. *Fool.*

His mother laughed. It was a dreadful, sneering tone that sent an icy vein of horror through him. "Are you still harping on about that? Nae, you'll be far too busy forming a family with your new wife to venture off into foreign lands."

"I dinnae..." Pain erupted in his chest, squeezing tight. Panic and dizziness overcame his senses. He stumbled to lean against the doorframe. "You said I—" It couldn't be. New wife? *He dared another darting look around the room. They were still alone. "What wife?"*

Sighing, his mother stood. "Hamish, you're thirty-seven years old. When I was your age, I was married, your brother was born and your sister was on the way." She clasped her hands before her, every inch the queen. "That is why I am holding a union contest for your hand."

Hamish doubled over, teetering on the edge of nausea as he struggled to keep back tears. Nae. *He pressed a hand to his belly, trying to still his stomach. How was this happening?*

The union contest. *He'd witnessed it with his siblings; a fight amongst currently eligible noblewomen from all the clans. But unlike his siblings, he wouldn't have a prospective spouse amongst the competition. Rather, he would be gifted to the woman who won his hand.* Like a trophy.

"Dinnae look so distraught," his mother snapped. "Your brother went through the same contest."

Hamish pressed a hand to his lips. Aye. *But Gordon had loved his wife. The union contest had been a mere formality for them, necessary only because his mother had deemed Muireall unfit to become the princess consort.*

But Hamish? Who would even have him? It was well-known that he had never had a wife, an unheard of thing at his age. Maybe the competitors would twig something wasn't right.

But if the expected suitors did *come? If someone won? What then?* Chaos. *He'd be despised. Outcast. Unsuitable as another link in the royal chain. His purpose of siring a child like his ancestors finally declared invalid. "You cannae—"*

"The first of the eligible nobles have already arrived. The rest will filter in over the coming week."

Hamish frowned. A week? *When the nearest clan was several weeks away? That could only mean she had sent the call before Darshan's arrival.*

Anger singed the fear from his mind. "You swore,*" he growled. He had thought this was retribution for his intimacy with the ambassador, but she'd been planning this before she even knew the wrong spellster was coming. "You gave me your word as queen that I would be allowed to marry in me own time."*

"I think we both know you didnae intend to ever keep your end of the deal, dear."

He glowered at her. No, he hadn't.

"Dinnae think I was unaware of what you've been up to. Becoming an ambassador? Of all the inane lies to weave. Nae son of mine is travelling to some far-off city to be some noble's bedwarmer. You will stay here and do your duty like any other Tirglasian prince."

"But—"

She strode across the room to halt before him, an imposing figure even if she came only to his chin. "The call has been sent. A few from the closer clans have already arrived. What do you expect me to do?"

"Call off the competition!" What difference would it make to the clans if the queen reneged the union contest? There could only be one

winner, so no one lost anything. "Tell them I'm nae ready for a family, that I might never be ready."

"You ken once the call has been sent, it cannae be undone."

He turned his gaze to the walls. "Aye," he muttered. Clans had fought over less. For the queen to renege the union contest was to invite civil war.

She clasped his hand in both of hers, her fingers colder than her ice-blue gaze. "I ken it seems unfair, but sacrifices have to be made to keep the land together. You've spent your whole life preparing for this; trained to defend your clan, schooled in case you have to take the throne. It's well past the time for you to settle down and have wee bairns like your siblings. Like I did with your father."

"But it's nae your life you're building, it's mine. I dinnae want it to be over."

His mother scoffed, jerking her hands back. "It's marriage, *nae a death sentence."*

That was debatable. "I ken what you're really after. You didnae even care which woman I marry." She never had been, thrusting every woman from the noblewomen who came to visit, to the youngest maid. "If it's the wee bairns you want from me, then why bother with the pretence of marriage? Why dinnae you just tie me to a bed and put me out to stud?" He was about as willing either way.

Gasping, his mother jerked her shoulders back. Her whole body strained to be taller than her spine allowed for.

Her hand came up, swift and sharp.

His cheek stung before he realised she had slapped him.

Hamish stared at her, struggling to see his mother amongst the naked rage blazing in front of him. He backed away, his hand pressed to his cheek. Warmth soaked through his fingertips. "You hit me." She had never raised more than her voice at him in the past.

"You brought it upon yourself. You're the one who dared to speak to me in that manner." Rather than follow, his mother stood her ground and pointed at the floor before her. "Now get back here."

His feet took him back through the doorway. Standing in the corridor, faced with a vision of his mother he'd never witnessed before, he fled.

Even in that, he had been hounded by her voice.

Hamish's hands shook as he raised his final arrow. His feet had taken him here, scuttling to the familiar like a roach. But even out here, in the heart of the only act that gave him some measure of control, he wasn't free of her.

And what exactly did he command? His skill with a bow? It lay shattered across the archery range. Stolen from him by… by…

The memory of the arrow he had loosed out in the forest filled his mind. The way it had twitched, veering off at an angle no trick archer could ever attempt—

Steady. Focus.

The arrow flew from his fingers, landing short.

Screaming, he lobbed the bow after it. Even that didn't make the blasted target.

Hamish raged up and down the line, throwing everything that his hands could get on down the range. Nothing he did mattered. He had nothing, not even his skill. He commanded nothing, least of all his life.

He *was* nothing.

Fury spent and, exhausted to his core, he leant over the low stone wall. Only an old, deeply aching sorrow was left. *What am I going to do?* He hung his head. What *could* he do?

Nothing.

"Now dinnae get me wrong," his father said. "But I'm sure it works better when the *arrow* flies, nae the bow."

Hamish jerked his head up. How long had his father been standing there watching him fail at the one thing he'd been good at? Did he know what his wife had done? Did he care? "Can you nae talk to her?"

"The bow?" His father scratched at his beard, a weak attempt at a jovial smile on his lips. "I dinnae think she'll listen to me, lad." He winced as Hamish levelled a glare at him.

"*Mum,*" Hamish clarified, certain his father knew exactly who he meant. Reclaiming his bow and another arrow, he returned his focus to the target. "Do you ken what she has done now?"

"You mean announcing the union contest for your hand? Aye." His father sighed. "I dinnae think your mum will listen to me any more than the bow. She's pretty dead set on this."

You better understand that, whoever wins your hand, you will *marry them.* His mother's final words echoed through his mind, digging their barbs into him.

Tears blurred his vision, but still he stared at the watery image of the target. There was a way out that involved him *not* letting the union contest come to pass. It was a path he had tried once before and so much of him didn't want to go through with another attempt. But marriage? It was no less likely to end in warfare than refusing. That left him with one action that was solely his to take.

I understand what you want from me, Mum. The bowstring snapped against his bare arm, taking off a thin layer of skin on its way.

The arrowhead struck dead centre on the target. He had one

chance.

And he knew precisely how to do it without a single scrap of blame falling upon anyone's shoulders.

Chapter 28

Darshan stared at the note unfurled and pinned on the table before him by two small weights. It was the reply from his father's trade council on the percentages they recommended for any textile beyond the desired linen. Most were as dismally low as he had expected them to be.

What was he going to do with it? Perhaps if he had the inclination to barter further, he would throw caution to the wind and strike a temporary deal that leant in Tirglas' favour. As things stood? Especially with Queen Fiona's ire at the supposed corruption of her son still strong...

He just couldn't bring himself to care for any of it.

Worse still, how was he going to explain all this to his father? *Sorry, I was too focused on getting a prince into my bed to care about trade.* Where would his father ship him off to next? Cezhory? The Independent Isles? Perhaps he would be of better use serving the dwarven hedgewitches. Most of them wouldn't even acknowledge a proposition, much less be lured by it.

Hamish managed. How? His lover seemed like such a reserved man, at least in comparison to past flings. What had Hamish said that had convinced a hedgewitch to—?

A door slammed open, jolting him from his musing. After being given the message, Nora had assured him he would have the library all to himself this afternoon. Who had invaded his privacy? And why? Was it some urgent missive from his father or the senate? Perhaps even from the trade council itself. Or something far sinister?

Abandoning the message, he peered around the bookshelf.

Hamish filled the doorway, a positively glowing example of divine work, his chest heaving with each ragged breath and his stance one of purpose.

" 'Mish." A quick cast about the room confirmed they were alone. "*Mea lux*, whilst your presence is always a welcome sight, I am—" Words failed him as the man stepped into the candlelight.

Those sapphiric eyes lifted. Dull and crushed. Pain moulded that handsome face, turning it ghastly.

"What is it?"

His lover silently wrapped an arm around him, firmly holding Darshan against that broad chest. Their lips met with none of the man's usual gentleness or wariness; just harsh desperation. A soft whimper escaped Hamish's lips. Far too much like a sob to ignore.

Darshan pushed back, patting Hamish's chest once they'd some distance between them. "As much as I appreciate the senti—"

"I need you inside me," his lover grated. "Now."

"No." Clearly, Hamish had been crying; those gorgeous eyes were rimmed in red. Darshan cupped his lover's face, trying to still him long enough to centre the man. "I would not dare to think of such things until you tell me what has upset you so."

Hamish shook his head, already reaching for his belt buckle. There was a numb quality to the action. Wherever his thoughts had gone, it wasn't on the task. "After," he mumbled.

"Talk to me, *mea lux*." Darshan clasped his lover's hands, pulling them from the belt buckle and to his lips. "I am here for you."

"Nae for much longer," his lover muttered, that red-edged gaze cast aside.

Try as Darshan might, the right words refused to make themselves known much less make their way to his lips.

Yes, he would only be here for the duration of the trade negotiations—they'd always known that—but if Queen Fiona refused to speak with him, then his time in Tirglas could become quite short indeed. *Not for another fortnight, at least.* That was the earliest any ship was heading for a Udynean port. At least, according to Nora's copy of the Mullhind docking schedule and that was only providing the appointed ship arrived here in due time.

Then he would return to the Crystal Court in Minamist. Whereas Hamish would be here, forced into his old way of life. Worse still, there was little either of them could do about that without having Tirglasian troops scouring the land or tailing Darshan back home.

"Tell me what is wrong," Darshan urged. "Maybe I cannot help with it, but that does not mean you need to bear whatever burden you do alone."

"*Help?*" Hamish all but growled. Rage and hurt fought for control across his face, darkening his eyes. "You already ken what I need from you."

"*That* is not happening. Not here. Not whilst you are like this."

Gods, he would never forgive himself if he even thought of taking advantage of the man when he was clearly distraught over something.

"Fine," Hamish spat. "If you willnae give..." He grabbed Darshan's hips, bodily lifting him onto the table.

Indignance had magic humming along Darshan's skin before he could think to use it. One blast of air was enough to send Hamish staggering back.

He slammed a shield around himself, keeping one hand outstretched to warn Hamish back should his lover attempt to rush him. What madness had taken over the man? "No one manhandles me without my permission and you are most certainly not in the right frame of mind to get that. Nor will I give my word until you tell me what is wrong."

Rather than move, or answer, Hamish stood between two bookshelves, trembling.

Just when Darshan thought his lover might not reply, Hamish slumped into a nearby chair. "Everything," he whispered. He laughed, a soft and mirthless sound. Broken emotion looking for an outlet. "It's all gone so wrong and I… I dinnae ken what to do."

Darshan shuffled closer, dropping his shield. "I take it your mother is no more inclined towards letting you leave?" He could see how that would indeed be a concern, but his lover hadn't mentioned anything throughout their travels that would've indicated any further barriers than those already in play.

Had conversing with Queen Fiona brought the situation back into the forefront of his concerns? Or was his lover now privy to new information?

Hamish shook his head. "Less so, if you can believe it. I—" His shoulders seemed to grow as he inhaled noisily. Whatever the case, the act appeared to give him strength. "I'm sorry. I dinnae ken what came over me. I just—"

Wanted to feel something. Darshan knew that feeling. It had become an old bedfellow of his a long time ago. He wrapped his arms around Hamish's shoulders, straddling one of the man's legs to get close enough, and squeezed.

His lover's arm snaked behind Darshan, drawing him closer. Not with the same desperate urgency as before, but just as firmly.

"Whatever is wrong," Darshan murmured against Hamish's temple. "You do not need to tell me now. But sex is most definitely off the table until we *have* talked."

Hamish lifted his head, wiping away the thin trace of tears from his face. "I also feel a little bad that you didnae get to see a bear on our way back." He stood, his face swiftly regaining the unflappable poise Darshan had come to witness during their travels. "How about I take you to one nae that far from here?"

"As in now?" Why the urgency? Was there something dangerous within the castle? To Hamish?

To me? The thought darted across the others swarming his mind like a bird across a pond, bringing with it a faint buzz of anticipation. It had been years since he'd come face to face with any actual danger. Was Queen Fiona planning on locking him away in a cloister like she had done with her own daughter? *I'd like to see her try.*

Tucking the thought neatly away in the back of his mind, Darshan cleared his throat and continued his current line of enquiry. "Why would we seek to leave when we have just returned?"

"Because now is the best time. Your things are still packed and we'll get a few hours of travel in. Maybe even get to see her emerge from her lair near morning." Something still rang hollow in his words. What had shaken the man so?

Darshan hummed, idly rubbing his moustache with a forefinger. Would removing Hamish from the palace free his lover from the cloud of whatever had put the pain in his eyes? A hurt that still lingered there despite the smiles. Or would it aid in shaking free the truth?

Only one way to know...

~ ~ ~

Hamish lay on his back, staring at the canvas canopy of the tent stretched above them. Leaving the castle had been laughably easy, involving no more subterfuge than leading their mounts out the gates whilst a crowd of others rode in. The guards had been too busy dealing with the newcomers to glance their way.

He had caught glimpses of what was to come amongst the new arrivals; flags with clan emblems that he'd only seen during his childhood lessons or at his siblings' union contests, and sombre-looking contestants garbed head to toe in mottled browns. Even if he had been willing to go through with the contest, he wouldn't see more than the woman's eyes until they failed or one of them was named the victor.

None of that mattered anymore. He was out here. Several hours' ride deep into pristine forestland. Only one law existed here and the Goddess was not hesitant about punishing those who dared to test its boundaries.

Darshan gave a contented sigh as he snuggled against him. Even bundled in his multitude of layers, a faint chill radiated off his hands. "Is it not dangerous to sleep so close to a bear cave?"

"It isnae *that* close." It would take a few hours marching through the forest on foot to get there as it was. He had considered camping closer still, but he'd a feeling Darshan would've baulked at such a suggestion. "Besides, tracking her will be easier with fresher marks."

His lover gave a thoughtful hum. Darshan had been making that sound so often over the past afternoon that Hamish didn't need any light to know the man's lips were pressed into a thin line. There'd be a slight twitch to the tip of his nose, too, which would've shuddered all the way to his glasses had Darshan still been wearing them.

Hamish braced himself for another of his lover's attempts to tease out the truth of what gnawed at him. No matter what happened, he didn't want what he had left behind them to mar this moment of stillness. Of just… being.

"It seems to me that you are far more at ease out in the wilderness than in the castle. Do you venture out here often?"

"Whenever I can." Everything seemed simpler. No impending union contest. No inevitable wedding. No one to make him feel guilty for his actions. Just him and his lover. "Although, they dinnae usually permit me to travel without a guard."

"What luck smiled upon us this time?"

Nothing. Any luck he might've possessed was just a cheap magical trick. Darshan had proven that. He had earned none of the accolades he'd been given.

"Me brother." No point in telling the man otherwise. Once Gordon got wind that he'd left with Darshan in tow, he would ensure his mother's guards didn't follow. "He convinced me mum's lackeys that our little hunting trip would be better served if they weren't crashing through the undergrowth alongside us." The lie wasn't his best, but certainly better than the truth that they might be tracked later.

"He is a curious man. Is he your comrade?"

"Me what?"

The cheek Darshan had laid on Hamish's bicep twitched. "I am unsure if you have a word for it. He helps you in your conquests. You… select what you deem as a suitable target and your comrade then basically assists in getting you laid via several means."

Hamish blinked. "You're right, I dinnae believe we have a word for that." Could he class Gordon as such? His brother certainly had some idea of what Hamish got up to during those distant times he'd spent in the dockside pubs. Did he assist more than keeping the guards away? "I dinnae think so." He couldn't imagine Gordon picking out anyone, not when his brother knew the fate of those caught with Hamish… *Treason*. Not a crime many came back from.

Just another reason to take the path he had chosen. How would the Goddess judge him for all the death he had caused?

"Truly? Well, I must confess I am not entirely certain what to make of him. He is the heir, is he not? Should he not be on your mother's side? Not that I am complaining. It is merely nice to know our allies."

"Gordon's on his own side." Always was. That his brother had decided his siblings were also part of that side was a blessing. "He's been at loggerheads with our mum ever since she forced the nearby cloister to disband." He was pretty sure that was due to there being an echo of his brother's older, deceased, daughter in Caitlyn's mannerisms.

Would his brother have had the same outlook on things had that man-killing mountain of a bear not taken his wife and eldest child? Would his mother care what Hamish did with his life had she not lost several of her grandchildren? Or would he always have been faced with her disgust over his lack of conforming to the path she had chosen for him?

No matter how much he tried, his mind wouldn't still. Never mind that the countless maybes and possibilities would all become inconsequential soon enough. Over and over, he had voiced his objection to the route he'd been forced down and if that wasn't enough for her to see what she was doing to him, then maybe tomorrow would finally get through. Enough to not set his nephew on the same path, at least.

Goddess, look over him. He wished he could've been a better example to Ethan, but this was their lot in life.

Darshan wriggled further up Hamish's side. "You have gone very quiet," he whispered. "Are you asleep?"

"Nae," he murmured. Sleep would not claim him tonight. Of that, he was certain. "Just thinking." His thoughts drifted to the dim memory of a conversation they'd had some weeks back. "You never did that vibrating hand trick, you ken."

"You did not ask for it."

He was correct there. Although, the matter of when had been a tricky one. Especially when they were on the road at first light through much of their journey. Hamish would often be asleep by the time Darshan was anywhere in proximity and likewise with the spellster. "There's always now." When else would he ever get the chance to experience being with someone he wanted as much as he did Darshan?

"Out in the wild? With the animals watching? I will pass on that."

"I'm nae suggesting we do it out there." He flung his arm wide to encompass the forest beyond their shelter. "We've a tent. How do you think your ancestors used to have sex?"

"Easy. In their homes. On a perfectly serviceable bed like normal people."

"And before they built those homes?"

"Then probably on board one of the ships." A small chuckled shook the man's stomach, pressed as it was to Hamish's side. "They are, technically speaking, *your* distant ancestors too. Or do Tirglasians not believe that all humans sailed here together?"

"The priests say the Goddess guided us to these lands from another." Hamish shrugged. "That's it."

"Nevertheless, I would prefer not to on the grounds that I am likely to wake the local wildlife. *And* I do believe I said such intimacy was only after you had spoken of what troubled you. Or did you think I had forgotten?"

"Nae really." He had hoped. It would make tomorrow easier if Darshan's attention was more on the bear and less on Hamish's actions.

"And? Are you still unwilling to confide in me?"

Hamish's insides seemed to squirm of their own accord. "On that subject, aye." Although, if Darshan continued to needle him, he might blurt out everything and his true reason for leaving the castle with just one man in his company would be for nothing. "But if you'll indulge me for a wee while, since neither of us seems ready to sleep, what parts of the old spellster legends are true?"

"What legends? Whose?"

He winced. Hamish had meant the old tales he had grown up with, but of course Darshan wouldn't know them, much less whether they were true. "Your people's, I guess. Can you do the same magic as the spellsters of old?"

Darshan gave a non-committal grunt. There was a faint shift of the blankets. Had he just shrugged?

"How can you nae ken?" Hamish rolled onto his side, seeking his lover's expression. But the twilight beyond their tent had well and truly slipped into darkness. "You're telling me nae a single person has ever tried replicating your legendary feats?"

His lover scoffed, bathing Hamish's face in his hot breath. "Of course they have *tried*. There are whole academy wings devoted to *trying*. But most of the feats my people speak about in awed tones were powerful. Terribly so. To attempt them without the right strength, or the precise steps, could tear you to pieces. It does not help that, for some, to even learn if you will survive is to actually attempt it. Few takers."

"We used to hear, when I was a wee lad." Back before Caitlyn was born, never mind taken to the cloister. "The storytellers in the market square recite tales of spellsters easily bringing people back from the dead." His mother had banned those stories from being told, within the confines of Mullhind, at least.

"Whilst few would not call it *easy*, such a feat is a common one that relies on a mixture of medical knowledge, willpower and magical strength. Like I did with that man at the cloister."

He thought back to the man Darshan healed from the brink of death. "But he wasnae *dead*, though." Close, according to his sister. "Spellsters cannae actually bring people back from the dead, right?"

Darshan hummed. "The recently dead? Yes, there are such cases where people have been deceased for over an hour and were revived."

"The people in the legends were several days' dead." Sometimes, the storyteller would substitute it for weeks. Often, it was a loved one and would end with some sort of sacrifice on the other's behalf.

"That sort of magic is... theoretically possible. There are always legends of this and that happening. People reappearing long after they were buried and yadda yadda. No actual mentions of how they appeared, of course. Just that they did. There is this myth that originated from my people's first encounter with the Stamekian nomads and how they will punish the unworthy by using their life-force to revive those who are."

"They swap the death of one for the death of another?"

"So the tale goes. Not many gift the tale much credit nowadays, but the idea does linger in a few debates. And I am certain if I asked around, I would find a few professors still attempting to determine if there was any merit to the act. They do believe the manner of how Stamekians treat their dead aids them."

"Do they nae bury them?" That was the Tirglasian way. Deep in the forest, if possible, so animals were nae drawn too close to the villages.

"I would think it is more along the lines of entombing their dead in sand. The dry environment is likely what preserves their remains."

A flush of heat took his face as he recollected the giant tapestry of the known world from which he and his siblings had learnt of the realms. The small empire of Stamekia was the farthest a person could head south before jumping into the ocean and, at least on the tapestry map, was mostly the fawn and taupe of arid land. "Right," he mumbled.

"My apologies, it is not much of a topic on which to gain sleep from. How about something a little lighter?"

They spoke all through the night on frivolous matters until sleep finally claimed Darshan. Hamish tried to follow suit, even if only so he could be alert enough to track the bear, but closing his eyes did little to still his mind. The best he could manage was just lying still beside his lover, listening to the man's steady breath, whilst the darkness grew old and faded.

Hamish sought to leave the tent only once the grey light of approaching dawn crept through the gaps in the entrance. He slipped free of Darshan's grasp and silently tugged on his boots.

At his back, Darshan slept on, seemingly oblivious to the new day.

He gently brushed back the hair from his lover's face and pressed a kiss to Darshan's forehead. *I'm sorry.* If it hadn't been for the spellster, he never would've known what it was like to love, both romantically and sexually, and have it returned, if not in full, at least in part with an honest echo of affection.

He couldn't force himself to take a path where such a feeling would never be possible, to be what his mother wanted. *I'm so sorry.* With luck, they would believe the spellster when he told them of how Hamish had been mauled to death.

Goddess willing, it would be a quick one. The bear might not be a known man-killer, but he had seen firsthand what such an animal could do to a person.

Darshan stirred. His eyelids slowly parted. " 'Mish?" Squinting, the man groggily groped for the little box that contained his glasses. "Is it morning already?" The words tumbled out, sleep-slurred and mostly Udynean.

"Hush." He caressed the man's cheek, absently running his thumb along the short beard that had grown over the course of their travels. "I'm just going outside for a bit. Go back to sleep." He could've roused Darshan further and have them on their way before dawn's light had finished filtering through the trees, but the spellster would need to be at his brightest if he was to get near the bear's lair on foot in one piece. And back to camp afterwards.

Those gorgeous hazel eyes fluttered shut.

Hamish slipped out into the last vestiges of darkness, pausing only to snap up his bow and a few arrows from his quiver.

The world under the canopies was swathed in grey light, enough to see by as he sauntered to the nearest tree, idly stringing his bow along the way. He slung the weapon over his shoulder before tending to the needs of his bladder.

The side of their tent caught his attention and his stomach twisted. *Just a little while longer.* Then they would head out, find the bear and...

He would have to be careful. There was no way to predict how Darshan would act once they reached the lair, let alone when Hamish put the last piece of their journey out here into action. It was cruel to use him like this, but he needed someone he could trust to be there, to bring back the news, to not know the steps he hadn't taken to avoid the beast.

The horses snorted, spooked by something in the bushes.

Hamish jerked his head around, cursing softly as he splashed his boots. Dealing with the rest of his business as swiftly as he was able, he hastened to the other side of the camp.

Mercifully, both pony and horse were still tied up. That they had trampled what remained of their feed into the ground and had an unusual interest in one patch of the forest did little to ease his concern.

He lowered Warrior's head, rubbing at the spots that typically had the pony sagging against him to no avail. "What's gotten into you two?" He peered through the trees, trying to make out anything in the gloom. It had to be something small. A bird or a rabbit or even a—

A hulking shadow shifted through the undergrowth. It moved with purpose, its back swaying ever so slightly from side to side.

Hamish slowly unslung his bow from his shoulder. There was only one thing in this forest big enough to cast a shadow like that. *You shouldnae be here.* The camp was several hours from its lair. They had made very little noise and had forsaken any meal that would require a fire.

Warrior tugged at the lead keeping him in place. Even Hamish's usually placid mare was giving freedom a good go.

Of course. The bear had caught the horses' scents. Well, that was his mistake.

He strode away from the horses, keeping the shadow within his sights. He was not about to let their mounts to come to any harm. If the animal didn't turn away soon, he would be left with no choice but to provoke it right here and hope his life was enough.

The shadow slowly became darker, gaining definition. The bear paused, standing up on its hind legs. Its short snout snuffled at the air.

Goddess, you crafted a beauty. The bear stood nowhere near as big as the man-killer he had slain in that village years ago, but the Goddess had certainly done just as good a job. He nocked his arrow, waiting for the bear to lower onto all fours before loosing.

The arrow sliced along the bear's side. Not ideal, but better than nothing.

Roaring, the bear loped towards him.

Hamish froze. He recollected the vision of his brother's wife after the man-killer had gotten the best of her. Broken and shredded. Barely recognisable. He had avenged Muireall's death. And that of his niece. Was this what they'd seen at the end? How much had they felt? Had they—?

The terrified screams of the horses echoed through Hamish's skull, uprooting him from his terror. *Shut up. Shut up!* He had to keep the bear's attention on him. *He* was the threat.

Taking a step back, he loosed another arrow. Then another. Wood tapped on wood as he shook, throwing off his aim.

He loosed the final one, hitting her paw. A lucky shot. He couldn't have missed if he had thrown the arrow.

Tossing his bow aside, he thumped on his chest. "Come on, then!"

A wall of muscle and fur slammed into him.

Hamish hit the ground. Air whooshed from his lungs. The bear's weight pinned him in place. Claws dug into his chest, piercing right through his thin shirt. A slobbering maw enveloped his sight, fastening onto his neck.

Pain finally caught up. It tightened his throat, struggling for release. Breathless as he was, his cry made little sound. Everywhere hurt. His chest was afire. His neck... The tepid flow of life pumped out across his skin. Was that crunching sound his ribs or—?

Quick as she had landed on him, the bear was gone. Torn from his person. Searing heat followed, flying over him. The orange blaze of fire filled his tear-blinded vision.

Dar...

The spellster wasn't supposed to be out here now. The bear... It—

The heat and glow of fire faded, leaving the world to grow increasingly cold and dark.

"Gods," Darshan blurted. "I should never have let you bring me out here." The words were soft, cracked and weary.

Hamish struggled to breathe. The cloying stench of burnt fur and charred meat invaded his nostrils. He tried again. His efforts produced only a gurgle. It was as if his lungs strained through swamp water.

" 'Mish!" Darshan's voice came brokenly. Closer now. "*No...*" Hands grasped him, frantically patting over his body. "Come now." Those same hands patted Hamish's cheeks. Words he couldn't understand poured from the man's mouth, jumbled with a mixture of Udynean and Tirglasian. "*Spiro!* Just breathe. *Aperi oculos tuos.* Come back to me."

Blackness sucked at his consciousness. Only a thin corona of white remained in his sight. Hamish drifted deeper on the current. No struggle, no floundering. Why fight? He deserved it. This death. Clean. Honourable. No one else needed to suffer for his flaws, for his inability to obey.

"I do not give you permission to die." Fingers pressed to Hamish's neck, tearing a fresh spasm of pain through him. "Do you hear me, 'Mish?" A warm jolt of magic pierced him much like the bear's tooth. "Not here. Not today. I shall not allow it."

He was vaguely aware of the stuttering beat pulsing through his head. Distant. Fading fast and unimportant.

Then gone.

Chapter 29

The terrified scream of a horse jolted Darshan from his fitful slumber. He sat bolt upright, groping for the little velvet-lined box containing his glasses. “Hamish?” he whispered. His lover would be able to determine the severity of a threat far quicker than himself.

A glance at the tussled blankets next to him revealed a marked lack of anyone.

Outside. With the whatever-it-was that had frightened the horses.

His fingers found the box. He flung aside the lid and fought with the square of silk holding his glasses captive. Hastening to tuck the wire earpieces in place, he burst through the tent flap and—

—clapped a hand over his mouth, barely containing his own cry of terror.

A bear, a small mountain of bloody fur and muscle, stood over Hamish’s inert body, its mouth wrapped around the man’s neck. There was no sign of his lover fighting back.

Gods. Tears fast obscured his view of the scene. He blinked them back, staggering forward. Was Hamish… dead? “No,” he mumbled. It couldn’t be true.

Unthinkingly, he raised his hand.

A blast of air tore the beast from Hamish’s body, spraying blood everywhere. Fire flowed from Darshan’s fingers, blazing across the clearing. It slammed into the bear, molten and lethal.

The creature fell in seconds.

He growled wordlessly at the smouldering lump. How had it happened? His gaze fell on the bow lying well out of Hamish’s reach. Several arrows dotted the forest. None appeared to have hit their mark. What had thrown off such a marksman? “Gods.” He halted beside Hamish’s body. “I should never have let you bring me out here.” If they’d stayed in the castle, then—

An answering gurgle came from the man.

Hamish still *lived*? He had thought for sure that no one could've survived such an attack.

" 'Mish!" Darshan collapsed next to his lover. *So much blood*. It poured from his neck and chest. Alive for the moment, but not much longer for the world. "*No…*" He ran his hands over Hamish, his magic dipping in and out of his body in search of the worst wound. "Come now." He patted Hamish's cheeks, hoping that would be enough to stimulate a response. "Breathe!" he commanded. "Just breathe. Open your eyes. Come back to me."

Whether through involuntary or conscious effort, the man's blue eyes rolled open. They stared at the canopy, glassy and vacant.

Darshan pressed his fingers to the deep-red wound in Hamish's neck, summoning his healing magic. "I do not give you permission to die." His power slipped into Hamish almost hesitantly, most unlike the draining pull from the last man he had healed.

He pushed harder. "Do you hear me, 'Mish? Not here. Not today." He clamped his teeth and grated through them, "I shall not allow it."

And yet…

Where was the tug on his magic, the parasitic pull of another's body feeding off his power? He should've been feeling the effects by now. Had he not—?

Was he too late?

Darshan lifted his finger from the wound, swiftly replacing it as blood erratically pumped out. *Too much.* The flow was ebbing—he could feel the wound shifting and growing smaller beneath his fingers—but it was all so slow. Hamish had already lost more blood than was ideal. His body wasn't trying to wrest all Darshan was from him because there was simply too little left to fight.

Darshan was going to have to do that for him.

Swallowing hard, he forced his magic a little deeper. *Careful.* A faint twitch was all it took to aid the thump of his lover's heart. Forcing the lungs to breathe was harder and required the greater bulk of his concentration. His lover's chest was a mess of lacerations and broken bones. If he could just fix a few, stop further blood loss by mending Hamish's chest, then maybe…

Control over his magic was ripped from his command as soon as the skin had knitted back together. Darshan swayed, momentarily stunned, then sagged over Hamish's still inert form.

His own body strained to keep up. His heart pulsed to the same erratic rhythm. He gasped open-mouthed, saliva shamelessly dribbling out. The mere flickering thought of pausing to swallow was lost in the battle to keep breathing.

Through each tremble and gut-wrenching breath, he struggled to regain control, to turn his magic towards what needed it most. The neck wound was sealed, it would be an ugly scar, but posed no threat to Hamish's life. His chest was whole, the ribs and organs beneath heeding Darshan's touch.

He was done. The injuries were gone. *Finally.*

So why did Hamish's completely whole body continue to drain him? His power funnelled into his lover like water over a cliff. But unlike a river, it wasn't endless. He needed to extract himself before it took a greater toll.

Keeping one hand on Hamish's neck, Darshan tugged his magic free. The second he did, the pulse under his fingers faltered.

Unthinking, he dove back in. This wasn't like any other healing he had done. There was no clear cause, nothing he could focus on. It dragged at him, sapped him of all thought beyond maintaining the flow of his magic.

It wasn't enough. Hamish needed more than Darshan had to give. Everything that made up his lover cried out for his strength. He was the air. He was power. Blood...

Life.

The wisp of a thought that could think beyond just existing fastened onto the previous night's conversation. *The legends.* There were theories, so many studies that had never born fruit, but all agreed that the power needed would be immense.

Had he the strength left to try?

Must. Letting go consigned Hamish to death, whereas continuing like this meant they would both die. Neither option was at all palatable.

But where would he get the extra life-force?

The bear? His head wobbled as he peered at the charred remains. *No.* Not even a spark. He'd been thorough there.

The horses? They'd need at least one once he was done. *If...*

With bleary eyes, he searched the clearing. Both mounts had broken their tethers. It was unlikely he could've reached them anyway.

Darshan licked his cracked lips. Maybe he was thinking about this all wrong. The legends came from a place where lifeless dunes stretched for miles. He was in the middle of a forest. They were surrounded by life. The ground pulsed with it.

A conduit. That was what he needed to be, not the source. Feed the life in the very ground through him and into Hamish.

He hadn't done such a thing before, not latching onto anything's life-force with the intention of taking. The idea of delving into plant life was entirely absent from any of his academic studies. Seeing anything more in the forest than wood and leaves was supposed to be at the core of dwarven souls.

He cringed from the thought, even as he dug his fingers into the soil. Udynea had her own legends of people skirting death—monsters who had worn the skin of humans as a thin disguise—and this, as much as it pained him to think it, came very close to what they'd done. *Just this once.* Just for him. *You can't let him die here.*

He wound a root of grass around his finger, careful not to let it snap under his touch. If plants absorbed what they needed through these strands, then he should be able to siphon what Hamish required back the other way. If he could just find the right focus to—

The fresh source of energy was like a slap in the face. The heartbeat of a new world thundered through his chest. The scream of a thousand—a million—voices roared in his ears.

Pain ripped through his veins and out his throat. The source fought him, necessitating that he actively tear the life from the surrounding foliage. It drew bile up his throat between gasps. Every inch of his body—from the root of his hair to the tips of his toes—felt afire.

But it was working.

Through the flashes of white and red blinding him, he spied the grass shrivelling as if it baked under a summer sun. The leaves on a nearby bush withered and fell, leaving only a stark, dusty twig. Like a plague, the circle of death spread, pulsing with his efforts.

It grew harder the further he needed to seek out life. Each heartbeat rippled through the dead foliage, the constant exchange from one blade of grass to the next exhausting him all the more. The screams in his head grew weaker with every ripple.

If only he could move... But no, he barely had the strength to remain upright. Anything more would be impossible without rest and he couldn't dare to stop until Hamish was beyond the crisis point.

The sluggish, ever-widening growth of the circle sputtered to a halt. Had he reached the limit of his range so soon? He clawed at the ground, using what minute strength he had in reserve to drag his arm as far from Hamish as he could physically manage. No matter how hard he stretched his magic, he could go no further.

Praying he had done enough, Darshan withdrew his touch from both the ground and Hamish. His body shuddered to his core.

He collapsed onto his side, barely able to keep his eyes open. His gaze fastened onto Hamish, seeing only the rise and fall of his lover's chest. *He lives.* Or breathed, at least. Only time would tell if he awoke. "Wake up," he commanded, the words barely a whisper on his lips. "Just open your eyes, *mea lux*. Please?"

Closer... Another shudder passed through him. *I have to get up.* Not possible. Much like the grass, his limbs buckled at the slightest pressure. He needed rest, to grant his body the time to repair what damage might've been done.

His eyes slid closed, very much against his will. The world was far too cold. *Please...* Even as he tried to lift just one eyelid, the absolute fog of exhaustion slipped over his brain, throwing him into dreamless sleep.

~ ~ ~

Hamish's limbs jerked involuntarily. Pain wracked his senses like lightning and fire rushing through his veins. Was this what being torn apart was like? *Must be.* He had thought for sure that bleeding out would've taken him first.

The searing pain burrowed deeper, gnawing on his bones. In the lull between bites, another thought shook free. Should he be able to think at all if he were dying? It had been sinking blackness and fog only moments ago, he was certain.

And yet, anguished screaming continued to fill his ears. His lungs hadn't the power to produce such a sound.

All at once, the pain vanished, leaving silence in its wake.

Hamish drifted in the dark. He was faintly aware of a presence to his right, but hadn't the strength or will to discover what. *Or who.* Hadn't he heard Darshan? Hadn't he attacked the bear?

Was the bear attacking Darshan? Was that what the screaming had been? Did his lover now lie dying?

Dar...

Battling against the snail-like reaction of his limbs, he rolled onto his side. Prone, he could move no further as a body-shaking cough took hold.

"Careful now," Darshan whispered, his voice thin and weary.

"What?" he croaked. Gunk filled his mouth. He spat out the glob of black muck to join a similar pile on the nearby ground and wobbled into a sitting position. All around him, the grass was dull and brittle. The very ground seemed parched.

"You are safe," Darshan continued, his voice sounding no stronger. "Healed."

Hamish's gaze lifted to where the bear lay nearby, charred and very much dead. "What have you done?" He patted his chest. His shirt was torn and blood-soaked, but the skin underneath showed no sign of injury beyond faint scars weaving through the hair. "You brought me back to life?"

"No." Darshan sat nearby, one arm draped over a raised knee. A sickly, pallid tint had taken his face. His chest heaved as if each breath was a great labour. "You did not die. A minor detail in the greater role of it all." He swung his hand in a limp circle. "You came close, but I pulled you back before then. Just as well, for I rather doubt I have it in me to push that far." His grin was one of forced gaiety. "Still quite the feat, if I do say so myself."

Hamish idly traced a finger along his neck as his lover talked. There were two smooth patches either side, one bigger than the other. A flash of the bear's teeth filled his thoughts and he shuddered. "You should nae have bothered," he murmured.

"Should not have—? What? Saved your life?" Darshan shook his head. "Were you taunting it by not firing directly?" He flapped a hand in the direction of the arrows littering the ground. "I know you are a better marksman than that. Anyone would think you wanted to die."

"I do," Hamish whispered. As soon as the words left his mouth, he wanted to push them back down his throat. Hunching his shoulders, he closed his eyes, not wishing to see Darshan's expression as he waited for the ridicule he had faced the last time he had tried. "I cannae do it anymore," he mumbled. "Living this lie. It was different before you came, I couldnae miss what I didnae have. But I ken what it's like now and I cannae go back."

Beset upon only by silence, Hamish slowly peered through his lashes. He half-expected to find himself alone with the bear carcass.

Darshan had leant back and now eyed him as if he hadn't encountered Hamish before now. But rather than the condemnation he had expected, all emotion had fled the man's face to leave only a heart-aching concern shining in Darshan's eyes. The little bump at his throat bobbed and he opened his mouth every now and then, but nothing came out.

Laughter, loud and mirthless, burst from Hamish's mouth. Of all the things to render the man speechless, he never thought this would be it.

Darshan wet his lips. His gaze flicked to the surrounding woods and back. Did he think Hamish might bolt like a skittish deer? "What happened to have you think this was a reasonable step to take?"

That hadn't been the response Hamish had expected. His last attempt had left him facing anger, accusations and, above all, his mother's disappointment. "You wouldnae understand. Naebody does."

Darshan sat silent and still for some time. Then, with a frown furrowing his brow, he scooted across the ground to halt only once the toe of his boot touched Hamish's, seemingly unable to summon the strength to move closer.

"What are you doing?"

"Waiting for an explanation." Darshan slowly crossed his legs and steepled his fingers. "With all due respect, you have lived in your current state for some time. To choose now speaks of a catalyst. I merely wish to know what that was."

Hamish huffed. He was tired of explaining himself. "What's the point?" No one ever listened.

"Well, I believe we have established I lack the understanding behind your reasoning to..." His gaze drifted over his shoulder to the deceased bear. "...to take your life. Refusing to even attempt an explanation seems counterproductive towards any sort of comprehension on my part. Trying can only serve to help."

Hamish remained silent.

Darshan took up one of Hamish's hands, linking their fingers. "Just talk to me. Even if I cannot fully comprehend what you are going through, I am still here to listen. To help you however you need me to."

"Help?" Hamish pulled his hand free. Darshan had said the same words back in the castle and seemed no less sincere. But how could he possibly help? "This is nae some wee matter. There is nae magical fix. You cannae just wiggle your fingers and make things better."

Darshan's gaze dropped. Although he didn't voice it, the hurt on his face was plain enough.

Great. He hadn't meant to lash out like that. Hamish wobbled to his feet, trying to put some distance between them. "I'm sorry. You didnae deserve that, this is nae your fault." He could blame the healing on Darshan, but not the reason they were out here in the first place.

Taking a step back had his legs dump him unceremoniously onto his backside.

"Slowly!" Darshan's hand was outstretched towards him, but he had made no attempt to move. "I rather doubt I am capable of healing more than a few scratches right now."

Hamish slammed his fist into the ground, the withered blades of grass crumbling beneath his fist. What had Darshan done? Was all this dead plant life his doing? *To heal* me*?* He squeezed his eyes shut. *Of course he did*. Darshan had pushed himself in healing that man back at the cloister. Why had Hamish thought his lover wouldn't go further with himself?

Tears trickled into his beard. He wasn't worth saving. "You dinnae even ken what it's like," he whispered. "There were times when me mum locked me up for days. Sometimes *weeks*. I'd lay there wishing, *praying*, there was a way—some method, even a spell—to fix this." He thumped his chest. "To fix *me*. All so I wasnae such a burden."

"You are not a—" Darshan's voice cracked. The inhalation he gave was tearful as was the blustery sigh that followed. "Any application of magic would be fruitless; there is nothing to fix. You are no more broken than I."

"Tell that to me mum."

"I would, if I honestly believed she would hear me. But..."

Scoffing, Hamish turned his attention the tree beyond where the bear lay. They were fortunate that Darshan's attack on the poor creature hadn't started a forest fire. "Me mum hears nae one but herself." Echoes of his brother's lamenting drifted up from the depths of his memory. "She keeps her own council and decides the kingdom's direction on a whim."

"Dangerous, that. Listening only to yourself."

"So you see why this—" He gestured between them with a chest-level flutter of his hand. "—cannae happen?" Not a damn thing between them. No matter how much he wanted it. "You were wrong. Every thought you had about having me in Minamist is wrong." He shook his head. "It's all wrong."

Darshan's gaze slid to the ground between them as he chewed on his lip. "If you thought us being together was wrong, then why persist? I told you that, if you did not wish to pursue anything, you only had to stay away. I would have understood your decision."

Dread bubbled in his stomach. "I remember."

"But you came to my quarters and agreed to continue on afterwards. Why?"

So many reasons. Because he'd been enchanted by the thought that he was still desirable, that thirteen years hadn't changed his ability to pleasure a man to completion, that maybe just the once he could be himself from the start. If he'd been in his right mind, he would've refused the offer, but he had always had a weakness for the intelligent, witty and handsome types.

But mostly, his actions had been fuelled by one fact.

"I did it because I wanted you." That was the reality, plain and simple. Ever since Darshan had kissed him in *The Fisherman's Cask*, then promised more within Hamish's own room, his loins had taken control of his senses. And he was glad for it.

"Then why—?"

"That doesnae matter anymore. Goading that bear was the only choice I had and you took it away. They would've been able to mourn me then move on." Just like they'd done with his siblings' spouses and their children. "Nae one'll miss me."

"What absolute nonsense," Darshan's reply carried little in the way of emotion, no heat, no pity. Just as if he'd stated a fact. "You think your mark on the world could be erased so easily? You are their brother, their uncle, their son. And even if what you say is true with them, there is still *me*."

"Is there really? *You* get to leave. *You* go home and I'm stuck here living the same life I was before you came." He shook his head, mirthless laughter huffing between his teeth. "Except it willnae be the same. It cannae be anymore. I'll be forced into a marriage I dinnae want."

"*Marriage?* Who to?"

Hamish shrugged and rubbed at his nose. "To whoever wins the contest of arms me mum's arranged."

"A contest?" Disdain warped Darshan's lips and wrinkled his nose. "She would see you handed off like a prize to the victor? This was what brought you to me yesterday? What brought you here?"

Hamish nodded.

"So run. We could find the horses and flee to the Udynean border. They cannot marry you off if you are not here."

"Find the—?" He twisted around to eye where their mounts had been tethered. *Gone*. The earth was churned, the surrounding foliage was either broken or shredded. The horses had fled in terror. "Even if we could find them." Unlikely, given that the horses were probably back at the castle. That would definitely rouse a search party. "I cannae leave. The answering clans are on their way, some have already arrived. If I'm nae here to be married off, then they could turn on me mum. Me whole family. Me wants are nae worth risking a civil war over."

Darshan nodded slowly. Perhaps he finally understood the predicament Hamish was in. "Do the other clans know you are not exactly... open to sleeping with a woman?"

He shook his head harder as if that would somehow make things clearer to the man. "Nae a soul." His mother would've seen any hint of such knowledge discredited. "If I told them..."

"Let me guess, that would also spark a civil war?"

"Aye. Me niece... me nephews..." He dug his fingers into his hair. "They're all so young, I cannae just toss their lives on the pyre." That was the fate that awaited traitors and false rulers. No burying amongst the wilderness, no chance for the soul to return to the Goddess' bosom. "All because I dinnae want to be with a woman."

Darshan's shoulders sagged. "No, I suppose that would be a bit much to expect of you." He rubbed at his temples, sunlight glittering off his rings. His gaze snapped up to Hamish, those hazel eyes surprisingly sharp. "But what about *your* life? Do you really think they care so little that they would rather you live a lie for their sake?"

Live a lie. His blood went cold at the very thought. It wasn't just the marriage he would have to go along with. He'd have to sire a child, learn to be someone he had never been, someone he had never wanted to be. But the alternative...

"Surely, if you explained the situation to the victor, she could be persuaded to—"

Laughing, Hamish buried his head into his hand. "To what? Be married to a man who has nae intentions of lying with her. You dinnae ken much about our marriage customs, do you?"

"I did not exactly come here to marry a Tirglasian, so of course not."

"Once we marry, a child is expected within the next two years. Nae child and the marriage is void. Whoever wins isnae going to be satisfied with a few years. If a child doesnae happen because I refuse to sleep with… me wife." A sour taste tinged his tongue as he spoke. Hamish suppressed a shudder and continued, "Then her clan has every right to attack."

"So you choose to throw yourself before a bear to escape all that? Death cannot be your only recourse. You could run without them knowing you live. What stops your brother saying you were mauled to death?"

If only it were so easy. His siblings had considered it in the past, after the incident with the dwarven ambassador. "The clans would demand to see a body." One with his brown skin and orange-red hair for starters. Factor in his height and build, neither one a bit modest, and it would be nigh impossible for him to fake his death with another in his place.

Darshan glanced over his shoulder. "Even then…" he whispered, the words fading as if he couldn't bear to think them let alone utter.

There are easier ways. He could've thrown himself from a tower or off a wall and over the cliff, but those ways would've brought suspicion to his family. His mother would've covered it up, as she always did when he acted in any way outside what she deemed appropriate. But her methods often ended with some poor soul dying for a crime they didn't commit. He'd no interest in dragging anyone else down with him.

"This was me only option. Death, a good clean death, would give me mum an honourable way to end the competition." Hamish hugged himself, rubbing the chill from his arms. He didn't want to die, but… "It was the only way I could be free."

Darshan snarled a few words under his breath. They didn't sound like any Udynean the man had taught Hamish, but he could guess they were curses. He spat plenty more into the surrounding forest and some in Hamish's direction.

"Dinnae be yelling at me in languages I cannae understand," he shot back.

"There is no freedom in death. Just darkness." In a burst of strength, Darshan all but launched himself across the space between them. He grabbed Hamish's shoulders, his fingers digging into the torn cloth as his weight dragged them closer to the ground. "Dying is never the honourable option. There must be another way out. I will not accept that it is a choice between that and death. I most certainly will not allow you to just… throw your life away."

Hamish folded his arms and stared incredulously at the man. "You willnae allow it?"

A flush of colour came to Darshan's cheeks. "I have grown rather fond of your presence. You being dead would put quite the damper on our friendship. And a rather poor friend I would be if I left you to this fate." He sat back, combing and ruffling his hair with one hand. "Give me a few days, a week at most. Let me talk to your mother, maybe I can…"

Hamish shook his head. A week would be too late. "She kens about us. It might nae be the original reason she's pushing for this stupid contest, but it's likely why she'll nae back down."

"Really? Then I think you are wrong in me not being at fault. It would seem that it is entirely my doing. If we—" Darshan frowned. "If *I* had controlled myself more and not pursued you, willing though you were, then this…" He hung his head, curls of dark brown hair falling to obscure his face. "I am sorry. I never meant—"

"Nae. She's been sniffing for a reason to do this. It was bound to happen eventually. If it hadnae been you, then something else would've seen her force me hand. I just ken what I'm losing now."

"I refuse to believe this is it."

"There's nae avoiding the union contest. It's designed to have nae way out." That was its purpose, to herd uncertain or indecisive men and women towards marriage.

"Except a violent, bloody death?" There was something mournful and dark lurking in those hazel eyes as Darshan peeked up from beneath his hair.

Goddess, forgive me. He had given no thought towards what witnessing would do to the man. How much had he seen of the bear's attack? All of it? What would his reaction have been had their positions been swapped?

Fresh tears rolled down his face. "You should nae have woken up when you did. You were nae meant to until… after."

Darshan laid a hand on Hamish's knee. "I am here for you, *mea lux*, in whatever capacity you may need me for. But if you think I am willing to stand by whilst you throw your life away, then I think you do not know me at all."

"I thought it would be quick," he mumbled. *More the fool am I.* He laid a hand on his chest. The scars would fade, eventually. How long it would take for the image of those teeth and claws to leave his nightmares was another matter.

Nothing but forward now. He couldn't stop the union contest. The only hope he had of being rid of this nightmare was to ride through it and find a means to escape being forced to live a lie after the victor had been decided. For now...

"We should head back." The guards would come for them sooner or later. He would prefer not being in this place when they did. Telling anyone the truth would only serve to restrict his movements further. He'd no desire to spend the better part of two weeks confined to his quarters like a disobedient child.

Chapter 30

They limped through the forest, aiming for the castle. It took some time to reach the road they had left behind yesterday afternoon. What had been a short distance on horseback was painfully longer on their own unsteady legs.

Unlike Hamish, who walked with the purposeful shuffle of the weary, Darshan could barely lift his feet. His passage through the undergrowth involved quite a bit of stumbling over tree roots, grass and even his own feet.

His stomach grumbled endlessly as they trudged. His body cried out for rest, for deep uninterrupted slumber. He fought the pull with every inch of his remaining strength. It would've been dangerous to heed such a call in the confines of the Minamist Palace. Out here, such a choice would be lethal.

His feet stumbled over yet another imaginary bump in the earth. He pitched forward, halted only by Hamish's steadying hands. Whatever life-force Darshan had poured into his lover, the man certainly had more energy than himself.

"You're ice-cold," Hamish murmured, hoisting Darshan's arm over his shoulders and continuing to walk resolutely through the forest. "You sure you dinnae want to stop for a bit? I could get a fire going."

Darshan shook his head. Even that small amount of movement taxed him. What he needed most was nourishment, something to replace what his magic had consumed to take the risk he had made. The measly scraps of last night's meal hadn't been near enough to fill his stomach never mind replace what he'd lost in healing. Hunting for more was out of the question, what with Hamish's snapped bowstring.

Only the castle could provide the amount that Darshan would require. Preferably in meat.

Hamish grunted. "We'll make better time once we reach the road. We're almost there. Just a few more steps." True to his word, the undergrowth parted to reveal the stretch of mud and gravel that made up the road they had ridden down yesterday. Hamish halted as they finally breached the forest. He stood on the roadside, his attention trained on something coming up the path.

The shadowy bulk swiftly turned into a retinue of mounted guards with Gordon at the lead.

Darshan's legs sagged at the sight, relief further sapping the little strength he clung to. Had the horses reached the castle so soon? Or had Gordon planned on heading a search for them anyway?

Either way, there appeared to be two spare mounts. At least they wouldn't be forced to walk or leave some of the guards behind.

Gordon's horse slid to a halt before them. "Thank the Goddess you two are all right. Your horses arrived at the gates midmorning, sweating and near exhaustion, you've got everyone back home thinking—" He all but leapt across the space between Hamish and his horse, stopping from fully embracing his brother only once his hands already had a firm grip on Hamish's shoulders. "Bloody hell. What happened to you?"

Hamish waved a hand, grasping at the blood-stained tatters of his shirt. "Just a bear." Brushing his brother aside, he escorted Darshan to the nearest riderless horse and assisted in him clambering aboard.

Any further questions posed to Hamish only had him glossing over what had transpired. Aye, he'd been attacked. Aye, the bear was responsible for his clothes being in tatters. Aye, the blood was his alone. And aye, the creature was dead, thanks to Darshan.

Gordon glanced at Darshan, disbelief over the whole story plastered across his face. But if he was looking for more answers, then he seemed content to bide his time. "You look like shit."

"Thanks," Darshan replied. "I feel like it." He slumped in the saddle. At least the horse didn't appear in a hurry to return to the stables. He rather doubted he had the strength to direct the animal, much less halt a stubborn beast.

"He needs food," Hamish supplied, hoisting himself into the only free saddle. "The sooner, the better. I think he almost tore himself apart trying to save me." A shadow passed across his face. He clearly still didn't think himself worthy of the effort.

A quick rummage through everyone's saddlebags produced little; a wedge of cheese with edges as hard as rock and half of a loaf that tasted like it had been baked last week.

Darshan devoured it all, right down to the final crumb. He'd need more, but this would shake the ghost of lethargy haunting his bones. He might even be capable of a little conjuring without passing out by the time they arrived at the castle gates.

Gordon swung his horse to march beside Darshan's mount as they began their journey towards the castle. The man gave only the twitch of a brow towards Darshan, his gaze flicking to Hamish and back.

Darshan replied to the man's silent query with a bow of his head, mouthing 'later'. Seeing Hamish back in the castle, ensuring his lover couldn't finish what he had attempted, was his first priority. He wouldn't speak of what had happened until then, certainly not in the company of unknown variables like the guards.

Velveteen twilight graced the sky by the time they reached the castle gates. Even confined in granite walls, Darshan didn't dare to leave Hamish's side as they entered the castle proper, much to his lover's consternation.

He would've followed Hamish into his quarters had the customary trio of guards not been waiting outside the man's door. They sneered at Hamish's arrival, a steely coldness settling into their eyes as they eyed Darshan.

Unperturbed, he leant against the wall and idly tapped the heel of his boot against the other toe. The guards seemed to be the same three that had invaded the guest quarters in the only time Hamish had lingered there. How hard would they try to stop Hamish from harming himself? Had they been ordered to keep him alive should the unthinkable happen? Or did Queen Fiona believe a dead son was better?

His focus slid to the door handle. How long had his lover been in there? Long enough to shed his bloodied clothes? Perhaps he hadn't gotten that far. What if he currently laid sprawled unconscious on the floor?

That final thought gnawed at him. By Hamish's own admission, the guards wouldn't check on him until dawn. Maybe not even then. Except he also needed sustenance. Perhaps not on the same level as Darshan, but it would be foolish for Hamish to sleep without something in his stomach. And Darshan had no idea of the effect his unorthodox magic would have on the man's body.

Darshan strode up to the door. He couldn't stand the idea of waiting whilst Hamish could be prone on the floor.

The guards slipped between him and the entrance before he could reach for the handle. "You cannae go in there," said the black-bearded man Darshan had already pinned as the leader. The man glared at Darshan as if spotting something slimy crawling out of a swamp. "Standing order of the queen."

Darshan straightened, firing back with his finest haughty look. They were actually serious? "I have no desire to break bones tonight." If he'd been feeling less drained, he wouldn't have bothered with such civility, but he would prefer not using what little of his magic he currently had at his command. “So I suggest you step aside now before I rethink that stance.”

The leader sneered at him. He’d barely opened his mouth, the creak of his first word passing his lips, when one of the other men crept up to whisper in his ear. The man’s eyes narrowed. He twisted to face his underling, seemingly seeking confirmation.

Well aware they still tracked his every move, Darshan tapped his foot. He made a show of cleaning his nails. It was an act that he usually did whilst the nails were already immaculate. Except this time, despite having scrubbed his hands clean with the remainder of their drinking water, dirt lingered in the crevices. Along with remnants of Hamish’s blood. “You have until the count of ten, gentlemen.”

The whispering stopped and the underling eyed him as if expecting a bolt of lightning up the arse at the next breath. The other guard also looked somewhat less sure about his orders. Even their leader had lost his cocky grin.

Darshan could practically read their thoughts. They believed he saw them as bothersome, annoying like fleas and just as easily dispatched.

He gave a little, slightly disappointed sigh. He truly had been hoping a fair warning would be enough. It seemed their fear of the queen’s wrath was greater than their qualms over personal injury.

“Wait!” the leader blurted, his hands held palms out before him. He backed away from the entrance, his lackeys following at almost twice the speed.

Unimpeded, Darshan marched into the room, throwing the door shut behind him.

Hamish stood near the bed, his head popping through the neck of his undershirt. “What the bloody hell—?” He stared at Darshan, panic widening his eyes. “Dar? What are you doing? You cannae be in here,” he hissed. “Me mum wouldnae allow—”

“I simply do not care what she wants right now. You almost died.” Maybe Hamish had. *For a brief while.* He didn’t wish to linger overlong on the idea, but it was a possibility. “So right now my only concern is for your mental wellbeing.” He crept closer, one hand pressed to the door lest the guards decided to enter. “How are you feeling?”

If Darshan were to judge by the mixture of confusion and distress on his lover’s face, no one had ever asked Hamish such a thing before.

“I’m just grand,” his lover muttered, tugging at his shirt. “And you dinnae have to tail me.”

“What is my alternative? What guarantee do I have that you will not find the means to make another attempt in the time I give you alone?"

"The means?" Hamish spread his arms. "With what? There's nae a thing here that'll cause a fatal injury and I cannae fit through the window."

Darshan stared straight ahead, trying with all his might not to even glance at the massive antlers hanging above Hamish's bed. If his lover hadn't considered just how sharp those points were, then he certainly wasn't going to give the man any options. "I am here for you, you know."

Grunting, Hamish hung his head. "You should've left me to die."

"Even if I did not want you, I would not have done that." His heart all but leapt into his mouth as he registered the words pouring out his lips. Had he really just blurted out an admission to having certain affections for Hamish? Perhaps his lover wouldn't notice.

Hamish paused in donning his overcoat. He settled on the side of his bed with a hefty thump. "What did you say?"

Was this really the place to unravel that particular snarl of emotions? *Certainly not.* They needed time. Hamish definitely didn't need Darshan fumbling through whatever he actually felt and *he* needed to sort out just what those feelings were before he blabbered any further. "I would not have left you to die under any circumstance."

Hamish shook his head. "Before that. You *want* me?"

Blast. So much for glossing over the gaffe by ignoring he had uttered a word on the matter. "I would have thought such a statement as old news. Of course I want you."

"As an ambassador in your court."

"As a lover." They might've had precious little time alone, but he had enjoyed just being in the man's presence. Did Hamish not think the same of him? It seemed unlikely, but so had what he'd attempted.

"More like a glorified bedwarmer," Hamish muttered, the words barely audible. "That's all I'm good for."

You mean more to me than that. Unlike most of the men he'd been with, he had spent more time in Hamish's presence clothed than not. And despite spending a fortnight sharing the man's bed, they'd done no more than sleep for two and a half weeks. This was his longest romantic relationship.

And that blasted bear had come close to ending it. All because—

Darshan swallowed, his breath coming only as a frantic rasp. He opened his mouth.

His stomach chose that moment to offer up its own opinion, echoing loudly up his throat. He clapped a hand to his mouth. His face all but burned against his fingers.

The ghost of a smile graced Hamish's lips. He rocked off the bed and onto his feet. "If you're going to follow me like a bad smell, then we should get you fed. You look ready to keel over, nae wonder you're spouting gibberish."

Darshan could only nod. Food and a chance to recuperate would be best before he attempted to dissimulate the feelings that had come to light in the wake of the past few hours. And figure out just what he was going to do with whatever conclusion he came to.

Making use of Hamish's washbasin, Darshan scrubbed his hands until they hurt. His bloody overcoat was a lost cause, best abandoned to the servants. Only when he was finally clean did they leave.

The guards made no movement beyond a crisp salute as Darshan exited the room close on Hamish's heels. They watched though, their dark eyes boring into Darshan's consciousness. Word would reach Queen Fiona.

He ground his teeth. For all his professions of not caring that the woman knew, he would've vastly preferred keeping her in the dark. Especially when it came to the truth behind the attack. *I must tell Gordon*. He had promised the man and Hamish trusted his brother. Perhaps, between the three of them, they could come up with a plan.

He lost track of their passage after the first set of stairs, his mind too focused on trying to determine just how he would explain the predicament to Gordon. He barely lifted his gaze from Hamish's broad back until the smoky scent of cooked meat tweaked his nose. Just where was his lover leading him to? The kitchens? That posed no risk of bumping into the queen, but—

The yawning double doors of the dining hall entrance greeted his questing gaze. Inside, the customary family table sat in the middle of an otherwise empty room. Much of Hamish's kin were already gathered, bar the ruling couple.

"I hope you dinnae mind the company," Hamish said, lifting one shoulder in an apologetic shrug. "But I figured since they'd all be eating..."

Darshan barely heard his lover, his attention almost wholeheartedly on the laden table. As it had been during the first night they had dined with the family, great slabs of meat dominated the platters. *Food*. His legs moved almost of their own accord, stumbling towards the feast.

The rest of Hamish's family must've been informed of the bear attack, for they asked no questions of their kin or Darshan.

He planted himself into the closest chair and began the methodical task of loading his plate with a piece of everything within reach. Some barely graced the plate before heading directly into his mouth. He chewed, humming appreciatively.

"Mum willnae be happy to see you here," Nora warned as he continued to pile his plate high. She eyed him as if a ravenous stray dog had wandered into the palace kitchens.

Darshan held up a forefinger in acknowledgement whilst he chugged down a mug of beer someone had placed within arm's reach. Wiping the froth from his moustache, he turned to the woman. "I shall only stay a short while." Long enough to take the edge of his hunger, then he would retire with his haul to his usual dining accommodations in the guest quarters.

His lover settled in the vacant chair next to Darshan. He eyed the doors they'd entered through as if expecting a pack of wolves to burst through them. "And just what is Mum doing?"

"Our parents," Gordon grumbled around a mouthful of potato. The man was sitting across from Darshan and specks of food flew dangerously close to his own plate. "Are busy entertaining the guests in the main hall."

Darshan slowed his chewing whilst he pondered that snippet of information. If the ruling couple were entertaining the few competitors who had arrived, along with their families no doubt, then why weren't the rest of the royal family also there? Was it traditional, or did Queen Fiona not want to highlight the possible absence of her two sons by having the rest in attendance?

Whatever the answer, Hamish seemed to perk up at the news. "So they willnae be eating with us?"

Gordon shrugged and returned to his food.

"Maybe," Nora replied. "Maybe not. You ken how Mum prefers nae to eat at public dos."

Waving his fork in the direction of his sister, Gordon swallowed and added, "But if she doesnae have even a wee bit of something, the clan leaders will get suspicious. Remember that time she was sick with Caitlyn?" Both of the man's siblings had barely nodded before he turned to Darshan. "I was just a lad of eight years and completed me first successful solo hunt. A few of the larger clans had joined us in celebrating and me mum just couldnae eat more than a weak broth without being sick. And I'm meaning proper sick. Like a dog after scarfing down too much jellied meat."

Darshan quietly shuffled the contents of a pie to one side, uncertain if he could eat it despite his questioning stomach.

Across the table, Nora wrinkled her nose. "The point Gor is trying to make—and doing a terrible job of it, unless he's after a re-enactment—is that the leaders from some of the bigger clans insisted that her refusal to eat meant the food was poisoned. She was forced to announce her pregnancy, far earlier than is expected, before they accepted the truth behind her lack of appetite."

"Aye," Gordon muttered. He rolled his eyes, the green shade twinkling in the lantern light. "As if the sight of us all tucking into the grub wasn't proof enough that it was nae deadly."

"Perhaps they thought you all immune?" It had been years since anyone had tried such a method with himself or his twin, but he remembered it well.

He'd been twelve and engaging in his first alcoholic drink as an adult. A slave, who had once belonged to a rival house, had slipped the poison into Darshan's goblet under the guise of a grape, although such a detail came after he had recovered. His healing magic might not have been used to mending himself, but it had seen to the damage swiftly enough. He could've done without being put through such immense pain, though. And blacking out hadn't done much for his burgeoning reputation.

Even so, all attempts on his life stopped after that. Now the only poison that touched his lips was the stuff he willingly imbibed.

"That's a lark and a half," Gordon managed through a rumble of laughter. "How would someone be immune to a dose of poison that's designed to be deadly?"

"Not being under the habit of questioning those who practise such techniques, I could not rightly say." Only the Nulled Ones would likely bother with such methods. Although incapable of being harmed by direct magic, they died as easily as other beings. Perhaps more so, given that magic was also ineffective in healing them. "But imbibing a small amount and gradually increasing the dosage over time seems like a logical start."

Gordon scoffed around a mouthful of food, gagging on it. He pounded on his chest, coughing and spluttering before regaining his breath in full. "That'd be like saying poking a few wee arrows at your chest will help defend you against one aimed at the heart."

"Nae really," Nora replied before Darshan could open his mouth. "More like being bit daily by a male arrowback spider, then being chomped on by the female." She drew her hands to either side of her face, her fingers twitching in a mimic of a spider's fangs, and made a noise like that of a stuttering serpent.

Gordon grimaced and shuddered, seeming to shrink to half his size. "Thank you," he growled, pushing his seat back from the table. "I wasnae planning to sleep tonight anyway."

The dining hall entrance swung open before Gordon could fully stand, admitting the queen and her prince consort.

Darshan froze, a mouthful of steak halfway to his lips. He should've anticipated this, should've kept note of how long he had lingered, but he'd been far too consumed with eating.

Across the table, Gordon plonked back into his chair. With his gaze darting all over the room, he quietly shovelled a few forkfuls of food into his mouth.

"Mum," Nora gasped, jumping to her feet. She shot Darshan a glance that he couldn't quite decipher but guessed was a warning. "I thought you were staying in the main hall with the competitors tonight?"

"And a mother cannot show interest in her children without inviting suspicion?" Her gaze settled on Darshan as she sat at her usual place at the head of the table. "I see we have consented to mingling this evening. I trust your little trip to one of our humble cloisters has returned you to your senses?"

Utilising every bit of experience he had mustered during his years within the Crystal Court, Darshan managed a neutral smile and small bow of his head. "Yes, things could not be clearer to me now, your majesty." Just this once, he wished spellsters actually had the ability to—what had Hamish once requested he *didn't* do to her?—turn people into slugs.

"Mum?" Gordon leant forward until he seemed to catch Queen Fiona's eye. He cleared his throat once she acknowledged him. "About the union contest?"

"We've a wonderful turnout, despite your brother's age." She cast her icy gaze in Hamish's direction before continuing. "And I dare say there looks to be a few barely permissible competitors amongst the lot. You'd do well to encourage them to try harder than the rest. They're more likely to bear you plenty of wee bairns."

"Well, isnae that just grand?" Hamish muttered behind a slice of bread. "I couldnae wind up with just any wife, but one damn near young enough to be me daughter. Just what I've always wanted."

Gripping his fork tighter than was really required, Darshan stabbed his meal.

Again, Gordon cleared his throat. "Is there any chance of you reconsidering?"

Darshan paused with a mouthful of fish resting on his tongue, lest his chewing drowned out any hint of a reply. At his elbow, he sensed Hamish also stilling.

Queen Fiona breathed deep. "The call has been sent, it cannae be rescinded. What else do you expect me to do?"

"Call off the gathering," Nora suggested.

Could it really be that easy? Chewing quickly, Darshan swallowed his mouthful and said, "You are the queen. Could you not merely tell the other clans that your son is not ready? Would he not serve you better as your ambassador in Udynea?"

Queen Fiona scoffed. "He has had more time than most to ready himself for this duty. And one of them is to sire children. Can he do that in Udynea?" Contempt pulled her thin lips tight. "I dinnae think so, nae whilst he's warming your bed."

Darshan slammed down his fork and leapt to his feet. If Hamish had an official position, then he'd have more worth in the Crystal Court than as some plaything. "I am sorry, but this is abhorrent. You know—every single one of you knows—he has no desire to go through with this. How can you just sit there and continue on as if you are not going to destroy his life?"

"Sit down," Hamish whispered, tugging at Darshan sleeve. "There's nae a thing you can say to change her mind."

"Hamish has duties here," Queen Fiona repeated. "Unlike those of other nations, Tirglasian royals take heed of their customs. My son will do his duty." She fixed Hamish with a piercing glare. "He *will* obey tradition."

"Obey *you*, you mean." Darshan couldn't help the sneer weaving its way across his lips.

"Of course, I am his mother. The only reason he lives is because of me."

"*Your son*," Darshan spat. "Would not even be here for you to hand over like some feast day trophy if it was not for *me* bringing him back from the brink of a death he wanted." As soon as the words had left his mouth, he realised how badly he had erred. He hadn't meant to say anything. Later, yes. But discreetly to Hamish's siblings so that Queen Fiona wouldn't be able to use the information to further herd her son.

"Dar!" Hamish gasped. Shock and hurt moulded his face.

"You mean that bear attack was you trying to take your life?" Gordon asked of his brother.

"A *bear*?" a young voice screamed.

Darshan whipped his head around to the other end of the table, where the children sat with wide eyes. He had rather forgotten their presence. *Stupid*. What had he been thinking?

"Is it true?" Sorcha snuffled. She clutched at the head of the bearskin draped over her chair. Although she was trying to put on a brave face, her chin trembled. "Is he going to die like Mum?"

Gordon slithered from his chair and scrambled to his daughter's side to envelop her in his arms. "Nae, me wee lass," he murmured, his voice cracking. "It's all done now. Darshan killed it and healed your uncle. Nae one's going to die."

"You..." Nora shook her head, her focus only on Hamish. "Again? You promised you were past all this."

His lover had made an attempt on ending his own life before? Rocking back on his heels, Darshan turned to seek the truth from the only reliable source.

Hamish ignored his sister in favour of Darshan. Those gorgeous blue eyes glistened with betrayal.

Only now he was faced with the outcome did the reality of what he had done flicker to life in his thoughts. *I'm sorry*. Hamish's attempt wasn't something that could be swept aside and forgotten, but he hadn't meant to blurt it out like that.

"Really now, 'Mish," Queen Fiona huffed. "You cannae even do that right? Have you nae shame? Look at how you've terrified your poor niece."

"You dare?" Darshan growled, his attention snapping back to the woman. "Your son has made it quite clear that he would prefer death over the future you have chosen for him. And rather than attempt to understand why and how he came to justify such a choice, you opt to berate him further for not fitting the mould you chose for him?"

Queen Fiona slowly rose from her seat. "How dare you speak to me in such a manner. You have nae idea—"

Darshan slammed his hands on the table. "I am nowhere near finished!" he snarled. The air around him crackled, the static charge lifting his hair. "There will be no trade agreement between our lands. I care not for what my father thinks on this matter, but you are an insult to your crown and your people. I refuse to deal with a ruler who would treat their own flesh and blood this way."

The queen sneered. "Rich words coming from a man with slaves."

The room grew hot, then icy. The stench of singed wood drifted in the air. Her son had tried to take his life and rather than focus on helping Hamish, she dared to throw a completely irrelevant fact in his face? His magic cried out to be used, to burn the source of his anger to cinders.

With a shudder that sapped his strength, he suppressed the urge.

"I do own slaves," he replied, keeping his voice low in an effort to contain his anger. "As do a great many of the Udynean nobility." It wasn't something he was wholly proud of, but he had never once denied it. "They are also treated with more dignity and respect than you display to your own child." He pushed off from the table, heading towards the door on unsteady legs. "I will depart these lands on the first ship headed for Minamist," he shot over his shoulder.

"That willnae be for another fortnight," Gordon said.

Darshan halted in the doorway. He knew that. The man had been there when Nora informed him. Did Gordon think Darshan had forgotten?

A fortnight. A lot could happen over such a time. Hamish could even make another attempt on his life. He would not allow that to happen, not in his presence. "Until then, I shall take my leave."

~~~

Hamish stared at Darshan's exiting back, then the door as the spellster left the room. How could he? Did the man even understand what he had done in blurting out the truth? All his freedom would be stripped from him. His mother would see he was accompanied within the castle as well as without.

He stood slowly, as if some part of his brain believed that would somehow keep people from noticing him. Maybe he could even reach his bed without anyone speaking. Maybe his mother would be lenient in light of the other clans milling around. Personal guards would look suspicious, especially to those who remembered the union contests thrown for his siblings.

"*Where* do you think you are going?" His mother's question rang through the room like a funeral bell.

Hamish hunched his shoulders. "To bed?" he mumbled. He should never have come down here whilst she was still awake.

"A grand idea." Gordon got to his feet before their mother could reply and gave his daughter a pat on the shoulder. "I'll walk you there." His brother glared at him, daring Hamish to argue the point.

Hamish merely waited for Gordon to catch up. No one else voiced their objection as they departed the dining hall. His brother was a better option than any choice his mother made; less restrictive on his part and more convenient for her to explain away. More of a brotherly discussion and less of an escort.

"Stupid, age-addled fool," Gordon grumbled. Although his brother sauntered at his side, Gordon still led the way, meandering through the lesser-used corridors where idle ears wouldn't be as much of a concern and their path was lit by the occasional lantern.

"You better nae be talking to me," Hamish snapped back.

His brother shook his head. "You *are* a fool, but *I* should've seen this coming. I should've realised what you'd do the moment Nora told me about the contest. You goaded that bear."

It wasn't a question, but Hamish nodded anyway.

"Did you go out looking for it, too?" Gordon barely waited for Hamish's answering nod before continuing. "How long has *that* idea been in your head?"

He shook his head. He couldn't give a definitive answer there. *Years, most like.* It seemed as though it had always been a whisper lurking in the back of his thoughts. Turning his concerns to keeping their mother's eye off his niece and nephews, off Ethan in particular, had stilled it for a time. He had a purpose there. But he had also thought him being corralled had been enough for her. *Guess I was*
~~~

wrong. Terribly.

They climbed a spiralling flight of stairs with Hamish at the fore as the space forced them to travel single file. A few servants scuttled off into the dark as Hamish reached the final step. Had they been warned to leave them alone? Or had his mother sent them to spy? *They're nae very good at it.*

Moonlight peeked in through the arrowslits adorning one wall, illuminating the way. If he peered out the holes, he'd be able to spy the courtyard and the main gate.

Falling back into step beside him, his brother gave a blustering sigh. "I thought you over doing this, that you'd worked your way through it. I thought you were happy." Gordon's lips pressed together. There was a certain look in his eyes. Not the shame of his mother, or the mournful distress that haunted Nora's gaze, but one glance from his brother was enough to tighten Hamish's throat and bring a wash of moisture to his eyes. "I see we all guessed wrong."

"I was—*am*—happy with Dar." For the first time in a good long while. Maybe in ever. "When I'm with him, it's like a weight's been lifted. I can be meself." Darshan expected nothing from him beyond what Hamish had to offer and, not once, had he seemed disappointed in the result. "I cannae imagine living without that feeling anymore. It hurts to think it." But that's what he faced, a lifetime of being something other than himself. "I cannae go back to lying just to please her. I'm tired of it." Listening to Darshan, hearing how it was in Udynea, just brought the feeling that much more to the forefront of his mind.

Gordon ran his hand across his mouth, huffing and mumbling into his palm. "You ken that you being with him was nae meant to be permanent. He'll leave for his home and that would be the end of it."

"Did you honestly expect me to just… let it go afterwards?"

His brother's lips all but vanished beneath his moustache as he pressed them together. "If I'd had the slightest inkling that you'd come away from this broken, I would never have let him near you." He peered at Hamish. "Why now? Isnae anything better than death? I ken you cannae run, but—"

Shaking his head, Hamish rolled his eyes. "You still dinnae get it. Nae even after all your help and attempts to understand over the years. The contest goes ahead, a winner is found and we marry. I'm then forced to live a lie."

"For one night, maybe. I ken that's nae ideal, but—"

"One night? *One?*" Again, Hamish shook his head. Maybe it had been that easy for his brother, but he knew more about that than he really wanted to. "Try *every* night until whichever woman wins me hand is pregnant. Every morning I wake up with her lying beside me.

Every gesture, every single time I open me mouth. Every breath. On and on, year after year until—" Terror pounded through his chest. He was right back in the forest, the drooling maw of the bear above him, not wanting to die, but begging for death to take him all the same. "Until one of us is dead," he managed.

What other way out did he have? What way wouldn't ruin more lives?

"What would you have done if Muireall hadnae won the contest when it was your hand being offered?" Hamish asked. Although not yet Gordon's wife, she'd been several months pregnant with their first daughter, Moire, at the time. Her family had howled about the indignity of making a couple compete for their right to be together, but they were a small clan wedged between two borders. Their cries had gone unheard.

"If she had lost?" Gordon shrugged, his interest seemingly drawn to the corridor's bare walls. "Maybe then both Muireall and Moire would still be alive." He rubbed at his nose, trying to hide a snuffling breath in the guise of a cough. "Why did you nae tell me the dark thoughts were plaguing you?"

"Because you would've stopped me."

A rumbling, mirthless laugh stole his brother's breath as they left the moonlit corridor for a narrower, dimly-lit passage. "You're damn right I would have. If I had thought for one second that you—" He shook his head. "I *thought* you were happy."

He had been until learning of the union contest. "Aye, the prospect of the man I love leaving far sooner than I want overjoys me." Hamish idly batted at the tassel of a moth-eaten tapestry forlornly attempting to brighten the corridor. Dust drifted from the threads. "I should've taken your advice. I should've run a long time ago, should've stowed away on some ship." The terror of being hunted down had kept him from trying. Surely no distance would keep his mother from him.

Then he'd be dragged back here and subjected to whatever punishment she ordered.

"The man you—?" Gordon slapped his forehead. "Goddess' teats, that's right. You said the same before we left for the cloister." His brother flashed him a look of pity. "You cannae still be serious about that."

"Why? Because he's a man? You dinnae think two men can fall for each other like you and your wife?" He sneered. "Do you ken who you sound like? I thought the side you were on was mine, nae Mum's."

Gordon slammed into him, ramming him against the wall. "Dinnae lump me with her," he growled. "You ken exactly what I mean. He's heading back to Udynea in a fortnight, to his home on the other side of the continent, and you—"

"You dinnae think I'm nae aware of that?" He shoved Gordon's shoulder, breaking his brother's hold on his clothes. "That it couldnae possibly have occurred to me that he'll nae want to stay in this hellhole a second longer than he needs to?" *A fortnight.* Hamish would be married before then, his mother would make sure of it. "That if I dinnae find a way out, I'll nae get to choose what happens?" He swallowed hard, fighting to stave off the dreadful constricting of his throat. "I'll be stuck. Alone. Just like you. Just like Nora."

Gordon's lips pressed together until they were no longer visible beneath the thick hair of his moustache. Anger lowered his brother's brows. His brother's eyes, dark in the dim light, bored balefully into him; a warning for him to silence himself.

"Except wait," Hamish blurted, pressing the heel of his hand to his temple. "I willnae be alone, will I?" He pushed himself off the wall to pace a few steps down the corridor, keeping his back to his brother. "Nae if Mum gets her way. I'll be trapped in a marriage I dinnae want, with a woman I could never love like she deserves. I ken it's selfish to want love over duty." He finally turned to face Gordon. "But am I nae allowed to be selfish over this?"

His brother stared at him in silence. Gone was the anger of smouldering coals brought to life. The pity that took its place was no less searing. "Are you *sure* it's love you're feeling, nae something else?"

"I think so." He didn't exactly have a reference, not beyond his siblings and their spouses. Even then, he had little idea as to what was mentioned behind closed doors. He knew what love was, of course. He loved his family—even his mother, for all her flaws—but this was different. Stronger. It touched something deep inside him that even his infatuation with the now long-dead stable master hadn't ever reached. "How did you ken you were in love with Muireall?"

Gordon shook his head. "You cannae use me to gauge you and Darshan. That's a path you've got to forge yourself." He took a few strides towards Hamish. Slow and methodical, like a trainer approaching a spooked horse. "I get why you're nae happy here. I really do. I think he does, too. And the fact he was willing to risk his life to—"

"I'm nae daft! I ken what he risked to save me." Darshan could've died because of him. He probably would have succumbed to the strain on their way back to the castle if his brother hadn't found them. *He should've left me to die.* None of this would matter, then.

The clans would've grumbled for a while, but ultimately understand there was no coming back from such an attack. They would've paid their respects and be on their way. "I just wasnae worth it," he mumbled.

"I'm sure he would disagree." His brother clasped his shoulder, squeezing tight. "We'll find a way out of this. Just promise me you'll nae do anything final."

Hamish inclined his head. What other option did he have but to carry on?

Chapter 31

Tendrils of fire poured from Darshan's fingers. The heat crackled in the night air as the fireball seethed before him. The cool breeze caressed the flames, twirling those at the opposite side to Darshan into a column of smoke and diaphanous fire.

It wasn't fair. Hamish's mother knew and she still pushed for her son to marry, to lose himself in duty. She knew and didn't care.

And there wasn't a damn thing Darshan could do to stop it.

It wasn't merely Queen Fiona he was furious with, but himself. *Fool.* He should've chosen his words more carefully. Why was it that even in trying to help Hamish, he wound up hurting the man? *I should've kept my mouth shut.* It hadn't been his place to speak of it. Not like that. Now, everyone knew what Hamish had attempted. And Darshan...

Well, he had gone and undone the one thing he'd been sent here to do. *Father's going to kill me.* Confine him to the palace's inner chambers, at any rate.

With a flick of his wrist, he hurled the fireball across the archery range, mutely watching as it roared through the air.

The fireball smashed into the ground before one of the targets. Molten rock and singed grass flew up, igniting the coiled rope that made up the target.

Darshan stood at the edge of the range, watching the fire burn. In his head, the echoes of screams invaded his thoughts. The noises hadn't stopped since he had brought Hamish back from the brink. Whispers. Impressions. Something not quite like a voice in the wind.

The target continued to blaze away. Just another example of damage he had inadvertently caused.

This whole disaster with Hamish was his fault, no matter what the man believed. If he had been more careful back home, had given some thought to the mess he might cause in sleeping with a betrothed man, then his father never would've sent him to Tirglas. If he hadn't come here, hadn't pursued Hamish, hadn't made the idiotic decision to kiss the man in public…

"Pretty sure that's nae what those targets were designed for."

Darshan whirled at the voice, a shield already wrapping around himself.

Gordon leant on the low fence separating the archery range from the rest of the training ground. "Easy there, your highness. I'm nae here to harm you."

"My apologies, for both the target and my behaviour in the hall."

"It was some display, I'll give you that."

"It was a simple case of the mouth moving before the brain could catch up." He shouldn't have stormed out, shouldn't have reacted in any fashion and certainly not have said the things he had. "I just—" His voice broke and he clapped a hand over his mouth. He could barely stand it, the thought of anyone being treated this way. Especially not someone he'd grown fond of.

"Judging by your outburst, things between you and me brother must be getting pretty serious." There was a hint of a question to the words, a tentative pry that dared not dig too harsh or deep.

"There need not be anything between us for me to find your mother's treatment of her son outrageous." This was his father with his urging for Darshan to have a son all over again. Why was everyone always so damn interested in what the next generation did?

"Uh-huh." Gordon nodded at the target still merrily burning away. "If we're going to talk, do you think you could deal with that first?"

Darshan turned his attention back to the blaze. The flames cast strange shadows on the far wall, like dark figures dancing in mockery of his folly. With very little effort, he contained the bonfire in a shield. The fire dimmed without fresh air, slowly dying as smoke filled the space.

"It's true, isn't it?" By Gordon's tone, he was more seeking for confirmation than querying Darshan. "About me brother attempting to take his life. When you said earlier that there was something you wished to discuss with me involving 'Mish...?"

"Yes, his attempt on his life was the topic." Darshan sighed. "I had no idea he had tried before though." Not until Nora had voiced it.

Gordon continued to eye the target remains, his eyes little more than faint gleams in the shadows. "It was also around the same time me mum tried to originally arrange the union contest for him, but I managed to intervene on both without her learning of it." He sighed. "Or so I had thought. This bloody contest is why she let us leave. It allowed her to sweep all the barriers aside. But I've been thinking.

The competitors couldnae have received the call and be here within the fortnight. Mum must've sent them before you even arrived."

Hamish had said the same thing.

"She expected Countess Harini." A reasonable thing to assume, considering the woman had meant to be the Udynean Ambassador before her tragic accident with an assassin.

"Aye. I can only assume me mum also expected the woman to accept an offer of marriage and be willing to compete." He shook his head, perhaps seeing the same folly in such a plan as Darshan did. "I should've seen it coming. She's been far too calm about all this."

"Calm? *That* was calm?"

"Believe me, you've yet to see her riled."

"She shows no concern for his wellbeing and I know, if he is forced to marry, he will try again." And this time, Darshan wouldn't be there to save him. "I cannot in good faith allow that to happen."

The memory of that bear pinning Hamish to the ground, of his lover's bloody body lying broken beneath the beast… It filled his mind to bursting.

Darshan shook his head, desperate to be free of the image. "I was almost too late to save him." Hamish's heart had stopped. It had been brief, but Darshan was sure of it. If he hadn't torn the bear from Hamish's neck when he had—

He didn't want to think about what would've happened, but he knew. *Just another claw, a deeper bite*. It would've been over.

"It's nae like the last time he tried," Gordon muttered. "He'd been miserable for months back then. I mean, sure, 'Mish is reckless and throws himself at whatever dangerous thing is at hand, but this is the happiest I've seen him in years. I did nae think he would make another attempt."

Darshan bit his lip in an effort to remain silent. A number of his half-sisters had died through what could only have been suicide. One had given birth to a son only months beforehand, and she'd taken her baby's life along with her own. Few of them had showed any signs.

Some hints registered only after it was too late.

"Me mum thinks you've placed some spell on me brother. Although, I suppose she will have changed her stance on that. Or accuse you of ensorcelling him into that bear's grasp."

Indignance stole his breath for a heartbeat. "I have most certainly not bewitched your brother," he snarled. If he had been at all capable of such, then Hamish would've been more likely to throw himself aboard a ship than before a bear. "That sort of magic does not work in such a fashion for long. Once direct line of sight is broken, it takes but a moment for the weakest of wills to clear their minds. Most who practice such abilities use it only in dire circumstances."

"But it *can* be done?"

"Not by myself. I have never been able to hypnotise people. It requires patience, concentration and a great many other minuscule stipulations, all needlessly taxing when I can simply order people to do my bidding. Hamish's mind is his own, you have my word there."

Gordon hummed, but seemed to accept the truth. "And you've made it quite plain how upset you are over what me mum's done to me brother."

"To put it mildly," Darshan muttered under his breath.

"I was wondering—"

"—if I will help stop this contest for his hand?" he finished for the man. "Certainly."

Gordon shook his head. "Stopping it isnae possible."

That was about what Darshan expected. Everyone acted as if the union contest was some immutable thing. "Because the peace between your clans is paramount to the wish of one man, I know." His gaze lifted to the tower ramparts, the walls that bordered cliffs. There were an awful lot of places within the castle alone where a desperate man could take his life. "Answer me this: Do you honestly think your brother would even make it to his wedding night?" No matter which competitor won, the outcome would be the same. "We both know the path chosen for him will do him no good."

"Do we?" Gordon straightened, indicating Darshan follow him with a jerk of his head as he ventured back into the castle.

Darshan trotted along at the man's side, forced to take two steps for Gordon's one. "I hope you are as trustworthy as your brother believes." He ducked his head as he spoke, a reflex of having to whisper to people far shorter than himself. "I rather get the feeling that trust was hard-earned."

"It was." Gordon peered out the corner of his eye at Darshan as they passed through a lit intersection. "He trusted me mum once, too. And he seems to trust you."

"But you still do not," Darshan said, fairly confident that was the direction the man was taking. "I understand, really I do. Entrusting the wellbeing of your brother to someone who is virtually a stranger? I would likely have the same doubts if it were *my* sibling."

Gordon wet his lips. He glanced over his shoulder, seemingly satisfied they didn't share the dark corridor. "He almost succeeded in his last attempt. Ate berries he had to ken were poisonous. Fortunately, we were nae far from the cloister at the time."

"And he has not sought to try since?"

Gordon shook his head. "Constant surveillance when he leaves his quarters. Nae weapons when he's alone. Anything to keep him from taking his life."

Not much of one. Whilst Hamish was distraught over the idea of being flung into a cloister, it seemed the man's life would've been better if that had happened. "Still, a little forewarning would've been nice." He might've been able to spot some hint of what had transpired in the forest before the bear could be roused.

"Aye, that was me fault. I didnae think he'd make another attempt with you nearby. He seemed stable enough journeying to the cloister." He sighed and wiped at the corner of his eye. "But I was wrong and he almost paid for that misjudgement."

"You might not have been as far off as you believe." After having listened to Hamish's every word all the way to the roadside, he had a fair idea of the reasons behind his actions. He didn't think they were called for, but he saw the steps leading to where they were now easily enough.

They trotted up a flight of stairs. It could've been the dimness of their passage, but he didn't recall walking this part of the castle before. Where was the man taking him? And would he be able to find his way back without alerting anyone?

"What if…" Gordon drawled. "What if *you* join the contest?"

Darshan came to a halt, all forward motion seemingly impossible whilst his mind sparked and buzzed. "*Me?*" Unable to see the man's face properly in the dim corridors, he formed a small ball of light to balance on his palm.

Gordon seemed wholly serious.

"*I* can compete?" Hamish hadn't mentioned anything about that. Surely the man would know who was eligible to enter the contest for his own hand. "I thought all the suitors were women?"

"Aye." It could've been the low light, but there seemed to be a gleam of humour in Gordon's eyes. "But the rules always remain the same of the competitors regardless if the hand being fought for belongs to a man or a woman. They request that only eligible nobles apply."

A small flicker of hope peeked into the darkness of Darshan's despairing thoughts. If he could compete, if he could *win*, then Hamish would be free to leave with him to Minamist. *Except…* "Your mother would never allow me to—"

Gordon bowed his head. Thick, auburn curls tumbled from his temples to obscure part of his face. "She would stop you." His gaze lifted, peeking through his hair. "But who said she needs to ken you're there until you've won? I've a few of me wife's belongings still packed away, including her clothes and the banner she competed under during the contest for me hand."

Darshan shook his head. Competing as himself was one thing. But, whilst he wasn't exactly a rough-around-the-edges kind of man, he would certainly get caught if he tried masquerading as a woman. "Would I not be a little conspicuous?" Darshan indicated the beard he had cultivated in the past month. "Even if I shaved and wore a dress, I—"

Gordon waved his hand, seemingly brushing the concern aside. "The competition requires each clan to present their suitors covered top to bottom." The man gestured from Darshan's head to his feet. "You're a mite bit taller than me wife was, but you're near the same build."

"I thought you did not trust me. Now you are asking me to secretly compete in what I gather is a rather serious rite?"

Gordon folded his arms across his chest. "I didnae think much of you at first, but you saved me brother from completing the worst decision of his life." He shrugged and let his arms fall to his sides before resuming his sauntering pace to whatever destination the man had in mind. "I think you're owed a bit of trust."

Darshan shuffled along behind the man, keeping the orb floating just over his shoulder to light the way. "You mean I stopped him from the outcome of one terrible choice and threw him into a worse scenario." Competing for Hamish's hand could be a step towards making it right. As long as he didn't get caught. "You seem sure of him even wanting to speak to me ever again. He seemed pretty angry." Not that Darshan blamed him. "Where is he right now?"

"Bed. Dinnae fash," he added, his cheek twitching as he shot Darshan a reassuring smile. "I've got people keeping an eye on him. And me brother's nae the type to hold grudges."

They had rounded a few more corners and clambered up two more flights of stairs before another thought came to mind. "What of your wife's clan? If I enter under her old banner, will they not dispute knowing me?" Were two competitors from the same clan even allowed? Darshan toyed with the end of his moustache. If he *did* compete, he would certainly need Gordon to fill him in on the rules.

"They probably would," Gordon conceded. "But her clan willnae be here. They refuse to let any of their women compete. After Muireall died and me sister's husband, Calder, drowned…" He shrugged. "Well, clearly our family is cursed." He pushed open a door leading to what appeared to be the man's personal quarters.

Unlike the starkness of the guest chambers or the barely lived-in state of Hamish's room, the walls here were adorned with various tapestries and weapons; although a few of the latter looked as though they'd been untouched for some time.

Gordon busied himself around the fireplace. Sparks flew from his flint as he lit a small fire.

"Are you certain helping me compete will be safe for you?"

Darshan asked once the fire was properly ablaze. "I have no desire to cause trouble for more people than I need to over this."

"Safe?" Gordon grinned, the expression stark in the firelight. "Nae bloody likely. Nae if me mum finds out. But you'll do what you feel is right anyway. I think that's part of his attraction to you. *That* and you've little to fear from our mum. It must be driving her mad, being aware of what you two were up to but nae being allowed to punish you like she did the others."

An unpleasant tingle trickled down his spine. "And what punishments were they?" Hamish had confessed that his incarceration after being found out in the midst of a deed was the usual response—and how Darshan hated that his lover considered it as normal—but the man had never mentioned the other party in his affairs being punished.

Confusion scrunched Gordon's face. "He didnae tell you? Nae even as a warning?" He settled on a stool set before a small writing desk. "Do you even ken she ordered the first man he was with slain?"

Darshan shook his head. Hamish spoke very little about his past exploits. And he had been given a clear enough signal that enquiring further would not be welcomed.

"Oh, aye. Nae that I'd cry over the bastard after what he did to me brother, but it's also been the fate of every man he's ever been caught with. Took us a wee while to figure out what was happening to them, being that they were mostly sailors."

"*Every* man?" Darshan echoed. Small wonder Hamish had shunned intimacy for so many years. Darshan didn't think he'd be capable of getting it up if he thought for one moment that it would mean the other person's death. Nor would he be surprised if that revelation coincided with Hamish's first attempt on his own life.

"Aye. Just as the old scriptures say." The man's mouth twisted sourly. "Me mum willnae deal such a punishment to 'Mish—or maybe she would have if our sister hadnae been a spellster, we'll never ken—but the men who, supposedly, led him astray?" He shrugged. "All I could do was help make sure he didnae get caught."

A sickening lump settled in Darshan's gut, forcing out a question even though he was sure he already had the answer. "What truly became of the dwarven ambassador?" Hamish believed the man to have been whisked out of the kingdom, but his lover had also been confined to his quarters during the days following their exposure.

Gordon grunted. " 'Mish told you about him, then. *He* did leave alive. Nearly joined the others, though. Thank the Goddess that Nora talked her out of it." Gordon slapped his hand down on the writing desk. "But what does a prince of Udynea have to fear? Even if you were nae as hard to kill as I suspect, having you disappear like the rest could only lead to war. Me mum may be quick on the temper, but she's nae stupid. She wouldnae risk having your *Mhanek* howling for blood."

"Thank the gods for small mercies." Although, he doubted he could count on one hand the number of people who'd be happy to see him dead. He scratched at his cheek, disturbing the short hairs that had grown during his fortnight journey to the cloister and back. "Is there a reason you brought me to what I assume is your quarters?"

Gordon peered at him. "The real question is: Do you ken how to fight?" He nodded at the glowing orb still hovering at Darshan's shoulder. "Beyond some flashy sorcery and fistfights?"

Darshan bit his lip. He relied quite a bit on his magic. More than he should, even by his father's standards. The *vris Mhanek*, according to his father, should be confident in defending himself even in times where the worst had come to pass and he was leashed. "Swords?" he offered.

Those green eyes pinned Darshan to the spot with a piercing look. "And how much training have you had?"

Far less than he should have. "I have… dabbled here and there." His twin boasted more skill with a blade than he, but she wasn't here.

Groaning, the man rubbed at his temples and stood. "That'll nae be good enough. Nae when you'll be up against seasoned warriors." He prodded Darshan's chest with one broad finger. "You're me brother's only chance of getting out of here without—"

"—causing a civil war?"

Gordon grunted. "Or another bloody hunt," he muttered, striding over to a chest. "If you're serious about this—about me brother—then you will train. You've a week before the last handful of clan competitors arrive, then it's only the trials."

"There is but three." He had no idea what they entailed, but how difficult could they be if someone without magic was expected to pass them?

"Aye and if you fail one, that's it. 'Mish loses. If you want to have any chance of winning this and keeping me brother from a short, miserable life, then you had better be in the training yard at dawn. Every day until the last of them arrives."

"Duly noted."

"In the meantime…" Gordon threw open the chest. It contained a few drab articles of clothing and a bundle of other objects wrapped in cloth. He gathered up a few articles and tossed them at Darshan's feet. "Let's see if I'm right about these clothes."

"Now?"

Gordon spread his hands. "You got somewhere else to be?"

Only his quarters if he didn't wish to further compound his actions by seeking out Hamish.

Donning the garb was a simple matter, although the headgear took a few attempts for him to get right on his own. Style-wise, it looked pretty close to what the men around here wore, if a little on the drab side. If he understood Gordon's chatting through the rustle of fabric, no clan had this sort of mottled dirt brown colour in their insignias, so it'd been adopted as a neutral.

Standing before the full-length mirror, Darshan eyed his reflection. The headgear had interested him when Gordon first unravelled the heavy scarf from the rest. Its length was now wrapped around his head in a manner that was eerily similar to the style worn by the desert tribes in Stamekia. With the lower half of the scarf covering his nose and jaw, he would've looked unrecognisable to his own twin.

Gordon stepped into view. He seemed to examine Darshan, his chest puffed out in clear self-satisfaction. "Seems like a near enough fit. How does it feel?"

Darshan rolled his shoulders, testing the limits of the attire. The loose clothing would certainly allow him to move freely. "It will serve its purpose. However..." He glanced over his shoulder at the man. "Are you certain about me wearing it? It did belong to your late wife and I would not want to sully it. I do plan to win Hamish's hand. To *marry* him. With all that implies," he mumbled as if the thought hadn't entirely occurred to Gordon. *Gods, that was awkward.* But then it had been quite some time since necessity had him pussyfooting around the whole 'I'm having sex with your brother' scenario, although the man had to be aware of what his brother had gotten up to over the years. "I thought men liking men was illegal here."

Gordon harrumphed. "It's nae illegal. Nae anymore. Just highly discouraged."

"People have died. I would say it is more than merely frowned upon."

In the mirror, Darshan caught the man's shoulders sag. "Aye, but that's me mum's overzealous response to the situation. They did have 'Mish in a compromising position."

No doubt that position had been with Hamish bent over a crate in some dark corner. And likely with his consent.

"It wasnae always like this. Once, even me mum was perfectly fine with the idea of men loving men. Right up until she learnt about 'Mish. After that, any man who looked too long at me brother was suspect and out to corrupt him. And those who dared to go as far as to touch him? Treason."

"I see," Darshan mumbled around the scarf. His breath bounced back at him, troublesomely hot. And the fabric, although soft, clung to his scruffy beard. He would need to shave if he didn't want to be driven insane by the constant irritation.

" 'Mish didnae tell you I was the one who found him the first time, did he?"

Darshan shook his head in reply, marvelling at how the scarf stayed in place. At least he wouldn't have to worry about it falling off at an inopportune moment.

"He was just a young man of thirteen and besotted with the castle's much older stable master, although only the Goddess understands why." Sighing, he rubbed at his chin. "The bastard used me brother then left him broken and bleeding in the hayloft. I only discovered 'Mish because he was sobbing."

Darshan fastened his gaze on his own reflection. He'd been of a similar age his first time. And he'd quite a few regrets about his choice of partner there.

"They had to send him to the cloister to be healed before he bled out where no man should bleed."

Daring to glance at Gordon's reflection, Darshan sought for a sign of the man lying. "If he was losing enough blood for it to be a concern, he never would have made it to your cloister." A week would've been far too long. "Or is the one we journeyed to not the closest?"

"It is, but there used to be one closer."

"Used to?" His thoughts turned to the ruin Hamish had pointed out to him weeks ago. His lover had said it was a cloister, but Darshan had assumed it to be an ancient structure time had degraded.

Gordon inclined his head. "A small one. It housed me youngest sister along with a few other wee ones from around Mullhind. 'Mish and I… we would visit her almost every day. Nora when she could, but Mum liked to keep her close."

"What happened to it?" He'd seen it only from afar and just bits peeking through the trees, but it had seemed like a once-sturdy structure fit for housing inexperienced spellsters.

"Me mum had it destroyed. She claimed all the visits and having magic so close corrupted 'Mish into his current path of only wanting men."

"That is preposterous," Darshan sputtered, whirling on the man. "Magic does not— It *cannot* do that. It is utterly impossible to alter such a delicate thing as the mind on a permanent basis." He knew that from personal experience thanks to his father's last botched attempt to persuade him into having a wife after failing at several other endeavours. "If you have the strength and skills, you can make a person hallucinate, you can even hypnotize them for a time, but it requires an active choice and a *lot* of effort. Even then, only a few are capable of such feats." And most would resort to mundane methods of cohesion.

"Good to ken."

Taking a deep breath, Darshan's thoughts swung to the one question with an answer he believed already resided in the pit of his stomach. "The stable master was the first she had killed, correct?"

Gordon nodded, his face grim. "Me mum had the man executed for treason whilst Hamish was recovering."

There was a touch of screwy reasoning there, given that the stable master had harmed a prince. "And I suppose she punished Hamish when he returned? Locked him away?"

"Nae at first. She thought he'd been led astray from his natural urges and, given the experience he had, that he wouldnae repeat the act. But it... changed something in him. He spent several years—I dinnae ken... three or four, maybe?—drinking and whoring himself out. He let all manner of man use him. Hurt him."

Isnae it supposed to hurt?

His lover's words rang through Darshan's thoughts, spoken what seemed like a lifetime ago. He had believed that to be the query of an inexperienced man. Now? "He was punishing himself," Darshan murmured.

Hamish might not have spent all his life being explicitly told what he felt was wrong, but if his mother's reaction to that kiss was normal... to be expected to play a certain role, having disappointment after disappointment heaped upon him when he gave into his desires... then the man certainly hadn't learnt it was right. He believed sex between men had to mean pain, yet he kept seeking out men he must've known wouldn't be gentle with him.

The very idea churned Darshan's stomach.

"That's possible. You ken, I've nae seen him smile so openly since we were wee lads. You're responsible for that." Clearing his throat, Gordon stepped closer. "And Muireall adored me brother like he was her own blood. She'd want the same thing I do. For him to be happy." He clapped a hand on Darshan's shoulder, squeezing. "So to answer your question on whether I'm certain about this? Aye, I am. I would even wager that, if me wife was still here, she would've thought of this far sooner."

"What happened to her, if you do not mind my asking?"

Gordon shook his head, a bittersweet smile lifting one side of his face. "Muireall was such a stubborn woman, always ready to defend her people. Have you noticed what adorns me wee lass' seat in the hall?"

Darshan nodded. The bearskin practically overflowed the little girl's chair. It was a hideous thing, covered in scars.

"That bear killed her mother as well as me older daughter, Moire. They were travelling back from Muireall's heart clan at the time, showing her parents their newest granddaughter. It was early spring and the monster was raiding nearby villages. She wouldnae have been me brave Muireall if she'd nae gone off to hunt the beast. First time she wasnae quick enough."

"My most humble of apologies."

Gordon offered him a small smile in acknowledgement. "Hamish saw to it that the bear didnae bother anyone again. Didnae tell anybody, of course, just rocked on up with that bear pelt for his niece. That has to be the last time Mum was ever proud of him." Shaking himself, the man gave Darshan's shoulder a brisk pat. "Now, about those." Gordon pointed at the glasses still resting brazenly upon Darshan's face. "How much do you see without them?"

"Very little, unfortunately." He had already resigned himself to the fact he'd be competing practically blind. There was no other choice. With his glasses on, he would be singled out immediately.

Cautiously lifting the scarf away from his ears, he slid the glasses free.

The world merged into wobbly impressions, the details of his own reflection all but impossible to pick out beyond the suggestion of a figure in drab colours. How difficult could the trials be? *Extremely*. He returned his glasses to their proper place. "I am unsure how well I will fair without them."

"You're going to have to try. If it's any help, me brother loves you." Gordon coughed loudly and added, "So if you're going to compete, it better not be you having a lark or you'll have me to answer to."

Darshan peered at the man's reflection. Gordon didn't appear to be jesting. "He... does?" Whilst he had hoped their affections for each other might grow to such heights, he certainly hadn't expected those feelings to be instantaneous. Maybe after a few months or years. Not now.

Gods. This was just like that cautionary tale his Nanny Daama so liked to tell, *The Winter Fox and the Red-breasted Weaver*. Hopefully, the outcome of this contest would be far happier than the one the two doomed mythological lovers went through.

Gordon frowned. "Did you nae hear the part where I threatened you?"

"Yes, yes, and you did so wonderfully. Honestly, this whole pulling together as a family really warms the heart. My sisters would have double-crossed me twice by now." Except for his twin, but she had different reasons to see he kept living. "They most certainly would have attempted to gain something from it. Probably my death. They are quite keen on that."

"And you want to drag me brother into that mess?"

"He will be safe as long as I keep breathing and I really have no plans to stop doing so anytime soon. Did you mean actual love?" His chest ached for the truth. He hadn't had much of a chance for quiet introspection on such a level but… the feeling resonated in him. So much stronger than any he'd had for any other man.

This would've been so much easier back home. *I would've—* What? Carried on this physical relationship unaware he had also delved into an emotional one? That his romantic affections for Hamish had grown alongside his carnal desires?

Was that what he felt for Hamish? *Yes.*

When, in the Highest One's good name, had he fallen for the man? *How long?* Somewhere during the journey back.

No. Earlier. On the cliff edge, with Hamish's silken voice purring in Darshan's ears whilst the sunset turned his lover's skin the colour of polished statues and his hair a dazzling ruby hue. *And his eyes.* The perfect shade of home, but warm and rich. And focused only on Darshan.

Shit.

I have to tell him. How could he not? And it was mutual. Wasn't it?

"Actual love?" Gordon echoed. "You mean the cow eyes and fairy dust feelings? Aye. He declared it not long after you arrived."

Not the same at all. Such a revelation did nothing to ease the tightness of his chest. "You mean he is infatuated with me." How foolish he was to think the feelings ran at any depth. It should've made him feel better that the prospect of losing wouldn't also mean having to leave behind someone who loved him, but it didn't because feelings ran both damn ways.

Gordon shook his head. "I've seen 'Mish infatuated, this isnae that. Were you hoping it wasnae true?"

Darshan shook his head. Of course he wanted to believe what the man said was the truth, but… *Shit.* It made the prospect of losing that much harder. He could've weathered having his heart cracked again, but not Hamish's as well.

I have to win. There was no other way. If he failed, Hamish lost right alongside him.

He would not let that come to pass.

Chapter 32

Darshan tugged the scarf a little higher across his face, surreptitiously shielding himself from the fog that had settled around the castle. The act allowed a tendril of cool air to slip beneath the linen. Even though his feet were growing numb with the cold, his breath was trapped by the thick fabric of the scarf and turned it into a veritable sauna for his face.

Women garbed in similar attire surrounded him on all sides, the last of the competitors having arrived just this morning. None of them had given his presence more than a passing glance. At least he hoped so. Deciphering expressions was difficult at the best of times without his glasses. To go only by eyes, that were so often dark pits in a vaguely oval face, was practically impossible.

Nevertheless, here he stood amongst the final handful of others that had trekked from the other side of Tirglas. To everyone's knowledge bar Gordon's, Darshan was here to stake his interest—going by Moira of the Dathais Clan at the man's insistence. He had trained the whole week leading up to this and just a stray word could see him outed.

Yet, no one had called out the anomaly in their group.

Now that he was amongst all the competitors, Darshan slowly became aware of how small he was in comparison to quite a few; not just in height, but also in the broadness of his shoulders.

The noblewomen back home spent much of their time lounging around and scheming from the comfort of their mansions rather than in a straight battle. Whilst just possessing magic consumed a great deal of energy—even more when actually used—and the general revelry at the multitude of soirées hosted across the empire took quite a chunk of energy, the rich food the Udynean nobility ate was more than the required extra amount and left the idle with a certain physique. Voluptuous, his twin called it.

Still, he had thought the women within Castle Mullhind had gained their bulk by way of labour or military training—or in the case of Nora, her bloodline—but this collection of Tirglasian noblewomen looked as if they'd been training their entire lives for this moment. Maybe they had. He wasn't exactly privy to all of Tirglasian customs, but this union contest seemed to be a commonality amongst their nobility.

The women milling around him straightened.

He swiftly followed suit. Gordon had told him little of today's proceedings, only that Darshan wouldn't be expected to fight just yet. That would come tomorrow. *With swords.* He sneered. Such a primitive weapon. Nobles in Udynea relied on their magic for battle, with a few eccentrics seeking out lessons in fencing. His father was one such man who'd tried to instil a similar mindset in his children to little avail.

"Welcome, dear competitors," a voice boomed across the courtyard.

Darshan stiffened. *Queen Fiona.* Although he couldn't see much of the wooden platform where the royal family sat—beyond a few colourful blobs—there was no mistaking that icy voice. Would she notice him? Surely he would be lost amongst the drab-clothed masses. By rights, only in his unveiling would his identity be made known. Unless he was forced to speak.

"By right of heritage and birth," Queen Fiona continued, "only those of noble blood may present themselves as competitors and fight for the hand of a Mathan Prince."

There was a pause. Was Hamish up there? Had that wretched woman really forced her son to face all these people knowing that he would have to marry one? Did *he* know Darshan was amongst the competitors? Had Gordon told his brother of their plan?

With Gordon having his training begin at first light and not stop until the last hint of day had departed the sky—and his muscles still remembered the bone-deep ache that came from overuse—Darshan hadn't seen his lover since the night of the bear attack much less have found the chance to speak with Hamish.

"I ask you all to forgive my son's melancholic reaction," the sweetness in Queen Fiona's voice was enough to make Darshan's teeth ache. "He recently took on a bear that has been tormenting the nearby forests and has yet to recover his humour."

Should've been in the Crystal Court. She certainly sounded like one of them with her half-truths.

"Whether you have come from prestigiously large clans or hail from a smaller one, you will be given an equal chance at my son's hand. However, as we all ken, there can be only one winner."

Rolling his eyes, Darshan subtly stomped his feet to work out the cold seeping into them. Did anyone honestly think more than one of them could marry Hamish? There had to be over fifty competitors, maybe even close to a hundred. He had no idea how many clans were in Tirglas. According to Gordon, the first trial would see the number halved by tomorrow evening and the second trial, an obstacle course through the forest, would leave just a handful.

"The rules of the union contest are simple," Queen Fiona continued. "Prove your strength and stamina in a battle of arms, your cunning and fleetness in a course of my clan's design and a final test that is customarily chosen by the prince himself."

Darshan shuffled a little closer to the voice. The colours atop the platform shifted, a vaguely human-shaped figure emerging from the fuzzy tapestry.

"I choose archery." Hamish's hollow voice boomed across the courtyard.

A soft gust of laughter escaped Darshan's lips before he could stop it. How in the world was he supposed to best Hamish's skill with a bow? Never mind that he hadn't used one for some time, he couldn't even *see* the target without his glasses.

"Make it through all three trials and his hand is yours," Queen Fiona cheerily finished. "Let the contest begin!"

Most of the women headed for the training grounds, either to battle an opponent for their chance to continue on to the next trial, or to watch.

Darshan shuffled along with the throng for a short while. He was to compete at midmorning tomorrow, although he wouldn't know the skill of his opponent until they faced each other.

He slowed as the crowd surged by what looked to be an alcove in the castle wall. Squeezing through the group, he sauntered along the outer edge, veering ever closer to that dark patch in the brickwork. Rather than a shadowy kink made by the wall and the storage building, it was a short alley leading to a door that few even within the castle seemed to know the truth about.

Gordon had led him here after a sword fighting session. The seemingly innocuous doorway opened out into a tunnel which led to the bottom of the cliff. There, the man had placed a tent nearby for Darshan's use. It currently held a small chest of his clothing. If he was quick, then perhaps he could nip down, change and return to watch how some of the competitors fought without anyone being aware of his movements.

With one hand on the door handle, he peeked over his shoulder. Gordon seemed certain that few would even glance this way, but if anyone caught him entering and exiting, they might—

The blurry outline of a person stood in the alley entrance. Even in the shadows, their hair was a vibrant, fiery shade of orange-red.

"Excuse me, me lady," a familiar voice said as the figure entered the alley. "You cannae go in there."

'Mish. Darshan took a deep breath. Time to test how well his disguise held up.

He turned to face Hamish. "Your highness." The higher-pitched tone he forced into his voice hurt a little, especially when combined with the natural roughness of the Tirglasian language, but he would hopefully only need to hold it for a short time. "How very irregular for you to be chasing a competitor. I thought fraternising with us whilst garbed thusly was against the rules."

"Aye and I apologise for putting you in this position, but you really shouldnae be—"

"Especially when you are rather less than recovered from being…" With his lover now close enough for Darshan to make out the man's features, he let his voice return to its normal range. "…almost dead."

Hamish's mouth dropped open. He stared for some time, almost uncertain, before leaning close and whispering a single word, "Dar?"

"Yes?"

"I've nae seen you since you—" He still wasn't close enough for Darshan to make out the minutia of the man's expression. "I thought me mum had sent you packing. What are you doing?" he hissed, pressing closer. "Why are you dressed like that?"

"I would have thought my attire would give away my intentions. But since you insist on having it made plain, I am attempting to save you from a loveless marriage."

"*You…?* You mean you're competing?" He stepped closer still, forcing Darshan to flatten himself against the wall or crane his neck up to see more than Hamish's beard. "You cannae—"

Darshan laid a hand on his lover's chest. Did Hamish tremble or was that himself? His heart certainly pounded wildly enough. "The way I understand it, you cannot object to this contest without causing a civil war, but there is no rule saying I cannot participate." He tried to peer around the man's bulk before giving up. He would see nothing without his glasses. "Is there anyone looking our way?"

Hamish shook his head. "This entrance is pretty secluded."

"Come with me, then." Swiping for the door handle until his fingers found it, he led the way inside.

~~~

Hamish halted in the doorway, not because he wanted to, but rather
~~~

due to necessity as Darshan had stopped just beyond the threshold. A small ball of light hovered over the spellster's hands as the man groped across the shelving that held the lanterns.

Feeling a little self-conscious of how an open door leaking unnatural light would look to anyone happening to pass this way, Hamish pulled the door fully shut behind him. The wood pressed against his rear, forcing him forward a half-step and into Darshan.

Darshan's back stiffened, likely not expecting an assault on his lower back from Hamish's groin. When the man didn't move, Hamish strained his hearing to catch any alerting sound of the unlikely chance of someone coming up the tunnel.

"*Mea lux*," Darshan breathed, the whisper of laughter riding in on the words. He sagged, leaning his shoulders back against Hamish's chest. "I hardly think here is appropriate."

Grunting, Hamish attempted to regain the lost space between them. The last he had seen of Darshan, the man had been adamant about leaving Tirglas on the next ship destined for the Udynea Empire. Now he was dressed in garb that mimicked those worn by the competitors and joking as if there hadn't been a week of silence between them.

He's competing. He couldn't be. There were rules. Men didn't compete alongside women, certainly not for another man's hand. How had he even managed to enter? How could he expect to win? What did he expect to happen if he did? Or if he lost?

Sweet Goddess... All that would be needed to turn the whole contest into chaos was for the man to unveil himself. Did Darshan know? Was he aware of how dangerous and foolhardy he was being pretending to be a competitor? And for what? He couldn't even seem to find whatever he sought for along the shelving.

Hamish cleared his throat. "What are you looking for?" With so many questions crowding his thoughts, this seemed the simplest.

"My glasses case. It should be along here." Darshan continued to pat the shelf as if the room was still dark.

The case sat just before one of the lanterns. The dark brown wood made it difficult to pick out from the shadows, but not impossible for those who knew what to look for. "Exactly how far can you see without these?" Hamish asked, handing over the case.

Darshan stretched his arm out before him, his palm flat as if it were pressed to a wall, and wriggled his naked fingers. "This far, clearly. Beyond that, I steadily lose details until it's all just coloured blobs."

"And you expect to compete when you cannae properly see your opponent?" A civil war. That was what the bloody man was going to start.

Darshan's jaw set into a stubborn line as he secured the wire frames over his ears. That determination echoed in his eyes when he glared up at Hamish. "I will manage. Same as I always do. Or did you think I have no experience attempting tasks without the advantage of regular sight?" There was a drop of venom in his tone, not acidic enough to mean much harm.

Hamish rolled his tongue, opting for silence. He had seen Darshan fumble his way around unfamiliar environments during their travels. Usually, it had been to relieve himself and he had stumbled into something along the way more often than not.

No matter how he tried, Hamish couldn't imagine the man winning a sword fight or traipsing through a forest for long without running afoul of something. If they hadn't noticed Darshan's addition to the union contest, then maybe they wouldn't notice if he also vanished. Especially this early on. "Dar—"

Darshan held up a hand. "Let us not speak here." Giving a curt jerk of his head, he descended the tunnel with the ball of light leading the way.

Hamish followed, running a considering eye over Darshan's outfit. It could've been the shadows, but the garb didn't just have the vague appearance of what the competitors wore. It was identical. "Where did you get those clothes?" If there was a woman tied up somewhere, they were going to be in more trouble than if Darshan's whereabouts were revealed.

"Your brother assisted me there."

"Me brother?" Hamish blurted. Now he was looking for the signs, the fabric did seem frayed. Old. "*Gordon? He's* in on this? For the love of—" He pinched the bridge of his nose. Of course this would have to be his brother's plot. That was how Darshan knew about this tunnel. Nora wouldn't have handed the Udynean a key, especially after the man's outburst at the dinner table, and none of the children were old enough to have access. "What has me bloody brother gotten you to agree to? What did he tell you?"

Scoffing, Darshan flapped his hands as if shooing a fly. "What makes you think your brother is involved any further than gifting me the appropriate garments? Why assume he did anything as crass as gossip?"

"Because you cannae have thought this up on your own. You dinnae ken anything about the union contest, you said it yourself." Whether or not Darshan acted alone now, Gordon would've been the one to bring this mad plan to the Udynean's attention. "What has me brother been doing?"

"Training me."

"Train—?" All this time? And with no word from either of them?

We'll find a way out of this. His brother's promise echoed through his mind. *This* was Gordon's solution? Throw Darshan into this manic press for Hamish's hand? Did he honestly think Darshan could win? That he would *want* to win?

"I thought you'd been kicked back to Udynea," Hamish mumbled. Whilst Darshan had arrived by ship, he didn't have to leave that way. An escort over land would take longer, but it would see him out of Mullhind within the day. "I thought—"

"That I had left you here to spend the rest of your life screaming on the inside or worse?" Darshan slowed so that they walked side by side. He had lowered the scarf from his face. Apparently, he had found time to shave with his busy schedule—one that didn't include informing Hamish of his intentions—and sported a style similar to the moustache and short, goat-like beard combo he'd worn upon his arrival. "Do you honestly believe I would choose to have you deal with that toxic woman who dares to claim herself as your mother alone?"

"Watch who you're badmouthing," Hamish snapped. "That's me mum. The woman who gave birth to me."

Darshan whirled on him, shock and indignance plastered over his face. "You will defend her after what she has done to you? That woman deserves a retribution fit for the gods. You owe her no allegiance, especially when she treats you in this manner." Regret dulled his eyes as soon as the words had left his mouth. "That was unworthy, my apologies. It is not my place to dictate how you interact with, or think of, your family."

"Well, you're right on that."

"It is just, seeing you having to hide your true feelings, the real you, from everyone. And then being forced into this, I cannot—" He hung his head and sighed. "If she were my mother, I would have disowned her long ago. I could never leave you here, even if I did not—" He turned from Hamish, lengthening his stride whilst rubbing at his neck and jaw.

Hamish attempted to catch up, surprised at the sudden speed.

"I think—" Darshan stilled as they reached the gate, stopping with a lurch that almost caused Hamish to collide into him. "Back in the woods," he whispered, clutching the thick iron bars. "Seeing the damage that bear had done to you. I realised then, I did not..." The words grew soft, almost hesitant. He peered over his shoulder. "I did not wish to lose you."

Hamish wet his lips, not sure what the man expected of him. "So you agree to compete for me hand?" Did he consider this as some sort of penance for his actions? "You do ken that, if you win, *I'm* your prize. You'd have to marry me."

"I am well aware of the terms, *mea lux*." Darshan turned, leaning back against the gate. In the dim light of his little globe, those hazel eyes were wide and glittering. “Is that a problem? I cannot account for his accuracy, but Gordon seemed certain you would be all for it. Are you objecting to this line of thought?”

Was he? “I just—” His mother could likely dredge up a dozen reasons for Hamish to refuse this offer, but he could think of only one. “You… you barely ken anything about me.”

“And those women likely know even less. At least with me, you know we are compatible.”

Hamish peered at the man. “Why are *you* doing this? You didnae have to get involved.” Yet here he was. Did the reasons behind Darshan’s actions even matter if the outcome saw Hamish free? *And yet…* Like a tree snake, a terrible new thought slithered through the scrambled nest of his mind and reared its head. “This isnae out of pity, is it? You cannae think you’ll get anything out of this.”

Darshan sighed. “Look, you said yourself that the only other alternatives beyond your death will lead to civil war. I know the rules; Gordon schooled me on them. I am more than qualified to compete. You cannot get any nobler than an imperial prince.”

Nae, you cannae. Although his mother would find plenty of other reasons to invalidate Darshan’s victory. She could even have him arrested, or at least try.

Would it matter then? If the man won, then everyone would know.

“As for what I get out of this?” Darshan continued. “I get you, do I not? Winning will see you free of all this, will keep you safe with me.”

Another way. Hamish leant against the wall to steady himself, his legs wobbling as the idea finally sank in. His bloody brother had done just as he had promised. “I—”

Darshan unlocked the gate and sauntered through. A tent stood nearby—shielding the tunnel exit and set slightly apart from the tents pitched by the other clans. It was to the back of this structure that the man strode and slipped through a flap.

Glancing around to ensure no eyes but those of the wildlife saw them, Hamish followed. The inside of the tent was quite sparse, carrying only the sort of essentials a clansman might require on a journey of this import.

Darshan had finished unwinding the scarf and was busy withdrawing his customary garb from a small chest. He glanced up from smoothing out his sherwani, meeting Hamish’s gaze. His body tensed in such a clear anticipation of a bad reaction that Hamish found himself mimicking the man.

“I had no intentions of becoming someone’s husband,” Darshan said. “Truthfully, the very idea of getting married was not something I was at all willing to entertain. Tying myself to someone I barely tolerated for the rest of my life sounded more akin to torture."

"Then why—?"

"I got to know you and—" He scratched at his jaw, remaining silent for what had to be an age. "The longer I am here, the more time I had with *you*. I started to consider that... maybe it would not be as bad as I had previously thought."

"To tie yourself to someone you can barely tolerate?"

Shock dropped his jaw. "No! That is not what I am trying to—" Darshan rubbed at his temple. He grumbled under his breath, snippets of words Hamish didn't understand but knew were of the Ancient Domian tongue. "*This* is the effect you have on me." He strode the few steps the width of the tent allowed, his hands fluttering. "Put me in the Crystal Court and I will know the exact words to say to charm any number of people, but stand me before *you*?" He chuckled, shaking his head. "I suddenly have all the eloquence of a tongue-tied goat."

Hamish knew the feeling. He had never considered someone might feel that way about himself, though.

Darshan stopped before him. He ran his hand down Hamish's chest, slowly as if soothing a horse. He remained silent for a while, that hazel gaze just meeting his. Searching. All jesting gone. "If you must marry someone at the end of this contest, then it should be someone you love."

Ice slid its way into Hamish's veins. *What* had his brother told the man?

"What I am trying to say is..." He laid a hand on Hamish's chest, the spot where his heart sat. "You are my light." The way he spoke. Soft and breathless. Almost as if he was saying a somewhat different phrase.

He cannae mean... Hamish's jaw soundlessly dropped open. Putting together everything Darshan had recounted about his homeland, the man likely meant exactly what Hamish believed. *Goddess, give me strength.* He must have it wrong.

Darshan chuckled. "Well, I thought it might have come as a shock, but I was not expecting it to leave you speechless." He frowned, the minute scrunching of thick brows. A spark of panic flickered to life in the faint twitch of his mouth. "Is it too soon? It is hardly some habit of mine to offer my heart to all and sundry." His gaze darted to the ground, then the walls. His hands lifted as if to twist rings that weren't currently on his fingers. "Or anyone before. But we are rather pressed for time."

He does mean... As desperately as Hamish tried to speak, no sound escaped. Even his jaw wouldn't do anything more than hang there. His throat tightened. His heart raced like a panicked doe.

A wisp of a memory surfaced at the declaration, the stable master, he'd whispered the same words. *Before...*

There had been others since then who had declared similar as they pounded him sore. Right before they were discovered, before he was dragged back into his room and they—

Died. His brother had tried to shield him from the truth, but he had learnt it years ago. He'd been like a plague amongst the sailors and ruffians who'd dared to accept his offer of a fun time. His mother had given the order, but he had delivered their death sentences.

" 'Mish?" Darshan peered up at him, that hazel gaze brimming with concern. "Are you—" His hand fell on Hamish's forearm. The warm buzz of the man's healing magic raced through Hamish and Darshan's worry seemed to shift. "Did I misspeak? Do you not use that phrase in Tirglas?"

"Nae like that," he whispered. Never had he heard any such words uttered with so much rawness or warmth. "But if it means what I think it does. That—"

"I love you?" Darshan suggested, the words coming easily. "That phrase is used back home as well, but for family. Whilst I would not shirk from having you join mine, what I feel for you is not the same love shared between brothers. If it makes you feel more comfortable I can—"

"Nae. I..." Hamish froze. "You actually love me?"

Darshan's gaze lifted. A hint of smugness curved the corners of his mouth for a moment before melting into a softer smile. "Did you think I was competing for your hand out of altruism? And why would I not love you? You are everything I have ever wanted in a husband, and I did not even realise I wanted to marry until I met you."

Hamish shook his head, trying to latch onto the words that escaped him. "How could you?" he whispered. "You've seen all that is happening, all that I've been put through, how could you possibly think *this* was a good time to tell me?"

Confusion clouded Darshan's eyes and wrinkled his brow. "This is the first time we have spoken to each other since we returned to the castle. When else could I have told you? Before I realised? *Mea lux*, I—"

"You said those words mean *my light*. You called me that the day after we had sex and every day onwards. Did you nae mean it then?"

"It is a form of affection and I meant it as such. I was perhaps unaware as to the depths that fondness ran at first, but my lack of awareness is no longer true. I am uncertain I could feel this way with another man and I am most unwilling to find out." Darshan grasped his hands, clinging so tight that the ring the man had bought him dug into Hamish's skin. " *'Mish*. I have said before that you are a good man, but I do not think you comprehend how rare a thing that is to find in the Crystal Court. Maybe it is a little selfish of me. I have been trying to go slow but—"

Hamish couldn't help the snicker that shook his body. "*This* is you going slow? By entering in the union contest?"

Darshan inclined his head, but not before Hamish caught a fond smile creasing the man's eyes. "It would seem I am not very good at it. The fact of the matter is... I messed up. I want to make it right."

"And trying to win me hand within a month of meeting me is going to do that?"

"I understand it likely seems like a leap to you, but when I saw that bear over you, the damage it had done..." He fell back to attempting to twist the still-absent ring on his little finger. "Every time I close my eyes, I see it. You lying there, bleeding with barely a breath to be had and even less of a pulse."

Shuddering, Hamish staggered back from the man. He squeezed his eyes shut. Never would he have thought that—

The bear's drooling maw filled the darkness in his mind. The smell of rancid meat invaded his nose. He could even sense the heat of its breath blasting across his face, freezing every muscle in his body.

He opened his eyes, but the image remained, drifting like fog over the real world.

" 'Mish?" Darshan took a few steps closer, his arm outstretched. Shock and concern battled for control over his expression, seemingly ageing him.

Hamish waved him back, relieved when Darshan halted in the middle of the tent. "I'll be fine," he managed, his voice tightening on the last word. He just needed time. Somewhere he could feel safe.

He shook his head, desperately trying to clear the scene from the forefront of his thoughts. It worked to some extent, although it left room for other concerns to make themselves known.

Could he do this? Stand idly by as another attempted to win his freedom for him? "Do you have any idea what'll happen if you win and finally reveal yourself?" His mother might be able to brush aside Darshan's attempt if he lost, but a win? Where she would have to accept a man marrying her son or stand before the clans and choose to ignore the contest's outcome?

"Will it matter when I have heeded the rules?"

"That's a load of bollocks, right there. Men dinnae compete against women." Not in any record he knew of. And he knew them all. "Me brother should've told you that."

Darshan scoffed. "Your brother thought it was fine and I am rather inclined to believe his lack of concern. Have you seen some of them? Up close as I have? Half of them are this tall." He waved his hand high above his head. "Some could likely pop a man's head clean off his neck with a flex of their arms no trouble. And I am certain there are a handful of others who could squeeze the brain from the skull with a twitch of their thighs."

The man could only be talking about those from the eastern clans, where riding through the mountains whilst herding their stock was a day's outing for them. The current rumour was they did much of their riding bareback.

Darshan shook himself. "My point is, I am somewhat at a physical disadvantage. So I doubt anyone can realistically claim I had the upper hand."

"Nae but there is your magic," Hamish pointed out.

"There is little magic I can do that would be useful in any of the trials and not also immediately give away my status as a spellster. Which I gather your mother would see as just as heinous a crime even if I were not a man."

He was right there. "Nae to mention me mum will claim that you snuck into the contest under the guise of a woman." And probably a fake name, now he thought about it. His mother would likely try to nullify Darshan's victory on *that* reasoning alone.

"I wear only what the other competitors do." Darshan tugged at the front of his drab-coloured shirt, the overcoat having already been discarded alongside the scarf sometime during their conversation. "Are they not disguised as well?"

"They do it to conceal their clan, nae their gender." How much damage would removing Darshan do? Could it be done quietly? Would the damage be enough for the other competitors to wonder if the prize was worth winning? Would the other clans seek revenge over the deception?

Darshan brushed the distinction aside with a sweep of his hand. "I have gone beyond caring over such trifling details. Your brother said there is nothing apart from your mother's stubbornness that can stop me from competing, so compete I shall."

"There is *one* thing. I could tell you nae to do it. To forfeit." It would mean letting the contest play out as he had been dreading only this morning, but it would also keep Darshan and the Udynea Empire out of whatever mess happened at the end. "Would you listen to me if I did?" Although, it could wind up drawing more attention. Maybe the only way to avoid chaos would be for Darshan to carry on, regardless of how Hamish felt.

Confusion twisted his lover's brows. "If the competition was fair, perhaps. But I am taking you from this place one way or the other. I will *not* leave you here to die. I simply refuse to let that come to pass." Darshan strode towards him, determination squaring his jaw. "I have trod the murky depths alone for so long that you blinded me when we first met, but I have basked in your light long enough to know that at your side is where I wish to be."

Hamish swallowed, attempting to clear his throat. Should his chest feel this tight at being faced with such an admission?

"But know this: losing you, returning home without my light in the dark, is not something I am prepared to go through. I cannot bear the thought of it. Whether you feel the same way or not, I just cannot leave without at least trying to—"

"I do." The words came out in a rush, almost breathless with fear. They hung in the air between them.

His lover had fallen silent, seemingly content to just stare at him with that hopeful little gleam in his eyes that served only to twist Hamish's stomach into a tighter knot.

Hamish hung his head. "I ken me brother spoke to you." Even without Darshan confessing to that, it was obvious. "The thing is, he certainly would've used how I feel about you as the carrot to get you where you're standing."

Darshan smiled. He held one elbow in his hand and stroked his chin. "And was he wrong? About your feelings?" There was a soft skew to his mouth, a certainty that he already knew the answer was in his favour.

"Whatever he said..." Hamish breathed deep. He was all but offering his heart on a platter to Darshan and still couldn't be entirely certain the man wasn't toying with him on some level. "It's true." He mimicked the gesture of pressing his hand to the man's chest. "You are my light," he attempted in Udynean, the words thick on his tongue.

Darshan winced, just the faint deepening of the wrinkles around his eyes. "Your accent is still atrocious." But he grinned. Beaming like the breaking of a new spring day after a month of winter storms. "Of course you love me. Everybody does." He laid his hand atop Hamish's keeping it firmly pressed to his chest. "I simply emit loveliness."

"Uh-huh." Modesty, too. "You think *I* sound bad? This coming from the man who still cannae use contractions in Tirglasian."

"They sound weird. But we shall need to work on your language skills some more, especially since I am taking you home." Such conviction ran through the words that Hamish couldn't help but grow giddy on that river of hope.

"Oh, aye?" He wrapped his free arm around the man's waist and pulled Darshan flush against him. "Am I going to need more of your native tongue?"

Laughing, Darshan tipped his head back. "Not letting that one go, are we?"

"Never, me heart," he murmured, nuzzling along his lover's neck.

A faint, contented hum flexed the muscles and tendons beneath the flushed skin Hamish was busily kissing. "That one is new. I like it." He pushed them apart a ways, eyeing Hamish. "Did you truly not realise it was me?"

"I thought the walk was a little familiar, but other than that?" He shook his head. Only the sudden change of Darshan's higher voice to the man's natural tone had alerted him to the truth. "It was you about to enter the tunnel entrance that finally tugged at me curiosity."

"I shall attempt to be a little more discreet in making use of the tunnel. And is my walk distinctive enough that I shall need to remedy it?"

Hamish shook his head. Few would've been in the man's presence long enough to notice, much less make the connection. And of those few, none would want to see Darshan exposed. "Would it make a difference either way?" Trying to affect another stance could draw just as much attention.

"Not really, if we are being honest." He cocked his head. "You still do not sound entirely convinced having me competing is a good idea. Surely, you would prefer I won over them."

Aye. A thousand—a million—times. "There just has to be at least a dozen reasons why this willnae work."

"I just need to take each trial as they come and make it through." He grimaced, seemingly from the core of his being. "That sounds terribly optimistic, I know. I blame you there."

"*Me?*"

"You make the thought of the future that much brighter." He caressed Hamish's cheek, his fingers threading into Hamish's beard as he lowered his hand to run tingling touches along the underside of Hamish's jaw. "My light in the dark," he whispered. "I warned you I was a selfish man and I certainly shall not let you slip away so easily. I want you to come home with me. I want you to be mine. Is that such a terrible thing to desire of someone you love?"

Hamish wrapped his arms around Darshan's shoulders, resting his cheek against his lover's forehead. It all sounded terribly reasonable. "Use your magic," he whispered.

"*Mea lux*," Darshan gasped mockingly, slipping free of Hamish's embrace. "Are you actually suggesting I *cheat*?" He grinned prettily, batting his lashes like when Hamish's niece tried to charm her way out of chores. "Or was that an insinuation that I cannot win honestly?"

"You dinnae have the luxury of losing." What guarantee did they have that Darshan wouldn't fail the first trial without magical aid?

None. Then what? Lead everyone to believe that allowing a man to compete was just some joke?

"Not the luxury now, is it?" The man's grin fell as his lips pressed together in thought. He gathered up his clothes, swiftly discarding a few of the articles. "If they catch me cheating, they will ban me from competing faster than if they discovered I am a man. I did not lie when I said there is little magic I can utilise to assist me in this endeavour. I might not make it through the duel tomorrow."

Something squeezed his chest. "Dar…"

"Do not mistake me for not dwelling on it," Darshan continued, his lover's words muffled by the undershirt currently being over his head. "There may be a few chances in my upcoming duel—" His head popped through the neck hole. "But I shall need some time to think on how to implement it and not be caught." He shrugged, tugging the hem of his undershirt into place. "It may be entirely unnecessary."

It had been some years since the last union contest, but Hamish recalled the brutality of the first trial well enough. Whilst it was rare for people to die, broken bones were a common outcome.

Darshan glanced up from exchanging the loose, drab trousers of a competitor's attire for a tighter pair from one of his off-white garbs. "I *did*, originally, come down here to change so I may watch the competition, so to speak, incognito but…"

"They'll be competing for some time," Hamish said, finishing the man's thoughts. One-on-one duels would continue all day and then tomorrow. Whilst watching the trials wasn't required of him, people still expected him to have an interest in the calibre of those competing. Mingling without blurting out his true feelings on the contest would likely be the hardest part of the next few days.

"No one knows we are here." Darshan stood, his trousers secured and his hand hovering over the sherwani he had laid out on the chest. "We could linger for a time, if you wish? No expectations, just conversing with a loved one."

"I'd like that." He had rather missed the velvety tone of Darshan's voice. Hamish settled on the pile of blankets that would've served as the man's bed if his lover had actually slept down here. They'd certainly given their all to the deception that Darshan was just another faceless competitor. "How about you start with what me brother's been teaching you?"

Chapter 33

Hamish lay still, content to stare up at the canvas tent whilst Darshan regaled him with the sword fighting techniques Gordon had drilled into him over the past week. He remembered his brother's training methods from their youth quite well. They'd been brutal, hands-on and often went for hours at a time. His muscles still ached with the memory of Gordon driving him around the training grounds with each attack and counter.

Apparently, his brother hadn't changed his tactics there.

Whilst his lover had chosen to lie next to him, Darshan seemed to prefer the simple comfort that came from using Hamish's stomach as a pillow. The man had also captured Hamish's arm sometime during their conversing and kept it in his possession by running his fingertips up and down Hamish's wrist. The sensation hovered on the edge of tickling. Coupled with his lover's voice as Darshan ran through the upcoming days, it was close to lulling him to sleep.

"In all honesty," Darshan concluded. "I imagine the last trial will be the hardest, given that I shall be shooting practically blind."

Hamish grunted. The final trial wasn't a customarily set task like the other two, for the very reason that it required the competitors draw even or best the person whose hand they were competing for in a skill they excelled at. "If I'd been warned beforehand..." He had chosen archery purely because few would be able to draw even with him. He had been hoping that number would be zero.

"Then what? You would have chosen something different? What could you have possibly picked that would have been in my skill set that the others would not excel at? Magic?"

"I..." That was a good point. He could've chosen a hunt like Gordon but, unlike the faith his brother had in Muireall's skills, there was no guarantee that another competitor wouldn't beat Darshan. "I dinnae ken." He could've taken his sister's route and demanded the final trial be a battle of languages. Like Darshan, Nora's seafaring husband had spoken a wide range. But that would've also run the risk of exposing Darshan before a clear winner was decided.

"We shall think of something."

"It'll have to be quick. Five days will go faster than you think." There were two days for the first trial, followed by one of rest to give those who had made it through a chance to recoup before tackling the forest run and the heart-gifting ceremony. Then the final trial. "At least I ken who I'll be giving me heart to."

Darshan gave a querying hum.

"Did nae one tell you?" He fished out a pendant from within his undershirt. The simple chain gleamed in the dull light. Hanging off the links was a heart-shaped ruby about as broad as the length of his thumb. Although his mother had commissioned the gem after he had survived his first year in this world, Hamish recalled only seeing the hearts of his siblings during their union contests.

She'd given him this one only yesterday. "See this?"

Darshan rocked his head to one side to appraise the jewel. His brows lowered in confusion, but he remained silent.

"After the last competitor finds their way through the forest, all those who make it through unscathed are lined up and I am meant to gift this to one of them." He ran his thumb over the ruby. The cut wasn't usually the type of style a man would wear. At least it wasn't ringed with diamonds like the one Gordon had gifted to his wife. Would Darshan object to wearing such a trinket?

"You bestow a favour part way through the trials? To what end?"

Shrugging, Hamish tucked the gem back beneath his clothes and laced his fingers behind his head. "Tradition. My choice is supposed to encourage the Goddess to bestow her blessing upon them."

"Then I best make it through the trials, had I not? Having a Goddess' will on my side surely could not hurt."

"Aye," he replied thickly.

"But you know," Darshan murmured, rolling onto his side to prop himself onto his elbow. "If you are going to insist on being sprawled on my bed like an offering for the Divine Agan..." He shuffled further upright, winding up on his hands and knees.

Laughter inadvertently snorted out Hamish's nose. "*Your* bed? As if you've ever used it." Seeing how well Darshan handled roughing it whilst travelling across the land, he couldn't imagine the man willingly choosing this cold pile of blankets over a bed in a warm room.

"We could." Grinning, his lover straddled his waist. "Right now."

Hamish lay there, well aware of how each breath shifted his

lover's weight. Still, he saw no need to push Darshan off him, although keeping his hands where they comfortably sat buried beneath his hair seemed equally as prudent. "Do you even ken what you want from this beyond having me in Minamist?" Did he *really* want Hamish as a husband? Or did he mean for them to remain no closer than lovers?

"In the moment?" One dark brow lifted suggestively along with a corner of Darshan's mouth. "Or in general?"

"Generally."

The cockiness in his expression melted away. "Not entirely," he whispered. "But I do know what I do *not* want to transpire and that is to lose you, to leave you here living a life others have dictated. That has to count for something, right?"

It did. Probably more than his lover realised. "And what, exactly, do you want from me?"

"So many things I know I cannot have." Darshan's hand glided up Hamish's chest, one finger gracing his neck before sliding downwards as his weight shifted off Hamish. "I want to be able to court you, *properly*. To gift you the ability to choose me as I have you. To hold you whenever and wherever I wished." His lover's hand slid along Hamish's stomach and onwards to his groin to slowly stroke him through his trousers to the accompaniment of Hamish's muffled whimper. "I want to empty myself into you every night," his lover breathed into Hamish's ear. "To hear you moan without fear of being caught."

Hamish rocked his hips, deepening the man's gentle movements. A soft, desperate little groan slipped out his lips.

"Yes," Darshan purred. "Just like that. But..." He withdrew his hand, a strange expression ghosting over his face. "I also want to just fall asleep in your arms and know you will be there when I wake."

Hamish tilted his head. "Me too." He'd had a measure of that during their trip to and from the cloister. He had missed such comfort in the days after the bear attack.

Darshan smiled back, care and desire softly skewing his lips. He caressed Hamish's cheek with the back of a finger, smoothing his beard. "And what I want above all?" He sat back. "Simply for you to be happy, to have the chance to be you."

He stared up at his lover, his throat and chest tight. Moisture pricked at the corners of his eyes.

"Is something wrong?"

"Nae," he managed, the word thick on his tongue.

"Are you certain? Forgive me, but you sound like you are about to cry."

I just might, yet. People always wanted things from him, expected him to act a certain way or be a certain type of person. To give his all without asking for anything in return. No one had ever let him just be *him*. "I love you," he whispered.

Darshan smiled, warm affection creasing the corners of his eyes. Even with only half the day being garbed as himself, his lover had rimmed his eyes with dark powder. "I believe we established that."

"Doesnae mean I'll stop saying it."

"I certainly hope not." Darshan pressed close. "And I *do* love you," he murmured, the breath of his words skittering across Hamish's ear. "I would never have found someone as sweet as you back home."

"Sweet?" Hamish gently pushed Darshan back until the man's face came into view. Lit only by the low light leaking through canvas and tree canopy, much of the man's expression was in shadow. Too much to know if he was merely joking. "I've nae been called that since I was a wee lad."

Darshan gave a low, brief chuckle. "Then a crime has been committed on your good character, *mea lux*. Everyone back home is always so obsessed with strength and power." He caressed Hamish's cheek, the rings adorning his fingers glittering with each tender movement. "Well, I have tasted both and rather find them wanting."

Hamish wet his lips, not quite sure how to respond to that. "What if you lose?"

Darshan scoffed.

"It is possible, even if you cheat." Which Hamish sincerely hoped the man tried only in small doses, especially if it meant using his magic. Anything that ran the risk of revealing Darshan's true identity wasn't worth it. "What will you do then?"

His lover remained silent for quite some time.

Doubt gnawed at Hamish's stomach. Maybe he was asking too much. It was one thing to win, to stand defiant just long enough for the trials to be considered as valid and his hand claimed. But if that didn't come to pass...

"If I lose?" Darshan grinned. "I shall simply spirit you away." He bent to kiss Hamish, his lips sweeping over Hamish's and halting as Hamish gave his lover little in the way of response. Darshan cocked his head, one dark brow lifting in query. "No? Afraid someone might catch us?"

"There's that." Not that the thought had occurred to him until the man uttered it. Few would opt to remain in this small village of tents whilst there were duels to observe in the castle grounds; even those competing tomorrow would be up there. On the other hand, there was always the chance someone could return and hear certain telltale noises coming from a tent that should've been empty. "But I'm nae really in the right frame of mind for fun, either."

His lover bent over him. Those hazel eyes narrowed behind the crystalline lens of his glasses. "And how have you been feeling recently? Still well in ourselves?"

Hamish shook his head. He knew precisely what Darshan was fishing for. *Like shit.* This morning was the first time he had been allowed any time alone beyond a few hours of sleep. "I'm better now that I ken you're competing." The possibility that his lover could do everything right and still fail did make him slightly queasy if he thought on it for too long, but there was nothing he could do about that except help where he could.

Was this how his brother had felt when their mum forced Muireall to compete?

Darshan sat back a ways, his lips pressed into a thin line. "I apologise for being so absent, it was not my intention to keep the nature of my actions from you. Especially not for so long. Your brother has kept me quite busy with training."

Sitting up, he wrapped an arm around Darshan's shoulders. "I've missed you," he whispered into the man's hair. He breathed deep of his lover's scent—the fresh rush of a breeze across the winter ocean and the sweet tang he now knew was of barely-constrained magic—committing the aroma to memory. "I thought you were gone, that me mum had exiled you." Or worse. Would she care if her actions brought ruin upon her people? Had she slipped that deep into her hatred?

Darshan's shoulders bunched slightly as he tightened their embrace. "She cannot touch me, you know. I will not disappear like the others."

A shiver ran through Hamish. He clung to Darshan, keeping his cheek pressed to his lover's shoulder so that he couldn't see the man's face. "What others?" he mumbled. Surely he was at the wrong end of the arrow with his thoughts. *He cannae mean—*

"The men you have been with during your youth?" The words were hushed, as if he was hesitant to finally utter the truth aloud. "I know they were quietly disposed of."

Hamish jerked back, letting his arm drop to support him. Darshan knew? *Obviously.* But he was still here. No attempt to leave. Quite the opposite. "And who told you that? Me brother?" What else had Gordon revealed? Just how far could he trust his brother to not go running his mouth off?

"He did." Darshan inclined his head. "He spoke a fair bit about your past." His gaze lifted, peering at him over the rim of his glasses. "Such as the state he found you in after your first time."

Anger and shame heated his face. How long had Darshan known about that? "Bastard," Hamish hissed. "I'll bloody kill him. It wasnae his story to tell."

His lover remained still, except for the slightest down-casting of his eyes. "No, but I am still aware of it. What do you expect me to do? Forget? The fact your mother has chosen to wilfully slaughter every man you have been with is not something that can be fast eliminated from the mind."

"*Every?* Is that what he told you? It was nae *every*. They didnae catch me with *every* man. But it was enough. It was too many." He scrubbed at his face. He'd little memory of most. To think he could've been the last thing they saw... "*One* would've been too many."

"It still does not change that I know."

Shaking his head, Hamish slowly slid out from beneath the man to sit cross-legged across the blankets from him. "I suppose not," he muttered. He couldn't ask Darshan to pretend he'd never heard without putting an extra strain on their relationship. His lover was already doing more than Hamish would ever ask of him.

"May I enquire as to when *you* were planning on informing me?" There was a sour twist to Darshan's mouth, but his eyes lacked a certain heat. He was annoyed, maybe even a little disappointed in Hamish, but he wasn't angry. "Would it not have been my fate if I had been anyone other than the *vris Mhanek*? Because that thought must have crossed your mind at some point."

"Only recently," he confessed. Before his mother had announced the union contest, he hadn't thought her willing to put the lives of the people at risk. "It could still be, if me mum's rabid enough." Having Darshan reveal himself at the final trial could even be the thing to push her over that line.

Darshan stiffened. What little emotion that'd graced his lover's face swiftly fled. "If she dares to try, she will find I am nowhere near as easy to have permanently removed."

"I think that's already clear to her." Hadn't his brother told her the consequences of a war with Udynea? He certainly hoped she remembered. Darshan hadn't exactly thrown his magical muscle around for the kingdom to marvel, but Hamish had seen firsthand what the man could do when wounded and lashing out on instinct. And there were plenty of stories telling of how dangerous spellsters could be if provoked.

He didn't want to think about what an imperial army of them could do to Tirglas if Darshan left here severely injured, especially in a way his magic couldn't easily mend. And if the *vris Mhanek* was to just... disappear?

Tirglas might never recover.

"I am sorry about Gordon," Darshan said, the emotionless mask dropping almost as rapidly as it had appeared.

Hamish shrugged, his thoughts sluggishly returning from the

vision of forests and villages falling like driftwood fortresses before a wave. "It wasnae your fault he ran his mouth off." And his brother was going to get such a clout over the head for it the next time Hamish saw him.

"And you would lay none of the blame at my feet? I could have asked for him to stop." Darshan folded his arms and peered at Hamish, clearly waiting for a response. "But then, you never offer me anything of your past without me having to tease out every word."

"And *you* are so open?"

Darshan rocked back onto his heels. "I have nothing to keep from you. Ask whatever you would wish to know."

Whatever? Hamish scratched at his chin. What did he desire to know about Darshan? *Everything*. He'd learnt a little during even the most frivolous conversation, but he wanted to know it all.

However, one thing did demand to be learnt above all else. "Tell me your first time." He caught a wince of apprehension flicker across his lover's face before Darshan could speak. "Fair's fair. You know mine, including how well it went, tell me yours."

Biting his lip, Darshan stared at the tent walls. "It has a somewhat less drastic ending for myself."

Hamish would've left it at that had he not caught the flash of shame peeking out through his lover's obvious discomfort. "How old were you?"

"Seventeen," Darshan whispered, closing his eyes.

"Who with?" He almost dreaded asking. But wouldn't he have been just as uncomfortable in talking about his time with the old stable master? *Probably*.

"Men back home tend to fall all over themselves to lay with me," Darshan babbled. "After all, I am the *vris Mhanek*. They are of the opinion that pleasing me could grant them a favour, despite the fact I have never actually done so for a single soul."

"Your first time," Hamish repeated.

His lover exhaled mightily. "He was... an elven man, not much older than myself." Darshan laid a hand over his lips as if trying to contain the admission. He glared at Hamish, almost demanding that he say something.

As a people, Hamish had never considered elves as sexually appealing. Those he had met were relatively lean and slightly skittish. Elven men like the guard Zurron were exceptions to the latter, but still not the sort he was drawn to. Clearly, Darshan didn't agree there.

That didn't explain why his lover sounded as if he spoke some great secret.

Hamish opened his mouth. "And—?"

"I know what you are thinking." The words came raggedly. "But he was sweet, gentle, softly spoken and… yes…" Darshan gave a weary sigh. "He was also a slave."

"That—"

"Do not dare to judge me," his lover snapped, jabbing a finger at him as he leapt to his feet. "I only learnt that last bit after the fact. That is my only excuse for what I did and, believe me, I know it is not good enough, but that is the truth of it."

"How could you nae have—?"

"—known?" Darshan finished. "Do you have any idea how many times I have asked myself that same question? That I have not berated myself over it? Because I have more times than I can count."

"Dar…"

Darshan shook his head, babbling in Udynean as he paced the tent. "I didn't know he couldn't refuse. *I* propositioned him. *Me*. The only time I have before you and…" His chin wobbled. "And he couldn't bloody say anything other than yes because I'm the *vris Mhanek* and he—" He clapped a hand back over his mouth but continued to mumble past his fingers. "I should have known. I should have considered it as a possibility." He hung his head. "I should have asked," he whispered.

Hamish waited for the man to compose himself. He'd been accused of luring people down the wrong path, of being possessed by demons intent on dragging him from the Goddess' side—typically by his mother—but it had never been implied that the other man hadn't been complicit.

Darshan lifted his glasses enough to dab underneath them. When he spoke again, the words had returned to Tirglasian and were devoid of emotion. "My first time involved me being with a man I can never be certain actually wanted me." He dropped his gaze. "No, I am still doing him a disservice. He had not the autonomy to refuse my offer and that means he could not have meant it when he agreed. There was no consent given, not freely." He lifted his head, those red-rimmed eyes all but burrowing into Hamish's as the man peered down the full length of his hooked nose. "I raped him. That I did not know until after does not excuse what I did. *That* was what my first time was like."

Silence continued to reign over Hamish's tongue. What could he say? He'd never considered taking a man, let alone by force. He couldn't imagine Darshan as being the type, either. To then engage in sex whilst believing the other man had been willing only to discover otherwise… no wonder he was upset relating it.

Darshan's shoulders sagged, all the fight seeming to drain from him. Grimacing, he tapped an idle little beat on his thighs. "I guess I shall leave, then."

"Wait." Hamish stood, hastening to his lover's side lest Darshan chose to flee. "You dinnae actually think that's true, do you?"

"Lack of consent to any act of a sexual nature means only one thing in Udynea. I assume it is the same here." Tears streamed down his cheeks, fogging the lenses. He took the glasses off, slowly drying them on the hem of his undershirt. "Gods, I have never told anyone about it. Not even Ange. I could not risk letting it be known. Such secrets I gift you." Darshan laughed, a trembling sound full of further unshed tears. "If we were in Udynea..." He donned his glasses, not quite pushing them into their customary spot. "Well, such a fine piece of information would see you set for a lifetime of blackmail material on me by now."

Hamish grinned, hoping a little show of humour would drag the conversation away from the delicate subject he had forced Darshan to speak of. "A whole lifetime, huh?" He shook his head. "You ken I'm nae going to do that."

Sniffing, Darshan rubbed the end of his nose with the back of his thumb. "Thing is. Even if you did, most would not care that he had been a slave. Him having a pair of pointed ears would be the greater gossip. The court would see it as shameful."

"Did you ever learn who he was?"

Darshan shook his head. "I am completely unaware of his name or even who owned him. He could have belonged to the empire just as easily as a visiting noble. As for what became of him? The mines, most likely. Especially if my father found out. He would not have risked such a scandal."

Hamish cleared his throat. "How did you learn he was a slave? Shouldnae him going 'master' have tipped you off? Or that he was elven?"

Darshan scoffed and rolled his eyes as if he'd heard the question several dozen times before. "Nobody says that. Not to me at least. I am *vris Mhanek* to all bar my family. It is considered an insult to address me otherwise in a formal court. And not all elves are slaves, although I am certain you have been told as such. The palace also employs a great deal of servants." His gaze lowered, shame darkening his cheeks. "I mistook him for one of them."

Was that really how blurred the lines were between servant and slave that Darshan could mistake one for the other?

The idea of elves living freely in the Udynean Empire was an easy one to imagine. Hamish had always assumed, especially after speaking with men like Zurron, that there were no free elves in the empire. Hearing otherwise was an odd bit of relief. If some were free, then maybe all of them could be liberated.

Another thought bubbled away in the back of his mind. One that sat a little closer to home. "The first night you came to me room?" he mumbled, still chasing the gossamer thread of his contemplating. "You asked for me consent?" Even when it was well obvious that he was amenable to anything the man suggested.

Darshan inclined his head. "I may not have the ability to change what happened, but I can ensure I do not repeat it." He rubbed at the back of his neck, a sigh whistling out his nose. "We should probably ascend to the training grounds."

Hamish scrubbed at his face. "Aye." He wasn't entirely sure how long they'd been down here, but it had definitely been too long. His mother likely had the guards quietly searching for him. "The clans will expect me to make an appearance. March the lines, watch a few duels, nod at the appropriate times." That wouldn't be too hard.

He hoped.

~~~

The dull thud of a blade hitting the ground was fast followed by the much louder objection of its wielder slamming into the compacted dirt. Swearing, the woman clutched at her shin.

Darshan winced in sympathy with the struck woman. That blow had been the heaviest he'd witnessed so far. Possibly enough to break bone.

They had gladiatorial sports back home, but fights where the objective was to hurt, and quite possibly maim, an opponent wasn't something he would willingly watch. Wrestling he didn't mind, especially when the match involved two men, but that was the limit of his enjoyment in such sports.

These bouts straddled the borders between the familiar sports of home and an almost warlike attempt at brutality. No one was in lethal danger. At least, that wasn't the intent of the bouts. The swords were the blunt practice ones from the castle's training armaments and blows to the head were forbidden, but they were still steel. And the garb the competitors wore offered little in the way of protection. Or maybe they wore chain mail beneath their overcoats. He would never be able to tell.

"One strike to red," a deep voice bellowed from somewhere along the far railing.

A mixture of groans sounded out amongst the louder ripple of premature jubilation from the crowd surrounding Darshan. Whilst the competitors' clans were naturally watching, so did a few others and a handful of locals; the latter being fresh from the docks by the
~~~

smell of them.

"Blue," the same thunderous voice boomed, "do you yield?"

Shaking her head, the injured woman waved off a group Darshan assumed to be of her clan, if not her immediate family. The blue ribbon tied around her bicep fluttered with the movement. That thin strip of fabric was the only concession anyone made to identify competitors, tied on at entry and removed after each duel.

The woman slowly clambered to her feet to stand before her opponent. She adjusted her scarf—being unveiled was adequate grounds for forfeiture and something he rather wished Gordon had warned him of earlier—before snapping her sword up and down in a clear ready signal to the judge.

Darshan's brows rose. She was truly going to try the final round after such a blow to her leg?

The crowd murmured around him, coming to the same agreement. Each duel consisted of three bouts in which to land the first blow, not even that if the victor was lucky the first two times.

"Begin!" that same voice ordered of the two women. "Victory either side."

Rather than rush at her opponent as she had first attempted, the injured woman opted to remain in place with her sword held low. Her red-marked rival paced back and forth in search of an opening. It seemed prudent. She had one point in her favour, same as her rival. It would take just this match to decide on who went through to the next trial.

Like operatic dancers, the pair slowly circled the arena; Blue due to her injury and Red because of her caution. Neither appeared willing to engage and risk losing. Or perhaps they both waited for that sliver of an opening in the other's defences.

"Come on!" yelled someone in the crowd. "Get on with it!" The cry spurred others to bellow similar sentiments at the pair.

Red lunged at her opponent, feinting. Their swords met each other mid-strike with a clang.

Blue held her place, barely twitching. It was hard to tell with only her eyes visible, but she seemed to wince. Was the pain of her injury too much for her after all?

Her rival attacked in earnest, giving Blue little time to block let alone properly counter. Red kept up her onslaught, haranguing her opponent towards a corner. If Blue was bailed up there, then that would be it.

Darshan leant over the railing, trying to get a better view of the pair around the shoulders of others who did the same.

With a burst of speed, Blue's sword slashed for her rival's chest. Red, clearly caught off guard, jumped back with a surprised shriek. It hadn't connected, but Red must've realised how close her error in misjudgement had been.

But Blue had the other woman on the defensive again and seemingly planned to make the most of it. Each of Red's swings grew more desperate as Blue forced her back one step at a time.

Harried, Red overshot and her rival's blade swung in a fluid countering move to knock the sword from Red's hand. With a yell, Blue swept her injured leg under her opponent, slamming Red flat onto her back.

Blue levelled her sword point at her rival's chest as Red went to pick herself up and gave her opponent an almost cheeky tap.

"Final strike to blue," the man bellowed over the roar of a crowd who already knew the outcome.

Just like that, the duel was over.

The crowd's cries were no less mixed than before, but they seemed to double in volume.

Their raucous quieted only when Red finally clambered to her feet and unwound her scarf to reveal a relatively young and pale face. Darshan hadn't thought Queen Fiona had jested about the age of some competitors, but this woman had to be in her late teens.

It's one less to worry about, he firmly reminded himself. The only actions he needed to be mindful of were his own.

"That was just a wee bit flashy," said a young and vaguely familiar voice.

Darshan twisted to find Hamish's niece and the trio of nephews standing at the railing not far from him. Their attention seemed trained on the competitors.

"And that limp is going to cause her all manner of trouble in the next trial. Would've been better if she'd lost," Bruce continued saying to the others. "She'll nae be able to dodge, never mind actually make it through the forest."

Darshan was inclined to agree with the oldest boy. The woman would hobble off to have her injury treated, naturally. But there were no spellsters nearby that could mend the damage enough to see her fit to compete at her best. No one beyond himself, at least.

"Good," Sorcha snapped, flicking the coils of her hair over her shoulder with a jerk of her head. "One less for Uncle Hamish to fash about. This is so unfair. I wish they'd all break their legs."

Darshan cleared his throat. "You really should not wish ill on your people, your highness. It is rather bad form."

The girl whirled on him, those stark green eyes widening to their fullest before she ducked her head. "I didnae mean it *that* way," she mumbled.

"Uncle 'Mish doesnae want this," Mac said, earning him a

susurration of shushes from the others.

"I know," Darshan replied. Hopefully, the rest of the children knew better than to shout their uncle's opinion on the contest to the world.

Darshan wandered through the crowd whilst the four children tagged along and offered up their opinion on each counter and hit. Other duels happened around them, most with little more than a few bruised egos.

How would his own duel go tomorrow? He had practised his hardest with Gordon, but the majority of these women moved with sharp precision. He couldn't match that, not with a sword.

A shield, even an invisible one, was obviously out of the question as were a great many other tricks. And he would have to remain vigilant to keep anything vaguely magical from notice. During his training, Gordon had teased that he seemed to rely less on his physical abilities and far too much on the dazzling flare magic gifted him.

Watching these women, he was bitterly coming to terms with the reality that the man was right.

Still, Hamish had said to cheat. And maybe a brief burst of subtle magic could aid him. A gust at the right moment to blind his rival in an attack. Or even the slightly riskier approach of bolstering his strength like the time he had hauled Hamish back in through the window.

Out in the arena, another winner was decided.

Darshan frowned, still lost in thought. Timing any magic beyond the instinctive would take concentration. How much of that would he be able to spare with the furious might of a Tirglasian warrior bearing down on him?

Not enough. And he certainly couldn't use the same trick twice without people finding it suspicious. He would have to win one point without such aid.

Darshan lingered at the railing whilst the children wandered off to watch yet another duel. He gnawed on the inside of his cheek. He should've thought of using his magic sooner, then he would've had time to practice such a feat. Sparring with Gordon wouldn't be at all possible now, not without earning attention.

"I hope the scamps have nae been bothering you," Hamish said, causing Darshan to look around for his lover.

Hamish stood not that far away, leaning on the arena railing.

"They were no bother." In truth, it had been somewhat of an education listening to how they would've countered particular moves. Perhaps he should've trained with them as well. The children weren't as impressive in stature as their uncle, but the two older ones weren't far off from his own height.

"Really? I hear they've been making right pests of themselves so far." Hamish tipped his head to one side. "You seemed a little uneasy in their presence."

"Did I?" After Mac's outburst, he had been waiting for the boy to voice even more of his opinion on the sort of person Hamish would prefer marrying. Mercifully, the boy had remained silent on that topic. "I do not mind the presence of other people's children. It is the thought of having my own that is mildly horrific."

A number of his sisters had learnt the unfortunate way that the Crystal Court was a hazardous place for a family, especially when they'd a killer within the bloodline.

Not that the court needed Onella's assistance in thinning the imperial family. He recalled little of his early childhood years beyond Nanny Daama's teachings, but the records on his twin and himself were rife with reports of assassination attempts. At least one from a governess his father had selected from a supposedly trustworthy few.

Hamish's brows twitched downwards before the man seemed to become conscious of the movement and smoothed his features. His lips parted, but that too halted.

Darshan's gaze drifted to their surroundings. There was nothing about the crowd that would spark an immediate alarm in regards to his proximity to Hamish. But that didn't mean there weren't any guards keeping the man under careful watch.

"I wonder," he said, ensuring his voice was loud enough for those nearby to overhear. "Does his highness have the free time to explain a few of the finer points in all this sword clashing?" He squared his shoulders and pretended to ignore the snickers his question garnered. Playing the part of the clueless noble was an act he had become well accustomed to.

If he couldn't attempt an actual practice with one Tirglasian prince to test how effective the magic attacks he had in mind would be, then he would have to settle with a theoretical conversation with the other and hope they were right.

Hamish smiled and stepped away from the arena railing. "I think I can manage a moment or two. How about a wee stroll whilst you explain what you find puzzling?"

Chapter 34

I *should've trained without my glasses*. He might've been less able to keep up with Gordon—he had barely managed as it was—but at least he would've been prepared for this.

He could see his competitor, in a vague sense of the word. She paced before him like an impatient hound, standing at perhaps half a head taller than himself and swinging her sword. But whilst he could identify the being before him as human in shape, the details were blurred and overlaid by other impressions that he couldn't pinpoint the source of.

Aiming with any precision was not going to happen. That didn't entirely rule out the idea of sending a dusty blast her way. It did limit its effectiveness, though.

He dared to glance at the closest railing. The crowd was a blur of shifting colours. Hamish stood amongst them somewhere. He squinted briefly, trying to focus on the spots of orangey-red amongst the crowd, before giving up. Maybe it was best that he couldn't be sure his lover was watching.

Darshan hefted his sword, testing the balance. The chosen weapons were clunky things in comparison to what he had briefly trained with back home. Even the Stamekians favoured the more graceful and swifter scimitars when magic wasn't an option.

"Competitors," bellowed that same deep voice he had heard all through yesterday's duels. "Begin!"

No sooner than the words had left the man's mouth, did Darshan's opponent rush forward.

Darshan jerked back. A shield sputtered around him, mercifully clear. *No, no, no*. He couldn't allow himself a sliver of magic, not until the right time.

Yet, suppressing the urge took a surprisingly great deal of

concentration. Certainly more than he had bargained on.

He backed away from the woman, his sword raised in warning. *I should've realised.* The usage of magical shields was rooted in instinct, like breathing or blinking. But however much having even a thin barrier between him and a training sword might stop him from being hurt, he couldn't risk it. Unless he was extremely lucky in not getting hit, casually shrugging off any lack of a reaction to a blow would draw the wrong sort of attention.

His opponent circled just beyond reach, her sword low and ready to strike at any opening. She feinted a few times, her blade darting this way and that as she tested his reaction.

Darshan mimicked her stance, keeping his balance on his toes. One thing he could do without rousing suspicion was to outlast her. His healing magic would see to it that his muscles didn't tire as quickly, but it would require a great deal of dodging. Any hit on her part would only make her bold. A hit on his could bring out her desperation.

He would prefer not to fight faced with either outcome.

Hollering from the crowd competed for his attention; bellows of encouragement to his opponent, cries for them to do something beyond dance around each other. He blocked them out. *If they only knew.* But he couldn't let that happen. Not yet.

Giving a roar that could've deafened a bear, his opponent rushed into his range. She swept her sword upwards, knocking aside his pitiful block.

Darshan gave ground, almost slamming into the sturdy railing hemming them in. He darted to the side and just missed clipping another rail before escaping into the centre of the arena. Exactly how had she herded him into a corner whilst keeping him none the wiser?

He shook his head. *Sloppy.* As much as he would've preferred otherwise, a change of tactics was clearly in order.

Daring to loosen his grip on the two-handed hilt, he focused on stirring up the air. Such magic was a difficult task to accomplish at the best of times. It always started small, the wisp of a current drifting from the lazy sweep of his fingers. He had to follow the puff of air out, force more of his magic into the breeze.

All whilst keeping a wary eye on his opponent.

He let the breeze roam the arena, sweeping wide to encompass the crowd in a vague circle as it gained intensity. *Not too obvious.* He backed up a little more, drawing his opponent with him, as the wind hurtled towards him. There was a patch of earth trampled bare by previous contestants. Was it enough? Only one way to tell.

With his back to the oncoming wind, he let the full strength of the gust drift low and sweep up. The wind whipped dust all around them, bombarding his back.

His opponent lowered her head. Had she been affected as he'd hoped? Hard to tell with her eyes in shadow. He'd just have to risk it.

Darshan lunged, aiming low. Collecting a leg might—

Pain lanced across his side. His breath whooshed out his lungs. The world flashed red.

He dropped to his knees, bent over and gasping. *More air*. The scarf inhibited him too much. He grabbed the edge, prepared to tear the fabric from his face. *No*. It was one blow. He still had a chance. Revealing himself now would ruin everything.

"One point to blue."

Darshan barely heard the call. He clutched at his side. Sharp pain dug into his chest with each breath, forcing him to breathe shallowly. Had he cracked a rib or—? *Yes*. His magic buzzed, steadily working to mend the injury, the drain more than bruised flesh or bone would warrant.

"*Red?*" their mediator barked, exasperation thick on his tongue. How long had the man been calling for a response?

Darshan lifted his head sluggishly. The world was slightly fuzzier now, his tears sapping the blurs of even more detail. He rubbed a hand across his face, clearing his vision as best as he could. Blindly, he faced the direction of the voice.

"Are you fit to compete?"

Breathing deep and wincing as a twinge hit his side, Darshan nodded. *It's just the first strike*. He hadn't given Hamish hope and risked throwing the whole contest into turmoil to bow out now. *How could I have been so foolish?* He should've waited, perhaps tried a second time, before reacting. Now he needed to win the next two rounds or—

Focus, you twit. Clambering back onto his feet, he marched into the middle of the arena and waited for the cry to begin the second bout of their duel. If he didn't train his full attention on his opponent, then he would be walking out of this arena defeated. *And exposed*. He couldn't let that come to pass.

His opponent, seemingly emboldened by her victory, hopped impatiently from one foot to the other. After dealing such a blow, she likely thought him easy pickings. She would've been right had he not his magic to lean on.

Darshan levelled what he hoped was a menacing glare at her. *No mistakes*. His healing magic still passively tingled through his body, not quite done with mending his ribs. Redirecting the energy to bolster the strength in his limbs took some concentrating, but far less than an initial summoning. He'd but a short window to use it.

"Second bout," the cry came. "Victory or even mark. Begin!"

He raced across the space between them. His sword snapped up, smacking the woman's blade aside before she could mount a proper defence, then down.

She scuttled backwards like a disturbed crab, barely missing incurring the same injury she had inflicted on him. Her left arm jumped, her grip loosening on the sword hilt. Was she used to fighting with a shield?

He feinted. Again, her elbow lifted that smidgen too high. And again, his sword swiped at her. *Too wide*. Even as he swung, he knew he had misjudged his aim. Too late to check himself. All he could hope for now was that she didn't—

His opponent let out a roar of pain.

She doubled over, the sword falling forgotten from her hands. He couldn't see anything wrong with them, but she cradled her hand nevertheless. Like Darshan, she wore gloves fashioned from simple brown leather. Meagre protection against a sword blade. Even a blunt one.

Had he broken her hand? The woman's howling certainly suggested something more serious than a bruised knuckle.

He had learnt from yesterday's duels that suffering a broken limb, even on the first blow, meant an instant loss. It wouldn't have been so back home, where such injuries could be healed in mere moments, but the Tirglasians seemed adamant that their spellsters stay beyond the reach of other folk. Even when it would've made life easier for them to have skilled healers nearby.

"One point to red," a voice bellowed over the woman's screams. "Someone check to see if her opponent's still fit to compete."

Two figures vaulted the railing and strode their way.

His opponent's hiccupping cries of pain abruptly shifted into one of rage. "That was a lucky shot!" she snarled. Her uninjured hand scrabbled for her sword hilt. With her weapon found, she used the sword as a staff to haul herself upright. "You dinnae deserve to win." She brought the blade up in one clumsy swing that Darshan easily dodged. "You're a bloody, dirty cheat!"

"*Blue!*" the voice snapped. "Contain yourself!"

Darshan backed up further. It *had* been fortunate for him that she'd chosen to deflect his sword rather than to stand beyond his reach and let the blade pass unimpeded, but that didn't mean he wasn't entitled to his victory.

"I'm fine," his opponent hollered. She waved the point of her sword at the people who'd entered the arena to check on her, warding them back. "It's nae broken." Even as she insisted, she shielded her injured hand with her body. "Announce the next bout and I'll prove I can still compete!"

Silence fell over the crowd. So singular in thought that Darshan fancied he could almost make out the words. *Will he let her fight again?*

It wouldn't matter if she won the duel as she now stood, she would fail once they reached the final test. Attempting archery with a broken hand would hardly yield the best result.

Darshan lifted his sword in preparation for an attack. Given her temper, she was likely to come at him with all the fury of a mother cow protecting her calf. He was close now, he couldn't risk dropping his guard.

"Victory to red," the mediator called out to the astonished yells and bleats of the crowd. "I've made me decision. I've made it, I said! Blue is nae fit to compete. Red wins. That's final."

I won? He staggered back, his weapon almost slipping from his hand. Naturally, winning had been the goal, but to actually manage it without his magic being much use… he hadn't expected it to be so exhilarating. It rather reminded him of his old training days with his sister, Anjali, and their Nanny Daama.

"Blue," the man growled, clearly having lost his patience with the woman. "The duel's over. You've lost. Remove your veil and return to your clan."

The woman begrudgingly obeyed, tearing the scarf from her face. She marched past Darshan towards the arena gate, bumping his shoulder along the way. "I hope you fall on your face, cheater," she grated. Her dark eyes flashed dangerously beneath the overhang of thick black brows. "A wee thing like you couldnae possibly swing that hard. Your sword's nae the same, is it?" She lunged at him.

"Me Lady!" the announcer roared. "Step down or be forced."

The woman ignored the man to favour of tearing Darshan's sword from his grasp.

Darshan scuttled back, one hand on his scarf. It was still held tightly in place. Would she dare attempt to snatch it from his head?

"I kenned something was up," she crowed, lifting the sword high. "It's weighted."

On the murky edge of his vision, Darshan spied the blurry figures of others entering the arena. The clank of chain mail reached his ears before he could make out their uniforms. *Castle guards.*

Darshan stiffened. If anyone amongst them recognised him…

The man stood between him and the woman. One grabbed the sword from her, hefting it even as he restrained her. "Nae it's not, lass." With one hand on her shoulder, he guided the woman away from Darshan.

Giving a sour grunt, she jerked out of the guard's grasp and strode off into the crowd mingling at the gate. Flanked by the men the whole way.

Only when she was well beyond reach did Darshan finally let his guard drop. He had made it through the first trial. *One down.*

Winning this contest seemed just a fraction more feasible.

~ ~ ~

Hamish gripped the rail. It was all that stopped him from rushing into the arena to embrace Darshan. He couldn't look too favourably at any one victory least it drew his mother's suspicion. *He did it.* His lover had bloody won.

His heart had almost given out when the sword had slammed into Darshan's ribs; an incapacitating blow had the blades been sharpened. Yet, his lover seemed well now. Had Darshan actually managed to heal himself so swiftly or had the blow simply not been as vicious as it had looked?

He hadn't missed the wind that circled through the crowd, moving like no breeze had ever done within the castle grounds. Had anyone else? *Nae likely.* No other spectators would be on the lookout for magic.

Making sure that he didn't seem any more pleased with the outcome than other duels he had witnessed today, Hamish worked his way along the arena railing. If he timed leaving, then he might be able to spend a brief moment in the tent with Darshan to ensure his lover was fully healed. And ask if the man was aware of what the next trial entailed.

He barely registered a figure striding into his path before bumping into them. "Sorry, I—"

They grasped his shoulders in a familiar hold, keeping them upright as they stumbled. "Steady on," his brother said. "Anyone would think you've places to be."

Hamish shook his head. *Of all the people to collide with.* Had Gordon been watching the outcome? He had paid only mild interest at the rest of the duels. Would his brother's attention on this one be noted as peculiar? "I ought to knock your teeth in."

Gordon's eyes widened to their fullest. "What did I do?"

"You ken exactly what you've gone and done." Hamish folded his arms. "Tell me, where do you think the Udynean ambassador is right now?"

"I saw him wandering the grounds yesterday, but..." His brother's gaze flicked to the arena, but both victor and loser were gone. He shrugged. "I'm sure he's around."

Hamish leant on the railing. "Closer than I think? I hear you've been keeping him occupied." He turned his head slowly as if the crowd didn't bother him. A fresh pair of contestants had entered the arena and no one seemed to be paying their princes much mind. Nevertheless, he lowered his voice. "And victorious."

His brother's brows rose. "Is that so?" He clapped an arm around Hamish's shoulders, gently turning him from the railing. "Did you catch that last one's wee tantrum?" He roared over the cheers from the crowd. "They nae looked impressed in being defeated at the first hurdle."

Hamish stuck to a curt nod in case his voice was drowned out by the cheers.

With a steady squeeze on Hamish's collar, his brother quietly guided him away from the arena. "How about I help you get ready for tonight's dancing?"

Hamish winced. The last thing he wanted to do was dance with the very women he was trying to avoid marrying. He had evaded mingling with them last night by feigning weariness. He couldn't get away with it again so soon. Not without the clans speculating on his health. "I can ready meself well enough."

"Right you are." Giving him a pat on the back, his brother turned to leave.

"Oh and Gor?" He grasped Gordon's middle finger, bending it back until his brother winced. "You let your mouth run off with your good sense again and I really will thump it back into place." He released his hold and continued walking through the crowd with Gordon keeping pace at his side.

"So I take it you *do* ken who's competing under the Dathais banner, then?" Gordon enquired once they were away from the bulk of the crowd. A few people still mingled between the arenas, but none seemed at all interested in anything beyond their own conversations or hurrying to watch a duel.

"You set Dar up under your wife's old clan?" he hissed. Some of the tension creeping into his body relaxed, replace by hollow dread. Whilst no one would think it strange for Gordon to witness how his wife's relatives faired in the contest, it also ran the risk of piquing their mother's interest with each trial Darshan completed.

One side of Gordon's shoulder lifted. "Their chief sent word that they'll nae send anyone else to the slaughter. I figured I could sneak him in without anyone howling, so I lifted the message before Mum could see."

"Hiding clan missives? Muireall would've kicked your arse for that." Hamish made a show of rolling up his sleeves. "But since she's nae here, I guess the honour's all mine."

Gordon shuffled sideways a few steps, his hands raised in

surrender. “Are you nae impressed with your big brother’s ingenuity?”

He was, but admitting that also meant having to deal with Gordon strutting around like a young rooster. “We have nae idea how badly Mum will react when she finds out.”

“We’ve got two more trials to concern ourselves with first.”

“And how much have you told him about those?” By the Goddess’ good name, he still hadn’t figured out how Darshan was supposed to navigate the forest run when he saw so little without his glasses. And if he got hit? “Have you even given a thought as to what might happen if he doesnae make it?”

“He’s smart enough to work out what the last trial entails, archery in Udynea cannae be *that* different. As for the other... I figured I’d see how he faired here first before bothering him with details.”

Combing his fingers through his beard, Hamish groaned. “Have you at least had him try his hand at archery?” How much experience had Darshan confessed when it came to wielding a bow? *Minimal.*

“Nae as yet.” His brother arched a brow in his direction. “Thought I might ask a master.”

Hamish let his breath out in a long blast. “Tomorrow morning, then. Bring the lads. We’ll school him on the forest run and archery at the same time.” With Gordon and his nephews at his side, no one would think twice on them vanishing into the forest beyond the clan encampments.

Of course, he’d be a fool to think he could get Darshan ready to compete against what would assuredly be skilled archers in a day. But if his lover lacked as much knowledge as he claimed, then he could teach him enough to have people thinking he wasn’t completely inept.

It wasn’t perfect, but it would have to do.

Chapter 35

Darshan wove his way through the crowd, his ears still ringing with the band's blaring. He had heard plenty of stories of how noisy Tirglasian music could be, but such rumours had done nothing towards preparing him for the monstrosity they dared to call an instrument one of the musicians had trotted out halfway through dancing. The wailing and screeching of beastly thing as the man blew into what looked to be a flute still permeated Darshan's senses.

Some forewarning to vacate the area before they had begun would've been nice.

He gave an almost absent nod to Gordon as he casually slipped by the man and ascended a winding flight of stairs to the mezzanine overlooking the castle's great hall. His feet tingled slightly at the new movement, his healing magic tending to the aches brought on by excessive dancing. One of the women had literally dragged him into a line that still cavorted.

A little notice on that also would've been helpful.

He halted at the top of the stairs. The mezzanine was cloaked in shadow. No one had thought to light the torches adorning either side of the space and the thick panes of the single window had darkened with age and a thin layer of grime.

A perfect place to harbour the person it currently cloaked in such darkness.

Hamish leant against the railing with his back to the sole entrance. His lover hadn't been here the whole time as Darshan had caught the man joining in during the less hectic dances. He had even seemed to enjoy the festivities, although apparently not anymore as the curve of his broad shoulders suggested a certain weariness with the display of dancers and music below.

Whilst it was tempting to heed the mischievous urge to surprise the man, Darshan took pity on his lover's nerves and merely cleared his throat.

Hamish spun. That gorgeous blue gaze alighted on Darshan for a heartbeat before widening and darting about the mezzanine.

"I do hope I am not intruding." Darshan's boots thumped alarmingly loud as he strode across the bare floorboards. "I thought you might like the company."

Seemingly convinced they were still alone, Hamish relaxed against the railing and shook his head. "You're blending particularly well with the shadows tonight." He waved a hand to indicate Darshan in his entirety. "Nae seen you in anything beyond pale colours before. It's an imposing look."

Darshan ran a smoothing hand over the black-dyed silk of his sherwani. It had a different, more modern, cut to the others; a little shorter and more open at the thigh. Bits of obsidian and jet had been woven into the dark embroidery and black pearls accented the buttons. *Imposing?* Not enough to stop women from approaching him for a dance. "I thought, given the nature of the celebrations, a sombre change of pace was called for."

"Few would agree with you on this being a solemn affair."

Indeed not, for the band continued on with their torture of that dreadful screeching instrument; harsh on his ears even at a distance. The musicians stood in the centre of the great hall whilst the dancers circled them in ever-widening rings. The dancers trotted a few steps one way, then the other, all in perfect unison. Their laughter and cavorting joined the clamour.

"You seemed to have enjoyed yourself down there," Darshan said once the cacophony of jumbled notes they dared to call music had stopped. "Although, your dancing was a little on the stiff side."

Hamish grunted. "I havenae danced like that in a good long while. Nae since Muireall died. Me dance partners were fortunate that I remembered the steps."

A fresh wave of music drifted up like a hazy melody. Familiar in tune, if not the dance the crowd had paired off to twirl to.

"Then perhaps you need a different type of partner." Darshan gently entwined their fingers and pulled them closer together. "One who will take the lead?" The faint aroma of the bitter alcohol his lover fancied reached Darshan's nose. Had he imbibed a few draughts for courage?

Hamish glanced over the railing. With the hall in full light, no one seemed to pay any mind to them; two shadows in the dark. Nevertheless, uncertainty clouded his lover's face.

"There is no one up here but us," Darshan gently reminded him. "I rather doubt anyone can see us from below and your brother guards the only entrance." Ostensibly, to keep any competitors from embarrassing themselves before Hamish. "I am quite sure we can manage a little dancing without causing a scandal." All night, he had yearned for just one twirl with his lover. A few steps in the dark was likely the best he would get whilst still in Tirglas.

That would change once he got Hamish home, even if he had to drag his lover out into the middle of the dance hall. He had grown so weary of keeping everything secret.

"*One* dance," Hamish whispered.

Darshan gently led Hamish through the steps, mindful of keeping any foray near the railing brief lest the unlikely chance the sharp eye of an elven servant actually caught them. His lover followed smoothly enough, allowing him to increase the speed with each four-measure beat until they'd caught up to the music.

Risking a little twirl towards the balustrade, Darshan glanced at the cavorting below. Last night, Queen Fiona's guards had been in full force. They'd shadowed Hamish, lingering in the man's presence like a bad smell. "I'm glad to have found you so easily. How ever did you get your mother's guards and escorts to leave you be?"

"Me mum called them off."

Shock almost had him mistiming a step. He recovered, sweeping them further from the railing. "How fortuitous."

"Nae really." He shrugged, seemingly unconcerned about the end to an issue Darshan clearly recalled the man panicking over just a few weeks back. "It doesnae matter anymore, nae now the union contest has begun. She kens I'll marry whoever wins before I risk a civil war."

Darshan gnawed on his lip. With the festive air in the hall, it was hard to imagine the dread hanging over this competition like a shroud. The bit that pained him the most was how right Queen Fiona was. If Darshan didn't win, then his lover would marry one of the others.

He just couldn't see Hamish living long after then.

"I've nae danced with a man before," Hamish said, drawing Darshan back from his thoughts. "Am I doing it right?"

Forcing a smile, Darshan swallowed the bile threatening to vacate his stomach. "I would never be able to tell had you not told me. You have yet to stand on my toes or anything else so ungainly." He grinned. "Unlike some of the others I have danced with in the past." So many of the men he chose were used to leading and it was often their first time in letting another take the reins.

His lover's soft gasp of laughter warmed Darshan's cheeks and creased Hamish's eyes. Not once did his gaze leave Darshan's face. His eyes almost glowed in the faint light. Like a fire burning through the night that refused to go out.

My flame. Darshan reflexively wet his lips. What was it his father used to say about eternal flames? "You know all those chaotic feelings people equate to love?" he mumbled, aware that his face was growing hotter with each word. "The fluttering, the sick to your stomach nervousness?"

Hamish bowed his head. "Aye, I ken that feeling well."

"My father used to say none of that happens when you are with your eternal flame." That was supposedly how a person was to know they'd found the right one. He'd never believed it possible until now. "You just feel warm, like basking on a midsummer's day. Only in *here.*" Darshan tapped his chest. "All the chaos in the world starts to make sense. You can live your whole life in darkness and never know what that is truly like until there is light to judge it by." He could see it all: the path, the choices, leading him to Hamish. "For good or ill, you are my flame."

His lover halted and Darshan's heart almost followed. Was it mere coincidence that they'd come to a stop near the doorway? Or did Hamish plan to leave? Had he pushed too hard? But his lover knew how Darshan felt.

Hamish bent his head.

Those soft lips brushed Darshan's and he gave not a second of thought towards answering in kind. The taste of bitter alcohol sat thickly on his lover's lips. Darshan cared nothing about that either.

His legs wobbled. He patted the air behind him. Was there not a wall somewhere nearby?

His fingers met the smooth surface of worn stone. Coaxing Hamish to follow him as he took a few steps backwards took little convincing. Through it all, their kiss remained the same; warm, tender and bursting with emotion.

Hamish broke the kiss first. They stood there, Darshan leaning against the wall and pinned by his lover seeking the same means of strength to remain upright. For a while, they merely shared silence and breath.

Then, like a giant and affectionate cat, Hamish rested his forehead against Darshan's. "This feeling has a name, then?" he whispered, his voice husky and raw. "So what *is* an eternal flame? Other than a mortal who got turned into a crown jewel?"

He remembered? Gods, he must've told Hamish that tale several weeks ago. Back when things seemed somewhat less complicated. "Araasi's lover was just the first Flame Eternal. The priesthood believes each person only gets one, that we can love others just as much, but there'll only be one soul we ever truly, deeply connect with."

"And you think that's *me*?"

"I know it is." How cold and parched he had been. How had he not have noticed it before? His whole life he'd been dying of thirst and hadn't even recognised it until stumbling upon this oasis.

Darshan stared out over the railing. Little could be seen from this vantage point, but he could hear the cavorting. "I am going to take you away from all this. I *will* win." Duelling one-on-one with limited access to his magic had seemed the trickier task. *Two more to go*. He just had to keep reminding himself of that and not think on how he wasn't quite sure what to expect from one and he was uncertain he could manage the other. "I am already a third of the way there."

A small smile tweaked his lover's lips, although there was a distinct lack of spark to his eyes. "You are. And I dinnae think I've congratulated you on being victorious in your duel." He laid a broad hand on the side Darshan's duelling opponent had struck him. "How are your ribs?"

Darshan rolled his eyes. Had the man learnt nothing from his conversations on healing magic? "They are completely fine. Did she break them? I believe so. *But—*" he swiftly added before Hamish could voice his concerns. "They were already fused back in place before I could take another swing." Admittedly, that was also due to the breather he had inadvertently managed to garner.

"I wish there was another way." Hamish scratched at the base of his neck, disturbing the chain holding the ruby heart he would gift to Darshan after the second trial was over. "I dinnae like the idea of you getting hurt because of me."

"I am fine." He gave his side a hearty thump with his fist. "See? Nothing." Unable to fully decipher Hamish's expression, Darshan pressed on. "What is the worst that can happen in the next trial? A sprained ankle?" *Or I get lost.* He shook the thought loose with a shake of his head and cupped Hamish's jaw. "I will be fine."

His lover nodded. Whether in agreement or reassurance, Darshan wasn't quite sure. "Of course you will be," Hamish mumbled as the skin beneath Darshan's fingertips grew steadily warmer. "I was thinking, since the rest of the competitors are taking tomorrow to recuperate, that you might be willing to join Gor, the lads and me for a little stroll through the forest. Maybe practice hitting a few targets?"

Darshan lowered his arms, gently returning them to dancing in a slow, meandering pace around the mezzanine. "Sounds prudent." Wandering unfamiliar forests with subpar vision was a risky ordeal. If he had a point of reference beforehand, then he might stand a chance of sticking to the appropriate section.

Hamish ducked his head, peering at Darshan. "And you're all right with the lads joining us?"

He cocked his head, dread quietly starting to bubble in his stomach. "Any reason why I would not be?" He hadn't done anything to make Hamish's nephews uncertain around him. "I rather missed their opinion on the duelling."

"Really? I didnae think you'd be all that keen on spending time with them." His gaze slid from Darshan to a spot far in the distance. "What with your lack of a desire to have bairns of your own."

What had he said about children that'd given the impression he disliked being near them? "I have plenty of younger sisters. Dealing with them takes a little more finesse than that rowdy lot. I—"

"But having your own would be—how did you put it?—*horrific*?"

Darshan gnawed on his upper lip. His preference to remain without a direct heir wasn't some clear-cut topic. And it was certainly not a conversation he wanted to have. Be it here or later on.

He had railed against his father's insistence of him siring children for so many years that refusing the idea was almost second nature. However, if the right opportunity, with the right person, presented itself? *Maybe.* It was dependent on so many other factors that he had barely given it a passing thought much less decent introspection.

"Dar? Did you even hear me?"

Jerked out of his contemplation, he stared up at Hamish. They had halted in the middle of the room. The music had stopped at some point. When? He wouldn't dare to guess.

"Forgive me, *mea lux*. It would appear my thoughts are unwilling to settle on anything more than light conversation." He shook his head. "The hour is late and this is a topic I would prefer not to talk about." Or even think on. "But is it not a bit premature to think of children?"

Why did he wish to speak on it? Did Hamish even think it would be possible for them outside of adopting? Not that the idea didn't hold some merit. It wouldn't satisfy his father's insistence on it being of Darshan's blood, but it seemed plausible enough on the surface.

Hamish bent to collect a tankard Darshan hadn't even noticed sitting at the foot of the railing.

Well, that certainly answers the question of when he last drank. Although, how many his lover had consumed was a far more pressing concern.

Hamish tipped back the tankard, shaking it to drain the last drop, and sighed in one blustery blast. "You're right. We should focus on getting you through the other trials and..."

"See you settled in Minamist?" Darshan finished when his lover's voice trailed off. "You are going to love it. The palace is set a little further back from the shore and we rather lack the imposing stature of your cliffs, but you can see the Stamekian shoreline on a clear day and—"

A new melody started up, livelier than the last and loud enough to jangle his hearing. Had those blasted shrieking instruments returned?

Still, Darshan took hold of his lover's hands. He probably had enough in him to twirl for a bit. "Care for another dance?" he asked as if Hamish's foot tapping to the beat wasn't answer enough.

"Do you want to lead this one, too, or should I?"

Grimacing, Darshan ducked his head. "I admit, I am unfamiliar with this dance. Lead away."

Hamish swept him into the middle of the mezzanine as the deep boom of a drum resounded through the great hall.

The dance started off quite simple. Although they held hands, Hamish remained at his side with one arm behind Darshan as they marched forward then back again to a steady, reedy tune.

In the distance, Darshan fancied he heard a voice calling out to the dancers below. Just as they'd done during that nightmare of sound and the crush of bodies he'd been unable to escape until finding himself here.

With one flick of his wrist, Hamish had Darshan twirling on the spot. He had taken perhaps three rotations before his lover grasped his hand and guided Darshan through a move akin to the four-step he had led them through earlier, only much faster.

The music picked up pace, the screeching of that dreadful Tirglasian instrument and the tattoo of drums overtaking the lighter notes. Hamish hooked his arm into the crook of Darshan's elbow and they cavorted in their little two-man circle as the music swelled.

Having been forced into a similar move earlier, Darshan was able to keep his balance a little better this time. The heady beat, a combination of drums and stomping boots, thundered through his body nevertheless. His own feet pounded out the same tune as he did his best to match pace with Hamish.

Magic tingled through his body, temporarily ridding his muscles of weariness. That would eventually take its own toll.

He lost all sense of time, barely registered the music fluttering between the heart-stirring pounding and the lighter trills of flutes. Each change demanded a different action, but he somehow managed to follow along with Hamish.

Despite the weariness threatening to gnaw at his bones, he couldn't help smiling. He had caught only glimpses of his lover dancing throughout the evening, but Hamish hadn't displayed even a fraction of the unadulterated glee that now adorned his face. Such a sight was his alone to behold.

Hamish grasped him around the waist as the music climbed its way to an almost deafening crescendo. He deftly guided them as they twirled across the mezzanine, growing ever closer to the wall opposite the railing.

The drums stopped with a single echoing bang just as Darshan's backside lightly connected with the brickwork surrounding the mezzanine's window.

Darshan leant back against the ledge, breathless. His legs wobbled at the point of collapse. "I should take you dancing more often." Getting caught up in the music was one of the best parts of Udynean soirées. The orgies that generally followed often being the other highlight.

Hamish chuckled. He also leant on the ledge, albeit with his arms on either side of Darshan. "As long as you're nae as distant in public as you were tonight."

"It appears I play my part as the uninterested foreigner all too well."

Another tune started up, soft and slow, clearly meant as a breather between more exuberant dances.

Rather than suggest they participate in a third spell of cavorting around the mezzanine, Hamish seemed content to merely stand. "It's nae that, you looked like your thoughts were out to sea."

"Did I?" His mind was abuzz with so much, it could barely steady itself for more than a few minutes. Perhaps if they were to retire to some place a little quieter. "Is there somewhere we can be alone?"

"We *are*."

Darshan shook his head. "Really alone. Just for a little while. It does not have to be physical," he added in a rush when Hamish's brow rose. He rather doubted he'd be good for more than just sitting there and that wasn't acceptable. "I just... I hate all this hiding." In a few more days, that would be over. Nevertheless, his nose wrinkled at the thought of having to continue this act for another moment. "There will be no more of it once I win."

"Aye," Hamish breathed, drawing closer. The scent of alcohol lingered on his breath, even after dancing for so long. "That would be nice." His hands roamed almost idly down Darshan's side.

In one clean move, Hamish fastened his hands onto Darshan's hips and hoisted him up until he sat on the window ledge.

"*Mea lux*!" Darshan managed on the wings of a gasp before his lover's lips were on him. Still, he persisted as Hamish drew back for air. "What if—?" Again, his voice was muffled by that sinful mouth.

Weaving a few of his fingers into his lover's beard and gently tugging was enough to garner Hamish's attention. "What if they discover us?" He didn't think Gordon would allow even his own mother to pass, but it had been risky enough dancing in the shadows. Surely, they'd be tempting fate to do anything more?

Grinning, Hamish swept their lips together in several slow kisses that tied Darshan's insides into a knot. "Then they'll ken I've already picked me a favourite." He pressed his hand against Darshan's chest. "Which I will announce once you make it through the forest course."

"No pressure, then?" Darshan quipped, rather conscious of the effect all this kissing was having on his nethers. *Not now*. If he could just extract himself with some dignity—

Hamish's hand slunk lower, cupping the steadily growing bulge in Darshan's trousers.

" 'Mish," Darshan breathed. "Are you drunk?" All the evidence pointed to such a possibility, although the same could likely be said of himself and he had imbibed very little in the pursuit of keeping his wits about him.

"A little," Hamish murmured, trailing his fingertips over Darshan's groin. "I think I ken exactly what you want."

Darshan remained still. As much as he wanted to entwine his fingers into his lover's clothes and tear them from Hamish's body, he steadfastly kept his palms firmly against the ledge. Being drunk was no invitation to paw at the man, no matter how much he believed Hamish would enjoy such reciprocation. "Please do elucidate."

Chuckling with a wicked delight that prickled Darshan's skin, Hamish slowly undid the ties to Darshan's trousers. "I reckon you're after a big, burly kind of man like meself to pin your arse against whatever surface there is and have their way with you." Hamish nuzzled at Darshan's neck, his breath hot. "Am I aiming close enough to the mark?"

Against his better judgement, Darshan tipped his head back. By rights, he should remove himself from the situation altogether, but he couldn't will himself to tug his lover's hand free of his trousers. "Dead centre, in fact."

"Is that all I am?" Hamish asked, the huskiness of his voice all but melting the last of Darshan's resolve. "A fantasy?"

"Only to begin with."

His lover rocked back. Even Hamish's hand shifted to rest on Darshan's thigh, allowing him a breath of reprieve.

"Was *I* not that for you?" he pressed.

Hamish's jaw tightened, but he remained silent.

"Neither of us had known the other existed for more than a few days before I kissed you." Gods, had it really only been the better part of a month since then? It felt more like a distant memory. "In all honesty, if things had gone the way they do back home, we would have spent one night, maybe two, together and that would have been it."

His lover offered up little more than a harrumph.

"And it would have been a terrible waste." He caressed Hamish's cheek with the pad of his thumb. "To miss knowing you, *mea lux*."

Hamish pressed his lips to the heel of Darshan's palm.

"So yes, I do imagine you doing those things you mentioned—and even the naughty thoughts still swimming through your mind that you dare not voice—but I fear it is only because I cannot imagine doing them with anyone else."

"Naughty thoughts?" Hamish whispered, his lips brushing Darshan's palm with every word. "Like *this*?"

Before Darshan had the wherewithal to grasp what his lover was doing, Hamish had already tugged Darshan's trousers down. The fabric pooled at his ankles, neatly trapping him should he dare to think of immediately vacating the area. His drawers were also swiftly worked down, releasing Darshan into the night air.

His lover's fingers, their grip firm but gentle, wrapped around Darshan's length.

He sagged against Hamish. "You might be a while there." Getting off on manual manipulation wasn't always a given. Darshan had to be very close to the edge first. Had they such time?

Darshan dared to glance at the stairway entrance. Would they hear anyone entering in time to not be caught?

Hamish chuckled, soft and low. "I dinnae think I will be." He cradled Darshan's jaw. His scarred thumb brushed along Darshan's cheekbone.

He obeyed the gentle request for him to turn his head and meet Hamish's gaze. A strange warmth flowed through him at the sight. He sat here, half naked, barely having Hamish's hands upon him.

Should he really feel so... loved?

"You are breathtaking," Hamish whispered.

Had this been any other time, any other man, Darshan would've been quick with a witty reply or flippant retort. He'd had plenty of men flatter him or speak his praises. But faced with such a vision of raw adoration...

Words failed him.

"Consider this as a reward for your little victory." Hamish sank to his knees. His breath ghosted across Darshan's exposed groin.

Darshan's lips parted, a protest on his tongue. Nothing escaped beyond a gentle groan.

Wetting his lips, Darshan rallied his senses for a second attempt. "And if someone hears us?" All it would take was for one moan to leave his throat a little too exuberantly and anyone could just wander up here to investigate. Not without barging past Gordon, of course, but there was little else to stop a person. He was not some exhibitionist, exposing himself to all and sundry. Not without a great deal of alcohol, at least.

"They willnae hear a thing if you're quiet." Hamish lowered his head. His lips closed over the tip of Darshan's length. He slid down a ways, not enough to engulf him, but it—

Gods.

Thankfully, the ledge supported his weight or he would've dropped. Darshan pressed his fist tightly against his lips, the rings digging into his skin. Silence wasn't his forte. Especially when the mouth in question was this damn talented and... *Magical.* Maybe it actually was. *Glorious and warm.* A talent that had been utterly wasted for so many years.

His lover's head bobbed in earnest, making good on his prediction that he was definitely not going to be at this for long.

Darshan bit hard on his lip, fighting to keep even a single moan from escaping. His breath panted through his nose. His head flopped forward, the light from the hall below further obscured by his hair. He shut his eyes, squeezing them tight.

When Hamish chose to swallow Darshan's length in its entirety, he couldn't stop the inelegant jerk of his hips.

His hands slapped either side of the window frame to keep himself steady. Magic flared through him. The stone beneath his fingers grew hot, groaning as he dug his fingers in. In the darkness behind his eyes, his head spun. Raw power continued to pour through his fingertips. Everything inside him grew taut.

Darshan tumbled over the edge like an avalanche.

He opened one eye, assessing the mezzanine for whatever damage he might've caused. Slowly, he extracted his fingers from the holes they had moulded into the window frame. It seemed otherwise intact. As did everything else.

Good. His body trembled, drained. He had almost expected to find he'd blown out the windowpane or the wall, or that the floor had caved in.

All acts he had inadvertently done in the past.

Hamish stood, half-tugging Darshan's clothes up with him. He pressed close for a chaste kiss. "Sleep well, me heart." Then his lover was off down the stairs before Darshan could think enough to respond, never mind make himself publically presentable again.

Darshan hastened to pull up his clothes. He rushed down the stairs after the man, still securing his trousers and barely halting in time to miss colliding into Gordon.

Of Hamish, there was no sign.

Well now. What was he to do? Chase his lover down or find a somewhat gentler pursuit to calm his still thundering heart? One thing was definitely certain, he wasn't going to sleep anytime soon.

Chapter 36

Hamish grumbled under his breath as he paced between the roots of the two giant yews, waiting for Darshan to show. He had specified morning. Hadn't he? Did the man not realise that meant daybreak? It was well past that now, although the forest floor still clung to grey light.

His fingers idly trailed across the yew trunk before he ground his heel into the dirt and marched back to the other yew. The trees were rumoured to be over four hundred years old and supposedly marked the spot where the young prince had lost the usurpers looking to destroy the last of his clan. Of course, the truth behind the tale was always a matter for debate, the story having become more myth than history.

Hamish tipped his head up as he passed the midway point between trees. The branches were gnarled. They wrapped around each other, eternally connected. *Until one of them dies*. Perhaps the connections forged through the centuries of growth would be enough to hold the other up.

"Do you think he's gone and gotten himself lost?" Gordon asked, neatly snapping Hamish's thoughts back to the present.

Hamish paused for a step in his pacing to glare at his brother. They had only been waiting in the forest for a short while. The fog hadn't even shifted from beneath the canopy. "He said he would bloody be here and he will come soon enough." Was his lover having difficulty getting to the tunnel unnoticed?

With Gordon's key in Darshan's possession, they had been forced to circle the cliff. But, in bringing his nephews along, their travels came with a plausible story of taking them out to practice their archery.

The three boys stood nearby, firing arrows at a tree one of them had marked with shallow slashes.

Hamish halted by the second yew, leaning against the trunk to watch the trio. They jostled each other between draws, sometimes biffing leaves or dirt to throw off their brothers' aim. *Just like we used to.* That little trick Bruce did to flick debris behind his back was almost identical to the one Nora had used on him as children.

Gordon joined him, his gaze swinging between the surrounding forest to the boys. "I ken this isnae something you want to hear, but I dinnae think he's coming."

Even as the words passed his brother's lips, Hamish couldn't help the twinge in his gut that maybe Gordon was right. Or maybe it was all the liquid sloshing about in his stomach. Waking had come with a dreadful headache, alleviated only by a jug of water and one of the cook's bitter concoctions that also left him with little desire for grub.

He took a deep breath. "Give it until midmorning. Dar's probably just held up." The spellster would have to avoid detection to the tunnel entrance, traverse it and then find his way through the forest without arousing anyone's suspicion. *If only he could make himself invisible.* Sadly, Darshan had already informed him such magic wasn't possible.

"You really are putting a lot of faith in him."

Tell me something I dinnae ken. Darshan could decide to back out of the contest with no one the wiser at any given moment simply by not participating. But... "He loves me." Surely if Darshan had any misgivings about competing, it would've been in the first trial, not now. "Said I was his eternal flame. I think it means he believes me to be chosen by the Goddess for him." He remembered that part of last night quite clearly. As if he could ever forget the golden warmth that had bathed his very soul at the confession.

His brother's brows rose. "He's *that* serious about it?"

Hamish nodded. At least, he hoped Darshan was.

Gordon rubbed at his jaw. "I suppose we can wait until the fog burns off."

They stood there, minding that the boys didn't get quarrelsome with each other whilst also continuing to keep the usual watchful eye for anything that might mean harm, be it an aggressive stag or a startled bear. Although, the amount of noise his nephews made would likely to scare off all but the most cantankerous of beasts.

The boys, seemingly bored with practising their archery on the same stationary target, had each taken up a fallen stick and seemed content to chase each other around the trees.

Where Mac failed to match his brother's with a bow, he was well capable of holding his own with a sword, even a makeshift one. The boy's crowing of landing the first strike echoed through the forest.

Gordon snickered as one exuberant hit shattered Mac's stick.

Undeterred, Mac tossed aside the remains of his weapon and launched himself at Bruce to wrestle his poor eldest brother to the ground. Ethan dared to valiantly attempt coming to Bruce's rescue and was dragged into the heap.

"Do you remember when Dad used to bring us out here?" Gordon asked.

"Aye." That had been back when they were all young and idealistic, when the idea of disobeying their mother's will was akin to heresy. When all four of them had lived under one roof. He lifted his gaze to the yew branches. "Caitlyn used to scurry up this tree like a cat."

His brother chuckled. "And Dad would always send Nora up to fetch her because she was the lightest." His wide grin almost split his beard in two. "But Nora always got stuck."

Hamish's chest bubbled with the laughter of a memory that'd grown soft around the edges with time. How he missed the innocence, stolen from him once his mother knew he'd never willingly find a wife.

His gaze slid back to the children. Ethan was still battling to free his elder brother's arm from Mac's grasp. "Do you ever wonder what'll happen to Ethan once Mum finds out?" How many years did the boy have before she set her poisonous sights on him?

Sighing, Gordon folded his arms. "Aye and I've been hoping it willnae matter when the time comes. But all this business with you and Darshan...?" He shook his head. "I dinnae ken what we can do. There's naewhere we can take him that she wouldnae hunt him down. Talking to her is useless. She's convinced her way is the only one."

"I've been thinking—"

"Thought I smelt burning."

He dealt his brother a hearty punch to the shoulder. He should've expected such a response. "About the sinking of *The Princess' Fortune*. What if it wasnae an accident? What if Mum—?"

"Our brother-in-law's ship sank in a storm. You cannae just have one form out of nothing. The Goddess was responsible there, nae our mum."

"Has it never struck you as odd that Calder, a man who was born to ride the waves, wasnae capable of steering his ship to a safe harbour?" There were a lot of things that could bring down even the most seaworthy vessel, but those who had been in the storm that had taken his sister's husband claimed the trade ship shouldn't have gone under as swiftly as it did.

Gordon frowned.

"Plenty of people survived. They talk, you ken."

"Sailors always talk," his brother grumbled. "They've enough time at sea to make up all sorts of stories."

"Similar ones about the same ship? *The Princess' Fortune* left Mullhind upright and hearty, yet people used to speak of it listing on the return voyage and I always wondered..." His voice dropped to a whisper. "Mum only cared she'd lost a grandchild. She wept over nae one else." Not Calder. Not even Gordon's wife.

His brother grunted, conceding the point. "Well, she never got on with Calder."

"I *do* remember the rows Mum had with him." The roar of a queen used to her words being law clashing against the bellow of a captain who hadd shouted over the sea herself. "Calder had a massive influence over Nora. He was the reason she saw more of our kingdom than just the royal clan lands."

"You're suggesting she gave the order to have her son-in-law killed? *Wilfully*? Dad would've stopped her if it were true."

"How? He hasnae the authority to overturn her orders." If he had been a king, then yes, but their mother was where the royal clan line came from. That was why she was the queen and not princess consort. "Mum already controls everything we do, where we go... who we marry. She cannae stand us choosing a path she hasnae paved." How much of a leap was it for her to decide how and when those who defied her died? She had already ordered the death of the men he had rutted with, why not Calder? "She was the same with your wife."

"Mum just didnae like how Muireall preferred to travel with just a couple of guards whenever she visited her old clan. And maybe she should've heeded Mum's wish to send a small contingent of guards with her. Maybe then she'd still be alive."

Perhaps. He doubted the presence of more guards would've stopped Muireall from attempting to slay the man-killer bear terrorising the village she had stopped at on her way through. "Have you forgotten that Mum made a pregnant woman compete in your union contest? That should nae have happened." Muireall confessed she couldn't have been more than four months along, but the thought of watching her duel still made him queasy. "Mum's even organising Sorcha's marriage. That's your daughter's life. The lass is barely thirteen. If anyone is to have a say in what happens to her, it should nae be Mum."

"You think I dinnae ken that?" Gordon growled. "What am I supposed to do there? Tell Mum she cannae have anything to do with her granddaughter and future queen?"

Hamish shook his head. "I thought you and Muireall were in agreement on an acceptable age for marriage? Didnae you want to wait until your girls were in their twenties?"

"Maybe I was wrong. Me eldest was old enough by tradition. She could've been home, preparing for a wedding instead of dying in some forest far from home. She should nae have been there and that is on me. *I* should've made her stay."

"Or have me in her place." Would it have mattered? Perhaps in their mother being less paranoid that something would happen to her grandchildren if they weren't kept under constant supervision. And maybe it would've shown the truth about her feelings towards those who dared to stretch her children's minds beyond the royal clan lands.

Gasping, his brother pushed off from the tree trunk to grasp Hamish's shoulders. "I would never want—"

"Mum would've." She had been almost disappointed when he had returned with the bear that'd taken the life of her daughter-in-law and granddaughter. "She would've preferred I had died to that bear than be involved with any man."

"That's nae true."

"But it *is*." He shook free of his brother's hold. "Mum forsakes those she cannae control. She would rather consider Caitlyn as having never existed because our sister has magic. She sees me as defective because I like men." And he had believed there was something wrong with him for so long until Darshan showed him the truth.

"That—"

"Caitlyn's *condition*—" Hamish all but spat the word. "—cannae be ignored or altered. Mine can. At least, as far as Mum's concerned." He had lost count of how many times she had attempted to negotiate with him, as if the right conditions would make him amenable to lying with a woman. "I'm tired of living by her rules. We shouldnae have to. She's our Mum, nae the bloody Goddess."

"But she *is* the queen. What sort of precedent would it set if we disobeyed her every order in favour of our whims?"

The wrong sort. At least, that was what his mother always proclaimed. Once, he would've readily agreed with such an answer. "What I have isnae a *whim*," he muttered. "I just want to be with him, to be *me* without having to look over me shoulder every other breath." Was that really such a bad thing to crave?

His brother grasped his shoulder and squeezed reassuringly. "This isnae the same and you ken it. She should nae have announced the contest, nae when she was aware how miserable it would make you."

"Then it is fortunate I am here, is it not?" a familiar voice piped up.

Hamish jerked his head around to find his lover standing nearby.

Heat rushed to his face like a bonfire. How much had the man heard?

Darshan held a practice bow awkwardly before him as if he had wandered into his parent's bedchamber. He wore the drab attire he had donned on their way to the cloister, likely in an effort to blend in with the rest of the castle inhabitants. The glasses kind of ruined the effect. "Should I come back later?"

"There is nae later." Over the man's shoulder, Hamish spied the boys huddled around the tree they had been aiming at earlier. At least they would've been less likely to have heard them.

"Where have you been?" Gordon asked. "I thought 'Mish told you the way."

"He had. I was merely taking the opportunity to arrange a few personal matters whilst I had the time."

Never one to be brushed off so easily, Gordon narrowed his eyes at the man. "*What* matters?"

Darshan held up his hand, the digits absent of their customary jewellery. "Nothing sinister. You can take the suspicious look off your face. It is just your mother is unlikely to be amenable to me winning."

"That's an understatement and a half," Hamish muttered. If only they could be certain of her reaction, then they would be able to plan better. Assuming the worst was the best chance they had.

His lover gave him a grim smile. "Quite. And rather than rely on her following with convention regardless of her feelings towards me, I figured it would be prudent to seek out back up measures upon which to fall."

"You went back to the trader's guild," Hamish said. If his mother reacted as badly as he believed, then having immediate access to funds would see them on their way to Minamist a lot faster. Although, the lack of a ship sailing anywhere near their destination for another week *did* mean leaving Mullhind over land.

Darshan bowed his head. "I did." There was a lingering bitterness to the words, warning Hamish exactly how the man had faired before Darshan could speak further. "Sadly, the woman I spoke to last time was absent and her successor is quite unwilling to loan me any further funds without my previous debt having been paid off."

"That is a wee bit unfortunate," Gordon said, his brother's falsely light-hearted tone doing little to lift Hamish's spirits. "But we've a slightly more pressing matter to get you through before then." He indicated the practice bow still held before Darshan as if it would somehow loose an arrow on its own. "Have you ever used a bow?"

Darshan regarded the weapon and grimaced. "Not since the hunting expeditions my father would take us on in my childhood. It is considered a commoner's weapon of choice back home. But I have seen both of you use them often enough during our travels. I am certain it will come back to me with practice."

Pursing his lips, Gordon's gaze slid to Hamish. His brother arched a brow at him.

Hamish could only shrug in response. If Darshan couldn't wield a bow, then he would be forced to forfeit the final trial.

"A day willnae give you much time to practice in."

Seemingly unfazed, Darshan slid an arrow from Hamish's quiver. "The method of use is a simple principle. Nock the arrow." He did the act smoothly enough. Not a clean movement, but better than most novices. "Pull back the string." Darshan's arm shook as he drew the bow to its full strength. There was a faint grunt and all was still again.

Hamish shuffled on the spot. He tried to remain silent, but the urge to instruct was too great to contain. "I wouldnae try to shoot with your arm like—"

"Nonsense. All I need to do is aim and..."

The arrow whistled through the trees, spinning in a pitiful arc before bouncing across the grass.

"Good job," his brother muttered, resuming his lean against the yew trunk. "If you were aiming for the ground."

Darshan whirled, glaring at Gordon.

"Your posture was wrong," Hamish said before the pair could start to bicker.

With a huff, his lover lowered the bow. "Do I tell you how to suck me off?" The acerbic tone in Darshan's voice stung a little. The man had never spoken quite like that before, at least not to him.

Behind Hamish, he caught the overloud growl of Gordon clearing his throat.

"Because I'm good at it," Hamish shot back, unable to let the jibe fall. "Unlike you with a weapon you've barely touched before."

"*You* show me how it is done then," Darshan snarled, thrusting the bow into Hamish's hands. There seemed to be a little more bravado in the action than it really warranted.

Was Darshan... afraid? He had displayed some uncertainty in his ability to make it through the trials, but little more. Did the prospect of losing gnaw at him as much as it did Hamish?

"*Well?*" Darshan pressed.

"I havenae picked up a bow since... since the bear." The only reason he'd brought one out here was more from habit. He wouldn't even have arrows if it wasn't for Gordon, for his mother had insisted all manner of sharp objects be kept from his hand.

The admission seemed to chip the haughty mask Darshan had donned. Grief and doubt radiated through the cracks.

"Gor?" he asked over his shoulder. "Give us a wee while alone, will you?"

Grumbling a few half-hearted obscenities, his brother sauntered over to their nephews. The trio instantly crowded their uncle, intent on gaining his praise all for themselves.

Darshan sourly watched Gordon's passage.

"All right, what's the real reason behind all this bluster? Did something happen last night that...?" His thoughts trailed off as he recalled what his brother had mentioned during their trek to this part of the forest. Hamish remembered only bits of last night's feasting and dancing, the rest drowned by alcohol. But his brother was adamant he had done something to fluster Darshan. "Did someone say something that could cause us trouble?" Had that someone been him?

His lover winced. An act he visibly struggled to cover up. "I have not the foggiest clue as to what you are referring to." Even as he spoke, a faint redness took the man's cheeks.

Hamish folded his arms and silently ran his tongue over his teeth. If he had said something wrong, then surely Darshan wouldn't have turned up at all rather than be surly about it.

His lover's gaze darted to Gordon, seeming to ensure the man was well out of earshot. "I availed myself of the archery range last night, before seeking solace in the library, and I—" Sighing, Darshan hung his head. "It shall not matter how many hours I practice or how well I attempt to aim," he whispered. "Without the aid of my glasses, I might as well be shooting blindfolded."

"Ah." He had considered that would be a problem, but he had also foolishly thought Darshan would have a solution. Hamish pulled at his bottom lip, tugging to one side and twisting back and forth between his fingers as he thought. "Can you see the target at all without them?"

Darshan looked back at where Hamish's nephews and brother chatted animatedly amongst themselves. "That tree they are standing before." He gently slid his glasses down his nose to peer over the tops. "The entire trunk is a fawn blur."

"But can you aim for it?" A blur was better than nothing. Aiming in the centre would likely get him a decent shot. Perhaps not the mark he would need, but it was a base to work on.

"I cannot even be certain how far away it *is*," he hissed.

"That willnae matter," Hamish said as he leisurely strolled towards his nephews' makeshift target with Darshan following. "There'll be one target to aim for. It'll be at one set distance. Each competitor will get one go."

Gordon twisted as they neared, eyeing them with a measure of interest before returning to herding the boys to the line they'd marked before the target.

Darshan screwed up his nose. "That hardly seems fair in itself. I would have thought an overall score. Surely, a poor competitor could win with one lucky shot."

"If that is the Goddess' will, then aye." Hamish agreed. There likely had been such occurrences over the generations. No one seemed to mind. "On the bright side, you'll ken exactly how good your aim will need to be."

"How so?"

Shrugging, he drew an arrow from his quiver and inspected the fletching. "The competitors go in reverse order of how they exited the forest run. Except..." He placed a finger squarely on Darshan's chest. "For the one I've announced as being me favoured to win. *They* go last."

"I would have thought the favoured one would go first."

"Once the others ken who he would prefer to win?" Gordon asked, joining them at the line with the boys. "Some may be accused of not performing at their best."

"Which is how they're expected to compete," Hamish added. He knelt before his nephews. "How do you lads feel about a little extra competition?"

"It isnae against *you*, is it?" Bruce asked, narrowing eyes almost as deep a green as his mother's at Hamish. "Because *you* always win."

"Even Uncle Gordon cannae best you," Mac piped up.

"Well," Gordon drawled, scratching at his neck. "I have done just that in the past. Back when your uncle was a wee lad and barely able to draw a bow, mind you," he finished with a wink in Hamish's direction. "But what I think your Uncle 'Mish is alluding to is a bit of friendly competition for our ambassador to gauge himself against."

"That I am," Hamish added with a bob of his head. He pulled out the arrows that were already in the tree and paced out the distance the trial's target would be placed at. "Here should be a good starting line."

Ethan gave a low whistle. "That's a fair distance for a novice. Are you sure you dinnae want us to start closer?"

Hamish shook his head. "If you think this'll test you lads, then maybe we've been going too easy on you." The distance was no greater than the length of the castle's archery range and the older boys could hit those with a substantial degree of success.

Bruce scoffed. "Nae hard for us. Right lads?" He stood in silence as his brothers shook their heads and exclaimed a similar opinion. "I'm more concerned for our competition." He arched a brow at Darshan, his lips twisting in an echo of his father's smirk. "I saw him trying. I dinnae think he has the strength to fully use his bow never mind send an arrow that far."

"You've a keen eye, lad," Gordon murmured. "Your dad would be proud."

Hamish glanced at the boy. Usually, mention of their long-dead father would elicit a stillness through the whole trio. Not this time. Bruce's face might've darkened slightly in embarrassment, but his chest was puffed out with pride.

The light seemed to dim as Hamish nocked an arrow, the air stilling like that morning outside the tent. *Just a wee bit of cloud cover is all.* There were no bears in this part of the forest. The boys would've cried out at the first whisper. His brother would've alerted them.

His bow trembled. Even knowing the true source of his accuracy, he hadn't actually managed a successful hit since that one in the castle range. Back when everything had started to go wrong.

Lifting his focus to the little circle carved into the tree trunk, Hamish breathed deep. It was hard to see how magic came into play. He barely needed to think on it. Was that part of the wonder in Darshan's voice over his skill? The effortlessness of it all?

He drew and loosed his arrow. The point hit precisely where he had focused. Dead centre.

"There's your target," he said, shouldering his bow. "Show us how close you can get. You too, Dar," he added with a jerk of his head.

The boys, ever ones for showing off, drew themselves to their full heights. It gave the added effect of adjusting their stances to be in line with their target.

Darshan stood beside them. He watched the boys' actions with what Hamish hoped was renewed confidence, even going so far as to mimic the way they stood. At least, to an extent.

Mindful not to pull too much attention to himself and let his nephews lose their concentration, Hamish sidled over to his lover. "Let them go first," he said, keeping his voice low. "Then we'll work on your form."

Darshan arched one brow in his direction, but gave no further indication of agreement.

One by one, the boys loosed their arrows. Whilst each one hit the tree trunk, only Bruce's managed to make it near the target.

"Good job, lads," Gordon said, clapping his hands. "Stay put," he added as they took a step towards the tree. "We're nae finished with this round. We dinnae want one of you scamps getting some extra ventilation." His brother rubbed at his face as if that somehow erased his poorly-concealed humour. He nodded at Hamish. "When you're ready."

Hamish laid his hands on Darshan's hips, intending on shifting his lover into a more suitable position. He froze as the body beneath his fingertips tensed. "Is something wrong?"

Darshan shook his head. "Unexpected is all. I assume you mean to criticise my stance?"

"*Improve*," he stressed. "You're capable in the draw, but this is a little different to hunting. You've time, for one. And your whole body…" Gently coaxing Darshan around, he lined his lover up with the tree. It was harder to imagine the distance without a properly marked point, but having Darshan train in shooting beyond the needed distance wouldn't be the worst thing. "You should nae be square on with your target."

"Understood."

"Your feet are best kept a shoulder-width apart." Rather than clumsily force Darshan to move, Hamish waited until his lover had shuffled into the appropriate position. "Keep your knees supple, that's also important for stability. You dinnae want them to lock." Out of habit, he bounced on the balls of his feet in the same manner his father had first taught him all those years ago. "The torso… you want it to stay centred and your back should remain straight. Like this." He stood beside Darshan and mimed holding his bow at full draw. "Arch in any direction and you've lost balance alongside power."

"I believe I grasp the concept."

"Good." If they could hammer in the basics swiftly, they'd have more time to hone Darshan's aiming abilities. "Now, aim for the tree and loose. Dinnae fash if you cannae make it. We'll come to that in a moment."

Pursing his lips, Darshan did as instructed. The arrow struck the tree low, just embedding itself into the tree roots. His lover winced.

"Nae bad," Hamish said.

Gordon scoffed. "It's bloody better than *your* first attempt. You couldnae hit the east side of the castle unless you were in a rage. Threw some good tantrums back in the day, too."

Heat took Hamish's face as he caught the tail end of Darshan's snicker. He glared at his brother, the promise of a slow death flashing hotly in his mind. "With the stories I've heard of your training, *you* were nae much better. At least me improvement came a wee bit faster than yours." Darshan would likely say the cause there was a product of this wisp of magic he possessed, but he fancied practice had a larger say in the act.

Gordon stuck out his tongue at Hamish before grinning broadly. "Let's see if he can do it again." He squeezed the shoulder of their closest nephew, who happened to be Mac. "You lot, too. There's nae such thing as too much practice. Now go fetch your arrows whilst you can." Ruffling Mac's hair, Gordon gave the boy a little encouragement in heading to the tree.

Grumbling, the other two boys followed their younger brother. They plucked the arrows free, including the one in the ground, and returned to their positions.

The four continued their attempts to match Hamish's mark. He went down the line, adjusting stances or grip as need be. Gordon joined in, focusing more on the boys and leaving Darshan's schooling entirely up to Hamish.

His lover was improving, but there still lingered a great deal of uncertainty of the task ahead of them. Hamish could see it in the tension of his shoulders and the wooden movements of his arms. Clearly, Darshan considered achieving their goal with nowhere near the amount of confidence he'd had at the beginning.

Maybe if they had more time. Why hadn't Gordon attempted archery training on top of sparring? His brother must've realised what task Hamish would choose for the final trial.

Hamish wasn't entirely sure if this was going to work. Darshan was right in that practice would only get him so far. If there was just a way for his lover to aim without seeing the target.

He stepped back after readjusting Darshan's grip to watch the four of them take their turns, idly tracking each arrow from bow to tree. *A simple arc.* This wasn't like hunting. The target didn't dart about. If his lover were to merely lift his bow that smidgen more, then the arrow's curve would do much of the work.

On the other hand, Darshan could need to adjust for the wind during the trial and there could be other arrow shafts in the way, maybe more than there was now. In which case, the arrow's direction would need to be adjusted so as to—

His lover gave a disapproving hiss and lowered the bow to glare at him. "You dare to try and wrest it from my grip?"

"How can I do…?" The question trailed off. Did he mean magic? He can't have been attempting anything there. Or had he? *Nae.* At least, he hadn't done so intentionally. "Could you feel it?" He bent closer and whispered, "Me magic?"

"Your influence on the arrow? Yes, I felt it vibrate through the fletching." A spark of hope ignited in his eyes. "Are you able to direct the arrow of another archer?"

"I'm nae sure. I havenae tried." He thought back to all the times he had helped his nephews train. They all seemed to improve a lot faster under his tuition than when he wasn't involved. "At least, I dinnae *think* I have."

"Let us see then." With a fresh surge of confidence squaring his shoulders, Darshan lifted his bow. "You aim. I shall loose on the count of three."

Hamish stood just behind Darshan. What the man suggested had merit and there was little harm in making the attempt.

The arrow tip gleamed on the edge of his vision as he focused on the tree over the man's shoulder. If he squinted, he could almost see a line trailing along the passage his mind envisioned.

"One..." Darshan pulled back on the bowstring and something deep inside Hamish drew taut.

Two... Hamish flexed his fingers. His own bow sat alongside their packs, but he could've sworn it was in his hands.

"Three," his lover whispered, releasing the arrow.

The point slammed into the trunk.

Again, his lover winced as if he had personally taken the shot. Then, Darshan seemed to become aware of what they'd done. "*Yes!*" he yelled in Udynean. He jigged on the spot, startling the others who likely had no idea what the man was saying.

The boys especially eyed his antics with a measure of alarm.

Having the arrow reach the tree wasn't an entirely new development as Darshan had managed it a number of times without assistance, just not consistently. That the shaft was nestled snugly against the arrow Hamish had loosed at the beginning was a whole other matter.

"I don't *need* to see," Darshan murmured, still in his native tongue. He whirled on Hamish, clasping his arm. "*You* can be my eyes." Those hazel eyes seemed to enlarge as fresh hope gleamed from behind the man's lenses.

Hamish's gaze flicked from the arrows to his lover and back. He scratched at his chin. "It could've been a fluke."

Grinning, Darshan nocked another arrow. "Then see if you can do it again."

They practised further. Every time he turned his focus away from the arrow, it missed. Not terribly, but enough to put the idea of Darshan winning the final trial on his own in doubt. When he *did* envision the path, the arrow always hit precisely where he aimed.

There were limits. He needed to stand behind the man for it to look natural. And, unlike when he was the one with the bow, he had to remain completely focused or the arrow wavered.

Before long, sweat started to soak his clothes. It wasn't overly hot, despite the lack of wind, but the trickle of moisture down his back and the beading across his forehead was undeniable. Was it a magic thing? Did this overheating happen to all spellsters? Or was it some sign that he was pushing too hard? Perhaps it would be better if he backed off for now.

Darshan glanced at him, his brow twisted in concern. The strain must've been obvious, for his lover merely nodded and continued to attempt the distance on his own.

Only when the entire contents of four quivers adorned the tree did they pause to consume the bread, meat and cheese Gordon had procured from the castle kitchens. His brother spoke little, although he would occasionally shoot a puzzled frown at Darshan.

The boys weren't so generous with their silence. They continued to talk, even whilst cramming more food into their mouths than Hamish had thought possible.

"I thought you hadnae handled a bow before?" Bruce queried, his voice tight with the strain of keeping the disappointment peeking through his otherwise blank expression.

Darshan, hastily swallowing a mouthful of water, opened his mouth. "Actually, I—"

"Was it magic?" Mac blurted. "I bet it was magic."

Hamish stiffened. Whilst the boy was correct, and they were likely to peg Darshan as the culprit, he wasn't sure if they had jumped to the conclusion because of the man's dismal first attempts or because it was obvious that magic that guided his arrows.

"It couldnae have been magic," Ethan protested before Darshan could utter anything either way. He fixed the man with a piercing glare. "Because then, it wouldnae have been *fair*."

"Cheating against *children*," Bruce murmured, sounding suitably aghast. The boy tut-tutted as though he were a man thrice his eleven years.

"Aye," Ethan added. "That's a low blow."

Mac stuck out his tongue and blew a long flatulent noise. "If *I* had magic, I would use it all the time. You would, too. Dinnae deny it. You're just sore you lost to him."

Hamish frowned. After Darshan had proved he had told the truth about magic running through Hamish's bloodline, his lover hadn't said a word about whether the rest of Hamish's family were spellsters or Nulled Ones. Any one of them could harbour a spark that would see them sent straight to the cloister. Or worse, be unable to be saved from illness or injury by some magical fix.

"Lads," Gordon sharply cut in. "Dinnae badger." The reprimand had barely left his lips before a chorus of apologies bubbled from the boys.

Hamish leant back against the yew tree they sat under. His mind sluggishly mulling over the trials.

Using his unique ability wouldn't come without its own risks. Here, he had relatively few distractions and no sudden gusts to compete with. Fortunately, he would be standing amongst the competitors to aim the arrow they must beat, so his presence there wouldn't be suspicious. Would they think it strange if he stood directly behind one? Would he need to mimic the move for each archer?

He gnawed on a thumbnail. He already planned to gift the ruby heart to Darshan. Surely showing concern over the possibility of the one who had gained his favour failing would be a natural one. Hadn't Nora been practically beside herself at the notion of Calder failing? *Aye.* Hamish might've been quite young when Gordon had married, but he'd a vague recollection of his brother being the same.

Ethan sat back, eyeing the yew tree. He'd been slowly chewing for some time, like a cow with its cud, and only now finally swallowed what had to be paste. "Do you think—since we're here—we could do the forest run?"

Mac bounced on the spot. "*Can we?*" Half-chewed crumbs of bread flicked out his mouth as he spoke. "*Please.* We havenae done it in *ages.*"

"I would very much like to see it," Darshan murmured, delicately brushing off the crumbs the boy had managed to spray onto his trousers. "Where does it begin?"

Gordon patted the yew trunk. "Right here," he replied around a mouthful of bread and cheese. "It'd be a bit hollow for you lads to attempt it without anyone aiming at you, but I dinnae see why not."

"We could play *root 'em out,*" Mac said, still bouncing. His brothers perked up at the suggestion. "Us against you three."

By the gleam in Gordon's eyes and the slight lift if his mouth, Hamish knew his brother already agreed to the idea. Still, he made a show of mulling it over, stroking his beard and humming. "I suppose that would be a good way to test your aptitude for stealth. A little better than sneaking into the kitchens at night," he added with a conspiratorial wink. "We'll give you lads to the count of—" He jiggled his hands as if comparing weights. "Let's say to twenty. That should be plenty of time for you scamps to make yourselves scarce."

"One," Hamish began, standing. "Two…"

Like a warren of flushed rabbits, his nephews scrambled to their feet and raced into the forest.

Darshan stood alongside Hamish. "It shall be safe for us to wander through? Are they not preparing it for tomorrow? Will they not notice our presence?"

Hamish shook his head. "Naebody comes here." Not often, at least.

"Nae until tomorrow," Gordon added. "Then everybody will." He swallowed the last of his meal and took a generous swig from the water skin. "The trial consists of a run through the forests along the hills just beyond those trees." He pointed over his shoulder. "Make it from here to a specified line on the other side without being hit and it's through to the final round."

Darshan peered at the forest, one brow cocked. "Hit by what?"

"It's nae dangerous," Gordon insisted. "Dinnae be concerned about that. I reckon if you keep that shield of yours handy, they'll nae be able to touch you. And you'll nae need to fash over being the first, either. You just need to make it through unscathed before noon."

"Your confidence in me is staggering."

"Except he'll need to remain inconspicuous," Hamish interjected. "Or the other competitors will ken there's a spellster in their midst. Do you think you'll be able to find your way without your glasses?" he enquired of his lover. "If you've been there before?"

A faint frown briefly touched Darshan's forehead. He lowered the lenses enough to peer over the tops. "Maybe."

"Maybe will have to do," Gordon rumbled. "I reckon that's long enough for the lads. Let's go flush them out."

Chapter 37

The section of forest lying beyond the two yews wasn't terribly difficult to navigate, if the runner was used to foliage and rough terrain. The task was more evading the men and women who would be hiding up in the treetops tomorrow. Others would line the crude rails on either side so that competitors couldn't completely skirt the area. All would be armed with small packets full of dye. Anyone who came out the other end marked was eliminated.

How well Darshan would handle the trial was a question Hamish didn't want to think on. Now that Gordon had gone off on his own path, the spellster crashed through the undergrowth, demolishing anything small in his way, be it the brisk skitter of a stone or the vicious stomp of winter-dead undergrowth. Curiously, he seemed to be avoiding any living foliage.

"You're upset," Hamish said. There was no chance the man was this clumsy and Darshan hadn't even attempted to skirt the small, reedy stand of broom that had yet to show any hint of yellow flowers.

His lover grunted and mumbled under his breath, the words too faint for Hamish to make out.

"What was that?"

Darshan huffed. "Of course I am bloody upset. Every time I think we will make it through this, another damn obstacle rears its head." He swatted a bush with the outer curve of his bow, seemingly wincing along with Hamish. "I hate it. How do you live like this?"

Hamish eyed the man's bow. It didn't appear damaged by the unorthodox usage. Fortunately, they'd had plenty more for practice purposes if it came to that. "Must be new for you, having to play along. I suppose the *vris Mhanek* gets everything he wants."

His lover snorted. "Evidently not or you and I would be on our way to Minamist by now." He slammed his foot down on a half-rotten stick, shattering it to pieces. "I should apologise for my harshness earlier. The stress of all this is overwhelming at times, but I should not have lashed out. Certainly not at you."

"I understand." Between his mother's goading words and the knowledge of what would happen should Darshan fail, Hamish had been hard-pressed to keep his own temper.

Another harrumph exited Darshan's nose. "Understanding does not make what I said any better." He halted, his hands resting firmly on his hips as he surveyed the surrounding forests. "So which way would your nephews have gone?"

"North, most like." That was the direction of the finish line.

Giving a considering hum, Darshan peered up at the canopy of branches and leaves. "The way we have been heading, then?" He resumed walking, taking a little more care of his surroundings. "Do you think they would veer much from that direction?"

Hamish shrugged. The boys knew their way around this place. His mother had insisted on all of them knowing the terrain should the worst befall the castle. Would Darshan fair just as well after one day? He would certainly have the advantage of treading these forests before the other competitors, but they were unlikely to require help to spy the move of a guard readying to lob dye at them.

Maybe he could stash the man's glasses case under a tree root near the beginning. But then Darshan would have to find it and store it again before he reached the finish line. What if he used one of the boys? Maybe two, so that the second could snatch the glasses back. All three would likely help if he asked, but what then? And how would he explain their absence to Nora? *Or Mum.* And if they were caught?

"*Mea lux?* Have we taken a wrong turn?"

Hamish jerked out of his contemplation. How long had he been standing here, keeping an eye out for the very nephews he now faintly heard chasing each other amongst the trees? *And me as animate as a log.*

Shaking himself, Hamish peered into the undergrowth and, spying nothing of note, continued to lead the way. "You ever wonder what our lives could've been like if we were nae like this?"

Darshan frowned. "You mean if I was not myself? Or if you did not have to keep an integral piece of you secret from the wider world? Which one are you trying to ask?"

"Both, I guess." He had spent years wondering about either scenario. In his darkest moments, he had even prayed that just one would be true, not caring which the Goddess chose to bestow upon him when either would see him free of his cage.

"For the former?" A sneer wriggled its way across Darshan's lips before being pressed into extinction. "I would probably be married by now. And no doubt knee-deep in heirs." Indifference, with a hint of loathing, tinted his words.

"You always talk about it with such disdain. Do you nae want bairns of your own?" It was a strange stance to take given he'd been so endearing around Nora's boys.

His lover sighed. "*Mea lux*, I adore you more than the sun, but do not ask me that again."

Hamish breathed deep. It wasn't quite as easy as that. "You nae answered me last night." Not properly. And certainly not to his liking. He had always been taught that it was customary to discuss children with a betrothed well before the wedding and he wasn't about to let it slide just because they were both men.

Darshan hung his head. "No, I did not."

He wasn't even sure as to the extent of their options when it came to children or if they would have the same ones in Udynea as they did here. "And we should be talking about it." And probably about a few other things, too. "Is it that you dinnae want to be a father or—?"

"Partially." He scuffed his boot along the ground, disturbing a mulch of rich soil and last autumn's leaves. "My father's insistence on me siring children rather dulled whatever glittering enchantment the idea had."

"Your father?" Hamish echoed. He had thought, after everything Darshan had said, that settling into the imperial palace at Minamist would be peaceful. But if the *Mhanek* wanted Darshan to have children, then Hamish doubted the man would be pleased to see his son arrive already married. Especially to a man. "What if your husband wants them?"

Darshan grinned, arching a brow. "So easily swayed to the idea of marrying me?"

Hamish folded his arms. He was in no mood for jokes. "I'm used to being surrounded by close kin. I ken that you winning the contest will mean you'll also take me from me family. I guess I sort of expected that we…" He shrugged. "That we'd somehow have wee bairns of our own. That's what tends to come after marriage," he mumbled.

Now he had said it out loud, it sounded stupid.

His lover's cocky smile faded. In its place came the stunned, slightly lip-parted, look of a man lost in fresh understanding. "If that is what you want, I suppose—"

"I kind of assumed *we* would want it, nae just *me*."

Darshan gnawed on his bottom lip. He stared out into the forest and twisted one end of his moustache.

"Why do you even want to marry me?" Certainly not for the usual reasons people in Tirglas married.

Those hazel eyes blinked up at him. "Because you are my light, my flame eternal. I love you." A flush of golden light seemed to glow around the man as he spoke. The Goddess' own timing in the gust of leaves and the angle of the sun.

Hamish's heart still fluttered at the sight. "But that's nae how it works here." Love could be a factor, granted, but there was so much more. "Children are expected after a wedding."

"I recall you stating something along those lines some time back. Two years, was it?" Darshan bowed his head. "I have never been this deep into a relationship. You are aware of that. And marriage? If you had told me when we first met that I would want to marry… I would have found the mere concept alarming."

When we first met. A month had passed since then. So much had happened that Hamish would never have been able to predict. He had been prepared for his mother to attempt an alliance between himself and a Udynean noblewoman. Instead, the Goddess had sent him the chance to fall in love when he'd thought it lost to him.

"Truth be told," Darshan continued. "I have no idea where we are headed or where I want to be." He brushed the hair back from his forehead, fisting the strands. "As for how to get there…" A sigh gusted out his lips, his shoulders seeming to deflate with the escaping air. "Back home, love in marriage, especially amongst the nobility, is a rare thing to have. Personal feelings are often pushed aside in favour of forming strong political ties and even stronger bloodlines."

"You get neither of them by marrying me. Me mum will never accept our marriage as anything but a sham." He wasn't even sure if she would recognise Darshan as the victor.

His lover shrugged. "If your mother sees no merit behind acknowledging the alliance it would make between our kingdoms, then I am afraid that cannot be helped."

I suppose. Perhaps his siblings would have better luck after Darshan was beyond his mother's sight. He doubted it, but it was the best chance until she was gone and Gordon took the throne.

"That being said, we do not *need* to have children to solidify such an alliance."

His stomach twisted at the thought. It wasn't just convention that made Darshan's statement a dubious one. "But *I* want to be a father." The admission was out before he could reel it back.

Darshan stopped midstride. His head snapped around, those hazel eyes wide.

"I always thought I would be," he rambled on, all the words pushing for their chance to escape. "Even as a young lad, I had believed it a path I could claim." The idea of sleeping with some poor woman his mother had picked for him, of dragging her through it all had been what'd stopped him from voicing his paternal desire to anyone else.

His lover remained as still as a deer looking for danger. The lump in his throat bobbed as he audibly swallowed.

Hamish scratched his nose with the back of a thumb. "I guess you're going to call me foolish and sentimental?"

Finally, something other than stark terror crossed Darshan's face, curving his lips into a watery smile. "There are worse things to be." His gaze returned to the forest whilst he toyed with his little finger. "Forgive me, *mea lux*, I had no idea you felt this way."

"That's why we needed to talk."

"Clearly. It is just—" A sigh sagged his lover's shoulders. "It is a lot to think on after everything else. If you would permit me the time to mull over the idea?" He clasped Hamish's hand. "And we shall have far more of it once these trials are over."

Did they? How much time did they really have to spare? He'd two more harrowing nights of sleep before Darshan's participation in the union contest was revealed. That couldn't be long enough to mull over the idea of children. "Dinnae think that means you can take forever."

The smile Darshan gave was a small one, creased with concern. He caressed Hamish's cheek. "It is not something to be considered lightly. There will be—" He grimaced. "—*obstacles* back home. But I shall consider it thoroughly. And I swear you shall have an answer before we set foot on Udynean soil."

Nodding, Hamish returned to walking through the forest. What obstacles could possibly prevent an imperial prince from being a father? Was the crown prince the only one allowed to sire heirs? It sounded like something the Udynean court would enforce. But then why would the *Mhanek* be concerned about Darshan choosing to not have children?

Hamish pressed his lips tighter together. If he let his thoughts wander in endless circles, allowed another word to slip free, he'd wind up bombarding Darshan with more questions that could have the man fleeing.

But his mind was nowhere near as cooperative as his mouth in staying still.

Were there other dangers in raising children in the imperial palace? *Assassins*. Darshan was only here because the previous ambassador had been killed. Surely, no one would attempt such a thing on a small baby. *They tried with us.*

Hamish felt along his head, to the scar buried deep beneath his hair. He'd been eleven when those ruffians had tried to slaughter him and Caitlyn.

Fire. His thoughts turned back to that fateful day. Most

considered of it as the time his younger sister had revealed herself to be a spellster.

He didn't remember much after one of the scunners had hit him from behind, but there'd been screaming. At first, it was just his sister's piercing cry, then the men as she unleashed the power of a furnace on the bastards. *And fear.*

Hamish rubbed his hands, which seemed hotter than they should've been. Not sweaty, just uncomfortably warm.

Darshan eyed him, but whatever caused the faint furrowing between his thick brows, he was seemingly content to remain silent.

He shook his head. *Best nae to think about it.* That'd been his father's suggestion all those years ago, perhaps it was for the best if he continued that stance. They'd been lucky. That was all anyone ever focused on. Perhaps it was the same in Udynea. Perhaps that was why Darshan needed time to consider.

Hamish dare not ask even that.

He led the way through the forest, silently pointing out tracks that indicated his nephews had split up. It made determining just where the rascals were a difficult one, but not impossible.

What he hadn't seen was any hint of his brother. Was Gordon scheming? Perhaps on a re-enactment of what a true forest run trial was like? Or did he merely tread the other side of the sectioned-off piece of forest in pursuit of his nephews in the same manner as they?

He cast a glance Darshan's way under the guise of adjusting his bow. His lover seemed to be alert enough to react to any harmless projectile Gordon might lob in their direction, if that was the goal.

But thoughts of his brother had him thinking on their talk as they waited for the boys to ready themselves for the day. "Apparently," he said, trying to keep his voice even. "That is, according to me brother—I should be discussing last night with you?"

"Should you?" Darshan gave a rich chuckle. "Gordon no doubt referred to the rather flustered state I descended the stairs in search of you. But he is a smart man and I am certain he already knew the cause did not stem from any disagreements." He cocked his head. "Do you even remember last night?"

Hamish tipped his head from side to side, his hand wobbling in a similar display. "Bits and pieces." He had a clear memory of the feasting and how much the women were intent on groping him whilst they danced in the main hall. Beyond that? When he had sought out the welcoming darkness and solitude of the mezzanine? "We danced and talked." For some time, although he remembered half of the conversation. But there'd been that same golden warmth as Darshan had declared him as his chosen. "And then I... kissed you?" By the way Gordon spoke, he could assume he'd made a right tit of himself.

"Did we...?" He let the question trail off.

"Have sex?" Darshan finished. "No."

A gust of relief expelled itself from Hamish's lungs. The confession clashed with the fragments of hot skin and the taste of his lover on his tongue, but it wasn't the first time he had dreamt such wonders.

"However." Darshan side-stepped a sapling as he spoke. "That does not exclude you dragging me to the window ledge and having your wicked way with my personage."

Hamish inhaled sharply enough to hurt his chest. "So that part wasnae wishful dreaming, then?"

Laughter erupted from Darshan, along with their chance of sneaking up on the boys should they be nearby. "Wishful dreaming?" he echoed between gasps for air. "Not unless we had the same vivid dream."

"Me brother gave the impression you were a wee bit disorderly and mystified." So much so that Hamish had wondered if he had done something wrong that he didn't remember.

"I was. But only because you decided to pleasure me then leave with just one kiss and a hearty 'sleep well'. You gave me no time to regain my composure, let alone the chance to reciprocate."

Hamish scoffed. "And what would you have done? It's nae like you could've draped me over the railing and had it off." They could've tried the floor, although his knees could already attest to its unforgiving nature. Never mind the fact he would've had to wait for Darshan to recover his strength.

Darshan rolled his eyes. "As if that was the only thing I could have done there." His gaze dropped. "Pretty sure I could deep throat that monster given time."

Hamish faltered for a step. There was no chance the man's focus could be on anything except Hamish's groin.

"What?" his lover chuckled. "You look as if no one has offered before."

To suck him off? Why would they? For most of the men he had propositioned, he had been a convenient place to stick it. The majority of them gave the impression that they'd rather not be reminded he was a man. For them to care about his pleasure was laughable.

Darshan gave a crooked grin, one brow cocking in amusement. "I know how well you can service a man orally and how the majority would be reluctant to forgo your magical mouth, but has no one really ever returned the favour?"

Hamish mutely shook his head.

"Truly?" Whipping his head around to peer at the forest, Darshan sidled closer. "Would you be disposed to participating in such an act? Whilst I might not have your skill, I promise not to disappoint."

"*Here?*" he whispered, his voice hoarse. One of the uppermost branches of the sapling they had just passed had been recently broken. Surely at least one of the boys was nearby. He tilted his head, but there was no other sound beyond their own boots crunching through the undergrowth.

His lover jerked his head back, his lashes briefly fluttering in mild surprise. "The thought of doing so in the middle of a forest had not crossed my mind, but if you are comfortable with the idea..." He arched a brow as the rest went unsaid. "Otherwise, whenever you desire."

"Well, now that's all I can think of." Whenever he'd done the act, even with all those men who'd grunted and moaned at his eagerness, not once had he considered what it would be like on the receiving end. Did they have time for what his lover was suggesting?

Smiling, Darshan clasped one of Hamish's hands. "Come with me." With a gentle tug, he guided them into a thick copse. "This should be adequate," he murmured, backing Hamish up to the trunk of a sturdy tree. A hunger Hamish had never witnessed took over Darshan's expression as his lover stroked Hamish's already semi-hard length through his trousers.

Hamish swallowed. His legs trembled slightly. He braced himself against the tree for good measure. "Actually, I'm nae so sure this is a good idea," he said, breathless. "To do it here, I mean. What if they find us?"

Confusion tweaked Darshan's brows. Those hazel eyes lifted, even as Darshan's palm continued massaging Hamish through his clothes. His other hand was deftly working on unbuckling Hamish's belt. "Are you afraid your brother will berate you?"

His brother? "Nae exactly." Hamish wet his lips, struggling to form words. If Darshan kept this up, he wouldn't have to worry about being found in the midst of anything. "If one of me nephews find us first..." He trailed off, already seeing the answer in the lack of fire gleaming within his lover's eyes.

"Blast," Darshan muttered. "That does put quite the damper on things. You are, of course, right. This is perhaps not the best time or place. Although..." With an impious twist to his lips, his lover practically climbed Hamish, stopping only once he straddled Hamish's hips. "I am not letting you take another step without a little something," he breathed, their lips not quite meeting. "It is a matter of pride."

"I love you," Hamish murmured, laying his forehead against Darshan's. By the Goddess, which one of them was sweating? "It's going to kill me if you go alone."

Darshan laughed, the sound small and breathless. "I am not going anywhere you cannot follow. I promise."

"That depends on how well we manage the next two trials."

"Then how about a kiss for my troubles?" Grinning wickedly, Darshan pressed close. "A nice chaste one that shall remind me just what I will lose should I not try hard enough."

The small gap between them was sealed before Hamish could think of a reply. True to his lover's word, the kiss was softly innocent. Or it would've been had Darshan not tightened his legs around Hamish's waist.

Two can play at that. He grasped his lover's rump and the man moaned against his lips in response. His legs wobbled at the sound. Hamish pressed his back against the tree in support. He sucked on his lover's lip until the majority was trapped by his teeth to the sound of a hushed whimper.

He ground himself against Darshan, groaning alongside his lover. Maybe... maybe they *did* have time. He had witnessed only a single sign of someone having come this way recently, but the noises had been much further from here than—

"Found them!" Ethan's voice cut through the haze of Hamish's thoughts.

The reality of the forest slammed back around him and heat flared across his face. The wisp of a curse tightened his throat, unable to escape his lips as more than a senseless grumble.

"By the Goddess' bleeding ears," Gordon barked. "Can I nae leave you two alone for a moment without you snogging each other's brains out? Or cannae you two find a room to grind against each other like frustrated dogs?"

With his body shaking in poorly-restrained mirth, Darshan bent forward until his lips brushed Hamish's ear. "He is fortunate to not have found us a little later," he whispered in Udynean.

Hamish barely had time to let the implications sink in—and just what would his nephews and brother have stumbled upon had they been delayed in discovering them even a short while later, anyway?—before his lover tipped back in his arms to shoot Gordon a charming smile.

"*There* you are," Darshan said, seamlessly switching to Tirglasian. "I was beginning to think we had lost you."

Gordon's face was carefully neutral, but his brother wouldn't look directly at them. Saying nothing, he headed back the way he had come. The boys tailed him. But not without Ethan shooting him a wide grin and whispering to Bruce.

Darshan snickered.

"It's nae funny," Hamish mumbled, his face growing hotter. Could he even release his hold on Darshan's backside without embarrassing either of them? His own trousers and overcoat should hide the obvious outcome of them grinding against each other—slow as it was in getting the idea that nothing further was happening—but Darshan's trousers were slightly more formfitting.

"Of course not." His lover laid a hand on his chest. "If it were one of my siblings, I would have been mortified to be caught in any sort of intimate act."

"But you're still laughing," Hamish growled, gently prising the man's legs from his waist and lowering Darshan to the ground. His lover's overcoat seemed long enough to avoid immediate embarrassment.

"Well, he is not *my* brother, is he?" Still chuckling quietly to himself, Darshan stepped back. "Are you going to stop leaning on the tree?"

Hamish tipped his head, resting it on the bark. "I'm nae sure if me legs will hold me weight just yet."

"Well, I—"

The nearing crash of something moving through the foliage caught his ear.

Hamish straightened. His bow was in his hand before he had finished righting himself. Was it another person walking through the forest or a potentially dangerous animal? His focus darted momentarily to the boys—who had taken a few steps towards the sound—as he nocked an arrow.

The trio seemed more troubled than scared. Should he order them back further? Or maybe have Darshan shield them? *Nae.* Not until he saw what they were up against. If there was a time for someone to try and cheat their way through, it would be during this trial.

A figure emerged from behind a tree, lightly trailing their hands across the bark.

Hamish lowered his bow. *Sorcha?* Although the girl was glancing over her shoulder, her face hidden by the windswept mass of auburn curls, Hamish had known his niece practically from birth. He could pick out every one of his siblings' children from a crowd.

" 'Cha?" Ethan blurted, rushing to his cousin's side. "What are you doing out here?"

Startled, Sorcha swung about. She tucked her hands at her back, instantly raising Hamish's suspicion. The girl wasn't usually one to cause trouble, but she also didn't tend to leave the castle without a family member at her side. "What am I doing? What are *you* all doing out here?"

"Gor," he called, hoping his brother hadn't gone far enough to not hear him. "We've got company."

To his relief, Gordon emerged swiftly enough, his bow in hand.

He'd barely joined them before his gaze settled on his daughter. "Lass, what are you—?" he growled. "You should nae be out here without an escort." He stormed over to kneel before Sorcha. "You've nae a weapon on you, have you? Isnae that what I *always* tell you?"

"Aye," she mumbled, refusing to look her father in the face. If she balled her hands any tighter, they were going to disappear altogether. At least she didn't seem to be holding anything.

Sighing, Gordon got to his feet. "I'm taking this lot back home. You two can carry on to the end, if you like." Clasping his daughter's wrist, he ordered the boys to follow with a jerk of his head and marched off in the direction of the castle.

"The finish line isnae far." Hamish took a few steps, halting beside the tree Sorcha had touched. Just beyond it was a small clearing marked by a row of broad-leaf ferns. All carefully cultivated. "See?"

"For the moment," Darshan murmured. He lowered his glasses, gently hooking one of the earpieces into the neck of his overcoat. "Shall we discover how well I can make it back to the castle without these?"

A gnawing hollowness took Hamish's stomach. Few of the competitors were going to make it through even without the impediment Darshan had to deal with. If only he could compete in his lover's place, but the rules against them competing for their own hand were explicit. "All right then, lead the way."

Squaring his shoulders, Darshan struck out for Mullhind with Hamish plodding silently behind him. At least he was off to a good start by facing the right direction. Maybe this wasn't going to be as difficult as Hamish had dreaded.

Please Goddess, guide his feet. Surely, it couldn't be that much to ask for. *Just for tomorrow.* He needed Darshan to get through the second trial unmarked. He could ensure victory from there.

Chapter 38

Darshan crouched next to a sturdy tree trunk. *Reach the ferns unmarked.* That was his goal. He had made it only a short way into the designated piece of forest before diverting to one side whilst the rest of the competitors raced on.

All this had seemed far easier yesterday, when he had succeeded in navigating to his tent by the castle tunnel. But then, he hadn't the added difficulty of people throwing objects at him or the uncertainty of when.

Without his glasses, the forest was an unending swath of green. He could make out impressions readily enough, although he couldn't be sure if the darker blobs he saw in the distance belonged to other trees or were just shadows.

At least he could be confident they weren't people. Not unless they had gained a statue-like talent for stillness. They were out there, though. He could feel it. A wisp on the wind.

Invaders.

Darshan shuddered. The whisper of—he couldn't quite call it words, but the impression of them—drilled into his mind. The ethereal notes grew stronger the deeper he pressed into the forest. Similar had happened yesterday when they had practised archery, but it had been more akin to a faint howl of pain. If he had time, he would've pondered on the cause.

In the distance came the occasional cry of his competitors as they were hit. Not dangerous—at least that was what Gordon had claimed—but judging by the screams reverberating through the trees, getting hit was an unpleasant experience nevertheless. *And an instant disqualifier.*

He strained his hearing, seeking any hint that he might be in danger. The far off rustle of a body stalking through the bushes caught his ear. Nothing closer.

This wasn't a contest of speed. As long as he reached those ferns at the other end by midday, time was a commodity he had enough to play with. Perhaps, if he waited long enough, the guards hidden in the foliage would run out of ammunition, leaving him with just the task of making it to the other side.

At least the headaches had yet to start. They would eventually, especially if he continued to strain his eyes like this. Such was always the cost of abandoning his glasses.

Another whisper of disturbed leaves, this time at his back. Was there another, more cautious, competitor lingering at the rear?

The muffled snap of a twig pressed into the earth heralded their closeness. There was definitely a presence behind him. Were they looking to waylay a few people on their way through?

"We ken who you are," a small voice declared.

Darshan hunched his shoulders. Only the faint familiarity behind the voice kept him from instant retaliation. Where had he heard it? "And just who would that be?" he asked, hoping the scarf muffled his voice beyond recognition. He spread his fingers, calling on his magic in readiness for an attack if need be. Perhaps he could knock out the tattler and be through the forest before anyone found them.

"The Udynean Ambassador," another voice replied, this one less familiar.

Well, that is rather unfortunate. Did that mean they were friendly? Darshan couldn't let anyone hostile to his task slip away after revealing such knowledge. Why track him down in the middle of the trial to announce their finds?

An acrid scent drifted on the breeze, carrying a clear message. *Danger*. The prickle of thorns scuttled up his spine, stabbing into the base of his skull. An image invaded his mind. Three figures hunched in the bushes, their bodies bending fragile branches and bruising leaves.

Darshan shook his head, trying to shake the image, but the howling dug deeper into his brain.

"We're here to—"

The image shifted. One of the figures had moved closer. *Danger*. The pressure in his head increased with the cry. Darshan whirled about, ready to unleash a blast of air that would knock the source of such pain unconscious.

And halted, the summoned power still dancing through his veins like needles.

Not danger. He knew those faces.

All three of Hamish's nephews peeked out from the bushes, their ruddy hair a beacon amongst the dark green foliage. They stood close enough that Darshan could clearly make out their identically smug expressions.

"We also ken that you're the one our uncle would most want to win," Ethan said.

"Is that so?"

The trio stepped out of their cover. All three were garbed in drab shades of green and brown. "We want to help," Ethan added with his brothers nodding along. "We've been running through this forest since we could walk, we ken these hills."

Darshan considered how easily the three of them had left behind not only Hamish and himself, but also their older uncle. Having three young pairs of eyes on the lookout as well as guiding him could only make the trial easier. "Does anyone know your whereabouts?"

"Mum thinks we're waiting at the finishing line with our uncles," Mac supplied.

"And Uncle Hamish said he would make sure everyone else thought we were with our mum," Bruce finished. He handed over a wooden case that looked suspiciously like the one holding his glasses. "He also said you needed these."

"I see." Flipping the case lid open, he found his glasses still neatly tucked into the velvet lining. Hamish had told the boys of their deception? And he had also sent them?

Darshan put on his glasses. The world once again had depth and definition.

He crouched next to the trio, peering over his shoulder as if he could spot anything untoward within the patches of green and grey. "So, what is your plan?" The gods knew his idea of scuttling through the undergrowth and hoping wasn't much of one. It was definitely improved now he could see, but not by much.

"It's simple," Bruce said. "Ethan'll guide you."

Over the boy's shoulder, his brother beamed.

Darshan couldn't help but be a little sceptical in the face of their confidence. "He knows where the traps are?" He had come across one, warned back by a ghostly whisper and a flash of men straining the strength of a tree's branches.

Ethan shook his head. "Nae that. Even the lobbers wouldnae ken their stations until they were given them this morning. But I ken the best routes to avoid any tricky spots. As for the rest..." He jerked a thumb at his brothers. "They'll scout ahead and warn us. Maybe even play diversion."

"What are the chances of you three getting caught?" As much as he appreciated the children's attempts to help, getting them into trouble would have quite the opposite effect.

"Slim to none," Bruce replied, shrugging. The boy's brothers seemed somewhat less confident of his opinion, but not enough to voice any doubts.

Truthfully, Darshan would've preferred a complete absence of risk. It was utterly ridiculous to place his chances at the hands of these three children, but the likelihood of him making it through the forest alone was far lower than the boy's estimation. "No time like the present," he mumbled, squaring his shoulders. "Did any of you happen to note any obstacles on the way?"

As one, the boys raised the hoods on their cloaks.

"Most of the dye-lobbers are further in," Bruce said. "We'll nae come across them for a stretch."

Dye? Was that what they were throwing? Something like the powdery balls of cloth the boys had attached to their arrows whilst they practised hunting with their kin? "Then, by all means, lead the way." With a low sweep of his hand, he indicated the breadth of forest stretching before them. A wisp of relief puffed out his nose as the trio started off in that very direction. At least he hadn't done something as crude as gotten himself turned around.

They crept through the undergrowth and hustled across open patches as swiftly as could be done once the path was deemed clear, always keeping as low as possible. Whilst the boys were certainly taller than the average child back home, encroaching on his own height when it came to the eldest of the trio, their stature was just that little bit lower to let them scurry along whilst stooped.

Darshan's back strongly objected to the stance. His healing magic thrummed through his lumbar region, having to soothe the area even as he subjected it to more abuse. It tugged at his already frazzled concentration.

At last, Bruce halted them at the base of a large tree where the trunk was surrounded by a loose cluster of budding bushes. He beckoned Mac forward, whispering to his youngest brother and pointing into the leaves and branches beyond whilst Mac shook his head and argued back with similar results.

Once they both seemed to be of the same mind, Bruce turned back to Darshan and his other brother. "There's a wee formation of lobbers set up in the trees just beyond." He jerked a thumb in the direction Mac still watched, but Darshan couldn't pick out anything different from the treetops. "We're going to get their attention on the eastern side. Take him west, keep him low. There's a ditch nearby. Be careful they've nae got someone stationed there. We'll meet up on the other side."

Ethan gave his brother a curt nod.

They waited for a short while as the two boys slipped out of the undergrowth and darted off into what Darshan assumed was an easterly direction. He tried to track them, but they vanished swiftly.

"Stay close," Ethan whispered, motioning Darshan onwards as he lifted a branch for them to crouch under. "They'll nae stay distracted for long."

Over the hushed crunch and rustle of their footsteps, came the faint exclamation of the nearby men. The sound was followed swiftly by a dull, and rather wet, *thwack*. Did that mean the other two were doing as planned, or was that one of the competitors?

Darshan risked a peek the way they had come. Nothing but green. And a buzz that carried on like the drone of an angered hive.

"I wish I could go with you," Ethan whispered, jolting Darshan from his fruitless search.

"And be miles away from your family?" he replied, keeping his voice just as low. He continued to follow the boy's footsteps closely, doing his best to step in the same places to reduce noise. "All the people who love you?"

Ethan froze for a heartbeat, then dropped to his stomach.

Knowing better than to hesitate, Darshan followed suit before daring to risk a peek at what had caught the boy's eye.

A man stood at the base of a tree not far from their position.

Ethan threw a rock off to their right, disturbing the undergrowth as it tumbled downhill. With the man momentarily distracted, they darted the other way. "What people?" the boy asked, apparently sure they wouldn't be heard. "Me grandma willnae love me once she learns about me."

Darshan hid his surprise in a scoff. Did the boy really mean what Darshan thought? "Of course she will."

"She doesnae love Uncle Hamish."

He bit his tongue, torn between placating the boy and the truth. "I am... fairly certain she does."

"She doesnae let him live as he wants, though." He hopped over a creek via a few suspiciously well-placed stones. "If she didnae ken, I'd understand, but she does and still insists on him doing things that make him sad. She wouldnae do those things if she loved him."

Darshan grunted noncommittally.

"Being away from me family *would* be really hard," Ethan conceded. "Especially if I went as far as Udynea. But I dinnae think it would be so bad if it meant I could find someone like you to marry."

Darshan pressed the veil closer to his face, muffling a chuckle. "A dear boy like you would not want to marry someone like me."

Ethan stopped abruptly beside a dense, green bush before dropping to his knees. At first, Darshan thought they were in the presence of another obstacle, but the boy whirled around to squint at him. His lips pursed as he jutted his jaw out. "You love me Uncle

Hamish, right?"

Spreading his arms, Darshan gestured to the clothing he currently wore. Was his participation in these trials not indicative of such? "Clearly, I hold enough affection for your uncle to go along with this madcap plan to compete for his hand."

The boy nodded as if expecting such a response. His face softened, a small smile lifting one corner of his mouth. "Then I *definitely* want someone like you when I'm older."

Darshan ruefully shook his head. If Ethan knew even a fraction of what Darshan had done, of what he'd been like in his youth, then he doubted the boy would be so quick with his declaration. Darshan certainly wouldn't have wanted a man like his younger self.

"Me brothers should nae be much longer." Beside him, Ethan fidgeted before adding, "If you dinnae win me uncle's hand, would you compete for mine?"

Caught off guard by the question, Darshan fought to repress a shudder, even though it felt terribly like a droplet of ice had tumbled down his spine. The boy was—what?—ten years of age? The very idea made his stomach roll. What was next? A query as to whether he would also proclaim himself a god like the previous emperor of the Stamekia?

Even with Darshan's face largely hidden by the veil, his silence must've been answer enough for the boy as Ethan hunched his shoulders. "I meant when I'm older. I've six more years before I'm of marriageable age, you ken."

That didn't make the thought any better. "I am twenty-three years your senior. I am certain you would connect more with someone your own age. You are young, you have plenty of time."

"Unless me grandma locks me up and kills all the boys I like."

Shock stole Darshan's breath for a moment. "What makes you think Queen Fiona will do that?" he asked, trying to keep his voice light. Gordon had been of the opinion that the children knew very little of what transpired when it came to their uncle and their grandmother. Clearly, they were more aware of the situation than given credit for.

"Because it's what she did to Uncle Hamish." He frowned out at the forest. A wave of moroseness seemed to take him, slumping his shoulders. "Everyone always acts like we cannae possibly ken all that she does to him. That we dinnae hear the guards or see how she treats him. But we do."

Darshan bit his lip. Due to the abundance of daughters his father had sired—by-products of his once desperate need for sons to take the throne should his heir die—whenever death stalked his family it was often from a sibling's scheming. One daughter in particular.

Onella had mellowed slightly with the birth of her son, but that made her no less dangerous. If he heeded Hamish's desire for children, she would be the one they'd have to tread carefully around. It wouldn't be the first time one of her targets had died in their crib.

Still, he was aware such a threat wasn't as commonplace even in other Udynean noble houses. "I am sorry you have been burdened with such knowledge. Children should never fear their elders, especially within their own household."

Ethan hunched his shoulders, his face growing darker. "It's nae your fault that she would rather me uncle was dead than living how he is."

"No, but I swear, this cycle of her hurting your uncle will stop come tomorrow." Once it was plain he had won this absurd contest, ensuring Hamish's safety would be his priority. No one seemed to know just how Queen Fiona would react and insisted he prepare for the worst.

They continued their wait in silence with Ethan fidgeting the whole time.

Darshan returned his thoughts to the buzz surrounding them. It wasn't as loud as when the boys had first made themselves known, but if he focused, he could make out individual melodies amongst the noise. Those soft notes buoyed the deeper thrums of something ancient. Older than himself, at least.

He laid a hand against the ground, compacting the grass. The pulse of life tingled through his fingertips. *Ignore it.* The stress of the day had to be getting to him. He was hallucinating, nothing more.

If he had been a dwarf, he would've said he had somehow reclaimed a portion of the old hedgewitch magic. But he wasn't. He couldn't even have dwarven ancestry and be a spellster. Those things just didn't mix. His very-much-human ancestors had thoroughly confirmed that in their quest to tear the unreachable power from dwarven hands. *Or maybe...*

Maybe after using such an untapped source of raw energy, he was merely more aware of its presence. That didn't explain the flashes of images or the whispers, but that could easily be stress warping his senses. *Not much longer now.* Just until tomorrow, then he wouldn't need to tiptoe around everyone.

When the other two boys arrived, their passage through the forest was more of the same skulking and waiting whilst Bruce and Mac drew attention to themselves. Then further scurrying past to the next safest spot to wait some more for their return. The time it all took trickled through Darshan's mind. How long did he have to reach the finish line? *Midday.*

He glanced up at the treetops during one of their pauses. The sun seemed awfully high.

Only once did he get spotted, resulting in a graze that surely would've been a hit had his shield not formed in time. He had discovered then that the projectiles weren't powder as he'd first thought, but thin sacks of coloured water that were designed to stain.

Eventually, the times between when the children would split up grew longer. He heard little of his competitors other than a few distant and surprised yelps. Even the forest seemed lighter, the canopy more open and the undergrowth less restrictive.

The boys halted beside the wide trunk of an oak, crouching amongst its exposed roots. Darshan took the pause as a chance to rest. They peered around the tree and shot meaningful looks at each other before shaking their heads.

"What is it?" Had they come across some particularly nasty little trap that they couldn't get around? "Trouble?"

"It's nae that," Bruce said. "We cannae go on the rest of the way with you, nae without being caught. But the end is straight ahead."

Darshan peered around the tree trunk. Through the gaps between the trees, he spied splashes of colour that could only mean a crowd. His chest tightened. Hamish would be waiting there with the favour tradition insisted he gift to one of the competitors. "Any obstacles I should know about?" He was so close to making it through this trial, it wouldn't do to trip up now.

All three boys shook their heads. "We've passed all the bleeding lobbers," Ethan elaborated, offering up Darshan's glasses case. "The forest run bottlenecks from here. It's just the finish line now."

Tucking his glasses away, he solemnly handed the case back. "Take care."

"You too," Bruce replied. "One of the cheeky sods might try to lob one at your back. So, keep a watch out."

"Noted." He would do well to keep a shield up until he was at those ferns Hamish mentioned yesterday. "Thank you for the assistance, I doubt I would have gotten this far on my own." With one hand on the rough bark, Darshan slowly circled the tree trunk until he was on the opposite side. Around him, the swathes of green and grey blurred dreadfully.

Darshan put his back to the tree and gathered himself for this final push. Who knew that spending the better part of the day avoiding people and skulking through the undergrowth would be so strenuous?

All that was behind him, now. *Straight ahead.* Simple enough, all things considered. A rather refreshing change of pace. *Pass through the ferns.* There was no other requirement for this task.

He focused on wrapping a shield around him. It took much of his concentration and a touch of finagling to keep the upper half relatively solid but also malleable to allow for the leaves and grass he had to walk through. All whilst keeping the barrier close to his body and transparent.

Completed, he tucked what little focus he needed to divert into the back of his mind. The shield would remain in place as long as he didn't attempt to alter its very particular construction.

Darshan swayed slightly as he left the tree's support and strode towards the crowd waiting near the finish line. What he wouldn't give to be able to slink off to bed after this, but there was the customary feasting and dancing to be had and he wasn't about to leave Hamish to face that alone.

Others emerged from the forest, mere shadows on the edge of his vision. He twitched at the appearance of each new figure, waiting for the moment that one tried to attack him. None dared.

The crowd grew more pronounced as people rather than blobs of colour. Their cries echoed through the forest, brash and infectious. Even though he knew none of the cheers were for him, he couldn't help picking up his pace. The closer he got, the harder it became not to bolt for the finish.

His legs almost gave as he strode through the ferns. He released his hold on the shield, letting it dissipate. He had made it. Not fully under his own power, granted, but what did that matter? Only the final trial stood between him and Hamish now. And with his lover directing the arrow, there'd be but one outcome.

A hand fell upon his shoulder. "Wait right there, lass," a deep voice boomed behind him with all the gravity of an approaching thundercloud.

Darshan stiffened. It took all his willpower not to retaliate. Even one spark, one flicker, of magic would negate all he had been through these past few days.

"Look," the voice commanded.

Heeding the instruction, he twisted to find the man holding him pointed at the back of Darshan's boots. Dark specks adorned the brown leather. It didn't look like droplets of moisture. Had he been hit? *How?* He could've sworn every inch of him had been protected right up to when he had stepped through that row of ferns.

The man wiped at one of the spots, transferring it to his forefinger. "Same as the others," he said to a grey-haired woman.

Terror stole Darshan's breath. To be undone by a few spots... Surely that wouldn't be enough to fail the trial. It could very well have come from another competitor dripping dye as they trudged through the forest to announce their failure.

But no one declared him disqualified or called for the removal of his veil.

The elderly woman shook her head, the thick cords of her hair swaying heavily with the motion. "What are these trials coming to that foul play is all too common?"

"Foul play?" he squeaked.

The woman gave him a hearty pat on the shoulder. "It's all right dear. Someone, possibly one of the competitors, has marked the underside of the ferns."

Darshan frowned. When would someone have time to set up such a trap? He had seen no one near here yesterday except for the children. And surely, the absence of ink on one competitor would single out the perpetrator.

She pointed to the row of women standing just off to the side. "Everyone with ink on their boots has been allowed into the final trial."

His stomach sank. *Everyone*. What were the chances that another would have Hamish's accuracy? If the competition in the final test had been whittled to a handful, he would've considered it a slim one.

"With *only* ink on their boots," the man growled, holding up a cautioning finger. "*Only*. Let's check you over, lass."

Darshan stood still, almost holding his breath as the man tugged and poked at the borrowed attire. When the man started tugging at the sides of Darshan's trousers, it took every fibre of his being to stare straight ahead and pray a certain bulge wouldn't make itself known from within the folds of fabric.

His gaze flickered to the group of competitors standing to one side. *Former competitors*, he silently amended. Even without his glasses, the rainbow hue of their clothes was obvious in a fair number. It helped that every single one had their veils down, if not having removed the entire scarf. As Hamish had proclaimed, the disqualified group seemed to be the majority.

What of those who *had* made it through? He looked about, spying a handful of women near the front edge of the crowd who appeared to still be covering their faces. *Eight in all.*

Would he make nine?

A hearty pat on Darshan's back jolted him into the present. "It seems the Goddess favours you," the man rumbled. "Go join the lot over there." He jerked his thumb at the women standing at the forefront of the crowd. "Dinnae dawdle, Queen Fiona is about to address them."

Darshan staggered towards the crowd. The other eight competitors turned to eye him as he joined their ranks. Any hint of irritation at his presence was hidden in a swathe of shadow, but he couldn't imagine they were at all pleased.

"My dear noblewomen," Queen Fiona said, jerking his attention to where she stood at the edge of the crowd. Hamish stood on her left, his fiery hair a beacon in the blur of colours. "You blessed few have proven yourself to be fleet of foot and as cunning as the winter crow. Tomorrow, one of you will lay claim to my son and take their place as a mother within our clan."

Hamish took a step towards them and paused. They'd been informed at the beginning of the trial of how he would bestow his favour upon one from those who had made it through. A simple thing that rational people knew bore no weight to the skill displayed in the final trial.

Darshan's heart thudded as Hamish continued to dither about. Could his lover not identify him from the line-up?

Whilst he made a bit of a show in sauntering up and down the line, as if the task of selecting the right woman was proving difficult, Hamish's brow twitched every time he walked by Darshan.

It eased the tightness in his chest some, but the impatient vein in him did grumble for the man to hasten things along.

Finally, his lover halted before him. With very little ceremony, Hamish lifted the necklace over his own head and placed it around Darshan's neck. "I choose you," he said, barely loud enough for anyone but Darshan to hear. "May the Goddess favour your arrow tomorrow."

Darshan bowed his head in acknowledgement. Everything hinged on his lover and his ability to utilise a talent that he had only begun to consciously control. If Hamish missed the target, if they didn't time everything right, there was nothing Darshan could do about it.

His hand went to the ruby heart dangling from its simple chain. The gem was still warm with his lover's body heat.

And far heavier than any mere ruby had any right to be.

Chapter 39

Hamish stepped back, watching alongside his siblings as both the disqualified and safe competitors dispersed with the crowd. Whilst he couldn't pick out Darshan from them now, he had spied his lover making his way across to the finish line earlier. And had almost had his heart fair jump into his throat when one of the judges went and clapped a hand onto Darshan's shoulder.

Still, his lover had made it.

He clambered into the saddle and nudged his mare to follow his parents and brother, also returning to the castle via horseback. They remained silent as they rode through the forest, but it didn't take much deciphering to know they also mulled over the outcome. Especially his brother.

Where had *the ink come from?* That question hadn't stopped tumbling through his mind since the first otherwise unmarked competitor had stepped through the ferns. Who could've done it? *Nae the lads.* Whilst his nephews might've been devious enough, they were also aware of Darshan's participation and that if the addition of oddly similar marks across all the women hadn't been spotted... then Darshan would've been disqualified alongside everyone else. *And exposed.*

Nora joined them at the other end of the forest, along with the children. Gordon swiftly caught them up on what had happened at the finish line, he eyed their nephews the whole time.

Whilst the boys looked innocent enough, and suitably shocked at the attempted deception of ink, he was certain they hadn't been at their mother's side this whole time. For Darshan to have safely made it through the forest without fuss and with plenty of time to spare, had to mean his nephews were successful in locating the man and leading him through the forest. If they'd also been behind the ink on the ferns, then they would've warned Darshan. *And thrown suspicion on him.*

Why even use ink in the first place? It was a sloppy choice. None of the guards had been provided anything of the sort, not even something of the same colour, and the coating beneath the ferns was too deliberately thorough to be a mistake.

His musing had gotten him no closer to a possible culprit by the time their horses reached the castle courtyard. The stablehands rushed out to collect the animals as everyone dismounted.

His parents lingered near the castle doors. Travelling via horseback had made the journey shorter than those on foot. For them to wait and greet the clans upon their return was the proper thing to do. Expected of him, too.

Hamish strode up the stairs and flung the castle doors open wide. It earned him a glare and an exasperated huff from his mother, but he was well beyond the point of caring what she thought of his actions. He would've dragged Darshan before the clan members and snogged the man if he wasn't so sure that acting on the impulse would lead to a civil war.

Unhampered, he continued storming down the entrance hall on his way to the library. It was one of the few places that had remained quiet and, more importantly, devoid of women attempting to cosy up to him. Perhaps he would get lucky and Darshan would pay a visit to the spot.

"Where do you suppose the ink came from?" Nora asked, sidling closer to Hamish and matching his stride.

He shot her a puzzled frown. "What makes you think I would ken that?"

Shrugging, she turned her attention to their surroundings. They were the same stone walls, faded tapestries and ornamentations that'd been there since before their births. "*You* didnae try to—?"

He shook his head before she could finish the question. There was no telling what their mother would do if he was caught attempting to rig the trials, but the other clans wouldn't look favourably on it.

Behind them, Hamish caught the tail end of his brother's grumbling. He twisted to eye Gordon. His brother's face was as dark as a thunderhead. "What was that?"

"I think it might've been Sorcha," Gordon muttered.

"Why would you think it was her?" Nora asked.

"What?" Hamish said almost at the same time as their sister. "Just because we caught her down there yesterday?" And she hadn't been carrying any tools on her that would enable her to coat the underside of every fern along the line. Was there even that much ink in the castle?

Nora's head had whipped around before the last word could pass his lips. The usual mossy green softness of her eyes had turned to shards of jade. "And what were *you* doing there?"

Hamish tilted his chin, peering down his nose at his sister. Whilst he'd a high degree of belief that Nora wouldn't immediately rat out Darshan if told the truth, there was always a nagging doubt gnawing at the edges of his certainty. She did spend a lot of time at their mother's side. "I was helping Gor mind your lads whilst they practised hunting over proper terrain."

Her eyes narrowed further until they were mere gleams of reflected light beneath her lashes. "I can *almost* believe that."

"It's true!" Mac blurted.

As one, they turned towards the boy.

In his self-absorbed musing and seething over current events, Hamish hadn't noticed anyone else tailing them, but all four of his siblings' children huddled in the middle of the corridor. At the back, mostly hidden by her cousins, Sorcha stood hunched with a fist firmly pressed to her lips.

With little more than the twitch of his head, Gordon ushered them all through the library entrance. A glance revealed it to be empty, despite a desk being laden with books. An overturned inkwell sat amongst the papers strewn across the desk. Tiny, blotchy bootprints tracked from the desk to the cupboard where other inkwells were stored.

Hamish tugged open the door, certain of what he would find. Rows of capped inkwells greeted him. He lifted one of the glass jars from the shelf. Although the design etched into the outer surface obscured much, it was clearly empty. He checked one of the squat, bronze bottles. Unsurprisingly, it also suffered from a marked lack of ink.

He opened his mouth to announce his find to his siblings, only to be cut off by a reedy sob.

"Why did you nae tell me?" Gordon asked of his daughter. He stood over the girl, his arms folded across his chest. Unlike their mother's fiery blasts of anger, his brother radiated tired disappointment.

Sorcha barely seemed to acknowledge her father's presence. Her head was bowed, her cheeks red and tear-streaked. "I thought—" She sniffed, wiping the back of her hand across her nose. "I thought you'd try to stop me. Uncle Hamish doesnae want a wife. He almost died." No matter how she tried to contain them, her tears wouldn't stop. "Just like me mum… me sister."

Hamish winced. Sorcha might not have been old enough to remember the family she had lost to the man-killer bear, but it didn't mean she wasn't aware of their absence or didn't feel it.

"Oh, me wee lass." Gordon knelt, his arms wide.

The girl jumped into her father's embrace. "I thought that, if everyone was marked, then they wouldnae have the next trial and, if they didnae have that, then Uncle Hamish wouldnae need to marry." She peered at him over her father's shoulder. "I just wanted to help."

"I ken you did," her father murmured. "But you could've caused a whole mess of trouble."

It likely wouldn't have been too bad once it was revealed to be a child's prank. The worst case would've had everyone exposed for the final trial. And that also would've meant Darshan being taken right out of the contest, if not the kingdom, especially once his mother found out.

"Could've gotten a certain someone disqualified," Bruce mumbled.

Ethan snorted in clear agreement with his older brother. "That would've been a grand shot, 'Cha," he muttered. "Having him booted fair out of the running."

Bruce nudged him, both him and his youngest brother having gone wide-eyed.

"Him who?" Nora asked.

Hamish shuddered. The question came quietly enough, but carried a winter's worth of chill.

"W-well, I-I..." Ethan stammered, staring up at his mother as if she had become some terrible demon from the old tales. "Did I say *him*? I dinnae ken where *that* came from."

With one brow cocked, she gave her son an unconvinced hum. "What have you two done?" Even though she continued to stare down all three of her sons, Hamish knew that question was directed more at himself and their brother.

"If we tell you," Gordon replied before Hamish could think of a plausible lie. "You cannae go squealing to Mum."

She turned her sharp stare on them. In the scant light streaming through the windows, the resemblance to their mother lifted the hairs on his arms. "Leave us," she ordered the children, who were quick to heed the command. Only once the library door was firmly closed did she speak again. "So you two are responsible for Darshan competing, then?"

Hamish's mouth dropped open.

Beside him, their brother sputtered. "Goddess' teats! How did you—?" He sighed. "Aye."

"I ken, because I pay attention to details, you dolts. He wasnae in the guest room this whole time and I couldnae find him elsewhere." She paced before the book-laden desk, snarling a few choice words just under her breath. "I cannae believe you two would—"

Hamish ducked behind Gordon as she continued to rant. Using his brother's bigger frame as a barrier seemed like a good idea. When

Nora got this angry, there was no predicting what she would do, but hurling objects at the root of her rage was always an easy bet.

Sure enough, the empty inkwell whizzed by his shoulder to clang off the wall at their backs.

Gordon dove for the nearest shelf of books, leaving Hamish to find his own shelter behind another.

"Are you both dense?" she demanded. "Do you have any idea what you've set in motion? He cannae compete."

"There's nae rule against it," Hamish mumbled. *Just convention.* He dared to peek around the edge of the shelving. She didn't seem any less angry, but the lack of a book flying his way meant she was calming down.

"That's nae what I meant. *You—*" She jabbed a finger in his direction, then in Gordon's. "Do either of you have any idea who he is?"

Hamish opened his mouth to reply. Out of all the Udynean Darshan had taught him, translating his lover's title hadn't been in any of his lessons.

"He's Darshan *vris Mhanek*?" Gordon ventured before Hamish could admit his ignorance. He still hadn't the courage to face their sister.

She stopped her pacing and, with one hand planted firmly on her hip, rubbed her temple with the other. "And do you understand what that title translates to?"

Hamish hung his head. On the edge of his vision, he spied his brother doing the same. It was a title? Why hadn't he considered that earlier? Especially when he knew *Mhanek* translated to emperor. "Imperial prince?" What else could it be?

"So, Darshan's a prince," Gordon said. "Mum already made us aware of that. Does it matter? Darshan being the emperor's son just means he has the credentials to compete."

Groaning, Nora rolled her eyes. "Did neither of you think to do even a wee bit of research since his arrival? You've been learning Udynean from him," she growled, rounding on Hamish with such ferociousness that he flinched. "What's *your* excuse?"

He hunched his shoulders. "I didnae think it was a title?" Whoever heard of a title coming after the name? The people didn't go around addressing him as Hamish Prince. "I thought it was honorific. Something to say he was the *Mhanek's* son."

"It *is* to signify he's the emperor's son. But—" She shook her head and grumbled under her breath words that he was certain she would've disciplined her own husband for uttering. "He's nae *a* prince. He's *the* prince. I looked into it, as per his last threatening suggestion."

"He *threatened* you?" Hamish blurted. "*When?* And why?" Darshan didn't seem like the sort of man to do so without cause, but his sister also vastly preferred negotiation and compromise to outright threats.

She waved her hand as if threats were something she dealt with daily. "It was right before you lads all shot off on your little two-week trip. Leaving me to mollify Mum, I might add." She shot them both a look she had definitely inherited from their mother. "But the thing is, the *vris Mhanek*? A *vris* is more than just a son of the *Mhanek*. He is the *eldest* son."

And only men inherited the Udynean throne, meaning Darshan was... *The crown prince*. But that couldn't be right. Darshan couldn't be the eldest son, because if that were true—

He swallowed, unable to think coherently on what would happen there.

"I dinnae ken how you managed it," Nora said. "Honestly, I dinnae want to ken. But you cannae have the bleeding heir to the Udynea Empire competing for your hand."

He turned from his siblings to lean against the bookshelf, infinitely glad that it was there. *The heir*. Somehow, hearing another say it made it all the more real. He should've known. It should've occurred to him that the Goddess was being too peaceful in allowing this farce to continue.

She didn't need to intervene because the natural order of their own laws would stop them.

"Why would they send the crown prince as their ambassador?" Gordon asked his face scrunched in genuine puzzlement. "That doesnae make sense."

The question set a surge of hope through him. *They wouldnae do that*. At least, it would've been unwise of the Udyneans. Harm was unlikely to come to an ambassador within Tirglas, but anything could've happened whilst they were at sea. There had to be an older sibling. Darshan had admitted to having around a dozen—

Sisters. Just a twin and a gaggle of half-sisters. All younger than him. Never had his lover mentioned any brothers, not even a younger one. *Why did you nae tell me?* Had Darshan assumed Hamish already knew? That he wasn't so ignorant?

Was that the reason behind Darshan's reluctance to speak of children? Because his lover knew that, eventually, he would have to answer the duty of siring an heir? He thought back to Darshan's words when Hamish had mentioned the idea of children. *Obstacles*. Hamish had presumed his lover referred to the usual barriers that kept two men from having children or assassins. But no.

Nora stared at him for a while, her brows knitting together in the middle. Without speaking a word to him, she swung her full attention to their brother. "It does seem rather sudden, though."

Hamish snorted. *That's rich coming from you.* Whilst his brother's courtship of his wife had been slow and long, Nora's had been anything but. Calder's ship hadn't even been at the port for a week before he had proposed, an act which had been promptly shut down by their mother—because of her insistence on a union contest rather than the shortness of time they had known each other.

Whereas Darshan had been here for a month. And what had Hamish learnt of the man? Certainly not that he was first in line to inherit a whole empire.

Gordon shrugged, the lack of concern rolling down his body as his shoulders fell. "So Dar's the type who falls deep and fast. I seem to recall someone else who did just that."

Nora's mouth twisted as she glared at their brother. "Calder wasnae an imperial prince. Or a spellster. How do we ken 'Mish is nae under some sort of magical influence?"

Inhaling sharply, Hamish struggled to voice his opinion of such a question. All that came to his lips were a few garbled splutters.

"I already hit Darshan with that question," Gordon replied. "He said it wasnae possible for him."

"You *asked* him?" Hamish finally blurted.

"And you believed him?" Nora asked of their brother before Hamish could get an answer to his own question. He was certainly going to need one by the end of this.

"Why would he lie? If Hamish was ensorcelled, then what would Darshan have to fear from telling me that?"

"I cannae believe you actually asked him if he had put a spell on me," Hamish snapped. He shoved himself into his brother's face, ensuring that Gordon couldn't easily dismiss him. What else had his siblings been stirring behind his back? "I'm nae a child, I dinnae need you watching over me every move."

"If I hadnae intervened, Darshan wouldnae have entered the competition and you wouldnae have the chance you do right now." Gordon sighed. "Which is none. You cannae marry him. Or more to the point, *he* cannae marry *you*. If he wins you're just leaving to become a glorified bedwarmer. That is nae what I had in mind when I suggested he compete for your hand."

"It's nae the worst outcome," Hamish snarled back. "Maybe it's different in Udynea. Maybe men can marry men without having to fash about siring an heir." With so many sisters, surely one of them had a son who could take the throne after Darshan. Or maybe—he hoped—Nora was wrong.

"Maybe," Gordon echoed, doubt etching itself into his face. He clapped a hand onto Hamish's shoulder, drawing them close enough to throw both arms around him. "But you deserve better, 'Mish. You should nae have to settle for second best."

"I ken," he whispered, patting his brother on the back. But if that was the only thing on offer, even if things went wrong once they reached Minamist and he somehow lost Darshan despite everything they had done, anything would be better than staying here and living a lie.

~ ~ ~

Darshan picked at the remains of what had once been a full loaf of bread, using the crumbs to idly mop up the gravy on his plate whilst his gaze roamed the main hall. Packed as it was with people chatting along their tables and the merry music that neatly drowned out much of their words, it was oddly comforting.

Soon, most of the tables would be pulled aside for dancing, and he intended to depart before then, but right now he lingered in pleasant company.

He had acquired a small table in a quiet corner of the room and had been quite alone until Hamish, then Gordon joined him. They chatted aimlessly enough with Darshan forced to pretend he didn't know frivolous detail from fact. It was a facade he was well acquainted with in using the Crystal Court's tendency to underestimate those they deemed weaker.

Darshan swallowed another lump of beef. "I was unable to see much from my vantage point," he said, ensuring his voice carried that little bit extra for the flapping ears he had spied congregating around the nearby fireplace. "What exactly *were* they throwing at the competitors?"

"Animal bladders," Gordon replied around a mouthful of pork crackling he had plucked from Darshan's plate. "Filled with dye."

Whilst Darshan already had an up-close and personal experience with the contests, he nevertheless feigned a suitably aghast expression. "Well, that would explain some of the more colourful faces." Although their attire covered much, a handful had the misfortune of being hit right in the head. The dye had stained a number of them quite thoroughly.

"Aye," Hamish rumbled into his mug, rather empty of ale judging by the echo. "The poor lasses got hit hard in that run. But what can you expect when you place people with good throwing arms front and centre?" He gave Darshan the barest trace of a wink and waved a servant over to refill their drinks.

"It is my understanding," Darshan continued, choosing his words carefully now there were closer ears to spread gossip. "That the prize in question picks the final trial." He swung to Gordon, outwardly displaying little care that this act brushed his back against Hamish's shoulder. "If you do not mind my prying, what did *you* choose?"

"Hunting. Me wife was good at tracking and the like. Swifter than most around here." He plucked another small strip of crackling, chewing slowly. "Figured it would be the best way for her to come out on top."

"You had people slaughtering animals purely for the trial?" It was one thing to hunt to ease hunger, but he'd never been one to do so for sport.

Gordon shook his head. "It wasnae a killing hunt. There was a black ram. I tied a charm around one of his horns and sent him off into the forest in the morning, they had to bring him back alive before sunset with the charm still attached."

Hamish gave a snort that seemed to be a mixture of amusement and annoyance. He tossed a piece of the hard bread crust at his brother, bouncing it off Gordon's head. "You're forgetting the part where she did all this whilst pregnant with your eldest lass."

"Forgive me," Darshan said before either man could speak. "She was with child *during* the time she was competing?" He frowned at Gordon. "*Your* child?"

Pride lit up the man's face. "That she was. Roughly four months in."

"There shouldnae have been a contest," Hamish muttered, glaring into his empty mug as if it had done him personal injury.

"Well, Mum thought different."

"She always does."

Darshan hunched his shoulders, suddenly conscious of just how much smaller he was in comparison to the two brothers. If either one decided to be physically violent with the other, sitting between them was a less than ideal position. "I am mildly surprised Queen Fiona has not attempted to see you remarried, Gordon," he said in an effort to divert their attention without being too obvious.

"Mum willnae do that," Hamish answered. "He's cursed."

Darshan arched a brow Gordon's way. "Cursed?" That wasn't at all the answer he had been expecting. Did Tirglasians still believe in such?

"Aye. After losing me wife and eldest daughter, Muireall's clan declared that any woman who married me would be cursed to a similar fate." He shrugged. "I dinnae mind. Could've been worse, Sorcha could've been labelled as the cause instead of meself. I can handle the slight easily enough, but it would've been a mite bit harder for her to."

"I am familiar with that sort of blight on one's character." His twin sister, thanks to the sheer happenstance of being born second, was considered to be devoid of a soul. For most, it meant death. Anjali only lived because their father refused to be rid of any link to their mother, even the one that had inadvertently killed her.

But the stigma still followed her, extending to everything she did. She was considered unfit for marriage. Her very actions held no actual weight unless Darshan validated them, the servants and palace slaves choosing to believe items just up and vanished when they knew those very items belonged to her. Even if his twin had children, they would be considered to have been born without a mother.

He hated it, never mind that Anjali seemed not to care and used it all to her advantage. But there was little he could do on his own to overturn a belief that had been held for centuries.

Visibly shaking himself, Gordon swiped the final piece of pork crackling from Darshan's plate. "But for a more serious question." He took a bite of his stolen morsel before waving the end in Darshan's direction. "Are you saving that for later?"

"The food you have so blatantly stolen? Evidently not now you have slobbered all over it." He slid his plate to one side to get it beyond the man's reach. "And I would thank you to stop your pilfering."

Giving a low chuckle, Gordon popped the remaining bite of crackling into his mouth.

Hamish tilted to one side, bringing his mouth level with Darshan's ear. "He means the crumbs in your little beard."

A faint warmth touched his cheeks in reply. With one hand, he carefully brushed off the crumbs. How ever long had they been there?

Gordon snickered. "I can tell you've not grown anything longer than a bit of face-fuzz before. You looked a lot more like a Tirglasian when you let your whole jawline grow out."

"I shall take that as a compliment." Having left his shaving kit back in the castle during their fortnight of travelling, he had spent little time getting a decent look at his reflection. The cloister had only afforded him the briefest chance to groom himself to a respectable standard and once they'd returned to Mullhind Castle…

Being greeted by a shaggy-faced being in the mirror had paled under the rigours of travel and the drain on his magic. Trimming it into a semblance of what he had originally arrived with had been somewhat therapeutic.

"It looks like you've tried to kiss a billy goat and made off with his beard," Gordon teased, nudging him with an elbow.

Darshan stroked his goatee. It was a strange sensation to have it longer than his face. Not entirely unpleasant. "I dp not intend to keep it at this length once I return home." Whilst he preferred his men to have a certain ruggedness about them, he had, like most of the male nobility, leant towards a more clean-shaven appearance.

"That's a shame," Hamish murmured. "I quite like it. It's a good look on you."

He smiled up at his lover, trying to ignore the fluttering warmth the man's words had infused in him. "I am sure that certain sacrifices could be made." If things went to plan, he wouldn't be some port in a storm for whoever sought to curry favour with the *Mhanek*. Growing out a beard because Hamish favoured the look was a trivial inconvenience in light of all he had witnessed the man suffer through these past few weeks.

"I see they're already lining up for a dance," Gordon said. The man had rocked back in his chair to give a disdainful look over his shoulder at the women clearly waiting for Hamish.

Hamish also looked over his brother's shoulder and groaned. "That's all I need, another night of being groped."

Frowning, Darshan peered at the clump of women. To a one, they seemed hesitant, almost scared, to come any closer. Would any of them dare if Hamish chose to stay put?

Gordon gave his brother a sympathetic pat on the back. "It'll be over soon."

"I thought you enjoyed yourself last night," Darshan said, deftly skewering a scant mouthful of roast beef onto the tines of his fork before it slipped into the range of Gordon's questing fingers. "You seemed to be having fun."

"As long as I stuck to dancing with the married women, aye it was a pleasant evening. But to be fair..." Hamish leant closer. "Nothing could compare to dancing with you the other night."

Darshan smiled, the bubbly heat in his gut slowly pooling in his face. That night *had* been enjoyable and not because of where it had wound up.

"This is me now leaving the conversation," Gordon mumbled into his mug before pushing himself away from the table and onto his feet.

Hamish scoffed, rolling his eyes. "Oh come on, now. I was just about to regale you with how they've their own version of the four-step. Although, I dinnae remember most of the moves."

Gordon gave a hearty, rumbling laugh. "I'm surprised you remember anything after the amount of drink you sloshed down." He shook his head, still chuckling. "But I best be off." He clamped his hand down onto his brother's shoulder. "Dinnae get into any trouble in the meantime."

"You ken me," Hamish quipped, grinning.

"Why do you think I said it?" Gordon shot back, holding his brother in a headlock and rubbing his knuckles across Hamish's head. He released Hamish almost as swiftly and, giving a nod to Darshan, slipped into the crowd accumulating in the middle of the hall.

The man's absence left the pair of them alone and, had this been anywhere in Udynea, Darshan would've made use of the fact in a more intimate manner than was considered most unseeming even back home.

Instead, he pushed back his empty plate and contented himself with nursing his drink; a red wine he had procured from the inner city market. "I wonder if you have the time to speak about your nephew. The middle one… Ethan?"

Hamish shot him a suspicious look whilst half-engaged in tending to the mess Gordon had made of his hair. "What about him?"

Attempting to still the racing in his mind, Darshan considered the direction to take the topic. Outright revealing another's preferences wasn't typically a done thing, but the idea of the boy suffering like Hamish wouldn't stop invading his thoughts. What harm was there in a more directly probing question? The boy's uncle would be the last person to lead Ethan into a dangerous situation. "Are you aware he is like us?"

His lover's brows shot up. His hands dropped, leaving the fiery orange-red coils sticking out in all directions. "He told you that?" he whispered.

"Not directly." A faint pressure eased itself from around his chest. Not that he had expected an explosive reaction. Whilst Hamish was certainly surprised, the shock didn't seem to come from a place of ignorance. "I take it you have known for a while?"

Hamish nodded. "As does his mum and brothers. In fact, I think only me parents dinnae ken. We've all managed to keep it hush from them and anyone outside the family." He bowed his head and murmured, "It's one of the reasons I havenae left."

One? How many threads bound Hamish to this awful life? "I thought you said you chose to stay?"

"I did. I chose to stand in the way, to protect him."

"But you could not have left anyhow." Not if what Hamish and his siblings had told him about their mother's insistence on her children remaining within the clan lands was true. "Being forced to do the opposite of what makes you happy is not a choice."

Hamish grunted, his expression souring as he shook his head.

"You know," Darshan said, hoping to bring a touch of levity to the conversation. "The boy offered his own hand in lieu of yours… should I fail tomorrow's trial."

His lover gave another grunt, this one slightly more amused. "For you? He can bloody get in line. I'll damn well fight him if he tries muscling in on a man thrice his age. Lad's got a lot of growing up before he can start to think of such things."

Darshan hid the smile tugging at his lips behind the guise of taking a sip of wine. He'd had plenty of matrimonial offers, from men and women, but none had declared their intentions of fighting another for the right. "There is no need, I assure you. I made it quite plain that my interests lie with older men."

"Damn straight," Hamish grumbled before taking a final swig of his drink. "What had him get that idea into his head, I wonder."

"Something about wanting someone like me."

Hamish stared silently into his empty mug for some time before fixing those stunning blue eyes on Darshan. "Do you think any of them might show signs of..." He dipped his head and whispered, "...magic?"

A considering hum stuck in his throat. Darshan attempted to wash it down with a mouthful of wine. "A month ago," he said, deliberately choosing his native tongue to keep their conversation for their ears alone. "I would've told you that if their magic hadn't made itself known, then it would amount to nothing. But after what you've told me..." He shrugged. "Anything could be possible."

"That's what I thought you'd say." Sighing, Hamish got to his feet. "I suppose I best get to dancing if I dinnae want Mum objecting to me preference to stay here and talk." Straightening his overcoat and visibly smoothing the strain of distaste from his features, Hamish bowed a formal farewell to Darshan before greeting the gaggle of waiting women.

Darshan gripped the edge of the table in an attempt to keep himself calm whilst watching Hamish dance. The vast majority of the women were alike in their single-mindedness. Their hands just a touch too accepting of where they landed and their fingers clearly digging in that little bit deeper than was proper.

Their attempts certainly weren't going unnoticed by Hamish, either. How they managed to remain oblivious to their dance partner's discomfort was beyond Darshan's understanding.

The pungent scent of scorched wood hit Darshan's nose. He hastened to stand and brush his soot-covered hands clean on a nearby napkin. Satisfied no one had witnessed the minor loss of control, he stalked across the hall for the exit. He would wind up doing something regretful if he lingered for much longer.

How he wished he could step out there, take Hamish's hand and dance as if such a tame thing wouldn't be viewed upon as some great scandal.

But if he did, if he showed one flicker of emotion towards the man that couldn't also be construed as mere politeness, then everything they had been through these past few days would be for naught.

"*vris Mhanek*," a woman called.

Curiosity turned Darshan's head and halted his feet. "Now there is a title I have not heard for some time."

The woman in question stood from her curtsey, her flowing wheat-gold hair artfully framing her round and flushed face. The ruddiness of her complexion failed to hide the smudge of blue dye streaking right across her nose and eyes. "Have you nae had a chance to dance with anyone tonight?"

"Not as yet, although I feel that stance is soon to change." He held out his hand before she could speak further. "Would you care to?"

Her face froze save for the hasty flutter of her lashes. She dipped another curtsy, grasping his hand. When she stood straight again, her face was no longer so stiff. "I would be honoured, *vris Mhanek*."

They twirled around the room, their feet barely keeping up with the quick beat. Whilst the woman wasn't as graceful as some of his previous dance partners, she was fleet enough to avoid being trodden on and seemed to know the moves well enough to not have to look down at every turn. Unlike himself.

On the edge of his vision, he spied Hamish still dancing with those he plucked from the seemingly endless line of women. Most of them would undoubtedly be those who, like his own dance partner, had failed the last trial.

"I hear you've negotiated new trade deals with our queen," the woman said.

He smiled to himself. It had been just over a month since he had set foot in this wretched land for that purpose. It seemed like such a simpler time. "Our negotiations are still in the process." Not that he fancied his chances of continuing down that path once the final trial was over. "Sadly, they stalled once this contest was announced."

"Really? They say you've been here for weeks. Surely some things have been finalised."

Chuckling, Darshan ignored the blatant attempt to garner information. "I see the gossip wheel runs just as smoothly here as in Minamist. What else does it say of me?"

"That you are..." She wrinkled her nose. "Or should I say *were* having an affair with his highness."

"Oh really?" He managed to hide much of his shock in a laugh. "Which one?" He had a fair idea, but no point in handing over any morsel that gossip could use to his disadvantage.

"Prince Hamish."

"*Him?*" His throat almost closed on the word. Had he been so uncaring towards the idea of hiding their romantic entanglement that he'd inadvertently announced the depths of it? "He is to be wed after this, is he not? It would be foolish on everyone's part for him to behave in such a manner."

"So you two are nae having it off? They say you kissed him in the first day of your arrival."

"The second day," he murmured, coming to a halt. "But that was an error on my part. I mistook his friendliness as something else entirely. Believe me, I am not having some clandestine affair with his highness." He could hardly call it secret when almost the entirety of his lover's family seemed to be aware of the situation. "Such things could lead to feuds and it would do none of our lands any good to embroil them in a war."

She seemed to consider his words, those dark eyes narrowing to mere slits.

Darshan drew all of his focus to this one woman. With his magic buzzing through his body in search of an outlet, a gentle tap to her temple with a finger would be enough to knock her out. He would need to time it in order for the act to look as though she had fainted. Perhaps if he—

"I must've heard wrong," the woman said, shrugging. She stepped back and gave him another curtsy. "My apologies, *vris Mhanek*. I meant no offence."

"And none was taken." He watched her passage as she left his side to flutter from one group of gossipers to the next. He would have to watch that nothing untoward reached the queen's ears before tomorrow's trial.

After that, they could gossip amongst themselves however they pleased.

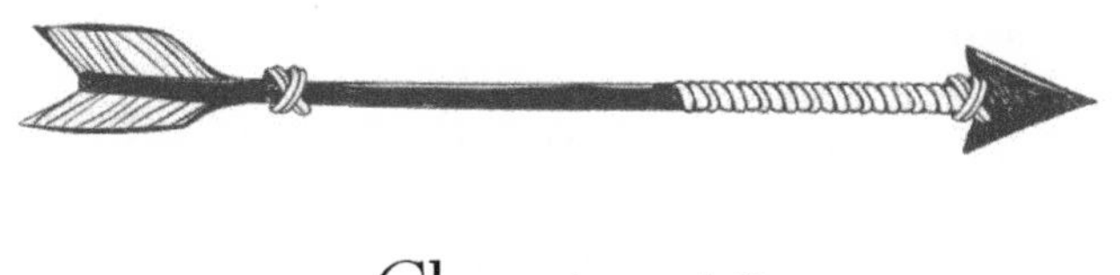

Chapter 40

Hamish sat perched on the edge of his bed, his face buried in his hands. It was the middle of the night. He should've been sleeping, preparing himself for the world to fall apart tomorrow. But even the Goddess would have no luck in seeing him succumb to something as simple as a light slumber.

The hollering of angry voices assaulted his ears. His family had been arguing outside his door for some time, but the shrill sounds were worse now that Nora had left the door open. He didn't recall her exiting his room. Where would she go? To face those in the corridor outside? He couldn't hear her amongst the others.

One voice rose above the rest. Not one of his family members, but no less difficult to deal with. The Goddess knew *he* had already tried to reason with her. "I demand you make me his bride." The woman's screeching sounded like an alley cat on heat. "You ken how they found us."

Hamish knew the exact circumstances his brother had barged in on. He had been bailed up in a corner in just his smalls whilst a pale-haired woman with a smudge of blue dye across her face tried to throw herself at him.

Others had arrived not long after, but none had been there for the worst of it. Of waking to find a strange woman sharing his bed, her hands inches from the hem of his smalls.

He shuddered. Nothing in the world would be able to scrub the image from his mind. He hadn't known that his mother had opted to leave his door unguarded since the first competitor had arrived. None of them had known.

It was just dumb luck no one had tried entering his room before now.

He should've done more than just stand there. He should've

pushed her away or bolted for the door. In his panic, his only concern had been in having the woman not touch him.

"It's the law," the woman continued.

Hamish hugged himself, softly rocking as dread settled in the pit of his stomach. He squeezed his eyes shut and silently prayed that no sound of agreement passed his mother's lips. He knew she was out there, as was his father. They all ignored him for now. Only Nora had come to check on him and she was gone, he hadn't even heard her arguing with the woman since leaving.

"Maybe that's true in *your* clan lands," Gordon growled. "But nae here. And certainly nae when it's a contest of skill and arms. One you've already failed." That had to be the fifth time his brother had made such a point. It should've been the end to the conversation. If Hamish had been a willing participant in the union contest, at least. If he had any interest in women, it still wouldn't have mattered if she opted to sneak her way into his bed after being disqualified.

Except their main barrier was less the woman and more—

"The young lady has a point," his mother replied.

Where his father could only mumble barely-audible opinions on the matter, his mother seemed hesitant to give any order that would see the woman—his molester, if he was honest with himself and the situation—evicted from the castle or imprisoned in Mullhind's jail. Even for the duration of the contest.

"You cannae be thinking of doing this to him," Gordon snarled. "After all your insisting that 'Mish abide by the rules of the contest, you cannae possibly be considering giving in to this ridiculous demand."

Although Hamish strained to hear any sort of response from his mother, only the heavy thump of his brother's pacing followed.

"If you saw nae need for the union contest to end when Muireall was in the running for me own hand," his brother continued. "And need I remind you she was *pregnant* at the time, then you shouldnae see a need to end it now."

As horrid as the idea seemed, Hamish could see a twisted reasoning behind stopping the contest here. His mother knew he wouldn't be at all agreeable to the consummation part of marriage. If this woman was willing to go this far, then maybe she would—

He couldn't even finish the thought before bile crept up his throat. He swallowed hard, tears burning the corners of his eyes.

"We were found *in bed together*," the woman repeated. Hamish could almost picture her lifting her chin to glare up at the very prince who would one day rule as king. The woman had to know, yet continued to insist she'd a greater standing by way of law.

Madness. Whatever clan she hailed from sat dangerously close to committing treason if this was what they taught their people.

"That's *nae* true," Gordon stressed. "And before you utter another falsehood, you were both clothed. *And* you were only there because you didnae follow the rules. You ken he didnae do a bloody thing to you."

The woman's voice became garbled sound as she seemed to struggle for an answer. "You!" she shrieked. "It's bloody true! You're—"

"*What* is *he* doing here?" his mother demanded over top of the woman's raving.

Hamish lifted his head. *He?* Did she mean Darshan? With loathing thick in her voice, surely his mother could mean no one else. But the last he had seen of the man was when they'd both left the dancing up to those with more energy and less sense. Darshan had even been bold enough to sneak a quick goodnight peck before they had parted ways to their respective beds.

"Never you mind him, Mum," Nora said, her voice far quieter than their brother's but no less incensed.

If she had spoken further or another had replied, Hamish heard little. His focus was rooted entirely on the figure standing in the middle of the doorway.

Dar...

Did he want the man here? Seeing him like *this*?

His lover's gaze drifted about the room, his expression neutral as he seemed to take in the assortment of clutter as if he had never seen the space before. Did he wish he was elsewhere?

Hamish scrunched himself into a tighter ball. How much had the man been told?

Darshan finally glanced at him, his features stiff with concern, before turning to Nora. "Who found him?"

"Gor did."

Hamish nodded slightly at his sister's reply. Ever since they were boys, Gordon's room had never been that far from his. That his brother had been awake enough to be alerted by Hamish's screams was a fact he would be forever grateful of.

Darshan arched a brow at her in silent query, but Nora didn't appear ready to divulge more without the man having to outright ask. She must've woken him with some sort of explanation involving Hamish for him to be here. Clearly, she hadn't given him much in the way of details.

Shrugging, she indicated Darshan enter and left them alone.

His lover sat on the bed. He glanced at Hamish, the sleep-ruffled mess of his hair hanging almost morosely in front of his face. His lips parted, only for them to close. He looked for all the world like someone desperately trying to think of the words to say and falling short.

What *could* be said?

Out in the corridor, no less muffled with the shut door, Gordon had barely paused in his arguing. “Nae, *you* are the one in the wrong here, sneaking into me brother’s room and right into his bed.”

“I was *invited*,” the woman snapped back.

Nora scoffed. “Whilst he slept?”

“He was nae asleep.”

“Me brother says otherwise.”

“So you’re the type to believe a man’s word over a woman’s.” An oily slyness took her voice. The sound trickled coolly down Hamish’s spine.

There was a hissing intake of breath. Hamish didn’t need to see his sister to envision the white-hot rage tightening her features. “What I believe is me brother. And I doubt he gave you a glance never mind an invite. How do we ken you were nae there to assassinate him?”

“Clearly not,” his mother answered whilst the woman gabbled incomprehensibly. “Otherwise he would already be dead. I think that we should listen to her without throwing baseless accusations.”

Like a crippled ship in the tide, Hamish sank his face into his hands. A single, snivelling whine shuddered through him.

Darshan gently laid a hand on Hamish’s back, cautious as though he expected the flesh beneath his fingers to pull away upon contact.

Hamish sagged against the man. More sobs shook his body. Not loud bawling, but whimpers that were almost ashamed to reach anyone’s ears.

Darshan pulled him closer, pressing a cheek to Hamish’s temple. He whispered soothing sounds—no words, just a constant drone of noise that blocked all but the loudest arguing—and slowly rubbed small circles into Hamish’s back.

The faint sheen of his lover’s magic-made barrier shimmered around them. Did it also lend a hand in the sudden silence?

All at once, Darshan’s whole body stiffened. His breath seemed to still, but his body vibrated. His grip tightened around Hamish’s shoulders, his lover’s fingers curling possessively into linen and wool.

“*What* are you doing?” his mother demanded, the usual sharpness of her voice softened by the shield.

Hamish lifted his head from Darshan’s shoulder to the vision of his mother filling the doorway.

Nora slithered into the room to stand before their mother. Her broader frame neatly blocked Hamish’s view. “More for ’Mish than you’ve ever done.”

"Go back to bed, Mum," Gordon insisted. "We'll handle this, same as always."

"I think I should be the one to do that," Darshan said before anyone else could utter a word. His grip on Hamish's shoulders tightened. "In all honesty, I am probably the only one here who can relate to this."

"Aye," Nora mumbled, scrubbing her face. "It is probably for the best."

Over her shoulder, Hamish spied his brother nodding. Even his father—having been little more than a silent hulk since his arrival—seemed to agree.

The long intake of his mother's breath before she spoke sliced through their collective murmurs like a sword. "He—"

His father laid a firm hand on his mother's shoulder. "Come on, lass. The last trial is due to be won in the morning. He's done as you've asked. Let him have this." He turned Hamish's mother, even as she stammered to object, and guided her out of the room.

Nora followed, giving a worried glance over her shoulder before shutting the door. They were…

Alone. No angry voices lurking on the other side of the door. No fear of being caught, of being locked away whilst Darshan was shipped far from here like disease-ridden cargo.

He was free of all that had plagued him for the first time in a good long while. *Until tomorrow*. Then he would be expected to play the same ruse he had been forced into for years.

Hamish flopped forward, his head in his hands. His father was right. Tomorrow was the last trial. Everyone would be waiting for a new addition to the royal clan to be named. *He* was supposed to be aiming at his truest for not only himself, but Darshan. He'd barely been able to manage the latter in the time given to them.

Could he do it also whilst sleep-deprived?

"I would ask if you were all right," Darshan said. "But I feel we both already know the answer to that."

"Aye." Even to his own ears, the word was cracked and shaky. Hamish lifted his head, peering out through coils of unbound hair. "But I feel a wee bit better now you're here." He took a deep breath, his whole body feeling as though it doubled in size. "I'll be fine. Glad I wear me smalls to bed, but fine."

Darshan's brows lowered. His lips twisted, clearly trying to keep his disbelief from displaying on his face. And failing drastically. He returned to rubbing Hamish's back. "You know I am here for you, right?"

Hamish nodded. "Have you really woken up with a strange woman in your bed?"

Grimacing, Darshan rubbed at his chin. "That was an outright lie," he mumbled. "But you needed quiet. I am afraid the only vaguely comparable scenario was the time my father sent two women to my chambers. They did no more than extend the offer of joining them when I discovered them fornicating on my bed."

Try as he might to avoid the cringeworthy image, it burrowed into his brain and ran its needle-like claws down his spine. Hamish hugged himself tighter. If Darshan's father was *that* desperate for his son to sire children, then perhaps Nora had the right of it on where the man stood when it came to royal succession. "Are—?"

His question was silenced by his lover giving him another hearty pat on the back.

"Speaking of bed, you need to rest. A lot of things hinge on tomorrow's outcome and keeping your focus sharp will require a clear head."

Hamish twisted where he sat, fingering the blankets. His limbs were leaden, but his mind endlessly tumbled over the event. "I cannae sleep." It wasn't merely the idea of doing so alone, for Darshan would undoubtedly stay if he asked. "Nae here. I just... cannae..."

Darshan nodded, his understanding expression remaining the same even as Hamish continued to ramble. "Come share my bed, then." His fingertips slid across Hamish's shoulder and down an arm until they were clasping hands. Linking their fingers, Darshan gently led the way to the door.

His lover's hand remained firmly joined with Hamish's as they walked through the corridors. They met not a single soul in their passage, even though Hamish was certain there would be the odd servant still up and about. *Or a guard.*

The guest quarters were warm. The embers of a burnt-out fire still cast a faint, red glow in the hearth.

Darshan strode across the room as if he had always lived here, lighting an array of candles set on the bedside table with the snap of his fingers. He flung open his travel chest with barely a touch and hauled out a small wooden box.

Hamish trailed after his lover, squinting at the sudden brightness. The light threw weird, wavering shadows upon the walls and glittered across the various glass vials and metal bottles his lover withdrew from the box.

He idly wandered the room, passing the dressing mirror standing tall in the corner near Darshan's travel chest. How long had his features seemed so tight and dark? The whole time? He glanced at the reflection of Darshan as the man continued to fuss with a vial of some powdery substance. *Nae wonder he's been thinking the worst.*

"Do sit down, *mea lux*," Darshan said as he returned the vial to the box and resumed his rummaging. "I shall not be long." He set aside a small glass bottle of dark powder to take up the mug and pitcher.

Hamish obeyed, shucking what little clothes he had managed to pull on once the woman had been distracted by his brother.

As soon as his backside was planted on the edge of the bed, his thoughts started to pace. Like a rabid boarhound worrying at a flock of sheep, his mind refused to let go of the troubles tomorrow would bring. "What are we going to do about the trial?"

Darshan set down the bottle he'd been pouring into the mug. "What do you mean? Nothing has changed." He frowned. "Has it?"

"Maybe." All manner of things could change what they had planned for. His mother could finally realise Darshan was participating, the woman who had molested him could announce her findings—even without knowing the truth about Darshan, throwing suspicion would be enough—or something even worse could rear its head. He didn't know. "Even with sleep, I'll be in nae fit state to focus and you're nae going to win without me."

His lover gave a grin that Hamish suspected was mostly bravado. "What sort of encouragement is that to give your chosen suitor?"

"I ken you're trying your best at a skill you've nae much practise with, but many of our people are good at hunting. They have to be. They'll hit the target, too." Maybe not dead centre, but that wouldn't matter when Darshan, for all his enthusiasm, hadn't been able to even once land a hit on his own. "And even if you did... me mum doesnae like the idea of you being near me."

Scoffing, Darshan returned to the mug. "*That* is quite apparent."

"I'm pretty sure that she's nae going to let you take me anywhere."

His lover continued to fuss with his concoction, humming softly. "Your mother is capable of confining her poisonous tongue when it is warranted, I witnessed that tonight. Maybe she will also see the benefits of having a son in the Crystal Court." Those dark brows lowered as he strode to Hamish's side with the mug. "But I *will* win and I *will* take you from this place." He offered up the mug. "Drink this."

Hamish peered at the contents, tipping the mug until the candlelight illuminated the cloudy water. The grainy remains of the dark powder floated on the surface. "What is it?"

"You need sleep."

"I dinnae think I can." Even away from his room, the thought of leaving himself in such a vulnerable state was unthinkable.

"Which is why you need to drink."

Hamish eyed the mug's contents anew. The man had made a sleeping draught? Steeling himself, he took a swig. Not an unpleasant taste. Swishing the remainder around to help mix the powder, he swallowed the rest. "How soon will this put me to sleep, then?"

"Not at all. Not at that dosage. But it should relax you enough to allow you to drift off on your own." He laid a hand on Hamish's shoulder, the pressure gently encouraging him to lie back on the bed. A few more of such actions and Hamish found himself neatly tucked beneath the blankets. "And do not worry about any interruptions to your slumber. I shall be here the whole time."

"I didnae think you'd be dancing along the eaves," Hamish murmured, the words sounding slightly drowsy to his own ears. He snuggled deeper beneath the blankets. His lids lowered and reluctantly opened. The dreamless dark of slumber beckoned him.

Another blink, even slower than the last. Darshan was right. He could close his eyes for a little while without anything untoward happening. *Just a wee while*. An hour would see him refreshed.

His lids slid closed. Hamish no longer attempted to fight their descent. The warm, welcoming darkness of sleep sealed itself around him.

He drifted, dreamlessly.

Safe.

Chapter 41

Hamish rolled onto his back and stared up at the ceiling of the guest chambers. How long had he slept? He peeked under his upraised arm at the window. The velvet blue of night still brushed the sky, but there was a flush of pink suggesting dawn wasn't too far away.

The faint crinkle of a page being turned caught his ear. Darshan sat on the other half of the bed with his legs stretched out. A globe of light hovered over his shoulder and a book sat open on his lap.

His lover glanced over as Hamish went to sit up, a faint frown lowering his brow before the creases morphed into ones of happiness. He carefully closed the book and set it on the bedside table. "I take it we are feeling better?"

Hamish nodded, warmth flooding his face. "Have you been awake this whole time?" Watching over him like a parent with a storm-shook child.

"I have dozed here and there, but for the most part, yes. Do not worry, I shall be fit to compete." He grinned, although the corners of his mouth wavered slightly. "And, once I win, I plan on taking you straight to Minamist."

"Sounds prudent." He didn't think his mother would allow them to stay for a second longer than it took for them to gather their things. If she gave them that small measure of grace.

Darshan chuckled breathlessly. "I actually cannot wait to see the look on my father's face when he learns that his heir finally married. He has rather resigned himself to the idea that I will not do so and—"

"So, it's true," Hamish murmured. "Your title, *vris Mhanek*? It means you're the crown prince." Small wonder the man's father despaired of his son chasing after men.

Mild surprise, mixed with a heavy dose of confusion, slackened his lover's face. "In a manner of speaking, I suppose so. Directly translated, it means *Eldest Son of the Great One.*"

Eldest. He let his arm thump back onto his forehead. Everything his sister had told him was true. Darshan had risked exposing his true nature, and quite possibly starting a civil war, for a future neither of them could have. The heir to the throne couldn't take a husband.

"Why did you nae tell me?" Hamish whispered, the lump in his throat barely letting him form the words. "Why wasnae that one of the first things you taught me?" Then he wouldn't be sitting here with his hopes shattered. He wouldn't have helped Darshan back himself into an impossibility.

Darshan's eyes narrowed. "Why do you speak as if this is new to you? I thought you were aware what *vris Mhanek* meant, that it was the one Udynean phrase you already knew."

He shook his head. "I thought it just meant prince." He should've known better than that. Darshan had never once made mention of any brothers. *Only sisters.*

His lover's lips flattened until his mouth was a thin, narrow slit barely distinguishable beneath his moustache. "My apologies for thinking they taught you anything about my people beyond the negatives. If I had known, I would have divulged it. I was hardly keeping the fact I am *vris Mhanek* a secret. How did you find out?"

"Nora told me after the last trial." Where she had dug up the information, he didn't know. "One thing didnae add up for us, though. Why would your father send his heir to the other side of the continent to negotiate trade?"

Darshan nonchalantly lifted a shoulder. "I told you that already. This was meant to be my punishment."

Hamish had vague memories of that conversation. There'd been so many things that had swamped the *Mhanek's* motive behind sending his son so far away. *To a land where men didnae lay with men.* He recalled the reason for that rightly enough. "For sleeping with a betrothed man." That had sounded barely plausible when Darshan had been just another of royal blood. Being the heir made the punishment seem even less likely.

"That part was the least of my father's issue with my actions." His lover's expression was akin to the looks Hamish would expect from one of his nephews after being caught doing something they shouldn't. "The feud I inadvertently caused rather upset generations of careful marriage arrangements. I think I may have cost an entire household to lose their estate. And possibly their lives."

"Marriages in Udynea are arranged?" It wasn't unheard of in some of the more rural communities, and he supposed the union contest could be viewed in such a manner, but marriages in Tirglas were typically done without formal arrangements.

"Not all of them. But everything in the nobility hinges on power. Specifically the strength you can call upon. Families with strong magical bloodlines unite to make them even stronger. That sort of union does not generally happen without a bit of nudging in the right direction. Most arrangements are made after the first display of a child's magic."

"Did *you* have a betrothed?" Would he be expected to confront them for Darshan's hand?

Darshan shook his head. "No one in my family was promised. My father is a rare example of marrying for love and he still carries a soft spot for it. He has helped settle spouses for a few of my sisters who sought marriage, but..." He briefly toyed with his rings before his hands slowly parted. "Once he wanted me to take a wife. Now, all he wants is for me to produce the next link in the chain."

An heir. Something Darshan just wouldn't get by being with him. Hamish rubbed the heel of his hand across his cheek. He'd been so close to believing this could work. "And there's nae one else to take the throne if you didnae have a bairn?"

"I am my father's eldest child and only son. The next in line, if I die today, is my nephew. Sadly, from my eldest half-sister." Disgust soured the normally sure line of his mouth. "Who would undoubtedly take great satisfaction in hustling her son to such a prestigious height."

Princess Onella. It had to be for Darshan to speak so disparagingly of the woman. The same person his lover credited the scar in his torso to. If she was willing to injure her own brother, then only the Goddess knew what sort of ruthless manner she had cultivated in her son. Certainly not the sort of person to leave an empire in the hands of. "You have to forfeit the union contest."

"I do *not*! And I shall not." Darshan shuffled around on the bed to kneel before him. "What has gotten into you?"

"You're the bloody heir to the Udynean throne," Hamish mumbled, hoping that would be enough. He should've known better than to think the Goddess would ever want someone like him happy.

"I believe we have already established that." He hugged himself, running one hand over the other arm as if struck by a sudden chill. "I thought I was your chosen spouse?" A queasiness took his face and, for a second, Hamish thought the man might just vomit. "Are you saying you do not want me because of what happened? Because the fault there does not lie with you."

"It's nae that at all, me heart." By the Goddess, his very soul ached at the thought of Darshan leaving his side. "But we— *You* cannae do this. You're the heir to an empire. You need an heir of your own." Such a requirement was even greater than for himself as a prince who was currently seventh in line. "Let's be realistic here, I cannae give you a child. You need a wife for that."

"This again?" Darshan huffed. Pushing the wire frames further up his nose, he peered down at Hamish as if his entire ancestry had been offended. "Well, I do not want a wife. I want *you*."

Hamish searched his lover's face for some sign that the man jested. Nothing. Of course there was nothing. Darshan had proven a multitude of times how much he desired Hamish.

Darshan chuckled. "Gods, if you could see the look on your face." He shook his head, a delightfully smug smile playing on his lips. "Allow me to make this entirely clear for you: I would not have put myself through this great malarkey if I did not find you so... compatible. And before you start rolling those stunning blue eyes of yours, I mean more than when we are fooling around." He shuffled about on the bed, planted himself before Hamish. "I love you far too much to leave you in this miserable place. I *am* going to win this, then I shall drag you back to my country like the savage I apparently am and marry the living daylights out of you. And there is nothing you can do to stop me." He bent over Hamish, pushing his face close. "What do you have to say about *that*?"

"Marry the living daylights out of me?" Hamish echoed. "I think some of that might've gotten lost in translation there."

"No, I do not believe so." He sat back with a sigh. "Look, I spent a little time in the library the other night. After we danced," he clarified.

"Even after I had...?"

Darshan grinned. "Well, I had to find some way to calm down afterwards. You did leave me so terribly flustered that, really, my only other option beyond my failed attempts at archery would have been to hunt you down and repay you in kind."

Although his lover continued to speak, Hamish was only vaguely aware the man's mouth continued to move. All rational thought had been engulfed by the mental vision of Darshan on his knees and orally servicing him in a similar manner. That tongue. Those lips. Would he feel the moustache? What—?

"Are you listening or am I merely airing my teeth?"

Hamish mentally shook himself, barely having the forethought to give a little nod. It was probably for the best that his lover hadn't taken that line of thinking. "I heard you."

The look Darshan shot was one of utter disbelief. Nevertheless, he continued, "My search led me to a small passage on Tirglasian customs. Wedding one's specifically." He sat back on his heels. "I understand that your Goddess is mostly concerned with bringing forth new life and her priests demand an understanding in the matter of children before vows are taken." He absently toyed with a ring before the fingers dropped to pat Hamish's leg. "You really do not need to concern yourself with it. I shall have it all in hand once the time to think of that comes."

"Except you havenae told me. It's very well saying you have ideas and that you need time to think them over, but you dinnae say what any of it entails."

Darshan bit his lip. "You are right, I have left that rather vague. In all honesty, I would need to return home first. There are people I would have to speak with before I could confirm anything and I do not wish to promise you what I cannot deliver. Suffice to say, there are ways that even your people would be capable of utilising."

"Speak to people? What about *this* person?" Hamish tapped his chest. He didn't need a promise that there would be children, if they ever came to that point, but they both needed to be sailing the same boat and that meant discussing it. "Having an heir is one of your duties as the crown prince."

Those hazel eyes widened. The faint remains of kohl around their edges making them stark. "Please, no," his lover whispered. "Do not do that. Do not sit there sounding like my father."

"Maybe he's right."

Darshan wrinkled his nose. His lips twisted as if he had swallowed something unpleasant.

Hamish probably would've given a similar look had someone told him that his mother really did know all the Goddess' secrets. Taking pity on his lover, he nudged the conversation in a slightly different direction. "I ken you dinnae like to talk about it, but have you ever given it any thought before?"

Giving a considering hum, Darshan's head rocked from side to side. "Once, I suppose. Back when I was young and idealistic. My father was a little more forgiving and less insistent then. I had met this man who was, in my father's eyes, perfectly capable of carrying a child to term."

Hamish scrunched up his nose. "What?"

A flicker of confusion creased Darshan's face. "You do not have—?" He sighed. "No, I suppose that sort of knowledge would be scarce," he muttered, seemingly to himself before continuing in a slightly louder voice. "Vihaan is *paalangik*. I…" He frowned. "I know no other word for it. He had the physical requirements to conceive and carry a child had he the inclination."

Not wishing to steer his lover off course now that he appeared willing to speak, Hamish silently waved the man on.

"Which was part of my point. He was a nice enough man, and we might have had something akin to romantic feelings for each other had we been left to ourselves. We were friends for some time before we attempted something deeper and…" Shaking his head, Darshan chuckled. "Honestly, we had barely gotten any further than a few chaste kisses here and there before my father—" Mentioning the man swiftly sobered him. "I knew Vihaan had no desire for children, that the idea of carrying one terrified him, but my father saw things differently. He never took Vihaan's feelings into account and, ultimately, it was too much. Vihaan fled the court and, I believe, he oversees one of his family's orchards near the Obuzan border." His gaze dropped. "I have not spoken with him since. I lost a friend because of my father's preference to focus only on the possibility of future grandchildren rather than our happiness."

"So what's going to happen down the road? If we marry—or even if we dinnae marry and continue as we are—" It seemed the option less likely to upset anyone in Minamist. He didn't mind remaining as Darshan's lover if he couldn't be the man's husband. "—and your father dies? You clearly dinnae want your nephew to inherit the throne, but do you really expect me to just stand aside whilst you—?"

Goddess, he couldn't even say it. The very thought made him sick.

"No," Darshan whispered. "There are other ways to become a parent."

"Adoption, you mean?" It wasn't generally a thing people talked about, but there were families who suddenly had one less babe to feed whilst another miraculously gained a member without the mother showing any signs of pregnancy.

"That is one, although I am certain that not only my father would baulk at the idea of me not having a least one child of my blood. What I meant is there are a number of choices and none of them require me to lie with anyone but you. One you would not be familiar with as it is… new."

"Didnae hedge. I ken it involves magic. Just tell me."

His lover stared at him, startled. "How—?"

Hamish laughed; a deep rumble that made his stomach ache. "The method of making bairns is as old as the land. The only way it could be new is if it's nae natural. That would mean magic."

Darshan slowly nodded. "A… little, yes." His lover's admission carried a heavy dose of caution, the tone not quite void of reluctance.

Magic. Something that would no doubt involve the two of them, otherwise Darshan could've done it far earlier. Taking a deep breath, Hamish blurted the first thought that came to mind, "Are you thinking I'll object?"

"Well, if you do not mind me saying so, you look rather aghast at the prospect."

"The way you've been acting, all the secrecy and deflection, I half expected to find you're planning on impregnating me." A horrid thought overtook all else as he spoke. "You havenae already done that, have you?" He had been feeling a bit weird the last couple of days. Slightly bloated.

Darshan stared back at him, those hazel eyes bulging. A snort of hastily-muffled laughter erupted from his lover. He bent over, grasping fistfuls of blanket. "Have I already done *what?*" he managed between fits of coughing and gasping.

"You dinnae have to laugh. I dinnae ken what a spellster's capable of."

Darshan grinned. "Not *that*." He crawled across the bed. "I do not think you—" He shook his head and threaded his fingers through his hair, scratching his scalp before fisting a great handful of dark curls. "Using magic on a living being is rather limited to what the body can already do naturally."

"Like a man taking on, and defeating, an opponent that should've been too strong for him?"

His lover scoffed. "That was a simple adjustment pertaining to my healer studies. It heals tears in the muscle at the same rate as they are torn. I cannot maintain it for long before it starts to take its toll." Darshan ran a finger up Hamish's chest, creating little spirals along the way. "But fortunately I did not have to."

Hamish mumbled what he hoped sounded like an agreement, his thoughts more focused on his lover's actions rather than the man's words. "Are other spellsters capable of making someone carry a child, then?"

"*Only* if you have the specific equipment that I am quite certain you are lacking. Besides..." His lover curled against Hamish's chest as if he wasn't lying near-naked on the man's bed. "If it was possible for one man to impregnate another, I would much rather take on that risk than leave it to you."

Hamish absently wrapped his arms around Darshan's shoulders. With his mind trying to figure out just how the conversation had landed here, he managed little more than a light, "Oh?"

"My healing capabilities would be enough to ward off most dangers and, perhaps, even keep me from dying. But that is not an issue." He took a deep breath, his chest pressing against Hamish's. "What I plan on doing is making use of a new procedure from Niholia. Quite expensive, although that is hardly a problem. The question is whether my sister would be willing to carry the child."

"Your sister?"

"My *twin*, specifically. I am assuming she has the relevant requirements. It is not something one generally asks people, not even siblings. If not, then I shall have to search elsewhere for someone suitable."

Hamish frowned at the ceiling. He had attempted to follow along with the explanation, but his trail of thought must've snagged somewhere along the way. "You want to impregnate your sister?"

His lover sat bolt upright, almost clocking Hamish with his head. His face was a mask of utter disgust. "I— Th-that's *the*... v-vilest..." he babbled in Udynean. He shook himself, brushing his torso as if bugs crawled over him. "*No.* Most certainly *not.* I intend to have Anjali carry our child, *if* she is amenable. The procedure is not without risks, but I trust her with my life."

"I'm nae sleeping with your sister."

"No, I—" Darshan grumbled and muttered to himself under his breath. "This is why I wanted to wait until we were back at Minamist. There are people who could explain this a lot better than I. Suffice to say, the process uses magic. You are correct there. It allows two people—of whichever combination of genders those people happen to be—to merge their bloodlines." He scooped up Hamish's hand, linking their fingers. "There are but a few who know all the finicky details on how it actually works, but I figured it was worth a try."

He ran his thumb across Darshan's. "You want to risk the future of having a bairn—your heir—to an experimental procedure? How many have been successful?"

Darshan shrugged. "All I know is that it started in Niholia with Tsarina Galina. She has a wife and is rather devoted to the woman. It took some years, but her people found a way for them to have a child that shared their blood. After the method was discovered, others followed. All women at first, but they eventually found a way for it to work with men."

Making bairns with magic. Hamish gnawed on the inside of his lip. The priests attributed such creations to the Goddess' will. *To depose her decree...*

He frowned. Were they? Niholians had their own deities. Perhaps one of them had led the way to this discovery? If the gods didn't want spellsters meddling, then surely they'd the power to stop them.

His lover eyed him, the faint flicker of uncertainty tightening his eyes and thinning his mouth. "Understand that I have no actual idea how viable it is. I hear the method for fusing the essence of two women is relatively stable, but two men?" He shook his head. "I am uncertain of the risks. I have kept all this to myself because I am attempting to dedicate my attention to the trials. I do not wish to lose you."

"And when your position demands an heir from you?" Hamish mumbled, still drawing the threads of their conversation together. "We do it via... magic? No sex with a woman required?"

"None at all." Darshan patted his hand. "But let us worry about one thing at a time. After can come... Well..." He offered a soft smile and a shrug.

"...after," Hamish finished, his gaze drifting to the window. The once dull glow of dawn had grown larger whilst they had talked. "I should leave," he mumbled, slithering his feet over the edge of the bed. "Get dressed. Let you catch a few winks."

"Actually, it is about time for me to depart for my tent." Darshan followed Hamish in standing. His lover paused in shrugging into his sherwani to rise up on his toes and plant a kiss on Hamish's cheek. "No matter how the trial goes, I swear I shall not leave you in a loveless marriage. Even if I have to steal you away."

Hamish chuckled. "Let's hope it doesnae come to that." The last thing they needed was an angry clan on their tail.

"Your secret will be out today, *mea lux*," Darshan whispered. "Are you ready for the world to know?"

His throat tightened. Only a scant handful outside his family was aware he liked men. Putting himself in a position for everyone to learn the truth was certainly a step up. A boulder-sized step. "Aye. As long as it means I'll still have you at the end of the day, I'm ready."

Chapter 42

I*'m so nae ready for this.* Hamish strode back and forth in what little space he had within the tent walls. His stomach bubbled. He hadn't expected to be so far from the castle, but the archery range had been deemed unsuitable. At least, as far as his mother was concerned.

She had arranged for a single target set in a nearby field. A decision she had apparently come to whilst he had been dreamlessly sleeping at Darshan's side.

Less of a chance for tampering. That had been her excuse upon his query. By who and how, Hamish still couldn't figure out. Did his mother think the woman who had snuck her way into his bed last night would stoop to other means? Or was she afraid Darshan would intervene?

His mother was out there right now, addressing the crowd, ensuring the clans and their competitors knew the rules.

"Will you stop pacing?" Gordon grumbled. Only his brother shared the tent, the rest having left to wait upon a temporary stage placed at the foot of the field. "You're giving me anxiety just watching you."

Outside, his mother continued to address the crowd, her muffled words failing to cut through his silent terror. Darshan already stood with the other competitors, waiting. Likely hoping no one would look too closely at him.

All whilst Hamish was forced to linger in here for the chance to gain his freedom.

"I cannae just sit here." Everything hinged on this one chance. If he failed to grasp the arrow as Darshan loosed, then it was over. "Was this how you felt when Muireall competed?"

A small, sad smile creased his brother's face. "Aye."

"What if he's discovered before it's over?" If his lover was unmasked whilst Hamish was in here, he wouldn't know Darshan had been found out until it was too late to salvage the day. "What if—?"

"It hasnae happened yet."

But there were more competitors before. Darshan could've gotten lost in the crowd as just another veiled face. Being one amongst nine gave him fewer opportunities to keep his head down.

"There are so many ways things could go wrong," Hamish mumbled. "I could make him miss. *I* could miss." Darshan had explained during his attempts to teach Hamish magic that, given the weakness of his ability, his emotional state could greatly affect what he was capable of. "One of the others could hit the centre. Or—"

"You're nae going to miss. You're good at archery. You'll make sure he hits the target." Gordon's conviction seemed to waver at the last statement. It had taken some convincing for his brother to grasp that Hamish's talent with a bow was in part due to magic. "And if one of the others matches you, there's nae much you can do about it."

"What if I cannae focus when the time comes?" Guiding another's arrow was all so very new. If he'd had more time to practice, then he wouldn't be left doubting himself. "If he fails? What then?"

Sighing, his brother got to his feet and clapped his hands on Hamish's shoulders. "I guess then we've nae choice but to let them ken about you two."

"I..." It was one thing to have his family know, but others? Even a handful of guards was as far as it went. Announcing it to all the clans once Darshan won was a big step, but to do that same thing with his lover disqualified? "I'm nae sure I can do that." Not with another as the victor.

"You'll be fine." Gordon squeezed Hamish's shoulder, holding him firmly in place. "Dinnae think on all the bad that could happen. Think on what you want."

"All I can think of is how everyone will ken soon." He had never imagined letting more than his family and a few quick flings know that he liked men.

"If you dinnae want to go through with this..."

"Then *what*? Have one of the others win? Force myself to be someone I'll never be?" There was no other choice. Not one he could live with. "I have to take this chance."

Gordon nodded. He opened his mouth, then swiftly shut it and cocked his head.

Hamish strained to make out the words amongst the droning beyond the tent walls. Had they just missed the call for his appearance? He held his breath as if it would somehow help him hear.

"They must be getting close," his brother mumbled, shaking his head. "Or I'm going senile. Maybe I should—"

Ethan burst through the tent flap before Gordon could take a step towards the entrance. He halted in front of them, doubling over and panting like a winded boarhound as soon as his feet slid to a stop. He waved a small wooden box at Hamish. "Take," he managed.

Hamish did as the boy requested. Peeking inside the box revealed Darshan's glasses nestled amongst a swathe of silk. "Where did you find this?" He knew where it should've been. How his nephew had gotten hold of it was a different matter.

Ethan shook his head. "Nae found," he replied between puffs. "Given."

"The person who these belong to gave them to you?"

With his breathing normal again, his nephew nodded. "For *me* to give to *you*, aye. For after, he said."

For when he's won. Darshan would need to expose his face and, even if everything went as they planned, the man would be vulnerable standing in the middle of a field without decent vision. Hamish slipped the case into his belt pouch, grumbling to himself as it barely fit. "Are they ready for me?"

Ethan nodded. "Me mum sent me over when you didnae show."

Of course. He'd been too busy fretting that he had missed the announcement. He grabbed his bow, fiddled with checking the string—an act he must've done a dozen times this morning—and exited the tent.

The roar of the crowd hit him with full force. A horde of people filled the field. Cheers and cries drowned out any other sound. Hamish acknowledged them all with a stiff nod and raised his bow to a renewed cheer from the crowd. In their eyes, they were witnessing the Goddess' selection of a new princess, not the disownment of a prince.

He strode towards the waiting competitors.

The women turned as he joined them at the mark—a simple length of rope pegged to the ground. Darshan stood off to one side. The ruby heart Hamish had gifted him just yesterday afternoon sat proudly upon his overcoat, gleaming in the midday sun.

Hamish glanced over at the temporary stage. Both his older siblings and their children sat in the shade of an awning, whilst his parents stood near the stage edge. His mother spoke, he knew that only because her mouth clearly moved.

He swallowed a sudden lump of uncertainty threatening to seal his throat shut. *I can do this.* He just had to block out everything else, focus only on the black circle painted in the centre of the target. The canvas draped over the target wasn't typical, but beneath it sat the usual lengths of straw, bound and coiled into a vaguely circular shape. Just like those used in the castle training grounds.

A steward trotted over. Her job would be to ensure that every loosed arrow bore no inherent flaws, as well as noting that no one stepped over the rope. Including himself. She handed him an arrow.

Taking a deep breath, Hamish nocked the arrow and loosed. *Dead centre.* Right where he had aimed. He didn't need to wait for the stewards at the far end to announce it. He could feel the rightness within his very core.

All he needed to do now was stay back and let the Goddess' grace dictate where the competitors' would hit the target until it was time for him to guide Darshan's arrow.

There appeared to be a sort of hierarchy amongst the women. They shuffled into a line and the first took her place at the mark. She lifted her bow.

Off-centre. Hamish averted his gaze before the urge to correct her got the better of him, but he already knew her stance was wrong. The arrow would land to the right side of the target if not miss it altogether.

"Disqualified!" The sound was nearly drowned out by the crowd's mixed response.

Hamish lifted his gaze at the call. Sure enough, the arrow had just managed to graze the target's edge.

Stomping her foot, the woman removed her veil to reveal a suntanned face reddened with frustration and embarrassment. As soon as she vacated the immediate area, another competitor took her place at the mark.

One by one, the other women took their turn. Some were little better than the first—one even missed the target completely and threw an almighty tantrum when she did—whilst two came fairly close to matching his shot. *That could be a problem.* They had to be from the clans in the north-eastern planes where the people hunted from horseback as easily as he did on the ground.

The last competitor of the eight women lowered her bow. She had failed to hit within the range of those closer to his arrow—the stewards nearer the target had already disqualified her—but she refused to give up the mark.

"My lady," snapped the steward. She stood off to one side, clutching the ninth arrow. Her ire was directed at the woman who still refused to move. "Your attempt has already been proven unsatisfactory." The steward strode towards the woman, squaring her shoulders in a clear anticipation of resistance. "I must insist you step aside and show your face or be subjected to force." She reached out, likely prepared to snatch the scarf from the woman's head.

The competitor whirled on the steward, the veil dropping as she shot the other woman a feral glare.

It cannae be. Hamish stared at the woman's face. He knew her. But then, he would be hard-pressed to forget the very woman who had spent several hours trying to convince his mother to have them married, especially after she had attempted to molest him. But hadn't she been removed from the contest? *Aye*. He quite clearly remembered her face being stained. How had she managed to scrub it off?

"What are you doing here?" the steward demanded. "You're already disqualified. And where is our other competitor?" She craned her neck around the woman as if another would suddenly appear.

"She is," the woman replied with a smirk, "nae fit to compete."

"What have you done?" Hamish growled. He'd no interest in having anyone but Darshan win this bloody contest, but that didn't mean any harm inflicted on the other competitors was acceptable.

Scoffing, the woman rolled her eyes. She planted her hand firmly upon one hip. "She's fine. She's even all snugly tucked up in her tent. She's just nae able to compete."

"Guards!" the steward bellowed. "Arrest this woman. Reckless endangerment of the competition."

"And send someone to check on the other competitor," Hamish added as two guards marched over to firmly secure the woman by her arms. "See that she hasnae come to any serious harm." He glowered at the woman. "We wouldnae want to add murder to this one's charges."

The woman's eyes widened. Her mouth opened and shut soundlessly like a stunned fish, but she was whisked away before she was capable of uttering a single word.

All around them, the mutter of the crowd increased with every breath. What would the guards find? Hopefully, the worst case would be the poor competitor trussed up like a felled deer.

Hamish glanced over his shoulder at the temporary stage where his mother now sat on a heavy wooden chair as if it were the stone slab of the throne. Would she insist on waiting for the actual competitor? Or, perhaps, a rematch? As things currently stood, all but two had been immediately disqualified.

There was just Darshan's shot left. He would have to hit pretty damn close to centre. Not, perhaps, land alongside Hamish's original shot, but doing worse than the next closest two would disqualify him and a draw with the others would only prolong the trial's end. They couldn't afford to have the stewards clear the target and demand everyone try again.

With a dramatic sweep of her arm, his mother waved them on.

"Final contestant," the steward bellowed. "Step to the mark."

Hamish shuffled a little to his left as his lover came forward. He breathed deep. This was it. *The last step.* All he had to do was focus and ensure this arrow landed in the precise spot without also looking as though anything other than the bow had sent the arrow across the field. *If Mum catches even a whiff of magic—*

He shook his head and returned his attention to the arrow Darshan now held at full draw. The sky between them and the target was clear, the breeze was slight and the distance no greater than when they'd practised. *Nae different to the tree.*

Except that this shot needed to best the others.

His lover's hand trembled. Even with Hamish's focus divided between the arrow and the target, the bow's juddering movements were clear. The tap of the arrow shaft against the bow's belly thundered through Hamish's ears. His stomach flopped with every scattered attempt to envision his own fingers holding the fletching.

Still, that tightness deep in his core vibrated. That line he could almost see between arrowhead and target wavered, but he could manage. All he needed was for Darshan to let go.

His lover would never make it alone. Even with his glasses, he hadn't the skill or strength for a full draw with such a bow. And if Darshan tried? Then one of the other two competitors would be the victor and *then—*

Darshan released the arrow, the snap shuddering through Hamish's body.

The world seemed to slow like winter honey off a spoon. The arrow sailed through the air. It wasn't a perfect arc. A little flat, a little off-centre. Such knowledge buzzed through Hamish, even before the arrow had reached the downward curve, much less reached the target.

It would be enough. *A close hit.* That was all they needed. It had worked. Not even the Goddess could stop it now.

The arrow passed the halfway point. He slowly prepared to let his hold on the arrow slip free and allow momentum to carry it onwards, then stopped.

Something wasn't right.

It was a slight change. The arrow had been travelling straight. Now it wobbled, growing…

Hot.

Hamish raced towards his lover as he relinquished his already tenuous hold on the arrow. He clapped a hand onto Darshan's shoulder. The man's body vibrated beneath his fingers. "Dar—"

A gasp from the other competitors drew his attention back up.

Fire sputtered along the arrow shaft as it continued the downward curve of its arc. Smoke trailed off the fletching, followed fast by flames. *Nae...*

The arrow hit. Hamish barely saw where before the entire target was consumed in a blaze.

Darshan whirled on him as the target continued to burn. "My glasses," he demanded, his hand outstretched. "Quickly."

Hamish fumbled with his belt pouch, withdrawing the wooden case and handing it over. "Was that you?" The question was out before the idiocy of asking caught up with reason. It had to be him. Who else would've had the ability?

"Regrettably," Darshan muttered, sliding the ends of the glasses beneath the scarf.

"*Why?*" Rage fought for dominance over his disbelief. The emotions bubbled in his gut, threatening to have him vomit hard enough to expel last night's dinner. "I had it."

"I know." His lover lowered the veil and smiled weakly. He looked as queasy as Hamish felt. "I panicked."

"What's going on here?" bellowed one of the disqualified competitors; a black-haired woman with a brown scar puckering her left cheek. She levelled a finger at them as if brandishing a sword. "Nae one said anything about a *man* competing. Who the hell are you?"

Clearing his throat, Darshan casually removed the scarf to bundle it beneath one arm whilst also stepping between Hamish and the competitors. "I am Darshan *vris Mhanek*." He paused, perhaps waiting for them to reach some sort of realisation.

Hamish winced. He had been expecting his mother to appear at his side any second since Darshan revealed himself. Perhaps she was far enough away that the man was unrecognisable without his usual glittering attire, but his voice travelled well.

He dared to glance over his shoulder at the temporary stage. His mother stood at the edge, held back by his father's grasp around her shoulders. Rage blazed across her face like a bonfire, but her mouth moved silently. For now. He was going to be in for a right bollocking once she had regained her voice.

When no one spoke, Darshan continued, "I am the crown prince of Udynea by virtue of birth and blood." That snippet of information gained a few glances between the women, but nobody chose to speak up. "For those of you who are unaware, I was sent to negotiate trade relations with your queen." He turned his head, that hazel gaze settling on Hamish. One corner of his mouth lifted. "I stayed to woo her son and win his hand in this contest. Which I believe I have just done."

"You dinnae ken that," growled the scarred woman. "Naebody

does." She jerked a thumb at the now-smouldering target. "The bloody thing blew up!"

"Goddess," another woman moaned, her milk-pale skin somehow growing whiter. "Did *you* do that?" She indicated the target with a shaky finger. "Have we been competing against a spellster?"

The other competitors shuffled back, as if putting distance between them and Darshan somehow helped. A few mumbles and mutters came from the group. Only a few were loud enough to hear.

"Surely the queen wouldnae let a spellster run amok," one said. "Nae during the union contest."

"It's a trick!" another proclaimed. "They wouldnae let a spellster compete."

Darshan scoffed. "I assure you, as unorthodox as it may appear, my inclusion is quite legal. And you have all been in my presence at one point or the other during this past week."

"That's hardly a fair match," the scarred woman grumped, pointing an accusing finger at him. "You had *magic* to help you. Whether you entered legally or nae, you should be disqualified."

"Magic," mumbled the ashen-faced woman—the one who had been shaking since the revelation that the target had ignited via magic. Her dark eyes rolled back as she slithered to the ground.

"Did *you* do that?" wailed one of the women—her face red in the scant patches between the heavy spray of freckles adorning her face. She pointed at the fallen woman.

"I most certainly did no—"

"Of course, he did," another woman cried out.

As a group, they scuttled back several steps. They muttered and whispered amongst themselves, quiet enough that Hamish caught only the occasional word.

Hamish dared to lift his attention to beyond. The fields were in chaos. The vast majority of the crowd seeking whatever exit could be had. Others milled about, seemingly torn between lingering to watch and fleeing.

Guards slowly filed through the crowd, spreading out in a wide circle around Hamish and the others.

Hunching his shoulders, he glanced towards the stage. His mother hadn't moved. She argued with his father, who seemed intent on keeping hold of her, but didn't appear to be ordering the guards.

"The rules do not forbid its use," Darshan interjected as the women's renewed grumblings grew louder. "And I thought it more than fair given that you all have full use of your vision whilst I had to do without these." He tapped on the frame of his glasses, scoffing as the revelation seemed to have no actual effect on the women's suspicious expressions. "If I had meant harm to any of you, I would have waited until the end."

"T-they—" spluttered the heavily freckled women. She pointed at the other two competitors who had been the closest to Hamish's arrow until just a few moments ago. "*They* were the ones who hit near enough to centre. One of them should be claiming Prince Hamish's hand, nae *you*."

"*I* dinnae want him," piped up one of the singled-out women, her blue eyes wide. "Nae if he's one of *them*."

Frowning, Hamish bit his tongue in an effort to keep from speaking. *Them*. Never had he heard the word spoken with such disgust.

"Neither do I," muttered the other woman. Still, she gave him a peculiar considering look, her eyes narrowed to slits. "Well, maybe for Isaac." She cocked her head to one side. "Is short and relatively hairless your only preference, your highness? Because I can probably convince me brother to shave."

Taken aback by the offer, Hamish struggled to find his voice. Was she really considering staking a claim to his hand and offering it to her brother in lieu of herself? Was that even allowed?

"Thank you for the generous offer," Darshan piped up before Hamish could form a response. "But I believe he is *mine* and I have no intention of giving him up." He clasped Hamish's hand, squeezing reassuringly. "By right of conquest, I claim the hand of Prince Hamish of the Mathan Clan."

The crowd stilled as his lover's voice boomed across the field.

"The hell you do!" his mother screamed. Whilst she still remained on the temporary stage—largely in part due to his father's grip on her arm—she looked ready to tear Darshan's throat with her bare hands. "Arrest him!" She struggled against his father's grip before imperiously pointing a finger at them. "Arrest that man! I want him flung into our deepest cell."

A three of the guards rushed forward, their swords drawn.

Nae good. Hamish stepped back, dragging Darshan closer to him. He had been prepared for a tirade. He was even prepared for her to banish the pair of them from the kingdom. But to call for Darshan's arrest? *Nae good at all.*

A shield formed around them in a filmy, flickering sheen of purple light.

Beyond the shield, the guards halted. They eyed the magical barrier and, with their resolve seeming to waver, turned back to the stage.

His mother urged them onwards. Even though no sound reached his ears, she was clearly raving.

Hamish stretched out a hand, brushing his fingers across the shield. *Warm and hard.* Like when his lover had enclosed him in a similar shield in order to keep Hamish from being rooted out by the guards; a time that seemed like years ago rather than a scant month. He hadn't been able to hear beyond the shimmering barrier's confines back then, either.

Whatever his mother was saying seemed to have little effect on the guards. If anything, they were instilling fresh panic in the crowd. The competitors had already vacated the area and the mass of quickly dispersing people poured out the field. If he strained, he could almost make out their screams.

"Dar, you need to stop." It was one thing to witness a target burst into flame, quite another to realise it was the work of magic, that the source stood in the middle of everything. And was also unwilling to bend to their laws.

His lover's brows lowered, merging with the upper frame of his glasses. "She ordered my imprisonment. *Me.* If you think I am going to let those brutes touch me—"

"They're nae going to lay a hand on you." There didn't appear to be a single guard standing who hadn't already joined the fleeing masses. *They're going to get an earful once Mum catches up to them*. To think of the skulking he had done over the weeks, and all Darshan would have needed to keep the guards away was to put up a simple shield.

"And how does opting to keep their distance exclude them from effectively turning me into a pincushion?" his lover shot back.

"I'm sure Mum wouldnae order them to—" He froze as a hand, too broad to be Darshan's, clapped onto Hamish's shoulder. *Gordon?* It had to be. Hadn't Darshan told him that his brother was capable of passing through the spellster's shields?

He turned to find his father looming over him.

"I think you two should head back to the castle," his father rumbled. A pair of horses stood at his back and behind them—

Hamish's gaze darted to where his mother was already planted on a horse. Not ready to bear down upon them in a burning rage, but being dragged away from the field by his sister's hold on the horse's reins. *How did they even manage to get her on a horse?* He doubted either sibling would dare to touch her. Had it been his father's doing?

"Lad," his father growled, the tone blanking all else from Hamish's mind. "Castle. *Now.*"

Nodding, Hamish grasped the reins as his father clambered aboard his own horse and left. He hastened to follow suit, barely registering that Darshan's magical shield had vanished.

"Man of few words, your father," Darshan murmured as he swung into the other saddle.

"Aye." He and his siblings had long learnt to listen sharp when his father was riled. *We well and truly fecked this up*. But what other way could Darshan have won the contest that wouldn't also have seen his mother spitting fire like a demon?

"What now?"

"You're asking *me*?" Hamish knew what usually happened once the final trial was won, but his mother wouldn't allow even the celebratory feast to go ahead, much less the wedding that should follow.

Darshan eyed the castle with a measure of consternation. "If we go in, there shall be only one entrance out."

Hamish nodded. There was the tunnel, but getting to it whilst tailed by guards would be tricky. And there was no guarantee that the key would still be wherever Darshan had left it. Or that the lower entrance wasn't suddenly guarded.

He fiddled with his reins, weighing the merits of leaving over obeying his father's decree. "We best be getting up there."

"I think this is a bad idea, but lead the way."

Hamish nudged his mare onward. He didn't want to think that Darshan could be right, but his mother could likely be beyond reason. And yet, a small seed of hope sat nestled within that. If everyone else was standing by him, they could make her see the truth. That, maybe, his mother wouldn't set him adrift because of who he loved.

Chapter 43

Hamish stared up at the entrance to the dining hall. His mother waited inside. Did his father and siblings also linger? *I hope so.* He could face her readily enough with Darshan at his side, but having them there as well would help immensely.

"It isn't too late to leave," Darshan whispered. His lover had slipped into speaking exclusively in Udynean from the moment they had entered the courtyard. The menacing presence of the guards milling around the gate likely had something to do with that. The man walked as if expecting an attack at any moment.

Hamish couldn't be entirely certain that Darshan wasn't wrong.

Ideally, this was the safest place for an ambassador, but he couldn't say whether or not his mother's senses had slipped enough to believe she could harm or contain Darshan without repercussion.

"I cannae just up and leave." He had to try and repair some of the damage. Maybe even give his siblings something to build upon to possibly smooth over any grumblings the clans might have about a Udynean nobleman participating in the contest.

Darshan squared his shoulders. His whole face seemed to grow stiff, once again donning that emotionless mask. "I understand," he murmured.

"Thank you." He gingerly clasped the door handle. If the worst was to happen, then they would be as good as trapped until either Darshan's magic took its toll or they managed to force their way out. "Just... stay vigilant."

The coolness of his lover's answering laugh prickled Hamish's skin. "Believe me, I'm already well there."

Hamish pushed open the door. Relief sagged his shoulders upon seeing his family. Not the children, but he wasn't going to be facing his mother with only the source of her ire at his side.

"You!" his mother screamed. She lunged at them, stopped only by his father's hasty grab at her waist. Whilst he effortlessly lifted her off the ground, her voice wasn't so easily contained. "You dare to enter this hall as if you are an ally? I looked the other way when you blatantly attempted to corrupt me son, but now you dare interfere with our sacred traditions? Do you have any idea what you've done?"

"*Sacred?*" Darshan shot back. "You are offering your son up like he is some... *trinket*." He took a few steps towards her, putting himself between her and Hamish. "And whilst we are on the subject, I won that contest."

"Won?" If his mother's eyes bulged any further, Hamish was certain they would pop out of their sockets. "*Won?*" Spittle flew from her mouth with each word. "You entered under another clan's banner. *That* little bout of deception alone makes you ineligible. You dinnae deserve that fecking favour!"

"Well I could hardly compete as myself. Doing so would rather defeat the purpose of everyone being anonymous, would it not?"

Rather than answer the spellster, she twisted to glare at Hamish's father over her shoulder. "Do you nae see what your laxity has allowed?" She indicated both Darshan and himself with a wave of her hand. "Are you blind? Are you going to just stand there and let him cheat his way to your son's soul?"

His father's gaze flicked between his wife and them. He lowered her to the ground, keeping a firm hand on her shoulder. "It's me understanding that he didnae actually cheat, so I dinnae see why you would think—"

"You mean nae one caught him," his mother scoffed. "He's a Udynean and a spellster, *of course* he bloody cheated. Probably killed the poor lass whose place he stole. Where is *she*?" she growled at Darshan. "What did you do with the woman whose clothes you wear?"

Hamish laid a hand on his lover's arm, hoping that simple gesture was enough to keep Darshan from doing something foolish.

"They're Muireall's clothes, Mum," Gordon said before anyone could utter a word. "*I* gave them to him. *I* put the idea of him competing into his head. The Dathais Clan wasnae sending anyone. He didnae cheat his way in. He went through every trial, just like the others."

Hamish swallowed the sickly lump building in his throat. Gordon might've helped Darshan, but he doubted his brother was aware of the spellster using magic in the first trial to bolster his strength. Or really understood how the messy business with the arrow hadn't been entirely Darshan's doing despite Hamish explaining at great lengths.

His mother shook her head. "Oh, ideas were certainly put into someone's head, but it was nae yours into his." She whirled on

Darshan, thrusting an accusing finger in his direction. "You bewitched them," she snarled. "You've cast one of your insidious spells and turned me whole family to your twisted way of thinking."

Darshan's whole body vibrated beneath Hamish's hand. "I have done no such thing." Shimmers of heat rose from his fists, but he kept them at his side. "There is not a spellster alive who can hypnotise a group of people."

"You admit it," she crowed, her face warped in malicious glee. "Nae as a group, but individually..."

His father turned his mother around. "All your children are doing is what you've always taught them to do: Stand by each other. You cannae ask them to change that nature just because the thing they are standing against is *you*."

Hamish stuck out his chest, welling pride stinging his eyes. His father was right. None of them had dared face her in the past, but now...

It was too much. She had made too many demands for them to back down.

"Even if the lad had used a little magic during the trials," his father added. "There's nae law against it."

She stepped back from her husband as if she had never seen the man before. "Of course there's nae law. It isnae there because our spellsters are *cloistered*." His mother spat in Darshan's general direction. "That's where you should be, locked away with all the others. I should've seen you put in one the second you stepped off that ship."

Darshan laughed coldly. "*Really?*"

That single word, softly echoing with the threat of eternal pain, lifted every hair Hamish possessed. He had always thought his mother to be the epitome of haughtiness, but Darshan's expression swept his mother's into the realm of a petulant child.

His lover took a few steps closer to Hamish's family, his movements like liquid. "Had I been the countess you had expected, I rather doubt that you would give a whit of care as to whether or not I had used magic. You fight against me winning only because I am a man."

His mother stood there in furious silence. If Hamish didn't know better, he would've sworn she was going to kill Darshan where he stood. It was a wonder she hadn't called the guard.

"Fiona," his father rumbled, tearing his mother's attention from Darshan. "If you think so poorly of Udyneans, then why did you accept the treaty?"

"I only accepted because it was made clear to me that refusing would mean war nae matter what they professed. I wished to spare all of you that." She whirled on Darshan. "Then *you* came along and stole me son's life."

Rage blazed across Darshan's face. "I—"

"Mum, *really*?" Nora snapped.

"You dinnae understand how these people think, dear," their mother ranted. "If I let him stay, if I accept this ridiculous claim and make him a recognised prince of Tirglas, then the next thing happening is you all winding up dead and Udynea has two thrones to plonk their greedy arses on."

"If we really wanted Tirglas," Darshan snarled, "we would have *taken* it. Or do you honestly think your defences would mean anything to our army? My father offered you peace."

"Of course you say that now," his mother roared. "What better way to see us lower our defences than act like the thought hadnae crossed your wee mind? Why else would your people send the Crown Prince of Udynea here?"

Hamish gaped at her. She knew? This whole time? Or had she only become aware of what his title meant after Nora told her?

The laughter that escaped Darshan's lips definitely had to be one of shock, or perhaps disbelief in what he had heard. "You *dare* to presume my actions? *I* am not the one here who refuses to accept Hamish exactly as he was born."

"*This*?" She gestured to Hamish, indicating all of him with a wave of her hand. "This is nae a circumstance of birth." The disgust in her voice twisted her features as she continued, growing monstrous. "It is a *disease*. You all see him rotting at the core and do nae a thing but aid the cause. Me own family... plotting against me, allowing their minds to grow sick with this *poison*."

"I cannae believe you still dinnae get it," Gordon muttered, shaking his head.

" 'Mish has found someone he loves," Nora added, her voice barely audible. "At least have the decency to concede that."

His mother turned from them to address Darshan. "Tell your father nae to bother sending another ambassador. I abolish any and all trade agreements. Your kind are nae welcome here. If your people set foot on these lands and—"

"*Mum!*" Gordon snapped.

Hamish gaped wordlessly, his breath stolen. He staggered forwards. She couldn't be suggesting what he thought.

"And... *what*?" Darshan's voice had grown cold. The whisper of danger hung in the air like an encroaching storm. He folded his arms, appraising her as one would a rabid boarhound. "You would truly rescind our offer of a peaceful alliance? Over your son's happiness?"

Slighting the *Mhanek* by slapping aside the empire's gesture of goodwill invited retaliation. Which would cause the clans to respond in kind. Which would see the forests burn and Tirglas swallowed whole. His home… His family… All of it would be ashes in the wind.

Unless Darshan was able to convince his father to ignore the insult.

"*Please*," Nora begged, clasping her mother's arm as if she were a child of five again. "Think of your granddaughter, think of me wee lads. If you actually care about our safety as much as you profess, then dinnae do this."

"I *am* thinking of them. This is me final decision. I will nae stand aside and let Udynea wheedle its way to our throne. Now go, all of you." She shrugged off her daughter and, without a single look Hamish's way, headed for the smaller hall entrance. "I must mourn me son's demise."

"*Mourn me?*" Hamish roared, outrage giving him voice. "When did I fecking die?"

The room fell silent, every eye on him.

His heart raced, thumping at his temples. "I cannae believe it. Even when everyone is telling you the same thing and you still willnae listen. You *never* listen. Nae when I first confided in you and nae now. You just keep insisting you're right. You were aware I didnae want this competition, that I'd chosen me path, and you still went through with it."

His mother lifted her head, jutting her chin at them. Every inch the queen. "Have you quite finished?"

Experience told him he should shut his face, but after decades of being forced to corral who he was, to *pretend…*

The years crowded his tongue, desperate to finally be heard. "If you had just listened to me, *understood* me, for even a heartbeat, you'd see that I ken what I want and that's *him*." He glanced over his shoulder, a small smile tweaking his lips as he realised Darshan stood right at his side. Adoration shone through those eyes that seemed to gleam every colour at once. "I love him."

On the edge of his vision, he spied his father rocking back, surprise wrinkling his brow. He twitched his head towards his other children, seeking confirmation from them, who gave it with a minute upward jerk of a head or an empathetic nod.

"And now you're threatening a *war*?" Hamish continued. "You'd rather bring death to our doorstep by slighting their offer for… What? Because he won? Because you cannae accept the truth? That, after everything you've put me through, I still willnae bend to your will?"

A soft gust of breath left his mother's lips. Not a laugh, not even the wisp of a scoff. He had only ever heard that sound the once, thirteen years back, and he had paid twofold for his insolence then.

"Why? *Why?*" She stormed across the hall, her anger echoing in each pounding step. "Because this is *wrong*. If you had ever listened to me, to *anyone*!" She spread her arms wide. "Then you'd ken that." Her face twisted with her ire and he was right back in her study, not quite two weeks ago. The first time she had ever struck him. "If you cannae see for yourself the harm *you* are causing, the danger *you* are bringing to this land by being with *him*. If you cannae be trusted to make the right choice, then I will make it for you." She reached out to grab him.

Her hand smacked into something shimmering.

Only now did Hamish notice the shield surrounding them. It was more a faint feeling in the air, a hum, rather than the visible entity he had witnessed in the field. Barely visible where her palm had collided.

"I will *not* permit you to lay a finger on him," Darshan hissed.

Hamish wasn't entirely sure she had heard the man. She stared Hamish down as if he was some sword-swinging madman. "You persist down this road," she snarled, "and you are dead to me."

Nora gasped. "Mum, you—"

"I'll nae have your influence poisoning me family any further."

"You want me to leave?" he demanded of her, knowing full well that she wouldn't answer. "Fine, I'm gone. I'll even play along with your daft game of pretending I'm dead." Hamish stepped closer, towering over her with the charge of the shield tingling along his skin. "But I want you to ken one thing before I do. I'm nae the poisonous one here. And despite what you want to think, I'm going to be living happily with a man who loves me."

Darshan firmly clasped Hamish's hand and squeezed.

With his heart thudding an extra beat, Hamish replied in kind. Feeling those slim fingers pressed against his skin gave him strength. He wasn't alone. Not anymore. "I'm marrying him. And when he inherits the imperial throne—and he will, Mum, you ken he's their bleeding heir—that'll make me the prince consort to the most powerful man in the world. And *you*? You'll still be bitterly living in decades gone."

His mother sneered. "I dinnae ken who or what you are, but *you* are nae me son."

"I think we both ken that I stopped being your son the day you decided I wasnae what you wanted in one." Rather than wait for a response, he turned on his heel and strode to the door.

Darshan followed at his side, their hands still clinging to each other.

Hamish's legs almost caved on him the moment he stepped through the doorway. He staggered a few steps before slumping against the wall. By the Goddess, what was he doing? What had come over him to speak to his own mother that way? *It would've been better if I had just left*. If only she would've listened.

His lover laid a hand on his shoulder, gently squeezing. "I—" He grew silent at the sound of approaching footsteps coming from the other side of the dining hall door.

Hamish straightened as the door creaked open to admit his siblings. Of their parents, there was no sign. Not even a whisper of his mother's acerbic voice. *It's over, then.* All those years… all boiling down to this. His exile.

Darshan bowed his head. "Forgive me, this was not how I imagined it ending."

"How else could it have possibly gone?" Gordon asked. "Did you think me mum would just accept it?"

Darshan's cheeks puffed out as he sighed. He scratched at the back of his head. "I had hoped she would find some measure of peace in her son's happiness."

A soft, weary chuckle escaped Nora's lips. "You would've needed the Goddess' intervention to pull off a miracle like that."

"Evidently."

"Come on," Gordon wrapped an arm around Darshan's shoulders, guiding him up the corridors. "You'll have to gather what you can carry via horseback. Both of you."

"I'll go see your mounts are still saddled and ready," Nora offered, hitching up her skirts and running off down the corridor before anyone could say a word.

"Horses?" Darshan mumbled. "But it will take months to leave Tirglas that way."

"Aye," Gordon said with a nod. "Unfortunately, your victory doesnae change the fact that the ship heading for Udynea is still nae in. If you were able to stay…" He trailed off with a shrug.

"But we cannot. I understand." Frowning, Darshan gave a curt nod. "Horses it is, then." He looked over his shoulder at Hamish. "Do not take too long gathering what you can, *mea lux*."

Hamish nodded, his pace faltering once his lover and brother were out of sight. Packing wouldn't take long; there were few possessions that he'd grown at all attached to and the rest…

Well, he didn't own the rest anymore. He had been disowned. No title. No clan. He was free to live as he saw fit.

If the Goddess willed it, that life would be with a man who didn't care he brought nothing but himself to a marriage.

Chapter 44

Hamish halted in the doorway to his room, taking in the gloomy space that had been his alone for three decades. *I'm never coming back.* Not once had he ever given the idea any merit. Never, in all his years, had he considered there would be a time where he'd be stripped of the right to return here.

Now it was a reality.

He rifled through his things, moving from shelf to drawer before kneeling at his chest of effects. His siblings would see to the rest of their gear, so he needed only to concern himself with personal items.

The chest carried nowhere near its capacity, but still too much to bring with him. Travelling by horse meant the amount of extra weight he could carry alongside the necessary gear was minimal. A pack horse could've allowed them to cart more, but they'd be lucky to get away with two mounts as it was.

He rummaged through the chest. What to take? Spare clothes, certainly. Items of value? He'd little there. Only a handful of things that bore sentimental weight. Absolutely nothing he owned had any monetary value beyond the silver ring Darshan had gifted to him.

Did he even have any money?

Something clinked at the bottom of the chest. He dug deeper into the rubble, his questing hands unearthing a small pouch containing a silver coin and a few copper bits. Enough for a night's stay and a meal at a moderately decent inn. He pocketed the coins and continued his search.

His gaze alighted on the box holding the phallic gift from Darshan.

Hamish had used it just the once. That'd been after dancing with his lover and turning Darshan into a panting mess of a man whilst they lingered in the mezzanine shadows.

Using the toy on himself had been quite the experience. Not as good as having the actual object of his desire inside him, but sufficient in a pinch. And not as risky as an attempt in smuggling Darshan into his room.

Udynea would hold its own set of risks, but who he slept with wouldn't be that big of an issue. At least, he hoped. He'd only Darshan's word to go on that everything would be fine once they reached Minamist.

Hamish sat the end of the box on the edge of the chest, resting his hands on the upright end and his chin on his hands. *What am I doing?* His mouth had run away with him whilst facing his mother, the weight behind his words only now starting to sink in.

I can go anywhere. Do anything. Marry anyone he chose.

There were limits, naturally. Having practically no money wouldn't get him very far, but he could subsist on the land long enough to get somewhere. And that was a start. He could settle wherever he liked. Not in Tirglas, perhaps, but there were other lands.

And yet...

Doing any of it all seemed rather pointless without Darshan at his side. But he couldn't expect the man to marry him. His lover would be a fool to not consider the ramifications of uniting himself to an outcast.

Darshan didn't even *need* a marriage for them to be together. They could live no differently as lovers.

Shaking himself, Hamish stowed the box into the base of his pack, alongside a few trinkets from his niece and nephews. A few more essentials joined them, such as string for his bow as well as his entire fletching kit; should he need to replace any damaged arrows. Normally, the kit would be without a knife, but still he had that on his belt.

Cramming his clothes on top, he turned to filling the chest with the rest of his things. He would leave the key on his person—same as always—but even if his siblings managed to transport what Hamish couldn't take with him now, it wasn't much of a guarantee. No one could've known his mother would boot them from the kingdom this swiftly. He doubted anyone could predict what action she would take after mourning her supposed loss.

Hoisting his pack onto his shoulder, he gave the room one final glance. Without the personal touch of his things gracing the nooks and crannies, his quarters seemed little more than a shell.

Not that it had been much better with the items there. Keeping things sparse had been a way to tell if something went missing as a boy. It had merely become habit.

Hamish strode out the door, nodding his final farewells to the two guards lingering on the other side. Gordon had ordered the duo there after the disqualified competitor tried her hand at molesting Hamish, but he hadn't expected anyone to still be here after the incident in the field. Certainly not the familiar faces that had greeted him, given that Sean and Zurron had never guarded the entrance to his quarters before. They'd usually be marching the walls.

Had that only been last night? *Aye.* He ached through to the bone and the day wasn't even over.

He burrowed his fingers into his hair, tugging at the coils, desperately hoping it would pull him from this nightmare. But no.

The corridors between his room and the guest quarters were devoid of all but the occasional servant. Each one scurried away once he was spotted as if he was a ghost. One man even squeaked and looked close to fainting as he staggered into a small supply room. Hamish had considered checking on the man—he hadn't heard the servant collapse—but decided against it.

Could it be that his mother had spread word of his apparent death? So swiftly? And with enough conviction that it was considered as irrefutable truth? Or had they been given strict orders to avoid him? With, perhaps, violent repercussions should they disobey.

Both seemed equally feasible given his mother's mental state. He had asked Sean and Zurron if either had heard of anything, but they'd been pretty much confined to that one corridor. They didn't even know Hamish had been exiled until he told them.

Hamish turned the final corner to discover the door to the guest quarters sat wide open. He halted, his ears straining to detect trouble.

The sounds within suggested only Darshan occupied the room. Perhaps his lover was having a problem in choosing what to leave behind. The man's travel chest *had* been packed to near bursting.

"If we're going to make good time before the sun sets," Hamish said, stepping through the doorway. "It'll be best if we—" The words died on his tongue as he took in the chaos that'd taken over the room. It looked for all the world like the chest had finally exploded.

A large pile of what had been Darshan's carefully-folded clothing now sat in a crumpled heap of silk in the middle of the room. The mound continued to grow as his lover threw more items onto it. He had changed out of the old competitor clothing and back into one of his more fanciful attires.

"You're nae planning on taking all of this, are you?" There was no way they could carry what had to be five distinct sets of clothing with them. And that didn't include the jumble of other items he was busily piling on top.

Darshan paused only to glance at Hamish before carrying on.

Shaking his head, he rifled through a bundle of parchment. A handful were shoved into his pack, the rest thrown on top of the pile of clothes. Pages fluttered in all directions.

Hamish picked up one that had skittered near his feet. Trade information adorned both sides of the parchment. Useless now. Tirglas would never accept any offer from Udynea whilst his mother still sat on the throne.

He released the sheet, letting it drift back onto the pile. Maybe they could try for an alliance once his brother ruled.

They were just fortunate to not have started the war his mother threatened.

"Stand back," Darshan warned, waving his hand over the stack of parchment and silk. Smoke curled from beneath the layers of fabric. A shield flickered to life around the pile, but the smoke seeped straight through the barrier.

"What are you doing?" Hamish demanded.

Flames continued to flick out from between the folds of clothing. They caught and swiftly burnt everything to ash.

"Getting rid of surplus baggage." With little remaining of his clothes, Darshan poked through the debris with a booted foot. "I refuse to leave behind anything of value."

"Dinnae you think burning everything is a wee bit on the dramatic side?" Hamish understood the desire to be rid of anything that might lead to the temptation of returning here—and the chance of Darshan's travel chest being smashed was far greater than Hamish's personal chest. However, setting what he couldn't bring with him on fire seemed like an extreme way to deal with it.

"Not really." His lover bent to pick up something small from the ashes, juggling it for a brief moment before pocketing the item.

"But your clothes—"

"I have what I currently wear and my warmer travelling attire is already packed. I can buy more if needed. Of course, such a task shall be easier once we reach Udynean lands, but I can make do with a few less in the meantime." He plucked several small stones from the ashes. "But I fear funds would be exceptionally tight without something to line our purses until we reach Udynea." He rubbed a thumb over one of the stones, revealing a ruby hue. "I am hoping your merchant guild will take these gems in exchange for spendable coin."

Hamish shuffled from one foot to the other. Acquiring more money beyond the small amount in his belt pouch wasn't something he'd been thinking of. Or even had the means to do without a lot of labour. "Thank you," he whispered.

"Thank—?" Darshan glanced up from collecting the gems and frowned. "For what? For getting you banished from your homeland?

For tearing everything apart and almost starting a civil war? For quite possibly ruining any chance of peace between our people?" He fisted his hair and continued to babble in Udynean, "Gods, what am I even going to tell my father? Or the senate? I shall be fortunate if he doesn't ship me off to Obuzan after this."

"I doubt he'd do that to his heir."

His lover scoffed. "There *is* my nephew. Or do you think my father would not have the boy nearby in the off chance that something untoward happened to me here?"

If Darshan had asked that question when he had first arrived, Hamish would've been adamant that nothing bad could've possibly happened to the man. But now that his mother had threatened so much? Attempted assassination seemed just as likely an option as everything else. "What I meant is thank you for standing by me." Whatever path his mother chose, Hamish doubted he would've had the courage to defy her without Darshan to support him.

His lover's eyes creased in a smile, but sadness lurked in that gaze. "Always, *mea lux*."

"I didnae think I would've had the strength to leave on me own. But I can now. You helped set me free." A weight seemed to lift from his soul as the words passed his lips, leaving him giddy. "I can go anywhere I want, do anything I wish."

"Not anything, surely." Dusting the soot from his hands, Darshan secured the pouch of gems to his belt. "By your laws, I won the right to your hand. I do believe that, technically, you are mine to take in marriage."

Hamish stilled, a strangely sick hollowness settling in his gut. He had planned to speak on the subject once they were away from the castle, but if Darshan was willing to bring up the topic now… "I ken what I said down there." What they had both said whilst tempers had flared. "But you dinnae actually have to marry me. I willnae hold you to that. It's nae like I'm much of a prize anymore."

"What if I want to despite all that?" Darshan clasped Hamish's forearm, his fingers almost hot enough to sear flesh. "You are still my light. Would you refuse me?"

Hamish shook his head. Refusing an offer of marriage would mean leaving Darshan's side, and he wasn't about to walk away from the man he loved. "But, seeing I'm considered dead and all, just what does marrying me bring to the table?" The bitterness of reality coated his words. Whilst the contest continued, he could pretend that marrying Darshan was a viable possibility. Normal. Not anymore. They both needed to face the truth there. "I'm nae saying we part ways, because I love you. But I have nae title. Nae clan. Nae ties of any kind." If his mother hadn't declared him as dead, then he could've brought the political link to his family to Udynea. "I have nae a thing I can claim as me own."

"That simply is not true." Darshan's hand slid down Hamish's arm to link their fingers. "And you *do* have something. You have *me*."

I do. Even having nothing beyond his name—and he wasn't even sure if he could still lay claim to half of it—Darshan would still be there. And his. "You dinnae gain anything by marrying me that you dinnae already have. There's nae even a dowry. It's just *me*." He could hope all he wanted that none of it mattered, but it did. It always would.

Soft amusement huffed out his lover's nose. "Do not sell yourself short, *mea lux*. *You* is more than enough. And dowries are to placate parents. I am not usually one to brag, but my father is already a very wealthy man."

He didn't know where the chuckle that escaped his lips came from, but it carried little in the way of mirth. "What good am I to you besides the obvious? I cannae be an ambassador to a kingdom who sees me as dead and you already have me willing enough to warm your bed."

Indignance tightened Darshan's features. "Do you honestly think I would have put myself through those trials if you meant no more to me than a place to stick it?"

Hamish shook his head. "I ken exactly why you competed. But me mum's disownment invalidates the contest." If Darshan had been a Tirglasian noble, such an act would've led to a feud between their clans.

"Meaning no binding claim to your hand should I change my mind?" Darshan scrubbed at his face and Hamish caught the mumbled words, "What is it about me that has people rejecting my offers of marriage? I am certain I have more than enough credentials to make me a good catch."

"You..." Hamish peered at him. "You've suggested marriage to someone in the past?" That sounded like something the man should've mentioned before now.

"Under *vastly* different circumstances, I assure you. I hardly think you would consider her as a threat to my affections."

"*Her?* Dar—"

Darshan waved his hand. "It was *not* one of my finest moments, but Rashmika is an old friend and I was trying to help her out of a dangerous situation. Her father was a rather influential man. He convinced my father to train her as my sister's handmaiden." He scrunched his nose, the act disturbing his glasses. "Her father used to beat her. Her magic healed the bruises, of course, but it was there in her eyes. I was just a young man, barely eighteen. Marrying me would have kept her safe. Just like it would keep you safe."

"And why would you need to be concerned about me safety?" Wasn't being at Darshan side enough for the Udynean people?

"Bringing you into the Crystal Court will upset quite a few people. Being a member of the royal household, even through marriage, comes with a certain level of protection from those not of our family."

Hamish's thoughts drifted to the scar on Darshan's torso. An arrow wound given to him by his own half-sister. "And what about those *within* your family clan?"

Darshan hummed noncommittally. "Most will fall into line immediately. Those who do not—" He shrugged. "Their actions would largely depend on my father's feelings over all this. Marriage to a *Mhanek*, or even his heir, is forever."

And yet, he had almost thrown away any chance of marrying for love. "Is that why this Rashmika woman refused you?"

His lover nodded. "She knew my reasoning, knew I had no physical interest in her. That, had I wed her, only her death would have freed my hand for another." One side of his mouth lifted. "She is happily married now, to a cousin on my mother's side of the family. I believe they even have children."

"And how do you think your father will take the idea of marrying me? Especially with how you plan to make bairns?" He couldn't imagine the *Mhanek* being at all happy about the trade and alliance deals falling through, but maybe he would be placated by the idea of a grandchild from his heir.

Grimacing, his lover sighed. "I honestly wish I knew. Any objections he has should be minor. Hopefully, I can mollify him on the important ones. Everything else?" Again, he shrugged.

"Fair enough," Hamish mumbled. They were definitely going to need to discuss how they faced Darshan's father, but it didn't need to be now and certainly not here. "We should get going."

Darshan combed back his hair, seemingly composed once again. "In a moment." Moving with deliberate slowness, he dropped to one knee before Hamish. "I suppose, all things considered…"

Hamish took a step back. "*What* are you doing?" There was only one reason he could think of for a man to be kneeling before him and they'd hardly the time for anything sexual, nor was this really the place.

"Hopefully, proving how serious I am to retain my claim to your hand." He grasped Hamish's fingers, holding them between both hands. "I was going to insist upon this before we reached Udynean borders, but now is just as a good a time."

Unwilling to reclaim his hand just yet, Hamish He shuffled on the spot. "For *what*?"

"I am unsure of your people's customs in regards to a proposal, so I am afraid you shall have to forgive my use of Udynean ones."

"Pr-proposal?" he managed. "We... we dinnae have..." Tirglasian couples didn't propose. They made arrangements, sought out the Goddess' favour and married only once an agreement on children was reached.

All of which Darshan had done.

Sweet Goddess...

How had he not realised that sooner?

"Still, I am only going to ask this once, so it would be less embarrassing for the both of us if you answer correctly the first time." He audibly swallowed and something about his face changed. The mask that he so readily slipped on had vanished, not even a thin veneer remained. "Hamish, will—?"

"Are you two ready?" Gordon's voice boomed down the corridor, growing louder as he approached.

Hamish had just managed to convince his body to face the doorway as his brother appeared.

"Why do I smell smo—?" Gordon froze, his mouth still opened. His gaze darted between Hamish and Darshan. "I..." He held up his hands. Only the Goddess could possibly understand what was going through his brother's mind. "I didnae mean to intrude. I'll just..." He pointed over his shoulder with both forefingers, backing up even as he mumbled a rushed, "I'll be in the courtyard."

Heat blazed across Hamish's face. "This isnae what it looks like!" he blurted after his brother. It was one thing to be aware that his brother knew Hamish was intimate with Darshan, quite another to have Gordon think he had walked in on such an act.

"I beg to differ," Darshan grumbled. "I am most certainly asking you to marry me."

"He wouldnae be thinking that you—" Shaking his head, he let the explanation go unsaid. He could do that once they were out of the castle. "You nae finished asking."

"I believe I just did."

"That... that wasnae a question. It's barely a statement." With a hint of an order, if he was honest. "And me brother doesnae think you're proposing, because we dinnae propose like this. He thinks you're about to suck me off what with you kneeling like you are!"

Darshan swiftly got to his feet. "I hardly think this is the appropriate time or place for *that*."

"You'll get nae disagreement from me there." Maybe when they were tucked away in some cosy inn room where they could rest and be guaranteed a bit of privacy.

"But I am serious about the proposal. I care not a whit about what you have or what political ties our people could have formed. I have never cared. Not when it came to being with you. I certainly have no need of a dowry. The only thing I would ever want from you is... *you.*" He once again clasped Hamish's hand in both of his. "You are my beacon, my flame eternal. I have no desire to return to the dark, I think we have both already walked through it for far too long."

Hamish frowned. It was true. He *had* had his fill of dark days. To return to where there'd be little else but more of the same? "We couldnae have that, could we, me heart?" he murmured.

"Then marry me." Darshan clung tighter to Hamish's fingers, those hazel eyes wide and glassy. "Please, Hamish of the Mathan Clan and light of my heart, say you shall be my husband?"

His throat tightened. *Damn you.* How was he supposed to say no to that? "Aye."

Watching the grin break across his lover's face was like surfacing after a deep dive. Darshan stretched up, coaxing Hamish lower with a slight push of his fingers against the nape of Hamish's neck to soundly kiss him. Then he abruptly pulled back, his brow creased. "I hope you are aware I shall hold you to that."

Fighting the urge to laugh, Hamish pressed closer. He cupped the back of the man's head, drawing them together so that their foreheads touched.

"*And* I plan to see us married before we leave Tirglas," Darshan continued. The warmth of his lover's lips brushed the tip of Hamish's nose as he spoke. "But first, we must head for the merchant guild." Gently slipping from Hamish's grip, Darshan shouldered his pack.

"You'll also have to find a priest willing to wed us." Hamish followed at Darshan's heels as they strode through the corridors. "Which could be a problem. Especially if word's got out to the city." It would already be shuddering at the outcome of the union contest.

What would the rumours make of his sudden eviction from the clan? Or would his mother insist on a proper mourning? One that would have the bells chiming all over the kingdom as word of his supposed death spread. She had done neither when it had come to shipping Caitlyn off to the cloister. His sister had just mysteriously vanished after the attack on their lives. Most had made up their own minds on what had happened.

"There is no rule that says the ceremony must be in Mullhind, is there?" Darshan halted just long enough for Hamish to catch up and walk beside him. "What of a temple in one of the border cities? Or a port? Surely, they shall be more lenient on two men marrying."

Hamish shrugged. "It'll take months to travel to the border." By then, his mother could've slipped her moorings entirely. Maybe even enough to order Darshan's capture, if not the man's death. "The southern ports would have us out of Tirglas sooner." Especially if they took a boat downriver and boarded one of the merchant vessels headed under the bridge at Freedom's Leap. That would put them on the water in little over a week and nearing the closest Udynean port within the fortnight, providing there was a ship headed that way.

Darshan squinted into the distance, possibly trying to think of the route Hamish saw quite clearly in his mind's eye. "I shall have to defer to your knowledge there."

"Why the rush to marry?" Was he afraid Hamish would change his mind? "I thought the danger was within your family."

"Yes. But it would be vastly safer for you to travel the breadth of the Udynea Empire as my husband than you could ever be as a mere paramour."

The courtyard was almost empty with just his siblings and two horses standing in the centre. Even the guards had vacated their usual posts at the gates.

Darshan stiffened briefly before taking the fore position. The air around them changed, the usual wind losing its customary sharpness. Another invisible shield? Did his lover think they were being led into an ambush?

Keeping a cautious eye on the empty ramparts, Hamish followed his lover as they trotted down the stairs. *She wouldnae order his death.* Not here. Out in the back fields of nowhere, perhaps, where she could blame it on bandits and the like, but not right in the middle of the castle grounds.

Still, the building tension in his shoulders refused to leave until they had reached his siblings. "Where is everyone?"

"Mum called them in for mourning," Nora answered, handing the reins of a small chestnut pony to Darshan. "We should be there, too, but we wanted to—"

Her words were muffled as Gordon enveloped Hamish in a hug. "Take care. Both of you. And *you…*" With one arm still wrapped around Hamish's shoulder, his brother dragged Darshan into their embrace. "You better take good care of me brother."

"Naturally," Darshan replied, the words warped due to his face being squeezed by Gordon's arm. Prising himself free, he clambered aboard the chestnut pony.

Giving his brother's back a final pat, Hamish swept his sister up in a similar embrace. "Dinnae let Mum get her claws into Ethan." As much as he wanted to remove his nephew from this place, to give him a chance to grow up where he'd be free to love whomever he chose, doing so would see guards hounding them all the way to the border. And they'd no guarantee that they would make it to Udynea with him.

"I'll try me best," Nora promised. A single tear slunk down her cheek. She hastily wiped it away. "Look at me blubbering like it's going to be forever."

Hamish cleared his throat. He had been trying not to think about all the people he would lose, but seeing his sister shedding the first tears he had witnessed from her in years...

He sniffed. He hadn't been prepared for this. "I'm going to miss you. All of you."

Gordon wrapped his arm around their sister's shoulders. "We'll miss you, too."

Hamish flung himself at them, holding them tight. "I love you. Both of you. I hope you ken that."

"We do," Nora replied.

"I just want you to ken in case..." He gave another sniff and attempted to clear his throat.

"We'll find a way to see you again," Gordon promised. "Somehow."

Hamish nodded. If there was a way it could be done, his brother would find it. "I just want to tell you, because I might nae have always shown it, how I appreciate all you've done for me over the years." It might not have always gone as they had planned, but they had shouldered so much blame together that it didn't seem fair to let them face their mother without him.

Darshan laid a hand on Hamish's shoulder. "We should leave whilst the guards are otherwise engaged."

Nodding, Hamish dried his face on his sleeve before swinging into his mare's saddle. She gave her customary impatient stamp of a hind hoof as he settled on her back. "Aye, lass," he murmured. "We're leaving." He didn't know if he would be able to bring her once they reached the river docks, much less aboard a ship, but it was comforting to have her on this final journey through his homeland.

He twisted in the saddle as his horse high-stepped her way towards the castle gates. "Let Caitlyn ken what happened, she'll fash herself sick if I dinnae show come summer. Give her me love. And the others, Sorcha, Bruce, Ethan, Mac—" Although he didn't need to, he rattled off their names. This could be his last chance to speak them. He wished he could've said it in person, but his mother likely insisted on having all her grandchildren at her side. "Dad, too."

"We will," Gordon replied.

"And Mum," he shot over his shoulder as his mare reached the gates. No one waited outside them. Even the road leading down to Mullhind was eerily deserted.

"Uncle 'Mish!" Ethan's voice echoed across the courtyard.

Hamish searched the surrounding walls, finding nothing, before dropping to eye the stables and storage buildings. If any of his sibling's children were within arm's reach, he wasn't sure if he would be able to let them go.

"Up here!" Sorcha bellowed.

His gaze lifted to the castle proper. His niece and nephews sat on the balcony high above the door, waving furiously. Had they been told the lie? If so, they clearly hadn't believed it. Or had they snuck around and been there for the truth?

Hamish raised his hand, his sight blurring anew.

One by one, they replied in kind. Voices, further garbled by echoes and an attempt to speak at the same time, bounced around the courtyard.

"Be good," he called up to them. "Stay safe. I love you." He watched them, his siblings and their children, even as his mare continued plodding away from them. He burnt their image into his mind; Gordon holding their sister tight, his niece and nephews clinging to each other. There was no guarantee that he would ever see any of them again.

It wasn't until they were out of sight that he repositioned himself in the saddle and took the lead for the city. His last ride into Mullhind.

Hamish gave the castle one final look over his shoulder. Had it always sat like a hulking beast on the edge of the cliff? "Do you think she'll ever change her mind?" His mother had been harsh on all her children for as far back as he could remember and abusive to him since his teenage years, personally putting him through a hell that even the Goddess wouldn't do. One he had finally fought his way free of.

But he was still her son. Surely she couldn't keep up the pretence of him being dead forever. Could she?

"She?" Darshan echoed, frowning. "You mean your mother? One can but pray."

Pray. That was precisely what she would be doing right now. For the salvation of a son who had yet crossed the threshold to the Goddess' side.

Maybe the Goddess would bring his mother clarity.

Swallowing the threat of fresh tears clogging his throat, he turned his back on the castle. If he started crying again, he wasn't sure if he would be able to halt them until he was a husk. "So, the merchant guild's our first stop?"

Darshan inclined his head. "Then we head south as per your suggestion." His lover had become subdued since exiting the castle proper. Hamish didn't blame him.

His gaze drifted to the southern horizon. Much of it was a haze of grey sky and green land. "I havenae travelled that way for years. I've had nae reason to. Nae since I was a lad with a bright future ahead of me."

Darshan stretched out a hand, clasping Hamish's. "It still is, *mea lux*. Even if we have to light the path ourselves, the future is no less bright for us."

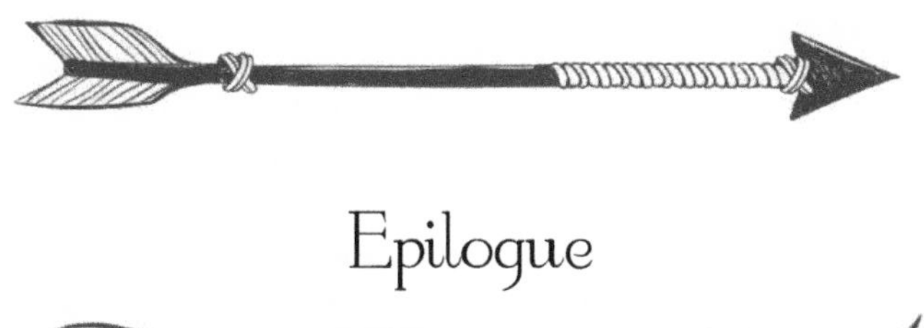

Epilogue

Hamish clung tight to the railing as another tumultuous wave smacked into the bow of the cargo ship. The briny scent of the sea filled his nostrils and the call of gulls was thick in the air, never failing to bring a lump to his throat for the home he had left behind no more than a fortnight ago.

He tucked a few wispy coils of hair behind his ear. Although the wind whisked the cargo ship along at a mighty clip, it failed to touch them thanks to the magic of Darshan's shield.

Hamish had been lured up here by the man in question, finally relenting to Darshan's eager insistence of leaving their small accommodations for the open air.

Darshan stood before him with barely a hand on the railing to steady himself. His attention was largely trained on the massive stone bridge spanning between two cliffs. "There it is," Darshan breathed. "Freedom's Leap."

Even though most maps showed only open ocean through the pass, the bridge connected one side of the strait to the other. It seemed spindly compared to the surrounding land, but the rocky formation had to be as wide as the ship was long.

"I've only ever heard of it," Hamish confessed. *This* was where the first of the nomadic elven clans fled what used to be part of the burgeoning Udynean kingdom—land that was now part of Obuzan. "None of Calder's cargo ever came this far south." And even if they had, his mother wouldn't have allowed him to take a journey that could potentially lead him onto foreign soil.

"Quite a feat of magic, is it not?" Darshan continued to gush, the words tumbling over themselves as he continued. "Legend tells that the first bridge the elves built tumbled into the sea. And took a great many of the Udynean slavers foolish enough to set foot on it." He laughed as if it was the folly of another empire.

"And the elves?"

Darshan sobered at the question. "Some escaped, I suppose. Where else would the tale have come from?" He nodded at the bridge. "They say the nomadic elves strengthen the magic keeping it in place during each crossing."

Hamish's stomach flipped at the thought of traversing such a structure. One wrong step would send a person plummeting into the water. Or worse, see them smashing against the cliff face.

"How did it become Obuzan?"

Darshan inclined his head, his lips pursing. "Through our sheer arrogance. Obuzan was a sect in the northern part of the kingdom that despised all things magic. When Udynea stretched herself to the east, that sect came snapping out at our flanks." He shrugged. "The empire could not fight on two fronts and annihilating our neighbours held more promise than returning to a place where resources were already depleted."

"You're very clinical about it."

Darshan gave another shrug, just as nonchalant as the first. "It was hundreds of years ago. Almost two millennia. Why get passionate over ancient history?" He cleared his throat, his gaze still on the bridge as the ship sailed directly beneath it. A few fist-sized rocks splashed into the sea not far from the railing. "I… um…"

If Darshan spoke further, Hamish certainly heard nothing over the pounding of his heart and the questions darting about his mind like gulls. Did Darshan's heart thump as heavily? How much crushing rock could his shield deflect if the bridge were to fail at this moment? Could it be stretched to incorporate the whole ship? Or would they sink along with everyone else regardless?

Only once the ship was out from beneath the bridge did he realise he'd been holding his breath. He took a few deep, open-mouthed gulps of air. That was definitely going on his list of things to never attempt again. Right at the top.

Darshan continued, his voice a little strained, "I would like to linger in the city once we reach the port. Send word of our travels to Minamist, speak to my banker about funds." He arched a brow in Hamish's direction. "And spend a night in a decent bed before we move on."

A bed sized for the pair of them would be far better than the cot that just gave Hamish enough room to lay flat on. Never mind their barely-successful attempt at doing anything except sleep.

"Maybe…" Leaning back, Darshan ran a finger up Hamish's forearm. "I do not know… Pick up where we left off?"

Hamish grinned. They had spent the better part of their first week freely exploring each other's bodies in the solitude of their tent, foregoing any actual penetration until Darshan had procured a small measure of oil at the riverside village. Sex whilst crammed in a cot hadn't been the easiest thing, but they had managed to varying degrees of success.

Whilst they had only attempted sex the once during their journey on board this ship—the cot being short enough that his feet couldn't make it onto the mattress—the time had been a memorable one. "And hear you roar again, me stag," Hamish teased.

Darshan's cheeks reddened. The shield faltered for a breath, allowing the chill wind to buffet them. "You are not going to let that one drop, are you? I *did* warn you that I get rather loud when things are going well."

The volume hadn't been a problem. The particular type of sound, however… Well, it wasn't one he would've expected to come from any man, especially not from one who seemed to keep themselves relatively under control during such intimacy. He supposed being the one riding for a change made all the difference. "It was cute."

"It was *not*. It was loud and boorish. And I think I might have woken the whole ship."

Hamish snickered quietly to himself. It couldn't have been the *whole* ship. The night watch would've already been awake.

"I have spent *years* trying to stop it." And yet, Darshan had still roared like a stag calling out in spring. He gave a disgusted grunt. "And it appears I was wrong in my belief that I had gotten it under control." He eyed Hamish suspiciously. "Anyway, I thought you found it… lacking a certain something?"

"I said it was nice," he murmured. And it had been. Not the mind-blowing pleasure Darshan managed to evoke when Hamish was the one doing the riding, but it wasn't as if he would mind repeating the experience. He'd just been surprised to find it wasn't as fun as the normal way they made love.

"Because *nice* was entirely my goal there." There was an acerbic tinge to the words. Surly. Just as he had been when Hamish first voiced his opinion.

"It's just nae a position I'd choose given the option." Not that he'd had such a choice in the past. Or the inclination. But Darshan had set the thought in his head and, with the man willing to excuse his lack of experience, trying before forming a proper opinion on the act had seemed fair.

One side of Darshan's mouth lifted. "It is perfectly all right, *mea lux*. Really. I can hardly fault you for having a preference." He absently patted Hamish's hand, his rings clinking against the sole golden ring sitting there.

Hamish's gaze dropped to the ring adorning his left hand. Several small orbs of dark garnet and shimmering pearls stared back. Unlike the cheap wooden band that now adorned Darshan's once bare finger—the one on his right hand that was meant for a wedding band—this piece had belonged to his lover. His... *husband*.

Darshan had sworn to pick out a piece with a style more appropriate for a wedding band once they were in Minamist, but this served Hamish just as well as any other ring. A quick resize at a jeweller working near the docks had seen it fit Hamish's finger. The middle left, just as was befitting Tirglasian marriage custom.

They had followed plenty of his land's customs in their wedding vows, too. They had waited until their last day in Tirglas before seeking out a priest. The ceremony kept brief and simple due to the necessity of not antagonising the man who had agreed to unite them.

The priest had been hesitant at first, protesting with all manner of scripture without alluding to the annexed passages, even as Darshan had loaded the man's hands with gold. It had taken Darshan stripping off one of his rings as extra payment for the priest to finally cave.

"I simply meant it is a pity you find it lacking," Darshan continued, dragging Hamish's attention back from the recent past. "I fear I shall certainly need another fix at some point."

"Oh, aye? A fix was it?" Well, Darshan had confessed to imagining the scenario since they had first kissed. Likely along with several others that he hadn't admitted to.

Darshan hummed. There was definitely a note of amusement to the sound. "Not right away, you understand. I might keep it for certain occasions." He waggled a finger in the air, the sunlight glittering off his rings. "No, actually. I shall need it more than that. Once a month would serve well."

"Only once?" Hamish found himself fighting to keep the amusement out of his voice. After the past week, it was quite the drop. But whilst it was a far better prospect than his previous arrangement of forced abstinence, he couldn't see Darshan adhering to his own declaration. Now they were away from the castle's endless watch on their movements, his husband had turned out to be a near-insatiable man.

"You are quite right. Once is far too long to wait. Twice would be more satisfactory, do you not think so?"

"What I *think* is I could manage sex more times a month than that."

"*What?*" Chuckling, his husband finally turned to give Hamish his full attention. "I do not mean *all* of it. I fully intend to be available for you to ride whenever you desire." He cocked his head. "Or does that arrangement not suit you?"

"That's a relief," he thickly replied. "Because I think you would've found me insisting if you stuck to a bi-monthly schedule."

"Do not let that stop you," Darshan said, his voice growing husky. "I would hate to be the only one taking the initiative there."

Hamish wrapped his arms around Darshan's shoulders and drew his husband closer. The world seemed to still as they stood there, their arms encircling each other, their bodies warmed by more than mere sunlight.

The strait opened out into a harbour roughly the size of the one that sheltered Mullhind. The ship veered south, heading for a city cringing in a small strip of land that the Udyneans had nibbled off the Tirglasian border centuries ago.

Land. He itched to already be there, to finally plant himself in a kingdom where his mother's word had no sway. He had been on a number of sailing jaunts with Calder, back before his older sister had even considered having more than one child. But they'd only ever travelled to Tirglasian ports.

This was foreign soil. *Udynean* soil.

According to Darshan, the port served as the bastion between the empire and Obuzan. The mountains running along the border played a heavy part in keeping the two countries apart, but those stone giants crumbled nearer the shoreline and there had been multiple skirmishes in this one spot.

Not recently, Darshan had made sure of that before procuring passage.

Hamish's heart leapt as the ship bumped against the pier. This was it. The first proper leg of their journey across the empire. Nothing left but to follow Darshan's lead.

The dock planks creaked and clattered under his foot no differently to those back home. When he breathed deep, the air was no less briny or pungently fishy. Nor was the chatter, now he understood a fair chunk of the language, any different. People still yelled at their underlings and merchants hawked their wares just as boldly.

His chest ached with the familiarity of it all.

But one thing was lacking. *Where are the guards?* This was a border city and of a size almost twice that of the port they'd left. There should've been people patrolling the docks if not the streets. Or did the threat of upsetting a spellster keep people in check?

They waited for their mounts to be unloaded and brought to them by one of the sailors. She bowed upon handed them the reins before returning to assist her crew in unloading the rest of the ship's cargo. The horses were already saddled and laden with their gear, a little on the lean side food-wise.

Hamish gave his mare a hearty pat on the shoulder as she blew into his face, pleased to see her again after the days she had spent stabled below deck. She seemed no worse for wear despite never having travelled aboard a ship before. It seemed he had worried over the possibility of leaving her behind in Tirglas for nothing. "Do you think they'll handle the warmer weather once we head south?"

"I am certain," Darshan replied, speaking entirely in Udynean. His voice rose as they left the dockside. "That the stable hands in the palace will keep them comfortable. But we could always clip their coats if they appear distressed on the journey."

They pressed deeper into the city, entering a busy market square.

This, too, looked no different to home. The vendors, the shops, even the people were common. Before their arrival, he had thought his clothes would have him standing out, but they were a close enough cut for him to blend in with the crowd. He supposed the similarity in terms of climate helped there.

Still, a touch of disappointment gnawed at him. He was in another kingdom, on the fringes, yes—the port city being not even a week's ride from the Tirglasian border—but it all looked the same.

Darshan jerked his head at a white-walled building on the other side of the square. "This way."

Hamish tilted his head as they passed through the building's archway and into a small courtyard. Was that music? It was difficult to tell over the chatter of the square at their backs, but he could've sworn his ears picked up the hushed beat of a drum—just audible over the quivering thrum and sigh of stringed instruments.

Were they headed for an inn so early in the day? He had thought for sure that Darshan would've sought out funds first. Or contacted his family in Minamist. Although, Hamish understood the urge to dither on the latter. Darshan couldn't be looking forward to explaining the mess they had made of the trade negotiations.

Nevertheless, he followed his husband's lead in handing over his horse's reins to a waiting stablehand and trailed inside, pushing aside a gauzy curtain.

The building's interior looked no less hazy, largely thanks to the men and women puffing away on long pipes. Thin plumes of smoke curled out one end, pooling in the arches and painted panels that made up the ceiling. Visions of pastures and mountains adorned the wood, the greens and whites stained a tar brown by the smoke. Hamish's eyes watered the longer he lingered in the doorway. His chest burned, but coughing did little to clear it.

The music he had heard came from a trio of elven men seated upon a dais in a corner. They swayed with each note, their surroundings lost to the sound. Being bare to the waist, the lantern light shone dully on their collars.

Slaves. He knew he would've come across them eventually—not perhaps this soon.

"What is it?" His husband had vanished from his side for the brief moment Hamish had taken to survey the room, but Darshan now stood before him with a frown furrowing the space between his brows. He turned his head, those hazel eyes searching the dim corner with the musicians before realisation slackened his face. "Would you like me to see them removed?"

Hamish shook his head. Whilst the idea of slaves was an unsavoury one, he couldn't expect them to be hidden for the benefit of him forgetting they were there. *I'd like to see them free.* Even as the thought surfaced, he knew it wasn't as easy as he had once thought. Darshan had spent a great deal of their journey on the water explaining the rules Udynea had about their most precious commodity.

A woman appeared from behind another gauzy curtain sectioning off a corridor. She trotted over and bowed. "How may we serve you today..." Her gaze darted over Hamish, and clearly dismissed him with a flattening of her lips, before turning back to Darshan. "...my lord?"

"Two cups of your finest blend," Darshan replied, lifting his left hand before him and almost idly rubbing his thumb over the ring on his forefinger. The ring bore a seal that only one man wore; that of the Udynean crown prince.

Gasping, the woman bowed even lower than before. "Right away, *vris Mhanek.*"

"My husband and I shall seat ourselves outside."

Hamish's throat tightened, any attempts at speech momentarily beyond him. *My husband...* They'd only been married a few days, how did the word fall so easily from Darshan's lips? His gaze darted to the woman, looking for the same hint of the distaste he had met during their time travelling down to the Tirglasian port.

If she thought strangely of them, she seemed to know better than to show it. "Of course, *vris Mhanek.*"

"Come with me," Darshan said, entwining their fingers.

Heat crept into his cheeks as Hamish allowed his husband to lead the way across the room. Not the inferno it once was, he was getting better at controlling it, but the eyes tracking their passage certainly didn't help.

The building's patrons lounged on either benches or nests of pillows piled high at their backs. A number of these latter folk were grouped around strange, bottle-shaped braziers with oddly flexible tubes, occasionally blowing more smoke out into the air. They all stared at him, likely taking in the plainness and travel-worn state of his attire.

"Did you have to do that?" Hamish muttered. Darshan had also flashed his signet ring to the ship captain, who had fallen over himself to accommodate them just like the young woman.

"One of the perks of my status."

Hamish frowned. "I hope you dinnae expect me to act like that."

"Of course not. I rather doubt they would respond in a similar manner anyway. The idea of the *vris Mhanek* having a husband would be unheard of." He twisted to peer at the entrance the woman had disappeared through. "Although, I suppose that will change rather rapidly now." Turning back, he grimaced. "And don't look at me like that, I plan to pay them. It's just nice to have the symbol recognised."

More gossamer curtains hung along the walls and between ornate pillars, some clearly framing off other entrances. Darshan parted one and stepped into a small, enclosed garden. A pond sat in the middle, its surface shimmering as orange fish swam in lazy circles just beneath the surface. Stone tables dotted the area between beds of flowers and drooping trees, the path to them marked out with wide slabs of stone.

A few people already sat at a table farthest from the entrance. They eyed Hamish and Darshan with great interest for a while, before returning to their conversation. Occasionally, one would look their way as Darshan made for a table on the opposite end of the garden, but they seemed disinterested. Was it the fact Darshan still held his hand that drew their eye? They couldn't know Darshan was their *vris Mhanek*. Or did they?

They briefly stumbled upon another table tucked behind a hedge where a couple of young men sat too engrossed in staring into each other's eyes to realise they'd been spotted. Hamish glanced back before the pair was obscured from view once again. They had to be in their late teens, yet here they were, more or less out in the open. He never would've dared.

Hamish settled at their chosen table. The middle had been hollowed out to set a little brass brazier inside. Darshan lit the coals with a flick of his fingers.

Servants passed constantly, always offering up cakes and bowls of small, powdered cubes that Hamish couldn't identify. He politely waved them away even as Darshan snaffled up several trays.

It wasn't too long before one of those trays bore two, small cups of dark brown liquid. Steam radiated from the contents as the servant set the tray on the table and, bowing low, left them without a word.

"You simply must try some of this." Darshan placed one of the cups into Hamish's hands. "It's a Niholian drink, very popular in most of the empires. They call it *kofe*."

Hamish lifted the cup to his lips. The sharp acrid scent assaulted his senses before he could take a sip. Nevertheless, he braved a mouthful.

Bitterness washed over his tongue. Hamish spat the liquid back into the cup and held it far from him as his body shuddered and his eyes made a valiant attempt to roll back into his skull. "Are you trying to poison me?" He set the cup down on the tray of a passing servant. It had to be some sort of prank, the *kofe* tasted only of ash and dirt.

"Hold on." Darshan ushered a nearby serving woman closer. After a few words in hushed tones, the woman returned with another tray sporting two cups, a pot of amber syrup and a bowl piled with what looked to be sand in colour and texture.

"I forget it can be a bit on the strong side to the uninitiated. I have been a constant consumer since my *Khutani*, but I am aware it can be an acquired taste."

Hamish eyed his husband's hands as Darshan busied himself with preparing a cup. He wasn't entirely sure it was a taste he wanted to acquire.

Darshan continued, seemingly none the wiser as to Hamish's hesitation. The *kofe* was poured from its pitcher into a silver cup with a long handle. From there, his husband tipped the foam into one of the two ornate porcelain cups before putting the rest onto the bed of glowing coals nestled into the brazier.

"The current trend is to have sweet foods with it—cakes, dates, candied fruit and the like—but I've always rather preferred it this way," Darshan said, his voice distant whilst his gaze remained intently on the *kofe*. He drizzled a generous amount of syrup into the silver cup, stirring occasionally and removing it from the coals only once the slightly paler brown liquid within had started to bubble. "Perhaps you will also find this a little more palatable."

Transferring the liquid to the cups that were already full of foam, Darshan set the silver cup down and lifted the porcelain cup in both hands to inhale deeply over its contents. Contentment lit his face. "Try it now," his husband insisted, offering up the cup.

Hamish bent over the table to take a sip without relinquishing Darshan of the cup. Bitterness still lurked in the aftertaste, but its edge had been smoothed by the familiar taste of honey and something even sweeter. Satisfied, he took the cup and tried another mouthful.

Licking his lips, Darshan slid over a tray of small pink cubes covered in white powder. "Now these are a purely Udynean dish from the south." He picked up a cube and popped it into his mouth, giving a decadent groan as he chewed.

Hamish plucked one from the pile. They were springy in a sticky sort of fashion, like a more solid form of the gelatinous gloop found in the poorer pies. Arching a questioning brow at Darshan, he followed his husband's actions by chucking the whole thing into his mouth.

The sweetness of the powder hit him first. He shuddered, reaching for the *kofe* to wash away the taste. He'd barely gotten the cup to his lips before another flavour worked its way through the oversweet powder. It was subtle and slightly floral. He rolled the cube around on his tongue until the powder was gone.

Rather than chew as Darshan had done, he let the cube dissolve, occasionally sipping at the *kofe*. Combined, they didn't taste too bad.

"Well?"

His gaze lifted to Darshan, who still intently watched him.

"What do you think?" An eager little gleam twinkled in his eyes. The same one Hamish had seen in his nephews when they were hoping they'd impressed him. "I did ask for them not to make the brew too strong."

Hamish lowered the cup and brushed at his beard to disturb any white powder that might have collected there. "It's fine. I've just been thinking." His gaze swept over their surroundings, taking in the quiet warmth of the garden. It was all very cosy and sweet. "We've nae places like this in Tirglas." A pub was the closest, but he'd wager they had plenty of them here as well. To choose a place that would be entirely foreign to him, to opt for this level of solitude—

He frowned. *Food, solitude and romantic company.* Hadn't that been the stipulations of what Darshan had called a date? But they were married. By Tirglasian standards, anyway. *If I get carted off by his enemies, I bloody swear…*

" 'Mish?" A thread of alarm wove its way through Darshan's voice. His gaze darted to Hamish's cup of *kofe*, but if he was concerned about its contents, he gave no other indication. "Is everything all right?"

Jerked out of his musing, Hamish cleared his throat and popped another powdered cube into his mouth. "Aye," he mumbled whilst idly chewing. "It's just a little strange."

Amusement and mischief gleamed in those hazel eyes as his husband grinned at him over his own cup. "If you think all this…" He twirled a forefinger, indicating the garden. "…is strange, then I simply cannot wait until I get you home."

Hamish returned to sipping the *kofe*. A warm breeze caressed his skin, the spicy floral scent it carried mirrored in the food. "With you at me side, I'm already there."

THE END

About the Author

Aldrea Alien is an award-winning, bisexual New Zealand author of speculative fiction romance of varying heat levels.

She grew up on a small farm out the back blocks of a place known as Wainuiomata alongside a menagerie of animals, who are all convinced they're just as human as the next person (especially the cats). She spent a great deal of her childhood riding horses, whilst the rest of her time was consumed with reading every fantasy book she could get her hands on and concocting ideas about a little planet known as Thardrandia. This would prove to be the start of The Rogue King Saga as, come her twelfth year, she discovered there was a book inside her.

Aldrea now lives in Upper Hutt, on yet another small farm with a less hectic, but still egotistical, group of animals (cats will be cats), and published the first of The Rogue King Saga in 2014. One thing she hasn't yet found is an off switch to give her an ounce of peace from the characters plaguing her mind, a list that grows bigger every year with all of them clamouring for her to tell their story first. It's a lot of people for one head.

aldreaalien.com

Lightning Source UK Ltd.
Milton Keynes UK
UKHW010115031121
393296UK00001B/208